Wings of the Morning

by David Beaty

Fiction

THE TAKE OFF
THE WIND OFF THE SEA
THE GUN GARDEN
VILLAGE OF STARS
THE WHITE SEA BIRD
THE HEART OF THE STORM
THE PROVING FLIGHT
CONE OF SILENCE
THE SIREN SONG
SWORD OF HONOUR
THE TEMPLE TREE
EXCELLENCY
CALL ME CAPTAIN
ELECTRIC TRAIN

Non-Fiction

THE HUMAN FACTOR IN
   AIRCRAFT ACCIDENTS
THE WATER JUMP
MILK AND HONEY
THE COMPLETE SKYTRAVELLER

by Betty Beaty

MAIDEN FLIGHT
AMBER FIVE
THE ATLANTIC SKY
SOUTH TO THE SUN
THE TOP OF THE CLIMB
THE SWALLOWS OF SAN
   FEDORE
LOVE AND THE KENTISH MAID
HEAD OF CHANCERY

As Catherine Ross

FROM THIS DAY FORWARD
THE COLOURS OF THE NIGHT
THE TRYSTING TOWER
BATTLEDRESS

As Karen Campbell

SUDDENLY IN THE AIR
WHEEL FORTUNE
THUNDER ON SUNDAY
DEATH DESCENDING
THE BELLS OF ST MARTIN

WINGS OF THE MORNING

DAVID and BETTY BEATY

Coward, McCann & Geoghegan
New York

First American Edition 1982

Library of Congress Cataloging in Publication Data

Beaty, David.
Wings of the morning.

I. Beaty, Betty. II. Title.
PR6003.E264W5   1982   823'.914   81-19467
ISBN 0-698-11141-9   AACR2

PRINTED IN THE UNITED STATES OF AMERICA

To Ted and Audrey – and for Sue, Carole and Karen

If I take the wings of the morning and
   remain in the uttermost parts of the sea;
Even also shall thy hand lead me: and thy
   right hand shall hold me.

If I say, Peradventure the darkness shall cover me:
   then shall my night be turned to day.
Yea, the darkness is no darkness with thee, but the
   night is as clear as day: the darkness and
   light to thee are both alike.

Psalms CXXXIX

BOOK ONE

First Light
1903–14

ONE

Amelia Jerningham had been born in 1886, but she regarded herself as a child of the twentieth century. And at five o'clock on the morning of 6 October 1903, she closed her bedroom door behind her, tiptoed softly past her older sister Victoria's room and along the polished galleried landing, in the sure and certain knowledge that she was about to become a part of the new exciting spirit of the times.

She had been awakened by her small alarm, tucked discreetly under her pillow, long before the cockerel crowed on the Home Farm. But to make doubly sure, for this was the day on which history was to be made, she had tapped her golden head four times on the pillow before drifting off into an excited uneasy sleep. A sleep broken by vivid dreams, a few fears and wild anticipation of the morrow, which was now today.

A cool day, as James had said it would be. Jerningham Hall was like the inside of the family mausoleum as she silently descended the curved staircase – a ghost herself, but a clever one – remembering to step over the third tread which was known to creak and which Stepmama had been known to listen for.

Downstairs, the reception hall was a rectangular lake of blackness relieved only by a faint sheen of light from the cusp of the old moon through the oriel-windows. The light glimmered on the gilt mirror over the Adam fireplace. Amelia hardly paused to glance at herself – a slight figure in a dark cloak, a pale oval face, her blue eyes black and shadowed, the light glinting on her piled-up hair. James had been insistent about that. No flowing tresses.

Now her second best feature (her eyes were her best) was primly pinned. Though never one to do entirely what she was told, even for James, Amelia had softened the effect with loops of ribbons that matched her dress. No doubt he would even object to her dress. It was velvet and frivolous. But Amelia had a great sense of occasion. Besides, James's carping was almost as delightful and much more frequent than his compliments, she thought, picking up the corners of her skirt and taking the six steps down to the kitchen two at a time.

She pushed open the green baize door to the kingdom ruled over by Hawkins, the butler, and Mrs Henshaw, the housekeeper. Inside the kitchen proper only the central stove remained lit all night. It gave off a pink glow which was reflected on the pans and kettles that hung on the wall, the forks and scoops laid out ready for breakfast-making on the scrubbed table, and lit her way to that most ill-favoured room of the house, the cold meat store from which her exit would be unnoticed.

Whitewashed and high ceilinged, the room was equipped with racks, meat-hooks and runnels in the stone floor where the blood could drain down.

9

Here the ventilation window catch was easy to open. What was not easy – what indeed was a labour of not inconsiderable love – was to negotiate her fumbling passage between stiff stinking carcasses of pheasant, hare and partridge.

At the end of the line hung a huge female hare with a distinctive splash of black on its back and the long teeth of old age. For years now, the gamekeeper had spared the animal. Out of respect for her once youthful cunning according to him, on account of the hare being a witch according to Sarah, the petty-maid. Following neither school of thought but needing some success while his hand was unsteady from the port, last week Mr Jerningham had shot it dead.

'Bad luck on t'house, Miss Amelia.'

'Rubbish, Sarah!'

'It ain't, I tell yer. The gipsies have seed it. Witch ter hare. Then hare ter witch. Regular as night and day!'

'What nonsense you talk, Sarah! This is the twentieth century! The age of enlightenment and achievement!'

Tucking her arms tight to her side all the same and avoiding the hare's glassy stare, the twentieth century child pushed open the window and thankfully drew in a lungful of the southwest wind. It smelled of the mown grass of the parkland mixed with the tang of the salt marshes. She could hear it rustling the brittle leaves on the oaks that lined the drive.

Fate was indeed being kind.

Amelia hitched her skirts above her knees and swung her legs over the narrow sill. Her stepmother, ever ready with her punishments and the undoubted ruler of the Jerningham roost, would have thrashed her if she had caught her now. But Stepmama and Papa had had a late night dining with the parents of Victoria's fiancé, the Honourable Henry Tyrell. They would not rise till ten. And by then it would be too late. All their aspirations for a gentleman just as suitable for Amelia, all their hopes of a double wedding, would have been dashed.

Pushing the window shut behind her, Amelia jumped on to the cobblestones of the stable yard. She didn't cross it directly but hugged its shadowy perimeter. Her own horse Pegasus gave a whinny of recognition as she fled hastily through the arch under the clock tower, dreading a sudden lantern or the challenge of a voice. She had at one time considered riding Pegasus over to the rendezvous. For he it was who had brought James and herself together. But a better, more modern, more silent means was to hand.

For Victoria's seventeenth birthday two years ago and for her own this year, each had been given a bicycle. They were housed in the gardener's shed against the vegetable garden wall. Victoria, sedate and proper, now busily preparing for her wedding to the second son of a peer, had never mounted hers. But even if she had wanted to do so, this would now be impossible. The wheels had vanished months ago – a fact not reported by the head gardener in return for a dazzling smile and a bottle of her father's port, a transaction made honourable by the role of those wheels, now pressganged into the service of History.

Amelia wheeled out her own bicycle, tied her skirt in a knot round her waist, mounted and went swooping like a bird down the long straight drive. She turned right at the lodge. Over the Solent, over Southampton Water, over the turf of the New Forest, the sky was still dark. But she could hear the faint uncertain pipe of the first birds. She pedalled harder. She must reach their rendezvous before dawn. Before James changed his mind. Not a job for a woman, he had once said. But she had proved him wrong, even made him *admit* he was wrong. She was quick, clever, deft. And where would he be without her bicycle wheels, not to mention the piano wire, the corset stays and all that petticoat silk?

A mile on, she turned left down a sandy track, wobbled over the ruts and stones and rounded a gorse bush. In front of her lay that wide stretch of flat turf. And at the far end, a lantern light, a black spindly shape with a tall thick-set figure beside it.

James March and his flying machine.

'James!' she called as she rattled over the last few yards.

In her fantasies, he would have come rushing to meet her, swept her off her bicycle and into his arms. But being James, he did no such thing. He lifted one hand in greeting and stood where he was.

Then she came nearer. Still shadowy in the half-darkness, he walked three paces forward so that she could dismount. And as if deliberately making the situation less romantic he called, 'Careful! Don't run into Ajax before we even begin!'

'I'm not late, am I, James?'

'Early if anything.' He spoke slowly and without emotion. 'Still a while before dawn.'

'Aren't you excited, James?'

'I can't let myself be.'

'I've been excited all night.'

He frowned as she began to unbutton her cloak. 'I told you to wear something suitable, Miss Amelia.'

'This *is* suitable! And don't call me Miss Amelia!'

'Amelia then. And it *isn't* suitable.'

'You only call me Miss Amelia when you're cross!'

'Or when you're tiresome.' He took her cloak. 'Or when I forget our different stations.'

He propped her bicycle against the pine tree beside him and flung her cloak over the saddle.

'*This*,' she held the velvet skirt wide, 'is the only kind of thing I have!'

'You have a riding skirt, Amelia. I've seen you in it often enough.'

'But it's far too bulky, James! I asked Stepmama to buy me bicycling bloomers but she said no. They are unladylike. And I am unladylike enough as it is.'

To her indignation, the dark head simply nodded. 'And now you're siding with *her*! And you know I loathe her!'

'I'm not siding with her. And I know nothing of the sort.'

Silently James began untethering the little aeroplane from the stakes that held it to the earth. Then he straightened and extinguished the storm lantern.

'Don't ask me *not* to come!' she said. 'Because I'm coming! You promised! You can't break your word!'

Smiling, he shook his head and put his finger on her lips. 'I'm not going to ask you anything of the sort. I'm just going to wish us luck.' He put his

11

hands on her shoulders and kissed her mouth lightly. 'If we succeed . . .'

'Oh, James!' She sighed. 'We're going to succeed, I know! You'll be rich! You'll be famous! There's *nothing* you won't be able to do!'

He smiled down at her sardonically. 'Even ask for the princess's hand in marriage!'

And though she knew that his tone was tinged with sarcasm, her spirits leapt. It was as if their soaring exuberance alone that day would have been sufficient to get them airborne.

The night was dissolving. Beyond the pines to the east came the first pink glimmer of that momentous dawn.

The light softly touched the swarthy almost gipsy-like face, the thick black hair above the dark blue eyes, as James bent over the little machine that was their creation. It glittered on the polished ash of the pusher propeller, on the white silk spread of the rectangular wings, one on top of the other, on the naked engine in front of the bamboo skeleton that led to the kite-like tailplane.

'Take hold of the starboard wing, Amelia! We'll push her out on to the slope!'

A kite was what had started it twelve years ago, a yellow diamond-shape for his eighth birthday. He had flown it not half a mile from here in a similar fresh breeze, watching its tail-waggling gyrations up into the sky as he paid out more and more line.

After that, he had spent all his spare time and what money he could on things that flew: bigger kites, balloons, model gliders, model aeroplanes driven by elastic and later by little petrol engines that he turned on his little lathe. Had he but known it, other men scattered over the world had been doing exactly the same thing for years: Pearce in New Zealand, the Wrights and Dr Langley in America, Karl Jatho in Germany, Mozhaisky in Russia, Ader in France.

Old Marsden, the village schoolmaster, a distant and impecunious relative of Mr Jerningham, his appointment a costless act of charity, had taught him well, trained him in design drawings. Marsden had need to leave his public school appointment because of some scandal involving the housemaster's wife, and was therefore prepared to accept a more humble and less scientific job than he was qualified for. All his skill and energy were lavished on the odd pupil like James who had brains and showed promise.

His father encouraged him too, helping him with the metal work and the sewing, for his mother would have none of it, saying it was not God's will to fly. Together his father and he had made their first full-sized glider, and James had nearly broken his neck on its first and last flight over Canford Cliffs. That was before the days of Amelia, before they had started to build this gawky angular baby that Amelia had christened Ajax – Amelia-James-Aircraft-Kiss – together in the secret workshop.

'That's enough, Amelia! She's dead into wind now!'

It was ironic, James thought, that while he and Amelia had worked to make this flying machine for which he felt certain the twentieth century would be memorable, Mr Jerningham had kept Jerningham village firmly anchored in Queen Victoria's departed reign. Choleric, hard-drinking and hard-pressed by creditors, to him daughters were an expensive nuisance. Maybe if he had been more liberal, if Amelia had been allowed, as she had wanted, to go to Oxford, she would never have taken up with James. And maybe if his own father hadn't gone off to the Boer War at Mr Jerningham's instigation, leaving him to look after the forge and take his place in the lifeboat crew, the friendship would never have ripened.

'What's that you're making?' she asked him on her first trip to the forge. Unlike the times that followed, Pegasus genuinely had cast a shoe and James interrupted his hammering of a thin strip of metal to attend to the animal.

'Oh, nothing you'd be interested in, Miss Amelia.'

'I'm interested in most things.' She eyed him pertly. Interested, yes. And not uninterested in him either, the little baggage, he thought. Until recently she had been away at school in Cheltenham, and he only remembered her distantly as a child.

'Well, let's take a look at that horse of yours first, Miss Amelia. Then I might show you.'

'Might indeed, damn you! *Must!*'

'Not must. If you say must, I won't show you at all.' He wiped his hands on a piece of rag, and walked past her, frowning. 'Which foot, Miss Amelia?'

'Right. Fore.'

He bent down, smoothing his hand gently over the horse's leg. Amelia tucked her crop under one arm and held the bridle. She whispered to Pegasus, but those bright blue eyes were on him. He could feel them as palpable as mischievous fingers, exploring, caressing. A baggage, not a doubt of it.

Slowly he lifted the horse's foot and examined it. There was still a torn bent nail in the hoof, and a tiny cut in the frog. He looked at her reprovingly. 'He's had a nasty knock.'

'That forest gate over by Darenth Wood.' Her chin went up. 'It's too high.'

'And you came at it too fast!'

'I didn't.'

'Must have done.'

'I don't need *you*,' she tapped his shoulder smartly with her riding crop, 'to tell me how to ride!'

His reaction was immediate. Still cradling the hoof, he grasped the crop with his free hand and sent it skimming across the forge into the different corner where his boy swept the shavings.

Amelia dropped the bridle and stamped her foot with rage. 'How dare you!' she gasped. 'Get my crop immediately! Bring it back this instant!'

James absorbed himself in extracting the nail. His heart beat with anger. Always quick in temper, he was nevertheless surprised at his own reaction. 'Pick it up yourself. Or leave it. Suit yourself.'

'I'll suit myself into never coming into this forge again!'

'And I'd suit myself into telling you to go now if it wasn't cruel to the horse.'

'God Almighty!' Amelia's cheeks were crimson. 'And I'll suit myself into telling my father!'

Distantly he realised that they were both behaving like children. Worse still, like children of equals, but he was too angry to think about it. He grunted derisively.

'I'll have you thrown out of the forge! You're only our tenants, don't forget! That'll be nice for your father, won't it? When he returns from fighting for his country. Evicted because he has a brainless oaf for a son!'

13

He stared at her furiously, longing to grab her by the shoulders and shake her till her pretty white teeth rattled for mentioning so airily what his mother most feared and he most hated. 'Well, I notice your father didn't go to fight for *his* country. And he's got a damned sight more of it than mine!'

The effect of his anger on Amelia was startling. She drew in her breath sharply and her lips remained parted. Her eyes widened. She took a step towards him. Then she covered her face with her hands. James immediately thought she was going to have one of those swooning fits which aristocratic young ladies were supposedly given to. Whatever she had, though, she would just have to get on with it. He was damned if he was going to take back anything or beg her silly pardon.

In the end, it was she who begged his. In a swift change of mood which he soon found out was characteristic, she dropped her hands. The blue eyes sparkled with suppressed laughter. 'I'm sorry,' she said with slightly exaggerated contrition. 'Your father is a very brave man. You have every right to be proud of him. And,' demurely, 'I shall pick up the crop, as you say.'

Immediately he was overcome with embarrassment. 'No, of course not, Miss Amelia.'

He put down the horse's hoof and rushed forward, trying to reach the dusty corner before her. They both bent to snatch at the crop. It was Amelia's agile fingers that managed to fasten over it first. Had he but known, that was the way it was to be – Amelia always that little bit faster. But all he knew then was that her face was close to his, her lips parted with laughter. And that had she been anyone else but Miss Amelia, he would have kissed her.

A little breathlessly she asked him, 'What's your Christian name?'

'James.'

'How old are you?'

'Twenty.'

'You look older.'

'That's because I work hard.'

She laughed. 'Ah, that's another provoking remark! You sound like one of those Socialists. You aren't, are you?'

'I'm not anything, Miss Amelia. Just a blacksmith.'

'Don't you ever want to do anything else?'

'Yes.'

'What?'

He held up the strip of metal on which he had been working when she came in. 'This.'

'What is it? Go on . . . tell me what you're making!'

'A turnbuckle.'

'What's that?'

'Part of an aeroplane.'

'And what's that?'

'A flying machine, Miss Amelia. I shall be the first man in the world to fly an aeroplane.'

'And where are you building this aeroplane?'

'In the old barn at the bottom of the forge smallholding.'

'Show it me.'

'No, Miss Amelia.' He turned back to the stove, 'I've work to do.'

14

'Show it me next time I come then.'

'All right,' he said to keep her quiet. There wouldn't be a next time, he felt sure, but she came back next day with Pegasus, and reminded him of his promise.

Diffidently, afraid that she would laugh, he led her out the back and through the orchard to the barn. 'There's not much to see, Miss Amelia. I've got the design and part of the frame. But that's about all.'

She stared reverently at the blueprint he had drawn on architect's cartridge paper and pinned on the timber wall, gazed wide-eyed at the skeleton wing made of bamboo, supported on woodcutters' trestles, touched with her fingertips his armoury of tools on the workbench, walked in silence to the far side where he kept what he wryly called his library – the textbooks, the periodicals, the clippings from magazines displayed on the wall. Leonardo da Vinci, Cayley, Lilienthal's *Bird Flight* and Chanute's gliders had been his tutors.

'But how did you know where to begin?'

'I read a lot,' he pointed to the books, 'and I watch everything that flies.' He led her over to the little glass case where he kept his sections of insects and bird wings. He handed her his magnifying glass. 'Would you like to take a look?'

She didn't shudder away. She examined his specimens thoughtfully.

'That wing section will have a sort of skin on it in the end.'

'Made of what?'

'Silk, if I can manage it.'

'But how will you get it all done? Won't it take ages? Won't lots of people fly before you?' And in the same breath, 'May I come and help you sometimes?'

He clamped his mouth shut at that and said tersely, 'No, Miss Amelia. Your parents wouldn't like it. Nor would I.'

She had come armed with a whole lot of trumped up excuses. Never had a horse suffered so with such ill-fitting shoes and such overgrown hooves. Each time she was allowed a glimpse of the edifice. Occasionally she made quite sensible suggestions. And then a month later she had come armed with a parcel of silk originally destined for petticoats. Under James's instruction, her deft little fingers stitched it into place over the wing-frame. From then on, it was assumed that when she came she worked. She displayed a remarkable aptitude and deftness that began to approach that of James himself. In initiative she often excelled him, producing Victoria's bicycle wheels as a Christmas present for the undercarriage. And then when there was the problem of how to make the silk on the wings sufficiently taut, she had come up with tapioca pudding, which was sometimes used by the maids to starch their lace caps. Two coats of tapioca drew the silk together tighter than a drum skin.

Her reward was to be allowed to accompany him on his Sunday birdwatch in the forest, to see the cygnets on the lake at old Cornford House, now deserted and overgrown and a haven for birds. Amelia had been insistent that she could and would come and that her parents would not object. Mr and Mrs Jerningham were too preoccupied with the expense of having Victoria presented that season to worry about Amelia. In any case, sketching flowers was a quite proper ladylike occupation.

Equipped with sketch pad and pencil, half a cold capon and two slabs of mint and currant pasty, Amelia had ridden to their rendezvous. She and James had picnicked by the edge of the lake and cast, as Amelia said, their bread upon the waters in the form of pastry crumbs. Then she had lain on her elbow in the sweet smelling spring grass. She had lifted her face up to him for the expected kiss. The sun was quite warm and the air very still like a held breath.

The reflected light on the water netted her face in a silver mesh. Just before he kissed her, he remembered thinking the net would be for him but at that moment he didn't care.

'You've kissed a lot of girls, haven't you?' she sighed when he finally released her.

'I'm not saying.'

'You don't have to. I can tell.' She stared moodily at the glittering water. 'Have you a girl in the village?'

He suddenly turned and cupped her face in both his hands and smiling said, 'Several.'

'Have you kissed them? Have you . . . ?'

'I'm not saying.' He stood up. 'But I'll say this. I'll not marry any of them if —'

And only to himself he added, 'I can't have you.'

From their observations on bird flight, on hollow bird bones, from kites and balloons and what others had written, the fuselage progressed well. But there remained one insuperable problem – the engine.

James knew exactly what he wanted. A firm called Tranmere of Southampton made light engines for pleasure boats. James had read all about them, had even been to the boatyard on the Hamble river to see if they had any secondhand stuff at a price he could afford. But they never had.

Then in July, just as Amelia was suggesting that she sold her ruby necklace, Fate had dealt him a trump card. At first it had not seemed to be anything more than a nuisance. It was a hot Sunday morning. His mother had gone to church grumbling apprehensively that he never accompanied her these days and that the Hall was bound to notice, when the lifeboat maroons went up. James cursed, put down the wing-panel he was gumming and dashed out of the forge.

It was downhill all the way to the lifeboat station at the estuary mouth, and he could do it in ten minutes. Even so, he had the farthest to come and the rest of the lads were pulling on their boots. 'A pc,' the cox had told him. 'In distress on Calmor rocks.'

James had taken his usual place forrard. It was high tide. There was a strong ground swell with a slight sea on top, and the double current at the estuary had been too much for the inexperienced sailor in a pleasure craft. It was soon apparent that the boat must have been going hell for leather – its bottom was ripped and it was wedged on the rocks, taking water fast.

The owners, a middle-aged couple from Birmingham, were weeping with gratitude when the lifeboat came alongside. As James lifted the wife over the side, she clung to him, begging him to talk her husband out of ever leaving land again. 'I wish the damned thing was at the bottom of the sea,' she wept. 'Promise me you'll make him see sense!'

'I promise,' James said.

He was as good as his word. That night at low tide, he rowed out to the wreck. The boat was just a broken cockleshell wedged in the fissure of the rocks by the weight of its engine. Carefully, James took out the screws, hacked the engine free, then tilted up the stern. There was a series of gurgles as the water flooded in, a cloud of phosphorescent bubbles. Then down she went.

A month's work on the damaged engine, and the flying machine had at last the power to get airborne. Three weeks later everything was ready for this moment.

'Shall I get on, James?'

He nodded. 'Tuck your skirt round you tight.'

'I will.'

She climbed on to the wing and lay down on the starboard side just in front of the engine.

'Petrol on!'

She put out her left hand and turned the tiny brass tap. Just below her, James finished off his checks. 'Are you ready?'

He had worked his way right round the machine. Coming up over the horizon the sun glinted palely on his face as he stood beside the propeller. 'Ready.'

'Switch on!'

'On.'

He swung the propeller with all his strength. A cough. 'More throttle!' he called.

Again he swung it. This time there was a kick and a whirring sound. A puff of castor-oil smoke materialised like a genie. He flung himself down on the quaking quivering wing beside her.

There were only two controls placed just in front of him. As he took hold of the joystick in his left hand and the throttle in his right, for the first time he permitted himself a wide, excited, almost schoolboy grin.

'Here we go!'

The engine roared. Then they were bumping forward – uneasily at first, jerkily, then gathering a lurching speed. Every roughness of the ground banged through her body, her teeth chattered, her feet were hot from the engine, her mouth dry with excitement. As the grass and the gorse shrubs whipped by, she kept fearing the frame was going to shake to pieces, that they hadn't glued it strongly enough, or stitched it enough times.

Then James pulled back on the stick. The nose went up like a horse at a fence. They seemed to be hit amidships as if the ground was giving them one last thump. She experienced a sudden indescribable sensation. A lightness of body and of spirit.

The earth fell away like a nerveless hand. The discomfort vanished. The banging quietened. They had broken through the Looking Glass into a different world. Entered a new awesome dimension. Touched, it seemed, infinity and eternity.

'James,' she shrieked above the weird screech of the wind in the piano wires. 'You've done it!'

It was as if the words broke the brief spell. Just as James turned into the sudden dazzle of the risen sun, a quick gust of wind tumbled Amelia's hair, plucked out the blue ribbons and sent them whirling, sinister as snakes, to be sucked round the spinning propeller.

17

The engine coughed. The left wing dropped. There was a frantic juddering as James tried to straighten Ajax with the rudder. Amelia felt the aircraft tilt sideways, slide dizzily, uncontrollably, till abruptly they crashed back to earth again.

Then nothing. She could remember nothing.

She still seemed to be flying in limitless space but in total darkness and in no aeroplane. Distantly she thought she could hear birds singing. She must be dead. She wondered if James had been killed too, and stretched out her hand in the darkness for his.

She came to, clutching a handful of heather. She could smell crushed grass, the fumes of burnt castor-oil, the scent of pine needles, and a smell that was peculiarly reassuring to her nostrils, that of James's leather jacket.

A light weight pressed on her chest. She half opened her eyes. James was kneeling over her, his ear against her chest. She was torn between curiosity and her desire to prolong the moment. She let out a little moan and fluttered her eyelids. James raised his head and peered searchingly into her face. His own was pale and streaked with oil, his eyes like dark blue flames.

'Are you hurt, Amelia?' He put his hand on her forehead, stroking back her hair. There was a lump on the side of her head just between her ear and her temple, which he explored delicately with his fingers. 'It must've knocked you out, but it doesn't seem too bad. Does your head ache?'

'No.'

'D'you feel sick?'

'No. Just sick about what happened.'

He shrugged. Then he ran his hands expertly over her arms and legs. Almost, she thought, with a little bubble of hysterical laughter rising in her throat, as if she were a mare. When his hands had slid down to her ankles, she sat up, rested her weight on her hands and squinted down.

Her dress was in ruins, her petticoat torn, her stockings so laddered that her kness emerged like small bruised apples.

'Does it hurt when I do that?' He clasped her ankle and rotated her foot.

'No.' She shook her head vigorously. 'It feels nice.'

He frowned and avoided looking at her. 'Can you move your toes?'

'I think so.'

'Then show me.'

Obediently she lifted her left foot and, blinking her eyes, trying to get her surroundings into focus, wiggled her toes. Her shoes had been torn off. She could see them lying by the aircraft. She supposed she must be shocked, but apart from a feeling of unreality, of not belonging, and a certain slowness of thought, she was not aware of it.

'If I scrape this piece of twig down your arm, Amelia, can you feel it?'

'Of course I can.'

'And you can see quite clearly? No blurring?'

'Quite clearly.' She put her hand on his arm. 'But what about you, James? Are you hurt?'

'Not a scratch.' He spoke brusquely. Angry with her, no doubt, and sick with disappointment.

'And what about Ajax?'

'I haven't looked yet.'

'Was I more important?'

'Of course.'

She sighed. He made as if to get up. 'So long as you're not hurt . . . '

'Oh, but I am.' She spread her arms wide. 'I'm hurt that it was all my fault.' Her eyes filled with tears.

'You mean the ribbons?'

She nodded.

'No, no, Amelia. They had nothing to do with it. I couldn't get the wing up. That rudder is no use. There must be some other control we need to use. And the engine was faltering anyway.' He smiled wryly, 'Stolen goods.'

'But you flew! No one can take that away!' As he bent over her, she threw her arms round his neck, pulling him down so that his lips were only an inch above hers. 'We were the first in the world to fly in an aeroplane!'

'You're sure you're all right?'

'I will be when you kiss me.'

Just as he put his lips on hers, she murmured, 'Of course it hurts just a little *here.*'

She began to unfasten the two remaining buttons of her bodice, and pushed down the lace edging of her camisole to show her small white breast. 'It's as if my ribs are bruised.'

She was not conscious of an actual desire to seduce James. But she desperately wanted the warmth and reassurance of his body against hers. It was as if now their lovemaking was inevitable and some older cleverer woman inside herself had taken over.

She guided his hand and it was not to her ribs. She shivered as his fingers touched her breast. 'You're not hurt at all!' he exclaimed, half-angrily, half-laughing, kissing her roughly.

He tried to end it there, but she clasped him to her, her mouth clinging to his, letting the warmth of her feeling somehow flow between them. His hands began to explore her body. They were capable and surprisingly tender and knowledgeable.

She gave a little hungry sigh and moved closer to him. She felt a sudden thrill of pain shot through with fear. Then it was like that soaring upward ecstasy of flight.

She had promised herself that the day would make history and so it was doing – though of a different sort and by a more tortuous and painful route.

Like the flight, Amelia's ecstasy was brief. It crashed to earth as abruptly and totally as the aircraft had done. She lay for a moment biting her lip. Then she scrambled to her feet and looked around her in a cold damp sweat of guilt and dismay.

The flying machine was in ruins. Their ambitions were in ruins. And she herself was in ruins.

Though it was not in her nature to despair totally, the shock of the last half-hour caught up with her. Her teeth chattered. She felt sick and dismayed. If she had expected words of comfort and love, they were not forthcoming. Perhaps James felt the same. Perhaps now he felt he would never find fame, never get away from being a blacksmith. He stood beside her, saying nothing. A new and heavy constraint had come between them.

19

In a curiously withdrawn silence, they turned away from the wreckage and tramped up the slope. There was no sound but the thump of James's boots and the rustling of her skirt on the grass. Still neither of them spoke. She watched him wheel away her bicycle from the pine trunk, regarding him with a stranger's eyes. It seemed a century ago, another existence almost, that they had first set out. Yet it must have been less than an hour. The sun was just above the pines. She wanted to ask James the time by his watch, always supposing his watch was still working, but she didn't want to be the first to break the silence. She didn't even speak as he draped the cloak round her shoulders. She nodded her thanks, looking searchingly into his face to interpret his mood, but his expression was closed up.

Holding the bike steady for her to step on to the pedal, he spoke at last – but superficially, not speaking to the real her. 'Are you sure you're all right?'

And when she nodded, he added in a low voice, 'I'm sorry. Very sorry.'

'About what?' she asked sharply.

'You know well enough, Amelia.'

She said nothing. Somehow it was all wrong that James should be sorry. Being sorry implied regret, repentance, wishing the act undone. It proved to her that the events of the morning had not drawn them closer together but had made them strangers.

'And I'm sorry about your aeroplane,' she said, in a cool stranger's voice.

'You make it sound . . . ' he began angrily and then broke off with a helpless gesture and tightened his mouth.

She waited a moment to see if he would say anything else, and when he did not, she pressed down hard on the pedal and wobbled off. She half-hoped he would detain her, ask her to say goodbye properly. But he simply strode a few paces beside her and asked, 'Shall you be able to get in all right?'

She pedalled harder and drew away from him.

'I don't give a damn!' she flung over her shoulder, hearing the words even then like little stones falling between them. The kind of words you picked up and stored and remembered, words which grew harder with the years.

She didn't look back to see his expression, but she slowed her pace, wondering if he would call after her. They had made no arrangements for their next meeting. No sound came from him. She reached the turn before the road and glanced quickly round.

He was a diminished figure, tramping head down in the direction of the wreckage. Just for a moment, she almost wheeled round and went careering after him. If only he had turned to look after *her*, she would have done. But he was totally absorbed in getting back to the wreck.

Squinting up at the sun she decided it must be close on seven. She would need a great deal of luck if she was to slip back to her room unobserved. And luck that morning had been conspicuous only by its absence. She cycled fast along the highway, pedalling for all she was worth. She paused at the lodge gates, put both her feet on the ground while she drew her hood over her head and her cloak tightly round her, vaguely hoping, if she was spotted, the lodgekeeper might think it was Victoria, out on some errand of good to the poor.

Had she not done so, she might just have missed the rider, approaching along the road towards her in the opposite direction from which she had come.

As it was, she heard the sound of hooves at a canter. Almost immediately, the rider rounded the curve of the park wall. They came face to face.

Sir Frederick Haybury, who had recently inherited the neighbouring estate, was as delighted by the unexpected encounter as she was horrified. He reined in his horse and dismounted, approaching her with a smile in which pleasure and admiration were most soothingly blended. He was tall and slenderly built. He had a thin face, a narrow high-bridged nose, auburn hair and golden eyes under sandy brows. He sported a small Van Dyck beard which had grown a shade darker and brighter than his hair. Altogether more foxy than the fox himself, Amelia had thought when she had first met him in the hunting field. But this morning, his pale skin flushed with the ride and perhaps the unexpected meeting, he looked more like Hals' portrait of the Laughing Cavalier.

'Why, Amelia!' He brought his horse to a standstill and leapt down from the saddle. 'How very fortunate! How delightful to meet you!'

'Indeed it is, Sir Frederick,' she agreed as warmly as she could.

He half-extended his hand, but she kept both hers firmly gripping the handlebars and planted her feet on either side of the bike, praying earnestly that her cloak would not fall open to disclose the state of her gown. 'It's rare,' she went on, smiling, 'that I meet anyone when I'm out cycling.'

'Nor I when I'm out riding.' He took a step nearer and looked down at her bicycle. 'They're much recommended, I understand.'

'For health? Oh, yes, indeed! And I can recommend them for pleasure.'

Her voice sounded a little breathless and over-enthusiastic, but he took that as an added kindness to himself. A manifestation that the pleasure of the meeting was not altogether one sided.

'And do you always ride so early, Amelia?'

'Oh, no, not always! But this morning I woke early.'

'Perhaps some morning, we could arrange . . . with your parents' permission of course . . .'

She nodded, vaguely smiling. She would have agreed to almost anything to be allowed to gain the safety of her room, to tidy and wash away and forget the events of the morning. Sensing her impatience and mindful not to push his luck too far, he turned away and prepared to mount. 'Meantime,' he smiled, 'you must allow me the privilege of escorting you to your door.'

'My parents . . . ' she began doubtfully.

'Naturally I wouldn't call. But I would like to accompany you. Merely up the drive to your home?' He swung himself up into the saddle, smiling down at her doubtful face. 'Come, let's race! Let's see who will be the faster, you on your bicycle or I at a walk!'

Always one for a race, she laughed eagerly. '*I* shall be the faster!'

'Then shall we have a bet on it?'

'You'd lose!'

'I'll take that risk!'

'Right!' She had already mounted her machine, not pausing for the bet to be named, which was just as well, because the drive rose steadily towards the porticoed house and she had not allowed for starting from a standstill. Besides, Sir Frederick's dun gelding had a long and capable stride. Although she was pedalling hard, Amelia nevertheless fell behind.

21

She arrived breathlessly at the forecourt, hot and clammy under her cloak. She dismounted and rested her bicycle against the stone entrance steps. Frederick smiled down at her flushed face. 'You concede defeat?'

'By a short head.'

'And the bet?'

'We didn't make one.'

'We didn't actually *name* it. But I'm sure you're sport enough to pay a small forfeit?'

She nodded doubtfully. Though she stood with her back to the house, she knew that the clatter of hooves and the sound of their voices had not gone unobserved. She flicked a glance over her shoulder at the treble rows of long Georgian windows, now glazed gold in the bright morning sun.

Then Sir Frederick named his forfeit. It was such a small undemanding one – permission to call on her that Friday – that she agreed to it immediately. Besides, she had found the encounter soothing and somehow restorative. She also shrewdly guessed that it would prove to be her one and only stroke of luck that day. A guess borne out by the fact that though by now the family was stirring, no one interrupted her passage back to her bedroom.

At luncheon, her parents' attitude approached the affectionate. Stepmama interrupted Victoria's discussion of her wedding plans to enquire of Amelia if she had enjoyed her ride. Her father complimented her on her bicycling skill. Amelia's announcement that, with her parents' approval, Sir Frederick would call that Friday worked like a magic talisman.

When Frederick arrived, Amelia's mood of mild gratitude towards him continued. By all the standards of her time, he was a good match. Well-born, rich, courageous on the hunting field, a clever Member of Parliament. He also appeared very amiable to women but had never been involved in any known scandal. And he made such manifest efforts to please *her*, in contrast to James who treated her roughly, used her and then despised her for it.

When, after tea, Stepmama suggested they might like a stroll in the garden, Amelia made no demur. She led Frederick through the rose garden and graciously gave him permission to pick one to put in her hair. She felt a little pang of anguish when he slid the stem through her topknot of curls where three days before she had sported the blue ribbons. But the anguish was brief, the sun was warm and Frederick's gaze ardent.

When he suggested they stroll further from the house towards the lake, she still made no demur. She allowed him to lead her into the willow arbour, agreed that they should rest awhile on the rustic seat. When he took both her hands in his and asked permission to kiss her, she almost laughed. And then, contrite at such flippancy, she offered up her face and closed her eyes.

The kiss had the excellent qualities of being gentle and soon done with. It was almost without sensation. It caused no galloping heartbeat, no unrefined cravings of her body, no heights, no depths, no guilts . . .

But it did most sweetly restore her to herself again.

TWO

That same Friday, the last load of bamboo, oiled silk and fractured metal was carted by James into the forge.

'So it came to nought,' Mrs March muttered to him over their evening meal. 'Just like I said!'

'What came to nought, Mother?' James asked her tersely.

'That,' she narrowed her eyes and her mouth worked sourly as if she were tasting vinegar, 'that *flying* machine of your'n!'

Ever since she had spied him bringing in the first load, Mrs March had mumbled darkly to herself. But she had not voiced her scorn so openly till that night. She could not communicate with her son, but she could feel him. She knew she could go just so far and no further with James. He had a quick temper and a fierce pride that frightened her. But that evening she also sensed his vulnerability. She could not remember when she had seen him so low and dispirited.

'I've not said anything before. I know how to hold my tongue.'

'You've made your feelings clear enough, Mother.'

'Why shouldn't I make them clear? It's unnatural.' What she really meant was that it was black magic, that only witches flew. 'You're not meant to fly. You're not a bird. You're a big heavy man.'

'I know what I am, Mother. I know what I can do.'

She said bitterly, 'You'll never learn.'

'Oh, quiet, Mother!' He shoved his plate away. 'It could've worked.'

'But it didn't.'

'Next time it will.'

James got up from the table, walked over to the fire and kicked a lump of peat back with the toe of his boot. He rested his arm on the mantelpiece and stared into the glowing embers, wondering if there would ever be a next time for the machine or for Amelia.

'An' when'll that be?'

'Sometime when I'm ready.'

'Sometime never!' She stood up and grabbed his plate. 'You wasting all this good food?'

'I'm not hungry.'

Mrs March, her head held stiffly on her neck, crossed the kitchen floor and scraped the plate into the pig bucket with noisy exasperation. She suspected, but she dare not give substance to her suspicions even in her own mind, that James was as upset by something to do with Miss Amelia Jerningham as he was about the flying machine. Amelia and James had been discretion itself, but Mrs

23

March was aware of Amelia's trips to the forge. Though she had not exchanged a dozen words with the girl, she had taken an instant dislike to her. In fact, she had disliked her long before she met her – from the day Amelia was born.

Mrs March had been born in the workhouse and brought up in an orphanage, which went some way to explaining her seriousness of character, her lack of frivolity or any expectation that life might be joyful. She had been given the name of Mollie Smith, that being, the master of the orphanage had explained, a suitable illegitimate name and though at the time the meaning of that was beyond her, it soon became clear that like most of the other inmates, she was a bastard. The orphanage was even more a workplace than the workhouse. Under contract to do laundry for hotels and hospitals, the inmates worked frantically.

James had not inherited all his dreams from his father, because Mrs March could remember one fantasy (though one only) that occurred throughout her childhood. That was of the sudden appearance of well-to-do parents – especially a mother – who would have discovered her as their missing child, spirited away by gipsies who came to the back door of the orphanage selling pegs and pots and pans.

When Mollie was twelve years old, this fantasy came the nearest it would ever get to reality. Mollie was paraded along with the other girls who had reached similar maturity before the wives of the local gentry. This parade took place twice a year, and promising girls were chosen to be petty-maids. She had lain awake the whole of the preceding night, not sure whether she was more terrified of being selected for some strange house inhabited by strange smart people in the strange outside world, or being left rejected in the orphanage, whose ills were numerous and cruel but which at least were familiar.

She had stared round-eyed at the smartness of the ladies, and early in the proceedings found herself chosen by the smartest and most beautiful of them all, the first Mrs Jerningham, an unpredictable, very young lady who inspired devotion amongst her servants and a fond exasperation amongst her equals.

Towards her, Mollie poured what was left of her pent-up devotion. Though she never rose to more than second housemaid, she remained in her service until she was twenty-eight, when James's father, years her junior, was summoned to Jerningham Hall to mend the guttering over the servants' sitting-room window. He had fallen in love with her serious face, her grave and beautiful eyes, so different from the willing village lassies. He was adventurous and jovial, clever and dashing, with a sense of humour and great inventiveness, and not a whit better than a lusty man of his age ought to be.

Perhaps by then she was too frozen in her ways to be melted by the warmth of his personality. She was a good and faithful wife. She kept an austere but spotless home. She sewed and cooked, could scald and smoke a side of pig, make brown and black pudding. But she rarely smiled and never laughed. Her great fear was that her home and independence might one day vanish, and that she would end as she had begun – in the workhouse.

'Did you try and fly with you inside it?'

'Of course I did, Mother. How else?'

'You might've bin killed!'

'Well, I wasn't.'

'With your father away like he is.' Momentarily she closed her eyes as though not to see the total insecurity of her world, 'You should tek more care.'

James didn't deign to answer. Both her son and her husband were men she would never hope to understand. They were clever and bold and had independent ideas. But they were humble working men and they ought to have been none of these things. The master of the orphanage, a religious man who starved and beat her into the ways of righteousness, she could understand. It was his place. She could even understand Mr Jerningham, who would strike her if she was clumsy and came of a night to the parlourmaids' room when he was so inclined. But he was gentry. No more should she seek to question their ways than she should question the unpredictable ways of the Almighty.

Thinking of the gentry brought her back to Miss Amelia. Besides the dangers of the flying machine, there was the danger from her. Mrs March had seen the way James looked at Miss Amelia. It frightened her like she used to be frightened of the sound of her own husband's footfall on the stairs. One familiar act, one laying of a hand by such as James on Miss Amelia and Mr Jerningham would have them all thrown out neck and crop without a roof over their heads.

At the thought of how fragile was her security on all sides Mrs March shivered, and immediately James came over and put his arm round her shoulders. She didn't like physical contact even from him, so she shrugged his arm off.

'Oh, suit yourself,' he said angrily, more irritable than she had ever known him. 'There's no pleasing some women!'

She shot him a hard straight look. 'It depends on the woman you seek to please.'

'You, for God's sake!'

'Oh aye?' she sniffed derisively. 'And don't take the Lord's name in vain in this house.'

He turned his back on her and returned to the fire, holding back his anger with difficulty.

'If you want to please me,' she went on, addressing his broad unbending back, 'you'll give up that foolish machine. If you've got spare time, mek something useful. Lamps, candlesticks, gates even.'

'No, Mother,' he said through gritted teeeth. 'I'll make no candlesticks.'

She mistook his quiet deadly tone for one of near mildness. 'All right then, son. Don't work in yer spare time. Enjoy yourself. There's some bonny girls in the village.'

James suddenly brought his fist down on the mantelpiece. 'Hold your tongue, Mother! Mind your own bloody business!'

James had recovered now from the first sickening disappointment of the crash. Given a bit of money and a lot of time he could eventually mend the machine. But neither time nor money would mend his relationship with Amelia. He had hoped every day for some word from her. She had always made the first move. Because of their differing stations, it had to be she who came to him. He couldn't march up to the Hall and ask to see her. He didn't dare to send a message even by the pettymaid Sarah, whose family lived on the other side of the green.

So he had just ground his teeth and waited, consumed with guilt about his own behaviour. In the cold light of subsequent days, it looked increasingly callous and brutish. He had taken unfair advantage of a young and innocent girl. Deflowered and despoiled a virgin. One so far above his station that her father would have had him horse-whipped. And he had done this monstrous act when the girl was frightened and shocked and in no condition to repel his advances. When she needed, indeed had every right to expect, his protection. No felon ever had a more ruthless prosecutor than that which James provided for himself.

But there were other times, when he was sick of staring out of the forge looking for her, when his mood seesawed, when his clever brain provided a very adequate defence. It reminded him that Amelia had been more than willing, might even be said to have encouraged him. But these moods and this defence did not last long, and he felt they were as contemptible as his taking of Amelia. He saw himself as she must see him – a rough-necked brutish oaf with a lot of imagination, a little talent and even less self-control. An oaf who would now never escape the forge in time to make his fortune and be in a position to marry her. It was indeed as his mother had said, sometime *never*.

Amelia was not interested in him or his eroplane. She was just amusing herself, as the rich sometimes did with the poor. Aeroplanes were different, he was different. But she had tired of both, and as soon as things might turn difficult, she had wanted rid of him. Her mother, the first Mrs Jerningham, had been like that. Or so his father said – a tease, a baggage. But Mr March had only dared to whisper such information to his son. The first Mrs Jerningham was the nearest thing to a saint in Mrs March's eyes.

James could still remember his mother's tears at Mrs Jerningham's death when he was three. She had died giving birth to Amelia. Though the rest of the village kept drawn curtains only till the funeral, the forge cottage curtains were drawn for a week. The mantelpiece he had his hand on now was festooned in black crêpe, and they all wore black armbands.

She had even insisted James went to pay his respects to the dead Mrs Jerningham, holding him up to look in the coffin as it lay on the catafalque in the flickering light of the candles.

'It *is* my business!' His mother came over to the mantelpiece. 'I'd like a grandson afore I die!'

It was as though his mother had sensed what he was thinking about. Now simultaneously they both remembered that scene seventeen years ago. And it was his mother's bitterness he found frightening.

'It's a pity,' she whispered hoarsely. 'It's a pity it wasn't the baby what died!'

A fortnight later, Amelia Jerningham did in fact wish she was dead.

Something had occurred – or rather not occurred – which sent her into the depths of apprehension and despair. Amelia, ever the optimist, studied the calendar, recounted her dates, tried desperately to make them different. But without success.

Sketchy though her ideas were on copulation and pregnancy she had heard enough from servants and the rare informed girl at Cheltenham to know that the one frequently followed the other with unwanted and unlucky regularity, and that the first sign of pregnancy was this.

'Oh, why didn't I think before that this might happen?' she asked her pale reflection in the mirror that Friday morning. James hadn't forced himself on her. She should have stopped and thought. But somehow she always suffered from this feeling that she bore a charmed life, that it would all come right in the end.

Now it was all coming wrong. And she had no one to talk to about it. Her stepmother was out of the question. She was a hard woman. James would be made to suffer with the utmost severity. So would his pale gloom-laden mother. God or the Devil alone knew what the Jerninghams would conjure up for them. Victoria was strait-laced. Nanny, who might have helped, had been found another post years ago.

Amelia was still sitting at the dressing-table, when Sarah came in with her tray of morning tea. Sarah was a stumpy round-faced twelve-year-old from Jerningham village. She was the middle child in a family of eleven. Brought up in a two-bedroomed cottage, she knew more about life than the most experienced girl of Amelia's acquaintance.

'Come over here, Sarah. Put the tray down on the dressing-table. No, don't go. I want you to brush my hair.'

The round face broke into a broken-toothed smile. Sarah put down the tray, rushed into the bathroom to wash her hands and picked up the silver-backed brush. They both understood that the invitation to brush Miss Amelia's hair was also the invitation to a little gossip. It remained only to find out what the gossip was to be about.

It was about pregnancy, about which unfortunate girls and women in the village were known to have 'fallen'. And what their symptoms were. Sarah, even at her tender age had already resolved that she would let no man touch her. She would sooner go into a nunnery or the workhouse. She had heard her father (and he was by no means a bad husband) at work in the next bedroom. She had heard the words 'I've fallen' so often in her lifetime that they were worse to her than any oath.

'Well, Miss,' she whispered in answer to the question from Amelia. 'There's me mother for a start. She reckons' – Sarah's eyes filled with tears; her mother was thirty-nine and tired – 'she's overdue. An' . . . she were retching . . . an' she got them grey marks . . .'

'Grey marks! Grey marks? *Where*, Sarah?'

'Under her eyes, Miss.'

Immediately Amelia's hand almost flew to those steely circles under her own wide and startled eyes. But with an effort of will she clenched her hands to her sides. Sarah, brushing absorbedly, avoided Miss Amelia's reflection.

'Is she upset? Your mother?'

'Oh, aye, Miss. She's gonna try the pennyroyal agin. Like the gipsies told her last time.'

'Pennyroyal. What's that?'

''Erb, Miss. Brings on the flux.'

'Where did your mother get this herb?'

'Mebbe from the gipsies. Mebbe from the forest. Mebbe from the 'erbalist.'

An expedition to Lyndhurst the next day on the pretext of buying gloves for a rout she was to attend with Frederick gave Amelia the opportunity to slip into Mr Seligman's, the herbalist.

Further enquiries from Sarah elicited the fact that her mother soaked the herb overnight in hot water and drank the resulting infusion in the morning. It worked, Sarah said, in a matter of days. Hope kept Amelia's spirits buoyed. She actually enjoyed the rout with Frederick. In his company not only did she escape her stepmother's watchful eye, but she could almost forget James and her possible condition. But the following Saturday, when the pennyroyal had failed to work its doubtful magic, she could not forget. More depressing still, Sarah returned from her day off visiting her family much relieved and bearing the good news that her mother was in great pain with the flux. The pregnancy, if pregnancy it had been, was over.

When Frederick called at Jerningham Hall that afternoon, he found a quiet, biddable Amelia. With her stepmother's permission he led her to the conservatory, that traditional, honoured background for proposals, and there, amidst the supposedly aphrodisiac scent of the lilies and camellias, asked her to honour him by becoming his wife.

Amelia gave him a vague abstracted smile in return, but it was all he seemed to expect. He broke off one of the camellias and asked permission to put it in her hair. Then, not dissatisfied, he returned her to Stepmama. The moment he left, Amelia ran upstairs to her room, took out the bottle of pennyroyal infusion from the back of her wardrobe, and drank the remains. But she was without hope now of it working. She knew she was pregnant. She had an inner certainty. She felt like a rabbit in one of the gamekeeper's traps – glazed with fright, unable to see which way to go.

She couldn't possibly tell James. She'd done him enough harm already. And anyway, how did she know that he wanted her? She couldn't stay at home unmarried and have the baby. Nor was she going to be able to get rid of it. What could she do?

In the end, the way seemed to come about inevitably. Frederick was assiduous in his calls, undemanding in their expeditions. She found it easier to be with him than under the sharp eyes of her stepmother.

That winter of 1903 was long in coming. There were golden days in November when the sun shone as warmly as late summer. Halfway through that month Frederick and Amelia went for a long ride in the forest. Sitting eating the lunch which Mrs Henshaw had packed for them, Frederick suddenly said, 'If we are to be married at the same time as your sister, you should tell me soon.'

'I shall tell you tonight,' she had answered.

It was almost as if she sensed the encounter to come. Halfway home, riding side by side on the outskirts of the village, they had overtaken a green and white painted cart that was all too familiar.

'Good afternoon, Sir. Good afternoon, Ma'am.' Despite his neutral tone, James had shot her a bitter look, staring at her with narrowed eyes till they had trotted past. She tried to feel an answering bitterness but she couldn't. She wanted most desperately to call to him. 'It is not as you seem to think!'

But then that would not have been true either.

She dug her heels viciously into Pegasus's side as if to squeeze the misery out of herself. The horse crabbed unhappily across the High Street. Frederick shot her a look of mild surprise, pressing his heels into his own horse to keep pace with her. Half a mile between the village and the lodge gates, she reined in, her mind made up.

She gave an exclamation of annoyance. 'I think he's about to cast a shoe.' She met Frederick's eyes innocently. 'Perhaps it would be safest to let the blacksmith hammer the nails in.'

At once he was all concern. He suggested she dismount and lead her horse or, better still, change mounts. But she dismissed both suggestions. She must speak to James. She would have preferred that Frederick did not accompany her, but could think of no way of getting rid of him.

James had only just returned to the forge and was donning his heavy leather jerkin. His apprentice was blowing up the fire with the long handled bellows. She saw his fists tighten as the two riders filled the entrance to the forge.

'Yes, sir?' He ignored her.

'Miss Amelia's horse!' Something in the blacksmith's manner irritated Frederick and he spoke imperiously. 'Take a look at the shoes!'

'I will if she'll get down, Sir.'

Immediately, Amelia stretched out her hand towards James for him to help her dismount. But he stepped back, wiping his hands on the sides of his trousers as if they were not fit to soil so delicate a lady's hands. Immediately, Frederick jumped down and it was he who took her hands.

Even so, Amelia still tried. She refused to allow anyone else to hold Pegasus's head, and when James came to pick up the front feet, she rested her cheek against the muzzle of the horse and said softly, 'James . . .'

'Yes, Miss Amelia?'

He straightened and squared his shoulders. There was a fixed cold shadow behind his eyes. His lips curled contemptuously.

'It is not . . .' she began.

Just for a moment, their whole future hung in the balance. One sympathetic word, one tender look, the smallest encouragement and everything would have been different. If he had only spoken to her, sent her the message she longed to hear in that secret telegraphy of theirs, she would have done a cartwheel of sheer joy, there right on the floor of the forge. Frederick, Papa, Stepmama, Victoria – she would have sent them all packing. She wouldn't have minded anything, no matter what happened – so long as he still loved her.

'It is not . . .'

'Yes, Miss Amelia?'

Daunted by his coldness and hostility, she gave up. 'It is not that foot,' she finished feebly.

He bent impatiently, and picked up the other foot. Then he said curtly, 'It is not any of 'em, Miss Amelia!' He addressed himself to Frederick. 'Nought wrong wi' them shoes! Nought but a bit of rough riding!'

Outside the forge again, riding chastened down the High Street, Amelia didn't reply when Frederick remarked, 'He's an impudent surly fellow, that blacksmith! I'm surprised your father tolerates him.'

She said nothing. Not one word all the way through the village and up the drive to the Hall.

But later that evening she gave Frederick the answer that he wanted.

THREE

That Amelia had been flaunting her eligible admirer in his face, James had no doubt. It was her way of telling him that she had found someone else; there was a much more suitable competitor for her favours.

To take his mind off her, he threw himself into repairing the aeroplane. He had worked out that the real cause of the crash had been the inadequacy of the rudder. There must be a third control surface, probably located on the wing. With carefully fashioned bamboo, he began rebuilding the frame. The patching of the silk was difficult – he had not Amelia's skilful sewing fingers. The metalwork he could do, but it was laborious and the allowed tolerances took hours to meet.

Certainly he had flown – but a short hop only, down a slope and without witnesses. If he could only get more time to work on it, he might still be the first officially recognised man to fly in a heavier-than-air craft. And if he did, then fame and fortune might still be his. Even at this eleventh hour, he might still win Amelia away from his rich rival.

Snow fell lightly on the last Thursday of November. 'Just like Christmas,' his mother said, making an effort to be cheerful as she set out the breakfast.

They had just finished their porridge when there was a loud clattering on the door knocker. She wiped her hands and hastened to open it. The postman's bicycle was leaning against the wall.

He handed her a letter with a South African stamp and an Army franking. She fled with it back to James, her face flushed, their recent coldness forgotten. She was a slow and unsure reader. She struggled with the letter, her pinched lips moving, her flush deepening.

'Here, son!' She handed it to James. 'Make sure it's what it seems to say.'

'Is it good news?'

'I think so.'

He shook the letter out. *Dearest wife,* it said. *This is to tell you that they are sending me home at last. I have my papers now and am off to catch a boat from Capetown. I hope you are well and the lad. I should be back in England middle January. Your loving husband.*

'Read it aloud,' urged his mother. For in her opinion if bad news travelled fast, good news was usually false. 'Mek sure it's right!'

He did as she asked. 'It's true, Mother! He's coming home!'

He threw his arms round her and this time she didn't repel his embrace. He felt as if a load had rolled off his back. All might not yet be too late. There was just the faintest glimmer of hope. His father was coming home and he would take over the forge again. At last he'd be free. He'd be able to leave home. He'd get himself in with people who knew about flying machines. He was young enough to succeed, to return triumphant. To claim, as he had said not altogether derisively, the princess's hand in marriage.

In their mutual joy, he had to sound one sober note. 'Of course, Mother, when Father does come back, I'll be going off. I'm going to strike out on my own.'

She didn't listen. It was rare that she showed such pleasure in anything. They would even have a supper. Keep the Christmas pig and celebrate his return. Invite the other villagers in. 'And we'll pray for his safe journey, won't we, son? There's a lot of sea between us still.'

'Of course we will, Mother.'

'Will yer come to church wi' me on Sunday then? Will you kneel side by side, so we can ask together?'

After a moment's hesitation, for James regarded himself as a freethinker and besides there was the danger of seeing Amelia, he said, 'If you'd like that, Mother.'

'I would, son.'

She actually almost smiled, as side by side three days later they entered the village church of St Swithin, and knelt on the carpet-covered hassocks. The church smelled of candlewax and chrysanthemums. Though they were early and the church half-empty, Mrs March knew her place, and they secreted themselves at the back.

Nevertheless Amelia saw them as soon as she came in. For a moment, her face went almost as white as the little fur toque she wore and her eyes burned bright. Sir Frederick Haybury had given her his arm, but she suddenly freed her hand when she saw James and tucked it in her white muff and went sailing down the aisle, her head held high and her sapphire velvet coat skirt whispering behind her. She was followed by her sister Victoria and the Honourable Henry Tyrell and Mr Jerningham with the second Mrs Jerningham. A family occasion indeed!

James whispered as much to his mother.

'That's because they're reading Miss Victoria's banns,' she whispered back. 'She's a good girl, they say, Miss Victoria. Just like her mother!'

Everything proceeded normally, except that Amelia seemed to be avoiding James's eyes. Mr Jerningham read the first lesson, the Honourable Henry Tyrell the second. And then just before the sermon, things began to go terribly wrong for James. It became evident why Amelia would not look at him as soon as the Rector began his announcements.

'I publish the banns of marriage of Victoria Jerningham, spinster of this parish, and Henry George Tyrell, bachelor of Knightsbridge. And I publish the banns of marriage of Amelia Jerningham, spinster of this parish, and Frederick Fitzpaine Haybury, bachelor of Haybury parish. Both for the first time of asking.'

Although on the morning of their wedding, the two brides had been told to sleep until ten, Amelia woke as the night sky began to pale. She could see the outline of the bare winter trees, swaying in a light wind. Her first thought was that it was good flying weather. Her second, with a dull disbelieving ache, that this was her wedding day. And the third, suddenly the most urgent of all, was that she felt sick.

31

She slid from her bed and knelt for a moment on the upholstered window seat, staring out at the movement of the poplars. Below she could hear the faint excited sounds of preparations from the kitchen. She tried not to smell what in previous days she would have thought was the fragrance of pastries and baked meats with which the house seemed to have become impregnated. But in a matter of moments, the swaying trees and the rich smells made her sickness worse. She tottered to the ewer set, sprinkled a few drops of water on her forehead and when that did not suffice, bent over the bowl, held her heaving stomach and retched as silently as she could.

The bowl was a fine one of Derby china, painted with cupids and cherubims. It had been a favourite one of her nursery days. But now she stared at those unreal cupids through watering eyes with loathing. Similar cupids spun from sugar decorated the huge cake downstairs. A great cupid bowl full of hothouse roses was to be the centrepiece of the buffet table. The seamstress had embroidered little cupids on the hems of three of her nightgowns. But love, Amelia knew, was not like that at all.

She dried her face on a towel, lit the gas, and padded through into the bathroom she shared with Victoria, to quietly sluice away the symptoms of her condition. Luckily, Victoria was too absorbed in her own future to pay much heed to her sister.

'There is some talk,' Victoria had whispered to Amelia a week ago, 'that Henry will be offered the post of Second Secretary at the Embassy in Washington.'

And now that future was a reality. After the wedding, they were leaving from Southampton in the *Empress of Russia* to go to America for their honeymoon.

Even two days ago when Amelia had fainted, both her stepmother and sister had regarded it as no more than the apprehensions and excitements and the tremblings of modesty before the wedding. Only Amelia knew better. Only Amelia knew that there would be no wedding today, for her at least, had she not known better. It was now Saturday, 19 December – more than two months since she had stolen out to meet James for the history-making flight. Now the only history that had been made was the oldest in the world. She was pregnant.

Too late and too little had been Stepmama's talk with the young brides yesterday afternoon. Stepmama, a cold woman in her late thirties, had married Mr Jerningham ten years ago, and having no children of her own, found their sexual enlightenment a disagreeable subject.

She had concentrated her talk on the niceties of society behaviour, the formalities of calling and card leaving in London. The necessity for a gentleman taking tea with a married lady to leave his top hat and stick and gloves on the drawing-room floor and not in the hall. The importance of the turned-down card corner. As for the marriage bed . . .

'I am happy to say you can leave that side of things entirely to your husbands, my dears. Your father and I have ensured that you marry men of breeding. All you need to know is that you do whatever your husbands wish. Your role is a passive one.'

Amelia knew very differently. Her role with James had been far from passive. But she kept her eyes lowered, her cheeks burning with what her stepmother hoped was maidenly modesty.

'Your cheeks are too white,' Victoria said, coming into the bedroom as Amelia dried herself. Victoria had just been laced into her stays, her long white silk stockings were clipped into place beneath knee-length knickers edged with broderie anglaise threaded with satin ribbon. 'Your skin will not become your gown, Amelia. Stepmama said it would be permissible to use a little rouge. Though not on our lips.'

'You look pale as well, Victoria. Very pale!' Amelia countered boldly.

Victoria rushed over to Amelia's mirror and stared at herself. 'Oh, dear!' She stroked her cheeks. Unlike Amelia, she was pleased about her wedding, actually liked her husband-to-be, admired Henry for his smooth courtly ways, so different from their father's, and earnestly wanted to look her best and be her best, and further his career as a diplomat.

'You're frightened, aren't you?' Amelia pressed home her advantage.

'A little, yes. One should be. For though Henry is a considerate man, I cannot look forward to . . . well, tonight.'

Amelia scrubbed her pale cheeks vigorously with the towel and said uncertainly, 'It'll be all right.'

'You're always so bold, Amelia. Too bold sometimes, Stepmama says. I think I might find it unpleasant. Many ladies do.'

Amelia shrugged and said nothing. From a long way away came the sound of carriage wheels, horses' hooves. Within the hour, the house guests would be departing for the church.

'I don't think I look forward to having children either, do you, Amelia? Though one should.'

'I do look forward to having children,' Amelia asserted. 'I look forward to that most of all! I want one straight away! As soon as I can!'

Victoria looked astonished. As always, Amelia was being quite unpredictable. 'I would have thought,' Victoria, said shaking her head, 'that you would not have liked to be tied down by children and childbearing.'

'Then you are quite, *quite* wrong, Victoria!' Amelia said with what conviction she could muster, 'I would like a child immediately!' And wishing to terminate this uneasy conversation, she looked critically at her sister and asked, 'Victoria, is that a pimple you have coming on your chin?'

Which possible horror, as she intended, sent Victoria squealing back to her room in panic, calling for her maid.

Her own maid arrived a few minutes later, coming into the bedroom with a little tray of tea. 'Did you bring some digestive biscuits as well?' Amelia asked hungrily. In the last few weeks she had developed an inordinate craving for these biscuits. A fact that had not gone unnoticed by the pettymaid.

'That I did, Miss.'

Sarah pattered through into the bathroom to pull the plug out of the bath and fold the towels and dry the soap. The biscuits were devoured by the time she returned.

'Are you 'appy, Miss?' Sarah asked hopefully, wiping her red hands.

Amelia shrugged. Sarah lowered her eyes and asked softly, 'Afeered?'

'No, certainly not!' Amelia felt a cold ache, but not fear.

'Not afeered of anything, Miss?'

'Only that I might be lonely. Among strangers. I'll miss you all . . .'

'Then tek me wi' year! Me petty year's a 'most up! Madam won't keep me after. She said so. Not wi' you and Miss Victoria gone. Oh, I know I'm rough, Miss. No lady's maid. But I could learn! An' I would!'

'You'd miss your family.'

'No. *Please*! I'd be summun yer could talk to. An' I need a new place.'

By the time the hairdressers arrived to arrange the brides' hair, it was agreed. Amelia, with her stepmother's permission, would employ Sarah as soon as she and Frederick returned from their honeymoon in Paris. Amelia was surprised how the thought of Sarah cheered her as the pre-wedding ritual swung into its climax with the donning of the gown.

'A perfect fit, is it not, Madam?' the dressmaker said to her stepmother as they both stood back to regard her. Another few months, Amelia thought, and she would have been bursting out of the satin and seed-pearl and lace creation. Surely she was right to act as she was doing! Act before it was too late. James wouldn't and couldn't marry her. No one would allow him, even if he wanted to. And in any case, that sort of man didn't expect to.

Amelia smoothed her hands over the bodice of her wedding gown. She had wanted this baby to die at first. But now her attitude had completely changed. She wanted it. She must keep it. It was all she had. Now it was the donning of the veil. 'Bring those top curls forward,' commanded her stepmother. Amelia's hair had been dressed in the style dear beautiful Queen Alexandra's had been for her Coronation. Society brides had copied the style since.

'May I pin the veil on to her hair, Madam?'

First the blue ribbons, then Frederick's camellia, now the long pins to secure the chaplet of orange blossom that held the veil were slipped into Amelia's thick gold hair. The veil descended over her face, hiding her expression, a curtain on an act. When it lifted again, she would be married. A new act would begin in the play of her already muddled life.

A knock sounded on the bedroom door. Hawkins announced to her stepmother that the first of the carriages was waiting. A conventional kiss blown from her stepmother's gloved fingers accompanied the conventional, 'You look entrancing!' Then her stepmother was gone.

The subdued busy murmur of the house quieted. Victoria sat while her maid tweaked fussily at her veil. Then their father came heavy-footed upstairs, his face purple with the exertion and the refreshments called for during such a sociable morning – so many house guests to entertain, most of whom he hadn't seen since his first wife's funeral. He smelled of port – or was it brandy? – and was gently swaying on his feet as he usually did. But he was smiling, which was less usual.

For once he was pleased with Amelia. Pleased she was marrying both title and money. No lady was expected to bother her head about money, but it was clear from violent arguments overheard and continuous gossip in the servants' hall that their father's finances were at a low ebb. Why else had Victoria's coming out been so parsimonious? And why was it tacitly assumed that Amelia would not be presented?

Arranging his daughters one on each arm, they descended the stairs. Behind them came Sarah and Victoria's maid, holding their trains high. 'And you need have no worry,' Mr Jerningham patted Amelia's hand. She in the end was marrying even better than Victoria. 'About that horse of yours. I'll see Pegasus is kept fit.'

He spoke indistinctly, slurring his words. Amelia barely listened, though it struck her she had never held a conversation with her father about anything except horses or her own inadequacies. She wondered of what she would speak to Frederick.

Downstairs in the hall, those servants not immediately engaged in the preparations were assembled to gaze up at the brides with cries of admiration. Cook clasped her hands while tears trickled unstaunched down her fat cheeks. Hawkins, who had served in the Crimea, stood to his decrepit version of attention.

Amelia didn't pause to glance at herself in the mirror that she had looked into those two long months ago. Mrs Henshaw was waiting with the bouquets. 'And there's a lucky silver horseshoe on each . . . Miss Victoria, Miss Amelia. With the compliments of the household staff.'

Outside, two plumed horses and a landau awaited the brides and their father. The two matched bays had been groomed till their coats shone like silk. Freshly shod (by whom, Amelia wondered) their hooves were as black as patent leather with oil and Stockholm tar. The leather and the brasses gleamed. From the grass verges, the Jerningham villagers waved at them. Up the path to the porch and into the church walked Mr Jerningham, a daughter on either side.

It was filled with smartly dressed ladies in huge feathered hats, and men in morning dress. All their faces were unrecognisable, relatives she had never seen or who were much changed. Friends, mostly their parents'. Some of the local gentry, vaguely familiar. The MFH and his wife. Somewhere would be Henry's aristocratic parents, aunts, his elder brother. Frederick, thank God, had few relatives – some cousins, and his old Aunt Sempner, rich and unpredictable, who had sent from London her excuses and what Frederick considered to be a most inadequate cheque.

The rector came halfway down the aisle to meet them. He smelled of macassar oil and mothballs and the violet cachous he used, so Sarah said, to sweeten his breath. Those smells mixed with the abundance of the hothouse flowers banked under the pulpit and that insidious scent of churches – old hassocks, old stone, old wood, death and decay.

But the music was beautiful. It lifted Amelia's feet and sped her forward till she caught sight first of Henry's stocky figure and beside him, Frederick. It was only then, as she saw Frederick glance over his shoulder for his first glimpse of her, saw his foxy alert profile, that she almost stopped dead in her tracks. Her father felt her resistant weight on his arm. And as he would have done to a shying mare, he pressed his body forward and hissed angrily under his breath, 'Come on, girl!'

Not that Amelia would have turned back. She stood, knees together to stop them trembling, while the rector droned through the double marriage service. She went through all the right motions, made the right low-voiced responses.

Only when it came to the words 'I, Amelia, take thee Frederick . . .' did she mentally but quite deliberately substitute the name 'James'.

It was a gesture, a crumb of bread cast upon the waters in the hope that some capricious God or Fate might, in another existence perhaps, bind those two names irrevocably together.

'And now Amelia . . . we are together for the rest of our lives!'

Frederick waved to the last well-wisher as the London train pulled away from the platform, brushed the rose petals off his immaculate shoulders and sat down opposite her to assess his prize.

She was, there wasn't any doubt of it, the most deliciously beautiful creature he had ever seen, combining the fragility of a Dresden shepherdess with the spirit of a thoroughbred mare. That first time he had laid his eyes on her out hunting nine months ago, furiously refusing to be blooded after the kill and galloping (corn-coloured hair streaming) up and away over the highest hedge, he had vowed to have her.

Get them young and lively and innocent and mould them to your needs, that was the advice laid down by none other than Edward VII when he was Prince of Wales, to his gambling, racing and womanising set. Had he not chosen his Alexandra at seventeen as immediately as Frederick had chosen his Amelia? And though he had been only on the outer fringes of the Prince's friends, no one was more assiduous in obeying all the Edwardian rules: discreet liaisons with mature married women with male children were perfectly permissible, and so was the bedding of maidservants. But no overt scandal! Not a word! In an age when birth control was imperfectly understood, the philandering season for marriageable young girls was permanently closed, for any such delight was as nothing to costly litigation over breach of promise, inheritances and disputed titles.

'Are you happy, dearest?'

She was looking at him in that set unblinking way, as if she hardly saw him at all. Her eyes looked very blue and pure under the sapphire velvet toque, her skin almost as white as the ermine of her muff. That was what she was. Pure and childlike and yet full of spirit. He would enjoy breaking her in. Of course she had a lot to learn. She knew nothing of the ways of society. But she had the dash and verve that all women in politics needed. His own bachelor Prime Minister's mistresses, Lady Elcho and Lady Desborough were women of spirit. So too were Asquith's wife and Lady Londonderry. To be a good political hostess, a wife had to have the dazzle to intrigue the powerful men of her husband's persuasion and the fire to demolish the ladies of the Opposition.

She nodded her head dutifully, 'Yes, Frederick.'

'Then smile, dearest.'

She smiled.

'I like going off on our honeymoon by train, dearest. Much better than Victoria and Henry on such a long journey by ship, don't you think?'

'Best of all,' Amelia's eyes suddenly sparkled, 'I would like to go off on my honeymoon by aeroplane!'

'Amelia,' he smiled tolerantly. 'What an imagination you have! Your nanny must have read you too many *Arabian Nights* stories.'

'I'm not imagining anything, Frederick. One day people will fly on their honeymoon.'

He opened his eyes wide, mimicking her. 'All the way to Paris?'

She took one of the pins out of her hat. 'Further than Paris. Much further! To the uttermost ends of the earth!'

He laughed. 'Well, Paris must content *us*. You are looking forward to it?'

'Oh, yes.'

By Paris the first night, which they were to spend at Claridge's, would be over. That was why she looked forward to Paris. She would know the worst. She did not think she could really contemplate such intimacy with Frederick, particularly as she was not sure if her husband would be able to discover that she was no longer a virgin. Sarah, whose family seemed to have experienced all human problems, had yesterday told her about her eldest sister, a girl of twenty who worked as an oyster opener in Lymington. Last year she'd wed a fisherman. But she was no longer a virgin. And a husband 'needed', as Sarah said, 'to see a drop o' blood'. Fearful of his anger, she had taken her oyster knife to bed and slit her thigh. It had gone septic and the poor girl had nearly died.

'It'd 've bin all right, Miss, if she'd used somethink like a pin. A clean hatpin!'

Now Amelia drew out a second pin. Frederick was smiling broadly. 'Even if we have to go to Paris by train and not a magic carpet?'

Amelia stabbed the pin forcefully into the hat, 'The idea of flying isn't preposterous.'

'Oh, yes, it is!'

Amelia waited, blinking her eyes rapidly while a cloud of steam drifted by. The engine thundered, the whole train shook. 'People *will* fly, I tell you!'

He threw back his head and laughed indulgently, hoping to tease her into one of her impassioned speeches, eyes sparkling, cheeks flushed. But she wouldn't be drawn. 'You'll see. Just you wait!'

Then she stared out of the window at the dark winter fields whipping past them.

'You'll be tired by the time we reach London,' he said at last. 'I hope Claridge's do us well.'

'How soon do we rise tomorrow?'

'The boat train leaves at nine. I have ordered breakfast at seven-thirty. In our room. And dinner tonight at nine.'

At the mention of dinner tonight, she closed her eyes. 'Would you mind if I had a little sleep now?' she asked without opening them. 'I was up early this morning.' She opened her eyes briefly to flick him another quick assessing glance.

'Of course! You would be excited this morning. Now you must rest! I'll wake you when we reach Waterloo.'

Surprisingly, she slept. She must have felt the speed and the rhythm of the train through her unconscious mind, for she dreamed that she and James were once again trying to get airborne. The machine kept jerking forward over the ground, refusing to rise, screaming like a half-dead bird. She was wakened by a hand on her arm. Looking up horrified, she stared into Frederick's face bending over her. 'We're coming into the station.'

She shook her head trying to shake the dream out of her brain.

'You look as if you'd seen a ghost.'

'I couldn't think where I was for a moment.'

'With me,' he said brightly. 'Now you will *always* be with me!'

She glanced outside. Darkness had fallen while she slept. They passed a square signalbox, bigger than she had ever seen. Yellowy gaslight glowed through its square windows. Frederick stood up. 'Here's the platform now, Amelia.'

There were rows of globes along the platform and figures hurrying with trolleys and baggage. She glimpsed great engines stopped against the buffers of other platforms, some letting off steam that curled and coiled like ghosts released. Hansom cabs were lined up ready, victorias, carts, drays, a steam car and a few motors. But above all there was noise. Voices, the rattle of wheels, the cries of newsboys and flower-sellers, the scream of engines, whistles. It was as if she had gone to sleep and wakened into another world.

She was thankful that Frederick knew his way about. In no time there was a porter bearing their luggage to a hansom cab. Frederick pushed his way through newspaper boys yelling unintelligible headlines, past vendors of lucky charms and handed her into the musty interior of a hansom cab.

'It won't be long now.' He put his arm round her. 'You have a lovely little waist, Amelia!'

He patted her face with his free hand and kissed her lips. He had a soft mouth and a moist one. As he kissed her, his tongue darted fast as a lizard's. She drew back. He released her and smiled fondly. 'You haven't been kissed very often, have you, Amelia?'

She shook her head. He tilted her chin, and outlined her mouth with his forefinger. 'It will be my pleasure to teach you how to kiss your husband properly.'

They were already approaching the brightly lit entrance to Claridge's. A high-hatted impressively uniformed commissionaire was standing on the lighted pavement. He strode towards them, snapping his fingers for the bellboys and the porters, who came running out like dark hounds from a trap.

When he said, 'Welcome, M'lady,' Amelia glanced round to see who was following them in.

'You! Silly!' Frederick caught her arm. 'That's *you* from now on!'

She remembered a piece of female wisdom whispered in the dormitory at Cheltenham, that a wife should be a lady in the drawing-room and a whore in the bedroom. At the time she had not known what a whore was. Now she did. And by marrying Frederick perhaps she counted as one.

'We've got the suite I wanted for you. It has a balcony.'

He followed eagerly on her heels out of the lift and along the corridor. A door was thrown open for them. The curtains were undrawn, and she could see the lights of London glittering beyond the long glass. Frederick had ordered the suite to be filled with flowers and iced buckets of champagne.

'It's lovely, Frederick.'

'And now a drink. A toast to us! Our future!'

Wine, dinner, the luxury of their surroundings and the fervour of Frederick's admiration restored her spirits and dulled her fears. Another bottle of champagne and she charmed him afresh with her gaiety.

'An early start tomorrow,' he said at last, gazing fondly at her white shoulders and the whiter swelling of her breasts above the sleek silk bodice of her gown. Her smile froze a little at the corners.

'I shall take a stroll,' he said. 'And perhaps smoke a cigarette downstairs.'

He was back within half an hour. She had put the perfume and the hatpin ready on the commode, undressed, brushed out her hair, donned the satin embroidered nightgown and was just climbing into the big double bed, when in he came through the door, holding the *Daily Mail* in his hand.

Seeing her already undressed, he looked somewhat disappointed, but he managed an indulgent smile as he advanced towards her. 'This will interest you, dearest.'

'Is it about us?'

'No.'

'What's it about then?'

'Ah-ha!'

She stretched out her hands, but he held it teasingly away from her, carefully folded so that she couldn't read it. It pleased him to see her twisting this way and that in the big bed, the sleeve of her gown, slipping off one shoulder, so charming and seductive.

'Please, Frederick, let me see!'

He held it high above her head. 'No.'

'Tell me what it's about then!'

'Your favourite subject.' He tapped her bare shoulder lightly with the rolled-up paper and then whipped it away from her sudden grasp.

'Flying?'

'Yes.'

'Really and truly?' She made a grab. He stepped back. She jumped out of bed and followed him. Pursued by her, playfully he began weaving between the chairs, behind the dressing-table, stepping up on to the bed and jumping down on the other side. When he felt his own excitement mounting unbearably, he pretended to stumble. She caught his arm. She was panting and breathless. He held the paper high above his head, his eyes fixed on her bosom, rising and falling so enchantingly above the lacy flurries of her nightgown.

'A kiss,' he said thickly. 'Then . . .'

She held up her face. He grabbed her to him. He kissed her throat, that delicate cleft between her breasts that so entranced him and then fastened his mouth over hers with a roughness and urgency that he could not restrain.

She struggled free. '*Now* show me!'

He gazed at her bemusedly for a second, intoxicated – the item in the paper, that amusing ploy, forgotten. Impatiently, as he began hastily to undress, he handed it to her and said. 'There!'

Above a tiny paragraph in the bottom left hand corner, she glimpsed the words *Balloonless Airship* and snatched the paper from him.

Then she read what the *Daily Mail* correspondent in New York had sent the day before: *Messrs Wilbur and Orville Wright of Ohio yesterday successfully experimented with a flying machine at Kittyhawk, North Carolina. The machine had no balloon attachment and derives its force from propellers driven by a small engine. In the face of a wind blowing 21 miles per hour, the machine flew three miles at the rate of eight miles an hour, and descended at a point selected in advance. The idea of the box kite was used in the construction of the airship.*

'Balloonless airship . . . box kite . . . flying machine . . . flew three miles . . . what nonsense!' Angrily she subsided on the bed. 'It's not true!'

Suddenly she crumpled the newspaper in her hand and flung it across the room. 'They weren't the first to fly!'

Frederick took not the slightest notice. He neither knew nor cared what she was talking about. All he cared about was getting out of his clothes and into that bed. His blood was up. He was ready for the kill. Roughly he clasped her to him. 'Frederick,' she said. 'Listen . . .'

He closed her mouth with his. He had intended to use her quite gently. To play her along with finesse. To rein himself in. But the little game had been too heating to the blood. He felt her wriggle and struggle, and try to pummel him. She gasped and cried out. And then suddenly she freed an arm.

The next moment, he felt a sharp pain as a long pin sank deep into the flesh of his left buttock.

FOUR

So the little animal bit!

He watched the white face framed against the window of the railway compartment – the same colour as the snow-covered French landscape creaking by and just as frozen.

She had hardly said a word since leaving Claridge's that morning. Neither had he. In an hour's time they would be arriving at the Hotel Rivoli in the Rue de la Paix, where they would be having dinner in the honeymoon suite that he had booked.

And then again they would be going to bed.

Of course, he knew she had spirit. He had wanted a young woman with spirit. A passive woman was dull in comparison and if truth be known, he had enjoyed himself. If he had been brutal, if he had in the end used her as he would a whore, she had only herself to blame. She had been taught a sharp lesson. It might be necessary to teach her another. And another yet. But that depended on *her*.

He studied her face, wondering what was going on in her mind. Just a little bit frightened of her husband was his interpretation of her silence. And that was as it should be. They were bound together for life now, irrevocably and indissolubly. She had certain duties and obligations to him and these would be obediently carried out according to his wishes. He doubted if she would try anything like last night again. If she did, she would regret it.

'We're just coming in to the Gare du Nord now.'

Only last night, he had said almost those same words to her as they steamed into Waterloo. What a world of change had happened since then!

'We are here to enjoy ourselves, Amelia,' he had admonished her in the fiacre. 'Not to sulk.'

'I am not sulking, Frederick.'

'Then what are you doing?'

'Thinking.'

There were roses in her suite. She did not appear even to see them. She made no comment on the delicious dinner and the iced champagne. Afterwards, she said she was a little tired and would retire early. He said, as he had said the night before, that he would go downstairs to smoke a cigarette and then come back to their room. Again, when he returned, she was in bed. This time when he took her, she remained totally unexcitingly passive.

For the next three days, the honeymoon continued in this fashion. During the day they visited the sights – Notre Dame, Napoleon's Tomb, the Eiffel Tower, the Louvre. At night, they retired early.

As Christmas approached and the coldness between them continued, he began to reconsider the ruby earrings, once his mother's, that he had brought along for her. Meanwhile the Ambassador, with whom he had an acquaintance, had heard they were on honeymoon in Paris and invited them to dinner on Christmas Eve. It would be her first high society function, and before they left for the Embassy in the Rue du Faubourg St Honoré, he gave her a talk about behaviour and etiquette. 'There will be a lot of grand ladies there,' he said, 'both French and English, keep yourself unobstrusive. Watch what they do. And remember,' he inquired, 'you are the newlywed wife of a Member of Parliament.'

She said coolly, 'You will have no cause to be ashamed of me, Frederick.'

That evening, she had put on a long gown of shimmering grey moire. Her fair hair glittered under the crystal chandelier in the reception room. Frederick had noticed that Frenchmen in particular turned their heads when she passed. But that evening she turned every man's head, including the Ambassador's, on whose right she sat.

On her right was a Monsieur Blériot, a rich manufacturer of acetylene lamps, who spoke only a little English. But she managed to hold her own with him in her schoolgirl French, helped now and then by the Ambassador. Halfway through the main turkey course, he heard Blériot mention the word 'turnbuckle'.

'Turncoat, Monsieur Blériot,' the Ambassador corrected, wanting to be helpful. 'Turncoat is the word you want.'

'If you will excuse me, Sir,' Amelia said. 'Monsieur Blériot is quite correct.'

'Never heard the word in my life, Lady Haybury!'

'It is the tightening mechanism on the rigging of an aeroplane.'

The Ambassador was most impressed. So were the other men. Monsieur Blériot was quite ecstatic with admiration. A beautiful woman to know so much about flying! In their halting mixture of the two languages they talked of nothing else. He had a friend, a Brazilian coffee-millionaire called Santos-Dumont, who was also mad about aviation, though unfortunately obsessed not so much with aeroplanes as flying pigs of airships.

After that triumphant evening, Frederick gave her the ruby earrings for Christmas after all. He had suddenly realised that he had married not only a beautiful woman but a potentially powerful political asset. Frederick's eyes were on the star of high office. With her beauty and intelligence, Amelia was certain to catch his Prime Minister's attention – Balfour liked women to have brains. A position on the Committee of Imperial Defence had been promised, but with Amelia's help there was no reason at all why he should not become a junior minister.

The honeymoon which had so nearly foundered became more agreeable. He showed her off at Maxim's and all the other expensive restaurants. He took her to theatres, concerts, parties. Together in the front stalls, they watched Belle Otero hanging high in her golden casket above the Folies Bergère girls kicking up their black-stockinged legs in the can-can. He took her to couturiers in the Rue de la Paix, sat on a plush sofa while she was bought ballroom dresses, tea-gowns, cloaks, and ermine stoles.

Coming along the Boulevard St Germain one afternoon, suddenly they saw ahead of them, weaving between the lime trees well below the level of the roofs, a strange silver monster with a gondola hanging below it, pushed forward by a funny little puttering propeller.

'It's Monsieur Santos-Dumont's pig!'

As they watched, the fat little airship manoeuvred round the corner, sank close to the ground and stopped outside a café. A dapper little man in a straw hat climbed out, tethered it to a tree as though it was a horse, and strolled inside.

Amelia's eyes were shining. 'Frederick, weren't we privileged?'

'Privileged?'

'To witness that flight! It's the sort of thing we'll tell our grandchildren about!'

Frederick smiled. He did not in the least expect to tell them of such passing stunts, but the thought of children and grandchildren and the continuity of his line pleased him. He even agreed to go inside the café with her and speak to Santos-Dumont about their meeting with Blériot at the Embassy. The upshot of that was an expedition to the Brazilian's airship station at Neuilly. Like his wife, the French, Frederick was beginning to find, really did take aviation seriously. And the germ of an idea came to him then that aviation might one day be quite useful to him.

At Neuilly they met Blériot again. Rather to Santos-Dumont's annoyance, Frederick thought, he accompanied them round the workshops and machine sheds.

'And now,' the little Brazilian said, leading the way to a red and white striped hangar, 'my *pièce de résistance!*' Outside was a flat grass launching ground and on it *Numero Neuf*, the motored balloon which had so fascinated Amelia. For an awful moment Frederick thought they were going to be offered a flight in the contraption. But fortunately it was not weighed up for flight.

'Observe my unique ballast, Madame! Water! Controlled by a tap! Harmless and versatile! The sand I keep only for altering the trim. And observe the bicycle-type steering, a great contribution to navigation!'

From the launching pad they went to the dope shop, where the fabric was treated, then to a shed where hydrogen was prepared from vats of hydrochloric acid and heaps of iron filings, and finally to the cold smelly engine workshop. 'Here, Madame, you will see something of great interest. Arrows! Arrows fitted with dynamite shot from an airship could sink a submarine!'

'*Non, non, mon ami!*' Blériot laughed gustily and shook his head, 'Airships, never! It is the heavier-than-air machine where the future lies!'

'That's what I think,' Amelia piped up, to Frederick's embarrassment and the amusement of the other two.

'Then you should come and see the aeroplane that I am building!'

So carried away was Amelia that when Blériot asked 'Have you ever seen an aeroplane, Madame?' she actually boasted, '*Oui!*' And in English, 'Once I helped to make one!'

Frederick chided her about that on the way home. But she laughed. 'It wasn't really a lie. I did once help to build a sort of aeroplane. A long, long time ago. When I was a child.'

'Ah, a toy! You were teasing them! How mad they are!'

Santos-Dumont and Blériot had obviously been charmed. And Amelia suggested Frederick could do worse than put some of his fortune into a French flying enterprise. And though Frederick was too shrewd for that, he was much more amenable to her second quite flattering suggestion that they extend their honeymoon. They were having such a splendid time. Paris had been good for them. They would take in the New Year and the festivities in mid-January and perhaps a trip to see Monsieur Blériot building his aeroplane.

After the uncertain start, everything in the end worked happily. He had been right to handle her as he had. He had broken her in with a firm and knowledgeable hand. The three weeks stretched to four. And on the way home, in the train between Paris and Boulogne, Amelia slipped her hand through his arm and whispered that though it was too early yet to be sure, she had reason to hope that she might be pregnant.

In Frederick's view it was the perfect end to the almost perfect honeymoon.

At the same time as the Paris-London express steamed into Victoria station bearing Amelia to her new life at 7 Park Lane, James was driving his cart into Southampton with a lightness of heart that he had not experienced for weeks.

Ajax's new airframe had been completed. It was stronger and lighter and would only have to bear his weight. The cracked crankshaft of the engine was still a problem, but he was pleased with the new propeller he had carved from ash, and which was inspired by the two-bladed sycamore seeds he'd studied rotating away from their parent trees.

It was a clear winter morning with the sky arctic blue and the Solent a sheet of unfired metal. He had meticulously cleaned the cart and harness last night. That morning he had fixed on the pony's head the festive three bells usually reserved for May Days and Harvest Homes. From the vantage point of Totton village, James glimpsed the fairest sight in the world – the single funnel and four masts of the troopship from South Africa at the far end of the dock basin. It was the key to his freedom.

Having laid his hands on every newspaper and journal he could buy, beg, borrow or steal, he knew now that all over the world individuals were trying to get themselves airborne. It was like a worldwide infection of single-minded people which no government would admit existed and which left politicians and experts quite untouched. He had read the piece in the *Daily Mail* that Amelia had seen. That was nonsense, he knew. But talking to an American sailor from a New York liner in the Jerningham Arms just after Christmas, he had found that Wilbur had certainly flown 852 feet in 59 seconds from a level start, not a jump from a slope as his had been. But there were other firsts – and very soon, James told himself, he would fly again, and this time would prove Ajax in front of witnesses.

Christmas for James and his mother had been frugal. The pig, usually killed for the festival, had been reprieved till last Friday. Then with half the bloodthirsty children of the village watching, James had performed his most distasteful task of the year. As head of the family, he had slaughtered the pig, drained it, and later chopped it up. The village children fought for the trotters, the tail and the bits his mother spurned. Then she wrapped a side of the pig in muslin and slipped it up on the wide chimney to smoke. A quarter she salted.

Tonight there would be a roast of a size not seen since Mr Jerningham gave the village a sick pig to celebrate the relief of Mafeking. Neighbours had left an abundance of vegetables, new baked bread, some butter, cordials, fruit and cheeses. His mother had baked raised pies and pasties. It was as she had slid the last one out of the oven all golden and crisp that she'd said bitterly, 'So you won't be stopping to sup many more'n these, son. When your father's home. You'll be off?'

'That's right.'

'Thought so.'

'Thought so!' he exclaimed angrily. 'You knew so! I've told you often enough!'

'For why?'

'For you know why! To make my way!'

'It's made here.'

'Not for me.'

'You've a good living. Better'n most.'

'Better'n some. Worse than others.'

'Worse'n the gentry, oh, aye, we know all about that! But your work's honest. An' it's here as long as you want it.'

'No, it's not, Mother. It's here as long as *they* say.' He jerked his head towards the Hall. 'And anyway, horses won't be wanted for ever.'

''Course they will.'

'Besides, *I* don't want *them*.'

'Don't let yer father hear you talk that way!'

'He'd say the same, Mother.'

'That he wouldn't. 'Tis his life.'

'Well, it's *not* my life. I want my life different.'

'Oh, we all know that! Flying up in the sky!' She drew a deep breath of tremendous scorn, and pursed her lips. 'Flying for a fall, if you ask me.'

Well, he'd risk flying for a fall, he thought, bowling along amid the thickening traffic. Four carts ahead of him was a steam dray. He raised himself up to see it better. A Frenchman called Félix du Temple had built an aircraft powered by steam. Maybe one day hot air would propel a flying machine, but he dismissed the idea as too preposterous even for him. Every day he looked at things, speculating whether they would fly or could be adapted to fly. Or if it was something whose nature it was to fly, like a bird, or a bat, or a bee, or a butterfly, *why* did it fly? Now he searched the traffic for the sight of a motor car. He spotted a green Bugatti, but it was too far away to have a good look. Petrol engines for aeroplanes were right at first, he was sure. Powerful petrol engines for forward thrust and an airframe shaped like . . . what?

As he drove up to the dock gate, he was turning over in his mind where he would make for first when he shook the dust of the forge off his boots. Bristol, where a manager of the Bristol Tramways had expressed his admiration for Santos-Dumont and the air-minded French and was urging other young men to follow suit? Or Dorchester where a man was going to cast himself off Maiden Castle Hill? Or Wales, where an aristocrat, the Honourable Charles Rolls, was pioneering petrol engines? Or London with its Royal Aero Club and its Royal Aeronautical Society? He had not made up his mind by the time he reached the dock gates.

'Ay,' a man in a peaked cap told him at the entrance gates. 'The lads've disembarked. Bin taken to the reception centre.'

When James asked him where the reception centre might be, he told him the drill hall beyond the end of the quay. He couldn't miss it, he'd see the Union Jack flying for our gallant troops' return. James saw more than that. As he got further down the dock, he saw the ship from South Africa was painted white with a big red cross on her side.

At the entrance to the hall was a sentry-box manned by a corporal with a beefy truculent face. He demanded James's name and business, waved him to the waiting line of vehicles. He told him the men would be released in alphabetical order, so by the look of things he'd have to wait another hour. He advised him to stand with 'that lot over there to see if you can recognise your particular person when he comes out'.

Two hours later James was still waiting, stamping his feet with the rest of the group, mostly women with shawls over their heads. He had been the witness of several tearful reunions. Half of the women hadn't recognised their menfolk. Some of the men had bandages over their heads. Dozens came limping along on crutches. Four had lost arms. A line of men, each holding on to the shoulder of the man in front of them, were being shepherded by two orderlies.

A clammy apprehension had already touched James's heart. But why hadn't his father said? He had been given to understand in his letters that he was being kept behind to train young blacksmiths for the units of the Regular Army that were being left behind in South Africa.

It was as well James had been warned by the red cross that this was a hospital ship. Otherwise, he might have let his father go by unrecognised. Somehow he had lost stature as well as weight. He had shrunk like a crab apple left out in the sun. The skin of his face had the same greeny-yellow colour and texture.

'Here, Father! Over here!'

James pushed himself forward and seized his arm, receiving such a blank look in return that for a moment James thought he had claimed the wrong man. Then he saw the pupils of his father's eyes were pin-pricks and their expression hazy. His father frowned, trying to focus. His own disappointment gave way to concern and pity.

'It's good to have you back, Father!'

'And good to be home, lad!' His father turned his face up to the small disc of white winter sun. 'There's no place like England, so yer mother was right!' Strange ominous words, James thought, from his adventurous father, as he helped him into the cart. 'Only a fool leaves England, son!'

'Why didn't you let us know you weren't so well, Father?'

'I've been all right till six months ago. As I told you, training the young lads. Then I got this thing and they put me into hospital.'

'What is it?'

'Nothing much, son. Didn't want to worry your mother.'

'Would you like to stretch out in the back?'

'Nay, son, nay! I want to look around me. See the green! Though I don't see so clear just at present. Some physic they give you.'

He clasped his arms round himself, shivering like a poplar leaf in the crisp air. James cursed his own thoughtlessness in not bringing a rug to wrap him up in. But he had been so sure that his father would return as he had left and as he remembered him. Strong, lively, jovial. When they rattled over the cobblestones near the dock gates, his father clutched his stomach.

46

'It gets me here, son. That's what they give you the physic for.' He gave a faint smile. 'Dunno which is worse.'

'Ah, well,' James said heartily, 'we'll soon get you right with Mother's good food.'

'Ay, that'll do the trick. She's kept well, ain't she?'

'That she has! Missed you though.'

'Aye.'

He lapsed into silence. 'Was it bad, Father?'

'Up and down. I wouldn't go again. A man wouldn't, like yer mother said . . .' His voice trailed away as if he was too tired to go on.

More to spark off his father's old interest than because he himself wanted to talk about it, James said, 'I'll be flying soon. My new machine—'

'Aye, your mother wrote me.' His father shook his head discouragingly without raising it. 'You're wasting yer time, son! Throwing away what you've got! Your future's in the forge.'

'But you always said—'

'I said a sight too much.'

'Adventure, you said.'

'That was before I knew what adventure were like.'

'And what *is* it like?' James demanded bitterly, jerking the reins as if speeding the horse would somehow speed him through the prison door he knew was closing. 'We read—'

'You read what they wanted you to read, son.'

'We read,' James said steadily after a moment, 'about the balloons at Ladysmith. You saw them, didn't you Father?'

But his father didn't answer. His head had sunk on his chest and he appeared to have dozed off. Dusk was falling by the time they reached the outskirts of Jerningham and his father hadn't spoken again. The sound of the horse's hooves and the rattle of the cart were awaited. Villagers carrying storm lanterns hurried towards the forge, their beaming faces upshadowed in their light like Hallow'en turnips. Suddenly the forge cottage door was flung wide. His mother's figure was outlined in the square rectangle of lamplight. Behind her in the kitchen, other figures could be seen bobbing excitedly. A feast for a returning soldier was better even than a wedding or a funeral. For there would be tales afterwards to listen to, a sing-song and maybe even trophies of the wicked Boers to be passed around.

Even out here, James could smell the roast pork and the spiky fragrance of apple and cloves.

'''Tis all ready,' his mother called excitedly. 'Pig's done to a turn! Josh's brought his fiddle.'

Then she took a closer look at the figure James was helping down from the cart. 'Best begin wi'out us for time being,' she called to the others. ''E needs to rest. James'll gi' me a 'and wi' 'im. Like he always does.'

Struggling up the narrow stairs, she paused to catch her breath. Shades of the workhouse seemed to be hot on her heels, almost catching her up. Urgently and angrily she whispered to James, 'There'll be no talk of your leaving yet awhile!'

James said nothing. He had lost Amelia, the chance of fame, and now freedom was going to elude him. He half-supported, half-dragged his father to the bed, then, waving his mother downstairs, began to undress him. His mother had stitched his father a new flannelette nightshirt and made up the bed with the linen given her by Amelia's mother. Slipping his father's arms out of the coarse army vest, James saw his father's body. There was a puckered scar on his shoulder that looked like a roughly healed shrapnel wound. Despite his muscular arms, his body was emaciated, the skin colour was unhealthy as his face. As he pulled the voluminous nightshirt over him, his father suddenly opened his eyes. 'I saw the balloons at Ladysmith,' he said. 'Always on the ground. Never up. No gas! No good! The war neither, except for them at home to read about in newspapers. Stay where you are, son! Keep your feet on the ground!'

Then, as suddenly, he fell asleep again. In the flickering lamplight, his face looked the colour of clay, the voluminous nightshirt more like a shroud.

It was a death all right, James thought – the death of his own hopes.

FIVE

'Aunt Sempner hopes to present you to their Majesties this coming season,' Frederick said six weeks later. 'Your name has gone forward to the Lord Chamberlain. I am delighted that Dr Poultney confirms your condition, my dear. But naturally it is imperative you be presented as soon as possible.'

Amelia bit her lip. It was almost the end of February and from the long Georgian windows of her upstairs sitting-room she could see the crocus buds thrusting up through the winter grass of Hyde Park. There was a faint green haze over the distant willows. The carriageways were busy with landaus and victorias. Nursemaids sat on the seats comparing their charges. The view was the best part of the town house. Amelia disliked its elegant formality. The huge high entrance hall with its ornate ceiling, its enormous crystal chandelier poised like a glittering nemesis and its highly polished floors.

'You'd like 'em less, M'lady, if you had to polish 'em,' Sarah whispered. Sarah had firmly established herself at 7 Park Lane by the time the honeymooners returned. The butler thought well of her, and was teaching her to speak his own version of the King's English.

'Frederick, I don't want to be presented,' Amelia said at last.

'What you want has nothing to do with it, Amelia. Presentation is a necessity. Like . . . like baptism. Without it, you cannot be received in the houses where we wish to be received.'

'Where *you* wish to be received, Frederick.'

Frederick's lips tightened. 'I naturally assume that *my* wishes are *your* wishes.'

'I never wanted to be presented.'

'Every right-minded lady wishes to be presented. Your parents should have initiated arrangements. I am merely repairing their omission.'

'I never wanted to be presented,' she repeated. 'And less than ever now.'

'If you are worried about its effect on your condition, then I will speak to Dr Poultney. Otherwise, I want to hear no more.' Frederick turned on his heel; Amelia remained silent. She prayed that the Palace lists would be full and Sarah loyally used the boiled chicken wishbone given her by Cook after broth-making to endorse that wish.

The lists were not full. Three days after Amelia had held her first soirée at 7 Park Lane, the gold-crested summons came. Lady Sempner was to present her to Their Majesties on 31 May.

'But I shall be showing by then,' she protested to Frederick.

'Then your dressmaker must disguise it. Your gown may be as loose as you choose, I understand. So long as it is white with a train. My Aunt Sempner will advise you.'

There followed weeks of preparation – dressmaker's fittings, orders for shoes and head-dress, the practising of the curtsey, interspersed with what Amelia regarded as the ridiculous formalities of card-leaving on the wives of Frederick's political friends, tea parties, and formal dinners. But London life had its compensations. From her sitting-room window Amelia and Sarah watched the rockets rising from Mr Brock's Fortieth Annual Firework Display. This year featuring, according to the advertisements, fine novelties from the Russo-Japanese war, a bombardment of Port Arthur, the destruction of the Russian torpedo destroyer *Steregustoni*. And at midday on 28 May across Park Lane they saw the Coaching Club meet just under the dripping leaves of the chestnuts.

'They remind me of Pegasus,' said Amelia pointing at Sir Philip Hunt's four matched greys. Pegasus and Jerningham seemed a long way away. She felt heavy and clumsy.

When the 31 May arrived, the dress had to be let out a whole inch, and the deep lace collar dropped forward to hide the unwanted curve. It was all rather like Amelia's wedding day again. The dressmaker was there, kneeling with her scissors and her pins. A taller, bonnier, more groomed Sarah watched as three curled ostrich feathers were fastened in her hair instead of flowers. The flowing veil cascading over the white satin dress, the pearls, the long white gloves, even the bouquet were reminiscent of her wedding. So was the stately descent before the servants' eyes to the waiting carriage.

After the rain of the previous days, the weather was warm and redolent of summer, the carriage open so that Londoners might enjoy the spectacle. The Park shimmered in the heat. The air smelled of crushed grass, spring flowers, the warm smell of horse-flesh, the tang of harness oil and tar, as a stream of gleaming carriages processed towards the Palace. Their way was lined with crowds gaping at the occupants, with hawkers selling flags and buttonholes and daguerreotypes of famous beauties, political lampoons, hot chestnuts and whelks.

A footman held a frilly white parasol over Amelia and Lady Sempner. Frederick, stiff in court dress, frowned as Amelia licked her lips nervously.

'No call to be nervous, gal.' Aunt Sempner's ancient face was so stiffly enamelled that she couldn't smile. But her bright monkey-brown eyes regarded Amelia kindly. 'Don't hurry your curtsey! Let 'em wait! You're worth waiting for, m'dear!'

'I feel so foolish,' Amelia murmured, putting up a hand to touch the feathers. 'I feel like a circus horse . . .' She began to laugh and then broke off quickly as she caught Frederick's expression.

They were turning on to the Mall now. The carriage wheels made a strange noise over the wooden blocks. At the far end, the roadway was incomplete, the carriage swayed. Frederick leaned forward to pick off a piece of grit thrown up on to the white silk covering Amelia's knees.

The crowds lining the Mall waved their Union Jacks, and pointed. Some clapped, but some eyed the plumed ladies that passed before them nodding and smiling, with derision bordering on hatred. What would James think if he could see her now? What was James doing at this very moment as she in her stupid tossing feathers passed through the gates of Buckingham Palace, then under the arch and to the carpeted steps, while the Band of the 2nd Batallion Scots guards played in the quadrangle?

What would he have made of these beautiful Palace minions in their satin breeches and brocade jackets, marshalling them into the ante-room and sorting them like cattle in order of precedence? Would he have raised a grim smile that she was taking his child into what was referred to with awe as The Presence? King Edward and Queen Alexandra sat in gilt chairs on the raised dais of the throne room surrounded by their Court – the Lord Chamberlain, the Vice Chamberlain, Gold Stick in Waiting, Silver Stick in Waiting, Ladies in Waiting. It was rumoured that Queen Alexandra would only appoint Ladies of the Bedchamber who were excessively tall so that her own daintiness was accentuated.

'I would be very suitable,' sighed a lanky girl behind Amelia in the presentation queue, as one by one their names were called. 'Though I wouldn't want the job for all the tea in China, even if I had the right name.'

Amelia paused to move up a place to the head of the queue. 'What is your name?' she asked the girl.

'Bettina Rolls. Otherwise Ballast.'

'Any relation of . . .'

'Oh, Lord everyone asks me that! Of course! Hence the nickname Ballast. That's all the Honourable Charles ever wants me for. Ballast for his damned balloons.'

'Are you interested in ballooning?'

'Not really.'

Amelia's name was called then, so the conversation came to an abrupt end. Gliding across what seemed an ocean of floor Amelia made her curtsey. Aunt Sempner had instructed her on no account to look either of Their Majesties directly in the eye. She had a vision of a bearded grandfatherly face, an appraising hooded stare. She stole a quick glance at Queen Alexandra to see if she was as beautiful as gossip said she was. But she wasn't really interested. All she could think of even when she was making her slow clumsy backward retreat was, what a stroke of luck on meeting the Honourable Charles Rolls's cousin! Never the one to let the grass grow under her feet, Amelia waited till the girl made her exit from the presence. Then she asked her humbly, 'Do you think your cousin would consider using me as ballast instead?'

A month later among the invitations for boating parties and garden parties, dinners and soirées, which poured into 7 Park Lane, came a brief note from the Honourable Charles Rolls inviting Lady Haybury to make a balloon ascent with him on 17 July. Frederick was due at Haybury that weekend. She would have the town house to herself. Amelia wrote an immediate acceptance to Charles Rolls.

'You'll likely be more ballast than the gentleman expects, M'lady,' Sarah said doubtfully, helping Amelia to fasten a net over the brim of her hat and under her chin. 'And what if the baby comes early, an' you up in the air?'

'Don't worry, Sarah! It won't! Look, the sun's shining! It'll be like going on the river in a punt at Henley. And you wouldn't worry about that.'

Indeed the day was calm. But the trip was nothing like Henley. Nor was the Honourable Charles Rolls anything like the gentlemanly punters of the boating parties Amelia had been to. He was tall, dark, handsome, moustachioed, blind to women and obsessed with flight and punctuality.

There was no need to send the groom to find him. He appeared by the Haybury carriage as soon as it arrived in the carriageway outside the Crystal Palace. The whole place was a hive of activity. All sorts of coloured balloons were tethered at the edge of Sydenham Hill. There were carriages and steam drays and crowds of people who had arrived by horse-drawn trams.

'Husband know you're coming with me?' Rolls asked as they walked across the turf towards a tall red and white balloon.

'Oh yes,' Amelia lied, as they walked past the big outline stands ready for the firework display, the cockfights, the cake-walk.

'Doesn't object?'

'Not at all.'

'No danger,' Rolls said. 'Don't see why he should.'

He asked her how she had come to be interested in ballooning and was enchanted to hear about her meeting with Santos-Dumont. The little Brazilian had recently addressed a meeting of the Aeronautical Society in London and had made a flight almost from the very spot where Rolls was now handing Amelia into the gondola.

Charles Rolls, Amelia was to discover, did everything with panache. Inside the gondola was a picnic hamper of cold game pie and iced champagne. He drew the cork of the first bottle as soon as they were clear of the hill and before they were too high. Then tilting a little from side to side in the uprising thermals, they watched a boat sail up the Thames, and drank a toast to flight. Sailing up and away from the shrunk city of London, its warm stone glowing in the afternoon sun, they rose over the smooth curve of the North Downs, over Surrey woodland and Sussex villages.

Amelia was entranced at the stillness, at the way she could hear dogs barking, train wheels clanking, men shouting. 'It's wonderful! I could go on for ever.'

'Sorry,' Rolls said, 'time to go home.'

That was easier said than done. The wind had dropped and they drifted for three hours before managing to get back to Sydenham just before dark. 'That's the trouble with these things,' Rolls said as he helped her out of the gondola. 'What I really want to do is to build powered aeroplanes. Here, are you feeling all right?'

'I'm feeling fine,' Amelia lied.

And though in the early hours of the following morning, Amelia dismissed her pains as too much game pie and champagne at too high an altitude, it was fitting and most fortunate that her baby should elect to be born after such an expedition. The balloon trip was obviously both the hero and the culprit.

As soon as she knew it was a boy, she resolved he could have no other name but Charles. On his return from Haybury, Frederick found 7 Park Lane lit up like the Crystal Palace itself. 'Dr Poultney tried to reach you at Haybury,' the butler whispered, appraising him immediately of the situation as he took his hat and gloves. 'But you had that moment left, Sir.'

'Is the doctor still with Her Ladyship?'

The doctor was still there but just leaving. He was bidding Amelia farewell as

Frederick reached the bedroom door. 'You have a fine son, Sir,' he boomed at Frederick. 'I congratulate you.'

'Is he strong and healthy?'

'Indeed yes.'

'But premature!'

The doctor paused for a moment. Then he put his hand on Frederick's shoulder. 'That, my dear sir, need not worry you one jot. You are in the best company. Our beloved Queen was prematurely delivered of Prince Albert at Frogmore after an outing on a sledge to watch the King ice-skating. He smiled roguishly at Frederick, 'You must ask your dear wife where she spent yesterday afternoon!'

But that could wait. Frederick was all eagerness to see his son and heir. He pushed past Dr Poultney's hired nurses, thrust aside Sarah, who was always under his feet, and pulled back the curtains of the cot. He saw a tightly swaddled baby, whose mouth even in its unformed state showed wilfulness and whose whole face resembled Amelia except that its half-closed eyes were inky blue.

He straightened and went to Amelia. Before asking her to what escapade the doctor had referred, he bent over and brushed her forehead with his lips.

'Thank you, my dear. You have given me a fine son. And you have given him your beauty.'

But there seemed nothing of himself in the child. No immortality for the Hayburys there.

SIX

Although Amelia would have liked to return to the good country air of Haybury after Charles was born, they remained at their town house, even when the season ended. Frederick's political career required closer contact with men of power and influence. To this end, he travelled to Panshanger in August for a week's grouse shooting with Lord Desborough. He had heard that Balfour was to be one of the party, and he sought a word in his ear about the vacant seat on the Imperial Committee. He did not press Amelia to accompany him.

And when Parliament reassembled, he left her for several weeks entirely to her own devices in her new role. Amelia mistrusted the nanny whom Frederick had engaged without consulting her, and acceded immediately to Sarah's suggestion that she be appointed nurserymaid to keep an eye on Master Charles and give him a little cuddle when the lah-de-dah nanny wasn't looking.

'I brought up the five that come after me,' she told Amelia. 'An' I didn't lose one. Not like her. When she was Nanny Bolsover, the youngest died of typhoid. Did she tell you that? I heard it in the Park when I wheeled young Master out on her day off.'

Disease was rife that winter – typhoid, scarlet fever, tuberculosis. The King himself had suffered bronchitis from the thick yellow fog that rolled in with the Thames and blanketed London, night after night. But the little season that December was a sparkling one, and Frederick expected Amelia to do justice to it and him. With the words 'Now it is time you became less of Charles's mother and more of my wife,' he escorted her, arrayed in her Paris gowns, to balls and banquets. They gave elaborate dinner parties. Frederick scanned the card salver each day to see if the right people were calling, and tried to educate Amelia into the subtleties of a political hostess. 'When you withdraw with the ladies, mind your conversation. Remember pillow talk! These ladies have powerful husbands. Always show me in the best light. Dersingham is also being considered for the Imperial Defence Committee. Some gossip against him would not come amiss.'

But gossip or no gossip, it was Dersingham who was appointed to the Imperial Committee, much to Frederick's chagrin. Nor did Amelia show herself to be as good as he would have liked with the politicians themselves. Certainly they thought her beautiful and charming. But she did not obey his dictum of being 'informed but not opinionated'. She took issue with Lord Curzon, her dinner partner at Devonshire House in January, when he declared that aviation was no more than a passing fad. And later on that same evening

Amelia was heard to remark sympathetically about the crowds of ill-clad and half-starved looking women who gathered on evenings such as this to watch and enjoy the arrival of the gentry in their magnificent gowns and their priceless jewels.

By the summer of 1905, Frederick's own efforts were not entirely without fruit. An election loomed. An election in which his own seat was so safe that he only paid a fleeting visit to his constituency. Frederick was promised junior office if Balfour's Unionists were returned with an even bigger majority. Campbell-Bannerman, the Liberal Leader, was not a popular man, and his wife was a plain shy woman – by no means powerful as a political hostess.

But when the elections came in November, Campbell-Bannerman and his Liberal Party were swept into office by a huge majority. Frederick began to feel that the snatching of the political prize from his fingers and the beginnings of days in the wilderness were somehow attributable to Amelia. Certainly the next event was almost entirely her own doing. She had taken to her role of mother almost as enthusiastically and foolishly as she had embraced aviation. Frederick, on the other hand, kept his ear to the ground and his nose to the political grindstone.

The Liberals were moving too fast and too furiously. The Unionists rallied for a possible turning out of the government, and Frederick's hopes of office returned. A whisper reached him he was being considered for shadow office, and not this time of junior rank.

This whisper gained added substance at the beginning of April with the arrival of an invitation to a ball given by the Marchioness of Salisbury, whose husband was the maker and breaker of political careers.

'Have a new gown made,' Frederick told Amelia at dinner. 'Isn't there some splendid woman Mrs Langtry patronises?'

'I don't really need a new gown.'

'Don't argue, Amelia. Do as I say. Who knows who will be present? Perhaps his Majesty himself. I wish to show you off.'

'I hate these affairs,' Amelia burst out suddenly.

Frederick dabbed his lips with his napkin and eyed her furiously. 'Sometimes,' he hissed across the table low enough for Pearson not to hear clearly, 'You astonish me. How can you not enjoy these affairs?'

'Quite easily,' Amelia said drily.

'Pertness, my dear, does not become you.'

'Then I will explain. I would prefer to stay at home.'

'With Charles?' he asked sneeringly.

'Just at home, Frederick.'

He went on as if she hadn't spoken, 'You spend far too long as it is in the nursery. Nanny has mentioned that fact to me. I will have no more argument.'

Amelia obediently said no more. From Aunt Sempner she learned the name of Mrs Langtry's dressmaker, the gown was ordered and the hairdresser told to come because Frederick had decided Amelia should wear his grandmother's tiara. Mindful of how precarious Charles's position could be if Frederick never came to love him, Amelia spent less time in the nursery, and that on Thursday when Nanny had her day off.

'He's growing into a lovely lad, isn't he, M'lady?' Sarah said fondly, on the

55

Thursday before the Salisbury Ball. 'Like you, but not like you. Bigger chin, M'lady. Like you made into a little man.'

Charles would be two in July. He was strong and big for his age. His most noticeable features were his stubborn mouth and his deep blue dark-lashed eyes. He had a quick laugh and a quicker temper.

'He'll break hearts one day,' Sarah spoke slowly sounding all her aitches, the way the butler had taught her. It was not only Pearson who made her mind her aitches. Nanny tutted audibly if she ever dropped one, remarking to no one in particular that she didn't know what the gentry was coming to, employing such staff. Sarah disliked Nanny whom she regarded as Frederick's spy. 'Even Nanny says Baby Bolsover was half his size at the same age and very sickly in comparison.'

'Don't tempt providence,' Amelia reproved Sarah sharply. Charles was so precious to her, she feared some act of divine providence snatching him away. The wheels of God ground slowly and might inexorably grind her to pulp. She was not particularly religious. James and she held similiar views. There was something beyond this life but what and where it was to be found, she didn't know. She had a superstitious feeling that there was some being who from time to time righted the score, and who tipped the scales of life against the sinner. She had been wicked. Wicked to James, wicked to Frederick, wicked to herself. Now she had lost James. But Charles was hers. Nothing must happen to him.

She knew only too well that infant mortality was terrifying high. Now with alarming clarity she could remember those sickly poems in all the magazines by Mrs Ball about infant deaths, about sweet sinless babies being gathered up to Jesus. Disease by which he could gather them were legion. At any time of the day or night, a child could begin to run a fever. Then, as quick as a flash, it was all over.

'I'l come with you to the Park,' Amelia said to Sarah impulsively, watching her dress Charles warmly for his outing. Though it was April, a cold wind blew, and the daffodils in the windowboxes this year were poor stunted things.

'Suit yourself, M'lady,' Sarah replied unenthusiastically. 'You'll be the only mother, M'lady.'

'I don't care. I like being out in the open. And I want to look at the other children.'

There was another sight she didn't at all like to look at. Just along the path by the lake, where Sarah had wheeled Charles to feed the ducks, stood a group of nursemaids, their heads close together in earnest gossip. They were watching another tall nursemaid, furiously pushing a large bassinet towards them.

Her gait was agitated, her pace so swift that her crêpe de chine headdress streamed after her. As she passed them, Amelia saw first that the expression on the nursemaid's face was half-demented, and secondly that the perambulator was empty.

When the hurrying nursemaid was out of earshot, the gossiping group interpreted for her. 'The little boy died, M'lady. Four days ago. Diphtheria. She's bin walking the Park each day since.'

The dreadful disease was assuming epidemic proportions. It was the change of the seasons, the city dust, the fogs, the old city drains that should by now be replaced. Whatever it was, the ground of Amelia's mind was prepared for disaster. The seed fell during the early evening of the Salisbury Ball. The gown of pale lemon taffeta was donned, her hair dressed round old Lady Haybury's diamond tiara, and Frederick had just appeared to take her to the carriage when Nanny knocked.

She bobbed an apologetic curtsey to Frederick and asked if M'lady could spare a moment. Master Charles was being stubborn about his supper, and for that matter had been stubborn about his food all day.

'Then let him go without. Put him to bed.'

'That would be my inclination, Sir.'

'Then for God's sake follow it. That's what you're paid for.'

'It's just that M'lady said to tell her . . . '

'I'll come,' Amelia said, hurrying to the door.

Frederick shot her a furious look, but did not forbid her to go. 'I'll allow you three minutes,' he said, perching himself on the edge of the sofa and taking out his watch.

Gathering up her skirt in both hands, Amelia jerked her head for Nanny to follow her. Accusingly, she said to the woman, 'He's ill, isn't he?'

'A little off colour, M'lady. He always is fussy and finnicky. If you give in to him, he'll . . . ' She threw open the nursery door. Sarah was sitting in front of the nursery fire, cradling Charles in her arms. His face was flushed, the dark hair round his forehead glued with sweat. Sarah looked up at Amelia, her eyes wide and frightened.

'I told Nanny to get you before now,' she said in a low voice.

'And I told you, young woman, I'm in charge here! M'lady has more to do than sort out childish tantrums.'

'It's more than childish tantrums.' Amelia bent forward and stroked his cheek. She could feel the heat of his body even before she touched him. His lips were a dark feverish red, his eyes half-closed. A pulse in his throat beat rapidly and jerkily.

'Tell Pearson to telephone Dr Poultney,' she said to Sarah, gently lifting Charles out of her arms. And to Nanny, 'Please inform my husband that with his permission, I will stay at home. Perhaps he will wish to come and see Master Charles for himself before leaving.'

She waited, her arguments marshalled, for the sound of Frederick's footfall. But when a footfall came it was Nanny's rapid tread. She came in with her eyes averted and a small secret smile of pleasure curving her lips.

'The Master is leaving immediately, M'lady. He told me to tell you he would see you on his return.'

Even up here, the furious slamming of the front door was clearly audible. The sound had a sharp finality, like a mirror breaking or a chapter ending.

At exactly the same time as Dr Poultney was sitting beside Charles's sickbed and taking his temperature, Frederick was sitting at dinner beside a dark-haired green-eyed beauty of the most unusual wit and charm. Her name was Lady Diana Nazier – the wife of Lord Nazier, old friend of the Salisburys and a power in the Unionist camp. Her husband had a chill, with all those damp river fogs. He had to be careful. She felt he would be better at home.

'Of course,' Frederick said.

He knew that Lord Nazier was old, but had no idea that his wife was so young.

'And what are you most interested in, Lady Nazier?' he asked.

'Politics,' she said promptly.

'Measles,' said Dr Poultney just as promptly, 600 yards away in 7 Park Lane. 'Sponge his skin with flannels wrung out in tepid water. Burn this for his breathing.' He handed Nanny some aromatic substance. 'Give him a couple of tablespoonsful of Fennings fever cure every four hours.'

'Will he be all right, doctor?'

'Oh, yes, of course, M'lady. He's young. But sturdy as they come. The fever will abate now the rash is out. Keep the lamps low. His eyes may hurt. And we must watch his chest.'

He brought out his stethoscope and listened carefully. 'Clear as a bell. No chest weakness is there in your family, Lady Haybury? Thought not. I know there is some slight tendency in the Hayburys. But not, it seems, handed on to this young man. I'll look in tomorrow. Now get some rest yourself, Lady Haybury.'

Three more hours and two spoonfuls of fever cure later, Charles's temperature steadied and then began to sink. Amelia agreed to return to her room. Nanny and Sarah would take it in turn to watch by the cot. She gave them strict instructions that she was to be called should there be any change. She undressed slowly, and slept fitfully. Shortly before dawn she must have fallen into a deeper sleep. She was wakened suddenly by a rough hand on her shoulder. Immediately she sat up, full of dread and asked, 'Charles? Is he worse?'

She could only see a shadowy figure, bent right over her that was neither Nanny nor Sarah. The grip on her shoulder tightened painfully. Breath that was heavy with brandy fanned her cheek. 'The child is sleeping. I met Nanny just now.' Frederick said thickly. 'It was a false alarm. A storm in a teacup.'

He pushed her back angrily on to the pillows. 'You could have come.' He climbed into bed. 'It was your duty. You put him before me, your husband.' His face hovered close over here, his hands gripped her shoulders and he shook her to punctuate his words. 'D'you know that? D'you know something else? I am glad you didn't come. I have begun to realise —' But he left the sentence unfinished, pulling her to him without warning. He took her roughly and with deliberate punishing cruelty. As she gritted her teeth and clenched her fists, she wondered if he was punishing her for putting Charles first.

Or because she wasn't the person he wished her to be.

SEVEN

The woman that stood framed in the lintel of the Jerningham forge had some claim to good looks and knew it.

'For the sweet love of Jesus . . . buy some firing before me back breaks!'

James looked over his shoulder, 'I've got my own firing.'

Regular as the seasons themselves, come Maytime a horde of gipsies passed through Jerningham. They were on their way to the Whitsuntide and spring fairs and the horse sales. They came into the forge to have their pots and pans mended, the axles and wheels of their carts seen to, and though they pared the ponies' hooves themselves, they wanted the blacksmith to shoe the bigger horses.

Besides the great basket of firewood she had lugged in, she had a sling-bag full of pegs and a handful of paper and wire flowers. She had stuck two crimson paper poppies in her hair, and seeing him notice them, she smiled. "Pretty, ain't they, Sir? An' if ye won't have me firing, will yer lady buy my pretties?'

'I'm not wed, thank God.' James tweaked a long slab of red hot metal out of the fire, laid it carefully on the cooler ledge and began hammering with a frown of concentration.

'Your sweet mother then, Sir?'

'She's busy upstairs with my father.'

The piece of metal was the left hand front mudguard of the Honourable J.G. Anstruther's crimson Daimer that had come off worst in an encounter with the gatepost of its owner's mansion. This was only one of three such cars, identical with the one in which HRH King Edward VII sped through the quiet country lanes, that James now maintained for Hampshire gentlemen.

He had no cause to love the gentry. No cause to love their deceiving daughters either. But their cars he loved and learned from. He learned not only about their engines and performance. In a copy of the *Tatler* left on the back seat of this same Daimler, he had seen two photographs of Amelia, one at Ascot and one watching the balloons at Ranelagh. She looked more beautiful and distant than ever. She had become exactly what she had said she would never become – the typical empty-headed society lady.

''E's sick, is 'e, yer father?'

'Yes. Very sick.'

'An' what does the old tail-puller say?'

'He doesn't know what really ails him.'

''Course he don't! But I do.'

James tapped the edge of the mudguard and shook his head. 'You can't know. You haven't seen him.'

'I seed 'im 'ere.' She touched her forehead, and then with another of her cunning smiles, ''E were a soldier? 'E fought a long way away?'

'That's right. Anyone could've told you that.'

'Could've but they didn't. I'll tell you sumthin' else. 'E'll get better.'

'When?'

'Next spring. Afore we come agen.'

'How d'you know?'

'I know most things. I know about you. More'n you'd like me to know.'

He put the last taps on the mudguard, took it over and laid it flat on the workbench, and then he turned round and regarded her with his hands on his hips, frowning.

'A handsome fellah like you. An' you're not married yet!'

'I told you so myself.'

'You didn't 'ave to. I knew. An' I'll tell yer sumthin' else. Yer won't get wed for many a year.'

'Never!'

She threw back her head and laughed. 'Oh, yes yer will! You'll wed!'

'We shall see.'

'An' yer'll marry rich.'

'I don't believe you.'

'Why d'you smile like that then, handsome? Ye'd like to believe me, wouldn't you?'

'No!'

She sighed. 'Can I sit down a minute? I'm that tired, Jesus knows!' And without waiting for his nod, she sat on the little three-legged stool James's father usually sat on when he was well enough to help him. 'I s'pose you wouldn't have a cup of buttermilk?'

'I might have.'

When he returned with the cup, she took it from him and seized his hand, turning it over till the palm was uppermost. He snatched it away, laughing. 'I don't want fortune telling!'

She laughed gleefully back. 'But I seed it!'

'You saw nought but grime and sweat.'

'I seed you'll marry your rich lady. Only it won't be 'ere. It'll be over water.'

'Away with you, woman!'

'An' your father, 'im that sits where I'm sitting now, 'e'll get well.'

'I'll believe it when I see it.'

'You'll see it! Start when the broom on the forest is yallerer than 'im.'

'Broom?'

'Aye, man, 'tis broom 'e needs!'

'How does he need it?'

'I'm telling you. Pluck it when the moon's full. Scald it. Give a draught of the liquor ter 'im. Nought else. Nought the old tail-puller gives 'im. Just the broom. That'll tek the poison out of 'im.'

James snorted disbelievingly.

'Then yer'll be free.'

'Perhaps.'

'That's what yer want.'

'Don't we all?'

'You more'n most. To be free as a bird.'

'You talk a lot of nonsense, woman!'

He picked up the belows. The fire was dying into grey ash at the edges. He blew the bellows hard, watching the tiny flakes of wood-ash shoot upwards towards the canopy. Hot air, how fast it moves! An idea glimmered in his mind. Could hot air ever propel an aircraft forward? Just by itself in a hot jet?

'I've told you good,' she said thrusting her pegbag forward and holding out her hand. 'Now you buy good!'

He handed her a penny. '*And* I'll have the pegs.'

She laughed admiringly. 'You're an 'ard man, Sir! But then you need to be. You've 'ard things to do. 'Arder than most.'

'Like what?' he asked, showing reluctant interest.

She smiled. 'Like killing.'

He looked at her sharply. 'Killing what? Pigs?' He laughed. 'I done that.'

'No, by sweet Jesus! Not pigs! Least only two-legged pigs!' Her face darkened and she spat. 'That's what were in yer 'and, mister! That's why yer didn't want me ter see it! You're a killer, sir! You'll kill and kill again! Only when yer've killed, sir, will yer marry the rich pretty lady like you dream!'

That summer, Amelia found herself pregnant again, and she was thankful that Frederick decided to pack her off to Haybury in the company of Nanny and Sarah, Pearson and Cook. Since the Salisbury Ball, he had been increasingly withdrawn from her, his concern mere politeness.

'You look pale, Amelia. Go to Haybury. I'll join you whenever I can. It's time we showed ourselves in the constituency.' Frederick had reluctantly accepted the joint Mastership of the South Hampshire Foxhounds, and though his constituency was as safe as houses, nevertheless it was time he diverted some of his attention towards it.

Sarah was delighted to be returning, polished and townified, to within calling distance of Jerningham. Her mother had never learned to write and her brother could pen only halting sentences, so she had received few letters.

'Mind you, M'lady, I hope it's right to leave the Master. He didn't look himself when he got home last night,' Sarah remarked darkly as Amelia prepared for her last engagement before their departure for Haybury – taking tea with old Aunt Sempner.

'Do you mean you think he's ill, Sarah?'

'Not *ill*, M'lady, no.'

'Not *ill*. Quite the opposite, my dear child!' Aunt Sempner replied from her satin-covered sofa in her Upper Brook Street house when Amelia asked her the same question. 'Full of health and vigour. Burning the candle at both ends. He'll have taken a mistress. Some actress. Some cast-off of the King's perhaps.'

She brought out a delicate cambric handkerchief and dabbed her boot-button eyes. Amelia's embarrassment added greatly to the pleasure of her company for tea. Lady Sempner swallowed a cucumber sandwich with enhanced appetite. 'Oh, he'll keep it discreet, never fear. You won't be ousted. Indiscretion would harm him too much. He's ambitious. And they're a sly lot, the Hayburys. His father and grandfather were the same. But you're a stupid gal to have let it happen.'

She was a stupid girl to have let many things happen, Amelia thought, as they arrived at Haybury on a baking August afternoon. The trees were in full dark summer leaf, the corn ripe. A lark sang too high to see in the blue unclouded sky above the sun-drenched parkland. She was suddenly filled with an ache of unsatisfied longing, of a sense of destiny frustrated by her own stupidity.

Even Haybury Hall which she had always liked failed to quench the feeling. She stood for a moment staring up at its rose-red brickwork, at the delicate treble bows on either side of the double entrance stairway. Built before Jerningham Hall, it was a Queen Anne jewel set on a stone balustraded terrace, its formal gardens edged by a ha-ha, then the parkland sweeping away to the distant glitter of the sea. But she would have exchanged it, given it away, for . . .

She drove past the Jerningham forge the following week on her return from visiting her parents to show them Charles. They displayed little interest, indeed seemed faintly surprised she had expected any.

'Frederick coming down, is he?' her father asked.

'He'll certainly be here for the hunting season.'

Her father grumbled that Pegasus was eating him out of house and home. Never seen such an appetite on a horse! And it was agreed that as soon as her confinement was over, Pegasus would come to the stables at Haybury. After that discussion, her father dozed off to sleep, her stepmother enquired about the gowns worn by the Duchess of Manchester, and some of the gossip about the Court which had leaked down to Jerningham.

Jerningham Hall estate was becoming increasingly expensive, her step-mother said in answer to Amelia's question. Her father drank more, Amelia must have noticed. The village was little changed. Marriages, deaths, births, the old blacksmith sick and useless. They would have turned him out long ago, but the son did his job for him, and surprisingly kept a civil tongue in his head.

There was no sign of him in the forge. A fire glowed as Amelia passed the open doorway. Sparks flew upwards. A horse waited tethered to be shod. But no one came to the doorway to see what carriage rattled by.

Frederick stayed up in London, unavoidably detained by growing political problems of land tax and social issues inspired by the new Liberal Prime Minister, Asquith, and his Welsh Warlock Lloyd George. But he arrived for Christmas and let the New Year in by accompanying Amelia to the Watch Night service at Haybury church and returning to dole out hot punch to the household staff. But for all that, the New Year did not come in auspiciously for the Hayburys. The first hunt of 1907 was on 5 January. The morning dawned with mist in the forest hollows and a light crisping of frost. And though the scent would be sharp, the ground still held the moisture of the wet winter months, so the going would be treacherous.

The meet was at Haybury Hall itself, and there was a fine following. Frederick was known as a hospitable host, and he intended to keep that reputation. Pearson and a footman brought out silver trays with the strongly laced stirrup cups, which Amelia helped to dispense. The huntsmen and whippers-in touched their caps, gave her the compliments of the season, and discreetly averted their eyes from her condition.

Her condition showed less this time than it had with Charles, and Frederick privately feared this meant the baby would be a girl. He had set his heart on another boy. Whatever it was, Amelia would lavish too much attention on it. But at least that would mean she spoiled Charles rather less.

'No sign of your father yet. Late as usual.' Splendid in his pink, Frederick leaned down from his horse. 'But no doubt we shall meet him down the drive.'

Someone made some remark behind his hand which Amelia didn't hear, and the gentlemen around him smiled. Then the huntsman put the horn to his lips and the whippers-in gathered the hounds. Frederick doffed his hat and they were off. From the steps Amelia watched them disappear before going back into the Hall.

The hunt was well beyond the lodge gates when Mr Jerningham came galloping up on Pegasus, purple-faced and irritable because his own horse had gone lame. Frederick gave him a cool good morning and Mr Jerningham took up his position beside one of his neighbours, still grumbling.

There was a view almost immediately. Determined that this should be a fast and challenging hunt, Frederick pressed his knees hard into the horse's flanks, and led them off at a fine pace, over hedges and fences, streaking across the forest.

Amelia was in the nursery when the news came. It was Nanny's day off, and Amelia had sent Sarah down to the kitchens to fetch some pieces of wood for Charles's toy goods train. It was all very cosy. A fire crackled behind the burnished brass guard, sending a suffused glow on to the polished linoleum floor. Her own worn rocking-horse had been imported from Jerningham as had the toy cupboard, and even her dolls' house. The same nursery clock swung its pendulum on the wall.

It was into this deceiving atmosphere of content and continuity that Sarah burst. 'Oh, miss! M'lady! Terrible news! It's him!' Her round eyes were wide. Her mouth trembled. 'He's just rode over.'

'Who has?' Amelia put down the toy train and rose clumsily to her feet. She rested one hand to steady herself against the nursery table. Already her heart had begun to race anticipating the dire news written all over Sarah's face.

'March. James March, Miss. The blacksmith, you remember?'

'Yes, yes! What about him?'

'He brought the news. He said to tell you gentle.'

'Then tell me, for God's sake!'

''Tis about your father.'

'What about him?'

'March said he didn't want you upset. But your father—'

Amelia clenched her fists and held them to her mouth. And then just as she was about to scream out at Sarah, she heard slow steps on the last treads, a footfall on the landing, the nursery door pushed wider, and there was James. They looked at each other down the years. She had already guessed from his face what news he brought. But she stared at him questioningly, her eyes asking him many other things. He looked the same and yet so different – thinner, older, sadder.

'I'm sorry,' she heard him say, just as he had said years ago.

Then it was as if the years between were a long dizzy drop. The floor tilted. James's figure receded and diminished. She heard a distant exclamation from

Sarah. Everything went dark. James rushed forward to catch her. Even in the darkness she was aware of his arms round her. When the faintness passed, she didn't immediately open her eyes. She lay with her head against his chest. She didn't want to hear what news James brought. She wanted to stay where she was, listening to his heartbeat, feeling his warmth, conscious of every indrawn breath.

Then she felt herself being laid down gently on the nursery sofa. She felt her hair being smoothed by a familiar touch. She shivered.

'Don't open that window so wide, Sarah!' James's voice said close to her ear. 'Here! Give me that glass of water. Now, the best thing you can do is take the child out of here. Go for a walk.'

Charles had begun whimpering. That sound made Amelia open her reluctant eyes.

'There! That's better.' James put his hand on her forehead. 'She's come round, Sarah.' He slipped a hand under Amelia's head and, reaching out for the water Sarah passed to him, brought it to Amelia's lips. 'Drink it steady. Just a little at a time. Put a cushion behind her, Sarah.' And looking gently into Amelia's face, 'I'm sorry I frightened you.'

'You didn't.' She sat up. 'I'm all right.' She reached out and squeezed one of Charles's fat little hands as he sidled up to her. 'I'm sorry,' she looked from James to Sarah to Charles, 'it was I who frightened you.'

'Come on, Master Charles,' Sarah said firmly in response to a meaningful look from James. 'There's nought wrong with your Mama now! Let's go and find some pine cones for her. You know she likes 'em.'

'Wrap up warmly,' Amelia said automatically.

'That we will, M'lady,' Sarah called with her head inside the nursery cupboard. 'It's a gaiters and galoshes day.' She came out with an armful of clothes, and began busily fitting Charles into them. James watched them silently, from time to time throwing a sideways glance at Amelia.

'Now, Master Charles, say goodbye to your Mama and to March. He'll no doubt be gone when we get back.'

When they had left, Amelia turned her eyes to James's face and waited. Stiltedly, painfully he told her that her father had been killed. He took both her hands in his. 'How did it happen?'

'At that same gate. Darenth Wood. He was behind the rest of the field. Tried to catch up I suppose. Took that gate too fast. Fell sideways. The horse on top. He wouldn't know anything, Amelia.'

'Was anyone with him?'

'That fellow from Lyndhurst Chase was just behind. He came for me. Your father was dead when I got there.'

Amelia said nothing.

'I brought him in.'

'Thank you.'

'I did what had to be done.' She nodded without comprehension. After several minutes of silence broken only by the ticking of the nursery clock and the shift of the coals in the grate James said slowly and distinctly, 'I had to shoot the horse.' He drew in his breath. 'Both back legs were broken, and he was . . .'

She nodded again and then suddenly looked at him and asked harshly, 'Which was it?'

'Yours,' he said steadily, holding her gaze levelly. 'Yours, Amelia. It was Pegasus.'

'Pegasus? Why him? Why was my father riding him?'

'His friend said something about his own horse being lame.'

'But he was mine! We . . .'

'You weren't there to ride him though,' James said gently.

'And you killed him!' Her voice was as accusing as her grief.

'Aye,' James said steadily. 'I killed him myself.'

'But did you have to?' Tears sprang into her eyes.

'I wouldn't have wanted a stranger to do it.'

Amelia suddenly became aware that she had been holding James's hands all this time, squeezing them, bearing down on them in pain, as nearly three years before she had squeezed young Sarah's hands when Charles was being born. She relaxed her grip, withdrew her hands, and as if this was his dismissal James straightened. 'I'll go and find your husband. You'll want him beside you. He was up at the front of the field. They'd got a kill. There was a lot of excitement. He mightn't know yet.'

'Thank you.' She tried to make herself look up at him, but she couldn't. It was unnatural and reprehensible to mourn the death of a horse at the same time as the death of one's father. But it was because it was James himself who had slaughtered Pegasus that she felt so unnaturally distressed. Pegasus was the instrument that had brought James and herself together. He was the symbol of their soaring hopes. Now the symbol, the underlining of the death of these hopes.

Twenty minutes later Sarah returned with Charles. And shortly after that Frederick came galloping home. He was shocked and tired. The fox had led them a dance to six or seven miles east of Haybury. They'd run him to earth on the new railway cutting. The dogs had their blood up. They couldn't be held. They'd torn him to ribbons. Just after the kill took place, the Jerningham blacksmith had ridden up with the dire news.

Frederick had been so shocked by this misfortune that he'd ridden home hell for leather, still clutching the fox's brush. A few youngsters had been waiting eager to be blooded. But he rode past them. His groom was hardly able to keep up with him. Both horses were scummy with sweat, their mouths foaming. He knew exactly where in Haybury Hall he'd find Amelia. He took the stairs three at a time, and wrenched open the nursery door.

She was seated in the rocking chair by the nursery fire with Charles on her knee. The firelight sparkled in her hair and glowed on her cheeks. 'I know already,' she told Frederick composedly. Then her eyes suddenly fastened on the fox's brush he carried in his bloodstained hand.

It seemed to her at that moment the physical embodiment of the day's sad and bloody doings. She shrank away from it. Jerked awake and following her eyes, the child let out a frightened yell. It was too much for Frederick. 'For God's sake!' he shouted. 'Stop that noise! You stupid, spoiled brat! Screaming and wailing at a fox's brush!' And rounding furiously on Amelia, 'When are you going to let me make a man of that child!'

Impatiently, not waiting for her to answer, he grabbed the child's shoulder, and snatched him off her knee. Before Amelia had time to more than rise clumsily to her feet, Frederick slid his grip to the back of the child's neck, and

65

taking the bloody end of the brush smeared it over the forehead, as he would blood a youngster in the field.

It seemed to have the desired effect. Abruptly Charles stopped crying. His soft lips tightened; his eyes blazed like blue flames.

The child had grown into a man.

A vast number of black-clad relatives descended on the Hall for Mr Jerningham's lying in state and the funeral. Many of them Amelia had met briefly at her wedding. But the ladies were hardly recognisable behind their thick veils, nor the men under their crêped hats. Still with her husband at the Embassy in Washington, Victoria was not amongst them, so Amelia and Frederick accompanied her father's widow through the public expressions of grief.

Charles was rigged out, on Frederick's orders, in a black Eton jacket, white collar with a black bow tie, black breeches secured below the knee with strap and buckle, black stockings, black low shoes and black hat. He sat, still as stone, between Amelia and Frederick as they drove to Jerningham Hall. The carriage was hung with black rosettes, silk ropes and tassels. The horses each wore three black plumes. Under the carriage rug, Amelia held Charles's hand tightly.

The day was grey and a wet west wind blew, but a queue of villagers had formed at the lodge gates, ready when the time came to follow them in. Her stepmother was waiting for them in the hall. She was swathed from head to foot in black. A thick black veil obscured her face. Even her handkerchief, which she held ready, was heavily edged with black. She rested a hand on each of their arms, and with Charles following reluctantly behind, slowly traversed the hall to the flagged and icy gun-room beyond, where the body lay on a raised dais.

The dais was hung with purple. Black curtains muffled the window. The only light was from the four flickering sconces at each corner of the catafalque. Four black-suited men guarded it. Amelia forced her eyes to regard the marble face that had once been her father. He looked as remote as the crusaders' effigies in Jerningham church, with his honours and badges carefully laid out on a white satin cushion beside him, far away from the reach of his marble fingers. Her own fingers sought those of her son and squeezed them.

'I shall lift Charles up so that he may look on his grandfather,' Frederick whispered to her. But she put her arm round Charles and moved him away as if she hadn't heard. She was suddenly aware of being watched. Through the darkness of her veil, through the smoking light of the candle sconces, she glanced at the four men. She saw they were all her father's tenants, and that the one facing her directly within touching distance was James.

The flames from the candle flickered in his dark blue eyes. Eyes like his but round and frightened looked up at her from the shadows.

'May we go now, Mama?' Charles whispered.

She looked from one face to the other. It was all too much. She began to weep, and not to be outdone, her stepmother lifted her veil and dabbed at her eyes. Frederick led them both into the fresh cold air outside. Charles was scooped up by a hovering twittering Sarah.

'Are you sure you should go to the funeral, M'lady?' Sarah asked as Amelia kissed Charles goodnight that evening. But she insisted. She had her own sense of duty. And James would be there. It might well be the last time she ever saw him. Sarah had picked up the latest villge gossip on her visit home. Mr March's health was improving. Rumour had it that James would be leaving the forge as soon as his father was able to work again.

'Is he getting married?' Amelia asked.

'No, M'lady. Going off abroad they say. America maybe.'

There was another sharp frost on the morning of the funeral. The ground was so hard that the hooves of the black-plumed horses struck sparks from the road, though they went at a slow walk through the village, past the houses with their curtains tightly drawn and the closed shops with black crêpe streamers over their windows.

The forge was shut. Black rosettes were nailed to the door. James's parents stood outside. His father certainly looked stronger. He stood bare-headed as the hearse passed, the cold wind whipping his hair. Mrs March lifted her veil to wipe her eyes. Just for a moment they met those of Amelia and exchanged quick hostile messages.

'Hypocrite!' Amelia thought. 'You never liked him.' But then few villagers had liked her father. Certainly James hadn't. She searched for him as the carriage wheeled round under the elms. There was no sign of him with the ostlers, marshalling the carriages. Then she saw him amongst the pall bearers, moving forward to slide out the coffin. The muffled bell was chiming from the church tower. A few crisp dead leaves drifted down, as the coffin was shouldered.

Amelia fell into step behind them, torn by contrary emotions. Why should James of all people bear her father to his grave? He resented Jerningham and its feudal society. He was intent on escape. Yet almost at once, the thought came to her that James was always near at hand when she needed him. And – her thoughts now racing through her mind – why should James bend his neck to his so-called betters who were so much less clever and resourceful than he? Till – the most dangerous thought of all – why wasn't it James there walking into the pew beside her, his shoulder that brushed hers, his arm on which her fingers rested as they processed after the service towards the family tomb?

Amelia closed her eyes to hold back the shameful tears as her father's body was laid to rest in the Jerningham mausoleum beside that of her mother. Small wonder that, as everyone said, the strain of the funeral brought on the pains. Amelia had hardly sat down to the over-rich funeral repast when the first dull ache began.

EIGHT

Arthur Haybury was prematurely born on 11 January 1907, and because of his weak state was immediately baptised. Prayers for his survival were said at Haybury and in all the neighbouring churches. Arthur was small, narrow-faced and pale. What hair he had was a thin haze of sandy red. But his features were well formed, and looking down on him, Frederick thought he had never seen a more beautiful child.

For weeks, Dr Randall mumbled uncertainly. Reluctantly he allowed Amelia to feed the child herself. She never left the baby and this time Frederick did not complain. He had, however, other things of which to complain. While Randall was still fussing about mother and child, Frederick became acquainted with the terms of his father-in-law's will and the mess in which Jerningham had left his affairs. He had some stormy meetings with old Mr Pearless of Pearless de Sangry, the Jerningham solicitors but that didn't alter anything – it was a pretty kettle of fish. Only Amelia's stepmother came out of it comfortably, with an annuity which would keep her very nicely in Biarritz where she had immediately made it clear she intended to settle.

'She's already got old Pearless negotiating an apartment out there. Can't wait to go if you ask me!' Frederick told Amelia a month after Arthur was born. She was, as usual, in the nursery, sitting by the window, gazing out as if in a dream. Nanny had taken Charles for a walk. Arthur was asleep in his cot. The ubiquitous Sarah, now grown well-fed on his good food was noisily washing something in the nursery bathroom. Frederick stood with his back to the fire.

'I know that old woman Randall doesn't want me to bother you with business just yet. But there it is. Someone has to bother and it can't always be me! You've got to know how your father disposed his property, such as it was, sooner or later. And then we can decide the best way to go about selling it. Property isn't all that easy to dispose of, y'know. Not the Jerningham sort. Talk of Land Tax,' he shook his head, 'has scared buyers off.'

'You haven't told me yet what my father left?'

'The money, such as it is, to your stepmother. He'd promised it would be hers. She'd made her plans. Jerningham comes to you and Victoria. But there's the snag. Apart from a sum of £500 each to you and your sister from your mother's money, there's nothing. No money to run it.'

'Does Victoria know?'

'Pearless wrote to her in Washington. But the diplomatic life occupies her now. She certainly doesn't want Jerningham. Who's to blame her? There's a lot needs doing. Sell or rent, she says. Leaves it up to me.'

'To us,' Amelia corrected him gently.

Frederick frowned. 'Don't split hairs, Amelia! Either way, Jerningham has got to go. Haybury is bad enough. We don't want two estates.'

'We have two sons,' Amelia replied promptly.

For several seconds Frederick said nothing. He stared down at the nursery rug, a deep frown drawing together his brows. The thought of Charles inheriting Haybury was bitterly distasteful to him. The thought of Arthur, if he was spared, having nowhere to inherit was even more distasteful.

'We would still need a considerable amount of money.'

'My £500 could go into it.'

'Useless! You have no idea of money, Amelia! None! No head for business. You may use your legacy to buy yourself a piece of jewellery. There's not even any of that coming to you. Or buy yourself a decent hunter. Replace the animal that dolt of a blacksmith shot.'

At the thought of the irritation and injustice of it all, Frederick slammed crossly out of the nursery. For a long time, Amelia sat staring out of the window at the winter-brown parkland and the bare trees of the forest beyond. She would never replace Pegasus. But she had an overwhelming desire to escape the confines of the house, to gallop at speed, to feel the wind in her hair and the cold whipping her face.

An idea for spending her money suddenly came to her. And never the one to let the grass grow under her feet, she hurried to her sitting-room, took out paper and pen, and wrote immediately to the Honourable Charles Rolls, asking if she might be permitted to buy one of his Silver Ghost cars.

Six weeks later, Mr Rolls delivered the motor car in person. He arrived in the middle of a windy afternoon. He was on his way from his workshop in Wales to help organise the Exhibition of Motor Manufacturers which was to be held at Olympia on 16 March, so if Lady Haybury, after he'd given her some instruction, would be kind enough to drop him at the station, he would complete his journey by railway.

The instruction was simple. You kept to the left hand side of the road. You steered by the wheel and you stopped by the brake. There was something called a gear level which could prove tricky. The lights were acetylene. Mr Rolls sat beside Amelia while, watched by Sarah and Pearson she steered the silver-grey car down Haybury drive. Inevitably she turned the nose of the bonnet towards Jerningham. She was a natural driver, Mr Rolls said. She took to it like a duck to water.

As they moved steadily down Jerningham High Street, Amelia hoped that James would watch them go by. But only old Mr March appeared in the doorway of the forge to see what the commotion was about. Disappointed, Amelia turned the car up past the shuttered lodge of her old home.

Already the drive looked untended. Her stepmother had left for Biarritz without leaving even a caretaker in charge. The façade looked more decayed than when Amelia had seen it last. Somehow she found herself telling Charles Rolls all about it. How it was to be sold or rented, how she would like to keep it but of what use could it possibly be.

'May I see it, Amelia? May we walk round?'

Hands folded behind his back, Rolls walked round the house and the stable block, the walled garden and the paddocks in silence. At one point he climbed on to a mounting block, and stared out at the glimmer of the Solent. Then returned to the passenger seat of Amelia's new car and said, 'Well, I know what I'd do if I had this place. I'd turn the stable block into workshops. I'd pull down the walled garden and make it a hard standing. The paddocks are flat so I'd make a grass runway through, and put a slipway down to the Solent. Then in a small way to begin with, I'd start building aeroplanes!'

'Building aeroplanes? Building aeroplanes at Jerningham? Have you gone out of your mind? And has that fellow Rolls gone out of his mind too?'

Frederick was naturally furious. He had raised no objection whatever when he had heard that Amelia had ordered a motor car. He had been understanding itself. Indeed quite a few of his Westminster colleagues were in possession either of a Rolls-Royce or a Daimler similar to the King's. And what was good enough for the King was good enough for Frederick. But that Amelia, ever one for fads and foolishness should be tempted into such a folly as to contemplate building aeroplanes was more than his temper could bear.

'We had a long talk,' Amelia said to Frederick. 'He stayed for dinner. Then he caught the last train to London from Brockenhurst. He really thought it through. It wasn't just an idle suggestion.'

'I consider it a monstrous suggestion!'

'But is it, Frederick, if you stop and think?'

It was the week after the car had been delivered and Frederick had duly admired it as soon as he had eaten the excellent dinner Cook had prepared for him. He might have known Amelia was up to something, as all his favourite foods – oysters, turtle soup, roast saddle of lamb and cranberry pie – followed each other till he was replete, his problems and irritations about Jerningham blunted.

Arthur too was stronger. He had gained weight. Randall had pronounced him out of danger. Then when Frederick had finished off a couple of glasses of port, Amelia had brought up this monstrous suggestion. She must have mistaken his horrified silence for interest for she plied him with the details this rich lunatic and she had worked out.

A man called A.V. Roe had been building aeroplanes for years under London railway arches, Rolls had told her. Another Englishman was also building small aircraft in a shed just across the river from Jerningham. He was making these craft with floats and planning to launch them for take-off on the river. It was all too much! Cloud-cuckoo land! Frederick had exploded with anger. He announced there and then that he was cutting his visit short. The next day he returned to the sanity of London and Lady Nazier's drawing-room.

On that Sunday afternoon, he found her alone. She had only recently returned from Marienbad where her husband was still taking the waters. Frederick had only twice met Lord Nazier. He was almost old enough to be her grandfather. But he was a life-long friend of old Salisbury's, of almost every politician, come to that. A force to be reckoned with.

Contrary to what Aunt Sempner thought, Frederick was not Diana Nazier's lover. He worshipped at her feet. She was his goddess, his lodestar. And he had no wish to offend her husband. But that afternoon, after Amelia had so irritated him, he threw caution to the winds. After only the barest of polite enquiries about her husband, he sat beside Diana and poured out his problem into her cool sympathetic ear.

70

Her lovely green eyes regarded him calmly. She smiled occasionally, shook her head from time to time, but heard him out without comment.

'Amelia has either taken complete leave of her senses . . . ladies have been known to experience madness after childbirth, I'm told.' Frederick accepted the little china cup of tea Diana handed him and sipped it gratefully. 'Or she does this simply to provoke me.'

'To provoke may come into it. She seems impulsive, self-willed, reckless,' Diana Nazier nodded her beautiful dark head. 'But she is also mad to try to build heavier-than-air machines. Aeroplanes will never have the luxury of gas-filled airships.'

'That's what I tell her. I suppose you saw that leader in the *Times*? I have the cutting here.' Frederick put two fingers in the vest pocket of his waistcoat and brought out the cutting: *All attempts at artificial aviation are not only dangerous to human life, but foredoomed to failure from the engineering standpoint.*

He handed it to Lady Nazier. She read it politely, while he studied the lovely line of her long white neck, the shape of her head under the shining folds of black hair, her long lashes. Handing the piece of newspaper back to him, she caught his look of uninhibited admiration and smiled faintly.

'Artificial aviation? Yes, they are perfectly right! But floating up in an airship or a balloon is a different matter, wouldn't you think, Frederick?'

At that moment, he would have agreed to any proposition she cared to make. She continued, smiling. 'On our way to Marienbad, my husband and I spent a pleasant week in Germany.' Impulsively she put a hand lightly on his arm. 'I thought of you, my dear Frederick, at Haybury with your many problems. Germany was so stimulating. I had the pleasure of meeting Count Zeppelin.'

'He must have been enchanted,' Frederick murmured.

'He is certainly a figure of great importance there. Idolised! We were of the privileged party who watched the Count make a flight on Lake Constance. Crown Prince Wilhelm was there too. I was presented.'

Frederick smiled admiringly, 'You move in exalted circles.'

Diana gave him a long challenging look that was more sensual and exciting than the most provocative glance from a lesser woman. She drew a deep breath, and said softly, enunciating each word with careful clarity, 'We could *both* move in exalted circles.'

He caught her meaning exactly. Theatrically, he dropped to one knee beside her and pressed her hand to his lips.

That night, he became at last her lover. He had been in love with her before she ever took him so graciously and sweetly to her bed. He loved her beauty, her wit, her shrewdness, her poise. But even had he not loved all these things, he would have fallen in love with her for that one night alone. Experienced as he was, he had known no woman like her, no other so sensual, so accomplished.

Lying in that warm lagoon after lovemaking, he thought how clumsy and unexciting she made other women seem, how naïve and schoolgirlish Amelia was in comparison.

And as if she had been reading his thoughts, Diana turned her head to him and whispered in his ear, 'If we are to be together more often, why not let your wife occupy herself with her foolish plans for Jerningham?'

The plans for Jerningham were drawn up after a protracted correspondence with Charles Rolls. *If your ideas on this are as splendid as your motor car*, she wrote to him, *we shall soon take off*.

Indeed as she drove his splendid motor car along the New Forest tracks, her foot pressed hard on its accelerator pedal, it did seem the ground might fall away and the car with herself inside become airborne. On those occasions she often imagined James was there, and up and away they leapt off the edge of the world.

She was in good spirits that April, hardly able to believe her luck. Though Frederick had remained in London over Easter not only had he given his consent to starting up at Jerningham, but had also agreed to invest a small sum in the little company. Victoria was amenable. The Honourable Charles Rolls also took a share. The company was formed with Frederick and Amelia owning one third of the shares each, while both Victoria and Rolls held a sixth. Frederick would be chairman, the others would be directors.

It all seemed a miracle.

Underneath his impatience, Frederick can be generous, Amelia told herself. He had not after all scorned her idea, had actually invested in it. He said he liked her enthusiasm and her energy, and there were, he had been told by friends in London, political possibilities in aviation – particularly in airships. The wife of Lord Nazier had been particularly interested in the idea of an aviation factory. She was quite an expert on aviation. They would have much in common. One day Amelia must meet her.

One day, Amelia promised she would. She took care to be particularly pleasant and obliging to Frederick. After all, he had been pleasant and obliging to her.

She even submitted to his lovemaking, which she had always tried to avoid whenever possible, with a meekness that surprised him. As he undressed Amelia in the cold Haybury bedroom and clasped her to him in the big four-poster, he whispered the secret that the government would certainly fall over Asquith's spring budget which reputedly contained the Land Tax and at last the Unionists would get in. 'There isn't a peer who'll vote for theft of his own inheritance. And when the government falls, we shall be in. Balfour has promised me a position as junior minister.'

He lay on his back after their cool unimpassioned lovemaking, breathing deeply as if already inhaling the sweet scent of political victory, while Amelia lay on her side, her back to him, thinking that he was as calculating in bed as he was in politics. It was all so cold. It made her feel not a person at all. More like one of the cows on the Home Farm that had been covered by the bull and put in calf. She began to fear a similar fate. Perhaps that was what Frederick wanted. Herself kept quiet with another pregnancy. Another Haybury son for the nursery . . . That she must avoid. There was so much to do. She had so many plans. She was relieved when Frederick suddenly relinquished his interest in the company for the time being and returned to London.

Above all, she longed to share her news with James, to get his advice. Only he would understand the real significance of what she was doing. More and more, she drove the Rolls round by the forge, but she never saw him. As well as all his other help, Rolls had promised to look out for a reliable designer and mechanic. But as April neared its chilly end and he had still not sent any names to her, a beguiling idea came into Amelia's mind.

It was still only an idea when on the last Friday in April she drove the Rolls across the forest to Motley Stud to look at a pony she thought might do for Charles. Returning in the late afternoon, she watched a skein of wild geese rise from Beaulieu lake, form their strange perfect V and arrow into the sunset. Memories, longings, overwhelmed her. She pressed her foot down on the accelerator, swung on to a cart track, and drunk with speed went roaring after the silent birds.

Grit rattled on the silver bonnet. The wind whipped her hair loose, filled her eyes with blinding tears so that, rounding another corner, she almost didn't see him.

Standing on the brake, swerving on to the turf, she stopped a foot to one side, just short of the horse's nose. The horse reared in the cart shafts till it was brought down by James's jerk on the reins. She heard him curse softly but furiously. Then for a full minute no one said anything. Amelia sat where she was, her hand to her mouth. The Rolls' engine hissed mildly. Then, satisfied that the horse was calm, James threw the reins over its head and jumped down.

'For Christ's sake,' he said in a low furious voice – low only, Amelia thought, so that his horse would not be further startled – 'what the hell do you think you're doing?'

'I've as much right to drive here as you have!' she said, her heart hammering.

'No, you haven't! *And* you know it! This is a track, not a highway. And coming at a pace like that, you stupid girl!'

'Oh, James,' she said suddenly, 'don't scold me like that!'

He shot her a quick suspicious look as if her change of mood pierced him. 'She's a beauty,' he said quietly. 'You've no right to drive her dangerously like that.'

'I thought you might have been worried about *me.*'

'No.' He looked at her directly with those deep blue uncompromising eyes. 'I gave that up nearly four years ago.'

He appeared not to notice her stricken silence. After several seconds, in which he walked round the car, looking at it carefully from every angle, he said casually, 'I heard you'd got a Rolls. I've serviced Daimlers and a Simms-Welbeck, but I think a Rolls might be even better.'

'How did you hear?'

'You passed the forge several times, M'lady.'

'Don't call me that.'

He looked at her keenly. 'It's what you are now, isn't it?'

'No.'

'Well, it's what you're supposed to be.'

'Not to you. Never to you, James. I'm Amelia. Half of Ajax.'

'That was a long time ago.' He paused, 'I also heard you'd had another son. Congratulations. I'm glad he's all right now.'

'Do you forgive me?'

'For what, M'lady? There was nothing to forgive.'

'Don't start that again, damn you!'

'Ladies don't swear.'

73

'You told me that the first time I met you.'

'That shows you don't change, Amelia.'

'You've changed.'

'Maybe I have.' He busied himself with the catch of the bonnet. 'Can I look inside?'

'Oh, yes! Please do! I'll take you for a ride in it, if you like.'

He twisted the corners of his mouth into a wry smile, and threw open the bonnet. He peered inside.

'Do you know how it works?' Amelia stood beside him leaning in, her arm brushing his.

'Of course I do. How else could I service them if I didn't?'

'Then tell me.'

'Why?'

'I might break down.'

'You'd get some man to come and help you.'

'Please, James! I really want to know!'

'Well, the petrol comes in here. That's the carburettor. A combustible mixture reaches the cylinders. D'you know what that means?'

'You know I do. I haven't forgotten.'

'Here's the cylinder where that mixture is compressed. And here's the magneto that makes the spark. The mixture ignites, expands and forces down the piston. It fires on all six cylinders. That turns the camshaft. 50 horse power . . .'

'More powerful than an aeroplane?'

'So far. But aeroplanes will have engines a hundred times more powerful.'

'You're joking!'

'No, I'm not.' He snapped the bonnet shut. 'Now let's have that ride! He'll graze for a few minutes there.' He jerked his head at the horse. She saw, besides the sacks of charcoal on the cart, some roots of still flowering gorse.

'I make a physic for my father.' James followed her eyes. 'Gipsy physic.' He smiled faintly.

'Does it do any good?'

'Well, he's better. And when he's fit again, I can leave. Put it like that.'

'And that's what you think has done it?'

He shrugged. 'It's possible. But then anything's possible.'

'Oh, James.' She slipped her hand through his arm. 'That's what I like! You make me feel *anything's* possible!'

'However, what isn't possible,' he said, gently disengaging her hand, 'is for me to take *her*,' he patted the bonnet of the Rolls, 'down a lane like this.'

'*You're* not taking her at all, James! *I'm* taking her. *I'm* the pilot this time.'

'No, you're not!'

'Yes, I am.'

'I've seen your driving!'

'I'll show you.'

Laughing she quickly began to climb back into the driving seat. He turned round and caught her arm. She tried to pull away. He put both hands suddenly round her waist and began to carry her, screaming and laughing and kicking, round the bonnet towards the passenger seat.

'Put me down, you wretch!' She kicked out, but he held her away from him.

Wriggling, pushing his shoulders with her hands, still laughing she caught a glimpse of the sudden vulnerability of his expression. Impulsively she threw her arms round his neck, and kissed his lips.

He dropped her like a stone. But not before she had tasted the sweetness of his mouth again. Avoiding his eyes, she climbed meekly into the passenger seat and folded her hands on her lap. In silence he started up the engine, backed the car, turned it in the first gateway and then eased it on to the road again.

'It was your fault, James.' Amelia said to his stern profile. 'For fooling around.'

'So it was. I should've known. I should have known *you*. But that's over, Amelia. *All* that, you understand. You're a married lady.'

'I understand, James.' She watched his foot gently ease down on the accelerator, felt the car smoothly surge forward. 'You're a good driver, James.'

He inclined his head. 'Thank you.'

'Don't you feel wasted being at the forge?'

He didn't answer. His eyes lifted from the road a moment towards the silvering of sea on the horizon.

'Don't you get tired of it?'

He still didn't answer.

'Now that my father is dead, aren't you worried? Frederick wanted to sell, you know.'

He turned the car left at the next turning, bringing them back in a circle to where they had begun. 'I haven't lost any sleep over it, Amelia.'

'But it would mean selling *everything*, James! Including the forge. What would your parents do?'

'I reckon I could provide for them.'

'How?'

'Never mind how. I'd provide.'

'But all your schemes to build aeroplanes?'

He eased the car gently at a walking pace on to the track where he'd left the cart, and at walking pace he brought the Rolls gently behind it to the whisper of a stop.

He put on the brake with a certain finality. 'My schemes will have to wait, Amelia.'

'But listen, James! They don't have to! And you don't have to leave Jerningham. Let me tell you *my* scheme.'

She poured it all out to him. He listened with his eyes fixed ahead, his hands resting on the wheel, his face inscrutable.

'And it isn't just for me, James. You've got a part in this too. A *big* part. We'll build Ajax yet. Oh, we're only starting off small. Not even as big as Santos-Dumont in Paris. We met him, you know . . . '

'On your honeymoon?'

'Yes,' she waved a dismissing hand and returned to her Jerningham plans. 'You could be manager, designer. We can . . . '

'What we *could* have done, Amelia, is finished.'

'It's not! Why should it be? We're young.'

'You had your choice and you made it.'

'I had *no* choice.'

75

'You've made your bed.'

'You sound like your damned mother!'

'And you'll keep my mother out of it! She's a good woman.'

'Better than me, you mean?'

'Perhaps. Life's too easy for you. You're bored. You're dissatisfied. So you and your rich friends take up the fad. Then you crook your finger and the local blacksmith —'

'James! How *could* you?'

'How could *you*? You think of *that*, Amelia, before you come offering me a job! A job paid for by your husband's money, eh?' He threw open the car door. 'What does that make me?'

'But why, James? Why couldn't we just be friends? Distant friends? Colleagues? Partners? Why couldn't you come and build Ajax at Jerningham?'

For answer, he put his hand on her shoulder and half-turned her to him. He kissed her fiercely, tenderly, passionately. It was a kiss that declared his love and simultaneously his total renunciation of it.

'That,' he said, releasing her. '*That's* why!'

NINE

James left home next day.

He humped all his possessions in his father's army kitbag to Brockenhurst railway station and caught the train to Farnborough. Having turned down Amelia's private patronage, his only hope now was the government. And the only flying they were doing was at the Balloon Factory at Farnborough.

There had been a row in the forge the night before. His father, his old strong self again, had shouted, 'What the 'ell d'you want to join the Royal Engineers for?'

That same question was asked when he arrived at Farnborough barracks by a recruiting sergeant with a face the colour of raw meat. James gave the same answer, 'To learn to fly.'

'What makes you think we'll teach you?'

'I saw a kite up as I came from the station.'

Disappointingly, it had looked identical to a kite he had seen behind a destroyer in the Solent four years ago. An aerial overhead railway led up into the sky, held up by an enormous box kite like a black bat with devil's horns, supported by four smaller bats at intervals along the wire, like intermediate stops to Destination Heaven. There was only one improvement – the wicker basket swinging below carried not a log but a man with bright red hair.

'If that's all you want, you best do it privately.'

'I haven't a penny.'

That was not quite true. He had six pounds and eight shillings.

'Then best take the King's shilling quickly, hadn't you, lad?' said the sergeant not unkindly, pushing a white form across the table. 'Make your mark there!'

'Sign, d'you mean?'

'So you can read and write?'

'Of course I can!'

'That's more than Colonel Cody, the kite-master can do.'

'But he's designed kites!'

'And other things.'

'He couldn't do that if he couldn't read and write!'

'Tell him, lad!'

'So if I sign up, I'll stay here flying kites?'

'You'll go wherever His Majesty says!'

'But I want to stay here!'

'You sign your name, and I'll see what I can do.'

'You see what you can do *before* I sign.'

The red face reddened further. 'Nobody talks to me like that! Nobody tells *me* what to do!'

'I'm telling you now what to do. Otherwise —'

'Who the bloody hell,' roared the recruiting sergeant, 'd'you think *you* are?'

One minute later James was back in the street, thinking that at least his father would be pleased. He began slowly walking away from the barracks down a cobbled street lined with lime trees, drawn towards that array of black bats as irresistibly as to a magnet. He was finally stopped by iron railings. Peering over the spikes, he saw a long stretch of grass on the right of which were a number of small huts beside a vast green-coloured shed. On the left were a dozen men in khaki manipulating the winch for the wire that held the kites.

'Christ! Sweet Jesus! God Almighty, but you sons of guns are slow!'

The words in a Texan accent came floating up to James, punctuated by the sound of galloping hooves. Round the corner of the nearest shed on a huge white horse came an enormous man with a theatrical moustache, long fair hair and a pointed beard. He was wearing twill cavalry breeches, brown boots, check shirt, a red handkerchief round his throat and a wide-brimmed cowboy hat on his head. Round his waist was a leather belt with two pistols in the holsters.

'Come on! Let out another 100 feet!'

This must be the kite-master . . . what was his name again? Cody, that was it! A dynamism like that of the kites now attracted him towards that figure on the prancing white horse. If he was going to get anywhere in this new venture, he would have to be bold. So with the same confidence as the horseman and the same panache, he marched round the railings, passed the sentry and walked through the open gates.

'Hey . . . you there!' shouted the sentry.

He stopped, turned, looked the man up and down.

'Your pass?'

'I'm a friend of Colonel Cody.'

The effect was magical. Just for a second, the soldier hesitated, taking in the cheap cloth coat, workman's trousers and black boots. Then he must have decided that such clothes were positively civilised beside the Colonel's own. 'All right.' He lifted up his arm to point. 'He's —'

'I can see him.'

James was through. He began walking briskly towards the other side of the winch, trying to decide what to do next. No one took the slightest notice of him. The figure on the horse went on bawling, the Engineers on the winches galvanised themselves to carry out the stream of orders. A steam tractor puffed over, engulfing the scene in a mist of acrid smoke. The wire from the ground to the cloud base swayed like a long thin snake.

And then suddenly, 100 yards away from the winch, there was a crack like thunder, followed by an anguished roar of American swearing. The next second, the wire itself, free of the winch, began whipping over the ground like a fire-cracker.

Shimmering over the grass, it passed within inches of James's left foot. He tried to stamp on it, missed, then flung himself forward, grasping the cold wire in both his hands. Immediately, he was pulled off his feet. Still clinging to the wire, he was dragged roughly over the grass.

Then all at once – total stillness. He was being hoisted up and up into the sky. For the second time in his life, James March was airborne.

He looked up and saw 1000 feet above him the red hair of the other men he shared the wire with above the rim of the basket. He looked down and saw the blur of moving ground twenty feet below. Men were running, holding out their hands. The steam tractor chugged, belching smoke. The big man on the white horse was racing across to the small wooded rise towards which he was drifting.

The wire he held was no longer cold but red hot. As the kites jerked him this way and that, it was scorching his hands. He felt himself slipping.

There were trees below him. If he let go now, he'd be all right. He couldn't hang on much longer. But if he did let go the wire, what would happen to the other man up there whose silhouette he could just make out, standing stiff and straight in the basket?

Now he was being swung from one side to the other. He could hear hooves, shouts, the hiss of steam. Just underneath him, he saw the man on the horse had reached the top of the rise. The next moment, he got up from the saddle, and standing on the horse's back gave one great leap and grabbed the wire just below James's feet.

With this enormous ballast added, the wild wire steadied.

Slowly James felt himself dropping. Slowly he sank to the ground, comfortably cushioned by the fat man under him. The next second, horses, tractor and Engineers were around them. The errant kite had been brought to a standstill, temporarily tethered to the flywheel of the steam tractor.

The large man wriggled free from underneath him. Close to he could be seen to have a very white skin and brilliant blue eyes. Astonishingly, he was laughing. He had thrown back his head. His long fair hair streamed halfway down his back. In between gasps of mirth, he was panting, 'Mighty fine! That was mighty fine!'

Then he sat up straight and held out his hand to James. 'Cody's the name,' he said in his slow American drawl. 'Samuel Franklin Cody.'

'James March.'

Just before they shook, Cody saw the blood on James's palms. 'Hey, you're hurt!'

He turned to the Engineers circling round them and shouted, 'Look at those hands, you incompetent bastards! If it hadn't been for James March here, Taffy Evans,' he looked upwards at the head and shoulders peeping above the basket, 'would be half way to heaven!'

After the winch had been brought up by another steam tractor and the kite again properly tethered, James was led back to Cody's office where his kitbag had already been brought. An urgent message was sent to the Balloon Factory for one of the women workers who knew about such things to come over and attend to his scorched hands.

'Lucky you were around, son!' Cody lit a large cigar. 'What was your purpose, beyond a free flight?'

'I wanted a job, sir. A job in flying.'

'A job in flying, eh? Well, what d'you know?'

Carefully circumspect, James avoided any direct mention of Ajax. Instead he concentrated on the kites he'd flown, the models he'd made, the glider he'd built, the Daimler engines he'd serviced.

'Fine! Fine!' Cody went on puffing at his cigar. 'Now, we have here at Farnborough . . .'

James had expected kites, gliders and balloons, but now Cody told him that in the big green shed he had seen from the road that Cody called 'the cathedral' was 'something secret', in which he and Colonel Capper, superintendent of the Balloon Factory, intended to travel the world. Better still, in Laffan's Plain just on the other side of the ridge where they had landed, was Cody's own workshop in which, he whispered to James, was something even *more* secret – his own aeroplane.

'In which, son,' Cody blew a huge blue circle of cigar smoke to frame James's face, 'I shall be the first man to rise from British soil in a heavier-than-air machine!' He tipped the cowboy hat he was still wearing to the back of his head. 'Like to work on that?'

Clearly against such competition, he could never win. James simply said, 'Yes.'

'Fine, fine! Ten shillings a week.'

'Twenty.'

'Settled at fifteen then. Ah, Mrs Evans!'

With a theatrical gesture, Cody rose from his chair and swept off his hat as a dark-haired girl in a long white dress came into the room. 'Come to attend to our hero! And who could be more appropriate? But for him, Mrs E, your better half would be picking up his harp!'

'Not Evans, sir!' She had a lilting Welsh accent and a flashing smile. 'Not that little old devil!'

'Pitchfork more like, eh? Well, see to James March's hands.' Cody began moving to the door. 'Have you anywhere to stay?'

James shook his head.

'Well, Mrs E here takes in lodgers.' Cody gave the girl a nudge. 'We've got a new recruit to the Business . . .'

James was to discover that positions in The Business, as Cody called it, were usually strictly reserved for his wife, his three sons, his relations and old friends. He was also to discover that everyone called Cody 'Colonel' though he had no Army rank.

'Does he tickle your fancy, Mrs E, as much as he tickles mine?'

Mrs Evans was already rubbing Dr Oliver's Burn Ointment on James's hands. Her warm brown eyes regarded him archly. 'He'll do, Colonel.'

Cody gave James a broad wink and said enigmatically, 'You couldn't have a warmer billet!' He opened the door. 'I'm off now to fix your job with Capper. After her ministrations, Mrs E can escort you to your new abode.' The door began closing behind the bulky figure. 'Taffy the Kite can bring you along in the morning!'

Mrs Evans's right forefinger rubbing in the ointment acted like a pestle to the mortar of James's outstretched palm.

'Ticklish, are you?'

'No.'

'Not hurting, am I?'

'Not at all.'

'Why is your hand trembling then?'

'It isn't.'

'Fibber!' She put her left forefinger to her lips. 'Naughty! You're as bad as Taffy the Kite!'

'Why do they call your husband that?'

'In Wales, you see, with so many surnames the same, a man is called by his Christian name and the name of the house he lives in. Like Dafyd the Mill, Peter the Farm.'

'But your husband doesn't live in a kite!'

'Ah, there you're wrong, James,' Mrs Evans said with a touch of asperity. 'An old married woman like me can call you James, eh?' Softly round and round went her finger on his palm. 'It's such a nice name!'

'And what shall I call you?'

'Why, Mrs Evans of course! Whatever next?' She suddenly dropped his hand. 'And since you are so fast, you shall stay Mr March!'

'I was only —'

The long eyelashes fluttered. 'You men are all the same!' She stood up. 'Now stop it, Mr March! *Stop it!* It's high time I took you home!'

She insisted on helping him carry his kitbag 'because of your poor hand'.

Decorously side by side, they walked across the grass, past the winch, now back in position. Mrs Evans was much too busy talking about what she did in the airship shed to spare as much as a glance for her husband aloft.

'We women work on scraping what's called goldbeaters' skin . . . that's the guts of an ox, isn't it awful?' She gave a little giggle. 'For balloons and – no I mustn't tell you what else,' she paused. 'Doesn't leak gas, you see.'

They went out of the main gate and along the outside of the iron railings past the Swan Inn. Just after the Queen's Hotel, she turned left down a small lane of terraced houses called Madeira Avenue and stopped outside number 16.

'Here we are!' She produced a key and opened the door.

Inside was sparsely furnished and scrupulously clean. She led him upstairs. 'This is your room, Mr March.' She pulled aside the lace curtains. 'It has a nice view of the front garden.'

A brass bedstead, a chair, a white wooden washstand and a cupboard.

'The rent is four shillings a week . . . bed and breakfast only, except on Sundays.' She put his kitbag down on the floor. 'When you're unpacked, you might fancy a cup of tea.'

A cup of tea extended to supper – bacon, egg and fried bread – 'just this once now, Mr March. You mustn't take advantage' – while she talked of her childhood in the Welsh coal valleys and asked him about his home and Hampshire and what he used to do.

The supper things were cleared away, and there was still no sign of the man of the house. Mrs Evans suggested a walk, 'so you can get your bearings'.

Outside was shell-pink and grey with the beginnings of evening. They walked together down the Farnborough Road, then along the towpath of the Basingstoke Canal that edged Laffan's Plain. All the time, James was conscious of that huge bat-eared kite with its four little attendant kites, diffused with red and gold from the last rays of the setting sun.

He stopped and looked up.

'He's been up there a very long time.'

'Taffy likes it up in the air.'

James's heart warmed to the tiny black silhouette in the wicker basket.

'He's practising for the King's visit next month. King Edward himself is coming to inspect the Balloon Factory.

'Surely your husband won't be up all night?'

'I'm sure I don't know how long he'll be up, Mr March,' she said indifferently.

'Won't he be hungry?'

'He's got some nice cheese sandwiches I made him.'

'Isn't he thirsty?'

'He takes up some liquid refreshment.'

'Doesn't he get bored?'

'He has a pair of binoculars.'

For the rest of the walk, James had the uncomfortable sensation of being scrutinised from above over every inch of the way. He was quite relieved to be back in the house again.

'I think I'll go up to bed now, Mrs Evans. I've had rather a long day.'

'Goodnight, Mr March. Sweet dreams!'

As soon as his head hit the pillow, he went straight off to sleep. Some time later – two hours, three hours, he had no idea – he was wakened by a weird high-pitched noise outside.

'Mae hen wlade fy nhadau yn annwyl i mi . . .'

'Land of my Fathers' was being sung in a slurred Welsh baritone.

Taffy the Kite had come down to earth at last.

'He's a crazy fellow, my husband, Mr March!'

James shifted himself into a more comfortable position in the horse-hair stuffed armchair of the front parlour at number 16. It was the second Sunday of his stay. Taffy was on duty, and Mrs Evans had invited her lodger to share a cup of afternoon tea. It was there on the painted table between them, poured from a china teapot into the best pink china cups.

James smiled at Mrs Evans to show he recognised she was joking and said slowly, 'You have to be a bit crazy to want to fly.'

'I'll second that, Mr March. They're all crazy at the Balloon Factory.' She sipped her tea delicately. 'Especially the Colonel. As for that chap with the goggle in his eye . . .' She turned her own expressive brown eyes to the ceiling.

'Colonel Capper . . . the superintendent?'

'Himself,' she nodded smiling. 'Well, you've only got to look at him! Real Komic Kuts. Lovely fellows, but crazy. Have you met Lieutenant Dunne? Well, you've a treat in store! You'll laugh! Well, perhaps you won't, because you're the polite kind, I can see. He always wears a boater and a white tie while he sends his funny models and gliders off Caesar's Hill.'

'I hear his little aeroplanes fly very well though.'

'Nobody knows. He's that secretive. A real case, like they all are.' She shook her head. 'And have you come across the Cody sons? Well, they're fine strapping lads. Handsome in an American way. But crazy! So's their mother, Leila. Well, I blame her as much as anyone. She fancies herself another Sarah Bernhardt.'

'Is she as fetching as Sarah Bernhardt?' James teased her mildly.

'Heavens above, no! But she acts a lot. In her husband's plays. Always the heroine, of course!' She stretched out a shapely hand. 'Here, let me give you another cup of tea!'

'I've had enough, thank you, Mrs Evans. That was very nice.' He put his empty cup down on the table. 'Mrs Cody helps her husband in a lot of ways doesn't she?'

'Oh, yes. She's travelled around with them. Looks a proper gipsy . . . though she's English. They give these plays to pay for his flying machines. She's got the bug just like the men. And what a bug, James . . . I may call you, James, mayn't I?'

'Of course.'

'And my name's Bronwen.'

'It's a pretty name.'

'Pretty is as pretty does, James.'

'It suits you, I'm sure,' James said after a moment in which she gazed at him expectantly.

'Oh, hark at you! You're a bit of a ladies' man, I can tell.' She shot him a sideways look from under half-lowered, thickly lashed lids. 'Now what was I saying? You make me forget . . . oh, yes, I remember. Would you believe, James, that my Taffy was as sane as you or me when I married him?'

James laughed. 'I believe you. And I *don't* believe that you drove him crazy, Bronwen!'

She contrived to laugh and pout at the same time. 'You're teasing me, James! I didn't mean that and you know it! You're a flirt! And a ladies' man!'

'That I'm not.' He got to his feet, still smiling. 'And now I'll tell you something, Bronwen.'

'Please do, James.'

'Your Taffy is still sane. Sane as you and still a good deal saner than me.'

'Well, well, well!' She stood up and began to put the china on the tray. 'Tell me what crazy things *you* get up to then, James!'

He began to walk towards the parlour door. 'Oh, nothing interesting.'

'I bet you could do interesting things if you wanted to, James!'

'I do want to.'

She put down the tray and came after him. She put a hand on his arm. She looked up at him ardently, her lips parted. 'What *interesting* thing do you want to do at this very moment, James?'

'Same as I always want to.'

'And what's that . . . James?'

'Build my own aeroplane and fly it.'

She took away her hand and pouted. It dawned on him as she rattled the china crossly, that perhaps he should look for digs elsewhere. But it was comfortable and clean and he liked the pair of them, and he was quite sure Bronwen was just an innocent flirt, far less menacing than someone like Amelia.

'You've got the bug all right.' Bronwen shook her head as she pushed the embroidered tea-cosy into a drawer. 'You'll just get worse! Before I've time to say Jack-Robinson or James-March-was-a-very-nice-chap, you'll be into all that crazy business with the rest of them!'

She was not so far wrong about the crazy business. After another month, James would certainly agree that crazy business went on at the Balloon Factory.

There was a cloak-and-dagger air about the whole place. Inside the huge green 'cathedral' was the secret monster that Cody had mentioned and everybody else talked about with bated breath. Lieutenant Dunne had something so secret that they were having to transport it to the remote Highlands to test it. And Cody, as well as his kites, had a box-kite glider on which he and his son flew from the rise at Laffan's Plain down Long Valley. In Samuel Cody's shed where James worked was a vast spider's web of an aeroplane on bicycle wheels, the evolution from his kites and gliders, looking exactly like a bat out of hell, particularly when Cody was sitting Machiavelli-like perched behind the controls.

'Only lacks a motor.' Cody told him in that slow American drawl. 'A real honest-to-God engine!'

Cody was short of mechanics, and James had been put on servicing a French 12 horse power Buchet engine that he gathered was to go into the glider to make it almost an aeroplane. In vain he approached Cody to get his permission to man the kites, fly the gliders and go up in the balloons.

'Mechanics,' Cody told him, 'are like gold.'

That was certainly true. To James's surprise he soon found out that he knew more about engines and design than anyone there with the exception of Dunne. Cody worked entirely from intuition. It was perfectly true that he was illiterate. A gleam used to come into those piercing blue eyes when he talked about his aeroplane, how far and how fast it would fly. But there was no worked out reason why it should fly at all.

'Suck it and see,' was Cody's philosophy with his kites, his balloons, his gliders and now his aeroplanes. Sometimes they flew. Sometimes they came a cropper. Then cheerfully up their master would get and try again. Four times he had fallen so hard into the ground that he got concussion. Twice he had been fished out of the sea.

James had a hard practical mind and a far more scientific approach. He had learned from his own experiments of the need for the curved camber on the wing and the wing-like qualities necessary in aeroplane propellers. What he still hadn't known was how to turn. The rudder on its own was inadequate. Clearly the wing would have to move but it couldn't go up and down like a bird's.

He now knew that Capper had been to America early in 1907 and had visited the Wright brothers. Capper had come back with the certain knowledge that in spite of the almost total ignorance about them in Europe, the Wrights had now certainly flown repeatedly for distances of two miles and more. They turned by means of a patent system they called 'wing-warping'. Since the American government had turned the Wrights down three times, Capper had also returned with an offer from them to put their planes and engines and all their inventions entirely at the service of the British government for £20,000. The War Office, however, had declared such aeroplanes a menace to the cavalry in battle, and the Admiralty had pronounced them of no practical use to the Navy.

So the offer had been refused. Nevertheless, James noticed that the aeroplane Cody was building used a system remarkably like wing-warping, though he had heard that the Frenchmen Voisin and Blériot were moving only the trailing edge tips of the wings which they called *ailerons* to achieve the same turning effect.

He urged Cody to adopt the French system as Amelia was doing at Jerningham. He also urged him to strengthen his aeroplane, pointing out that the wings and the vast elevator that protruded forward like a proboscis had only single wire bracing. But neither Cody nor anyone else wanted to know. Indeed to urge caution was to ally oneself with the legion of disbelievers in flying. That made up 99.9 per cent of the world. At Farnborough, there wasn't the time for worrying. It was all part of the game to take risks. Cody inspired enthusiasm about the Balloon Factory. Everybody – even the usually conservative Sappers – appeared to be in some glorious race for the most tremendous prizes.

And he had supposed he was all alone, James thought as he walked back to Madeira Avenue, the evening before the King's visit. He and Amelia had worked out that flying the first aeroplane would be his path to fame and fortune. So had others – Count Zeppelin dissipating his private fortune, on the airships that bore his name, Santos-Dumont financing his aircraft from the profits of his Brazilian coffee plantations, the Wrights ploughing bicycle profits into aeroplanes, Blériot realizing his aerial dreams through acetylene lamps. And Cody – the way Cody financed his flying ventures was certainly the most bizarre of the lot.

That night *The Klondike Nugget* by S.F. Cody was playing at the Aldershot Empire, and Bronwen insisted on going. Taffy the Kite was still at the camp preparing for the King's visit, but he had told Bronwen that he would be greatly obliged if James would escort her in his place. So after kippers, bread and butter and tea, James had taken her to see it.

To his surprise, the large theatre was crowded. Led determinedly by Bronwen, they managed to get seats at the back, just before the crimson curtain went up on a courtroom scene, where Cody as the wicked sheriff was trying to get both the huge golden Klondike Nugget ('made from two bricks wrapped in balloon skin' Bronwen whispered) and the heroine Rosie Lee (played by his wife Leila) from the hero (played by his son Leo).

'Lynch him!' shouted Cody, and suiting the action to the words, threw a noose round Leo's neck. With much choking and gasping, the rope had actually been seen to tighten, when suddenly there came the thunder of drumming hooves. In through the celluloid of the court room window leapt the faithful Redskin brave, played by Cody's nephew on Cody's own white horse.

The audience was electrified by such an apparition, as indeed was James. The occupiers of the favoured front seats cowered. At the back, Bronwen threw herself at James. Her arms fastened round his neck. 'Oh, I am frightened!' She pulled his face down to hers and arranged his arms so that they had to hold her. 'Tighter, James! Hold me tighter!'

She could hardly bring herself to look at the rest of the play except from the shelter of his right arm. Even so, she kept hiding her face in his waistcoat. The play proceeded at a frantic pace. There were leaps from chasms, log cabins blowing up, Mrs Cody ringed by knives thrown by her husband. Mrs Cody having cigarettes between her lips put out by bullets from her husband's gun, horses galloping up the aisles, smoke, fire, pandemonium. James's concentration on the brilliance, ingenuity and daring of the scenic effects was somewhat distracted by Bronwen's wriggling and squirming.

By the grand finale when the hero on horseback with the heroine across his saddle leapt over a wooden bridge collapsing in flames, Bronwen was almost draped round his neck, her tear-damp cheek hard against his.

'I did enjoy it, James,' she said, still clutching his hand as they walked home. 'No, you don't have to let go my hand. Taffy won't mind. And I'm still frightened. It was that good. Everyone liked it, didn't they?'

Everyone did. And this was where the money came from to finance Cody's aeroplane, since the British government weren't interested.

'At least they gave him a standing ovation!' James said, thinking of the wildly cheering audience, and then as number 16 loomed in the yellow gaslight, 'I wonder if Taffy's home?'

'Not him,' said Bronwen, her grip on his hand tightening.

But to James's relief he was. Sober, too. He was sitting on a stool in the kitchen blacking his boots. 'Not half going to be a do for the King tomorrow, man! The spit and polish! Let's hope it's a sunny day!'

25 May 1907 was overcast with a fresh northeasterly wind. Not at all the sort of day for a garden party, although it was evident that the visit of King Edward VII and Prince Fushini of Japan was regarded as such by the authorities.

James stood with Bronwen Evans and the other factory workers behind an immaculate line of Royal Engineers – one of whom was Taffy – watching the procession. The King's scarlet Daimler led a long line of cars and carriages filled with men in top hats and morning suits and ladies wearing elegant dresses and feathered hats.

In the last but one carriage, James suddenly recognized the gingery face of Frederick Haybury. With a painful leap of his heart James saw beside him a lady in grey. She had her face turned away. A large osprey plume hung from her hat. It *must* be Amelia, James thought, getting up on the tips of his toes and stretching his neck to get a better view. It couldn't be anybody else. Then the lady in grey turned her head and meeting his intent eyes, smiled graciously upon him without the slightest sign of recognition.

It was not Amelia. The lady in grey had a pale oval face, eyes of electric green, hair as black and shiny as the carriage coachwork, a beautiful head perched on a high and haughty neck. James felt a hot tide of outrage, anger, relief and disappointment sweep over him. His eyes followed the carriage till it disappeared amongst the marquees that had been set up on Laffan's Plain.

'I saw you!' He felt the handle of an umbrella tap him lightly on the face. 'I said you were a ladies' man!'

Wondering who she was, James escorted Bronwen across the grass to stand with the lesser mortals ringing the royal party. Frederick and the lady in grey, he noticed, had managed to secure a place at the King's right hand.

The first event was a demonstration of kite flying. Under the awning of the huge bat-eared master-kite and its five attendants, up went Taffy in the wicker basket. But the attention of the royal party was more engaged by the balloon *Thrasher*, tethered waiting to take off.

The northeast wind had freshened and the balloon was twitching on its trail rope. Seeing Cody standing beside Capper, James went up to him and said, 'Isn't the wind a bit strong, Sir?'

Kites appreciated wind. Balloons did not.

'Strong, March?' Cody smiled. 'Just right for a nice quick trip!'

'But where to, Sir?'

Both Cody and Capper thought that a huge joke, and while they were still laughing, the two Engineer lieutenants in the balloon, Martin-Leake and Caulfield, took off and smartly disappeared over the southwestern horizon – never to be seen again.

Taffy remained, high over everybody, swinging in the wind. But the royal eyes were now focussed on the flag-decorated 'cathedral'. The huge doors had been thrown open and the most important of the Balloon Factory's secrets stood revealed in all its glories. An ugly blunt nose. A big fat piggy body contained in a corset of four thick black bands under which hung what looked like a canoe. A French Antoinette engine powered her two propellers.

So the big secret is simply an airship, James thought. Something Jules Verne's *Clipper in the Clouds* had shown as no match for the as-yet-not-invented aeroplane in 1897. Something that Count Zeppelin had built six years ago. Something even Santos-Dumont had now given up, saying to propel a dirigible balloon through the air is like pushing a candle through a brick wall. Presumably the British government, late as usual, felt it was being left behind, and this was how they intended to catch up. But if James was disappointed, the royal party was not. The lady in grey had edged forward to stand beside the King. James heard her say, 'Are you interested in airships, Sir?'

The bearded head turned. For seconds the humorous eyes held steady on the beautiful face. Then with a twinkle, 'Very!' There was a pause, 'She is very beautiful. And what is she called?'

Bustling up from behind, Frederick said, 'Lady Nazier, Sir.'

'Thank you, Haybury, for that introduction.' The King's head gave an amused little nod in the lady's direction. 'But I was referring to the airship.'

'She has no name, Sir,' Colonel Capper told him.

'Then I christen her —' The King's eyes remained steady on the beautiful face. '*Nulli Secundus*.'

'Second to None!' breathed the lady in grey. 'Sir . . . what a marvellous name!'

'The *Nulli Secundus*,' said Capper, 'will leave at ten thirty am tomorrow, 5 October 1907, fly round St Paul's Cathedral and return to the Balloon Factory.' He gave one last glare through his monocle at James. 'There will be no more argument about *that*!'

'There's a strong wind forecast,' James pointed out. 'Just as strong as when *Thrasher* disappeared.'

The frown on Capper's forehead deepened at this reminder of the sequel to the King's visit. Bits of wicker, ends of rope and strips of torn goldbeater skin had been washed up at Exmouth – that was all. Nothing more was ever heard of the two Royal Engineers who had been on board.

'But from the opposite direction,' said Capper.

'What difference does that make?' James answered. Capper was known to have a very erratic sense of direction in that his flying logs almost invariably showed his courses were 180 degrees out. However nobody questioned him just as they had not questioned him three weeks before when the airship had made one short flight 100 feet above the common, watched by half the population of Farnborough. That five-minute flight ended in the engine stopping and a quick descent, but this Capper considered an adequate proving flight, and nobody questioned that either. For the trip next morning, James had been recruited to start the Antoinette engine – he and Cody were the only two strong enough to swing the twin propellers.

Just before the briefing broke up, James did ask, 'Wouldn't it be best to wait till evening, Sir?'

But Capper simply said, 'No, March. Everything tomorrow will proceed as arranged.'

Everything did. At ten, led by Corporal Crossby and Lance Corporal Evans, a squad of Engineers slowly guided the airship out of the 'cathedral', each holding on to a rope. Capper and Captain King, the balloon instructor, got in the gondola.

At ten twenty, James and Cody swung the propellers. On the third try, the engine caught. Cody stepped on board. Capper gave the signal. The man paid out the ropes. Foot by foot, the airship began to rise.

At ten thirty exactly, the airship headed northeast still dangerously low, its trailing ropes almost touching the chimneypots of Farnborough. James watched till it disappeared behind the gasworks still on course for London. He heard afterwards that the trip was uneventful. The southeast wind turned up as forecast and gave the *Nulli Secundus* a fast trip to Buckingham Palace, where King Edward and Queen Alexandra viewed her from the balcony.

From 7 Park Lane, Frederick and Lady Nazier saw her turn almost symbolically towards Whitehall. 'To our future, Frederick!' Diana raised her glass.

Watched by vast crowds, *Nulli Secundus* circled St Paul's. The cheers could be heard in the gondola as Capper turned southeast to fly home – slap into a headwind of 29 knots, three knots below the airship's top speed.

Inch by inch, it reached Clapham Common. There at 200 feet, it became stationary. For an hour, engine flat out, it hovered. The wind gave no sign of abating. Gradually Capper realised that she would never get home.

High above London in the sunshine, she made a marvellous landmark. James momentarily looked up at her as the Daimler truck he sat in with Corporal Crossby and Lance-Corporal Evans and six Engineers tore through Wimbledon in hot pursuit. The wind started to increase. Fighting a losing battle, *Nulli Secundus* started to go backwards.

At ten to three, Capper gave up the struggle and turned the nose round away from the headwind. Reaching the high glass structure of the Crystal Palace on Sydenham Hill, he stopped the engine and slowly brought the airship softly down on the bicycle track. Capper, Cody and King got out of the gondola to the cheers of the crowd, and set off back to Farnborough in the Daimler, driven by James, leaving Corporal Crossby and Lance-Corporal Evans and the Engineers to picket her down and guard her.

Britain, Mistress of the Air! the banner headlines of the evening newspapers screamed, as the *Nulli Secundus* uneasily rubbed the underside of her plump belly up and down on the cinders of the bicycle track.

Next day, it began to rain. Water soaked into the goldbeater skin, weighting it down. For the next four days, the *Nulli Secundus* became the Crystal Palace's main attraction as half a million people swarmed to see her, lying tethered to the ground.

On Thursday, the wind became a gale. Four picketing stakes gave. The *Nulli Secundus* began wobbling, turned tail up, started gyrating. Corporal Crossby opened the valves to bring her down, but the hydrogen came out too slowly. The last picketing stake left the ground. As the free airship began to ascend, Corporal Crossby took a knife and leaping up in the air, ripped the envelope to pieces. With a noise as loud as thunder, the airship deflated into a piece of torn skin.

That was the end of the *Nulli Secundus*. Or so it seemed. But as Taffy Evans remarked when Bronwen was all that winter lamenting the waste of her handiwork, 'It's an ill wind that blows nobody any good.'

Cody was always quick to seize an opportunity. He obtained permission to use the Antoinette engine from the crashed airship. James and Charlie Lucan, Cody's fitter, overhauled and fitted it. Watched by jeering newsmen, Cody spent much of the spring and summer of 1908 doing taxying trials on Farnborough Common.

What was this 'grasshopper airman' supposed to be doing in his 'moving machine'? asked the newspapers. When was this pseudo-Colonel, going to be locked up? Who would rid Britain of this mad American?

TEN

'No wonder Rolls wanted rid of him,' Frederick jeered when he saw Eustace Wilkinson. 'He looks half dead already!'

'He didn't want rid of him, he has the highest opinion of his design work,' Amelia corrected, 'Mr Wilkinson needed to come south. He has a weakness of the lungs.'

'Consumptive, I shouldn't wonder. I shan't want to come too near him. But appoint him if you must. The board is agreeable. I only hope you don't regret it.'

Amelia appointed Wilkinson forthwith. She never regretted it, though at first she felt sorry for him. Eustace Wilkinson, a tall stooping man in his middle forties with thin untidy grey hair and a clean-shaven cadaverous face, did indeed look half-dead. He did not disguise the fact that he was consumptive, though his complaint was not highly infectious. His only hope was to live by the sea. And the more clement weather in Hampshire had made him forsake his senior job at Rolls-Royce in Derby.

'He's a visionary,' Amelia told Frederick a month after Eustace Wilkinson had taken up his appointment and installed himself in the small room at Jerningham that used to be the sewing-room. Adding to herself, 'He's far more clever than James. Older and wiser. More educated, more experienced, more patient.' She had recognised in Eustace Wilkinson a yearning to create flight and an obsession to succeed (though for different reasons) as strong as her own.

Amelia's obsession to succeed had rapidly transformed Jerningham Hall. The main rooms had been made into offices and designers' studios, though with an idea to the future entertainment of buyers, Amelia had kept the drawing-room and dining-room as they were. Upstairs, the bedrooms had been turned into bedsitting rooms for an office manager when he was appointed, and a first-aid room.

Outside, a curved French Bessoneau hangar had been erected on the edge of the lawn down to the Solent, together with an engine shed and a hutted fabric workshop. The stables had been gutted to provide a carpentry shop. A store stood where the walled garden used to be. In the studio, Wilkinson had talked to Amelia about her ideas and had painstakingly drawn a blueprint for the resurrected Ajax. He had been intrigued both by the design and surprised by the fact that a woman should show so much enthusiasm for flying. On that score, Amelia had pointed out that there were dozens of women trying to take to the air. And she laughingly bet him that it would be the young women aviators who captured the public imagination in the end.

As for the name and the design, they were something dreamed up through trial and error by a friend and herself, she said. That Wilkinson assumed the friend to be Charles Rolls himself didn't really matter. What mattered was that he accepted the design with enthusiasm, though he incorporated ailerons for turning.

'I'd like a more powerful engine too, Ma'am. A Green 50 hp. It's British, as you know. And it's the most powerful and best.'

Eustace Wilkinson also suggested that their new venture should be called Ajax II, and insisted that before work on the prototype commenced, a model must be built and successfully flown. 'If you're going to fly, Ma'am, you have to learn to walk before you try to run.'

Inevitably progress at Jerningham was irritatingly slow, while all over the world like some sleeping giant flexing itself, aviation stirred. In 1906, Santos-Dumont had flown his *No 14 bis* and been hailed in a France oblivious of the Wright brothers as the first man to fly. Blériot had flown his *Libellule* for 140 metres.

Despite other people's achievements, Eustace Wilkinson would not be hurried. By the spring of 1908, a fruitful respectful partnership had developed between Amelia and her designer. Pained, angered and baffled by James's rejection, Amelia sustained herself with a dream of revenge.

She would be the first to achieve success. Before, it had been James's success she had worked for. She had always wanted to share the Jerningham factory with James. Now it was her own success and his disappointment she wanted. Her tiny factory which James had spurned would build the first British heavier-than-air machine to fly. She had heard that James had allied himself with a travelling showman by the name of Cody and his actress wife rather than work for her. This man financed himself by some sort of wayside mummery and circus acts. Well, much joy was James likely to have of it!

She knew from Frederick that aviation was still regarded in the highest circles as no more than a sport for the rich, a more exciting form of horse racing. And that even Farnborough, upon whose periphery James and Cody appeared to have settled themselves, was under constant threat of abandonment. Come that day, James would return, cap in hand, begging for employment. She would not give him any prodigal's welcome. She would make him sweat every inch of the way.

'I am happy to say that every position in this establishment is satisfactorily filled,' she would tell him. 'And I could not wish for a better designer/manager than Mr Wilkinson.'

By the autumn of 1908, James had not returned to seek her employment, and the ranks of the aviators were swelling. Knowledge of the Wright brothers' achievements had burst upon a formerly disbelievig Europe. Wilbur was showing them that they still led the world with record flights of one hour and nine minutes from Camp d'Avours in France and altitude records of 115 metres. The Kaiser continued to shower his favours on Count Zeppelin, and in sceptical England, the *Daily Mail* put up the sum of £1000 for the first flight across the English Channel.

On 10 October 1908, Wilkinson's model was ready for trials, but that weekend Frederick had invited guests for a shoot on the marshes near Haybury. They were politicians and diplomats and Amelia's presence was needed. She forbade Wilkinson to launch the model until she herself could be present. Then the weather was too boisterous and another few days went by.

Thus it was the 19 October before the trials could begin. The morning dawned almost like a summer day. The air was still. The high dome of the sky cloudless. The moorland was filled with lark song and the cries of the seagulls. Hastening to the factory after a light breakfast, Amelia found Wilkinson waiting.'Well, Ma'am,' he said. 'This looks as if it might be the day!'

Together they took one last appraising look at the fragile silk and metal model, powered by a scale miniature of the Green engine. Then they shook each other solemnly by the hand as they watched Wilkinson's trainee, a Southampton lad called Tim, carefully wrap it in sheets of felt and load it into the back of the Rolls-Royce.

Fifteen minutes later they had driven to the test launching area in the far southeast of the parkland, and unpacked the model. With the changeability of the Solent weather, a light sea breeze had sprung up. Not enough to turn the gently undulating waves into white caps, but enough to make it, as Wilkinson said, perfect flying weather. It brought in the nostalgic smell of the salt marshes mixed with the scent of gorse and heather. Just for a moment, standing beside him, as he tinkered delicately with the ignition of the engine, Amelia was reminded of that other morning of perfect flying weather, now five years, a marriage and two children ago.

Then the little engine puttered. Amelia was enveloped in a cloud of castor-oil fumes. The frail contraption went bumping forward into the modest wind. And then gently, sweetly, inevitably as a bird, it lifted, gained height and soared.

'It's flying!' Amelia's cry seemed to echo down the years. She jumped up and down. She watched the little model grow smaller and smaller. Then, as the engine ran out of fuel and the plane came gracefully down to the ground she thought, I have triumphed over James.

It was after they returned to the factory and were back in the office that Tim pulled the morning *Southampton Echo* out of his pocket and said shyly, 'It's a big day for British flying altogether, M'lady.' He thrust the newspaper into her hand. 'Just look at that there!'

For the first time, aviation was front page lead news. *First powered flight of 1390 feet from British soil,* she read in bold black headlines.

In small print below was an account of Cody's flight from Farnborough on 16 October. There had been a crash, due to the need to avoid trees but nobody had been hurt. Then in small print at the end, *the engine was installed and serviced by Charles Lucan of London and James March of Jerningham.*

She read the account twice before handing it to Wilkinson. She waited to feel the joy of the morning drain out of her. To feel anger and jealousy surge in its place. She felt the colour drain out of her face and her heart beat faster. But the emotion that quickened her was neither anger nor jealousy.

It was the most overpowering sense of pride and joy.

'Well, Ma'am, that goes to show it can be done! It *is* a great day for aviation!' Wilkinson drained his glass and handed on the newspaper to Lyle, the engine fitter. 'And our machine will be better than Cody's.'

Amelia had insisted that a bottle of champagne should be brought up from the small stock of wine that still existed in the cellars and they were drinking both to their success and Cody's.

'Are you having another glass?' asked Smith, the office manager.

But Amelia was already halfway to the door. 'There is an errand I have to do,' she said, favouring them all with a dazzling farewell smile. She patted Tim's arm as he leapt across to open the door for her. 'Finish the wine!' she said to them all. 'It's you who deserve it!'

Then she was in the car and accelerating down the long drive. She drove exultantly towards the village. All her anger with James was forgotten. He had achieved success and she was delighted. Radiant. She stopped outside the forge. The fire was bright and sparking. Mr March was stooped over it bending a piece of red hot metal.

He put it down and pulled off his goggles when he saw her. He seemed unsurprised, almost as if he had expected her. Under her self-imposed dictum that she wouldn't visit the sins of the son on the father, Amelia had put a considerable amount of factory business in Mr March's way. But even without that, he would never have felt the intense dislike that his wife did towads Lady Haybury.

Amelia didn't make any pretence of calling to discuss work. She simply said, her cheeks flushed and her eyes bright. 'You must be very proud!'

'Aye, M'lady. We are that.'

'Did you know about it beforehand?'

'We knew they'd had a shot at it back in May. But we've just read it in the papers today, same as,' his lips curved into a smile of shielded pride, 'everyone else.'

'There will be a great deal of excitement in Farnborough, I expect,' Amelia said.

'Aye, M'lady. There will that!'

'He lives there, doesn't he?'

'Aye. Has done this past twelve month and more.'

'Can you give me his address, please?' She smiled. 'I would like to send him a telegraph message. Of congratuation.'

'That would be very civil of you, M'lady,' Mr March said after just the faintest but discernible hesitation. 'He has lodgings at 16 Madeira Avenue. With a Mr and Mrs Evans. A nice respectable couple, James says.'

All the time he had been talking he had been patting his pockets, feeling for a pencil. Having found one, he walked over to the wooden shelf with the stool underneath it that he used as his writing table, tore off a sheet from the notepad, and wrote laboriously. He handed her the paper. 'There, M'lady. That'll find him.' He smiled. 'I don't suppose the lad's ever had a telegraphed message before in his life.'

But James, Amelia thought, would have to wait for that doubtful pleasure. Nothing would do except seeing him in person. She climbed back into the Rolls, and without knowing exactly where Farnborough lay, pointed the car's expensive nose northwards and began homing on 16 Madeira Avenue with the speed and unerring instinct of a bird.

The door was opened by Bronwen Evans. She took two astonished looks, first at the elegant figure on her well-scoured doorstep and secondly at the elegant car parked outside and decided there was some mistake.

She was quickly disabused.

'Mrs Evans? Good afternoon.' The voice was unmistakably well bred. The shapely lips parted in a smile that disguised their owner's suprise. A surprise almost as great as that of Bronwen Evans.

On her journey to Farnborough, Amelia had visualised the Evans as a stout couple, middle-aged and homely. The woman would cook James's meals, mend his clothes, mother him. One look at Mrs Evans's hot brown eyes convinced her that whatever other services she offered James, mothering was not amongst them.

'I'm Mrs Evans, yes.' The girl spoke suspiciously in a sing-song musical voice, 'Good afternoon to you.' Then she waited for Amelia to state her business.

'I believe Mr March lodges here?'

'James?' The girl's round face broke into a coy smile. 'Oh, yes, he lodges here all right!'

'My name is Amelia Haybury. May I see him please?'

Mrs Evans's smile faded. Before she replied, she looked Amelia over slowly, her eyelids half-lowered to just the safe side of insolence.

'Pleased to meet you,' she said at last. 'And oh yes, indeed, you *could* see him, but he isn't here.' She appeared to make up her mind about something. 'But you can come in,' she said, throwing the door wider. 'You can wait for him. He shouldn't be long.'

She took a step back into the small spruce hall and jerked her dark head for Amelia to enter. A steep brown-painted staircase covered in a narrow drugget led up from the little hall.

'His bedroom is just at the top,' Mrs Evans said, smiling secretly to herself. 'You can see the door. It has a very pleasant view of the garden. He likes that, James . . . Mr March does.'

Amelia made no comment. Mrs Evans opened a door on the right and waved Amelia into what was obviously the parlour. It smelled clean but closed up. The room had a small square bay window covered in lace curtains tightly rodded at the top and bottom. There was a Landseer print of the Monarch of the Glen over the fireplace. The empty grate was filled with a pleated pink paper fan.

'Do sit down, Miss!' She waved Amelia towards a red armchair, its back covered in an embroidered antimaccassar. 'Make yourself comfortable. He shouldn't be long. His last words to me were "Bron, I promise you I won't be late for tea." I was just about to get it.'

'Please don't let me keep you from what you were doing.'

The mention of tea reminded Amelia that she was both hungry and thirsty. She considered if Mrs Evans might offer her some refreshment. But her hostess perched herself on the edge of the opposite armchair. 'Oh, it won't take a moment,' she said. And then 'Do you know our James well then?'

'Quite well.'

'He never mentioned you might call.'

'He didn't expect me.'

'Never mentioned you at all, come to that.' The bright brown eyes travelled over Amelia, taking in the expensive clothes and the undoubted beauty of the youthful face. And just as suspiciously, just as resentfully, Amelia's eyes surveyed Mrs Evans. She would put her age at twenty-five or six. Not much older than James, if at all. She had a good figure, which looked well even in the plain fawn dress. So well in fact that she made Amelia feel overdressed. Mrs Evans had a fine rosy skin, a very mobile saucy mouth and a way of looking sideways out of her eyes that men would find provocative.

Having looked her fill, Mrs Evans asked with a pert smile, 'Is it business or friendship you've come on?'

'Oh, friendship,' Amelia said and then added, 'I hope.'

'To renew a friendship, is that it?' Mrs Evans's sing-song voice enquired insidiously.

Opening her mouth to remind Mrs Evans that it was none of her business, Amelia tightened her lips. There was something about James's landlady that put her on her guard. She would make, she thought, a bitter enemy. And yet from the set of Mrs Evans's mouth, from the glitter in her eyes, it was apparent she was already that.

As if to disarm her, Mrs Evans threw back her dark head and laughed merrily. 'I can see what you're thinking! What a cheek! It's nothing to do with her. Now be honest! Weren't you, dear?'

She leaned forward and put a small hand on Amelia's knee. 'But it isn't cheek really. You might have been dunning him for money, dear. Or wanting him to come into service. I can tell you're a lady. And you might be from that horrid place where he lived. He hated the people there. He told me.'

When Amelia didn't answer, she went on, 'Then again, James has had his name in the papers. You get all sorts trying to tag on. Even society ladies. We get a lot down here at the Balloon Factory. Real nobs. I work there, so I know.'

'What do you do?'

'Oh, nothing very important. Fabric work . . . on goldbeater skin. And I used to be in charge of first aid. That's how I got to know James. I dressed his hand that first day. But then he'd have told you about that.'

'No.'

'He doesn't seem to tell you much, dear. Does he write?'

'No. We don't correspond.'

'I know *you* didn't send *him* letters. Otherwise I'd have seen. No scented letters.' She laughed mischievously. 'I say to him, "James, if ever I smell Attar of Roses or Parma Violet on pink and purple notepaper, it goes straight in the privy." I don't mean it, of course! Being married . . .'

'And Mr Evans? He's —?'

'Oh, he's here too, of course. Very much so! A lance-corporal in the REs. Jealous, too! Welshman are. Very possessive. But he's very fond of James. And naturally, he doesn't know how James feels about me.'

Amelia gritted her teeth and did not ask the question. She pulled off her gloves to give herself something to do.

'Go on!' Mrs Evans invited. 'Ask me how he feels! You're just being ladylike and you do't have to be. You're married yourself, I notice.' She nodded at Amelia's hand. 'So you know what men are like. You'll understand.' She smiled meaningfully. 'Yes, indeed! Anyway, I'll tell you. He's in love with me. James told me he'd never, never been in love like this before. He's had girls, yes. What healthy man of his age hasn't? It wouldn't really be right not to have.

But they haven't meant anything. Never wanted to settle with one. Now he's met me . . . and he does. But I'm married.' She held her hands in front of her surveying the offending left hand with its heavy gold ring, and sighed shaking her head. 'He said . . . "Bron, if only I'd met you five years ago" . . . that would be before I was married, you understand . . . "Mr Evans wouldn't have got a look in."'

'The situation must be very difficult,' Amelia said with frozen lips. 'I'm surprised James . . .'

'Doesn't move out? Yes. We had considered it, my goodness, yes! But he knows how to keep his feelings to himself, does James. Even when Mr Evans is on nights. There's only been one occasion. No, I tell a lie, two, when . . .' The colour of her rosy cheeks deepened. 'Well, none of us is perfect, I say!'

Amelia said nothing. She stared transfixed at the smiling face wreathed in reminiscent smiles. Then she stood up. 'I think perhaps I've waited long enough.' She looked at her half-hunter. 'I have a long journey.'

'Oh, must you go?' Mrs Evans smiled warmly. 'It was ever so nice to have a little chat. Shall I tell him you called? Or will you come again? You're welcome any time.'

She opened the door of the parlour, then squeezed past Amelia to release the catch of the front door.

They each knew there would never be another time.

Each recognised the other's jealousy. Each knew a skirmish had taken place. And each knew that Mrs Evans had won.

'It's jealousy, M'lady!' Sarah began. She came knocking on Amelia's sitting-room door as soon as she returned to Haybury from the town house, and asked if she might have a quick word in M'lady's ear.

'Very well, Sarah.' Amelia sighed. She was tired after her two months in London. There she had held the political dinners Frederick set such store by, the soirées, the luncheons designed to help slide the Unionists in. She had now returned thankfully to Haybury as election hopes receded.

'Who is jealous of whom?' she asked adding, as Sarah drew a deep breath, 'And I don't really think you ought to gossip.'

'Gossip! Me, M'lady? May I be struck down dead if I ever gossip! This isn't gossip. This is the truth. Master Arthur is jealous of Master Charles. Gets him into terrible trouble. Tells tales. If I've sung it once to him, I've sung it a score:

Tell tale tit,
Your tongue shall be split,
And all the little dogs in town
Shall have a little bit.'

'Thank you, Sarah.' Amelia put up her hands to her ears. 'You don't have to go through all that. Children often tell tales. Didn't you ever?'

'No, M'lady. Never!' She set her puggy mouth. Amelia believed her.

'And if it wasn't for me sticking up for him, Master Charles'd be in hot water all the time. He does bad things does Master Arthur! Then he blames Master Charles and Nanny Haybury punishes him. That's the gospel truth, M'lady.'

A truth of a different gospel, Nanny Haybury's was told to Amelia when the boys were brought down to the drawing-room before dinner.

'I fear I have a poor report to give of Master Charles,' Nanny pursed her lips. 'He is wilful and disobedient. He is unkind to his little brother and insolent to me. Sarah, of course, spoils him.'

A kinder but still adverse report was given the following morning by Charles's governess, a cleryman's daughter called Miss Potter, whom Frederick had engaged for Charles in January. To Amelia's shame, she had hardly exchanged more than the time of day with her in the months since she arrived. She took her meals in the schoolroom. She was shy and quiet. She told Amelia with a catch in her voice that much as she hated to worry a lady for whom she had such a profound admiration, she must tell her that Charles's rejection of all her efforts to get him to read had driven her almost to despair.

Despite these domestic problems, despite Frederick's attitude to her, despite her longing for James, Amelia herself did not despair. She threw herself into her work at the factory. Ajax II was progressing and Eustace Wilkinson read with envy that an Englishman called A.V. Roe had made and flown a small paper-winged biplane. The Wrights, now fêted throughout Europe, were teaching the Germans to fly. Not to be outdone on heavier-than-air machines, Santos-Dumont was producing his *Demoiselle*.

Then halfway through June, Amelia read in the *Aeronautical Society's Journal* that a Women's Air League was to be formed. 'What did I tell you, Eustace?' Amelia pointed the advertisement out to him. 'The women will be famous yet.' She resolved to attend that first meeting in the Courts of Art on 29 June 1909.

On the morning of that day, she drove the Rolls to Brockenhurst station and caught the train to Waterloo. A hansom cab conveyed her to the Courts of Art building in time for the meeting.

A number of smartly dressed women were already in the hall. They looked more like a meeting of the Poor Law Guardians than a group of intrepid aviators. Amelia knew none of them. There was a platform set with a table and nine chairs with nine sets of water jugs and glasses.

Amelia was glad when the ladies of the platform filed in. Lady O'Hagan made an impassioned speech from the chair declaring 'Our objects are to disseminate knowledge, spread vital information to the Empire of air supremacy. We are organising an educational campaign to collect moey to build' – she paused dramatically – 'an all-British airship built by British mechanics of British materials!'

The applause from the floor was deafening. But it was airships they were cheering, not aeroplanes. Amelia realised that she had strayed into the airship lobby. Life was a series of opposites and conflicts. In politics, Tories and Whigs. In aviation, aeroplanes and airships. In love, James and Frederick.

She had nothing *against* airships. After all, she herself had fallen in love with Santos-Dumont's little plump pigs in Paris. But she did not believe that they could ever compete with aeroplanes, and was resisting Frederick's pressure that they should start building them at Jerningham. 'If we do, we can expect finance if not from the government at least from private sources,' he had told her. 'I have that on the highest authority.'

Amelia's eyes travelled over the faces of the audience, listening intently to speaker after speaker. Who, she wondered, was this 'highest authority', for certainly this must be that financial source to which Frederick was referring?

The chairwoman rapped her gavel, 'I call on Lady Violet Beerbohm-Tree to propose the motion.' Perhaps *she* was the 'highest authority'.

'I propose that this meeting warmly approves the formation of the Women's Aerial League and pledges itself to support it by every means in its power. Already we are collecting money for airships and this should be followed by a fleet of British airships – more airships than all possible combinations of countries. And the quicker they are built, the better, so that we get supremacy of the air to complement that supremacy of the sea which has been England's boast since navies were!'

Amidst cheering, Major Baden-Powell who had flown balloons and kites in the Boer War seconded the motion.

After him, others rose to add their support.

'And now before I bring the meeting to a close there is one illustrious speaker I know you all want to hear.' The chairman looked to the far end of the table on the platform, 'Diana.'

A slender figure in lavender watered silk rose. Her dark hair was piled up under an elegant grey hat. Though Amelia could not see her face, she spoke in a voice which throbbed with theatrical conviction of her subject. She *had* flown in airships, particularly in Germany with Count Zeppelin. 'Such experiences were quite unforgettable,' she told them all. 'There is no finer or more beautiful or more efficient way to travel than to fly in an airship.'

'Thank you, Diana, for your knowledgeable support. And with that memorable speech from Lady Nazier ringing in our ears, I will bring our proceedings to a triumphant close.'

Lady Nazier – the name immediately impinged. Amelia craned her neck, caught sight of a long white neck, an elegant pointed chin, pale cheeks ad luminous green eyes. So this was Frederick's friend and political mentor! She had imagined her older and certainly less beautiful. This too, no doubt, must be his 'highest authority', Amelia followed her with her eyes as she left the platform with the other ladies, and watched while she was surrounded by friends and well-wishers and escorted out into the hall.

Amelia hurried out in the forefront of the chattering crowd. And there, standing under the glittering candelabra, talking to the commissionaire, was Frederick. He was in evening dress, and there was about him a smiling air of expectancy. As the lecture-room doors had opened, he lifted his eyes from the commissionaire's face and regarded the ladies eagerly as they emerged.

Amelia was half-hidden by a stout lady in brown. About to lift her hand to him, she dropped it again. There was something in his facial expression that was not for her; that indeed told her the last person he would want to see would be her. She stayed hidden behind the lady in brown. Then Frederick saw Lady Nazier. He pushed his way towards her and took her hand. He raised it to his lips. He said nothing. But his face said everything for him.

Though she had no right to, Amelia found that look so painful that she turned away and walked to the noticeboard to hide her face and herself. Like that, she wiped her eyes, and when she blinked them open again, she found herself staring at a bold yellow poster.

It was of a girl so like herself that she might have modelled for the artist. She was slim and slight and of medium height and fashionably dressed, and she was staring up in rapt attention at a golden sky where curious looking aircraft disported themselves.

Across the bottom were the words, *Grande semaine d'aviation de la Champagne. Rheims 22–29 Août 1909.*

The poster spoke to her condition. James didn't want her and neither did Frederick. She was probably born to be unhappy in love, lonely as her double, gazing skywards. But there was still the air. She would help conquer that. Be its mistress. She would go to Rheims – and James and Frederick could go to hell!

ELEVEN

Frederick raised no objection to Amelia going to Rheims. Not only would he accompany her himself, but Lord and Lady Nazier would join their party.

Suddenly aviation was *in*. On 25 July Louis Blériot flew the Channel from Calais to Dover in a monoplane at 45 mph. The newspapers were full of such names as Wright, Santos-Dumont, Voisin, Glen Curtiss, Latham and Farman. The champagne-producers in an effort to stop falling sales had switched from sponsoring motor racing to flying at Rheims.

In their own way, the politicians and the military were also switching their interest and sponsorship towards flying. The French President was to attend the Rheims meeting, along with several of the crowned heads of Europe, including perhaps King Edward himself.

'Lloyd-George will be going,' Frederick told Amelia. 'So will General French. It is most important we should be seen there. You will like the Naziers. Lord Nazier is one of our most valued elder statesmen.'

Lord Nazier was certainly elderly. Quite the oldest man she had ever seen, Amelia thought, as two weeks later he and his wife entered the Pullman carriage on the special overnight train at Victoria station. His Lordship's face and skull seemed carved out of ivory. His thin body was swaddled inside a long black ulster with a black Persian lamb collar. Supported on the arm of his valet, he followed his lovely young wife in.

Close to, Diana Nazier was even more striking than when Amelia had glimpsed her at the Women's Air League. Her skin was pure and creamy white, her eyes a dazzling green. She was wearing an emerald velvet coat with matching toque, which showed off both to Frederick's unconcealed admiration.

Introducing Amelia and Diana, he held Diana's hand affectionately, 'I can wish for nothing better than that you two should be friends,' he said sentimentally.

'I am sure we shall be *great* friends,' Diana whispered, her eyes unfriendly, her voice a low husky contralto. Her husband's was cracked with age, but the eyes under the hooded lids were still shrewd and kindly. From time to time as the train sped them south to Dover, Amelia felt those eyes on her face studying her. She was quite glad when he retired, again on the arm of his valet, early to the sleeping car.

They arrived at Rheims shortly after breakfast. Despite the fact that it had begun to rain, a band was waiting at the station to greet important visitors, in front of whom the station master paraded up and down in top hat and tails.

'Vive l'Entente Cordiale!' he cried, conducting them to their waiting carriages.

There were red, white and blue streamers across the cobbled streets.

Someone had nailed up flags on the arches of the Mars Gate. Even the statue of Joan of Arc in front of Notre Dame Cathedral was braided with bunting.

The Hotel République, where Frederick had arranged for them to have four magnificent rooms, was full of important looking foreign visitors and excited rumours of even more to come. The hotel stood between the river bank and the canal. There was a terrace at the back planted with rosebeds from which a flight of stone steps led down to the towpath.

Despite Lord Nazier's age, he declared himself in need of no more rest, and insisted that he wanted to go straight to the race meeting.

'And who shall you be putting your pennies on, m'dear?' he asked Amelia as the driver of their motorised taxi pulled up behind a long queue of coaches, cabs, victorias and drays waiting to get into the airfield.

'Colonel Cody if he's here,' Amelia replied.

'He won't be here,' Diana Nazier said. 'The man's a charlatan. In any case, heavier-than-air . . .' she pulled down the corners of her mouth.

'And what about you, Frederick, m'boy?'

'I shall let Diana guide my choice. She'll find some balloonist for me to back.'

The hooded eyes regarded Frederick for just one second too long. 'Yes, I expect you will let her do that, m'boy.' Then smiling like a foolish old gentleman, he asked their driver what he would be backing.

'Ah, M'sieur Blériot!'

'Odd name for a horse,' Lord Nazier gave his cracked laugh, and stared out at the pelting rain.

'It is *not* a horse race meeting, Philip! It is an *aviation* meeting!'

'Well, well, well! Bless my soul! But it looks exactly *like* a horse race meeting.'

He cleared the glass with his silk handkerchief, and pointed to the grandstand and the public enclosure and the President's box. All so exactly like a horse racing stadium that it seemed unnatural for there to be no horses, no jockeys. There was even the track with its fou4 turning points – a high red and white tower at each point, their tops almost disappearing in the heavy grey overcast.

'Ah, there they are! Now I see 'em, m'dear!'

On the track itself as they got closer could be seen thirty-eight fragile and bedraggled steeds – Farmans, Blériots, Voisins, Wrights and a Curtiss, but not a single British aircraft – waiting for the race to begin.

'Beats me,' Frederick said, 'how they get all these crowds.' He stared at them crossly as they surged past, slithering and sliding in the mud. 'Just to see aeroplanes!'

'They have come, m'boy,' Lord Nazier squeaked as they reached the President's enclosure and took their seats under the striped umbrellas re-served for notables, 'to watch 'em crash!'

'Oh, I hope not,' Amelia cried.

'It's true.' Lord Nazier nodded his head several times. He turned his old eyes to view the 300,000 spectators scattered under umbrellas over the muddy plains of Bethany. 'Public hanging or public crashing, human nature doesn't change.' He transferred his hooded gaze to Frederick, 'Am I not right, m'boy?' But Frederick had his opera glasses to his eyes. The race was beginning. One after another, the little aircraft were taking off. Banking wildly, their oiled silk wings weeping with water, the little Voisins and Farmans rounded the towers, jostled each other, crashed into the mud, tipped on their noses. The crowd sighed.

The whispered question went round, 'Has anyone been killed?'

Ambulancemen kept running around with casualties on stretchers. Spindly fire engines struggled manfully through the mud. By lunchtime, there was nothing worse than a broken leg. Lots of broken aeroplanes, of course. By the time they had eaten their lunch of lobster and turkey, washed down with vintage champagne provided by the champagne companies, the pile of broken spars, bent wheels, torn silk and cotton just beyond the hedge was as high as a house.

Diana Nazier finished off her champagne and shuddered, '*Who* would fly in an aeroplane after seeing *this*?'

'I would,' Amelia answered promptly.

'I wouldn't if I were you, m'dear,' Lord Nazier said. 'What if you got up in the air and never came back? What would poor Frederick do then?'

'What indeed!' Frederick echoed rather hollowly. 'But she won't get the chance.'

She didn't that afternoon. The ground was too wet. Next day was worse and all flying was cancelled. Carriages and motor cars were stuck and had to be hauled out.

There were meetings and small parties at Rheims where Amelia met a number of notable airmen and asked questions. Ailerons, she found out from Santos-Dumont in her schoolgirl French, were certainly preferable to wing-warping – he after all had invented them. A man called Samier advised her to build monoplanes – naturally, for he was racing a Voisin.

There was no sign of James. Wednesday was brighter, and Amelia managed to get down to the aeroplanes, where again she chatted with Blériot, who had already crashed once. Ferber showed her the controls of a Farman, with a huge horn like a sledge stuck forward under the wheels to slow it down, and said in reply to her question, 'No one from the Balloon Factory is here. Cody's certainly not bringing his Army Aeroplane Number One. A pity, for I wanted to meet him. You underestimate him in England.'

Farman won the long distance prize with a 3½-hour flight. A Wright crashed, narrowly missing the judges' box. Two more Voisins dived into the ground with a sound of cracking bamboo and tearing silk. But miraculously nobody was killed.

'Still two days to go,' said Lord Nazier. 'Keep hoping, Diana!'

The sun shone warmly on that Friday and the champagne corks popped louder. Everyone was in the best of spirits. Three Voisins all rounding a turning tower one on top of the other, their wings inches away, roused a huge gasp of apprehension which turned to an admiring cheer when all three straightened out safely.

Glenn Curtiss beat Blériot in the speed trials, averaging 46½ mph. There was total silence from the French crowd as the Stars and Stripes was run up the flagpole. Then there was the passenger-carrying race. Henri Farman with two men bunched behind him had just landed. Amelia was walking back from the judges' box after finding out that his distance was a new world record of 6.2 miles when she was seized by the arm. Looking round she recognised the moustached Samier.

'Mademoiselle!'

From his mouthful of fast French, she gathered that she was being asked to be the second passenger in his Voisin for a try at the Farman record.

'Mais oui!'

'Mille mercis!'

Samier threw his arms around her and began showering her with kisses. The next moment, he was lifting her up on to a wing as yellow and varnished as a Chinese parasol, and setting her down on one side of the engine. He whipped off his scarf and tied her bonnet firmly under her chin. Then after his assistant had produced a length of rope, he bound up her skirt from her thighs to her ankles.

'Pour la modestie, mademoiselle,' he said gallantly, climbing up behind the controls.

He touched his arms and shook his head, a message Amelia took to mean she wasn't to touch him. Then his assistant swung the propeller and, with a loud guffaw, the engine caught. Everything was obscured by a great cloud of castor-oil smoke. It got up Amelia's nose, into her throat and stung her eyes as the little Voisin began bumping over the rutted grass to the starting point.

There they stopped. Samier throttled back the engine. The castor-oil smoke cleared. Amelia turned her head to the left in order at least to smile and say hello to her fellow passenger before they took off . . . and found herself staring into the face of James March.

The smile froze on her lips. She opened her mouth. Anything she said would have been inaudible because now there was a sudden deafening roar. The Voisin began lurching over the grass, the wind blowing harder and harder in her face.

A tree loomed ahead. The hedgerow at the far end of the field came closer. Then just like a grasshopper the Voisin jumped.

Again that ecstasy of flight came over Amelia. Just for that moment, six years rolled away and she was back in Ajax with James. They were rising in the crystal air – but now it was not the New Forest she could see but the Plains of Bethany and the towers of Rheims cathedral.

Then the earth tilted, as skidding and sliding they rounded a turning tower. Abruptly straight again, they approached the grandstand. She could see Frederick and Lord and Lady Nazier looking up at her.

Again the wing tipped. They dropped almost to the ground, then soared again. The earth sizzled and spun. Circling dizzily, they were being whirled on some gigantic merry-go-round, faster and faster to the tune of the whistling wires. Swiftly a tower bore down on them. Samier took it too close. Amelia actually saw the black and white stripes knifing into the wing tip.

There was a crack. The horizon did a cartwheel. Suddenly the sky was filled with bamboo bits and yellow rags.

Then she was falling. She felt a hand – James's – grab her and hold her away from the hot engine and the still whirling propeller. The next moment, she was rolling down the wing, trussed up like a chicken, flinging out her arms to slow herself.

Then there was no oiled silk left. With a thud she had connected with something hard. A jazzy green whirled round her. Stars appeared in front of her eyes. She heard a voice say in a French accent, 'Are you all right?'

And herself reply, 'Perfectly all right! I always land like this!'

'Terrible business, m'dear! Thought you were a goner!'

In the subdued rays of the late afternoon sun, Amelia reclined on a chaise-longue on the hotel terrace. Lord Nazier sat beside her, sipping the large glass of brandy he had demanded after all the excitement of the day.

He had come up with Frederick as James and the pilot disentangled her from the remains of the Voisin and into one of the prowling ambulances. The Frenchman's friends had also descended on the scene, sweeping the pilot and James away before Amelia had gathered her senses.

'Your first flight and you crash!' Lady Nazier had sighed as the ambulance threaded its way back to the hotel. 'Surely that brings home to you the danger and foolishness!' Then turning to Frederick, 'And that should show you how terribly unwise it is to invest in heavier-than-air machines!'

Even in the chilling surroundings of the interior of a French ambulance, even with the aftermath and shock making her teeth chatter, Amelia had managed to gasp out, 'Rubbish!'

Lady Nazier had not deigned to reply. She had been in fact all sisterly kindness as they raced dramatically with klaxons howling back to the Hotel République. She had lent Amelia her maid to run her bath and lay out fresh clothes and take off the torn and muddied ones to be cleaned. When a doctor was summoned, she had held Amelia's hand while he examined her (though there was no need) and personally promised the doctor (though he hadn't asked her) to ensure that Amelia rested and had no more excitement. And when callers came to enquire after Amelia, she had given instructions that they should leave their names and be sent away.

'Even though you are lucky to have broken no bones, you mustn't think of coming to the Mayor's reception this evening,' Frederick ordered.

'I wasn't thinking of so doing,' Amelia murmured. 'But please don't give it up on my account. I am quite happy to stay in the hotel.'

Immediately Lord Nazier said he had had no intention of going either. Seven o'clock was his dinner time, nine o'clock was his bedtime, and he wasn't going to change his routine for any reception, even if the French President and Lloyd-George and the president of the Board of Trade, Winston Churchill, *were* going to be there.

Neither Lady Nazier nor Frederick tried to dissuade him. 'Amelia and I will keep each other company,' Lord Nazier said, 'like two old soldiers. Frederick, you can escort Diana to the reception for me.'

So it was all arranged. At six thirty, Lady Nazier, resplendent in a Worth gown of apricot mousseline with a silver lace collar, kissed the top of both their heads, and then offered her hand to Frederick.

Before leaving, Frederick gave Amelia a pile of cards. 'Here are your callers. You may wish to write to some of them. I haven't been through them all. There are one or two from the Press . . . you can throw those away. Blériot and Santos-Dumont have sent cards. I have put those at the top.'

But the card she sought was halfway down . . . *James March.* And below the name, in James's small simple handwriting *Twice is too much.*

After dinner, sitting in the garden, she still held the card in her hand as the evening sun crept under the fringe of the umbrella and almost blinded her. She and Philip Nazier chatted about Rheims. He told her about the Cathedral of Notre Dame where kings and queens of France were crowned and consecrated with the oil of the sacred phial believed brought from heaven by a dove.

He finished his brandy. Eyes closed, he breathed deeply as if savouring the sweet heavy scent of the river mixing with the roses that lined the drive. She felt an unusual melancholy sweep over her. James had left his card and been sent away. Now she would not see him. The very stillness of the summer air seemed to hold an almost poetic renunciation. The golden sky was so like that poster – the gathering clouds, those few words written on a card, the ill luck she seemed to bring James. Her eyes closed painfully.

A shadow blocked out the slanting rays. She opened her eyes and saw him.

James noticed the quick change of expression in her eyes and his face flushed. 'I came to see how you were, Amelia. They told me I'd find you out here. How are you?'

It was Lord Nazier who answered. 'She's well, m'boy.' The hooded eyes opened rheumily one at a time. 'And who are you?'

James introduced himself with, 'I was the other passenger in the aeroplane.'

'So you were.' Lord Nazier stretched out a withered hand. 'Thought I'd seen you before, m'boy. Any ill effects?'

'None, thank you.'

'And how do you come to be at Rheims?'

'I work for Colonel Cody, Lord Nazier.'

'Oh, yes! The mad American flyer!'

'He couldn't come, so he sent me.'

'Well, sit down. Pull up that chair! Amelia would like a bit of company.' He closed his eyes. After several minutes, he said, 'She's lonely. I'm no company for a young girl. And she's had a nasty shaking. You cheer her up. Take no notice of me.'

Strangely enough after a few seconds, it didn't seem as if he were there at all. James leaned forward and said softly to Amelia, 'It was a bad moment. I thought . . .'

She smiled, knowing what he thought, and said happily, 'I didn't have time to think.'

'Well, you kept your head.'

'Only just. It was you who got me out of danger.' She stretched her hand and touched his fingers. 'Thank you.'

He shrugged in embarrassment and looked from her hand clasping his to Lord Nazier's closed eyes, 'Where's your husband?'

'At a reception. The one at the Town Hall.'

'The Mayor's? Oh, yes, I know.'

Amelia lowered her voice. 'Lady Nazier, his wife, went too.' James took another look at Lord Nazier's ancient face.

Amelia whispered, 'She's much younger. Years and years. And very beautiful.'

'Poor old buffer,' James said, remembering the lady in grey at Farnborough. 'Why poor?'

'No reason. To be so old, I suppose.' And then embarrassed at this whispered conversation, 'Could we take a walk? Do you feel strong enough? It might do you good.'

'Oh, yes!' Amelia stood up all eagerness. 'I feel wonderful! We could stroll down by the river. Those steps at the far end of the terrace lead down to the towpath.'

'Will he be worried if he wakes? Will he think I've kidnapped you?'

She laughed softly. 'He won't wake. He never does apparently,' and bending over Lord Nazier called, 'Philip?'

'Lord Nazier?' James called a little louder. There was no answer except a deeper breathing and the suspicion of a snore.

'I'll leave him a note, just in case.'

Amelia wrote on the back of one of the caller's cards, and propped it on the table. Then, with James's arm to support her, they crossed the terrace and descended the mossy cool of the towpath steps. The setting sun, unhampered by any obstruction flooded the river and turned it into a molten tide of bronze and gold. It was edged with silvery grey willows that trailed the surface.

Amelia's mood, exaggerated by the shock of the crash, somersaulted from melancholy to ecstasy. James was beside her. James loved her. She knew it now from that expression on his face when she had opened her eyes and seen him standing there. She knew it by what he began to say but could not say, up there on the terrace. And knowing that James loved her was everything. It was like the flood of sunset light – melting, gilding, disguising everything. In her euphoria she almost forgot her jealousy of Mrs Evans, her anger over his rejection of her job.

Almost, but not quite. She raised her hand on his arm as they turned down the towpath, and asked half-teasingly, half-severely, 'James, are you having an affair with your landlady?'

He dropped his arm, put both hands on his hips and stared at her in astonishment. 'My landlady? Here?'

'Of course not *here*! Your landlady in Farnborough!'

'Mrs Evans?'

'Yes.'

'How d'you know about her?'

'Never mind how I know! *Are* you?'

'Not so much of the never mind, Amelia! Don't ask impertinent questions and then demand an answer! How do you know,' he frowned as he repeated his question, 'about Bronwen?'

'Oh, it's Bronwen, is it?'

'Yes, it's Bronwen!' He began to walk on scowling, not offering his arm. A barge chugged by, leaving a feather of black smoke in the evening air and a smooth wave of gold green water that slapped on to the bank and fizzed over the towpath.

'Well, I know because I called. Didn't Bronwen tell you?'

James looked surprised and despite himself, gratified, 'At number 16?'

'Yes. Number 16.'

'When did you call?'

'After Cody's flight. To congratulate you. She asked me in. She seemed to think . . .' Amelia's anger returned. She finished indignantly, 'She said . . . you and she . . .'

But now she tried to remember them, Mrs Evans's words had not been all that positive.

'Mrs Evans,' James said sternly, 'is a married woman.'

'And what difference does that make?'

'How can you ask? A lot!'

'Lady Nazier's a married woman,' Amelia said, bridling at James's tone.

'That's her business and her husband's.'

'You're wrong,' Amelia stamped her foot and almost wept. 'It could be mine too!'

Tears of anger and self-pity and frustration that had nothing to do with Frederick filled her eyes and spilled down her cheeks. 'Just because he's taken her to the reception?' James said much more gently. 'Of course she couldn't mean anything to him. Beside you, she's nothing.'

He could not seriously believe that Frederick had more than political interest in Lady Nazier, but he was moved by Amelia's distress. He pulled her over to one of the iron and wood seats along the towpath. Long overhanging fronds of willow almost hid them from view and sent soft shadows over his face. His expression was concerned again. Her tears flowed faster. She shook with sobs. He put his arm round her shoulders. She clung to him. He brushed the top of her head with his lips. She held up her face, her cheeks wet, her lips pathetically parted. He kissed them gently. She responded with a fierceness that took him by surprise. He felt the warmth of her body through the thin dress. Their kisses became more urgent, dizzier, almost frantic.

Just for a moment, he almost forgot where they were and who she was. For that moment they tottered on the brink of what he told himself afterwards was disaster. Then, with a supreme effort, he pulled himself away. He stood up so abruptly that she felt as if part of her own body had been amputated.

'I'll take you back,' he said coldly, clenching his fists to his sides.

'Take me back!' She echoed, the pain of his rejection changing swiftly into fury. 'You're a bastard, James!'

Some of his mother's horror of that word had rubbed off on to James. 'Don't ever call me that!'

'I hate you, James! I hate you . . . you pious bastard!' She stood up. 'Oh, it's all right with your Mrs Bronwen Evans!' She imitated Mrs Evans' sing-song accent. 'But it's *not* all right with me!'

'No, by Christ!' She had rarely heard James blaspheme. 'And you should know it!' He meant to add even in his anger *and you should know why.*

She swept past him hissing, 'Don't take a step with me. I'm going back alone, damn you!'

She picked up her skirts in her hands and ran along the towpath like a schoolgirl, her hair coming loose, her shoulders heaving. He watched her till she reached the steps. She was breathless by the time she climbed to the hotel terrace. Lord Nazier was still sitting in his chair. She thought his eyes were open and upon her until she reached the table and saw that he still slept.

Her note was still in place. As she subsided on the chaise-longue, she reached out and scrunched it up. That small sound seemed to wake him. He looked for a moment at the long shadows on the terrace flagstones and then at his watch. He exclaimed it was time they went in. His half-closed eyes appeared not to notice her disarranged hair or her tear-stained face.

'I had a splendid sleep,' he said. 'Did you, Amelia?'

She nodded.

'Never woke once.'

'Nor did I.'

'I had a dream that some unknown man came and swept you away. I wondered what on earth I would say to Frederick!' He paused. 'But it was only a dream.'

'Yes,' Amelia said emptily. 'Only a dream!'

TWELVE

'My, my, my!' Bronwen sighed over roast beef lunch, a month after James's return to Farnborough. 'As I was saying to my Taffy in bed last night, Rheims didn't do you no good, James!'

Her Taffy, all spitted and polished and ready for afternoon duty, swallowed a corner of Yorkshire pudding and nodded sagely. Then he winked and asked, 'Was it the champagne then, boyo, or too much parlyvooing with the mamoiselles?'

'Both, if I know James,' Bronwen said, adding slyly, 'though miladies is more like it. James doesn't go in these days for common or garden mamoiselles.'

'Oh, indeed to goodness!' Taffy laughed uncomfortably, as he always did when he played foil to his wife. He pushed back his chair. 'You must tell us about it some time, James boyo.' He bent down and kissed the top of Bronwen's head. 'Well, girl, I must love you and leave you. Duty calls!'

James was aware of his own ill humour, but told himself it was because of all the government help being lavished by the French and Germans on their aviators, while the British only poured scorn on their own fliers. But the real cause, as he perfectly well knew, was Amelia. Rheims had brought home to him how unsuccessful he had been in forgetting her. She was as much a part of him as his own right arm. And the years had sharpened rather than numbed his need for her. He tried pushing her to the back of his mind, but she kept returning like some persistent ghost refusing exorcism. Now to make matters worse, a ghost with that cold fixed shadow behind her eyes, that tightening of her vulnerable mouth that made him fear she was as unhappy as himself.

'What's happened to your tongue, James?' Bronwen asked when her husband had departed.

'Nothing.'

'You're still cross with me, aren't you?'

James smiled faintly. 'Wary.'

'Call it what you like. Cross I say. Cross I didn't say your smart ladyfriend had called.'

'You should have.'

'Maybe I should and maybe I shouldn't. I seem to remember she told me not to.'

'I doubt that.'

'Well, I don't. She's two-faced, if you ask me.'

'I didn't ask you.'

'Oh, snap my head off if you want to! Well, maybe she did and maybe she

109

didn't! You're just too . . . oh, sorry I spoke again out of turn.' She stood up as James pushed back his chair. 'Now where are you off to? You're not on duty!'

'I told you before. I'm going to timekeep for the Colonel. He's testing a new modification.'

'Oh, what a waste of time it all is! A lovely day like this. I thought you and me'd go to the park. Come back for a cosy tea. You know I like you, James. It's just I don't like to see some stuck-up lady make a fool of you. 'Cos that's what she's doing! She as good as told me! Honest! If you really want to kow why I didn't tell you, *that's* why. I was so disgusted! I said the less James hears of this talk the better!'

As she told the goldbeater girls afterwards, at that point James lifted her bodily and moved her out of the way. His face was like thunder. Bronwen wasn't letting him get away like that. She nipped smartly out and into the little hall. She spread herself against the front door, arms outstretched.

'No, I shan't let you go! You're not going out of this house all cross again! Come on! I've said I'm sorry! Let's kiss and make up!' She closed her eyes and held up her lips.

The faint click of the back-door latch made her eyes fly open. She banged furiously on the window as James leapt the garden fence and went striding down Madeira Avenue.

'I had to fight him off,' she told the goldbeater girls next morning. 'He was like a man possessed! Well, it stands to reason! He was a blacksmith. He's got a body like iron! And now the Colonel's taught him to fly, he's going to win all the prizes at Hendon!'

There Bronwen was romancing as usual. Cody's planes were much too precious (and too easily smashed) to teach anyone to fly. In fact, only two Englishmen at that time knew how to fly – and one of them wasn't Cody because he was still an American subject.

1910 altered all that. And there were changes in politics too. Lloyd-George's land tax budget was thrown out by the Lords, and in January another general election, on which Frederick placed high hopes, was called. His hopes were dashed. Though the Tories gained 100 seats, Asquith still remained in power. Not only was there no chance whatever of office for Frederick, but the Liberals were now planning to undermine the position of the landed gentry by drastically curtailing the power of the House of Lords.

Only the serious illness of the King in May forced a truce. A true Edwardian wife to the last, Queen Alexandra summoned her husband's last mistress, Mrs Keppel, to his bedside as he lay dying. His son, soon to be George V told him, 'The two-year-old plate at Kempton Park races. It was won by your horse, Witch of the Air!'

The King gave a last chuckle. 'I am very glad,' he said.

The nation mourned the King's death with genuine sorrow. Asquith said of him, 'He carried well the title by which he will always be remembered – the peacemaker of the world.' Nevertheless after the ostentatious funeral attended by all the crowned heads of Europe, his nephew Kaiser Wilhelm took the opportunity of sounding out the French on the possibilities of a combined attack on Britain.

At Ascot that year, all the ladies wore black dresses, black hats decorated with black feathers, and carried black parasols. James's mother hung the forge with black crêpe and bunting. Sarah bought a pair of black gloves and stitched a black ribbon on her Sunday hat.

The new King was quite different from his pleasure-loving father, though just as interested in flying. The world's first airmail was flown from London to Windsor with newspapers describing his magnificent coronation in Westminster Abbey. Shortly after his coronation he visited Farnborough to watch the flying. He delighted Cody by constantly addressing him as 'Colonel'. Cody had by now signed his naturalisation papers on the bent back of the Doncaster town clerk at Britain's first aviation meeting on the racecourse.

Aviation began to explode. Aerodromes sprang up. Flying schools started. Model aeroplane clubs flourished. Prizes were offered. Dozens of Englishmen flocked to France to get their 'ticket' and to Amelia's irritation a society beauty, Mrs Beauvoir-Stocks, was declared the first woman pilot in Britain, though Leila Cody had been the first to fly. At Jerningham, things went very slowly. Wilkinson was frequently sick and Frederick always parsimonious. The engine failed as Ajax II took off on her maiden flight. For months afterwards Frederick put every difficulty in the way of its rebuilding.

Moore-Brabazon, not Cody, won the £1000 Round Britain prize. Cody also tried for the new £10,000 *Daily Mail* London-Manchester prize, ordering special fireworks from Brock's to mark his route. These fireworks were made to explode at 300 feet and emit red smoke and a small parachute with a red flag attached. Unfortunately after fifteen minutes' flying, Cody's engine petered out and he had to make a forced landing. Against fierce competition from Grahame-White who took off in the light of car headlights and flew through the night, the prize was won by the Frenchman Paulhan in the same sort of Farman biplane that Amelia had flown in at Rheims.

The races were watched breathlessly by tens of thousands. No longer was flying the sport of the rich, but the latest thrill of the ordinary man. Long queues of people paid £2 for a three-minute ride at Brooklands – sometimes ending in the neighbouring sewage farm when the engines failed on take-off – or at Hendon which was now staging flying carnivals that rivalled the yachting at Cowes and the ballooning at Ranelagh.

And then, suddenly, the fun-loving aeroplane showed its sinister side. It was a warm July day and the aviation meeting at Bournemouth was packed. 'I shall expect to see you waving from the stand.' Charles Rolls had telephoned Amelia. 'And I'll give you a flip when I've done my stunt!'

True to form, Rolls took off in his Wright Flyer and zoomed over the grandstand so low that everyone, including Amelia, ducked their heads. Then the spectators cheered as at barely 40 feet the aircraft roared on. Amelia saw it a heartbeat ahead of it happening. She saw the nose being pulled up sharply but not responding, the rear elevator snap. The cheering died abruptly. In silence, the crowds watched the Wright Flyer plunge into the ground.

The silence was followed by tumult. Everyone was running to the broken pile of wreckage. Everyone was talking and shouting. There was the ringing of ambulance bells. Somewhere a woman screamed. Then Amelia saw far ahead of her, tearing head down like a bull across the grass, the bearded figure that she knew from the newspapers to be Colonel Cody.

He was the first to reach the wreckage. She saw him pull a piece of wing aside. She saw him kneel down. Then she saw his shoulders heaving. Saw the tears streaming down his face as he spoke to the ambulancemen. The crowd respectfully held back. There was nothing to be done. The mutter went round that Charles Rolls was dead. The men took off their hats and held them against their chests. He was Britain's first aviation fatality.

Amelia walked back to the car and sat for a long time in anguished silence, before determinedly starting up the engine and turning the nose of the Rolls towards Jerningham.

1911 brought a further glimpse of the sinister side of flying. In a sudden war with the Turks in North Africa, the Italians used Blériots for aerial reconnaissance and dropped small bombs made from hand grenades. In that same crisis, Britain and Germany moved perilously close to war. Shouting down Frederick Haybury and the rest of the airship lobby in the House of Commons, the naval Dreadnought lobby chanted, 'We've got four! And we want four more!'

'Look at that!' Bronwen pointed to a piece in *Aldershot News* of 3 April 1911. 'Colonel and Mrs Cody being piped aboard the new dreadnought in Plymouth. He's a lucky fellow!'

'Lucky,' James thought wryly, glancing at the photograph. Well, maybe he was. He had miraculously survived a dozen accidents seemingly as severe as that which had killed Charles Rolls. And to ensure his luck continued, Cody kept a black cat as a lucky mascot, a horseshoe over his workshop door, never flew on Fridays, abhorred 13 and on no account would allow anyone to wear green.

'It must be ever so nice being Mrs Cody these days! Hobnobbing with important people.'

'I don't suppose she likes it all that much.'

'Oh, don't you! Well, I would! I'd like to be piped on board a dreadnought with the sailors lined up all stiff to attention!'

James unhooked his jacket from the back of the door and laughed out loud.

Bronwen frowned. 'I'd enjoy it more than wearing me hands down to the knuckle, doing housework! Not to mention skinning me fingers scraping horrid balloon stuff! Not to mention scrubbing Taffy's sweaty shirts, and mending his socks! Just pick up that paper, James, and turn the page! Oh, give it here! I'll do it for you! There! On page three. A silly suffragette chaining herself to the railings! Well, do you know what I'd say to that silly suffragette? *I'm* chained to the kitchen sink and nobody cares! Nobody takes a picture of me! And if they was to send me to prison, I wouldn't know the difference! In fact, I might think it was paradise!'

'Bronwen!' James shouldered his way into his jacket. 'You talk a lot of rot!'

He said it half-teasingly, half-exasperatedly. But with the suddeness of a tap being turned on, Bronwen burst into tears. James glanced at the clock. Compelled to delay his departure for the airfield to comfort her, he patted her heaving shoulder and said inadequately, 'I didn't mean to upset you!'

'Well, you have!' She dived into her pocket, produced a lace-edge handkerchief and dabbed her eyes. 'And it isn't the first time! You're always upsetting me these days. Taffy's noticed too. You're ever so different from what you was. Ever so high and mighty! Success has gone to your head.'

'But I haven't had any!'

'Not in one manner of speaking maybe. But in another you have, being with the Colonel.'

'That's not the same thing at all. It's *his* money. *His* effort. *His* design. I'm glad for his sake. But I'm not interested in reflected glory.' He found himself getting angry again. All the old frustrations came surging back. He seemed destined to go in circles. 'I'm a good mechanic,' he was speaking to himself rather than to Bronwen, 'and a good blacksmith. But that isn't exactly setting the Thames on fire.'

'But it's the beginning, James. Remember that picture in the papers of you slapping the Colonel on the back, last New Year's Eve when he won the Michelin Cup? And him with his beard all white with frost? 1910 went out with a bang. I said then to Taffy, 1911's coming in well for James.'

'Maybe. But that was him, Bron. Cody's doing. He had to stay up there for four and three quarter hours. Not me.'

'But you're young still. If you pushed yourself forward a bit more, you could be well . . . properly famous. You could get invited to places, with the Colonel. And you know how to behave when you get there. You're not an old stick-in-the-mud like Taffy.'

'Taffy's all right,' James said, preparing to leave. 'They don't come any better than Taffy.'

'"Course they don't.' She gave a sudden little smile. 'He said near the same about you the other day. He's ever so fond of you. But he's sensitive is Taffy, and he said something else.'

She paused and blinked her eyes.

'Well?' James said impatiently. 'What?'

'He said it's a pity now when the Colonel's doing so well that *we* don't see something of it. Go to one of the shows when he's flying. He must get some free tickets. We could cheer him on. Taffy would like that. And it would be a real nice change for *me*.'

James promised to do what he could. It seemed a small price to pay for the stowing away of the lace hankie and his escape. Besides, Cody was only too keen to swell his audiences.

When three weeks later, the programme came through for the air show at Hendon, Cody handed James two spectators' tickets. 'For your landlady and her spouse. You can drive them in the Simms-Welbeck if you want to, James. We'll need it for the spares. It'll make a nice day outing for them.'

Bronwen began her preparations immediately. She bought a bolt of shot blue silk from the draper's in Farnborough, and with her skilful fingers fashioned a dress that would not have disgraced Ascot. She trimmed a matching hat and sewed a ruff of the material round her parasol.

'It may be cold,' James exclaimed as Bronwen threw open the door of number 16 to him, and he saw her dressed in her finery. He jerked his head behind him at Cody's open Simms-Welbeck.

'Whatever else I am, James, I'm not cold!' Bronwen hitched a corner of her voluminous skirt to show the multiplicity of her petticoats. 'Besides,' she slipped her hand through his arm. 'I've got *you* to keep me warm!'

'You've got Taffy.'

'Oh,' she sighed. 'And that's what I thought, too, but he's got himself on

113

duty. More's the shame on him!That sergeant of his. Proper beast, and my Taffy's a pushover. Never stands up for his rights. Sent a message round while you were up at the field this morning.'

'So he's not coming?'

She shook her head. 'He said not to let it spoil our fun. And he's given me some money to spend and . . .' she pulled the door of the house shut behind her ' . . . and what are we waiting for?'

Two hours later they were in the thick of it. Two minute units in a crowd of 50,000, strolling amongst the candy-striped tents at this huge aerial circus.

'I don't think I've ever enjoyed myself so much,' she said, slipping her hand through James's arm. 'I feel a proper toff! A real lady! You're a handsome fellow, James. You could pass for a real gentleman.'

'I don't want to.'

''Course you want to!' She gave his arm a shake. 'Everyone wants to! I wonder if people wonder who *we* are?' She nodded graciously to strangers listening to the brass band as the little aircraft came almost within touching distance, making all those smartly hatted heads bow in a swathe like so many cornstalks.

'Oh, it's lovely!' Bronwen clapped her hands. 'Like a seaside fair only up in the sky!'

The sky was clear blue and the sun shone and the exploits were ever more daring. There were obstacle races and aerobatics and people clowning around with mad contraptions that couldn't get into the sky. Those that did get up flew so low and slow that the spectators could see the pilot's face and everything he was doing. And there was even a strange chap who got out on the wing and started fiddling around with a spanner while the aircraft just wobbled on. The air was filled with the honking of car horns, the neighing of horses, the clang and putter of aero engines and the whistling of wings. It smelled of crushed grass, caster-oil and petrol, horse dung, hot sugar and roasting chestnuts.

Now they were watching the wing-walkers on the Deperdussins, nonchalantly dipping their feet into empty space. Then the clowns fighting in the sky and pretending to fall when the commentator urged them on. Just before they took tea in the striped refreshment tent, they watched Hamel in a Voisin and Grahame-White in a Blériot, only inches apart fly round the flagged pylons of the ring.

'It's better than a circus, James! Better than the flying trapeze!'

'You wait till the Colonel comes on!' James promised her. 'He'll steal the show!'

He had already reported in at the Cody tent with the spares. Cody was surrounded by his sons and had bidden him go off and enjoy himself with his pretty little friend. This he was doing, despite the fact that he had a strange disturbing feeling that Amelia was somewhere near. He half-expected to feel her hand on his arm and hear her voice.

As dusk fell, a circlet of Chinese lanterns ringed the flying arena. The dark shapes of aeroplanes now flew overhead rimmed in different coloured lights. Then a vast black silhouette of a battleship was suddenly illuminated by a battery of searchlights.

'Oh, James! What are they going to do now?'

'They're going to bomb the battleship,' James said, as the bands struck up with sea-shanties.

'Oh, do let's stop and watch! We don't have to go yet surely?'

Out of the twelve rows of spectators' chairs, there was only one vacant seat right at the front.

'This'll do, James!' She led the way. 'Sit down!'

'No, you sit down.'

'You can't stand up in front, silly!' She gave him a quick push. 'You sit down and I'll sit on your knee! Everyone else is doing it!'

Perched elegantly on his knee with her parasol in her right hand and her left arm draped round his neck, they waited for the show to begin. And as they waited a Farman emerged very low out of the darkness, blazing red, white and blue in the beams of the searchlights.

A well-known handsome face was spotlit. The crowd cheered.

'Who's that, James?'

'Claude Grahame-White.'

'He's a good looker, isn't he? My, my! A real ladykiller! Ooh and look! There's a lady behind him!'

James had already seen and recognised her with a strange lurch of his heart. As the Farman zoomed only feet above them, Bronwen shrieked, 'It's your lady friend, James! *It is*! Wave to them!'

Jumping off his knee, she waved her parasol. Round came the Farman again, lower this time, with Grahame-White leaning over the side to wave back to the enthusiastic parasol. James cringed. Amelia wouldn't be able to recognise either of them with all the lights blazing in her eyes. But as always with Amelia, he had that terrible certainty that she could sense his presence as he could sense hers.

'Look, James! Mr Grahame-White's coming back again!'

Worse than that, to the delight of the twelve rows of spectators, ever the showman, Grahame-White set the Farman neatly down in front of them. He cut the engine, jumped down on to the grass, and helped Amelia out. Then pulling off his long gauntlets, he began shaking hands with the spectators.

Bronwen waved ever more furiously. 'Amelia!' she shouted. 'It's me! Over here!'

No, James thought, No! Dear God, make them go off in the other direction!

But Bronwen's voice was penetrating and urgent. Claude Grahame-White turned. Never able to resist a pretty face, he came smiling towards them with Amelia beside him.

'Amelia,' shrilled Bronwen staying firmly on his knee. 'You'll never guess who I've got here!'

Curious heads turned towards them. Bronwen stuck her parasol in the soft trodden grass as if anchoring herself by it, put her right arm round his neck like a noose and wriggled her bottom on his knee with possessive relish.

Abruptly James detached her arm, pushed her aside and stood up. 'Hello, Amelia,' he said, meeting her blazing blue eyes.

She nodded frigidly. 'James.'

'Are you enjoying the show?' he asked lamely.

'I can see you are.'

115

Bronwen darted James a reproachful glance and rubbed her arm as if he'd bruised it.

'Aren't you going to introduce me to your pretty friend, Amelia?'

'Mr Grahame-White, Mrs er . . .'

'Evans. Bronwen Evans. I've heard ever so much about you, Mr Grahame-White. I admire you ever so much.'

'Then I hope we shall see more of you.'

The ordeal could only have lasted a minute or so because Grahame-White had to get over to the ring to ride, as he called it, a Blériot for the battleship-bombing. But to James it seemed to last hours. If he put out a hand he could have touched Amelia's. And if only she had met his eyes, surely he could have signalled something. But she didn't. When she was compelled to look in his direction, she fixed her gaze on a point just above his head. Nor did she offer him her hand when she left.

An angry Bronwen watched them go. 'I hope you realise you've ruined my parasol,' she said, showing him the bent tip. 'Pushing me aside! As if I was a sack of coal!'

'It's just the ferule. I'm sorry. I'll get you another parasol.'

'Oh, thank you very much! With what would you buy it, might I ask? Besides, that isn't the point! The point is, you were very rough and rude. Not a bit gentlemanly. Not a bit like Mr Grahame-White! And what about your horrid stuck-up girlfriend . . . '

As James bit back his reply, Bronwen was interrupted by the commentator announcing the last item. One by one out of the darkness came the sound of engines starting up. One by one into the air they went – Cody, Grahame-White, Hamel Parke. Round and round they flew over the illuminated battleship.

Then down came Cody, flew directly at the centre of the silhouette and dropped four white sacks. Immediately the battleship was covered in the smoke of bursting flour bags. The crowd went wild. The bands played 'Rule Britannia'. Bronwen forgot she was angry with James and hugged him hard.

And as one by one, the little aeroplanes swooped down, dropped their load and zoomed away, as the black battleship gradually turned white, neither the crowd nor the Lords of Admiralty who were also in attendance that night saw it as a lesson that one day aeroplanes would sink battleships . . .

Merely as a beautiful spectacle, the perfect climax to a perfect day.

Bronwen remembered her anger as soon as they got home. She sulked for a month. Meals were served in offended silence. Taffy's favourite pudding and James's breakfast kippers disappeared from the menu.

'You seem to have upset our Bronwen,' Taffy was moved to say after a disappointing Sunday lunch of skilly followed by sago pudding. 'Say you're sorry and make up, there's a good boyo!'

More for Taffy's sake than his own, for he had already begun looking through the Rooms Vacant column in the *Aldershot News*, James called in at the draper's the following Friday. Cody was a prompt paymaster when he had the money, and James had at last a few shillings to spare. He bought a very pretty blue parasol, had it wrapped and carried it home.

Bronwen was cutting out Christmas cards in the kitchen. She looked up as James came in and then pursed her lips and began gluing on some cut-outs.

'Pretty,' James said.

'Thanks , I'm sure.'

'This is for you.' He handed her the brown paper parcel. 'It's a new parasol.'

She unwrapped it, eyed it critically, half-opened it and examined the pattern, clearly not greatly taken with it.

'It'll go with your nice dress.'

'I s'pose so.' She put the parasol down against the kitchen table as if she'd lost all interest in it. 'Near enough.'

'And I'm sorry.'

'For what?'

'For upsetting you. For being rough.'

'Did Taffy tell you to say that?'

'Of course not!'

'Bet he did! Bet he'd tell you to do anything just so as he can get his favourite grub. Proper pig he is! Doesn't care about me! Nor do you, James March! Throwing me off like a sack of flour! I don't want ever to wear that dress again I said to my Taffy.'

'You told him, did you?'

''Course I did.'

'Didn't he mind you sitting on my knee?'

'Did he hell!'

'I wouldn't have *my* wife sitting on anyone else's knee.'

'Oh, James! I bet you'd be ever such a jealous husband. But Taffy isn't. Honest! I've done much worse than sit on men's knees!'

'Bronwen!'

'Well, it's true. Oh, I fancy *you*, James! I've told you often enough!'

'Well, don't.'

'And if you hadn't bin brought up so mealy-mouthed, you'd have taken what was offered!' She gave a high hard laugh. 'But you don't need to think you're the only pebble on the beach! You're not the only man to tickle my fancy!'

'You're talking rubbish again, Bronwen! You're a silly girl! You live in a dream. Taffy should take you by the hair of your head and thrash you! And then scrub out your dirty little mouth!'

'Taffy and whose army?' She put her hands on her hips. 'He wouldn't dare to lay a finger on me. He knows I've had other men.'

'I don't believe you.'

'It's the gospel truth!'

'Then he should bloody well see you don't.'

'Oh, hear who's talking about dirty mouths now! Mr High and Mighty. The friend of Lady Loose and Flighty.'

James grasped her by the shoulder. 'Don't you dare call her that!'

'I've called her it. And that's what she is! She's a loose woman!'

'By Christ, she isn't!'

'She is. Everyone knows that. People talk. She's not interested in flying . . . something else beginning with . . . '

She gasped as she saw the furious expression of his face. Lifting her hand defensively, she suddenly struck out and brought the open palm hard across his cheek.

His head jerked back for a moment. He bit his tongue. His temper blazed. Picking her up with one arm, he subsided on to the kitchen chair, dragging her with him. She squealed and struggled across his knee. Cards and cut-outs went flying.

She made an effort to scrabble for the parasol but his arm was longer. He snatched it, lifted it and brought it down hard on her bottom. She screamed each time in outrage. 'And that's what Taffy should've done a long time ago!' he said at last, pushing her from him.

For a moment she stood in front of him, her eyes half-closed. Then she flung her arms round his neck, pulled his head down and kissed him wetly on the mouth.

'Take me,' she said urgently, 'Take me now! Please! I want you so! I'll forgive you if you take me now!'

For a second, his lips responded. His blood surged dizzily. Physical desire almost overwhelmed him. Then furiously he pushed her away, rushed out of the room and wrenched the front door open.

Taffy was just coming up the path with a big bunch of yellow chrysanthemums in his hand.

THIRTEEN

'To celebrate,' Taffy said, putting the chrysanthemums into Bronwen's arms.

'What the hell's there to celebrate *here*?' she asked sulkily.

'The birth of the Royal Flying Corps, my love! You see before you no longer Corporal Evans of the Engineers, but Corporal Evans of the RFC. Motto . . . *Per Ardua ad Astra* . . . which being translated for the uneducated means "through hard work to the stars".'

'If that was true,' Bronwen said. 'I've reached the stars already.'

'Give over, Bron! Drink to the RFC! And you, James man! I've got a half-bottle of gin in my pocket!'

As far as celebrations went, Cody was still having his share. He had again won the Michelin Cup and £1000. And he was busy building a monoplane to win the Military Trials at Stonehenge aerodrome in four months time.

It was at Jerningham that there was nothing to celebrate at all. Wilkinson had suffered further bouts of ill-health and Ajax II still had not flown. The company was simply losing money all the time and Frederick was more hostile than ever to the Ajax project.

Nevertheless in the middle of April 1912, the fat buds of the daffodils were beginning to burst and there was a promise of warmth in the air to which Amelia's volatile and optimistic spirits were beginning to respond. Wilkinson's health, she was telling herself, would improve with the sun. Ajax would at last be completed, would take to the air, would be acclaimed. Orders would flood in.

After that last spectacle at Hendon, she had given James up to the tender mercies of that little Welsh flibbertigibbet who certainly would have him. But Frederick in London was certainly preferable to Frederick at Haybury. And she had dear little Arthur. And above all, she had Charles . . .

There was a knock on the library door. One glance over her shoulder at Mr Symes's face when she bade him enter warned her that bursting daffodil buds were no guarantee of better times. Charles's tutor, a middle-aged man with a leonine head but rather disappointingly short legs, was pale with anger. His pepper-and-salt whiskers bristled with it. He bowed stiffly to Amelia and bade her good morning as she turned to meet him. He murmured that he trusted she could spare him a moment as the matter was of the most extreme urgency.

Then he closed the library doors weightily behind him and advanced ponderously, pointing to his chest. There on his white shirt front up as far as his collar was a huge blotch of ink.

'I thought you should see for yourself, Lady Haybury.'

Amelia nodded several times and then asked hopefully. 'Was it an accident?'

'No, Lady Haybury. It was no accident.' He drew in a deep breath. 'It was a deliberate act of aggression.'

'By Charles?'

'Yes, Lady Haybury. Another of his misdemeanours. And this, Lady Haybury,' he slipped a plump hand into the inside pocket of his jacket and produced a long white envelope which he placed on the library table between them, 'is my resignation.'

Amelia was panic-stricken. When Frederick heard of this there would be hell to pay. 'Please,' she said, pushing the envelope like a counterbetween them. 'Take it back, Mr Symes. Reconsider. There are other measures. You have beaten him, I hope?'

'Until my arm aches, Lady Haybury.'

'But you are still angry.' She held up her hand as Mr Symes seeme about to interrupt her. 'And rightly so. But anger is a bad counsellor. You've told that to Charles yourself on occasion. I will, of course, replace the damaged shirt. And your suit, for I see your waistcoat is splashed too.'

There was some ink on the pepper-and-salt whiskers, but she could do nothing about them except try not to smile. She was a bad mother to even think of smiling, let alone have to bite the inside of her cheeks lest her mouth curl upwards. No wonder Charles misbehaved! She was immature, as Frederick told her, even though she was almost twenty-six.

'If this were the first time, Lady Haybury, I would agree. Anger is indeed a bad counsellor. But there is such a thing as righteous indignation.' He pushed the envelope back towards Amelia. 'And there is nothing wrong with that.'

'But consider —'

'This is not, after all, the first instance of your son's misbehaviour.'

This time there followed a catalogue of Charles's misdoings from the smashing of Arthur's rocking-horse (another deliberate act of aggression) to the episode Lady Haybury would recall when he had driven her own Rolls-Royce down the drive and dented the mudguard. There was the disgraceful incident of the banana skin and Lady Sempner, the occasion last Guy Fawkes night when Charles had stolen out to join the village bonfire celebrations, the rocket he had brought back with him and detonated in the servants' sitting-room, the common rat he had introduced as a pet and kept in a box in the nursery bathroom, and the bad language he had used to Nanny when she had caused that same rat to be destroyed.

All this on top of Charles's general disobedience, insolence and disinclination to learn. 'Despite my qualifications – I am as you know Messrs Gabbitas-Thring's most qualified tutor – and my sincerest efforts, he has scarcely a word of Greek and only a phrase of Latin.'

'He is more mechanically than classically minded,' Amelia said tentatively, pushing the envelope towards Mr Symes's side of the table.

'Of that I would not know. Though if he is, it will be of very little use to him in his walk of life. What I *do* know is that Charles has a good deal of knowledge of matters of which he should be ignorant.'

Amelia bit her lip and said nothing.

'He associates too much with the servants – the grooms and the gardeners especially. And Nanny tells me —'

'I am not interested in gossip, Mr Symes.'

Especially not any gossip Nanny had to impart. She had never liked Charles. Never liked Amelia, come to that. Nanny had always been on Frederick's side. She had been horrified last year when Amelia had begun taking Charles to the factory with her. He loved the models of the aircraft, loved helping Wilkinson's riggers with the stitching and stretching. He had a mathematical mind and was a quick learner – so long as it wasn't formal teaching. That he hated. Just as he hated all authority. Nanny had told innumerable tales to Frederick and earned Charles as many beatings. But still Charles didn't learn.

'I simply can't communicate with him,' Frederick had said repeatedly. 'We enjoy no common ground.'

Nanny agreed. She had remarked (not in Amelia's hearing, but in Sarah's) that Charles, with his dark brows and hair and eyes of such deep blue that they sometimes shone black, looked like a limb of Satan. And that if it hadn't been for Master Arthur, she would have followed the governess's example and left the Haybury employ.

For Arthur, his ginger curls now paled to gold that haloed his pale face and perfect features, looked exactly what he was. An angel. Like those illustrations of Victorian nursery poems about the deaths of infants. Nanny always thought of him as the child in Mrs Carey Brock's moral poems. Arthur touched Nanny's dried-up heart as no child had yet done. She spoiled him accordingly. So did the housekeeper. So did Cook.

In the opposing camp, Sarah was fiercely devoted to Charles. The grooms and the gardeners treated him as one of them. And in some odd way, the young boys exercised a strange divisive power over the Haybury household which was to grow stronger with the years. A power which Frederick's infrequent visits exacerbated. For rarely did a visit end without Charles being thrashed and Arthur indulged, Sarah furiously arguing with Nanny, the head groom censured and Frederick and Amelia further apart.

I am a failure, Amelia thought, staring down at the library table and the white envelope which Mr Symes had once more pushed towards her. I am a failure as a wife and even more as a mother. The Jerningham factory is a failure. Ajax will never fly. And it is obvious now that no amount of pleading will succeed in changing Mr Symes's mind. I have failed in that, too.

'If it is a question of salary —' she tried as one last attempt.

'I have already been approached,' Mr Symes told her, 'by a nephew of one of my first parents. A gentleman in His Majesty's household.'

'Will you at least stay until I find another tutor?' Amelia begged cravenly. And with Mr Symes's grudging promise, Amelia sent a groom round to inform Wilkinson that she had been called away to London on urgent business.

'I may be back tonight, but I doubt it,' she told Sarah. It was Nanny's day off and she should, she knew, have punished Charles, but she was filled with the urgent necessity to have the matter settled before Mr Symes's resignation came to Frederick's ears. Frederick was not greatly taken with the tutor. He had appointed him on his impressive qualifications rather than on his personality. A change might even be for the better, Amelia thought, as she climbed into her Rolls-Royce and pulled down her driving veil. She decided on impulse that it would be pleasanter and perhaps quicker if she drove all the way to London.

The road took her through Jerningham village, past the church and the forge. The pollarded willows were lightly hazed in green bud. James's mother was sitting in the doorway of the forge cottage, plaiting rushes. An old woman's task. The sunlight gave her face an ivory translucency. She looked tired and sick. Amelia almost stopped to talk to her. But as she hesitated, the old woman looked up. Her eyes were hard as stones. She hates me still, Amelia thought. Perhaps James does, too.

She pressed her foot down on the accelerator, taking the corner sharply, then righting the car, and pressing even harder on the accelerator for the long stretch of road across the forest. The wind blew in her face. She found herself thinking of those faraway days when she used to pretend that James sat in the seat beside her. Twice she neglected to look at the signposts and lost her way. And despite her frequent and heavy use of the accelerator pedal, it was four thirty before she reached Marble Arch. Though she was thirsty and would have liked to call at 7 Park Lane for tea, time was important, so she drove directly towards the educational advisers' offices in Victoria.

News of her problem had already preceded her. A white-haired gentleman in a high collar and dark morning suit informed her with kindly pity that Mr Symes had already written at length about Master Haybury. They spent a somewhat fraught hour going through a list of possible tutors, none of which appeared to be immediately free. There was the possibility of one young man, recently qualified, who might be available in June . . . they would contact Lady Haybury if the candidate offered himself. Meantime perhaps Sir Frederick would like to interview some of the others.

The sky was grey by the time she left the offices, and the warmth had gone. The lamplighter was moving slowly down the sidestreets, touching the lamps into hissing yellowy white incandescence. Motor cars, hansom cabs, electric trams and horse-buses trundled people homeward.

Amelia herself felt a reluctance to go to 7 Park Lane. Frederick would most likely be out at the Commons but if by any chance he was home, she would immediately have to explain the reason for her presence. To postpone the inevitable, to try to marshal in her mind, rehearse the explanations for Charles's behaviour which she must offer Frederick, Amelia took herself to Gunter's, next to the Bath Club.

Amongst the tinkle of china and silver there was much chatter of the coming season, one of the first since the Court came out of mourning, and speculation as to how greatly the King, or more importantly the Queen, would change the style of the Court.

'And will the new season find *you* still buried in Hampshire?' an elderly voice croaked in her ear. Aunt Sempner's silver-headed cane was laid peremptorily on her arm. And almost in the same breath, 'What brings you up, gal? Does Frederick know you're here?'

Helping her into the gilt chair opposite, Amelia shook her head. Lady Sempner's monkey eyes at first registered surprise. Then the enamelled face broke into a thousand porcelain cracks of inexpressible delight. She murmured something under her breath which sounded like, but could not have been, 'Serve him right!'

Aunt Sempner allowed Amelia to buy her another tray of tea and some carraway cake. She enquired after her great-nephews and before Amelia had time to answer embarked on the latest gossip about Mr Asquith's outspoken wife, Margot. But then she refused Amelia's offer of a lift, and shooed her home.

'Quickly, gal, quickly!' She gave a strange knowledgeable chuckle. 'If you hurry, you'll catch —' In mid-sentence she had stopped a hansom, climbed inside and was gone.

Puzzling over her odd behaviour, Amelia drove the Rolls-Royce slowly down Park Lane. The lights were on in number 7. She parked the car in the rear mews yard and let herself in through the back door. Walking up the corridor, she found the hall deserted. The salver was empty of calling cards. The butler did not appear to hear her. Then she remembered that Wednesday was his day off. She walked up the circular stairs without encountering any of the servants.

Her sitting-room was in darkness and the curtains were undrawn. No fire burned in the empty grate. The room was excessively neat and smelled of camphor and cold, as if she were never again expected back, had almost ceased to exist. Suddenly she felt almost frightened. Her feelings somersaulted. All at once, it was imperative that she found Frederick. She hurried along the corridor to his bedroom, and with only a perfunctory knock turned the handle and threw open the door.

The room was softly lit by a single table lamp. The glow of a coal fire flickered on the high ceiling, sending weird shadows on to the plaster ornamented nooks and crannies. A man's head rose from the pillows. The firelight pulled out his nose and peaked his head and exaggerated the dropping open of his mouth.

Frederick's astonished outraged face gaped at her. His eyes glinted angrily. A mass of dark hair lay fanned on the pillow beside him. Amelia saw Lady Nazier's pale pre-Raphaelite profile slowly turn full face towards her. Still maintaining her calm, Diana sat up, unhurriedly fastening the satin bow of her bodice.

'Amelia!' Frederick sounded furious and reproachful. 'For God's sake! What are you doing here?'

Side by side from the bed, they both stared at her, Frederick indignant, Diana Nazier disdainful. It was all too much. Now Amelia knew why Lady Sempner had looked so maliciously pleased.

'What in heaven's name, am *I* doing?' Amelia shouted. 'What the hell are *you* doing?'

And rushing forward, she grabbed a handful of Diana Nazier's beautiful hair and pulled and twisted it till its owner screamed. Then with the open palm of her free hand slapped both her cheeks.

The other woman retaliated immediately. She scraped her long nails down Amelia's face. She seized the velvet lapel of her jacket and wrenched it till it tore. They were well matched in size, in youth and in anger.

Then Frederick intervened. He took hold of Amelia roughly by the shoulders and with her arms gripped behind her back held her captive.

'Now Diana, you shall pay Amelia back in her own coin! I give you my permission. Slap her as she slapped you!'

Cleverly, cool and calm again now, Lady Nazier shook her disdainful head. 'You behaved like a Billingsgate fishwife,' Frederick said, when he had returned from escorting Diana Nazier home. 'I was ashamed of you.'

'And *she* behaved like a whore!' Amelia said, fighting a rearguard action now because somehow Frederick had by her act gained mastery. 'I was ashamed of *both* of *you!*'

'That's enough!' Frederick held up his hand. 'I will not have Diana spoken of slightingly.'

'Slightingly! It isn't possible to slight her! She is what she is. An aristocratic whore!'

'A loyal friend, that's what she is! And you knew of our friendship!'

'Friendship!' Amelia grimaced. 'Is that what you call it?'

'It has ripened into something more than friendship certainly. Something that you were not prepared to offer.'

'You never asked me!'

'Never asked? Does a husband have to *ask*? In so many words? Are you as immature as that *still*, Amelia?'

'With words or without words, you didn't ask!'

'Then you must be blind and deaf and spoiled! You've had too much of your own way! Now you object because I have come to this . . . arrangement, this association . . . which most wives would accept with dignity.'

'I couldn't.'

'Precisely!' Frederick gave a little smile of triumph. 'Precisely why I didn't tell you! Because you lack the maturity to deal with the situation.'

'And would you have the maturity to deal with it, if it were the other way round?'

'I don't understand you.'

'I think you do. If *you* found *me* in bed with another man.'

Frederick made a little gesture of distaste. 'The situation is not the same.'

'I think it is. Exactly the same!'

'But what you *think*, my dear Amelia, and what happens to be the case are two entirely different things! It's a known fact that men . . .' he broke off and shrugged. Then resumed, 'I don't propose to go into all that now. The subject is painful and delicate. But let us say it is a fact that men are allowed a certain latitude which their wives cannot be allowed.'

'Why not?'

'I've told you, we shan't go into it! I can't envisage such a situation arising with you. If it did, I would have to deal with it according to the merits or demerits of the case.'

'You are a pompous —' Amelia began angrily.

Then she bit her lip. Nothing would be achieved by ranting at Frederick. Any loyalty he had had towards her was gone long ago. Maybe any feeling too. He had demonstrated quite clearly that his affections lay with Diana Nazier. She was his new paragon. Perfect in every way, while Amelia was the failure. All she had now succeeded in doing was to bring the situation out into the open and make it worse.

'And you, my dear Amelia, if we're engaged in name calling, are as spoiled as your elder son! You're perfectly happy as long as you're allowed your head! You want to stay at Haybury. You want to build aeroplanes at Jerningham. Aeroplanes that, alas, do not fly and for which I supply much of the money. You've been told by brains far better than yours and mine that such a project is

124

useless. Doomed to failure. That gas-filled airships might one day be useful, but aeroplanes, *never*! Yet you persist! On the other hand, you don't like the political life, so I'm left to fend for myself. So long as you have all you want, *I* don't matter.'

'I didn't say that.'

'Your actions have said it for you.'

Amelia said nothing.

'What help, for instance, have you been in my career? What help on the other hand has Diana been? And now, you haven't told me what brought you up to town in the first place? Did you hear a rumour? Gossip? Has Aunt Sempner been talking to you? Did you hope to catch us?'

'No, no!' Amelia covered her face with her hands, 'I'm not like that! You should know!'

Finally, under the most impossible circumstances with Frederick as implacably angry as only a man can be who has been discovered in *flagrante delicto,* he made Amelia confess her reasons for coming up to London.

He could not have desired a better scapegoat. All his pent-up fury was directed against Charles. 'That's it then! This is enough! I won't be made a laughing stock! I shan't engage another tutor! I don't care what you have said to the agents! I shall countermand your instructions. You have no right to give them. Charles shall go to school! And I shall choose a *rigorous* establishment! One that can lick him into shape! I shall arrange he begins there immediately!'

A school was selected near Marlborough that specialised in dealing with difficult boys. The fees were reasonable; the discipline harsh.

'The very place,' Frederick told Diana Nazier with satisfaction, 'to turn Charles from a mother's boy to a man!'

When Amelia took him there two days later in the Rolls, he put on a cheerful face for her benefit. On the journey, he chatted about flying and the factory. They stopped for lunch at an hotel in Salisbury. Just afterwards, as they began climbing up on to the Plain, she heard a low clattering noise. Pointing ahead and to the right of them, Charles shouted, 'That's a Cody III!'

A biplane with two rudders on the tail booms and a couple of bicycle wheels hanging underneath, looking like a vast bedraggled raven, was struggling against the north wind.

'Got a Green engine, Mama . . . same as Ajax!'

The Rolls began to gain on the apparition, now skimming some trees almost on their beam. Amelia had a glimpse of a figure in a white coat, crouched up at the front, naked to the winds.

'Mama, it's . . . yes, it's Papa Cody!'

Effortlessly the car overtook the aeroplane. Just before the thing disappeared behind them, the figure raised an enormous cowboy hat in salute.

'How d'you know it's Cody?'

'That hat, Mama! Whoever else could wear it?'

'And why d'you say *Papa* Cody?'

'Oh, everyone calls him that. Papa or the Colonel.'

'Is that the plane he's entered in the Military Trials?'

'One of them.'

So that was James's employer and that contraption was what he preferred to

Ajax to work on!

Amelia put her foot hard down on the accelerator. The clattering became fainter, finally stopped altogether. There was nothing now but the sound of the wind whipping over Salisbury Plain and the hum of their own engine.

'Well,' Amelia said with triumphant finality, 'Ajax won't have any trouble beating *that*!'

FOURTEEN

'We're going to win, boys!' Cody roared across the shed at Laffan's Plain every morning. 'Against our three aeroplanes who else has got a cat in hell's chance?'

The Cody II had taken up four passengers at the same time; the Cody III won the Marie Tempest Cup at Hendon; the new monoplane Cody IV was nearing completion. Practically penniless because of the cost of his aeroplanes, Cody was now giving flying lessons. He was taking up a pupil, but became anxious close to the ground and, leaning over the man's shoulder, he pushed the control column forward.

Cody II hit the ground, threw them both out and staggered pilotless into the air before disintegrating on the banks of the Basingstoke canal. Seeing the crash, Frank Cody bicycled wildly home to warn his mother and collided with a large dog. Husband and son were carried in to Leila Cody, one after the other on stretchers.

'We're going to win, boys!' Cody roared from his sick bed. 'We've still got two planes left!'

The minute he was up again he was flying the monoplane, while a pilot called Harvey-Kelly flew Cody III. Coming in to land from that formation, less than a month away from the Military Trials, Harvey-Kelly clipped a tree coming in to land.

'We're going to win, boys!' Cody roared at the despondent. 'We've still got the monoplane!'

A few days later, practising tight turns, the big Austro-Daimler engine cut. Cody glided down to a forced landing in a meadow and hit a cow. In the bits and pieces of the wreckage, the cockpit seats were upside down. And the maker's labels were painted bright green!

'That's what it was!' Cody roared. 'Nothing else! We're *still* going to win!'

'What are we going to use for an aeroplane?' asked one of his workers sadly.

'We've got pieces of *three*,' James answered. 'All we need is elbow grease and a few spares from other people.'

'I hold with that, James!' Cody roared approvingly. 'Now, are we going to win, boys?'

'Yes!' they all roared back at him.

James and Cody drove all over England in the Simms-Welbeck tourer, looking for spares.

The fact that all they had managed to obtain from the Bristol Aeroplane Company that day were two Bosch magnetos and a drum of bracing wire hadn't depressed Cody. As he drove he sang, honking his horn in accompani-

127

ment, bidding James join in. Just past Marlborough, he suddenly said, 'What've we got here, James?'

Ahead of them a figure was standing in the centre of the road.

Cody pulled the car to a stop.

The figure scurried round to the driver's side window. Wearing his long red-lined cloak and vast stetson as usual, Cody turned to look to his right at the youth outside.

Difficult to tell his age, James thought, but he was certainly tall. Something about the eyes and the way of holding his head touched some painful chord of his memory. He looked well fed and, though his clothes were covered in dust and he had taken off his jacket and rolled it in a bundle, well dressed too.

'Could you possibly give me a lift, Sir?' His voice was what James would call 'well off'.

James studied the boy with narrowed eyes. 'Why do you want a lift?'

But the boy took no notice of him. He was staring at the driver. 'Sir . . . Sir!' His voice now was certainly boyish, shrill with enthusiasm. 'You're Colonel Cody, aren't you, sir?'

Probably because of his long sojourn in the wilderness, Cody got an enormous pleasure from being recognised. He beamed at the boy. 'I am.'

'I know all about you, sir,' the boy licked his lips shyly. 'I've seen you flying. And a chap at our . . . I mean a chap I know . . . had a ride with you at Hendon!'

'Pleased to know you, son.' Cody took his large right hand off the wheel and proffered it to the boy, who leaned forward eagerly to wring it.

'Why do you want a lift?' James persisted.

'Why does he want a lift?' Cody snapped. 'Why do we want to fly? He wants a ride . . . a ride in a Simms-Welbeck!' He reached behind him to open the rear car door. 'Hop in, son! You're welcome!'

'Thanks awfully.' Eagerly the boy climbed inside, dropped his jacket on the seat and with a tired sigh settled his head back on the leather upholstery.

James gazed at him thoughtfully in the mirror. 'And where are you making for, son?'

'Farnborough.'

'You don't say!'

'Well, anywhere would be a help. A mile even.'

'I guess we can take you further'n that. It so happens we're making for just that place.'

'Farnborough? Oh, gosh! That's ripping!'

'And where are you *from*?' James asked him levelly.

The boy hesitated. Then, his colour deepening, said 'Guildford.'

'Do you like Guildford?'

'Not much.'

'Do you work?'

'Odd jobs. That's what I'm hoping to get at Farnborough.'

'What sort of jobs?'

'Sweeping. Cleaning.'

'And you've done that sort of work before?'

'Oh, yes, Sir.'

This time, James swivelled right round and said crisply, 'Let's look at your hands! Come on! Turn them over! Palms uppermost!'

He inspected a pair of square capable palms that were as pink and soft as a girl's. He saw a little inky lump on the second finger of the right hand where the boy had tightly clenched his pen, rather as he had himself done years ago in Jerningham church school. No amount of washing and scrubbing totally eradicated it and to this day, though it was no longer stained, he still had the hard little lump. 'You're just a schoolkid!'

'An' what if he is?' Cody demanded in the boy's defence.

But James took no notice. 'And what's your name?'

'John.'

'John what?'

'John Smith.'

James gave him a long piercing stare, and then as if tiring of his nonsense, reached across swiftly and seized the rolled up jacket. Before the boy had time to grab it back, he turned the collar down to disclose the name tape. Afterwards, Cody couldn't for the life of him decide which face had looked more horrified, James's or the lad's. Certainly, Cody had driven over half a mile before James said stonily, 'Charles Haybury. That's this bad lad's name!'

And then it all came out.

Charles hated and resented Frederick's choice of school. He didn't like the boys or the masters. But it was the freedom of the open spaces that he most missed, and the night before he had climbed out of a bathroom window and taken to the London road, determined as Dick Whittington to make his fortune, preferably as a flyer.

As that same road now whipped by under their wheels, Cody and James listened. Cody alternately wagged a genial admonitory finger and shook with gusts of laughter. 'I've heard all this before! You're the spitting image of my three sons!'

An immediate rapport had started between them. Cody began yarning about his big plane. The boy listened raptly, hero worship shining out of his eyes, though every now and again he saw the man Cody called James watching him in the driving mirror, and then nervously he looked away.

And yet as they reached a small market town with a wide cobbled high street which James announced as 'Odiham', it was Cody who turned round and said, pleasantly but quite firmly, 'You gotta go back, son! You know that, don't you? There's no other way.'

From anyone else, even from the man called James, Charles would have stubbornly refused. He'd probably have asked the man to stop the car or even jumped out if he wouldn't. But from Cody it was different. Besides it was said so warmly, as if Cody had really thought about it. Charles had always recognised his mother's love, but it was the first time that a man, and a heroic man at that, had actually seemed to mind what happened to him or have any feelings about him at all.

'You just figure it out,' Cody went on. 'They'll get the police after you if you don't watch out. If they found you with us, we'd be accused of abduction. An' think of your parents! They'll be worried sick! Your mother'll be crying her eyes out!'

'She's too busy,' Charles whispered disloyally.

'You stupid young pup!' James snapped. 'You need a good hiding!'

129

'And you'd get a beating when they found you. And a school worse'n the last.'

Charles blinked his eyes and said nothing.

'Besides you reckon you wanna be a flyer?'

'Yes, Sir.'

'Well, then you *gotta* go back to school!' He winked at James. 'You won't get anywhere if you can't do sums. Angles, that sort of thing.'

'Geometry?'

'Geometry, yep. Calculations. What are your sums like, son?'

'Pretty good.'

'Like sums, do you?'

'Yes, Sir.'

'What about books?' Cody again winked at James who very well knew and often worried about the great man's own illiteracy.

'I read a lot, Sir.'

'There you are then! You're halfway there! You go back to school. Grit your teeth. And when you leave, you come to me and God's honour, I'll give you a job! I'll teach you to fly myself . . . so long as you go back now! Do you an' me strike us a bargain?'

An hour later, Bronwen Evans was peeping out of the carefully pleated net curtains of her parlour window when to her delight she saw Cody's car draw up.

She had many times suggested that James should bring the great man for a meal. She was eager to impress him with her cooking and her housekeeping, for she knew that James held him in the highest possible esteem. She was eager, too, to hear of their latest exploits and perhaps to spend the evening in some mild convivial celebration.

For who knew where such an evening might end?

She was surprised however to see that the car carried three occupants, and before rushing to the kitchen to put on the kettle, she watched a tall young boy step out and follow the two giants, James and Cody, towards the gate. She assumed they had taken on an apprentice and that they might even wish her to put him up. She had already decided she would refuse, though nicely – because three again would be a crowd – by the time she flung open the welcoming door.

He was a rather surly looking lad and he reminded her of someone. Then Cody put his big friendly hand on her shoulder and said, 'Mrs Evans, I want you to meet a friend of ours, Charles Haybury.'

And *then* she knew who he reminded her of . . . Lady Haybury. She almost said the distasteful name aloud, but just stopped herself in time. She smiled roguishly at Cody. 'I quite thought you'd taken on an apprentice.'

'And in a manner of speaking, you'd be exactly right. So we have! But not right now. He's got a bit of schooling to finish off first.'

Naturally he took Mrs Evans into his confidence about the plan he had worked out in the car. A plan designed to get the boy back to school with the minimum of upset and punishment. It was no surprise to James, but of some to Cody, that the boy was in terror of his father. The school, Charles was sure, would have discovered he had bolted, and would have telephoned to

Haybury. But his father was in London and it was unlikely they would telephone there. His mother would keep quiet, for a while at least.

'Just so long as Sir Frederick Haybury doesn't find out,' Cody confided behind his hand to Bronwen. 'I guess the lad'll get away with it!'

Bronwen looked over the rim of her teacup, thinking all the time how much the boy reminded her of his spoiled and pampered mother – the shape of her eyes, the long lashes, the haughty set of the head. She disliked him more than she could say. She resented, too, the amount of time Cody and James were prepared to spend on him. Actually proposing that after they had been to the airfield to report back and fit the spares (while she gave the brat a good square meal), they would drive him back to the school and make their representations on his behalf in person.

'Why not just put him on the train?' she asked as they all sat around in the parlour.

'Because we wanna make sure he gets there.'

'And because,' James smiled his rather deprecating smile, 'the arrival of such a well-known hero as Colonel Cody will soften up the headmaster.'

Bronwen looked from James to Cody to Charles. 'Well, all I can say,' she tried to disguise the tartness in her voice with a smile, 'I hope you're honoured, young man! And that you won't do anything so silly again!'

'I won't,' he said fervently.

She darted him a bitter look. 'Bet you do!'

Behind his hand, Cody whispered to Bronwen, 'James knows the lad's family. He don't like the Pa, but the Ma's a real honey. In the aviation business too. So we gotta do something for him!'

It was a sentiment that Bronwen Evans most wholeheartedly now echoed. If James thought the mother such a honey then of course she would do something for the son.

James's last words to her as he and Cody left for the airfield served to strengthen her resolve. 'We'll be back for him in a couple of hours. Feed him up, Bronwen! He hasn't eaten since yesterday!'

She thought about what she would do for young Master Haybury very carefully while she prepared a delicious high tea of ham and eggs and mushrooms and tomatoes. Then waving aside the boy's thanks, she said, 'And now if you'll just excuse me a moment, I have to make a call on a neighbour at the end of the road.'

The neighbour at the end of the road was a telephone booth. It took her only a few minutes to find the London telephone number of Sir Frederick Haybury and even less time for the operator to connect her. Good fortune was with her. The butler informed her that Sir Frederick had just come in, and though he was reluctant to allow her to speak to him, he changed his mind when she informed him that young Master Charles had run away from school and was now at her house and in her charge.

An hour and a half later, the deed was done. James and Cody returned to find Charles gone.

'You could have knocked me down with a feather,' Bronwen sighed. 'Here this great big Daimler drew up! Chaffeur-driven an' all! And out this toff gets. I wondered who in the world it could be! The lad was in the kitchen luckily, otherwise he'd have bolted again, I fancy. Sir Frederick brought the chauffeur in with him, just in case. I offered them a cup of tea, but they wouldn't stay. They were ever so nice. What was that, James? How did they find out? How should I know? The police I suppose. What I *do* know is he's a cheeky young cockerel! D'you know, Colonel, he had the nerve to say their Ajax would beat your Cody into a cocked hat!'

FIFTEEN

Phoenix-like, Cody V emerged from the fragments of the ashes. Twenty-four hours before the Military Trials began, the completed aeroplane was wheeled out on to Laffan's Plain.

'The winner!' Cody announced. 'Boys, we've done it!'

A real prehistoric biplane monster in James's opinion, not much different from Cody's Army Aeroplane Number One of four years before. If Cody was going to win on that, he'd have to drag it through the air himself. Cody flew as though he were riding, James thought next day, watching the ungainly pair go bumping over the grass. He watched the flapping white coat balanced on that girdered flying bridge gradually turn grey as Cody swung the nose westwards towards Stonehenge aerodrome.

'Hell of a wind,' said the other mechanic. 'Hope he makes it!'

'Oh, he'll make it all right,' James said. 'More to the point, will we?'

The Cody brothers had gone with their mother and two of the seamstresses in the car. All the other workers were following by bicycle. For the trip to Stonehenge, James had borrowed Taffy's and the wind was dead against them all the way to Amesbury.

Puffed and tired, they stopped for a late lunch at the fork of the road below the ancient circle. Finishing his potted meat sandwiches sooner than the others, James walked up the slight rise to get a better view of the Stonehenge circle when a puttering noise up in the sky made him look upwards. A blue and white monoplane was flying in from the southeast – pretty low too. As it came closer, it struck a familiar note.

He had now had five years of what could be called an aircraft apprenticeship with Cody, and immediately he recognised the nice clean lines of the machine. Far smaller than Cody's, it looked modern where his looked ancient, and there was something aristocratic about the neat cut-away fairing round the engine. The fuselage with its single tail had a French streamlined look, and the wings, though not as sharp as Dunne's, had a definite arrowhead.

He was immediately impressed. That was the sort of plane he would build. Cody wouldn't have a chance against it. As it flew over, he glimpsed the name painted boldly on the underside of the wing. Ajax II.

Of course, he thought. No wonder it looked familiar! Just as Cody V resembled Cody I, so Ajax II resembled that first Ajax that Amelia and he had built together. Amelia was bound to be coming. Soon he would be seeing her. Immediately he got back on his bicycle and began to pedal up to the aerodrome. But then he ran into a long jam of cars, bicycles, carriages and tricycles. When he finally got inside the field, the first thing he saw unmis-

133

takably towering above everything else was the gawky top wing of the Cody V. And just beside it, was the small smudge of blue and white which was Ajax.

As he threaded his way between a Voisin and a Blériot, their ground crews already at work, he saw Sarah emerging from the cab of a lorry, dressed decorously in her Sunday best.

'Hello, Sarah.'

'Good morning, March,' she said, immediately putting him on the same level as herself.

'I didn't know you were interested in flying.'

'Sarah has come to keep an eye on Arthur.' Amelia stepped down from the lorry, dressed in a light blue blouse and knickerbockers, followed by a tiny boy with an angelic face and ginger curls, followed by Charles.

'Hello, James.'

'Lady Haybury.'

Arthur gave him a smile, but Charles replied to his nod by looking right through him.

'I saw Ajax fly over. It has beautiful lines.'

'Glad you think so.' Her eyes travelled over the large spider's web of Cody V without enthusiasm. 'Is this what you've been working on?'

He said levelly, 'That's right.'

Men started unloading packing cases off the Jerningham factory lorry. With her two boys trailing behind her, Amelia went over to the trestle table where Cody was laying out tools and spares.

'I'm Amelia Haybury, Colonel Cody,' she said. 'I have to thank you for being so good to Charles.'

'Glad to know you, Lady Haybury. I watched you come in just now. You've got a fine aircraft there.' Cody suddenly saw Charles, 'Hello, son.'

'Hello, Sir.'

'Why so bashful? You were bold enough three weeks ago, eh?'

'He was a naughty boy, Colonel. But for you, I don't know what would have happened to him.'

'What did happen, son? Was it painful?'

'Not specially.'

'Serves him right,' Arthur said piously.

'So it does,' Amelia echoed as if she didn't mean it. 'My husband . . . '

'Beg your pardon, Ma'am, but that was what I was planning to avoid. I was going to deliver him to the school and explain.'

'So Charles told me. But you shouldn't have troubled yourself.'

'No trouble, Ma'am. Anyway the plan didn't work out. Unfortunately someone —'

He didn't elaborate. But it was very evident during the next few days whom Charles believed that someone to be. He deliberately avoided James. Amelia and Arthur had rooms in the Bustard Hotel just north of the field where Cody and his wife, and numerous other competitors, were staying. James and the rest of Cody's team lived in a packing case. And just beside Ajax, Charles had pitched his boy scout's tent in which he slept.

The first test was a climb to 1000 feet. Accompanied by RFC observers, Cody did it in three minutes, Wilkinson in Ajax in six seconds less. But the French machines beat both of them, and so did Sopwith and De Havilland in a Royal Aircraft Factory BE2.

Then came the duration test of three hours and a climb to 4500 feet. Cody and Wilkinson had no trouble completing it. But there were two incidents. Parke, flying an Avro, suddenly started diving, then went into a spiral like a twisting leaf. Just when everyone was certain he would crash, the Avro pulled out. Quite how or why, Parke had no idea, and for years afterwards there would be arguments as to what caused it and what stopped it. Then a golden Mersey monoplane at the top of the climb seemed to stop in its tracks. Up went both wings – then off they came as though being pulled out by the roots. The figure of a man fell hurtling down, followed minutes afterwards by the fuselage. Amelia took both boys promptly away to the hotel. But next day, Charles was back, helping secure Ajax to the ground in a rising southwest wind.

The next test was high and low speed. Ajax clocked in 83 mph and won it. Its low speed was 48 mph which was well up with the leaders. It now looked, with only six competitors left in the race that Ajax was going to win. Certainly it was well ahead of Cody V. The Avro was out, getting bogged down in the taking-off-and-landing-in-a-ploughed-field test. Then the wind blew up even stronger. The weather worsened. Heavy rain and gales pulled at the flimsy aeroplanes tethered to the flattened grass. A Voisin coming in for the landing test turned on its back. Pilots who had flown told of big bumps, upcurrents that sent them soaring into pitch-black clouds, pressures that forced them inexorably towards the earth. Watching Cody being thrown all over the sky, James suddenly saw that the uncharted currents of the air could be far more dangerous than those of the sea. Cody stopped in 45 yards by means of the first air brake – a chain that pulled his tail-skid hard down till it acted like a spike.

Then Wilkinson went up. The southwest wind was gusting 40 mph. Against the grey clouds, the little blue and white blob danced – rising and falling in the terrific gusts. James watched it inch round the airfield, turn into the wind and come unsteadily back towards the ground. At 100 feet the left wing dropped. Wilkinson got it up again smartly. Steadier now, Ajax was approaching the hedge, when suddenly a gust must have lifted the tailplane. The fuselage twisted as the nose dived.

James was already running towards it when seconds later there was a sound like thunder. Bits of blue and white were flung up into the air. There was that sudden silence that James was beginning to learn was always the aftermath of a crash. Then struggling out of the broken fuselage came a lanky rather stunned figure – Eustace Wilkinson, miraculously unhurt.

Towards evening of that same day, a senior RFC officer came up smiling and handed over a long buff envelope. Not only had Cody won the British division prize of £1500 but also the International division's £4000.

All hell then broke loose in the Cody camp. Singing and cheering started. The band of the Wiltshire Regiment, bugles blaring, drums beating, escorted them into Salisbury to receive the freedom of the city.

James followed with the other jubilant Cody workers to the Town Hall. Standing on the steps, Cody triumphant, the idol of the journalists, promised, 'Now we'll win the £5000 Coastal Seaplane Prize!' The crowd went wild. The band played 'See the Conquering Hero comes'.

Standing right at the back, James suddenly became conscious of a lorry trying to push its way through. Stepping to one side, he caught a sudden glimpse of bits of blue and white aeroplane, a broken propeller, a battered engine.

And squeezed all together in the cab with the driver were Wilkinson, Amelia, Sarah, Charles and Arthur.

SIXTEEN

'If Cody can rebuild his aircraft in a month and win the Military Trials,' Wilkinson said, 'we can rebuild Ajax, fit floats and beat the new Cody seaplane for the Round Britain £5000!'

It was easier said than done. A handful of men can achieve wonders in a corrugated iron shed – provided they're left alone to get on with it. With the rebuilding of Ajax from those pathetic blue and white scraps, everything seemed to conspire against them.

First, that winter Lord Nazier fell seriously ill. As a result, Frederick spent all his time up in London helping and sustaining Diana. He could not spare the time for a company board meeting needed for urgent decisions on Ajax.

Then the Parliamentary Aerial Defence Committee and the Committee of Imperial Defence (Frederick was a member of both) came out in favour of airships. The *Daily Mail* had financed an airship hangar at Wormwood Scrubs, and Lord Jellicoe, now First Sea Lord, having flown in a Zeppelin, demanded airships for the Navy. Orders were given. The Farnborough Royal Aircraft Factory began to build three. Vickers re-opened its airship workshops. And Connaught Engineering, which had bought Rolls's Jerningham Aviation shares, tried to obtain subcontracts for ballooning work.

In contrast, aeroplanes that year began mysteriously breaking up. Fenwick, Hamilton, Gilmour and Hotchkiss in England and others in France died because their monoplanes collapsed in the air. Rogers-Harrison in the Cody V, Parke of the famous twisting dive at Stonehenge, were both killed. The French and British governments banned the building of monoplanes.

Last but not least, Diana Nazier asked, 'What is the point, Frederick, of producing something that will not be *allowed* to fly?' To Wilkinson's chagrin and Amelia's disappointment, the rebuilding of Ajax proceeded at a snail's pace.

Things in the Cody camp remained cheerful. In the hut at Laffan's Plain, the vast 60-foot span seaplane with its 100 hp Green engine began to materialise fast. Cody formed a company, Cody and Sons Aerial Navigation Ltd, with an issue of 50,000 £1 preference shares – joining Bristol, Sopwith, Avro and Short in the building of British aeroplanes. He was also busy designing a plane to cross the Atlantic for the *Daily Mail* £10,000 prize.

The only person in the camp who was not happy was James. Cody VI was even more antique than Cody I. Still the same high-fronted elevator, still wing-warping instead of ailerons, it looked more like a vast metal cobweb than an aircraft.

On 6 August he accompanied Cody and a friend down to the new Naval seaplane station at Calshot, taking Cody VI's three floats in the company lorry. The idea was that Cody would fly the plane (fitted with wheels) from Farnborough and land on the beach beside the Solent. Then the floats would be fitted and Cody VI, now a seaplane, would have its first water trials.

At Calshot, they met Lieutenant McDougall, the Scottish engineering officer, who accompanied them to choose a suitable spot for Cody to land. Since Cody and his friend were having lunch at the station, James got his employer's permission to take the lorry to see his parents at the forge.

Are you ever coming to see us again his mother had kept writing in all her letters. They were delighted at his unexpected visit, hurt that it was only for an hour but mollified when he told them he would be back next day to supervise the Cody VI seaplane water trials and hoped to be staying with them.

Cody and party left later that afternoon and were back at Farnborough before it was dark. Next day, James was up early. Before he flew with his son Leon down to Calshot, Cody had promised to give a flight to a keen young officer of the 20th Hussars. Lieutenant Keyser brought a friend, Evans, the Hampshire cricket captain.

The first flight was uneventful. Then just as Leon left his brother Frank's side to take Keyser's place, Evans asked if he could have a trip. Cody could never refuse a would-be flyer. 'Of course!' he roared. 'But it'll have to be a short one!'

Leon got out. Evans got in. Cody opened up the throttle. James watched Cody VI lollup into the air. Like a vast butterfly, it was pinned against the blue of the sky. It floated airily round in a circle, then began a slow dignified descent back on to Laffan's Plain.

Lower and lower it came, its rotating propeller shimmering in the sun. Then just above a little wood, it seemed to hesitate. Seconds later, it gave a lurch forward. Its wings went up and folded together vertically.

Out fell a white-coated figure, and a grey one. In terrible slow motion, they were twisting round and round as they tumbled into the trees, followed by the remains of Cody VI.

James, Leon and Frank raced to the wood. Leon and Frank flung themselves on the white-coated figure, crying, 'Oh, Dad, Dad, Dad!'

James, stunned and sorrowful himself, left them to their private grief and began to lift the lifeless body of Evans. By an ironic coincidence, Evans's socks were green – the only thing that the fearless Cody feared.

Cody, the sky crusader, had said, 'When my time comes, I hope my death will be swift and sudden – death from one of my own aeroplanes.'

Death had granted him that.

But death had also taken Cody's enterprise. There was no future now for any of them at Laffan's Plain.

None too willingly, next day, Frederick came down to Jerningham to discuss the future of Ajax.

The situation was just as unsettled and worrying at Westminster. Rumours of war and fear of the Kaiser filled the columns of the newspapers all that spring and summer while thoughts of the likely political impact of a war had filled Frederick's mind. Lady Nazier, though frequently called to the bedside of her mortally sick husband, had pointed out that if war came a coalition would be inevitable. Frederick must make his voice heard more frequently in the

House, ask questions about the military and naval use of observer balloons and airships so that his name would spring to mind when vacancies arose in a wartime coalition cabinet.

By August when Parliament recessed, Frederick had chalked up three questions and two quite lengthy speeches. And several times Lord Nazier had seemed on the point of slipping peacefully and sensibly away, and twice fought back, opened his eyes and asked his valet to read him the latest in the *Times* newspaper.

It was the *Times* newspaper that Charles clutched in his hand when Frederick came into the Haybury drawing-room window gazing out at the rose garden.

'She's at the factory,' Charles said in response to Frederick's question. 'She left early. There was some important call she had to make.'

Frederick was astonished to see that the boy's eyes were bright and his lashes wet as if with recently shed tears. He assumed that Charles and his mother had had a row, which he hoped had not been in front of the servants. He was even more suprised when Charles, not usually the one to volunteer any information, blurted out, 'He's dead.'

Frederick assumed he meant Lord Nazier, though of course if he had thought about it he would have realised Diana would have telephoned him immediately. But that first mistaken assumption made his heart race, and the question long pushed to the back of his mind leapt intriguingly to the forefront . . . what would Diana want to do now that she was free?

'Let me look.' Frederick reached for the newspaper. 'When did it happen? Is it in the obituaries?'

'It's on the front page.' Charles handed him the *Times*, pointing to the headlines – *Ex-American aviator killed in aeroplane crash over Farnborough. Seaplane breaks up in mid-air. Big military funeral planned for 'Colonel' Cody.*

Frederick read it twice to make sure that this was the item of news which Charles found of such interest, and scanned quickly down other columns to check there was no mention of Nazier. No, it was just Cody from Farnborough, the dashing hero of schoolboys who was dead, while Nazier still clung on.

'I never cried at your age. I'm sure your little brother Arthur wouldn't cry even at *his* age.'

Frederick began stumping out of the room. Charles was a strange boy. An incorrigible boy, his headmaster said of him, on whom the harshest punishments made not the slightest impression. And yet here he was in tears over an ex-American cowboy! Not at all like him. Not at all like Arthur.

Just as Frederick opened the drawing-room door, he looked back.

Charles was staring out of the window, his half-averted face spotlit in powerful sunshine. Like motes of dust dancing in such a powerful searchlight, the actual minutae of his face were now suddenly revealed. Not just the arrogant hold of his head. Nor the mutinous mouth. But every detail and all of him. The sunlight was a lamp held up, exploring a dark corner that subconsciously Frederick had always known was there, uncovering a nagging suspicion.

Now that suspicion exploded silently in his head . . . he is not my son.

It was the following month that Lord Nazier died in his ninetieth year, and

139

Frederick was called upon to console the widow. He it was who smoothed the arrangements for the funeral and who secured Lord Nazier's due mead of praise in the obituary columns, indeed contributing one himself which drew attention to their shared interest in aviation.

Frederick had been constantly at Diana's side. More so than discretion those days allowed. Aunt Sempner on her usual September visit to Haybury, drew Amelia's attention to the matter. 'You'll have to try to put a stop to it, my gal! There was a piece about them in the gossip column of the *Mirror*.'

'I never read the *Mirror*,' Amelia said loftily.

'I'll show you.' Aunt Sempner dived into her old-fashioned reticule. 'I have it here.'

Amelia paced up and down the sitting-room floor. 'I don't want to see it.'

'Suit yourself, gal! So long as you warn him! Times aren't what they were, you know! Their Majestics are far stricter than poor dear Edward. Less fun too, but there you are! You take the rough with the smooth.'

'It isn't like Frederick to be indiscreet,' Amelia clenched her hands, not so much in agitation as in indecision. Ever optimistic, a beguiling thought came to her that now that Diana Nazier was free perhaps Frederick would agree to a divorce. James remained unmarried. And Sarah had heard a rumour in the village that as Mr Cody was dead he might be coming home.

'Frederick's very taken with the Nazier woman.' Aunt Sempner's eyes shone. 'She's a fine looking gal. Clever, too!'

'Do you think he wants to marry her?'

'Why ask me, gal? In any case, he can't. He's got a wife already.'

'But there's divorce now.'

'Unthinkable! Remember dear King Edward . . . divorce is too indelicate a subject ever to mention in front of ladies.'

'Why?'

'Men don't want it. Frederick's set on a political career. He doesn't want to commit political suicide like Parnell. Can you imagine Diana Nazier as Kitty O'Shea?'

At that very moment, Lloyd-George was pressing Parnell's memoirs into the hands of Frances Stevenson, his secretary and mistress. Mr O'Shea had cited the Irish political star as co-respondent. After the divorce, Parnell had married his Kitty, but it was the end of him politically. Frances Stevenson took the point that divorce would be the end of the Welsh Chancellor of the Exchequer.

Amelia could not rest until Frederick answered that question himself. Weeks went by before he showed himself again at Haybury. But certain problems in his constituency, mainly due to the greater militancy of the Socialists, necessitated his personal appearance. After a difficult public meeting, he arrived at Haybury just before dinner in a mood of mingled irritation and elation. He poured himself a stiff whisky, and as so often these days, avoided Amelia's eyes.

The meeting had been tiresome, he said. He had been constantly heckled. At one time it had seemed the platform would have to retire, even though there were two lady speakers present. Amelia was sure that Diana Nazier was one of them, because there was about Frederick an aura of masculine sexuality that she found disturbing.

'Was Diana one of them?' Amelia finally asked.

'Of course she was! That's why I was so damned annoyed. She spoke well. But some louts kept shouting her down!' He darted a sudden sharp look at Amelia. 'Any reason why she shouldn't be there?'

'I don't know,' Amelia replied softly. 'You tell me.'

'And what sort of answer is that?'

'Only that it appears other people suspect what I know to be true. There was a piece in the gossip column.'

'Oh, Lord, I know about that! That means nothing. Who told you? No, don't bother, I can guess. Aunt Sempner. She never liked me, the old crow! Well, it's nothing to do with her. I hope you told her to take her gossip back to where she found it.'

'I asked her if she thought you wanted to marry Lady Nazier. Now that she's free.'

As soon as the words were out, Amelia was afraid. It was as if she had disturbed a needed stepping-stone, said what was best left unsaid. For a moment Frederick looked almost young again. He held his gingery head in his hands. Then he said hoarsely. 'Yes, well, I can't, can I?' And as Aunt Sempner had done, he added, 'I have a wife already.'

There was no mistaking the frustration and regret of his voice. Amelia felt a sharp pang of remorse. She longed to make amends. She it was who was at fault. She should have told James. She should have defied her parents and refused to marry Frederick. Yet even now few people of her class married for love or even for a powerful physical attraction. But suddenly it seemed as if she had been given a second chance. Her father was dead, her stepmother abroad and uninterested. Victoria and Henry were now in Panama. Her sister's letters spoke of little except the exigencies of Foreign Office postings and their disappointment that there was still no child. She never asked about Jerningham.

'Divorce isn't as unthinkable as all that,' Amelia said, sitting on the arm of his chair. 'Mrs Langtry divorced her husband.' She began enumerating the society divorces on her hand. 'So did Mrs Wallace.'

'Is divorce what *you* want, Amelia?' Frederick asked softly. It was as if suddenly they were friends or fellow-conspirators. But his eyes as he looked into hers were blank and cool and devoid of friendship.

'If that's what you want,' Amelia said carefully.

'I must discuss it with Diana. It's an enormous step. I shall need at least a week to think it over.'

It was nearer a month before he gave her his decision. A month in which her hopes burgeoned painfully. Hope was like a tree. There was not just the main trunk but all sorts of fruitful branches suddenly springing out of it. Not only would Frederick agree to a divorce, but James would return to Jerningham for good. He had been seen by Sarah driving his parents in the direction of Lymington. He was out of a job, Sarah said. He was going to try to stay in the area because his mother was so poorly. Now Amelia would offer him a job again. Between them, their success was assured. She began to talk to Wilkinson about him, and though he expressed the opinion that a man as qualified as James March would get dozens of offers, Amelia remained hopeful that this time it would be hers he would accept.

During the last weekend of November, Frederick wrote summoning her to the town house to discuss certain matters. It was a curt note and from it she could not deduce what his decision would be. The day was moist and misty. She could hear the mournful sound of the foghorns from the Solent as she drove the Rolls towards London. There was a thick yellow pea-souper in the city that slowed her down to a crawl. She had set out in a buoyant mood, but somewhere along the way her confidence had left her.

In the library of the town house, Frederick was alone, standing with his back to the fireplace, a glass of whisky in his hand, a morose expression on his face. 'It's no good,' he said thickly without preamble. 'It wouldn't work. Diana and I have discussed it. We are totally agreed.'

'Why wouldn't it work?'

'Because of my career. We're too much in the public eye. We've gone into it carefully. We've talked to a number of people. They agree. Divorce is political suicide. Especially now. Things could go this way or that at the moment. I have far too much to lose. And Diana would lose her good name.'

Till that moment, Amelia had not been aware of how high her hopes had been. She felt a sickening sense of disappointment which quickly turned into anger. 'And what about me?'

'What about you?'

'What have *I* got to lose?'

'Nothing, so far as I can see. You have in fact everything to gain by remaining my wife. It is Diana and I who are making the sacrifice.' His face reddened with anger. 'It is we who are to be pitied. Not you.'

'I don't want to be pitied. But I don't want that sort of marriage. I don't want to be married to you if you want her. It's humiliating!'

'A divorce would be far more humiliating!'

'For you.'

'For all of us. Think what the gutter press would make of it! And come a coalition or a successful new election, it would totally rule out cabinet office.'

'And what if *I* want a divorce?'

'What you want is irrelevant.'

'Damn you,' she clenched her fists. 'It is *I* who have the grounds!'

'I doubt that! I doubt that very much! Certainly not without my co-operation! I haven't deserted you. You have only my . . . regard . . . for Diana.'

'Only regard?'

'No . . .'

'I saw you, remember! I could drag her name through the mud!'

'You could,' he paused. 'But you won't.'

'You can't stop me!'

'Of course I can! You are so naïve!'

'So are you if you think you can stop me!'

'Let me tell you, Amelia, you will not breathe one word against Lady Nazier. Not one! On the contrary you shall make her your friend.'

'I'm damned if I will!'

'You *will*!'

'If you don't want to marry her, stop seeing her!'

Frederick drained his glass and shook his head. 'I shall see her as often as I choose. And you also will see her as often as I choose. You will be as restrained and co-operative as Queen Alexandra.'

142

'Never!' Amelia stamped her foot. *'Never!'*

'Unless you do, my dear . . . Unless you promise, I will . . .'

He left the sentence unfinished, went over to the sideboard, re-charged his glass and sat down contemplating.

'You will *what*?'

'I will pay a visit to my solicitors.'

'For what purpose?'

'For my estate. My will. The disposal of my property.'

Amelia said nothing but she felt a little twist of apprehension.

'As it stands, *Charles* will inherit Haybury.'

'Of course,' Amelia said boldly, but an icy fear had gripped her heart.

'Yet this is quite wrong, isn't it?' He seized her shoulder and shook it. 'Isn't it? *Isn't it?* Answer me! *Isn't it?'* His narrowed eyes watched her expression like a fox its prey. And when all the colour had drained out of her face and her eyes no longer defiantly held his, he said slowly, 'Now I know that Charles is not my son.'

SEVENTEEN

Frederick took his revenge.

At the next board meeting he tabled a resolution 'that the building of aeroplanes by the Jerningham Company shall be abandoned in order to concentrate on airships and balloon construction'.

Subcontracts for non-rigid airships had been obtained for Jerningham from the Admiralty, largely due to the persistence of Lady Nazier.

Those voting for the resolution: Mr Pearless, acting on Victoria's behalf, complimented Lady Nazier on her dedicated work for the company; Cannaught Engineering; Sir Frederick Haybury, chairman.

Those against: Lady Haybury.

At the time of the board meeting, Wilkinson had been up at the Royal Aircraft Factory to try to interest them in Ajax. Not that it was much good. There was still the ban on the monoplane. The government were giving orders only to French aircraft or to its own planes like the slow BE2 – supposedly the ideal military vehicle since it provided such a steady platform for reconnaissance, the only role the War Office and the Admiralty visualised for aeroplanes in war.

He returned to Jerningham depressed and disappointed, only to be greeted by Amelia with the news that Ajax II was to be scrapped. He was stunned. 'Is the factory to close then?'

Amelia shook her head. 'We've got subcontracts for airships and balloons.'

'Ye gods! Are we to be gassed out by the stinking insides of oxen?'

'So it seems.'

'And so it seems,' he explained bitterly, 'they have lost faith in me!'

'Of course they haven't! But you know the government ban on monoplanes.'

'Yet Prévost won the Schneider Trophy in a Deperdussin monoplane!'

'And the Deperdussin company went bankrupt.'

'But Ajax is far better! She'll win next year's Schneider Trophy! You're not going to throw all that work down the drain now she's ready?'

'I'm as sorry as you are, Eustace. But that's the board's decision.'

'Not before her speed trials surely?'

'There's no point now.'

'But they know I've just been waiting for the weather! I'd planned to go up today. Surely we should find out her performance! She's a world-beater, Lady Haybury!'

She smiled. 'I'm sure she is.'

'Well, then! You're sure she is! I'm sure she is!'

'And the monoplane ban?'

'They'll have to lift that soon!' He straightened his shoulders determinedly. 'Have I your permission to take her up?' Amelia hesitated, then nodded.

'Shall you watch?'

'Well, my husband's down here. I promised to take him to Brockenhurst to catch the two o'clock London train.'

'You've still time to see the take off.'

She looked at her watch. 'Just!' She got up from her desk. 'Well, Eustace . . . let's go!'

Together they walked along the corridor, descended the same stairs she had tripped down so airily ten years before into the same hall now stripped of all its pictures and fine furniture, out into the fragile sunshine. Side by side, they walked past the carpentry shop, the fabric room, the engine shed, on over the long lawn-smooth landing field down to the new concrete slipway.

The seaplane was standing in a trailer. Carefully, two mechanics in hip-high rubber boots eased her down the slipway till she floated far on the water and held her steady for Wilkinson to board. As he climbed into the cockpit, he patted the blue monocoque fuselage. 'You'll see for yourself what she can do! And you'll have my report on your desk first thing in the morning.'

One of the mechanics swung the engine. It caught first time in a cloud of castor-oil smoke. With a veil of bubbles behind the floats, slowly Wilkinson taxied forward. A southerly wind was chopping up the Solent. He turned directly into it, waved to Amelia on the shore and opened up the engine. Trailing a thick white wash, Ajax II slid easily forward. The propeller shimmied the air into a crystal ball. Up came her floats out of the water. Up she climbed, higher and higher, effortlessly into the blue sky.

Head right back, shading her eyes, Amelia watched. That climb was faster than anything she had ever seen. She waited till he had disappeared behind cumulus puffs over the Isle of Wight. Then folding her arms, she walked thoughtfully back over the grass to the Hall.

You never knew. Things were always changing in aviation. If the figures in the final report *were* fantastic . . .

She looked at her watch. Time she was on her way to the station. She was just getting into the driver's seat of the Rolls, when there was a great roar and Wilkinson flashed just above her.

That was the last time she saw him alive.

Only the two fitters, still standing on the slipway, saw what had happened. For an hour, they had watched him, now inches above the sea, now high in the sky, turning, twisting, circling, climbing . . .

And then suddenly – he dived.

This was no ordinary dive – that was the first thing the mechanics noticed. The wingtips were going round and round like little cars in a merry-go-round. They actually twinkled in the bright sunshine as Ajax came nearer and nearer to the earth.

Stressing her to the utmost, the fitters thought. He'll pull out soon. Any second now . . .

But he still came on down. Still turning. Still diving. The plane got bigger. It wasn't more than 300 feet, heading vertically towards the Beaulieu river. Now they could hear a high screaming sound, sharp as a falling shell.

'Come on, Wilkie!' one of the fitters muttered.

But there was still no sign of the dive ending. Lower and lower and lower . . .

'Pull out!' the other fitter screamed at the top of his voice. 'For Christ's sake, *pull out!*'

Wilkinson's body was retrieved from the river marshes with difficulty, but the seaplane remained, half submerged in mud and reeds. Immediately he heard the news, Frederick returned from London but refused point-blank to have anything more to do with Ajax. Let it rust and rot! Let the next spring tide sweep the rubbish off the mudflat down to the bottom of the Solent!

Amelia had no heart to resurrect the aircraft either. She had no heart to begin all those years of experiment again. She felt keenly Eustace's loss; she would never be able to replace him, not just as a designer but as a friend.

'Diana's right! She's always been right!' Frederick reiterated at dinner two days after the crash. 'The future is in balloons and airships! Look at the Germans with their Zeppelins! We're well shot of Wilkinson and his designs!' He frowned and raised his voice. 'Amelia! Are you listening to me?'

'Yes, Frederick, I am.' She hesitated. 'It's just that, while we are talking of Wilkinson, there is another thing —'

'Not some dependent?'

'No, no. He had nobody. Nothing.'

Indeed the rooms where he had lived at the far end of the Jerningham east wing had remained singularly devoid of personal possessions. Just a few clothes, a set of drawing instruments, a marine sextant, a small architect's drawing table and in the right hand drawer of that table, a letter to Amelia.

It was about the contents of this letter that now she spoke.

Wilkinson had a horror of being buried alive; writing of this in his letter, and telling her that he belonged to a cremation society, he asked that he be cremated and his ashes scattered in the Solent.

Frederick would have none of that either. An ordinary decent funeral at Jerningham church, yes. But if she wanted anything new-fangled, Amelia could dig into her own pocket. Look at the expense! Look at the difficulties! The Solent wasn't consecrated! And anyway, the Church of England didn't approve of cremation. It was in contradiction of the Nicene Creed. In any case, the fellow would have no way of knowing if he was under the ground or under the Solent!

It seemed natural under the circumstances for Amelia to turn to James; he had returned to Jerningham the month before. Since there was no more work at Farnborough, after he had helped clear out the Cody hut on Laffan's Plain he had said goodbye to a silent Taffy and a tearful Bronwen and had come back – to his parent's delight – to help his father in the forge for the time being. He had written off to the Bristol Aeroplane Company and Sopwith Aviation and other aircraft manufacturers, and had had a word with McDougall about a possible job at Calshot.

Amelia contacted him; she needed him now. James could always find his way round difficulties. And according to Sarah, some of his lifeboatmen friends had their own small craft. The following afternoon, having retrieved the casket containing Eustace Wilkinson's ashes from the Crematorium,

Amelia drove to the landing stage at Buckler's Hard. James was waiting in the borrowed boat. The only noise was the puttering of the motor as they set off into choppy water.

Near the mouth of the Beaulieu river the sun came out. The tide was strong and ebbing. Over on the left, the little blue wings of Ajax showed up clearly against the brown mudbank.

Sitting in the stern, Amelia watched James's averted profile, trying to guess what he was thinking, trying herself to think of poor Wilkinson and the tragic waste of their joint effort. It was the beginning of her despair. Life after all seemed no more than a handful of ashes. All endeavour was useless.

'Will this suit, Amelia?' James spoke his first words gently to her. 'Shall we leave him here?'

She nodded. She felt cold and numb and sick. She had no idea how it should be carried out. She had little idea of Wilkinson's religious beliefs, if indeed he had any. He had always seemed such a pragmatist, devoted only to his obsession to create flight. And now he was nothing. A speck of dust in a waste of water. A wrecked aircraft as a headstone. She lifted the casket, opened it and tipped the contents into the broken water, saying what she remembered from funerals. 'In sure and certain hope of the Resurrection!'

Overhead, the seagulls, white as the wind-driven clouds, wheeled and cried with unbearable mournfulness.

As James turned the boat for home, Amelia threw the casket over the side and her face crumpled. Keeping his right hand on the tiller, James slid closer to her, and put his arm round her shoulders. She turned and buried her face in his sweater, crying as she could not remember crying since she was a child.

He made no attempt to stop her convulsive sobs. When she dried her eyes, he said slowly, 'You'll salvage Ajax, of course. That's the resurrection he'd want. And that's the resurrection you can give him.'

She shook her head violently. 'No.'

He held his head sideways to study her face.

'Why not?'

'Because I've no money.'

'You shouldn't let that stop you.'

'I've no heart.'

'Don't be so stupid! That's no way to talk!'

'But it's true!'

'Well, don't let it be true! You've got a good aircraft there.'

'Then why did it crash?'

'These early days . . . ' she knew suddenly that he was thinking of Cody. 'Crashes happen. We learn . . . and we go on.'

'Well, I'm not going on! The company's got a contract for airship work.' James snorted angrily. 'Don't let them take it on!'

'I can't stop them.'

'Not long now, and they'll be screaming for aeroplanes! You believe that, don't you?' He looked at her reproachfully. 'You used to!'

'But I've no designer, no manager!' She stopped suddenly. Her eyes brightened. 'I suppose you wouldn't consider it, James?'

'Consider what? Working for you? No, thank you.'

'Working *with* me.'

'For you, you mean. Not even for *you*. For your husband. He's the paymaster, isn't he?'

'I suppose so.'

'Well, then. That's why.'

'But there are other reasons, aren't there?'

He signed impatiently. 'You know damned well there are, Amelia! You're not a fool!'

'I've been a fool,' she said in a low voice. 'I've been a fool from the beginning!'

For a moment, he took his hand off the tiller, and put it over her mouth. 'Hush, Amelia! What's done is done.'

Her eyes filled with tears. She stared past him at the distant view of the spindly wreck on the mudflat. 'And I'm still a fool,' she went on as if James hadn't spoken. 'I should never have let him test it!'

'It's a good aircraft.'

'It's finished.'

'No!'

'I tell you it is! I don't want it! Frederick doesn't want it! Nobody wants it!'

'*I* want it.'

'You! Why? Why do you want it? It's a wreck.'

'I'll build it up again.'

She looked up at him fixedly for several seconds. Beyond his shoulder, she could see the landing stage looming into sight. But the strong ebb tide still kept them battling slowly towards it.

In an altered voice she said, 'All right, you can have it. But there's a price?'

He glanced at her sharply, 'What?'

She didn't take her eyes off his face. 'A kiss,' she breathed. 'Kiss me! Kiss me properly, and Ajax is yours!'

For a moment she thought he would refuse. James could be awkward and pig-headed and sometimes as strait-laced as his mother. Then she saw his dark blue eyes soften. He bent down suddenly and kissed her parted lips.

She threw her arms round his neck and kissed him with all the ache and hunger of the last ten miserable years.

His whole future suddenly did a somersault. Of the firms who had replied to his letters, the offer from Bristol was the best and he had pretty well made up his mind to accept it. But that meant working under a designer, simply being a glorified mechanic – basically what he had been with Cody. As soon as he realised Amelia was serious, all that had changed.

He bicycled over to Calshot. He found McDougall in the hanger, working on an old Antoinette engine. He explained the situation.

'But we'll never get it out of the mud!' McDougall spoke slowly with a thick Scots accent. Like the old Antoinette, he always took some starting, but once he was on the move there was no stopping him.

'I'll borrow a motorboat. The lifeboat, if necessary.'

'Wouldn't be worth salvaging!'

'That's what the Ajax company think. But that mud'll have cushioned the fall.'

'Then where'd you put it? Where'd you work on it?'

'Here!' said James firmly.

'Here?' McDougall was horrified. 'In Calshot?'

He raised every difficulty. It was Royal Naval Air Service property. James was a civilian. He wouldn't be allowed.

'You've always said you're short of civilian aircraft mechanics. I'll sign up so long as you let me have a corner of the hangar to keep Ajax. After all,' he pointed out, 'even the Army raised no objection to Cody building his aeroplanes on their property.'

Eventually McDougall got the idea. He became filled with the same excitement as James. The connection with Cody, the need to outdo the Army, the inspiration of actually helping to build something that flew combined together to make the idea irresistible. He moved.

'The hangar is half-empty. That south corner now, if you can pack it in there . . .'

He moved faster. 'No need for your motorboat. We'll take a Navy tender and a couple of matelots.'

He was now moving faster than James. 'And you can give instructions to our mechanics.' He winked. 'While you're building her.'

They went out that afternoon, four of them with every tool they could think of. The Solent was overcast and the sea was as grey as the sky. The little blue tail sticking high in the air looked like a ship's pennant on a stubby mast.

The tender made heavy going through the reeds of the saltflats. Twice they ran aground and had to get out into the water and heave the boat forward. When they finally did reach the scene of the crash, they first collected the pieces of the wings that lay scattered all round, carefully stowing them on board.

Then they began digging.

They were still digging five hours later, but all the engine was uncovered and they had started to clear the shaft of the broken propeller. James had been quite right. The soft mud had blanketted the fall, and though the damage was substantial with luck it would be repairable.

Eventually they managed to get the engine into the tender. The fuselage and tail followed, leaving behind a large hole oozing seawater that gradually filled up. Just at dusk, they returned to Calshot and stowed the wreck in the hangar.

Next day, James signed on as a civilian mechanic and in the evening began to work on it. The damage to the engine was worse than he had expected. The crankshaft was broken and the main bearings had to be replaced. A new propeller had to be bought. So had silk, bamboo, wire, struts, undercarriage wheels as well as new floats – so that Ajax, like the Cody VI, would be able to operate from both land and water.

In the quarrel with the Army, the Navy had finally split away from the government plan, establishing its own flying school at Eastchurch and buying its own planes from private companies, rather than from the Royal Aircraft Factory. They had ordered from Sopwith the Bat Boat, the only plane almost to finish the Round Britain Seaplane Race circuit, which poor Cody had hoped to win. James and McDougall were pinning all their hopes on the Admiralty buying Ajax.

The church bells of the New Forest joyfully rang in the new year of 1914, and still Ajax II remained in pieces. There were times when James became desperate that he could ever bring it back to life, there were so many parts to make and buy. He lived at the forge, cycling over to Calshot early in the morning to do Navy contract work, finishing up with a long stint on Ajax in the evening and often well into the night. He never once saw Amelia. Only the products of the factory – big sausage-shaped balloons latticed by ropes that hung above the Jerningham fir trees on still days.

Bit by bit, Ajax II began re-emerging. It was a revelation that the germ of this design – the sweptback wing, the sharp cut on the tail, the tapering line of the fuselage – was inherited from the old Ajax that he and Amelia had built all those years ago. Certainly there were many improvements that Wilkinson had made – the strengthening of the struts, the clean fairings behind the propeller and the big 100 hp Green engine –nevertheless there the old Ajax was. The old design contained all that he had learned from Pilcher's and Chanute's kites and Lilienthal's gliders, just as in Cody's kites could be seen those of Harcourt, and in his aeroplanes the shades of the Wrights and Curtiss.

That spring and summer, it was hotter than anyone could remember. Sunshine flooded the forest, and in London the social season was particularly brilliant. The balls and routs lasted all night. The theatres were packed. At His Majesty's, Mrs Patrick Campbell and Sir Herbert Tree were rehearsing a play by Bernard Shaw called *Pygmalion*. In April, Pixton won the Schneider Trophy in a Sopwith seaplane with a French Gnome rotary engine at a speed of 86.78 mph – *quite as important, Le Temps said, as that shown by the Germans in capturing the world's duration and height records.*

James read of Britain's single aerial triumph in the *Southampton Gazette*, only disappointed that it hadn't been Ajax. On 9 June he read a much smaller piece in the same paper, reporting that a madman had shot and killed the Archduke Franz Ferdinand, heir to the Austro-Hungarian throne, and his wife the day before in a Serbian town called Sarajevo.

A castle of cards had been touched. Other cards began falling. On 28 July Austro-Hungary declared war on Serbia. On 1 August, Germany declared war on Russia. On 2 August, Germany demanded right of passage through Belgium, whose neutrality Britain had guaranteed. On 3 August, Germany declared war on France. On 4 August, Britain issued an ultimatum to Germany.

As the British Prime Minister's wife and her friend, the German Ambassador's wife, clung together in tears, comforting each other with the thought that the Kaiser would not be so mad as to reject it, the twelve hours grace given with the ultimatum ticked by.

BOOK TWO

Red Sky in the Morning
1914–18

ONE

5 August 1914 dawned hot and still. At first light, James had taken Ajax out on to a glassy Solent to do its first water-taxying trials. Coming back to the Calshot slipway just on nine, he heard the maroons going off.

'What's going on?' he shouted at McDougall.

'Air raid.'

'*Air raid?*'

The engineer officer tossed a newspaper into the cockpit. 'Take a look at that.'

James read the thick black headlines of the Foreign Office statement. *Owing to the summary rejection by the German government of the request made by His Majesty's Government for assurances that the neutrality of Belgium will be respected, His Majesty's Ambassador at Berlin has received his passports and His Majesty's Government have declared to the German Government that a state of war exists between Great Britain and Germany as from 11 pm on 4 August.*

In fact, that air-raid warning was a false alarm. But the Germans had already begun methodically carrying out their Moeltke plan, known by British Intelligence for years, bombarding Rheims and invading Belgium. 'Poor little Belgium!' was the cry as thousands of young men rushed to the war as though to a dance, frightened only that it would be over by Christmas.

The 63 serviceable aeroplanes of the Royal Flying Corps – all with French engines – limped off to France: there were two fatal crashes on the way. Their purpose was solely reconnaissance. A pilot who fitted a Lewis machine gun to his Farman was immediately reprimanded and ordered to remove it.

The British Expeditionary Force also hurried across. The Germans were stopped at Ypres. There General Moeltke advised the Kaiser to make peace. He refused. Instead of being over by Christmas, the Great War became a stalemate of mud and blood and millions of casualties.

James went on working at Calshot with the Navy, in the evenings and weekends tuning and checking Ajax in preparation for the first flight. The day before he planned to get airborne, a regulation came into force forbidding passage through the airspace above Britain to anything except RFC and RN flying machines. McDougall made it immediately clear that though Ajax could remain in the Calshot hangar, under no circumstances could he allow James to take off.

So off he went to join the RFC as a pilot. 'Have you your flying ticket?' an Army captain asked him at the Kingsway headquarters.

'No, but I have a lot of experience with aeroplanes.'

'Tell me about it.'

James told him, but the captain was unimpressed. 'Can you ride a horse?'
'Yes.'
'How old are you?'
'Thirty-one.'
The captain made a long face. 'And what are you doing at present?'
'Helping my father in the forge.'
They offered him a job as a blacksmith. He promptly turned it down and returned to Jerningham, to the delight of his father. 'Don't join anything, lad! That's my advice!'

So James's life went on much as before. As McDougall relented so far as to allow him to taxi on the Solent ('After all,' James pointed out to him, 'it's only the sky that's restricted'), he spent many hours in Ajax on the water, getting to know its behaviour in different weather conditions, every now and then, when he was round the corner from Calshot so nobody could see him, lifting Ajax a few inches up into the air and flying just above the surface for a couple of miles before putting her down again on the water. He was pleased with her speed and manoeuvrability. In this way, he taught himself to take off and land – indeed to fly.

The Ajax factory was now on contract work for naval airships. Huts and hangars were being erected. Dozens of new employees were taken on. Everywhere else in Britain, the gay Edwardian-style life continued as though there were no war on. The Prime Minister and his Cabinet had no real idea how to wage it, but then neither had the Kaiser. There was very little blackout. No shortages. No conscription. Plenty of good food, plenty of good wine and whisky, plenty of money, plenty of parties. The Café de Paris and all the other nightspots of London boomed. Everybody said that the long *Missing* lists were exaggerated and the boys would soon come safely home.

The feeling in London was that the war was a new kind of sport. The first aerial duel resulted in an Allied fighter shooting down a German plane with a rifle, as though it were a pheasant. Even the arrival of a Zeppelin over Norfolk towards the end of February 1915 was pretty innocuous. Nobody thought that London could be attacked. Devil though he was, the Kaiser would draw the satanic line at bombing his cousins in Buckingham Palace. And nobody had any idea that a Dutchman called Fokker was at that moment perfecting a machine-gun that fired through a plane's propeller, and having been turned down by the British, had sold his invention to the Germans.

Then poison gas was used by the Germans at Ypres. Fifteen days later, a German U-boat sank the *Lusitania* off Cork. Amongst more than 1000 dead were 124 Americans. The Kaiser, everyone now believed, would stop at nothing. And sure enough, just over three weeks later came the Zeppelins in force. Bombs were dropped on the East End. Fifteen civilians were killed. The Kaiser's scruples, if they existed, had been overcome by Count Zeppelin and by the need for battle news more propaganda-worthy than the monotony of trench warfare. The Count personally directed the attacks and coined the battlecry *Gott Strafe Engländ*.

The British, impervious still to the menace of the skies, were unprepared. Civil defence was supposed to be organised by the Admiralty, but nothing had been worked out. The sight of the huge silver cigar shapes in the moonlit sky produced at first astonishment, then excitement, then as the bombs were thrown out of the gondolas, a wave of fear and anger.

At nightfall, thousands rushed for the Blackwall Tunnel and the underground stations. There was real concern in the House of Commons that panic would result in the crushing to death of hundreds, and a direct hit on a packed shelter would be a major disaster. 'It has reached a dreadful pass,' Frederick spoke later that week, 'when on British soil a British coroner rightly sees fit to bring in a verdict on a civilian of wilful murder against the Kaiser. Our government should hang its head in shame at such unpreparedness! What will our lads in the trenches feel when their families at home are under fire? I will tell you . . . anger against the Kaiser, yes! And anger against this government!'

In the upper echelons of society the anger was muted. The Zeppelin raids coincided with the height of the season – albeit a watered down season because so many young escorts had flocked to the Colours, so many society matrons had turned their homes into private hospitals, and so many debutantes were rolling bandages and knitting socks and nursing. But there were still dinners and parties and handsome officers on leave to be entertained.

A Zeppelin raid in 1915 was like black manna from heaven. A spine-chilling cabaret, the awesome accolade to any party.

No sooner did the hastily assembled guns begin firing in Hyde Park and the Mall, than the stately doors of Mayfair were thrown open. Out rushed the debutantes and their escorts to find the Zep. Carriages were summoned. A deathly hunt-the-slipper began.

'I hope we see a Zep,' Charles remarked hopefully as he and Arthur and Amelia drove to the town house from Haybury on 13 October. It was their half-term holiday treat. There would be shopping for clothes and tuck-box replenishment at Harrods and Fortnum's, followed by the theatre and a music hall.

'I'd rather see a Zep raid than the theatre,' Charles said.

'Well, I wouldn't,' Amelia said shortly.

'Nor I,' Arthur smiled his sweet seraphic smile. Amelia eyed him affectionately. He had grown very little. He still looked fragile. Amelia feared he would be bullied at school on his first term. She was full of maternal anxiety.

'You're a namby-pamby,' Charles turned on his brother. 'And a swot! Fancy actually wanting to go to school!'

'It should be good fun. And I wouldn't run away if it wasn't.'

'Well, Papa says . . . '

'Quiet,' Amelia said. 'Both of you! You're old enough to know better! Especially you, Charles!'

Charles's mouth set mutinously as it always did at any criticism. He stared out moodily at a platoon of Seaforth Highlanders marching through the Park, bagpipes skirling, drums beating.

'How long d'you think the war will last, Mama?' It was his most constant and irritating question. On warm afternoons like this Amelia could tell herself that the war would be over soon. It would remain distant. It would not touch them. James had been rejected from the RFC, the boys were far too young. Frederick had got himself a job at the War Office. But underneath, she knew differently. Since Eustace Wilkinson had crashed, she had a melancholy feeling of inescapable doom, not just for herself but for everything she touched.

'Years,' she said sadly.

'Till I'm old enough?'

'Probably.'

'Not till *I'm* old enough, I hope,' Arthur smiled.

'They wouldn't want you,' Charles snorted. 'You're the size of an organ-grinder's monkey.'

'Brains are better than brawn.' Arthur put out his tongue.

They bickered until Amelia brought the Rolls to a halt in the mews yard of 7 Park Lane. Frederick was waiting. But not for them. 'I thought, my dear, we'd do things slightly differently this year. I've invited Diana Nazier to dine with us. And she has a box tomorrow for *La Bohème*.'

'She is one of my most favourite persons.' Arthur smiled dutifully up at his father. 'She was awfully decent at my birthday. We had her box then. It was topping!'

Following Frederick through into the library, while the boys went upstairs to their rooms, Amelia said, 'I thought this was the one occasion we were *en famille*?'

The family trips to London had begun in the year Charles ran away from school. They were an attempt to paper over the widening marital cracks so that they would present themselves to one another and the outside world as a family. Frederick replied suavely, 'Diana Nazier *is* one of the family. I thought I made it clear that she should be treated as such.'

'As your mistress?' A sudden anger that had little to do with Diana Nazier made her cheeks flush. 'Is that how I'm to present her to the boys?'

'As a loyal friend and trusted adviser. The boys' friend and adviser, too. *Your* friend.'

'Not mine!'

'Oh, yes! *Yours!* Very much so. Jerningham's. The factory's. Do you really think Jerningham would have got all those lucrative contracts without her?'

'Yes.'

'Then you'd be wrong! Again! You're usually wrong. Diana on the other hand is usually right.'

'I don't want any damned contracts from her.'

'But I do. The firm is mine, too. The bills are mine. And I'd be a wealthier man today if I'd listened to her instead of you.'

'You didn't listen to my ideas for long.'

'Too long!' He drew in his breath. 'But that's all over and done with now. The present and the future are the important things. There's a war to be fought.'

He shuffled through the papers on his desk and selected one which he read through with a gratified smile. 'I have recently been co-opted on to the Committee for the Defence of London.'

'Do you know anything about it?'

'No other wife would ask such a question.' Frederick's eyes glittered balefully. 'Any other wife would congratulate her husband.'

'Diana Nazier will congratulate you.'

'She does better than that. She advises. Helps with her knowledge of Count Zeppelin. She is invaluable to me.'

Lady Nazier's knowledge of Count Zeppelin was the main topic of conversation at dinner. After a few minutes devoted to flattering enquiries which she

156

made of Arthur about school and hobbies, she spoke about the Count at length. She had been one of the first ladies to fly in his airships, she told them. She had stayed at his *schloss* in Bavaria and had been introduced by him to the Kaiser and Prince Wilhelm.

'Are they frightful bounders?' Arthur asked.

'The Kaiser is ruthless, certainly. Edward never liked him. Never invited him to Sandringham. But he hasn't got horns and a tail as the Press portray him. I found him courteous and chivalrous and perfectly charming.'

'Even Huns have the sense to find Lady Nazier irresistible,' Frederick said.

A look of naked hatred flickered in Charles's eyes. Even Arthur seemed surprised and discomforted, looking anxiously from Frederick's face to Amelia's. It was almost with relief that Amelia heard the pop-popping of the Hyde Park guns. Nothing would satisfy Lady Nazier but that they drive round in the carriage and find the Zep. 'We shall regret it if we don't! This is history being made!'

The boys supported her wholeheartedly. It would simply make the weekend, give them something to talk about at school. Frederick supported her slightly less enthusiastically. Amelia's protests were overruled.

'No one at school has seen a Zep raid yet, Mama,' Charles urged. 'No one's been there when the bombs actually dropped.'

'Come!' Lady Nazier had already assumed Amelia's role and rung the bell for the maid.

'Stay at home if you prefer,' Frederick said coolly. 'We four shall go. It'll be something for the boys to remember all their lives. I can't think what has come over you, Amelia. You used to be so adventurous!'

It was impossible to explain to him that not only had she now two hostages to fortune in Charles and Arthur, but that she also felt a deepening awareness of ultimate tragedy. 'The bombs have killed dozens of civilians, Frederick. You said so yourself; 28 last week.' She looked at the boys. 'Children amongst them.'

'We'll dodge them,' Charles shouted, rushing to the window. 'The searchlights are up! Hurry, Mama! Put on your cloak! Oh, my God! There he is! I can just see him. He's coming this way! He must have followed the river up! Now he's turning!'

Charles was out at the front of the house before the coachman had brought the carriage round. The pavement was already crowded. All the houses along the lane had their front doors open and their occupants, caught like themselves in the midst of dinner, darted around excitedly on the steps and the pavement and in the small gardens, clutching feather boas and wraps and cloaks over their evening dresses.

'I didn't want to lose sight of him,' Charles subsided breathlessly into the carriage beside Amelia. 'Can you see him, Mama? Isn't he a splendid sight? They're bigger than I thought.'

High above the outline of Big Ben, high above the little red sparks of anti-aircraft shells sailed the huge dirigible cigar-shape. The sharp nose was suddenly caught and silvered in a searchlight. Other searchlights fingered the sky blindly. Then another one caught the airship and formed a cone with its predecessor with the Zeppelin balanced on the peak. Puffs of white gunsmoke

157

broke below her – too far below. On the Zeppelin came, in and out of the searchlight like a big silent shark in moonlight water above the silvery snake of the Thames.

All around them, carriages and motor cars were hurrying into Park Lane, accelerating towards Marble Arch. Pedestrians shouted and pointed. The guns sent up a futile fire. A man in a steel helmet urged them to take cover. The Zeppelin was at an angle now, floating across the extreme southwest corner of the Park, its nose still pointing north, the rosy red of its engines glowing on its underbelly and on the night cloud.

'Where's he making for, Frederick?' Lady Nazier leaned out of the carriage window. 'The munitions factory at Kilburn, would you say?'

'Probably. Or Watford Junction. But there's no telling. Just coming in to slaughter,' Frederick said working himself into a rage. 'Keep those lights at a minimum, Grant!'

But there were lights everywhere. The street lamps were dimmed, but houselights illuminated the pavements. Chestnut roasters were out in force, the glow of their stoves reflecting on the pavement like the Zeppelin engine on the clouds. 'Up the Edgware Road,' Frederick told Grant. 'Don't get too close to that victoria in front! Give ourselves some room to manoeuvre.'

Now the Zeppelin was coned in three searchlights. Looking up, Amelia saw the long gondola underneath and the black silhouettes of men. The great silver shape turned, its attendant pilot fish of ineffectual gunfire bursts following. Then the searchlights lost it.

'Take this road to the left,' Charles shouted. 'I can still see it.'

Having evaded the searchlights, the Zeppelin descended over the meaner streets of North London. She was a shape, just darker than the sky half a mile ahead of them.

Then simultaneously two things happened. A pub door opened with a sudden crack of white light and as it opened, a bomb dropped. Then another. And another. There were three deafening crashes followed by a furious rattle of anti-aircraft fire. The horses reared. Grant shouted. Frederick pushed Lady Nazier to the floor, and lay on top of her. Amelia threw her arms round Charles and Arthur. There seemed to be a long stunned silence. Then someone outside in the street began to scream. Grant must have opened the carriage door. They descended stiffly. A crowd had gathered on the pavement outside the pub. The glass from the window and door of the pub had been blown out. The air smelled dusty and foul.

'There ain't nothing yer can do, guvnor,' a man said as the crowd parted to let them through. 'He's a goner.'

Amelia found herself staring in the same direction as the rest of the group. On the pavement spotlit in the lights from the broken pub window, lay a small twisted form. At first she thought it was a child. She made a movement forward, and someone – a stranger – put a restraining hand on her arm. Then she saw the boots and the trouser legs, and the gnarled upflung hands. And after that she saw the empty place and the scarlet stump of neck and just on the edge of the wooden pavement, the old man's head.

She didn't know how long she stared, unseeing. She was blinded with anger and sadness.

'Cut clean orf,' a fireman shouted to his mates. 'A goner! More to do in the

158

next street! Water main's hit. No houses, thank God! But pavement's lifted.'

Dazed, Amelia tried to push her way back through the crowd, but it was growing every second. When she at last saw Frederick, he was almost at the carriage. He was half-carrying Diana Nazier. Grant had come forward to help him. Charles was holding the door open. Arthur appeared to be crying.

'You'll have to find your own way,' Frederick told Amelia. 'Diana has fainted. I must see her home.' And to Grant, 'Let her stretch out on the seat. Give her air!'

'We'll walk back to the main road and get a hansom,' Charles said as the fireman began shooing everyone away from the scene. An ambulance had come up. The ack-ack fire was dying away.

They picked their way along the sidestreets. The darkness was chequered with excited lights, as people held back curtains to peer out, swung lanterns, called to one another from open doorways. The streets stank of sewage. Halfway to the main road another water point had been fractured. The whole of the wooden pavement had lifted like a pie-crust. They walked in stunned silence. Gone was the boys' excitement. They looked white as ghosts.

'That's what war is really like,' Amelia said, when they arrived back at 7 Park Lane. 'Don't ever forget that! War is beastly! Cruel! Unjust and obscene!' All her anger and frustration and horror was suddenly directed against Charles. 'For God's sake,' she shouted at him, 'stop wishing you could go to the war! Stop asking how long it's going to last! Stop wishing you were older! Stop wanting to grow up!'

But Charles grew up that night. His first words to Amelia sitting alone at the breakfast-table next morning were, 'Papa not back? So he spent the night with Lady Nazier, I suppose?'

159

TWO

The Zeppelins came over regularly that autumn. Bombs were dropped on the East Coast. There were sightings in November over the Channel and more attacks on London.

Public indignation reached panic proportions. The Asquith government was attacked for having no plans to protect civilians. Men in the uniform of the Royal Flying Corps were set upon in Piccadilly for staying on the ground. Vast sums were offered by private firms – like the peacetime cups and prizes for the victors of air races – to the first man to shoot a Zeppelin down over England.

'And you always saying that Zeps are no use!' James's mother kept saying.

'Nor are they.'

'Aeroplanes don't do much against 'em!'

'They will.'

'How?'

It was no use trying to explain to his mother, and he didn't try. The trouble was that the power on the French rotary engines fell off dramatically at height. The RFC planes couldn't reach the Zeppelins majestically cruising at 20,000 feet. Nor were the pilots trained in night flying. Nor were there adequate instruments for flying through cloud and darkness. The Ajax with its 120 hp in-line supercharged engine might reach them and he was willing to take his chance on night flying. If only he could get hold of something to bring Zeppelins down, he wouldn't mind having a go himself in spite of the government restriction.

Cody had had a weird idea of lowering a wire with a weight on the end and cutting the Zeppelin fabric in two – not in James's view one of his happier inventions. But bullets were no good either. Dropping bombs on them weren't much better. Warneford had been lucky over Bruges – the only British kill of a Zeppelin so far. Bombs were beyond James anyway. What else was there?

That 5 November, watching the children dance round the bonfire on which a straw-stuffed Kaiser instead of Guy Fawkes was roasting, suddenly he realised. His mind had gone back to that last time at Hendon four years ago when he and Bronwen had watched Brock rockets spurting from aeroplane wings.

Next day, he bought up every remaining rocket in the Lyndhurst store. On both sides of the Ajax cockpit, he fitted simple metal holders and inserted six metal-tipped rockets on sticks. On one of his taxying trials at dead of night, helped by a young matelot, he took his miniature arsenal with him. On a lonely stretch of the Beaulieu river he lit the six rockets on the lefthand side of the cockpit, and was gratified by the sudden *whoosh* and the multitude of white stars bursting a couple of hundred feet above his head. Thereafter on all taxying trials, he took his rockets with him – but saw no sign of a Zeppelin. He consoled himself with the fact that nobody else did either. The airships would be staying in their sheds till the moon waxed brighter.

Meanwhile McDougall tried to persuade him to fly Ajax to Farnborough (with his special permission) so that the Royal Aircraft Factory could test it. But James knew they would give it the thumbs down unless they had special pressure on them. They would only pass government aeroplanes like that tortoise the BE2 on which the RFC were being slaughtered by the fast Fokker. Even big private enterprise firms like Vickers and Sopwith had trouble getting government contracts. James had learned enough from the showman side of Cody to realise that to succeed Ajax had to be launched with the Cody panache in a blaze of publicity. And what better blaze than a burning Zeppelin?

Stealthily, he would creep over the waters of the Solent and up the Beaulieu, sometimes lifting off for a short flight as the moon waxed. Slowly it fattened into a Zeppelin moon. Any time now and they'd be over again.

The days passed one after the other and they did not come. On the night of 26 November he had no great hopes of seeing anything. There had been a light fall of snow. Slowly in the moonlight he taxied over to the first of the three lighter buoys that served him as a flarepath. Then he opened up the throttle. He heard the soft hiss of water on the floats and the whistle in the wires. One red light went by, then another. Up came the nose. There was the slightest bump, a shimmy in the tail – and then suddenly there was nothing but the night air, cool and black, and the subdued but not blacked out lights of Southampton disappearing under the port wing.

He climbed. The cloud thinned. Now all that remained of Hampshire were tinfoil flashes of moonlit lakes, half-covered by ragged tufts of Turkish towel. Ahead he could see the snake of the Thames like a silver buckle on a belt joining Essex to Kent, a caterpillar of a lighted train crawled below him towards the giant glow-worm that was London.

He caught his breath, lost in the sheer wonder of flight – the fabric wings bellying like sails, the murmuring of the engine, the slight rocking of the fuselage like a punt on the water. Only the night and a handful of stars for company, and on the eastern horizon, a black battalion of cumulonimbus.

He edged southwards. Better keep away from the rough stuff. Night flying on a thermometer type airspeed indicator, an aneroid altimeter and a bubble-gauge of an attitude indicator was bad enough. He wanted no pillow-fight with bumpy clouds. He would do a couple more climbing turns, a final altitude test and then he would go back home. Things could hardly be more peaceful. No sign of enemy activity tonight.

Only cold – icy cold, colder than ever as he climbed. Passing 15,000 feet, he took off his gloves, blew on his fingers. Back inside, momentarily they enjoyed a frail warmth, but in his fur-lined boots both feet had turned to ice. The engine was warm, the exhausts bright yellow and smelling of roast chestnuts. Power dropping off now, controls a mite sloppy, approaching her ceiling . . . And then suddenly he saw it. Like a white maggot from an oak tree, a fat snub-nosed shape was emerging from the black trunk of cumulonimbus above him.

'Zeppelin!'

He shouted out the words to the wind and the stars, as he began to climb. Others had seen it now. Little red sparks appeared in the blackness far below. Two searchlights criss-crossed the sky.

The air up here was thin and cold. He was breathless now, gasping for air. Leisurely, lazily, malevolently, the airship still wallowed above him. He could make out two gondolas below, the skeleton of metal girders beneath the fabric – now no longer boneless, but menacing, sharklike, purposeful. Cloud came up then, and he dodged behind it.

James put on right bank. Sluggishly the port wing rose. Everything moved in slow motion like one of those flickering cinematic films he had seen in the new Southampton cinema, as he tried to manoeuvre underneath the belly. The searchlight was a nuisance, flickering into his eyes. As for the gunfire, the shells were bursting far below.

A streak of punctuated yellow dots came towards him from the top of the envelope. A machine-gun platform was up there – he could see it. And more tracer bullets were coming from both gondolas. He turned out of range. On no account must he dive too fast, get into a Wilkinson death dive.

The Zeppelin was accelerating. He could actually see the skin, silvered by searchlights, palpitating in the moonlight. The next moment – stealthily, quietly – it had slipped out of sight into a cloud. Fearful he had lost it, James climbed up into the stuff, felt it break like spume all over him. Flung upwards and sideways in the violent aircurrents, he lost all sense of attitude, felt momentarily as though he was upside down. He heard the propeller screaming, then, hazily ahead, he saw a looming monster smudged in grey.

He pulled hard back and kicked on the right rudder. His propeller raced inches away from the wet streaming skin. He seemed to be climbing up a smooth mountain, actually saw through the moonlit mist the ghostly faces of the men on the top, actually heard the machine-guns. The next moment, he was rolling away, down, down, down out of the cloud back into the night.

Above him, the airship crept across the moon like an eclipse.

Now was his chance! *Now* while they were shaking themselves free of their jolting in the cloud! The Zeppelin was directly above him, hiding him in its own shadow.

He throttled back. Taking his time, he positioned himself perfectly. For a full minute in that strange vertical formation, they flew like friends. Holding the matches and the joystick in his left hand, James struck a match with his right. It went out.

He tried another. It didn't light.

The third flared beautifully. Just as he was lighting the six rocket fuses on the left side of the cockpit they must have seen him, for he heard the rak-rak-rak of bullets, followed by a *whoosh* as the rockets rose.

Feverishly he lit the six fuses on the right, felt the rockets leave, was looking up into the darkness when the night sky erupted above him. He had a moment's picture of dazzling lava pouring out of tangled girders. A hot hurricane was blasting into his face. And then he was over on his back and diving.

He was aware of nothing then but the Ajax's dive turning into a crazy whirl to the shrill tune of the overspeeding propeller. This is Wilkinson's death dive, he thought. This is what happened to Parke and all the others – wings

162

spinning round and round like a top.

He watched the needle of the altimeter unwinding. 12,000, 10,000, 8000 . . . He looked at the bubble – hard over to starboard. They were spinning clockwise.

He put on full left rudder. No difference.

He pulled back on the stick. The spin tightened. 5000, 4000, 2000 . . .

Above him the night had turned to day. Below him, a false dawn was floodlighting the countryside.

He looked up hypnotised by the elliptical sun burning above. He let go of the stick, his left foot stopped its pressure on the rudder. The sight was awesome. Ablaze from nose to tail, the Zeppelin was being blown south to the Channel.

Suddenly he was aware he was no longer spinning. Ajax had righted herself. A little slow perhaps, so he put the stick right forward. And immediately he had full control again.

So that's all there was to it! Don't try to get out of the dive. Dive faster and put on opposite rudder. There was nothing the matter with the design at all. Spinning was just a natural manoeuvre following a stall.

Now he saw fields, trees, roads. Gently he eased back. Slowly the nose came up till once more he was level, and he set course back to the Solent. Five minutes later, his three lighter buoys beside Calshot winked out a dim red welcome.

The real welcome waited till he was down and taxying – and then he had seen nothing like it. Speedboats, naval pinnaces, even a destroyer, were moving towards him, raking him with searchlights. When he came up to it the slipway was alive with people – Navy, reporters, police, soldiers, everybody – McDougall included, and thank God not looking horrified, but beaming from ear to ear.

He was carried shoulder-high to the hangar. After the cheers came the questions. How had he done it? Wasn't he breaking the law? Was it true the RFC had turned him down? Did he realise that tomorrow he and his Ajax would be world headlines? Why had the Jerningham Ajax managed to shoot down a Zeppelin while other planes had failed?

James March was not a showman. Normally quiet, normally undemonstrative, on this occasion he recognised what was wanted. Smoke, fire, banging guns, leaping steeds, yawning gulfs, villainous Zeppelins and heroic aeroplanes – in a nutshell *The Klondike Nugget* in real life. Panache, bravado, colour, assurance, that was what the country needed, just as much as Amelia's Ajax needed advertisement and publicity.

On his performance pivoted Ajax, the Jerningham company, his entrance into the RFC, his future – *everything*.

Wryly remembering the complete lack of publicity for the Wrights twelve years before, and not without a certain sense of irony, James rose to the occasion. 'There I was at 20,000 feet, when suddenly I saw —'

Colonel Samuel Franklin Cody would have been proud of him.

Amelia was proud of him. As paper after paper headlined James's victory, as Lord Northcliffe's press wondered long and loud why it had taken a civilian pilot – one turned down by the RFC, they would have their readers note – and an unknown little aeroplane to shoot down the terror of the moonlit night, the

Zeppelin, Amelia wondered if she might go and congratulate James in person. The forge, Sarah told her, was besieged with reporters and photographers. Several villagers, including Sarah's father, had been interviewed for reminiscences of the hero's childhood.

Amelia had no wish to push herself through the throng, and had not decided what she would do, when two things happened almost simultaneously. She had an irate telephone call from Frederick direct from the House of Commons, expostulating that the now famous Ajax was not this fellow March's at all, but the property of the Jerningham Aircraft Company and nobody else.

'You forget, Frederick, I gave it to him. Or I gave the wreck to him.'

'I don't forget, for the simple reason that I never knew.'

'You neither knew nor cared. Let the tide take it out, you said. You had no further use for it.'

'Nevertheless, there was nothing on paper. Legally it is ours. It will now be exceedingly valuable. Contracts will come in.'

'But . . .'

Frederick hung up with an angry exclamation, and Amelia had scarcely replaced the receiver on the library extension when Sarah came bustling in importantly and excitedly, 'It's him, M'lady! Mr James March! How he got away from the forge without the reporters seeing, I'll never know.'

She glanced behind her to see if James was following. Then she smiled, and shrugged deprecating her own excitement. 'He's waylaid. He came in through the kitchen. The gardener's lad and the groom were in having a mug of tea. They asked him for his autograph. You should've heard him laugh! But I wouldn't be put off. I made him give it me.'

She patted the pocket of her crisp white apron. Then James appeared, rather flushed over his cheekbones, an embarrassed smile curving his lips. But for all that a somehow more confident, much older James.

Immediately Sarah closed the door behind her, Amelia put her arms round him. He held her tightly and lovingly but didn't try to kiss her.

'Oh, James,' she said, 'I am so proud!'

He said nothing for several seconds. They stood in the middle of the library floor, simply holding on to one another. Somehow in those moments, she knew his feelings – not just for her, but for the whole awesome business of the war he had now entered. He didn't have to tell her about the Germans he'd seen on the gondola whom he had killed. She knew his revulsion as well as his triumph. Then James said, 'It's a good aircraft.'

'It's *you* I'm most proud of. *You!*'

He released her gently, and pulled out a chair for her. 'You mustn't be. You've no cause to be.' And implicit in his tone, 'You've no right to be.'

'But you have cause,' he went on, as she sat down, 'to be proud of Ajax.'

'It would have been nothing without you.'

He dismissed her remark with a shake of his head. 'It's Ajax I came about.'

'Do sit down, James,' she waved him to a chair. 'You make me feel uncomfortable.'

He smiled at her tone, recognising wryly the cause of its sudden petulance as clearly as she herself recognised it. She was disappointed that he hadn't come to see her on this momentous occasion simply for her own sake.

When he had perched himself on the edge of a leather chair opposite her, she

164

asked, '*What* about Ajax?'

'It's yours, Amelia. Or rather,' he went on using words so similar to Frederick's, 'it's Jerningham Aircraft's.'

'Nonsense!' she said roundly. 'I gave it to you!' And then with a teasing smile, copying his manner, 'Or rather I sold it to you for a consideration.'

His blue eyes crinkled up, their expression softened. 'Well, whether you gave it me or sold it me, Amelia,' he drew in his breath. 'I'm giving it back to you.'

'Nonsense!' she exclaimed again. 'I'll not have it back! It's yours. It would have been at the bottom of the Solent if it wasn't for you. You did all the work and the testing. You took it into action.'

'Even so, it's yours.'

'It was yours in the beginning.'

'If you want its pedigree,' he smiled, 'it's yours and mine and Wilkinson's. And I found why he crashed. The reason for that spinning dive. No need to fear it now. I told you it'd be his resurrection. Now maybe I want it to be mine.'

'What d'you mean? You don't need it. You're riding the pig's back, as Sarah would say. Everyone's applauding you. Just you see, the Royal Aircraft Establishment will examine Ajax.'

'They've already asked for trials. I heard this morning.'

'There! I'm right! You'll actually get money from the government to build Ajax. You've done it, James! I'm so pleased!'

'But I don't want to build Ajax, Amelia!'

'You must! You've always wanted to! Right from the beginning.'

'There's something else I want to do first. Something else I heard about this morning.' He leaned forward and took her fingertips in his hand. 'You know the newspapers made a lot about my wanting to join the RFC, and being turned down?'

'Yes,' she said stonily, knowing now what was coming.

'Well, the Press campaign has had its results. This morning I received a letter,' he paused, 'offering me a commission in the Royal Flying Corps.'

Amelia said nothing. She stared at him, her eyes frosty, her mouth set.

'Aren't you going to congratulate me, Amelia?'

'No.'

He didn't ask her why. And after long moments of staring out at the grey November sky, she exclaimed bitterly, 'I know the casualties, don't forget! How could I congratulate you? Even Frederick is horrified by them. You must know what the average life of a pilot is. You heard what that MP who's a pilot, Pemberton-Billing, shouted in the Commons at Asquith, didn't you?'

'No, Amelia, I didn't.'

'He shouted that the BE2s and the RE8s are powerless against the Eindekker! That the British pilots are called Fokker Fodder!'

Tears streamed unchecked down her face at those emotive words. In a studiedly calm voice James replied, 'All the more reason to have Ajaxes built.'

'Oh!' She clenched her fists, thumped them on the arms of the chair and exclaimed wordlessly. Then she said, 'Just when things seemed to be going better!'

'How *can* they go better,' he asked her sternly, 'while the war's still on?' His expression was closed up. 'I know what I'm going to do. You're not to argue any more, Amelia. I'm not making Ajax. Do you understand? If you won't have Ajax back, then I shall transfer it to the Royal Aircraft Factory.'

'God forbid!'

'Well, then?'

She stared down at her folded hands for a moment, then she looked up at him, and asked, 'What sort of price would you expect?'

'Nothing,' he said gruffly.

'Nothing, James? Nothing at all? For all your work? Your expenses? Nothing?'

'There is just one thing.' He stood up and as if the request slightly embarrassed him, avoided her wide-eyed expectant stare. 'I'd like you to promise . . . '

'Yes, James.' The beginning of a smile touched her lips.

'That my parents will never get turned out of the forge. It's just in case anything happens to me.'

'Oh, James! How can you talk of it? I can't bear it.'

'That's what I'd like you to promise.'

She swallowed and said, 'Of course. I promise you that.' Then, holding up her face to him tearfully, 'Are you sure that's your full price?'

He cupped her face in his hands and brushed her lips with his and said, 'There's no such thing as price between you and me.'

THREE

Five days later, James left by train for Stonehenge aerodrome to begin his RFC initial flying training. His father saw him off at Brockenhurst station on a pink hazy morning that held a hint of frost. There were gipsies camped near the railway track on the flat heath beyond Lyndhurst, their fire glowing blood-red against the low ground mist. A woman squatted amongst a brood of children, peeling what looked like hazel bark.

Suddenly he remembered the gipsy coming into the forge all those years ago. He saw her face, heard her voice, 'You'll kill and kill again! Only when you've killed will you marry the rich pretty lady like you dream!'

He had already begun to kill. He shuddered, remembering again those black figures in the gondola, the huge orange-red explosion, the figures blown away like charred paper. Now it looked as though he'd go on killing. Killing was what he had to do. And what of the rest of the gipsy woman's clairvoyance, a voice he hated inside himself asked? What about Amelia?

Climbing into the Crossley tender, he answered his own question derisively. What sort of superstitious fool was he, to take notice of a fortune teller? There'd never be anything closer between him and Amelia. How could there be? But there was Ajax. And he took some strange comfort in that.

As the Crossley turned into the camp, he felt a variety of emotions – excitement, apprehension, keenness to get up into the air again, determination to succeed. He had no desire to kill, but it was that or be killed.

He soon found out that you didn't have to wait till you got to the Front. The killing started immediately. The Maurice Farman Longhorn, nicknamed Rumpetty, looked like a bilious yellow ghost from Rheims. The instructor crouched over the only pair of spectacle controls, with the pupil holding on to him from behind in a lover-like embrace.

The instructors were supposed to let the pupils hold the stick. But they were terrified of their charges. And the 'Huns', as the pupils were called because of their propensity to kill instructors were terrified of stalling the aeroplane.

Not without reason. 'Top speed 58 mph!' James's instructor yelled at him on his first flight. 'You're a dead man at 57!'

Once in the air, he said grudgingly, 'Now put your hands lightly on the spectacles below mine . . . *lightly* I said, Hun!'

After the Ajax, it wasn't flying. It was flopping around like a big eiderduck, the wind billowing out the wings like sails and the earth below almost stationary.

James's reputation as a giant-killer had preceded him. The RFC didn't like having its arm twisted, and every effort was made to take him down a peg.

'Now we'll come round for a landing.'

Squinting over the instructor's shoulder, James saw the half-full long white stocking of the wind sleeve. He lined up with its wind direction to the right of the line of pupils sitting on oil drums, waiting their turn.

'Can't you see there's a chap trying to land ahead of us?'

James had been keeping an eye on the Longhorn since turning up wind. As he manoeuvred behind him, he suddenly saw the aeroplane in front break up in the air, crumple like matchwood and sink to the ground where it exploded in a yellow flash.

'Stuff the nose down!' his instructor shouted frantically. 'More throttle!'

They were too low. James tried to move the elevator back, but the instructor's grip on it was like a vice.

The wheels banged hard on the ground, slowly they came to a stop outside the instructor's hut.

'You made a bloody awful landing!'

James gritted his teeth and said nothing.

Still visibly shaken, the instructor climbed out.

'Off you go, Hun!'

Taking off alone over the still burning Rumpetty, James felt an immediate feeling of release and relief. Like a truant escaped from some horrible school, in a glorious feeling of abandon, he went where he wanted and did whatever came into his head.

For an hour over the woods and hills of Wiltshire, he played with the monstrous bird. Then on impulse he slipped south to Hampshire and the forest. Before he had reached Jerningham, halfway along the road from Beaulieu he spied an unmistakable silver Rolls.

He put the stick forward and came low. Amelia was driving. He saw her take her hand off the wheel, point upwards and then rest her hand on the arm of the dark-haired man beside her. James banked away and climbed north. He was no longer in the mood for playing.

Back on the ground again, his fellow pupils congratulated him on his solo; he just gave a brief nod and walked away.

He did six more hours on Rumpettys and then he was sent off to Dillington on the Sussex coast, with the instructors' best wishes, to learn to fly the Morane. A French fighter monoplane reputed to be a killer – of its own pilot.

In fact James found the Morane just like Ajax to fly, featherlight fore and aft, capable of out-turning anything, armed with two machine-guns firing through propellers protected by metal deflector plates.

Not only did he like the Morane, he liked Basil Beaumont, the chief instructor, a plump little man with sleek black hair and come-to-bed eyes. 'You've got to show the Morane who's master, James.' Beaumont told him, 'Same as with any other woman!'

And every morning, his invariable greeting was, 'Come on, James! Up we go!' And up they went indeed – two little red and white Moranes soaring into the sun, sideslipping, looping, diving, rolling, stall-turning off the climb into an Immelmann dive.

'Never fire till you can see the whites of his eyes, James! Tuck into your prey so close, no other Hun can shoot for fear of hitting him! *Look* as though you mean business! Attack from his *home* ground where he doesn't expect it! Out of the sun if you can! Never reverse turn in a dogfight! And never, never, *never*, try to dive away, or you're a gonner!'

Despite such an apparently bloodthirsty streak, Basil Beaumont was a very civilised man. 'I am not interested in killing anyone,' he said. 'All I am interested in is saving my own and other pilots' skin.'

There was no master-instructor-dog-pupil relationship at Dillington. Instructors and pupils spent most of their time together, either flying or in the village pub.

They damned the government. They damned Royal Aircraft Factory aeroplanes. They damned RFC High Command for their lunatic policy of deep offensive patrols over the enemy lines and for not providing pilots with parachutes. They drank to their enemies, Boelcke and Immelmann. And then they talked flying-women-flying-women-women-women.

'Flying is a disease, James. Induces stress and strain. A woman is the cure.' It could have been Dr Beaumont prescribing Pink Pills for Pale People. 'I shall get my Welsh biddy to sort you out a woman.'

James knew that Basil had installed a girl in a little end-of-terrace house beside Dillington church – 'A little widow, James. They're the best because they know the ropes.'

Many of the other instructors had done the same. When the Dillington supply had run out, they had raided London, where women, even though they had still no vote, had come into their own in other ways. The city abounded in little teashops with discreetly curtained alcoves, where attractive young waitresses in black bombazine and frilly caps and aprons served China tea and toast and other delicacies on request. For the richer and more discerning tastes, there were luxurious establishments where a wide variety of women were paraded by the madame for the customers' personal choice. The Dillington instructors rarely returned empty-handed.

And it was Beaumont's ambition that James should become one of his instructors. He had been up to Central Flying School, obtained his wings, and returned with an *Exceptional* endorsement.

'Sheer waste at the Front, James, a pilot like you! And good teachers are scarce. HQ needs to be told I want you at Dillington. You'll settle here, whether you like it or not! All we need to do now is to find you a woman. And I shall get my Bronwen to sort you out one.'

There were, of course, thousands of other women called Bronwen. And they would, of course, be Welsh. And hundreds of Bronwens, of course, could live near Farnborough, from where rumour had it he had imported his. All the same, James avoided the environs of Dillington church. Pressed to 'come home for a bite' he always declined.

And then on a lovely June morning when the roses were out and James was lying outside the dispersal hut in the fragile sunshine, Basil called through the open door, 'Give me a hand out with this.'

James got up from the grass. 'Sure.'

'This' turned out to be an enormous tin trunk.

Basil had already hold of one end. James took the other, and staggered to the door. 'Have you got a body in here?'

They reached the green Bugatti. James was walking away, when Basil called out, 'Hey, I'll need some help when I get home! It's too heavy for Bronwen.'

It wouldn't be the same Bronwen, James thought, as the Bugatti skidded at high speed through the town, it *couldn't* be . . .

But it was. He saw the dark hair at the end of the passage as they staggered through the front door, Basil calling out, 'Bron'.

Then he saw those well-remembered brown eyes.

Basil must have seen the look because he said, 'She recognises you, James. That's fame for you! James March, Zeppelin killer . . . this is Bronwen.'

'How are you?'

'I am all right,' she said very carefully. 'And how are you?'

'I'm all right too.'

They put the trunk down in the passage. 'What've you got there, Basil?'

'Just books, Bronwen.' They went into the lounge. 'And now go down in the cellar and get us a bottle of the Châteauneuf, that's a good girl.'

Obediently she trotted off, returned with the bottle, three glasses and a corkscrew on a carefully polished silver tray.

'I've got her well-trained, as you see, James.' He began uncorking the bottle. 'Sit on the sofa beside Bronwen, there's a good chap!'

Tight against the cotton frock, he could feel the warmth of her body.

'James is going to be our new instructor.'

'Oh no, I'm —'

'But what a bachelor like him needs is a girl! You must find him a nice girl, Bronwen!'

There was a microscopic silence. Then she said, 'I should think a fine man like Lieutenant March . . .' another microscopic silence '. . . would have found . . .' a third silence '. . . a *woman* already.'

The little episode was over in ten minutes. On the way back to the aerodrome, James asked Basil, 'What happened to her husband?'

'Shot down in a balloon over Ypres, James.'

Poor old Taffy, he thought. But Bronwen seemed to be happy. With a bit of luck, she might even get Beaumont to marry her. And as for instructing, he never wanted to do it anyway. He told Beaumont so three or four times that week.

'You *are* going to instruct, James. It's all arranged!'

'No, Basil. I —'

'And Bronwen has found a woman for you.'

'She can't have done!'

'She has done. She's told me so!'

She certainly had – herself.

A letter was given to him by his batman on the last day of June. 'Delivered by a young lady's hand, Sir.'

. . . *you will no doubt know now that poor Taffy was killed in action. I thought you had a wife, James, but now I know you haven't, you and I can marry, just as we always wanted . . .*

Fate is a strange thing, the way it suddenly intervenes – for better for worse, for richer for poorer . . .

That same afternoon, Beaumont called through the door of his office to James lying on the grass outside. 'Those bastards at HQ! Whenever I ask for anything, they give me the opposite.' He emerged furiously waving a signal flimsy. 'Look at this! The swine are taking you away!'

After embarkation leave, Second Lieutenant March to ferry Morane 3362 to St Omer on immediate posting to 188 Squadron.

On four days' leave at Jerningham, James found the village already changed. The factory, like every other manufacturer of aircraft in Britain, was booming. Jerningham simultaneously prospered and sorrowed, and found itself in the grip of rapid change. Families, according to his mother, were breaking up. The butcher's son had been killed at Verdun. The harness maker had shut up shop and volunteered for the Hampshire Yeomanry. Several village girls had gone off to work in munitions, Sarah's sister being one of them. They came home sometimes at weekends, swearing like troopers and setting their little brothers and sisters a terrible example.

Those villagers who stayed were, despite the war, better clothed and fed than they had ever been. They had more money in their pockets. His father said he'd never wrought so many fancy candlesticks in his life before. Anyone that had a spare room (and some according to his mother who hadn't) took in lodgers – mostly the mechanics that worked up at the factory. Mrs Mounsey, the postmistress, whose husband was now in the Navy, was very friendly with hers, and had been seen in the Jerningham Arms with him, and at a theatre in Southampton.

Up at the factory, James's father told him, six new sheds had been erected in the park, and four more were planned. There was a new office complex and a new road across the park being put down for the lorries. Every day, as James saw for himself, lorries made their way through the village to and from the factory. The verges and the hedges and the lower branches of the elms outside the church were browned by the fumes of this alien traffic.

'Go down the cellar both of you,' James ordered his parents, 'the moment you hear the air-raid warnings sound. All this expansion up at the factory will make the village a military target.'

At the factory and in the village, the only target that concerned them was the monthly output target. Jerningham was excelling itself. It had become a feather in Frederick's political hat, and a powerful weapon in his hand. Frederick's war record, as Lord Derby, the Secretary of State for War, pointed out on his appointment to the Joint Air War Committee, could hardly be bettered. Not only was Sir Frederick chairman of a company producing a type of aeroplane that the Admiralty and the War Office were literally fighting to possess, but he had turned his town house into a convalescent home for RFC officers, retaining only a small flat at the top of the house as a *pied-à-terre* for attendance at the House of Commons.

The Park Lane house was only one of half a dozen homes run by a ladies' committee chaired by Diana Nazier, who still found time to put on *tableaux vivantes*.

'Divine,' Frederick had told her she looked as Athene in a classical tableau in St James's Park, taking her in the flat still in her goddess's green robe. Tireless in her efforts for him and for the country, Diana held dances for charity and organised parties of ladies to roll bandages and knit socks and balaclavas. Whenever he could spare the time, Frederick took senior Army and Navy

171

officers to Jerningham to inspect Ajax's progress. Necessarily, they had to be taken separately, as Henderson (for the Army) and Balfour (for the Navy) were engaged in a bitter fight with each other for the control of the air.

The War Committee collapsed in May under the strain and Lord Derby said that the only solution was the fusion of both Navy and Army services into one. In a storm of controversy and contention, the Air Board took its place. And on this, too, Frederick managed to get himself a seat.

All this competition was very good for business. Contracts for Ajax were signed impartially and equally with the War Office and the Admiralty. Balloon and airship work continued. Amelia was always looking for extra staff. Goldbeater girls were as scarce as the proverbial gold dust. Diana Nazier had suggested she might recruit some East End women for Jerningham, but Amelia had curtly refused any assistance from that quarter.

Numbers employed up at the Hall, his mother told James, had topped 300. They had a scheme to train girl mechanics. What would happen next? It was another of Lady Haybury's queer ideas, of course.

The only sign of Amelia that James saw was the silver-grey Rolls-Royce. Walking with his mother on the last evening of his leave, he saw it approaching the Hall gates along the Haybury road. It was driven by a dark-haired good-looking man in a tweed suit, the same no doubt whom James had seen from the Rumpetty.

'That's Mr Cummings, Lady Haybury's designer.'

'He's young.'

'But ever so clever they say. Got ever so many qualifications. I'm surprised he's by himself.' His mother's voice was sharp with meaning. 'He's usually got Lady Haybury with him.'

'And I'm surprised,' James felt himself suddenly consumed by a bitter and irrational resentment, 'that he isn't at the Front!'

Next day, he caught the first train back to Dillington.

FOUR

Early next morning, still bitterly resentful of Cummings, James took Morane 3362 off Dillington Aerodrome, flew over to Eastbourne and lined up with the shaft of the huge white arrow cut in the grass of Beachy Head pointing east to St Omer, the RFC headquarters and aircraft park.

No matter the wind, hang on to the course the arrow gives you. That was RFC navigation.

It worked. He arrived slightly south because of the northerly beam wind, landed softly and taxied over to a crowd of Sopwith Pups and BE2s.

Scrambling out of the cockpit he walked over to the headquarters tent, and reported in. There was a Crossley tender, he was told, just outside the main gate which would take him to Blaize Farm where 188 Squadron was stationed.

Beside the corporal driver, the tender had only one other occupant, a round faced youth with baby blue eyes, a girlish mouth, and blond hair. On the breast of his RFC uniform was attached a pair of pristine new wings.

If ever there was an example of Fokker fodder, James thought, he was looking at one now. His resentment against Cummings deepened. Cummings stayed at home dancing attendance on Amelia while boys like . . .

'What's your name?' he asked, sitting down opposite the youth.

'Barford Reynolds.' The youth spoke with an American accent, but quite unlike Cody's, the only other American James knew. 'My friends call me Babe.' He extended his hand.

'I can't think why,' James gave a small smile. The youth smiled engagingly back. He had a surprisingly hard grip, and a reassuringly strong chin. A lad of contradictions, James decided. 'Are you American?'

'Yes, sir. But I trained with the RFC.'

'What on earth possessed you to come?'

The youth shrugged.

'I hope you know what you're letting yourself in for.'

'Oh, I've been around, I guess.'

'But for how long?'

'Nineteen years and eleven months. I aim to make it to twenty-one.'

'Then you'll need thirty times the luck of the average pilot,' James said, worried by the youth's naïvety.

'Jesus wept.' Babe's blue eyes widened.

'And goes on weeping.'

The American smiled with the superiority of extreme youth, 'I guess it's gonna have to get better.'

'Not before it gets worse.'

The American shook his head slowly at James's pessimism. Smiling he said, 'I'll make it. As the Good Book says, the Lord looks after fools and drunkards.'

'It says nothing of the sort,' James snorted. Babe Reynolds would need looking after, that much was certain. And in the absence of the Good Book's promise that task would probably be his. He stared out of the window. They were turning off the main road now on to a narrow bumpy track that followed the bank of the River Lys. He stared out at the slow moving grey of its waters.

In a moment or two they both spied a wind sleeve, then six curved canvas Bessoneau hangars. Just before they reached a large red brick house, one after the other five Moranes came in over the hedge-top and landed. The driver announced, 'Blaize Farm. 188 Squadron HQ.'

A batman came out to collect their bags and conduct them to room 8, a small one at the back of the farmhouse with a couple of trestle beds and a view of the orchard. The apple trees were in bud. For a moment, James stood staring at them, wondering if this insouciant ignorant youth would be still alive when the apples came.

'The office is on the first floor, that way,' the batman said, 'Major Calthorpe is expecting you.'

James led the way up some ricketty stairs. From a door at the end of the landing appeared another boy who introduced himself as Major Calthorpe. He took them into a room lined with filing cabinets and long-legged Kirchener nudes cut from *La Vie Parisienne*.

'Take a pew!'

He asked about their hours on Moranes. He brightened at James's sixty-one, but made a face at Reynolds' two.

'Have a cigarette?'

Neither of them smoked. The young Major lit one and inhaled deeply.

'Our main opponent here is Boelcke's staffel in Fokker Eindekkers.'

He appeared to be waiting for them to make some comment. When neither of them said anything, he asked, 'How does that strike you?'

Babe said, 'OK.'

The Major looked at him sadly and inhaled deeply again.

'Fortunately, we're on stand-off tomorrow. You better take a couple of Moranes up and get your bearings.' Then he leaned back in his chair and called out, 'Grandpa!'

A plump red-faced man with thinning grey hair came in from the next office through the open door.

'Couple of new boys. March and Reynolds.'

He smiled and shook hands.

'Grandpa's our recording officer. Writes up combat reports. He'll chalk up all those' – he gave them rather a forced smile – 'Fokkers you're going to shoot down.' He looked at his watch. 'Drinking time already! Everyone'll be down at the Café de Paris.' He leaned across for his cap. 'Coming, Grandpa?'

'Not tonight.' James saw a shadow cross his face. 'Some letters to finish.'

They piled into the CO's car, and bumped away from the farmhouse towards Merville. Long shadows of poplars striped the fields. The town was badly bombed. 'Not exactly like its London namesake.' Calthorpe slowed to a stop in the main square. 'But the women are not exactly offputting and the wine is tolerable.'

174

It was packed. The atmosphere was dusky and thick with cigarette smoke. Three candles flickered on a marble-topped table. The floor was wet with wine.

'*Garçon, trois fines.*'

'*Oui, Monsieur.*'

Suddenly they were surrounded by oily leather coats and battered caps. 'The boys.'

A string of introductions were effected. A man of about twenty-seven with a leathery brown skin and a broken boxer's nose, held out his hand and said in an Australian drawl, 'Maddox.'

'Mad Maddox,' his friends chorused.

A blonde curled round the neck of an Irishman named Paddy Craig smiled seductively at Reynolds. '*Américain?*'

'*Non, mam'selle.*' Babe blinked his eyes innocently. '*Je suis Français.*'

She pouted. '*Li – ai – re!*'

Everybody laughed.

A brunette slipped her arm round his waist. '*J'aime les Américains!*'

'*J'aime les Françaises,*' Babe replied.

She stood on tiptoe and kissed him. '*Quel galant!*'

'And you, *mon vieux*,' a plump girl with milkmaid's blue eyes asked James. '*Pilote?*'

He nodded. He was thinking that her eyes were almost the same colour as Amelia's, but they lacked the strange sweet depths of hers.

'The farmer's daughter,' Calthorpe whispered. 'Name of Françoise. Bounces higher than a Morane.'

'*Vous avez une femme?*'

'She's proposing, old chap! Be careful!'

'*Tu es si serieux! Je suis très jolie, n'est pas?*'

'He doesn't understand French, Françoise! *Garçon, trente-et-un fines!*'

The wine flowed. The atmosphere became thicker. More girls arrived.

'*Vive la France!*'

'*Vive Boelcke!*'

'*Vive me!*'

The hangar doors opened.

' . . . nose dropped. Straightaway into a spin . . . '

'It was a Fokker, I tell you!'

'. . . gave him a long burst. Closed right in. Then the bloody Lewis jammed!'

' . . . a DFW. I saw it hit.'

' . . . he half-rolled. But I had him in my sights and . . . '

A wrestling match started. Someone poured a bottle of wine over Paddy Craig and all the girls started licking it off his cheeks. Babe Reynolds was upended and slung from one to the other like a rugby ball. James kept a wary eye on him, but he seemed to be enjoying it. Bottles hurtled against the wall. Babe caught one, put it to his lips and drained it.

Bit by bit, James collected the past history of 188 Squadron. Calthorpe had only been the CO for a fortnight. There had been a Major Driver before him, a South African before him. The room they were occupying in the farmhouse had belonged to two Canadians – both shot down by Eindekkers over the weekend. Those letters Grandpa was writing . . .

175

The blonde was sitting on Babe's knee, stroking the back of his neck. *'Quel age as tu, mon petit?'*

'Cent-et-un.'

'Li – ai – re! Tu es Bébé! J'adore les Bébés!'

There were rooms upstairs. Couples were disappearing. A man called Daly who had been drinking Vichy water all evening went over to the ricketty piano in the corner, and began thumping the tune of the 'Tarpaulin Jacket'. Everyone roared out:

> A young aviator lay dying
> And as in the wreckage he lay . . .

Above the din, Calthorpe was shouting out hints to James and Reynolds on the Eindekker. 'Remember he has two guns. Slower than the Morane. But lighter and just as manoeuvrable. Don't for God's sake let him get on your tail!' He was drinking wine by the tumbler now. 'Don't ever let him see you're afraid of him!'

> . . . take the cylinder out of my kidneys,
> The connecting rod out of my brain . . .

'Most of our work is escorting BE2s over the Somme to photograph. The Huns rarely come over here now, but as soon as we're over their side, you'll see them . . . real circus, all brightly coloured red, blue, green, silver . . . looping and rolling and gambolling like new born lambs, waiting for us . . . '

> . . . from the small of my back, take the camshaft,
> And assemble the engine again . . .

'The Morane's all right, of course. We're lucky to have Moranes. When I see those poor chaps in BE2s and those pusher monstrosities FE8s, Christ, how I damn the Royal Aircraft Factory and thank God for the French! Ajax, that was the aircraft you were flying when you got that Zep, wasn't it? Seems just what we need here!'

'The Jerningham factory hopes to be in production soon.'

'Good! *Garçon, trente-et-un fines!'*

It was getting late; the candles were burning low. In spite of the horseplay, the roaring of the songs, the drinking and the swaggering, and the boasting of 188 Squadron's exploits, James sensed underneath the uncertainty. Not fear, but a resigned fatalism. They know the Fokker Eindekker is better than the Morane, he thought. They don't really believe that over a term they've got a chance. And they're a bit apprehensive of the Morane itself. All those stories of it being dangerous have left their mark.

' . . . be careful not to take a Morane vertical.' Calthorpe conscientiously still doing his stuff to save their necks. 'And no aerobatics, mind!'

The bottle-breaking had stopped. Two of the girls were asleep, huddled against the oily leather flying jackets. From the piano now, a yearning hymn-tune note was coming.

. . . when this bloody war is over
Oh, how happy we shall be . . .

The *patronne* was shutting up shop. Everyone was trying to get a lift back to the farmhouse in Calthorpe's car.

' . . . no, Paddy, ladies first. New boys second! Drunks last!'

Eventually eight bodies crowded in, half-hanging out of the windows. Two more lay on the roof, Françoise, the farmer's daughter, was spread half on James and half on Babe's knee. Springs squeaking, slowly the car moved off.

Goodbyeee . . . don't cryee
There's a silver lining in the skyee

Intermittent moonlight spotted the road. It shone on the bend of the river, on the curved canvas Bessoneau hangars, on the solitary wind sleeve, on the row of silent Moranes.

'Time to get up, Sir!'

James lay in the soft warmth with his eyes closed for a few seconds more, listening to the batman clattering along the corridor, Reynolds' bed creaking, the rasp of a match, the pop the oil lamp made when it was lit.

'What's the weather like, Babe?'

'OK.'

James swung his legs out of the feather bed and began dressing. Three pairs of socks, vest and trousers pulled over his pyjamas, tunic and Sam Browne, feet into thigh-length sheepskin boots. He grabbed his Sidcot flying suit, two pairs of silk and one pair of furlined leather gloves, scarf, balaclava, helmet, goggles and loaded revolver and followed Babe downstairs.

Calthorpe and Mad Maddox were already halfway through breakfast.

'Escorting six photographic BE2s at 11,000 over Pozières beyond the Somme,' the Major said, 'Babe leading on their left. You, James, on their right. Maddox and I'll guard your tails.'

The new boys' position, the lot of the inexperienced. The American caught James's eye and smiled. For the last week, that had been their role. Get some more hours in on the Morane. Get your bearings over the French countryside. It had been in many ways an idyllic existence. The sun had come out. When they weren't flying, they were stretched on deckchairs in the orchard under the apple trees. Most mornings they joined the others after the dawn patrol, swimming naked in the grey waters of the Lys.

The same insouciant attitude to life continued. Two Moranes crashed on landing, but nobody was killed. Even when Paddy was shot down in flames over Hunland and the Germans came over and dropped a note to say he'd been shot down by Boelcke in his blue Fokker and had been buried with full military honours, the squadron considered it quite an honour.

James downed his coffee and stood up. 'Ready, Babe?'

'Yep.'

In the darkness outside, the four Moranes were waiting. Over in the east, there was a faint glow of pink and yellow. Everything seemed very still. James strapped himself in his plane, started up, taxied forward with an Ack Emma on each wing. They took off two by two, new boys first, climbed to 11,000 and found the chocolate-coloured BE2s. Then they formed up and flew over the lines, solemn as a church procession.

It had grown rapidly lighter. Underneath, James could see bottle-green woods, yellow slabs of pockmarked clay, the zigzag of sandbagged trenches, barbed wire, shell holes. Ahead four Hun observation balloons were being rapidly drawn down.

A sudden loud cr-u-um-p. The Morane's wings shook. A puff of white smoke had appeared on his left, followed by another. James kept moving his head, left, right, up, behind. Still only the BE2s on his left and Calthorpe behind him. Pozières – a shattered village beside a muddy stream.

The BEs' leader, white streamers trailing from his struts, began a slow turn to the left. James turned with them. The next second, he heard the rattle of machine-guns, saw a star-shaped crack on his windscreen, glimpsed behind him Babe chasing the red Eindekker off his tail. Then it was a mad merry-go-round of dancing colours – chocolate, red, white, blue, silver.

A round blur of propeller was coming head on at him. Just before he fired, he saw the curved wingtips of a Morane. On his left, he felt the slipstream of a BE, swooping inches above him. Then there was a sudden lull. The BEs began heading for home. James turned west with them and landed back at Blaize Farm.

The BE2s had all returned. But one Morane was missing. With a sinking heart, he saw there was no sign of Babe. James spent a miserable half-hour pacing up and down, listening for the sound of an engine.

Then he heard it. Unmistakably a Morane. It materialised out of the clear sky and landed with more speed than style. Apparently Babe had become involved with a red Eindekker.

'Why didn't you keep with us?' Calthorpe was furious, 'As I told you?'

Babe shrugged, 'I guess I couldn't get away.'

'You could have broken off!'

'He wouldn't let go. No, Sir! No way.'

'You're no bloody match for them. Just remember that. Christ, these Boelcke boys are good.'

Babe hung his head and said, 'Amen!'

'He could have got to you on your first bloody patrol!'

'But he didn't. The Lord looks after . . . '

Calthorpe cut him short with, 'Inexperienced pilots like you the Huns have for breakfast! Next time we go up, *you'll* . . . ' He became aware of the recording officer behind him, 'Yes, Grandpa?'

'Merville battery on the telephone, Sir.'

'What about?'

'A red Eindekker. They saw it crash in flames.'

The news travelled fast. Guarding the stairs to their bedroom was the farmer's daughter carrying an enormous bouquet of flowers with a note – *Félicitations au Lieutenant Reynolds.*

Next day, Reynolds got another Eindekker, then two more a week later. And after each victory, a bouquet of marigolds appeared by his bed from the farmer's daughter.

Bit by bit, James learned the origins of Babe's skill. He came from a rich oil-owning Ohio family. For his eighteenth birthday he had been given a Curtiss biplane. With this, to the disgust of his family, he had gone into the flying circus business – stunt flying, wing-walking, aerobatics, he'd done them all over every big city in America.

He was also a fanatic on gunnery. Shooting, not flying, brought a plane down he told James. Both of them spent hours on a makeshift firing range they rigged up at the bottom of the orchard. Last thing every night, they both worked on their machines, tuning up engines with the fitters, adjusting the wires with the rigger as delicately as a violin, going over their guns with the armourer, examining the ammunition for duds, checking the deflector plates on the propeller blades for damage.

Most days they flew both morning and evening. Babe's score mounted. But it was not till the last day of June that James shot down his first German – and then it was only a lumbering old Halberstadt.

Now the roads round Blaize Farm were clogged with ammunition lorries and marching men. It was no surprise when General Trenchard suddenly arrived in his staff car, sat on his shooting-stick under the apple trees with the squadron gathered around him and told them that in the next few hours there would be a big attack on the Somme, in which they would be supporting the British Fourth Army.

Next morning, the squadron took off in three vics of five. At exactly seven o'clock it was as though the grey mud veined by trenches below them exploded. From 11,000 feet James stared down through the heat haze at what looked like a vast cotton field. He could actually see the howitzer shells, feel the rush of air, hear them sobbing like porpoises before they did their death dive, and the thunder of the explosions. Then the landmines went off like volcanoes erupting.

Fifteen minutes later, he saw thousands of little figures like ants moving forward. The next moment he and the others were in a dogfight with a dozen Eindekkers.

That day both Babe and James shot down two German fighters. But the squadron lost three Moranes, as 188 Squadron flew inches above the trenches, trying to differentiate khaki uniforms from grey.

So began the Battle of the Somme. A few yards of ground were gained that first day at the cost of 100,000 British casualties.

For the next four months, the fighting continued. Some days, 188 dropped 100–pound bombs on gun emplacements. Some days, they escorted photographic reconnaissance BE2s. Some days they were given their heads and allowed to roam in Hunland, strafing trenches, shooting down observation balloons, machine-gunning aerodromes. But the lines on the ground didn't advance. And the squadron lost more aircraft.

On 15 September, 188 were ordered off on a secret job, guiding tanks and reporting their position to HQ.

From 500 feet, James stared fascinated at the lopsided diamond-shapes hauling themselves out of shellholes and through barbed wire on their caterpillar tracks, firing 2.2 shells from swivelling turrets. Flers-Courcelette, Combles and Thiepval were promptly captured by infantry following behind them. But there were too few tanks, and the advance was not maintained.

The stalemate continued. As autumn approached a brilliant all-red Albatross began to make a deadly appearance. A woman was flying it – that was the first rumour – a German Joan of Arc. *Le Petit Rouge* was what the French pilots called it. Then a name was on every RFC flier's lips – Manfred von Richthofen, the Red Baron.

With the new name came a new technique. Vast circuses of 50 planes swooped down on the British Moranes, BE2s and Sopwith Camels.

188 Squadron fought back, but losses were heavy. When the November rains bogged the battle down in a sea of mud, Allied casualties were 600,000. The Germans had lost 369 aircraft, Trenchard had lost 782. Of the pilots in 188 Squadron in June, now only Calthorpe, Babe Reynolds and James March remained.

The evening that the continuous gunfire ceased and a hush fell over the Somme, Babe shot down his fourteenth Hun – a black-and-white Halberstadt.

That night, James woke up at the sound of the door opening. Soft footsteps tiptoed down the passage towards the wing where the farmer's family lived. Looking across the room, he saw glowing in a jam-jar the marigolds of Babe's fourteenth bouquet.

But the American's bed was empty.

FIVE

It's in high places, son, as well as low. What goes on in Jerningham these days, I'd blush to write! The girls showing their ankles, laughing and drinking even on Sundays, the men all shirkers from conscription. One of them was wearing a white feather a lady had given him as if it was a buttonhole! The noise is that bad at the Arms no one can sleep of a night. And up at the Hall last week, Lady Haybury had a dance for the aircraft workers. They were at it till four in the morning – she waltzing, they say, with her Mr Cummings. The terrible casualty lists don't seem to bother them. I counted nine black armbands in church last Sunday. But Mr Bingham preached a lovely sermon about our Victory on the Somme.

With her letter, his mother as usual had enclosed a number of newspaper cuttings. He read them, lying on his bed. The first was of a sermon Canon Newbold had preached in St Paul's Cathedral on how the nation was going to the devil, committing sins which could not with propriety be alluded to from the pulpit.

Another was a complaint from General Smith-Dorien on the scanty clothes of chorus girls and songs of a ribald character in the music halls. The troops did not want this sort of entertainment, the General asserted. Indeed he was the recipient of numerous complaints from the troops themselves. The Devil, he concluded, had entered the soul of the country and we would never again see the Garden of Eden Britain was before the war.

'For some,' James said, crumpling up that one and throwing it in the wastepaper basket. 'For some!'

As was her wont, his mother had included an uplifting poem which seemed to contradict her earlier moral pessimism,

> And bless that land whose gracious hand e'er opens wide her door,
> To welcome in the widow wronged, the orphan and the poor.
> Where lurks the coward base who shirks to to strike the righteous blow,
> For English hearths and English graves against the foreign foe.

On the back there was a newspaper cartoon of Asquith and Haldane being kicked out of office under the title *Petticoat Government*. The war was in dire straits. After intrigue and counter-intrigue, Lloyd-George had taken over.

Her last cutting, a large picture headlined *The Brave Cardinal of Rheims* showing an old man standing in a shaft of light through that magnificent rose window. Underneath was the caption, *Cardinal Lucan who refuses to leave his beloved cathedral. The Germans shelled it for three days after their Verdun defeat.*

Rheims! Just for a moment, James closed his eyes and was back there on that golden sunlit 1909 evening with Amelia again. For a moment he allowed himself to remember her fierce kiss, the taste of her tears, the warmth of her body. 'What's the hold up, James?'

Babe was calling up to him from the bottom of the stairs. He and Calthorpe had just come back from St Omer in the Crossley in a state of some modest jubilation. Their purpose in going there had been to beg for Ajaxes to replace their ancient Moranes, now no match against the Albatrosses of the Richthofen circus. They got no replacements, but they were told that both of them and James had been awarded the DSO and now they were off to the Café de Paris for a combined celebration of their decorations and Christmas.

'Coming now.'

Calthorpe drove with James beside him. Most of the squadron pilots on stand-off, together with Françoise, were squeezed into the back. But for James, the evening for many reasons was not a success. The laughter and the horseplay seemed strained. He would, like the other two, have traded the decorations for aircraft which would match the Red Baron's. He thought of the unrealistic attitude at home compared with the reality here. And he thought of Amelia and their own unrealistic dreams.

'One thing, James,' Calthorpe said as they returned rather more sober than usual. 'Things are bound to get better in 1917.'

But they didn't. Calthorpe was posted to HQ at St Omer. Babe Reynolds was given command of 87 Squadron at Vert Galand. James found himself in charge of 188 Squadron and a lot of new pilots.

Once the winter thawed and the weather improved, Richthofen's circus operating from Douai began shooting them down like newly fledged pheasants. Abruptly, the whole gentlemanly attitude of the air war had disappeared. April that year was called Bloody April; hundreds of RFC pilots and observers were killed. The one bright gleam of hope was that America declared war on Germany. But few believed that American forces would arrive in time. Meanwhile night after night, tight-lipped, James wrote what words of comfort he could to the relatives of those green young boys in England.

The blood was not only shed in France. The big Gotha bombers had taken over the destructive work of the Zeppelins, which rarely made an appearance now. Once British aircraft were fitted with superchargers to get them up to 20,000 feet and explosive bullets like James's firework rockets, had been invented which ignited the highly inflammable hydrogen, the airships' war was over.

The Gothas were much more lethal. On 25 May 1917, twenty-one of them, flying in tight formation, each equipped with three machine-guns to ward off fighters, made a daring daylight raid on London.

Finding the city shrouded in morning mist, the Gothas dropped their load of 600 pounds of bombs apiece on a busy street in the centre of Folkestone. It was crowded with families doing their shopping; 200 people, including 37 children, were killed. A furious attack on the government immediately ensued.

'Public opinion will force the government to act, Lady Haybury,' said the good-looking young man sitting opposite Amelia in the Jerningham design office the following Monday morning. 'You mark my words. They'll allocate priority to Ajax.'

The prototype Ajax fighter had flown, but due to hold-ups on materials everywhere, they were slow in production. At Jerningham, Amelia had

182

decided the factory should still go on working during the morning of the Whit holiday, though the afternoon would be free for those who wished to go to the annual Whitsun Tide, which had taken place at Haybury for hundreds of years.

'I have learned to mark your words, Ronald,' Amelia smiled gently and affectionately. 'You tell me to often enough.'

It was indeed the new designer's favourite phrase. As if he knew he was clever, but lacked enough poise for his words to be given their true weight.

In the year since the board had appointed him, Ronald Cummings had gained a good deal of maturity. But he was still fresh and enthusiastic, and at times engagingly dogmatic. When the orders for Ajax began to come in, Amelia had no Charles Rolls to turn to, so she had advertised in *Flight Magazine*. The first man appointed had lasted only one month. Coming out of an aeronautical meeting a richly dressed lady had handed him a white feather. He had joined up under the Kitchener recruiting drive six weeks later. Her re-advertisement had brought Cummings, one of the assistant designers at Sopwith, to her. He was twenty-two at the time of the appointment, a graduate of London. He was a slim compactly build man, with dark brown eyes, and a wide intelligent mouth. He had elderly parents living in Westmorland, but no other family, and few friends. Amelia had taught him how to polka and how to waltz and how not to show when he felt shy and uncomfortable. He was devoted to her. Neither wild horses nor white feathers would drive him from Jerningham.

'And what does Sir Frederick think of these raids?' Ronald asked her.

'He hasn't said. But he'll be as appalled as we all are. Where will it all end?'

Ronald Cummings shook his head. 'But you are not expecting him today? For the Tide?'

'No.'

'Shall you go yourself?' And after a pause. 'The locals tell me one of the family usually goes.'

'Probably.'

'In that case, Lady Haybury, may I . . .'

He flushed an uncomfortable red. However poised he had become with other people he was still vulnerable with her.

'You may, Ronald,' she smiled. 'In fact, I'd be glad of your company.'

'I suppose *my* company wouldn't be enough,' Sarah said, aggrieved, as after lunch that day she donned a straw hat decorated with marigolds and yellow ribbons. It was part of country tradition that everyone, especially the young-sters, had new clothes for Whit. Sarah, the recipient of Amelia's cast-offs was dressed to kill.

She was now twenty-six. She had grown into a bonny woman with humorous hazel eyes and a firm mouth. Years ago, Amelia had despatched her to a Harley Street dentist who had worked wonders with her teeth. Sarah had many admirers – Burton, the Jerningham butcher among them, much to Cook's delight in these days of shortages – but she knew what dirty beasts men were and kept them all at arms' length. It was a pity Master Charles would have to grow into being a man, she often said. But he'd be the exception.

Nevertheless she had no objection to the admiring glances that came her way as she followed her mistress and Ronald Cummings round the fair.

Perhaps because of the state of the war, perhaps because of the free refreshment, more crowds than ever had come this year.

There were all sorts of entertainments – swings, a carousel, a rifle range, a coconut-shy. There was a boxer offering a golden guinea for any man who could fight him for five rounds, a two-headed lamb, an ape-man, a performing bear, a fire-eater, and half a dozen fortune tellers' tents.

'You could hardly believe there's a war on,' Ronald Cummings smiled, as Amelia pressed a crown into Sarah's hand, and told her to go off and enjoy herself.

'I can believe there's a war on,' Amelia said shortly.

Two nights before, when a strong southwest wind had been blowing, people had heard the faint but terrible reverberation of guns. Now her eyes were irresistibly drawn to the black armbands so many people wore on their new Whitsun clothes. And from them, as they strolled further, to the long queue of people waiting outside the fortune tellers' tents. As the casualty lists lengthened, the clairvoyants had flourished. And not only did they acquire new converts, but they also acquired fraudulent mediums who preyed on the bereaved.

'I've been in, M'lady, to Princess Azdenia.' Sarah rushed up to her an hour later. 'She's a real gipsy. And she's ever so good. She told me all about my mother dying. And my father marrying again . . . though I knew he would, I must say. She said our Jenny would marry again. Rich, this time. You should go. I've never seen her before. But she's good . . . she said ever such nice things about me. And there aren't so many waiting now.'

'You mark my words, they'll tell you a load of rot,' Cummings smiled indulgently as Amelia handed him her smart parasol to hold, and pulled her veil tightly down over her face. 'Or as they did with Sarah, they'll tell you what you know already. That you're beautiful, successful, rich. That you have everything in the world.'

He was wrong. The wizened gispy sitting behind the star-spangled table was old and shrewd. Amelia was aware of coal-black eyes studying her as her own eyes accustomed themselves to the dusky interior. The tent was lined with black material spangled with a travel worn moon and fraying stars. The tent smelled of whisky and violet cachous. The gipsy woman wore an Indian-like garment, a headscarf stitched with gold coins; when she spoke it was with an Irish accent. She requested a shilling, dropped it in a tobacco tin on the table, and took Amelia's hand.

She grunted and sniffed over it, sighing, closing her eyes, opening them suddenly wide. Then she held a smoky crystal ball in her hands, tightly at first then gesturing over it as if waving its unwelcome visions away. She looked intently at Amelia and said in a hoarse voice, 'He ain't dead, my pretty. That's what you wanted to know, ain't it?'

She had probably said the same to a hundred women that afternoon, but Amelia said as if hypnotised, 'Yes.'

'But he'll die, my pretty. Sure as you sit here, he'll die.'

'In the war?' Amelia asked humbly.

'In the war? Oh, aye. What else? But not yet awhile. The war'll give him ter ye for a while. Not long. Then the war'll tek him from yer.'

Amelia drove home to Haybury Hall almost in silence. She did not ask

Ronald in for a drink. She went early to bed but not to sleep. She dozed and dreamed and wakened from violent nightmares. Always the same nightmare. James crashing in an aircraft in a distant alien place and herself powerless to reach him.

Two weeks later in broad daylight, the Gothas penetrated to London itself. Londoners were horrified to see the bombers flying in a diamond pattern over the hazily sunlit city. Frederick hardly liked to leave Diana's side. Tons of bombs fell near London Bridge and Liverpool Street station, on East Ham, Islington and Bermondsey. Schools and houses, factories and offices were hit. Among the 574 people killed were 144 children. At an emergency Cabinet meeting, orders were given to expand the RFC from 108 to 200 squadrons.

When a similar Gotha raid followed on 7 July, public indignation amounted to hysteria. RFC officers travelling to the new airfields defending the capital were mobbed. Fists were shaken and stones thrown at ministerial cars. Hostile crowds gathered in Whitehall. When Frederick and Diana lunched at the Commons that Saturday, the talk was of nothing else. The Cabinet was meeting that very afternoon. The corridors of the Palace of Westminster seethed with excitement and agitation. Rumour was rife.

The casualties, rumour said, were greater even than in the previous raid. When it became known that Sir William Robertson, chief of the Imperial General Staff, had been summoned to the Cabinet meeting and that General Haig had been recalled from France, there were even rumours of surrender.

By a not quite fortuitous chance, Diana and Frederick met Sir William in the corridor after the meeting. Sir William had an eye for a beautiful face and Diana Nazier had a slight acquaintance with him. 'You look so strained,' she said sympathetically. 'Was it very dreadful?'

The Chief of Staff mopped his brow, 'You would have thought,' he said bitterly, 'that the whole world was coming to an end!' So it seemed. The impossible had happened. Not only was flying a reality, but so were those deadly battalions of the air. Death could rain down at any moment on the heart of the Empire, on women and children and unarmed men. The sun appeared to be setting on civilisation.

But for Amelia, opening a telegram in her office that evening, it was the dawn of an Indian summer day.

The telegram was from the War Office. It informed her briefly that a squadron of the RFC would occupy the airfield at Jerningham forthwith. At key places over Southern England squadrons of the RFC were arriving from France to defend the homeland and to allay public anger and disquiet. A two man committee, consisting of Lloyd-George and the South African General Smuts had been appointed in haste and alarm by the Cabinet to look into the Kingdom's air defence, and to try belatedly to deploy resources properly.

The number of the squadron was not stated in the telegram, but before Amelia had time to hope, the lorries of the advance party began trundling in with stores and ground equipment. Tents were put up, latrines dug, a drogue erected and the extended runway outlined with paraffin lamps. A signals' van, two fire tenders, a field kitchen and three ambulances followed.

'It's 188 Squadron,' Ronald Cummings put his head round Amelia's office door. 'Equipped with Moranes. I've just had a word with some of the ground crew. They've had a helluva mauling in France. Practically none of the seasoned pilots left.'

Just before a heavy sultry dusk, the Moranes flew in. Amelia telephoned Cook at Haybury and told her to keep dinner. Then she and Ronald Cummings watched the aircraft glide in from over the Solent. The sun had just set. One by one as the Moranes approached, their propellers caught the vanished rays and spun the fiery light into glittering webs.

'Shall we go and welcome them?' Amelia suggested lightly. 'It would be nice, don't you think?'

Her heart raced and her legs felt weak. She had no reason to suppose that James was still with 188 Squadron, she told herself. They never corresponded. She relied on Sarah's gossip, and her visits to church when she was always relieved to see Mrs March not dressed in black. The war would give him to her for a while, the fortune teller had said. Amelia wished she'd never visited her tent. Yet even without the fortune teller's predictions, she had a strange uncanny sense of James's nearness. Deliberately she slowed her steps as she and Ronald Cummings walked towards the newly erected squadron record tent.

Thunder clouds were building up over the Solent. The air was suddenly still. Sounds carried with that resonance before a storm – the whine of metal on metal, the grate of a saw, an aircraft engine running up and then faltering, men shouting, the fall of a hammer on a tent prop. The smell of newly turned earth mixed with the petrol, burned castor-oil and dope. The sounds and smells were of no great beauty, and yet just before Cummings lifted the tent flap, Amelia knew she would remember that moment for ever.

Cummings stood beside her as she blinked her eyes in the smoky light inside the tent. Everywhere Amelia looked were khaki clad strangers, laughing, smoking, drinking beer out of tin mugs. James, she told herself, sickened with disappointment, was not amongst them.

Then a broad pair of shoulders suddenly turned. James's eyes met hers above the heads of the rest of the squadron. He put down his mug and pushed his way towards her. She stayed where she was, unable to move. It was as if they had never been parted, and simultaneously as if she was seeing him and falling in love with him for that first fresh undimmed moment. Yet her first words after she had introduced him to Ronald Cummings were, 'You've changed.' Adding, 'You're so sunburned.'

'It was a hot summer,' he smiled grimly.

Despite his sunburn, he looked thinner and haggard. Even his heavy frame seemed to have fined down. His eyes were shadowed with experience. But he was relaxed with Cummings and his manner was easy. In a darker arena of life, he had acquired a sophistication more durable and less frivolous than they would ever have.

'Anyway, you don't change, Amelia.'

'I would hardly have recognised *you*.'

She knew that wasn't true. She would have recognised him blindfold. The spark was still there between them. She was almost afraid to touch him. 'I hope you'll come over to Haybury for dinner,' she heard herself asking him coolly. And as coolly he accepted, only his eyes betraying that he regarded this as anything more than the lady of the manor inviting the squadron CO to dine.

From then on, everything fell into its predestined place. Hurrying home ahead of James who promised to drive over in the squadron Crossley, she sent Pearson down to the cellar to bring up Frederick's best wines and brandy. She made Sarah rearrange the bowl of roses on the dinner table. She donned her best moiré dinner-gown.

She raised her glass and touched James's. 'To your homecoming!'

Then, warmed by the wine, made reckless by the long drawn-out suspense of the war, she told him about Frederick and Diana Nazier. She told him the truth but not the whole truth. She omitted all mention of Charles. James seemed unsurprised. He sat for a long time twirling the stem of his glass, staring at the polished mahogany of the table. 'You'd suspected it, of course?'

'Yes. But I didn't *know*.'

'And now that you *do* know?' He looked up at her levelly, 'Shall you divorce him?'

Dear James, she thought, everything is so unequivocal, so black and white to him. 'Do you want me to?'

'Yes.'

She threw truth to the winds, 'Then I probably will.' And in the same breath. 'Will you stay here tonight?'

He smiled. 'If you want me to.'

Arms round each others' waists, they went up to the big four-poster. He made love to her with a mingled fierceness and tenderness. When the threatened storm broke with midsummer fury, it seemed a part of their own tempestuous union. The lightning flickered through the curtains, threw strange shadows on the ceiling. After a while, they lay side by side watching them, drowsy, satiated and at peace as the last rolls of thunder rumbled away.

A spell of brilliant weather followed the storm. The Solent gleamed in unbroken sunlight. It was the weather for Gotha raids. At four o'clock that afternoon Jerningham RFC base became fully operational. The workmen linked the squadron telephones to the new headquarters set up at the Horse Guards in London. At five o'clock, there was a practice scramble. The klaxon sounded its three horns. Gulls and guillemots, mallards and peewits rose screaming from the grasslands and the saltflats, their clamour drowned by the noise of warming-up aircraft engines.

Everyone that wasn't actually employed getting the planes into the air spilled out of the huts and the tents, shading their eyes against the sunlight. Clumsy figures in flying kit lumbered towards the Moranes which the mechanics had manhandled on to the runway and started up.

A white Very light soared into the air. Immediately there came the sustained roar of 18 aircraft taking off together. Airborne, they formed themselves into a vic. Amelia watched them until they dwindled to the size of a skein of wild geese, then specks, then nothing at all.

They returned half an hour later, scrambled again and returned.

Tomorrow, James told her as they dined that evening, they would begin regular patrols. In between times they would be stood down. As Cummings had told her, the men were anxious to get up to London. According to James to see their families or take in a theatre.

'According to Ronald Cummings,' Amelia said, 'they're looking for women.

Prostitutes.' She eyed James teasingly.

He was not amused. 'You shouldn't,' he said as his mother might have done, 'talk like that, Amelia, to a boy of his age!'

She flushed.

'And what made you choose such a young fellow, come to that?' he asked her crossly.

His jealousy reassured her. She threw her arms round him. 'Because he was the only designer I could get. The one I *really* wanted refused to come.'

She brushed his lips with hers. He kissed her with mounting urgency. Then suddenly he held her away from him.

'Amelia,' he said huskily, 'I don't like this way of doing things. You *must* get a divorce. Promise?'

She was spared the necessity of answering. Across the hall in the library, the telephone could be heard faintly ringing. James leapt to his feet and had hurried over to answer it before Pearson, now slow of foot and hard of hearing, could get there.

When James returned, he had already picked up his cap from the hall and was turning it apologetically in his hands. Just for a second the old shy James was visible in the assured one like vanished youth in a wrinkled face. Her heart melted with love.

'Sorry, Amelia. Could I ask you to drive me back? We're to be on readiness as from two am.'

They drove in silence through the moon-bleached countryside.

'Are you remembering?' she asked.

Did he remember, she wondered, that was the heath where they had tried to fly the first Ajax, that stretch where they had crashed? The forge he could not forget nor the spire of the church, nor the gates at the empty lodge.

'I was remembering all right, Amelia,' he said at last as she pulled up at the front entrance of the Hall. Lights leaked out between the shutters. '*You* remember too, Amelia,' he said standing on the running board, 'remember what I said about getting a divorce. Things won't be right between us till you do!'

They were. Everything between them was right. It was wicked perhaps, she thought, in wartime. But as the summer days became a dazzling week, Jerningham took on a festive holiday air. Not all the men had gone to London to seek out women. Dozens of them had telephoned, written and telegraphed their families. And these families descended on Jerningham by car, by train, by horse and trap, many finishing the journey from the station on foot. They canvassed the village for accommodation. Expansive in her happiness, Amelia threw open the spare rooms at Haybury Hall.

The lodge, too, was used and some half-derelict cottages. Stacks of square mattress segments were loaned by RFC stores. A communal open-air kitchen was set up. The bakery in Jerningham did a roaring trade. So did the shops. Like Amelia, the village made fiesta before the onset of winter.

Jerningham Hall revived too. The officers held a party in the sitting-room. The sergeants held another in the old kitchen. The other ranks put down wood planking and danced in their tents. Charles was furious that the school summer holidays had not yet begun. Rather touchingly, Arthur wrote to ask her if she was all right on her own with all those soldiers and aviators. Dear Arthur! She wrote back affectionately and reassuringly.

Every day, the squadron patrolled at 15,000 feet. They had their designated beat from the Solent to Folkestone, looking for Gothas. They were not allowed to leave it except to attack bombers. They had practised Gotha attacks, perfected formation flying, devised tactics – but had seen nothing, while the Gothas penetrated to their targets in cloud.

'They'll send them back pretty soon, you mark my words,' Ronald Cummings said hatefully on the Wednesday. 'They're screaming out for them at the front. There's talk of a big push at Arras.'

Sometimes in the quiet hours of the night when James was on readiness, Amelia found herself unable to decide what to wish for. That the bombers shouldn't come. In which case he would be sent back to much heavier fighting. Or that they should come and perhaps James be killed.

The days when he was stood down became the best. 'Shall you take me to see your mother?' she asked him on the second Thursday.

He shook his head. 'She's old and cranky, my mother. Set in her ways. Thinks the morals are going to the dogs. Best wait till things are . . . more settled.'

Instead they took a picnic to the lake at old Cornford House where years ago they'd watched the earliest flight of the young swans. This time James provided the food from the officers' mess. Amelia parked the car on the road and they walked the rest of the way. The afternoon was hot and still. Nothing except the occasional stirring of a bird moved the yellowing rushes. Grasshoppers jumped from under their feet. Kingfishers flashed over the lake in dazzles of emerald and blue.

It was too late in the year to see baby cygnets. They were almost fully grown, grey, in-between adolescent. 'Like we were,' James said as they lay side by side on the dry coarse grass of the bank, watching the smooth V of their wake on the glassy water.

'But we're still the same, aren't we?'

'I suppose so.'

She rolled on to her side, rested her elbows on the ground, cupped her chin in her hands and studied his face intently. The sun felt warm between her shoulder blades. In a moment, they would move effortlessly and naturally towards one another. Her happiness would be total and complete.

A faint doubt niggled. 'You only suppose so? Does that mean you've changed?'

'You know it doesn't, silly.' He broke off a grass stalk and gently stroked her cheek with its feathery head. He said, half-mockingly, 'Anyway, *you* change a little, Amelia.'

'How?'

'You get more beautiful.'

'You're teasing me! You're not the dewdrop-giving kind. You must be teasing me!'

He shook his head. He pointed to a pair of fully grown swans, white and magnificent, with wings alert to strangers, sailing regally past the bank. 'That's us now. Those two.'

'Ah,' she bent forward and kissed his cheek, then the hollow of his throat.

'Swans mate for life.'

Before he pulled her tightly to him, he stared searchingly into her eyes. His own looked very blue in the sunlight, intent and piercing. 'That's why you must get a divorce,' he kissed her lips. His hands moved over her body.

'Oh, yes,' she shivered to his hands. 'Yes. Yes. Yes.'

'You agreed you would get a divorce.' A different James sat opposite Amelia at the dinner table the following evening. A more troubled, quite uncompromising James.

He had told her not to wait at Jerningham for him. He had made his own way to Haybury on a squadron bicycle, after the afternoon patrol. An abortive one again. They had seen nothing but naval vessels and a few permitted fishing smacks, and what looked like a battered convoy moving in. Yet while they performed their abortive patrols, there were rumours of a setback on the Front, clamour in the newspapers for more effective prosecution of the war, and talk in the mess of heavy RFC losses.

James felt restive and ashamed. He had called in again at the forge on his way to Haybury. He had bought some whisky for his father and some chocolates for his mother. She had aged almost beyond recognition. Even her tongue had lost its edge. Though she talked with some of her old fervour about the men of the village who had gone to the war, while Amelia kept her young fancy man at the Hall.

'Keep away from her, son!' she said as she kissed him goodbye. 'She'll bring you nought but trouble.'

'The trouble is,' Amelia said, putting down her spoon. 'I haven't really had time to think.'

'Haven't had time! Don't be ridiculous!'

'Well, I haven't.' Her cheeks flushed.

'That's not true!' He was angry now. 'I told you straight away. Get a divorce. You said yesterday, that you would.'

'It's just . . .'

'Oh, stop hedging, Amelia! You're such a compromiser! You don't know what you want! You can't tell me you've not had time to think. You made a stupid marriage. You must have often thought of divorce.'

She shrugged helplessly.

'After all this,' James went on in a low voice, 'surely you don't intend to carry on as before?'

When she said nothing he asked more sharply, 'Well, *do* you?'

'Frederick,' she said keeping her head bent and not looking at him, 'would never agree to a divorce.'

'So you *have* had time to think about it?'

'Yes.'

'And asked Frederick?'

'Yes.'

'*When* did you ask him?'

'Years ago. When I found out about Diana Nazier.'

'And he refused.'

'I've told you, yes, he refused.'

'He doesn't want to marry her?'

190

'So it would seem.'

'Yet you let me . . .' he began and broke off making instead some remark about the morals of high society.

Amelia pushed back her chair. 'You sound exactly like your mother.' She folded her arms and stood in front of him, an arm's length away.

He shot her a bitter look and went on, 'I could sound like worse people. *Make* him agree.'

'That's easier said than done.'

'If we are to continue, you *must*!'

She thought how impossible it was to tell him about Frederick's ultimatum about Charles. And here was what sounded like another ultimatum from him. 'Is that an ultimatum?'

'It is.'

She was caught – caught between them.

'Understand this, Amelia! I won't have a hole-and-corner affair! I won't be some society lady's lapdog!'

'And that's how you regard it?'

'What else? *You* tell *me*? If you won't make your husband free you, what else am I?'

She was too overwrought to find the right words, too angry to throw her arms round him. Instead she said, 'You have a low opinion of yourself and of me.'

'What else can I have? You want to have your cake and eat it. You won't give up your husband and his position. But you'll use his bed with me. What does that make us?'

She reached down and picked up her untouched glass. She dashed the wine into his face.

'I think you're saying,' she said, 'that it makes me a whore! Now get out of here! I never want to see you again, as long as I live!'

She threw open the dining-room door. She didn't even glance at him as he left. But she had already seen enough. Her aim had been poor. Most of the wine had been dashed on to his tunic and shirt front. There it spread in a dark red stain as if she had shot him through the heart.

That stain haunted her all night. She lay tossing and turning, drifting off into uneasy sleep. But in the morning, she awoke, resolved. She must see James and explain everything as best she could to him. Halfway to Jerningham, she heard the distant sound of engines, and a few minutes later out over the Solent, she saw the distant shapes like a skein of wild geese.

At the airfield itself, all was packing and flurry. The squadron, Ronald Cummings told her with relish, had been immediately recalled to the Front.

191

SIX

Back at Blaize Farm, James found a mood that matched his own. Now there was no more saluting German aircraft, no more dropping wreaths and messages on Hunland airfields. The mood was desperate, bitter, him or me. But for James there was an added spur. He flew and fought to prove himself to himself again.

His behaviour at Haybury had offended that innermost core of his being, an austerity and integrity, which was as necessary to his life as his love for Amelia. He had taken her believing her marriage was dead, that she would obtain a divorce, and that he did not steal like a thief into some other man's bed. Her refusal so to do had made him that, a thief and an adulterer, and worse showed him that she did not love him sufficiently to cut herself away from Frederick and her comfortable way of life. That he was her plaything, that her family and position came first, not him. Fighting was the only balm to his disillusionment and self disgust.

As soon as the circus formations appeared over the horizon, James dived into the centre of them. Then he would come as close as an adder to bite the victim that was in some strange way himself. The enemy pilot would be hypnotised by his slow nerveless progression even before he pulled the trigger on his machine-guns. Twice to the delight of the ground crew and his own indifference he landed with a German's blood on his windscreen.

Then as his score mounted and his self disgust eased, anger and revenge remained. Revenge for young Thwaites, standing up in his cockpit, his flying clothes on fire. Revenge for Brown, actually jumping from 10,000 feet. Revenge for Farquhar trapped in a spinning Morane. Revenge for Frederick and his possession of Amelia . . .

By the winter of 1917 he had killed and killed again. Eindekkers, Halberstadts, Fokkers, Albatrosses spun smoking into the ground. But there was one German aircraft that continually eluded him as effectively as Amelia – a bright gold Fokker triplane that once a week flew over the British lines taking photographs, flaunting its lone presence by streaming smoke.

That was called a vapour trail, the meteorological officer had told him the first time he took off to attack. The triplane must be flying very high.

How high James had not realised till the power on his engine began fading, his climb slowed and stopped. And there he was, flapping about at 19,000 feet with the gold triplane still above him, calmly and boldly carrying out its photography.

He stripped the Morane of all weight except one gun. Again and again, he tried to reach it. Again and again he became stuck in thin air, ice-cold himself

192

and gasping for breath, still 2000 feet below the triplane.

He tried a Camel and the new SE5 with the same result. There was only one aircraft that would have the height to do it – Ajax. And he kept up a continuous verbal bombardment of Calthorpe at Amiens to get 188 re-equipped with them before the expected German offensive in the spring.

At home, news from the Front dominated the closing of the year. Held them like puppets on strings, it seemed to Amelia. Especially her, scanning the lengthening casualty lists making contrived visits to the forge, ostensibly for this to be soldered or that to be rivetted, but really searching for news. They'd had a few letters, Mr March told her, but James didn't say much. He was well, and that, he supposed was all his mother and he needed to know. Leave? No, he hadn't mentioned leave.

Every night she lay in the big double bed praying, willing that James would come once more, so that she could explain to him. She conducted a bargaining, bartering dialogue with the Almighty. Only let James return so that he knew why she couldn't get a divorce and she would mend her ways, be devout, uncritical. For James to be killed now, irreconciled to her, would be like a Catholic dying outside a state of grace.

Honouring her side of the bargain, she took to going to church every Sunday. The church was always full but there was so much black. And even in little Jerningham, so many to pray for. The family of Able Seaman Albert Baines, once the cox of the lifeboat, the grocer's son killed at Poperinghe – on the rector droned and feverently they prayed, week by week, wondering which dreaded names they would pray for next.

Once Mr March showed her a photograph taken at an airfield called St Marie Cappel. Then James was moved up to the Arras. The next time she visited the forge, Mrs March came hobbling in on a stick. In a voice as dry as gunpowder, she told Amelia she had cut out a letter from the *Hampshire Gazette*. Lady Haybury might like to read it. She handed her a square of newspaper. It was headed *Average life of pilots at the Front now three days*.

'D'you think that's true?' she asked Ronald Cummings.

'Only with the inexperienced ones.'

'And the experienced ones?'

'The longer they survive the better their chances. It's like everything else. You get the hang of it.'

She flashed him a grateful smile. 'Besides they've had pretty rotten equipment. D'you remember the song the squadron sang when they were here?'

She shook her head. 'I never heard it.'

'Well, I won't treat you to a rendering. But the tune's "And they called it Dixieland", and it's about the Factory BE2s.'

'Soon they'll have Ajaxes.'

'The lucky ones.'

It was the cue for her to work harder than ever. The orders came steadily in. During October, the Cabinet established the War Priorities Committee. Powerful men served under the chairmanship of General Smuts. Frederick became one of its political secretaries. There was talk that a separate Air Force might be formed, and though Field Marshal Haig opposed such an innovation and the idea turned the Admiralty apoplectic, the committee was agreed on wanting more aircraft and balloons. And Diana Nazier was assiduous in her pursuit of orders for what she called 'Frederick's factory'.

'The danger is always of strikes.' Cummings sighed. 'You've heard of the strike at Woolwich?'

'I've heard.' Amelia said, 'But that's dreadful and dangerous work! Ours isn't.'

'Ours is more precision work. More taxing.'

'Perhaps. But we keep such good labour relations.'

'Nevertheless you can't expect the staff to work all hours.'

'We can if we pay them enough.'

Amelia made that her philosophy. Work double for double pay.

'And what is *your* incentive, Lady Haybury?' Ronald asked her just before Christmas. 'What is your double pay?'

'The prosecution of the war,' she answered lightly. 'Anyway, I might ask you the same.'

'But you would already know the answer.' He smiled quietly. And then seeing her faint flush, went on to ask her if her husband and sons were coming to Haybury for Christmas.

'The boys certainly. They can't wait. Don't let Charles pester you! He can be a terrible nuisance.'

'On the contrary, I enjoy having him around. I think I'm a teacher *manqué*. He shows real aptitude. He'll be a designer himself, I shouldn't wonder.'

'He wants to be a pilot.'

'Don't they all? Anyway he can just about fly already.'

'He's hoping the war will go on another four years.' She looked at Cummings half-humorously, half-seriously. 'Charles and I pester the Almighty with contrary pleas.'

Ronald smiled. 'The Almighty will give judgment to you, I think.'

'Oh, I do hope so! Though Charles will be heartbroken if he misses it.'

'The Navy takes them at thirteen.'

She shuddered.

'And how about Arthur?'

'Not him. He doesn't want the war to go on. He's a quiet soul. He fights with Charles but is good with everyone else. I never quite understand him. I'm sure he's thinking, but I never know what. I never know what he's feeling come to that. Perhaps I don't spend enough time with either of the boys. Arthur much less than Charles these days. I'm a neglectful mother.'

She tried that holiday to make up, to repair her own maternal image of herself. But circumstances were against her. On Christmas Eve, Frederick arrived at Haybury Hall accompanied by Diana Nazier. The five of them descended to the depleted servants' hall for their Christmas Eve party. Frederick was on his best behaviour, enquiring about Sarah's sister, now working in munitions. About her uncle, a prisoner in Germany, and Gower the footman whom no one seemed to know about except that he'd joined the colours under Lord Derby's recruiting drive. He shook his head over Addison who had returned from the Somme with shell-shock, and they drank a toast to Peterson who'd been mentioned in despatches. He congratulated Cook on managing such a spread with rationing so tight. And he told them all, as one close to the heart of government, that the tide had turned. This would be the last Christmas of the war.

Lady Nazier also radiated charm and a rather fearsome confidence. She had brought a Christmas present for Arthur. A silver model of an airship, made by Mappin and Webb, and so perfect in detail that there were six tiny figures in the minute gondola, and even – though only to be seen with a magnifying glass – dials on the instrument panel in front. There was no present for Charles.

'Well, Arthur, do I get a kiss in return?' Diana watched his manifest delight, her green eyes glittering and amused.

Arthur threw his arms round her neck and kissed her mouth with uncharacteristic warmth and spontaneity. Somehow Amelia felt it as a rejection of herself.

'I hate that woman,' Charles said when Amelia came to his room to say goodnight.

With the adults, the niceties were carefully preserved. Lady Nazier retired to the guest suite in the west wing. Frederick lay down beside Amelia in the big four-poster. They lay awake, talking like polite strangers.

'Yes', he said in answer to Amelia's question as to how things were with him in London, 'I am content. My enterprises prosper. Politically, I carry considerable weight. Life is treating me well.'

'Diana is looking lovely. She makes you happy, doesn't she?' Amelia paused and then suggested softly, 'Would you not wish now . . . ?'

'To divorce?' Frederick heaved up in bed. 'Unthinkable! Their Majesties have let it be known they will not receive divorcés. It is out of the question! Now more than ever!'

The Christmas meal was constrained. Charles ate and drank in silence, occasionally resting his dark hostile glance on Lady Nazier. Not entirely oblivious of it, she devoted herself to Arthur, gave him her most enchanting smile and rapt attention. Did he enjoy the theatre? How refreshing in a boy of his age! And had he seen the great *Chu Chin Chow* at His Majesty's? The London theatres were carrying on sturdily, despite the occasional Gotha raids. *Romance* was at the Lyric. And at the Globe, where as Arthur knew she had a box, was a play called *The Willow Tree*.

It was decided over the plum pudding that Arthur should accompany his father to the flat in the town house when he returned there on Tuesday. Charles was not invited. He would not have gone even if he had been. As soon as Boxing Day was over, he cycled to the factory. He spent the remainder of the school holiday in the production sheds and the hangars or watching Cummings at work in the design office.

'He's got himself a few rides up aloft in visiting aircraft,' Ronald told Amelia. 'Though low be it spoken! You're not supposed to know!'

'I would sack whoever took him up on the spot, Ronald! So don't do it again!' She sighed. 'All the same, he's enjoyed his holidays.'

The day before they ended, Charles decided to devote himself to his mother. He came to her office, sat on her desk, drank her coffee and shared her lunchtime sandwiches. 'Mama,' he said, brushing the crumbs off his knee on to the floor. 'Are you busy?'

'Yes, very. Why?'

'I thought you and I might take the Rolls for a drive on the forest.'

'I would love to, my darling, but . . . '

In the weeks that followed she was never to cease to reproach herself. 'Besides,' she went on, 'I shall have to take the day off to drive you to Paddington to go back to school tomorrow. Then I shall have to take the day off on Friday to meet your father and see to Arthur. I tell you what I'll do though! I'll let you drive the Rolls through the forest tomorrow.'

But with the strange cussedness of Charles, he declined her offer. He sat in the passenger seat beside her, arms folded across his chest, hardly speaking. Like that, withdrawn and frowning, he looked so like James.

'Why do you keep staring at me?' he demanded suddenly, as she accelerated over the flatness of Hounslow Heath.

'Was I? I'm sorry. It's just that you remind me of someone.' He didn't ask whom. He just shrugged his shoulders, and returned to his own thoughts.

In the booking-hall at Paddington station, he said suddenly. 'Let's say goodbye here, Mama. It's embarrassing in front of all the chaps, kissing one's mother at the barrier.'

She smiled tenderly, lifted her net and held her cheek up for his accustomed peck. He put his arms round her and hugged her to him. Into her ear he whispered, 'I love you, Mama! More than anyone in the world!'

She sped home, touched and oddly happy. Two days later, just before she left Haybury Hall for the factory, she was summoned to the telephone. The Matron of Savernake School was enquiring about Charles. He had not arrived for the commencement of term. Was he in fact ill?

And while the first shock of panic broke over Amelia, Sarah brought in the morning's mail. She must have read the postcard. She always did. She had placed it on top of the pile. Even before Amelia lifted it, she saw her aghast expression.

Postmarked Ashford, the card was in Charles's handwriting, addressed to Amelia only. *I've changed my name and joined up. Don't try to find me.*

It was signed *Your loving Charles.* And in a PS *I meant what I said.*

James held the letter for several minutes before opening it, turning it over and over in his hands.

Amelia's handwriting conveyed a powerful impression of her. It was almost as if she stood in front of him, and he was trying to read her face. A quick irrational hope made his heartbeat quicken. She was writing to tell him Frederick had changed his mind, that he now desired to marry Lady Nazier and that a divorce would be agreed.

Why else would she write? Why else?

He suddenly found himself ripping the envelope open, and unfolding the letter with an unsteady hand. It was a long one. His hopes strengthened. But it began formally *My dear James*, and casting his eye quickly down the close-written page for clues, the name Charles recurred too often for it to be a letter of reconciliation between them. Or indeed a letter of hope at all. Odd words leapt out at him. *I'm sorry, despair* and perhaps most hopeless of all the phrase *you as my friend.*

Ironically, it was not until he opened that letter that he realised how piercingly he loved her. After the formal opening, Amelia came straight to the point. *I write to you because I am in such despair. Charles has run away from school ostensibly to join up, and I do not know to whom to turn, except to you as my friend.*

Frederick and I have made every possible enquiry at every possible level. But if he has joined up, he has done so under an assumed name. There are thousands of youngsters joining up. Frederick thinks he may have enlisted in the Navy as a midshipman. But knowing his passion for flying, I feel he would try to get into the RFC. Do they employ Army personnel on the airfields? Frederick says he would get into the Army more easily. As you may remember, he's under age, but he's tall and looks well over it. He's fit and strong and reasonably intelligent. You and Colonel Cody were so good before when he ran away, and I'm sorry to burden you with this when you yourself . . .

It was a sentence she didn't quite finish. She went on with another one. *I wondered if perhaps you would look out for him, make a few enquiries. I have visited every recruiting centre in Southern England, every airfield, been to every ministry. I'm sure I'm right that he will try to work around aircraft. I'm sorry to turn to you yet again. Charles is very dear to me.*

In the whole of the letter, there was no mention of anyone else who was dear to her.

James tried Vert Galant first. There he found Babe Reynolds had left 87 Squadron. No one knew where he was. Then he tried St Omer and Amiens HQs. As soon as he landed after the dawn patrol, he took the Crossley down the winding rutted lanes to Poperinghe, Armentières, Ypres, Bethane, Arras.

Nothing.

Then he tried the Army. He went up to the battalion HQs, had a word with the officers in the trenches and the reserve camps. He was given to understand that he was looking for a needle in a haystack. Lots of boys under age had come into the forces. Conscription was working none too well. There were numerous shirkers, despite the women's efforts with white feathers. The recruiting offices didn't look too closely or ask too many questions.

He wrote to Amelia, trying to sound not too discouraging. After five weeks without a sign, he tried the Navy, going all the way up to Dunkirk and inquiring at the RNAS depots.

Then the last Sunday in February, Calthorpe rang up from HQ. James was to go south to Toul first thing in the morning to discuss a new joint offensive with the 103rd Aero Squadron of the American Expeditionary Force, made up of former members of the famous American Lafayette Escadrille.

'Can't you send someone else?'

'Sorry. Trenchard is insisting on you.'

'But you know our first Ajaxes are supposed to arrive tomorrow! I want to be around to see they do.'

James's pressure had at last obtained a fulfilment of HQ's reluctant promise that 188 Squadron would be re-equipped with Ajaxes.

'I promise you they will be.' Calthorpe paused, then as an added inducement went on, 'You'll find Babe Reynolds there, James. I've just heard he's one of the flight commanders.'

James hadn't seen Babe for over ten months. Leaving word that he'd be back next day, James drove down to Toul where Babe showed him round. The Americans were flying DH4s with American-built Liberty engines. After talking tactics for a couple of hours, they adjourned to the bar and then went to the Mess hall for dinner.

'Special treat today,' Babe told him. 'Especially for you.'

197

The meal started with French vegetable soup. Pheasant followed, beautifully succulent, with bread crumbs, stuffing, vegetables and all the trimmings.

'What d'you think of it, James?'

'Excellent!'

'Compliments of Corporal Smith.'

'Your cook?'

'Our righthand man more like. Our provider. Bagged these pheasant from the back seat of a DH4.'

'With you flying?'

'Yep.'

'Smith's a good shot then?'

'Better than me.'

'That I find hard to believe.'

'Lot of things about Smith you'd find hard to believe. You hear this, James, that boy –'

For the rest of lunch, Reynolds talked about Corporal Smith. He had belonged to an artillery unit of 5.5 howitzers stationed five miles to the east of Toul who had come along with a number of others to give the Americans a hand in getting up their camp. During the visit, he had got talking to one of the air mechanics. The American soon found out that he knew a lot about airframes and engines. This knowledge the American had imparted to Babe Reynolds, and an arrangement had been set up with the gunners' major to borrow Smith for the time being.

Henceforward Smith had simply been taken over on the American strength. Not only that, he had trained himself in gunnery and regularly flew as Babe's observer on DH4 patrols. Not only that, going forward to the trenches on his half-day to see his friends in the gunners, he had rigged up a field observation balloon with an 'observer' made of straw in full uniform with 200 pounds of gelignite in the basket. Attached to the towing rope was an electrical wire with a button on the end of it. Sure enough, an Albatross saw the balloon, swallowed the bait and dived. At the crucial moment, when the German opened fire only a few yards from the defenceless balloon, Corporal Smith pressed the button. There was a flash, a noise like thunder – and balloon and Albatross descended in flames together.

'Pity you didn't meet him when you arrived this morning, James,' Babe said. 'But he's off to Vert Galant looking for spares. Still, we'll see him this evening at the Lion D'Or . . . You'll stay for dinner won't you?'

James said he would. In the afternoon, he took up a DH4. As a bomber he found it fast, but it was heavy on the controls after Ajax and the Morane. After dinner that evening, they walked down to the estaminet in the village. 'No doubt you have found a replacement for Françoise?' James asked him.

Babe smiled. 'That girl jest couldn't be replaced, but I have an understudy or two. Oh, by the way,' he added as they reached a crumbling stucco edifice, 'I warn you, things get hectic.'

They went down six steps to a dark cellar lit by candles. A dozen girls were sitting at tables with Americans. Six more were dancing to a small band. The air was filled with cigarette smoke and the reek of spilled wine.

'Cognac, James?'

'Please.'

They drank, a serious little group to one side of the bar, while the hilarity went on. Babe introduced a number of the squadron. They stood awkwardly talking to James, all the time clearly wanting to get back to the fun.

'Seen Corporal Smith?'

'Oh, he's around sir,' they all said vaguely.

A bottle hurtled across the room. Two Americans started fighting, sprawled on a marble-topped table.

'They're a great crowd,' Babe said as a glass came crashing down like a shell and splintered all over him. A dark-haired girl came up and put her arm through his.

'This is Toni . . . '

He bent his head and whispered into her ear.

She nodded. 'I try.'

She left. Minutes later, she came back with a pretty redhead, who draped her arms round James and insisted on kissing him.

The evening progressed. The wine flowed. The girls giggled. The laughter got louder. Just after midnight, suddenly Babe said, 'There's Corporal Smith!'

James followed the direction he was pointing. Candlelight was flickering over a thick-set figure in khaki sitting at a marble-topped table in the far corner, animatedly talking to three American airmen and a blonde. As though he was suddenly aware that he was being watched, the soldier stopped talking and looked straight across the smoky gloom to the bar.

James threaded his way slowly and deliberately between the tables over to the far corner. From under thick black hair, smouldering eyes regarded him belligerently.

James stopped at the marble-topped table. 'Hello, Charles,' he said.

SEVEN

'You were tough on the kid! Real hard-down mean! Now he's gonna hate your guts!'

James hadn't argued with Babe Reynolds's verdict on his handling of Charles. Nor had he told Babe that Charles for some reason already hated him. He was satisfied that he had done what was best for the boy, though Babe railed long and loud against his having Charles escorted back to Savernake School as though he was a prisoner, and ringing up General Trenchard at St Omer HQ to report the incident.

James didn't attempt to explain. The Ajaxes had arrived, and he was far too busy giving the squadron conversion training on this new and yet strangely familiar aeroplane with its swept back wing and far more powerful Rolls-Royce engine.

To the relief of the Army, low cloud muffled the battlefield and there was no sign of the gold triplane. James, impatiently awaiting its reappearance, received a letter from Amelia thanking him. Charles had been received back by the headmaster surprisingly mildly, mainly due to the fact that a letter from no less a person than General Trenchard had preceded him. For this, she supposed, she and Frederick and Charles must again be grateful to him.

It was a cool, formal letter. The inclusion of Frederick's name somehow made it abundantly clear that she had not changed. The ultimatum he had given her had long since expired. She wanted him, but not enough to divorce Frederick. Her letter went on to say that the factory was very busy.

Frederick, he had read in one of his mother's newspaper clippings, had been created Companion of the Bath in recognition of his services to the new Air Board under Lord Cowdray, so *he* must be doing well both politically and financially. Bitterly James thought, how could he ever expect Amelia to divorce Frederick for someone like him? And hard on the heels of that bitter thought, that it was up to him now to sever the relationship.

Other unwieldly relationships were being severed that wet spring. The RFC ceased to exist. By recommendation of the Smuts' Committee, the air arm was taken away from both the Admiralty and the War Office (to their fury), and the Royal Air Force was created on 1 April 1918. The change made little difference. The pilots of the RFC and RNAS had always got on well, in direct contrast to the bickering and power-seeking of their superiors. An Air Ministry was established at the requisitioned Hotel Cecil.

That same April, a huge German drive was made on 50-mile front from Arras to La Fère. 188 Squadron retreated to a field 20 miles west of Blaize Farm and lived uncomfortably in tents. They were regularly harassed by Richthofen and his circus. But still there was no sign of the high-flying gold Fokker triplane.

And then, on a dark April morning, through a crack in the cloud-covered sky, suddenly James caught sight of a tiny gold speck. Within seconds he was inside the cockpit, the propeller was turning, and as lightning veined the black cumulo-nimbus thunderheads, he eased Ajax off the sodden grass.

Immediately he was smothered in damp grey cottonwool. Bouncing up and down in the uneven air, compass going round in circles, turn indicator gesticulating wildly, he had little idea which way up he was, let alone whether he was closing in on the tripe. Only the erratic movement of the altimeter needle gave him reassurance that at least he was climbing.

At 13,000 feet he suddenly came out into sunshine. He was flying in a chasm between two vast cliffs of cloud. And there, high above him, still busy taking his photographs through breaks in the storm was the golden triplane.

Tucking himself into the wispy edges of the cumulus, like a climber on a rock face, half invisible, he scrabbled up higher. It had become very cold. The wires glittered in sudden shafts of sun. Beginning to feel breathless, he looked at the altimeter.

19,000 feet. The cloud tops still towered above him. Veils of vapour broke off and drifted like molten lava from a volcano down over the Ajax.

21,000 feet. Now he was gasping for breath. The Ajax was staggering, wallowing, falling back in the thin air. Anxiously he saw a film of the mist muzzling the two Browning guns lying over the engine cowling ahead of the windscreen. At full throttle, the Ajax was flopping around like a wounded duck, and still the triplane was flying steadily and stately above him.

22,000 feet. And now, suddenly the pilot of the triplane saw him and immediately wheeled round in a half-roll.

James pressed the button on the stick. There was a reassuring clatter and a stream of tracer bullets. The triplane turned over on its back, seemed on the point of spinning – it was a trick. Seconds later, he came up from behind Ajax.

Rak-rak-rak.

James saw the bullets tearing into his wings. Kicking on full rudder, he dived, then pulled back sharply. But the triplane was already on him, both Spandaus spitting fire.

He heard the engine cough, falter, then the nose started dropping. Oil covered his windscreen. The needle on the altimeter accelerated anti-clockwise.

The next moment, the storm enveloped him, tossing him all over the sky in a frenzy of fury. Smoke filled the cockpit. He could smell burning. That his first fight in Ajax should end like this saddened and sickened him. Dizzy with lack of air, half-choked with fumes and smoke, he felt that this whirling descent from the heights symbolised the end of all his hopes. And now he saw flames leap from the engine. Flattened by the slip-stream, the yellow fangs crept over the engine fairing and began spilling into the cockpit.

Next moment, he saw his flying clothes were on fire. He could feel the heat on his legs, heard the roar of the flames like the forge furnace under the bellows. He kicked the stick right forward trying to blow the flames out, slapping his legs with his thick yellow gloves.

It was no use. He was a living torch as Brake and Leefe and an unknown German airman close to Blaize Farm, had been. He remembered the grey-black incinerated skeleton, the rags of burnt cloth. He would be that if . . .

He reached down for the revolver in his boot. Better to finish everything off quickly. He had expected to die. There was now nothing to live for anyway. He had the revolver half up to his head. He clicked over the safety catch. His fingers were already curling on the trigger, when suddenly he stopped.

If he was going to die, then he would die fighting. He had struggled and fought all his life. He could not suddenly give up now. He threw the revolver down on the floor. Blinded by the smoke, he forced the aircraft down into a hurtling dive. He could hear the roar of the engine, the high crescendo of the wind in the wires.

The wings would be off in a minute. He could feel them flapping. But the smoke was dispersing. Now through the stinging greyness, he glimpsed trees, a road, parkland, the ruins of a village, then a flat stretch of cornfield not 50 feet below him.

With all his might he pulled at the stick, felt the nose respond, the wings flatten. The next moment the Ajax hit the ground. He was out of the cockpit in a flash, slapping at his burning clothes, running through the stalks of winter wheat. Seconds later, there was an enormous crump behind him, and the whole gloomy countryside was lit up by the yellow and red flames of the exploding aircraft.

Gasping for breath, his legs weak and burning, he reached a wood of firs. His uniform now was only smouldering. He beat out the last sparks, and looked round for clues as to where he was.

This was no ordinary wood – not just trees and mossy banks. Lines of gun muzzles, howitzers, tanks, big field guns, caterpillar-tracked troop carriers, a railway line on which there were trucks with vast guns, far bigger than anything on a battleship, on which someone had chalked one word . . . Paris.

He had fallen well behind the German lines. This was an armaments park of enormous proportions. The Germans were not defeated, like everyone was saying. They were going to have another huge push like the one that started the war and capture Paris.

He began running again, but now he felt dizzy. He could hardly see where he was going. Sick with pain, he struggled through thick undergrowth. Then he heard voices, and looking back saw a slight figure moving towards him. There was another figure behind, a huge one, holding what looked like a pitchfork, as though it were a bayonet.

He was dashing for the shelter of thick rhododendrons when suddenly through a blur of pain and rising unconsciousness, he heard a woman's voice calling in English with the slightest French accent, 'It's all right . . .'

'So after all I am a prisoner,' James said aloud, partly to decide whether or not he was still alive.

He was in some sort of cellar. There was a small window high up with an iron grille over it. What illumination there was came through grey and filtered, but he could almost swear that some time he had seen a great cone of artificial light blazing through it on to his face. He could still feel it on his eyelids trying to force them up. And once surely, when his ears had been full of noise, tramping feet and voices, he had managed to open one eye, and the cellar had been crowded with Germans. One of them had put a hand on his shoulder, and even in his dream or his unconsciousness, James could remember screaming in pain.

He looked down. The shoulder was bandaged. So was the left side of his face. He raised his head from the pillow. The walls of his cellar had once been white washed but now were scaly and crumbling. The floor was stone flagged. He lay on an iron bedstead. The mattress was hard, the blankets grey army type. But his pillow was covered in a clean slip and there were sheets, thin and carefully patched. Beside his bed was a small wooden chair and against the wall a table with a carafe of water on it. It was too good for a prison. The Germans must have been the figment of a nightmare. His hopes soared.

There was a thick oak door over on the extreme right. In his nightmare, he had heard the sound of that door being kicked open, a woman's voice speaking rapid French, and men's hideous laughter.

Where in God's name was he?

He tried to struggle out of bed to reach the door. But his right leg dragged, and before he had got both feet on to the floor, the door opened and a woman came in. She looked like the woman he had glimpsed distantly in the wood. She was slight, with straight brown hair, tied in a loose knot like a young girl's. The shape of her face had a certain beauty, but it was sallow and lined and desperately thin. She could have been any age between twenty and fifty.

'Major,' she waved him back into bed, and then bringing the chair closer, sat on its edge and peered into his face. Her brown eyes had abnormally large pupils giving the impression they were coal-black. 'How are you feeling?'

She spoke English with that same French accent and he smiled with relief.

'Pretty good, thank you.' And then in a rush, 'Where am I? Who are you? What day is it? What's happening? The last thing I remember were lines of German guns. Are you going to hand me over? You realise what'll happen if you don't?'

She held up her hand. It was small and square and toil-worn. 'Please! Let me do the talking, yes? First, I am Marie de Saguenac. I am French. It is now Tuesday. You have been . . .' she waved her hands, 'unconscious . . . feverish . . . like this for three days.'

He interrupted her to ask, 'And where are we?'

'In the Boche lines. The village of Courcy. I shall not hand you over. I would not hand anything to the Boches. Nor do anything for them, except kill them. They came here first in 1914. The Allies took it back two years later. Last week, it was lost again. My husband . . .'

She broke off and drew a deep breath. For a full minute she kept silent. Then she went on, 'As you saw in the wood, the Boches are preparing an advance.'

'Then they'll be even more on the alert.'

'Yes, Major.'

'They'll come here. You must not try to hide me.'

Instinctively he began to push back the bedclothes. She put a hand restrainingly over his. 'Major, they have already been.'

So it had not been a nightmare!

'And what did you tell them?'

'That we saw the burning aircraft. Boche or Allied, we did not know which.'

'*We*. Was that your husband? The man who grabbed me?'

'With the pitchfork? No.' A ghost of a smile touched her lips. 'That was

François. He used to work as a gardener here. Now we have no gardens. Nothing. The whole estate is razed. François saw you coming down. He ran to see if . . .'

'If I was alive?'

'Yes. You were lucky. You crashed in what once was the parkland.' She dipped her hand in the pocket of her apron and brought out a much thumbed map. She turned her chair round so that they could look at it together, spreading it on the rough grey blanket. 'We are here.'

'The château?'

'It was once a château. Now no longer.'

'Quite close to Rheims.'

'Twelve kilometres. It is said the Boche intends to attack from the bridge here. They will take Paris before the Americans arrive.'

James said slowly, 'They will kill you if I stay here, Madame.'

She struggled.

'You have done enough, taking me in.' He looked at her thin figure and asked, 'How did you get me here?'

'François carried you. He is strong. He stays here to help me.'

'To do what, Madame?'

'To survive.'

'Hiding me will not help you to survive, Madame.'

'Perhaps not.' She gave that faint ghostly smile again. 'But it gives purpose to my life while I do survive.'

'Nevertheless as soon as it's dark, I shall leave.'

'No.' She put her hand on his arm. 'You will endanger us more if you do. Much more. You will stay here till further orders. You are not the first Allied fighter to be here. It is arranged. In Courcy, we have friends. All Courcy hates the Boche.'

'What if they come here again?'

'It will be as before, when they came. I told them you are my husband, whom they half-killed when they shelled us last week.' She lowered her eyes to her hands, twisting them nervously in her lap. 'They saw how it was with you with their own eyes. One of them shoved his rifle butt into your torn shoulder. They were satisfied. In any case, it was true.'

'True, Madame?' James asked gently.

'Quite true. Except that you . . . you were killed.'

For a long time James said nothing, then putting his hand over her nervously twisting ones, 'Your husband was killed only last week? In the shelling?'

'Oui.'

'I'm sorry.'

She clenched her fists, her whole body trembling. 'I am not the only one. Most of Courcy has lost someone.'

'But surely,' James said after a while, 'the Germans know of your husband's death?'

'No, Major. They know nothing. Why should they? We tell them nothing. They care nothing for what we suffer.' She spat out the words. 'You . . . he was buried in the ruins of what used to be our private chapel. François buried him. We told no one. We had not even a priest.'

'Why, Madame?'

204

'We wished his papers and rations. It is often done. We wish to survive. We have no heir. I am all of him that is left. He would wish me to survive. You will take his papers. You will become him.'

'I hardly speak a word of French.'

'There is no need. You are wounded.'

'What was your husband's name?'

'Pierre.' She closed her eyes momentarily, 'He was a good man. He hated the Boche.' She clenched her hand and held it against her thin chest. 'He hated the Boche with all his heart! I also! I hate! I do this for him too, you understand? Soon we will see how well you can walk on that leg. You were lucky. It was not crushed. Merely badly burned and bruised. Indeed,' she gave that faint faded smile as if she had forgotten how to smile properly, 'you are covered in bruises. You have a cut on your back which I stitched. Your head also.' And still speaking in the same dry brisk tone, 'You will spend the rest of your stay in my room here . . . yes, it is the cellar but there are no rooms left standing! Now I will fetch for you some food and then you must get some sleep.'

She returned a few minutes later with a bowl of soup, a hunk of bread and some Brie. The soup was aromatic with herbs and delicious. She watched him eat greedily, her dark eyes bright but inscrutable.

She slept that night on a palliasse on the floor. Twice he woke from feverish dreams to feel her hand on his forehead and to see her bending over him. Once he woke himself with his own shouting.

When she brought him his breakfast of porridge and goats' milk, she asked, 'Who is Amelia?'

He said nothing.

'You shouted her name. Is she your wife?'

'No.'

'Have you a wife?'

'No.'

She sat on a corner of the bed. 'If they find you they will shoot you. They will say you are a spy.'

'What about you?'

'That would not matter to me.'

'It would to *me*.'

Abruptly she changed the subject. 'The latest news François has heard is that the Boche are making final preparations to advance.' The news made him more desperate than ever to get away.

The following morning he felt much stronger. He insisted on getting out of bed. He shaved and asked for his clothes. His uniform had been destroyed, she told him. She produced a suit of her husband's to wear, and a silk shirt. They fitted well. Pierre had been a fine man, she said, of the Major's build.

That evening she led him out of the cellar, and up staircases that ended in nothing but the twilight sky. The air was soft and warm and still and a few stars shone. Momentarily he was reminded, painfully, of walking on the terrace with Amelia last summer at Haybury.

Artillery sounded like approaching thunder. Nostalgically the French-woman pointed out, 'Here was the dining-room. And over there, just where that piece of wall is, was the drawing-room,' her voice became momentarily youthful, no longer a flat monotone, till she gripped his arm and whispered, 'and there, Major, near where you stand, by that was a window, there he was killed.'

Later, the three of them ate their supper of some stew in the cellar kitchen. For a long time, she conducted an earnest conversation in French with François, interspersed with long dark thoughtful glances in his direction.

Finally she said to James, 'It seems, Major, that it will be in three days' time that you go. It is arranged. If you are strong enough, François will take you by the river to the next house along the escape route.' She smiled her faint reluctant smile, 'You must rest well these next three nights.'

Yet he had scarcely dozed off to sleep, before a hand pulled back the quilt. He woke to see Marie bending over him, her thin face upshadowed in lamplight. 'Are the Germans here?' he whispered hoarsely.

She put her finger to her lips, and turned to douse the lamp. In its last dwindling rays, he saw she was naked.

'Please,' she said, resting her knee on the mattress. 'Please.' She touched his face. 'Let me come in.'

EIGHT

The night they left the Château de Saguenac was pitch black and raining. No lights, nothing – only the sound of François' feet over the moss in the woods, the rustle of dry leaves, the occasional crack of a twig gave James the clue where to follow.

'So this is adieu, James,' the Countess had said, as together they made the last preparations in the cellar. 'This will be the last time we will see each other.'

There was no point in conventional expressions of hope for the future. They had met and they had come together when there was no future for either of them. They were parting under the same circumstances. The war looked like lasting for ever. The chances of James surviving it were few indeed. And the next push and the next bombardment would be likely to knock down those few stones of the château still standing and obliterate her with them.

To James, it was as though those days were a mysterious interlude, a ghostly existence in a ruin five hundred years old. A not unpleasant existence, but a sad one. And Marie herself was unreal, withdrawn, belonging somehow to another age, when the world was different from this one.

'A dream,' she had called it as he held her in his arms that last time. A dream as different from his lovemaking with Amelia as shadow from substance. When they woke, the dreams would be gone. And if they didn't wake, so much the better. Now, standing by the door, shielding a candle with her fingers, she was only a grey shadow already merging with the night.

'François will take you to Vigny,' she had told him. 'That's five miles along the line. There you will stay till it is safe for you to go further. Finally you will reach Berry-au-Boc. That is the front line. Near there you will be escorted over to the British lines and safety.'

François led the way through the woods and across a heath, skirted a river, finally reaching a small farm half-hidden in a valley. There James was handed over to an elderly woman who ran it, and François immediately departed to get back to the château before moonrise. All day, he stayed hidden in the hay barn, being brought food and drink till it was quite dark and the second leg of the journey could be started. Twice they saw columns of lorries and guns, but the old woman was as adept as François at avoiding them.

That night he was hidden in a village bakery. The last stage of the journey, his new host told him, was the most dangerous. They would be skirting the German lines at Berry-au-Boc and going on to the foothills of the Chemin-des-Dames ridge. A cave leading right under the slope had been further excavated so that it emerged in the British held lines to the north of the river Aisne. It had been a very quiet sector, but lately there had been large troop build-ups. The cave entrance was in a thick wood, but this had recently been filled, as at the château, with guns and ammunition. Troop movements were many. It would be difficult to avoid detection.

In the event, they had little difficulty. Not only was the night dark but the foothills and the woods were filled with mist. As the baker led him unerringly forward, James could hear continuous sounds of lorries, horses' hooves and marching men, but they hardly glimpsed one German soldier.

By midnight, they were in the cave crawling on their bellies under overhanging rock. An hour later, James thought he felt a tremor. A hundred yards further on, the earth began shaking. When they finally emerged into a cornfield, the sky was alight with bursting shells.

The two of them stayed in the cave for the next two hours. When it became apparent the bombardment would continue all night, James persuaded the baker to get back home while there was still darkness. There was bound to be a lull in the shelling next day. He was in the Allied lines. He would easily be able to contact British troops.

When dawn came next morning, it revealed nothing but desolation. Two hours afterwards, it was not British but German troops he saw, advancing down the Chemin-des-Dames ridge and moving forward. The German offensive had started.

For the next three weeks, James was caught up in a mêlée of refugees moving westwards, victorious German troops and Allied prisoners. He reached the town of Fismes only to find the Germans there already. He hid in haystacks, barns, ruined buildings. He ate what he could from scraps he found in abandoned homes. All round were lorries, guns, carts, fleeing human beings. Twice DH4s came over low down and dropped bombs on an advancing column of German tanks. He got down to Fère along the railway, hanging under a cattle truck. There he saw the huge guns he had seen in the château woods, moving along the railway track towards Paris.

The French refugees told him the Germans would be taking the capital the next day. They were only 55 miles away from it and 65,000 Allied prisoners had been taken. The French government was tottering. The Boche were going to win the war after all.

That evening he reached a thick wood. Exhausted, he was about to lie down and rest when once again, intense firing started. Figures were moving all round him now in unfamiliar uniforms. This was it, he thought. This was the end. There was no chance of escape from here. He had been seen anyway. They were coming towards him holding rifles with fixed bayonets, shouting to him to surrender. But not in German; they were shouting – he could hardly believe his ears – in something like Cody's accented English.

The Americans had arrived.

Only 40 miles from Paris, the 2nd and 3rd Divisions of the American Expeditionary Force stopped the German advance dead. At Château Thierry a US machine-gun battalion successfully defended the river Marne crossing, while to the west General Omar Bundy won the bloody engagement of Belleau Wood.

Fed, rested, medically examined, James was taken by ambulance to RFC HQ at Amiens where the first person he saw was Calthorpe. 'We'd given you up, old chap. Posted you missing, believed kilted. Come and have a drink.'

James spent a week in hospital at Amiens, though he kept on telling them that he was perfectly all right. The inhabitant of the next room, he found, was Basil Beaumont. He had been with 56 Squadron on the new SE5 fast biplanes with the gun that could shoot upwards into the belly of the Huns and had been jumped on by what seemed to have been the whole Richthofen circus. He had now a 'Blighty one' in his left leg and they were sending him home the next week.

He was far from sorry. 'Flying's fun but fighting's foolish,' he told James. 'Besides, I want to get back to the wife.'

'The *wife*, Basil?'

'Hadn't you heard I was married, James?'

'Not a word! Congratulations!'

'Thanks, James. We're very happy, Bron and I.'

'Bron?'

'Yes, James . . . short for Bronwen. You met her! Don't you remember?'

They had a few of what Basil called 'thrashes' in the Amiens estaminets, taking no notice whatever of hospital regulations. Then Beaumont left to catch the boat for Dover, and James reported to Calthorpe that he was perfectly fit to go back to 188 Squadron.

'No, James positively not! You're staying here at HQ. All you're going to fly for the next few months is a desk.'

So it was from the ground that James saw the last few months of the Great War. He saw the big Handley-Page four-engined bomber drop 1650-pound bombs, the largest ever. He saw an American ace called Eddie Rickenbacker shooting down the triplanes of the big German circuses. He saw the American General Mitchell do what Trenchard had tried to do with six squadrons on the Somme and swamp the German air force in an air offensive of 1000 planes. He saw the last Battle of the Marne begin.

He was in Paris when the Germans who had pursued him from Chemin-des-Dames to Château Thierry were themselves surrounded. He was a liaison officer attached to the American Aero Squadron, and in this capacity followed them to Rheims – actuallyin the front line for almost the whole war and battered beyond belief.

Seeing the ruins and the desolation, he was again filled with anxiety for Marie. He had no illusions that but for her he could be dead. But what about her? What had happened to her and François in the German push and in the even more terrible Allied counter-offensive? He had to visit a unit in Berry-au-Boc the day after he arrived. After it was ove, he drove the staff car those fifteen miles further east.

Shell holes, ruined buildings, wrecked trucks, bodies of cattle – there was nothing but desolation, nothing he recognised until suddenly, rounding a rutted corner, he saw fir trees still standing and recognised the wood into which he had crawled after Ajax crashed.

He slowed the car and looking closer, saw the slight rise where the wood had been cleared and what had once been lawns climb up towards the ruin of the château. He brought the car to a halt and stared up at the ruins. Either distance or more recent shelling had reduced them to what looked like no more than a cairn at the top of a scarred and blasted hill. Even the woods at the bottom of the hill were scorched and ripped. He looked around for signs of what must be a drive leading off this road to the château, not sure even if he found it that he would want to find whatever lay at the top.

When he discovered what seemed to be the drive, it led between half-demolished stone portals, past the foundations of all that remained of a lodge, past flowerbeds full of weeds. There was a broken plinth for a vanished statue, a shattered urn, and near a shell crater, a dead horse. The carcass was rotting. Why hadn't François done something about it? He began to have a premonition of what he was going to find at the top of this winding shell-pitted drive. Why hadn't François come out with his pitchfork? Why was there such an air of total stillness and lifelessness?

He had seen so little of the ruins before he left, but surely they had been shelled recently again. Dust particles, the smell of rubble seemed to hang in the air. And surely, the stone staircase Marie had taken him to the top of had now vanished? And why this silence? Not even the birds singing or the rooks cawing. Slowly, hoping that at every yard François would appear and challenge him, James picked his way over the rubble to the cellar door.

He knocked. There was no answer. He knocked again. Finally, he touched the heavy latch and tried to raise it. The latch lifted easily. The door swung inwards. The room was almost as he had left it, the chair, the table, the bed. Marie was sitting on the edge of the bed, her elbows on her knees, her head held in her hands. She looked for a moment as if she'd been killed where she sat, in that posture of defeat and despair.

'Marie?'

He went over and knelt beside her. She slowly raised her head and stared at him uncomprehendingly, like someone shell-shocked.

'Marie,' he said gently. 'Do you not recognise me?'

'I recognise you.' She nodded several times, and smiled wanly. Tears sprang to her eyes, and she took a corner of the old brown smock she was wearing and dabbed them.

'Are you not glad to see me?'

She nodded. 'Glad and relieved.'

'Where's François? He was not keeping very good watch.'

'He was killed,' she said shortly, 'getting food.'

'And you've been living here all alone?'

'Of course.'

'For how long?'

'I forget for how long. Time is nothing.'

He got to his feet. He would take her in the staff car to HQ, see she was put up in some comfortable place behind the Allied lines. Get her properly fed and looked after.

His mind was filled with plans to repay her in whatever way he could. He took both her hands, and tried to pull her to her feet. But though her hands and arms were still very thin, her movements had lost their agility and her body seemed heavy and clumsy.

He looked from her thickened body to her agonised face. Then the truth hit him like a bullet.

Marie was pregnant.

NINE

'How soon before the lads are back, M'lady?' Sarah asked, as they stood side by side, surrounded by the rest of the staff at the front door of Haybury Hall.

It was 11 November 1918, one minute before eleven am.

'Soon,' Amelia whispered, and put her finger to her lips for silence. Almost immediately the silence was shattered. From the ack-ack sites at Jerningham and the coastal batteries came the salute of guns. There was the hoot of tugs, the sirens of the big ships in the Solent, as everything afloat joined the chorus. Then came a waterfall of rejoicing bells. The church bells of Haybury, the more distant ones of Jerningham and from further back in the forest, the peal of all the village churches and chapels.

The Armistice was signed. Peace had come. Amelia embraced all the staff, thanked them, commiserated with them, murmured hope to those who had relatives still missing. For she knew their sorrow. No matter how long she lived she would never forget the moment she knew James was missing. For days she had felt uneasy and restless. And then passing the forge on that last Saturday in May, she had caught sight of James's father. She couldn't see the expression on his face, his back was towards her. But there was something in the bent shoulders, something in his stance that told her as clearly as if he'd shouted it aloud. James was either dead or missing.

She had stopped the Rolls and gone inside. 'At least,' she had said humbly, minutes after Mr March told her, 'he's missing. It's better than . . .'

'Missing, believed killed, M'lady. We've got to face facts, his mother and me. Missing behind enemy lines. And his aeroplane burned to a cinder.' He shook his head. 'A pal of his flew over.'

The following morning at Matins, James's name had joined that dreaded list to be so earnestly prayed for. For the next three weeks, Amelia assiduously attended every service which the Reverend Bingham held. And each weekday on her drive from Haybury to Jerningham, she slipped into the church and prayed, implored and tried to bargain with the Lord. Spare James, let him come back, then I will leave Frederick if necessary and tell James everything. Each day she dreaded seeing the curtains of the forge cottage drawn, or black crêpe on the door. Each Sunday she dreaded seeing Mrs March dressed all in black. Those weeks convinced her that she could not live without James.

Then halfway through the fourth week after James had been posted missing, Mr March had actually waylaid her. He'd rushed into the street as the Rolls came towards the forge, waving a piece of paper in his hand, and laughing and crying at the same time. 'The lad's been found. Thank God. Walked right through the enemy lines.'

211

Now surely, Amelia told old Pearson, whose younger son had been missing since Jutland, now surely the missing would be found. There were so many thousands. They couldn't all be dead.

It was what most of the population of Britain believed. Their men would now return. They couldn't all be lying rotting and unburied or hanging on the barbed wire gnawed by rats, as the pessimists said, in the mud of Flanders. They would be found in friendly farmhouses, wounded in some hospital, taken in by monks or nuns against the glorious day when the Germans unconditionally surrendered.

The last few days had been agonies of suspense. The great American sweep on the 50-mile front above Verdun was just over a week old. But Austria had already surrendered and the Americans swept on, seizing the heights of Sedan, as the French and British took Maubeuge and the Canadians took Mons. The war was over. Germany had been brought for ever to her knees. Everywhere hope stirred as the celebrations exploded. Teams of ringers kept the church bells pealing. Everything drinkable was drunk. People danced in the streets, put up bunting, hugged and kissed, held hands, sang 'Auld lang syne', 'Rule Britannia', 'God save the King', 'Keep the home fires burning' and all the wartime songs.

They besieged Buckingham Palace and demanded that their sovereign and his family appear on the balcony. The British public's love affair with the Prince of Wales had already begun. It was known he had insisted on going to France. They cheered the family to the echo. But most of all they cheered the little prince. They rolled women like barrels down the sloping platform of Waterloo station. They let off fireworks right through the night, and burned effigies of the Kaiser and Little Willie.

In Jerningham and Haybury, the celebrations were slightly more decorous. State business kept Frederick in London. His advice was being sought on the disposal of the German flying machines. Hermann Goering of Richthofen's squadron had been ordered to deliver the circus machines to the Americans. This he had flatly refused to do, and taken them to Germany instead.

There were a dozen other matters on which Frederick made himself useful. So the free beer barrels were rolled out under Amelia's authority, the yellow lemonade crystals bought in Southampton, and sticky buns made in the local bakery.

But the real celebration should take place, everyone agreed, when the lads came home. As Sarah said, they had all been safe enough really apart from the odd Gotha raids, in their little neck of the woods. They'd been prosperous too with the aircraft factory. But the lads had had hell. They were the ones that should be feasted when they returned to the promised land fit for heroes.

Amelia could not have agreed more fervently. The day of the celebration was fixed for the first Saturday of the bright New Year of 1919. The year of hope.

'They'll find things changed,' Sarah said. 'The lads,' as she helped Amelia stitch bunting.

'We'll all find things changed, Sarah.'

'You never said a truer word, M'lady.' All the same, Sarah glanced at her mistress curiously. Lady Haybury had spoken with such pleasure of things changing. She who had so much to lose by change. 'It'll be a different way of life. The lad's aren't going to be content just to go back to their old jobs.'

'Always supposing there are the jobs.'

'And look at the mutinies! Who'd have thought the German Navy would mutiny? Or the French Army? And the revolution in Russia, M'lady! What are ordinary people coming to? Let's hope we don't have none of that here!'

'But as you say,' Amelia stitched the last triangle of blue on a string of bunting, 'There will be changes. Peaceful ones, I hope.'

'Like women getting the vote,' Sarah smiled. 'And getting into all those smart professions.' She lowered her voice. 'And not having children when you don't want them. Like that Dr Stopes says. I wonder if my mum . . .' she sighed. 'Ah, well, it's no good wondering. It's too late.'

'I think women altogether will get a different deal, Sarah.' Amelia drew her breath in before saying softly, 'More independence. Easier divorce.'

Sarah bit off the thread with her teeth and said non-committally, 'Well, I hope you're right, M'lady.'

If she saw the way the wind was blowing, she gave no sign. They went on to talk of the preparations. Congratulated themselves on selecting a convenient date. Arthur and Charles would be home from school, Frederick had promised to try to be there.

Frederick was well pleased with the way the war had gone for him, but disappointed it had ended before Ajaxes could be produced in vast numbers. Amelia's mind was made up. She would talk to him again. She would point out how things were changing – morals, conventions, priorities. And when James came home she would tell *him* everything. The war, her agony when he was missing had convinced her, if indeed she had needed convincing at all, that she could not live without hope of James.

'I can't think why you are so excited, Mama,' Charles said when the boys broke up for Christmas. 'It isn't as if you've had anyone actually in the war!'

His face darkened as it always did at the mention of the war. His escapade was still a raw wound. He had not quite forgiven her for her part in it, though his special hatred was reserved for Frederick and James. Perhaps, Amelia daydreamed, in this new changing revolutionary world, they could all three run away together. James and Charles and herself. But the daydream stumbled at Arthur. She loved him too.

Her main hope was that Frederick would find it impossible to live any longer without Diana by his side as his wife. Frederick was now on speaking terms with the Royal Family. King George and Queen Mary, known to be strait-laced, might feel such a liaison should be regularised.

'But the two villages have given so many men,' Amelia said in answer to Charles. 'And so many young men are returning.'

'So many not,' Charles replied shortly.

'Well, you were in the war, darling. And you're back. I want to roast the fatted calf, or the fatted pig, I should say, for that.'

She put her hands on his shoulders, smiling at him tenderly, but he shook off her hands. 'I was kicked out. Humiliated. Made a fool.'

'But you'd done so well, my love!'

'I'd have done much better. I'd have made a name. You spoiled it all. You're so possessive.'

He had never spoken to her like that before. She put her hands over her ears. And then when he stopped shouting, she said, pale-faced, 'I shall pretend I didn't hear you.'

'Oh, Christ, Mama,' he shouted flinging himself towards the door, 'So you will too! Pretend! That's what you do! You don't know what life's like at all. Because you don't want to! You're so old-fashioned. So out of date. You don't understand!' He grasped the handle of the door. 'But understand one thing! I'm not coming to hand round the free ale and baked bloody meats. Certainly not if that bastard's going to be there.'

'Which bastard?'

'Major March. Or I suppose now he's got some RAF rank like squadron leader.'

'You should be grateful . . .' she said in a low controlled voice when he interrupted, 'Well, I'm not! You may be, but I'm not!' His face puckered almost as if he was about to cry. '*Is* he coming?'

'I have simply no idea. I am not in communication with him. Ask his mother or his father. I know nothing of his movements.'

Though she spoke the truth that she knew nothing, it was not because she hadn't tried to find out. She paid a visit that very day again to the forge about the spits that were needed for the roasting of the pigs. They had no news of James, though they had painted the cottage and Mr March had wrought *Welcome home* and *Well done* in iron ready to place over the forge door. But James had been hurt and in hospital, and then he was liaising with the Yanks, and he was never one to write even when he could.

A dozen men returned in mid-December. James was not among them. Christmas came. Frederick and Diana graced the Haybury repast. Lady Nazier was full of excitement about an airship project she was interested in. A consortium was being formed. With luck, Frederick and she would be invited to go on a delegation to find out what could be appropriated from the Zeppelin factories. Because of this it was unlikely Frederick would come again for the homecoming celebrations. He did, however, take a polite interest in Amelia's preparations. He gave permission for her to dig into her pocket for a five-piece band, and even agreed that each child should receive a Victory mug fired at the little pottery at Poole.

Everything was going splendidly. Just before New Year another batch of men arrived home. The London stations were crowded, the papers said, with our returned lads. They'd hoped to get most of them home for Christmas, but failing that for the New Year.

Then on the last day of 1918 the long awaited good news came. 'I've just heard, M'lady.' Sarah came into Amelia's room with the morning tea. 'From the gardener's boy. Squadron Leader March is back.'

'Did he say how he looked?'

'No, M'lady. Just that he was back, safe and sound.'

Wonderful words! Safe back! Amelia lay for a moment savouring them, letting relief and happiness wash over her. Then she was up and bathing, choosing her dress, urging Sarah to be quicker with her hair.

Their estrangement, their parting words were forgotten. It was the end of the war, peace, the beginning of a new era. Even strangers embraced. She got into her car without waiting for breakfast, and drove to the forge. The welcome sign was up in place, and the villagers were fastening swathes of red, white and blue bunting right across the street. Amelia jumped out of the car, slammed the door, then stood for a moment in the entrance to the dark cave of the forge.

Her heart beat thickly and unsteadily. What would he look like? What would his first words to her be? She saw his father bending over the embers of the forge fire. He must have been smiling dreamily to himself for as he turned, his face was still wreathed in smiles.

The smile somehow froze. 'Good morning, M'lady,' he said, coming towards her, rubbing his hands clean down the sides of his apron, 'and a fine one.'

'A wonderful one. I hear he's safely back. Have you told him about the celebration?'

'Oh, aye. Yes, thank God.' He paused. 'They're both arrived safe.'

'Both?' Amelia was still smiling. Had his good mother gone somewhere, crippled as she was, to meet him? Or had James brought home a friend? The more the merrier!

'Yes, both, M'lady. It was quite a shock to us an' all. But a pleasant one! A very pleasant one! James married while he was out there, M'lady. A French girl! A grand lass! He didn't want to leave her behind. So he stayed to bring her home.'

BOOK THREE

The Noonday Sun
1919–39

ONE

'Times have changed, Amelia! Can't you get that into your head?'

Frederick was irritable, frustrated, angry. He was convalescent now from his attack of the virulent influenza that had killed and was still killing so many people. He had caught it on his last trip back from the peace conference at Versailles. Diana Nazier had realised as soon as she met him at Victoria that he was a sick man, and had sensibly packed him off to Haybury in her own chauffeur-driven Daimler, away from the damp and fog of London.

Now he sat in his silk smoking-jacket by the fire in his bedroom at Haybury awaiting Dr Randall's daily visit, his eyes on the clouded February skies outside, his expression bitter. He had just tried to tell Amelia that the Ajax side of Jerningham must close down, and as usual Amelia was arguing and suggesting instead that Ajax be entered for the Schneider Trophy race in September, the first to take place since 1914. She was dangling in front of his nose the carrot of the King's interest in flying, and the possibility that His Majesty himself might attend.

'Unlike some people, munitions manufacturers, black marketeers and those rascally uniform-makers up in Yorkshire, I've come out of this war a poorer man.'

It was not strictly true. He had come out of it a poorer man than he would have wished. As far as Frederick was concerned, the war had ended far too soon. If it had gone on for another year, with the contracts Jerningham had already received for Ajax from both the Navy and the Royal Air Force, then Frederick would have come out of the war with considerable wealth.

'Even if you haven't made money, Frederick, you've advanced politically. Without the factory, without Ajax, you would never have got on to the Air Board in the first place.'

'How very disloyal of you to suppose that!' Frederick's face went an angry mottled red. 'You'll be saying next that my royal appointment is due to it, too!'

In that of course, damn her, she might have been right. King George was interested in aircraft. The young Prince of Wales had been to France and inspected the R.F.C. But Amelia had no right to imply . . .

Diana Nazier would never have provoked him like that. She was the only woman who deserved the vote, he had told her weeks ago after the bill to enfranchise women had been passed. She never argued, never lost her temper. Any temper that had been lost recently had been his.

'You are getting to be rather jealous and possessive, my dearest,' she constantly chided him. His jealousy was natural. Diana was a widow of great beauty and wealth and opportunity. Her admirers were legion. By the end of the war, she had laughingly told him, no less than thirty-six eligible men, most of them it is true young officers who by now alas were dead, had proposed to her. One for every year of her life.

Frederick longed to be able to regularise their position, but as he steadily climbed the political ladder, divorce became even less acceptable. He had now been made a Silver Stick-in-Waiting to King George. He and Queen Mary were almost as strait-laced as Queen Victoria had been. And these days Frederick was haunted by the fear that the King, or worse the Queen, might hear of his affair with Diana, or that Diana might tire of the arrangement and marry someone else.

'But being an aircraft manufacturer,' Amelia went on doggedly, 'gave you political status. You can't deny it. It gave you the authority to speak as an expert.'

'Those days, Amelia, are over.'

'Those days are just beginning! People will still want to fly.'

'Not in the foreseeable future. Not by aeoplane. There simply isn't enough comfort. Who wants to freeze up in the sky with castor-oil over their faces? If passengers desert the ocean-going ships, it will be for *airships*, where they get the same civilised comfort.'

'They'll get it eventually from aeroplanes.'

'What arrant nonsense you talk! The only possible future in the air is with airships like Zeppelins.'

'Diana Nazier's favourite project!'

'Don't sneer at Diana! Nor at airships! The government wouldn't have put money into R34 if there wasn't a weight of informed opinion behind it.'

'Governments have done stupid things many times before.'

'But this isn't one of them. And next month, God willing, I shall travel up to see our airship R34 at East Fortune. If she makes a success of her maiden flight, then I shall certainly get subcontracts for Jerningham.'

That of course brought Amelia round full circle again to Ajax and the Schneider Trophy. 'Don't you see Frederick, that the same goes for Ajax? If Ajax wins this year's Schneider Trophy race we will get orders. Think what prestige that would bring! Please, Frederick? It's only a matter of a few months. *Please.*'

She almost went down on her knees. To prevent herself doing anything so undignified, she walked to the window, ostensibly to see if Dr Randall's trap was coming up the drive. But the drive was empty. As empty as her own future, she thought. First James. Now Ajax. She had lost James for ever. It was six weeks since she had heard of his marriage, but she couldstill not reconcile herself to it. Her optimistic nature had led her to believe that James would wait, that the miracle would happen, that Frederick would suddenly want a divorce, and that she would be free. Now James had deserted her. Sarah had told her that James's wife was beautiful, a French comtesse. Worse still, she was a Catholic, so the marriage was indissoluble. No divorce. No hope.

'I shall not go to the Welcome Home celebrations,' Amelia had announced to Sarah on her return from the forge, after Mr March had told her of James's marriage. 'So stop pressing that wretched dress!'

Sarah had continued her task doggedly. 'You'll *have* to go, M'lady.'

'Have to, Sarah? Did you say *have* to?'

'Yes, M'lady. Otherwise . . . '

'Otherwise *what*, Sarah?'

'Otherwise it'd look funny.'

'You get above yourself sometimes, Sarah.'

'Yes, M'lady.'

'I don't ever want to hear your advice again! Do you understand? It is not worth hearing. You do not know what you're talking about. And I shall *not* go.'

'No, M'lady.'

She had gone; Sarah was right, she could not do otherwise. It was her duty. It was expected of her. They were all waiting for her under the greeny-yellow hissing gaslights of Haybury village hall. It was an ordeal of unimaginable pain.

'Dear Lady Haybury,' the Reverend Bingham had whispered to her. 'You will, I hope, consent to lead the dance?'

'Of course.' She had assumed that he, the Rector, in Frederick's unavoidable absence in Paris, would partner her. But no, as the band on the platform had struck up, the Reverend Bingham continued, 'We thought it very appropriate dear Lady Haybury, that our local war hero . . . '

Amelia hardly heard what the Rector said after that.

Something to the effect that the Squadron Leader should have the honour of leading off the dance with her, since his wife had been unable after her long journey to accompany him to the hall. She was only conscious of the Rector turning to smile, to draw someone towards her. She was aware, acutely aware, of James.

James, clasping her loosely and decorously, waltzing her on to the floor. James's face, pale as a ghost's in the gaslight, his eyes shadowed, his mouth set. She was aware of her own shameful longing for him. Yet when she had looked directly up to him, and he had bent his head to hear what she whispered, all she had been able to manage was, 'How could you?'

And then his own reply, delivered through tight lips hardly above a whisper but thunderous in its condemnation, 'How could *you*?'

Frederick's voice broke irritably into her consciousness. 'There is no need to snivel over Ajax, Amelia.' She had not been aware till then that she was crying.

'I shall consider holding off stopping work altogether until the Schneider Trophy race. But if Ajax has no success there —'

Frederick was interrupted by the ormulu clock chiming four, and punctually after a brief knock, Sarah edging through the doorway with a tray of tea.

'Randall's late!' Frederick exclaimed. 'He's usually here to take my temperature, hold my wrist, tell me not to drink port, and then stay to eat and drink my tea.'

'The doctor's delayed, Sir,' Sarah glanced at Amelia, her eyes shielded. 'He telephoned just a few minutes ago. He'll be here shortly.'

In silence, Frederick watched Amelia pour his tea. Staring moodily into the fire, he ate a buttered scone. When Dr Randall finally appeared, he asked testily, 'And what excuse have you for neglecting your most important patient? Has someone died?'

Dr Randall shook his head. His grey whiskers parted in a sentimental smile. 'No, Sir. None of my patients has died today, I'm happy to tell you. One was born. I've just come from there. The Squadron Leader's wife. Their first-born.

221

Such a happy occasion. Gave birth not an hour ago.'

'You know he was the damned blacksmith here, don't you, Randall?'

'I do, Sir. And now he's the local hero. *And* bought Cornford House! Not a bad little property with that lake.'

'Well, times *have* changed! I've been trying to convince my wife of exactly that. Working men coming back from the front with a few pips on their shoulders, and imagining they're as good as we are!' He drained his cup and set it down with a clatter. 'The working class is getting above itself! There'll be trouble before long, I shouldn't wonder. Do you know, Randall, that not one of our female servants who were released for munitions has come back? Time was when they were queuing up for a servant's job at the Hall. This is what giving them the vote did. And time was when *you* wouldn't have kept me waiting for the blacksmith's wife.'

'She is a delicate lady, Sir Frederick.'

Frederick snorted.

'And how is the baby?' Amelia asked in a stifled voice.

'Fit and well, M'lady. A beautiful little daughter! Perfect! Lovely face. Not many new-born babes you can say that about.' He smiled sentimentally again. 'No doubt one day she'll break some hearts!'

And already, Amelia thought, leaving the bedroom, she has broken mine. She was surprised at the strength of her own feelings. A sense of unutterable desolation swept over her. She fled along the corridor to her own bedroom, and flung herself on her bed, face down. Why did the birth of James's daughter so affect her? Was it because it made his marriage to the Frenchwoman so much more solid and secure? Was it because some part of her had hoped it was a marriage without love? That it hadn't been consummated? Was that how she had deluded herself?

Or was it because of James's real first-born? Because of Charles?

TWO

Charles was the last person on Frederick's mind as he travelled down by train to attend the Jerningham board meeting on the last Thursday in July.

Diana Nazier had very affectionately seen him off at Waterloo. They had gone up together to Pulham in Norfolk to see the triumphant return of the British airship R34, after her double crossing of the Atlantic. The airship had at last been shown – after its disastrous war performance – as the queen of the peaceful skies.

Who would travel in noisy open-cockpitted ex-bombers or even in ocean liners when they could achieve the speed of the former with the luxury of the latter? For ten days afterwards Frederick and Diana had dined in the highest political circles on the story of the R34's arrival and their conversations with Captain Scott. Two days afterwards a subcontract for balloon fabric work for the R38 had been mysteriously manipulated out of the Air Ministry by Diana. What matter if Winston Churchill, the new Secretary of State for War and Air, was busy cutting down the RAF from 280 squadrons to 28? What matter if the Army and the Navy had gone back to quarrelling over the dismemberment of the RAF and the eating of the pieces? What matter if aircraft manufacturers had been reduced to making bathtubs, or like Graham-White selling surplus armoured cars with Rolls-Royce bodies to the war-profiteers? Now a Department of Civil Aviation had been set up under Sir Sefton Brancker, Jerningham would help to build the airship links for the all-red-route of the British Empire.

What was on his mind, as he blew Diana a farewell kiss from his first-class carriage window was . . . who was she off to dine with now? Wonderful though she had been this last fortnight, he sometimes felt that she wasn't completely satisfied, that really their relationship was just a little too pre-war – particularly now she was free to marry anybody.

The Prince of Wales himself was setting a new style. Having met petite and pretty Mrs Dudley Ward down a cellar in an air-raid during a party given by a Mr Ernest Simpson's sister, hardly a week passed when he was not with her. The gossip was that he could certainly marry her. Attitudes to divorce were rapidly changing. George V was getting on in years; a new king would bring new ideas.

But of course that might be many years yet. And meanwhile . . .

He couldn't help again feeling, when Amelia met him with the Rolls at Brockenhurst, that the problem would have been solved altogether more quickly and in a more dignified way if the flu epidemic had carried her off as it had so nearly carried him.

All through the board meeting that afternoon he had pondered that question. What would have happened if now he had been as free as Diana?

Impatiently he agreed that the money should be made officially available for Ajax to enter the Schneider Trophy – but added the rider that if nothing came of it, the Ajax project would be shelved permanently. He was already regretting his vote when they returned to Haybury for dinner. During most of that meal he sat silent. Then he went up to the library where the evening post was waiting on his desk. There were only two letters. The one with the Harrow postmark he opened first. Arthur's report described him as having settled into the school extremely well.

He opened the other buff envelope. It was Charles's school report. He picked up the long ebony ruler from his desk and rolled it between his fingers, as though to smooth out the wrinkles and excrescences of his increasingly complicated life. Then he rang for the butler. 'Would you please ask Lady Haybury and my sons to kindly step into the library?'

Three minutes later, the door opened and Amelia led the way in, very much on the defensive. 'You wanted to see us, Frederick?'

He twiddled the rule round faster. 'I do, my dear.' He turned his head to give his youngest a special smile. 'Arthur, your report, I'm delighted to say, is very good.'

Arthur relaxed. Amelia did not. There was a long silence.

'Charles —'

Frederick held the report by its lefthand corner as though it was something defiled. 'Have you any idea what this is?'

'I can guess.'

'Have you any idea what it contains?'

'I can guess.'

'*How* can you guess?'

'Because Holmes always was a stinker.'

'Exactly what your headmaster thinks of *you* . . . though he puts it rather more politely.'

Frederick got up from the desk and holding the ruler in his right hand and the report still in his left walked over to the mantelpiece.

'Position in Greek, bottom! Position in Latin . . . bottom.'

'But I was top in maths.'

'Conduct . . . disgraceful!'

'So is he.'

'Come over here!'

Charles stayed where he was. 'Didn't you hear what I said? *Come over here!*'

Very slowly, Charles walked over to the mantelpiece, followed by Amelia. Arthur stayed by the door.

'You have spent your entire term, according to your form-master, obsessed with those damned silly American flying boats and Alcock and Brown in their bomber!'

'But they crossed the Atlantic! That's history!'

'Not a thing did you do! You are lazy! You are insolent! You are continually breaking bounds.'

Frederick had flushed an angry purple. 'I presume you have been disciplined?'

'What does that mean?'

'Thrashed, sir!' Frederick shouted. 'I take it you have been thrashed?'

Charles's face went white. 'They wouldn't dare!'

'Wouldn't they, by God!' He was in a paroxysm of fury. 'Put out your hand! Immediately!'

'Frederick!'

'You keep out of it, Amelia! The young puppy's got to be taught a lesson.' Frederick raised the ebony ruler. 'I'll —'

With a contemptuous little smile, Charles put both his hands behind his back. Amelia rushed between them, but it was too late. With terrific force, the heavy ruler slammed across Charles's face, cutting his left cheek wide open.

It began to bleed profusely. Charles stood quite still. Frederick tossed the ruler back on to the desk. 'Not a penny more will I waste on your education! Out! *Get out!*'

Just as slowly as he had walked to the mantelpiece, Charles now walked to the door. Arthur had already disappeared through it.

Alone with Frederick, Amelia was unable to speak. Her whole body trembled. Her lips felt numb. After what seemed minutes, controlling herself with difficulty, she said, 'If you won't pay his school fees, I will!'

Frederick raised a derisive eyebrow. 'With *what*?'

'With the profits we'll make when Ajax wins the Schneider Trophy!'

The night before the Schneider Trophy race, Amelia went late to bed. She was nervously excited, unable to unwind. So much depended on it – though not, Charles had told her often enough and bitterly enough, his continuing education. After the row over his report, he had written off to the airline Air Transport and Travel at Hounslow, and after a series of interviews had got himself the promise of a mechanic's apprenticeship in October.

'If Ajax wins, you won't need to take the apprenticeship up,' Amelia told him. 'I'll have the money to send you wherever you want to go.'

'That's where I want to go. And that's where I'm going. I hope you win, but it won't make a damn of difference to me.'

He was so stubborn. So like James. He couldn't wait to leave. She lay staring up at the ceiling in the big bedroom at Haybury. The same ceiling James and she had stared up at those two long years ago.

James had been invited three months ago to address his old village school at Jerningham on the first Empire Day of peace. Sarah, whose little niece was Britannia in the usual pageant of the member countries, had told her all about it. How James hadn't given the sort of speech they expected, all about the war and the Empire and how wonderful it was. That he'd listened with a funny little smile to the children chanting:

Today's the Empire's birthday,
The 24th of May,
Salute the Flag, salute the King,
On glorious Empire Day!

And then he'd talked to them about flying, and that he wanted every boy and girl to be determined early to pursue the career they wanted. He'd told them about the Schneider Trophy race that would take place off Bournemouth

225

sands nearby, and the R34 about to fly the Atlantic. Britain, he said, would rule the skies as certainly as she ruled the seas.

The RAF were not making an entry, so why his interest in the race? Amelia would have liked to think his interest was because of Ajax. Ajax owed as much to him as it did to Cummings or poor Wilkinson, and certainly much more than to her. But mostly she wanted him to be interested in Ajax because it was their joint effort, their link with one another.

This interest in the totally RAF R34 was more obvious, now he was staying on in the service. But the story that had captured Amelia's interest – as it had that of King George himself – was that of the airship's homing pigeons, carried in case of distress. While in New York, one escaped from its cage. It beat the R34 home to England, winging its way over 3500 miles of tumultuous ocean.

That was the story Amelia hugged to herself that pre-race night. Those small wings triumphing over that trackless ocean – as tomorrow Ajax must triumph.

Earlier that evening, Amelia had gone down to the hangar with Cummings for a last look at the Ajax that had been selected and groomed for the race, as one might visit the stable for a last look at a challenger, and had run her fingers down the thin blade of its wing.

Ajax was the only monoplane in the race. Cummings had made a practice flight round the Needles, clocking in a speed of 160 miles an hour – far faster than the Sopwith or the Supermarine Sea Lion flying boat or the Avro. The French and Italians, too, had only biplanes.

'Those wings slice through the air,' Cummings told her, 'You mark my words, we're going to win!'

Just before she left the office to return to Haybury, the designer handed her a picture with the words, 'Tomorrow, I intend to present you with the real thing!'

It was a coloured drawing of the Schneider Trophy – a romantic piece of sculpture cast in gold. It was of a young man's head just visible in a curling sea wave, being kissed, held up, about to be drawn into the skies by a winged golden-haired goddess.

When eventually she did fall asleep, Amelia dreamed of that trophy. But she was not looking at it – she was inside it. And it wasn't anything cast in gold. The waves were real and tumultuous and menacing. And the face that looked up was James's. The winged golden goddess wasn't there to pull him out of the waves – only her mortal self, struggling through mountainous seas. And then just as she reached James, his face disappeared and there was nothing but an ocean and sky of enveloping grey. She woke with her heart pounding and a feeling of imminent disaster. The bedroom was still shadowy. She looked at her watch.

Six thirty-two . . . yet it was still quite dark outside.

Strange, she thought, her window faced east and by now the sun on such a still day should be shining right into her eyes. She got up and walked to the window. It was not black outside at all. It was grey, slowly turning white.

Thick fog blanketted everywhere.

'They won't cancel.' Cummings said with determined cheerfulness. 'You mark my words, they can't!'

Ghostly figures in the fog helped him up into the cockpit, and pushed the aircraft down into the flat calm water. Standing at the top of the slipway beside Charles, all Amelia could now see was a smudge of cottonwool.

'It'll clear,' Charles said, squeezing her arm, 'by the time we've had breakfast, the sun will be out!'

Frederick had gone to Paris on a conference on the aftermath of the now signed Versailles Treaty and German reparations. He had taken Diana and she had specially asked for Arthur to accompany them, much to his delight. They had gone by train and boat, much to Charles's disgust, instead of by ex-bomber of Air Transport and Travel Ltd that had just begun a two and a half hour London-Paris service, one way ticket £21.

Breakfast wasn't exactly a cheerful meal. Charles did his best, but Amelia talked abstractedly, her eyes on the fog peering and pressing against the three long windows of the dining-room like poverty, famine and pestilence themselves. No sun had appeared by the time breakfast was over, but word came through by telephone from the organisers that Ajax had safely taxied round Hengistbury Head and was moored near the Royal Aero Club's yacht *Ombra* anchored off Bournemouth pier. Cheered by this, Amelia and Charles set off in the tender.

Visibility ahead was only a few yards, the fog rolled and swirled over the oily water. Sounds came distorted, the putter of engines, the tinkle of mast-bells, the mournful regular note of fog horns. Skilfully Charles steered round the salt flats of Lymington, under the shadowy cliffs on to Bournemouth beach which was packed with an army of ghosts expectantly waiting for the race to begin.

Finding Ajax, still as stone in the glass-calm water, Charles moored at the same buoy, and they chatted to Cummings, all the time hopefully looking for an improvement in the weather. A sudden roar overhead made them look up. The snub-nosed snout of the Fairey seaplane made a momentary appearance, then there was a splash as it alighted. Next came the French Spad that practically overturned a rowing boat. Aeroplanes and bathers became mixed up. The Italian flying boat accidentally beached itself amongst children building sandcastles.

By one o'clock the weather improved. Charles happily munched sandwiches, Cummings made a pretence of eating one, but Amelia was too dry-mouthed to swallow a crumb. At three o'clock, the white pall of fog shimmered as if the sun were about to break through. But the race hadn't begun and no one seemed to know what was happening. Charles took the tender round to the yacht *Ombra* and Amelia went on board to find out. She was told by a harried race official that the start had been postponed till six. Among the officials on the yacht and the representatives of the competitors there appeared to be one long argument.

Then Swanage – one of the turning points – suddenly became visible across the bay and there was a flutter of excitement. The committee of the Aero Club immediately decided to start the race, even though the pilots protested that the weather was still not suitable for flying.

Almost at once, Nicholl took off in the Fairey and disappeared; Hawker refused to go in the Sopwith. Cummings in Ajax took his place. Amelia's heart lifted as she watched him roar off into the fog.

'Good luck!' she called after him.

The Supermarine flying-boat went next. Then Hawker changed his mind and went off at full throttle. He had scarcely vanished into the fog, when Nicholl in the Fairey returned, having abandoned the race after looking at the weather conditions around Swanage. Hawker also returned and in a towering rage both pilots boarded *Ombra* demanding the race be abandoned.

The Supermarine flying-boat had completely disappeared and was later discovered to have upended in the sea, tossing out the pilot who was rescued by motorboat. But Janello in the Italian flying-boat still went on and so did Ajax. Now there really was a good chance of winning. Amelia found herself a vantage point in the stern of *Ombra*, gripping the railings, scanning the sky, listening for the familiar sound overhead of Ajax's engines as Cummings completed a lap. Once, twice, three times . . . her heart was in her mouth. She clenched the rail so tightly that she could no longer feel her fingers. Then a voice just behind her said quietly, 'He's doing well.'

For a moment, she didn't trust herself to turn, certainly not to speak. The excitement of the race was transmitted to this meeting with James. The race became simultaneously nothing and everything. Nothing compared to the torment, the excitement of seeing James again. Everything because Ajax was theirs, their joint venture.

No other person in the world would want it to win as much as she did, except James. No one else would understand. No one else's excitement could match hers. Nothing else but Ajax battling to win could overleap, wipe out the bitter circumstances of their last meeting. And for Ajax to win the race with James beside her would be symbolic of some continuum however tenuous between them.

When she forced herself to turn her head, she saw James holding a stopwatch in his hand. She had hardly looked at him during that painful waltz at the Welcome Home. Now her eyes travelled hungrily over him. His muscular body was fined down somehow by the well-cut blue uniform. Under the peak of his cap, his face was half-shadowed. He looked years older than his age, she thought, assured, commanding even, yet with the same familiar expression round his mouth and in the deep blue eyes. A James infinitely dear and known, yet somehow more desirable and remote from her. It was as if the Almighty had chosen some special punishment for her, worse than anything the gods had visited on Tantalus, to make her need and desire James more each time she saw him and yet simultaneously to take him further and further from her.

All the anger and reproach she had stored up against him which had so warmed and sustained her these last eight months evaporated. She felt weak and foolish and a girl again. 'You look rather intimidating,' she said.

He smiled. 'It's just the uniform.'

She shook her head, 'I doubt it is.'

His smile deepened. 'I doubt there's any uniform in the world that would intimidate you, Amelia.'

'You sound regretful.'

'No, far from it.' She thought he said the word, 'Proud,' but she was not sure. Cummings suddenly roared very low above them, so low that she caught a flash of the slender wings.

'Damn,' James said, 'I forgot to time that and it was a fast one.'

He punched his watch, not looking at her.

Neither of them spoke. It was as if in that brief silence before Cummings roared overhead again, they had slipped through some crack in time, back to their old eager relationship again.

'Six minutes 57 seconds!' James shouted exultantly above the noise of Ajax's engines. 'At this rate, Amelia, he'll do it.'

Somehow she had stopped holding the rail and was gripping his free hand tightly with both of hers. Scenting victory, Cummings was outdoing himself. Ajax appeared and reappeared overhead in ever swifter laps. 'Faster by twenty seconds! That's it!' He put his hand on her shoulder. 'Amelia, you've done it!'

'James!' She threw her arms round his neck, *'We've* done it.'

She closed her eyes as he kissed her gently on her forehead. It was a moment of infinite, unbelievable happiness. Behind them on the yacht they could hear the excited clamour of megaphones. Someone was announcing Ajax had landed safely in the fastest time and was the winner. Someone else was shouting in Italian, another in French.

'We'll go down to the bar to celebrate,' James said softly. 'We'll crack a bottle of champagne together, and then . . . '

She knew what 'and then' meant. And then we shall go our separate ways. Yet it wasn't total renunciation. Somehow they had something. They had shared the triumph. The Ajax project, their love, too, perhaps went on.

Then just as the barman opened the champagne bottle there was some sort of argument between officials, much coming and going, head shaking and brandishing of papers. It was announced that the judges on the marker boat which was the turning point at Swanage had not had sight nor sound of either Ajax or the Italian Savoia.

Nobody knew where in the fog they had turned. The race was declared null and void.

THREE

After that sad fiasco, three-quarters of the Jerningham factory was closed. Two of the bigger sheds and six rooms in the main building were prepared for the promised subcontracts for airships. The Ajax project was shelved and the one surviving Schneider Trophy aircraft was banished to the smallest hangar by the slipway. There she was to remain year after year, as financial panic gripped the government, the aircraft manufacturers and the workers and the euphoria of peace gave way to the bitterness of unemployment and poverty.

The Welsh Wizard flitted from one trouble spot to another to smooth them with his charm. Lloyd-George and his government had been elected as the winners of the war when the blood was hardly dry on the battlefield. Squeeze the Germans till the pips squeak, cried the British public almost as vehemently as the French, make *them* support *us*. Take their equipment, their resources, their ideas, their land, their money. Make sure they never rise again!

Lloyd-George, once the supporter of aircraft, now wanted to hear no more of them. The RAF was cut to a tenth of its former size. Aircraft manufacturers went bankrupt right and left. Not many were as lucky as Jerningham in landing airship subcontracts. Amelia was also lucky to be able to keep the goldbeater girls from the village, among them Sarah's niece. She was lucky also, she knew, that Ronald Cummings stayed. 'You can try him,' Frederick said. 'If he want his job at half his salary, more fool him.'

He had decided to be a fool. 'You mark my words, before the end of the decade there'll be passenger aircraft with more carrying capability than those fat pigs of airships!'

Charles had left. Early in October, he had given her that particularly sweet smile, told her not to worry and had gone off to his apprentice job, living in digs near the tiny Hounslow grass airfield.

Just as the embryo warplanes had had to struggle against official disbelief, now it was the turn of the baby airliners. Churchill had declared, 'Civil aviation must fly by itself. The government cannot possibly support it in the air.' Others saw its future. The Smith brothers flew their Vimy bomber to Australia. The Postmaster General gave airmail to AT and T and allowed their DH16s to fly the Royal Mail pennant. The King and Queen of the Belgians flew to the newly opened airport at Croydon to attend the wedding of Lord Curzon's daughter to the up-and-coming MP, Oswald Mosley.

Thanks to Cummings's training, Charles was soon servicing the new eight-seater DH18s that AT and T used on the Paris service. Now in a cut-throat fare-slashing battle with the subsidised French service and Handley-Page, the money he was paid hardly covered his subsistence. But he twice got flights to

Paris, and to Amelia's relief seemed to be settling down. Then AT and T went bankrupt. Charles got a job with the Handley-Page airline. Then Handley-Page went bankrupt. Charles did not tell Amelia, but kept writing cheerfully while he tramped round London offices trying to get a job.

No one wanted to know about aeroplanes. Airships, yes – he was promised a job in the airship shed at Cardington, but just before he went to Bedford, suddenly on 24 August 1921 there were headlines in all the evening papers.

R38 breaks up over Hull.

Of the 65 people on board, mostly Americans to whom the airship had been sold, 62 were killed.

The breaking up of the R38 was the biggest tragedy in civil aviation so far, and was long to be remembered.

At that time, discussion was going on in Haybury as to how best to remember the million British dead of the Great War. All over the country towns and villages were beginning to build war memorials, engraved with the names of their local dead, and though neither Frederick as their lord of the manor, nor James as their local hero had shown much interest, Haybury and Jerningham did not wish to be outdone. The Rector telephoned Amelia to say that the Squadron Leader's wife had kindly offered the hospitality of Cornford House for a meeting on the proposed war memorial which he hoped either Sir Frederick or Lady Haybury, or better still both, would be kind enough to attend.

Government business kept Frederick in London. Amelia felt she could not do otherwise than put in an appearance. The dreaded meeting with James's wife could no longer be postponed. I've postponed it for too long as it is, Amelia thought, as Sarah helped her dress for the meeting. She probably thinks that I've snubbed her. I've perhaps made an enemy of her.

Aloud she asked Sarah. 'You've met her. What is she like?'

'The Comtesse de Saguenac?' Sarah's lip curled as she bobbed a derisory curtesy. 'Or Mrs March? Well, I didn't really meet her. I only saw her when I took my niece Rosie to ask if she'd like her as a nursemaid. She was all right, I suppose. But distant. Maybe that's because she's French. Anyway she didn't want our Rosie. And Rosie'd rather be a goldbeater girl. Mrs March said she wanted a French nursemaid.'

'Is she very pretty?'

'The nursemaid? I don't know. I shouldn't think so.'

'Don't be awkward, Sarah! You know I didn't mean the nursemaid!'

'Oh, *her*. Well, she's quite handsome. In a dark way. Sallow. Dark eyes. But you'll see for yourself, M'lady. Beauty's in the eye of the beholder, as my poor mum used to say. Handsome is as handsome does. I've heard village folk say they can't think what he sees in her. An' I have heard it said, he married her because she saved him from the Hun. Or that he married her for her money. A big estate, they say, in France. But his mother, old Mrs March, says he married her because he worships the ground she walks on.'

'She would,' Amelia said, fastening on a bracelet, and picking up her small clutch handbag.

Sarah opened the door for her. 'Watch how you drive, M'lady!'

The new gate to Cornford House stood welcomingly open. A variety of

231

emotions assailed Amelia as she drove up the freshly macadamed drive. Gone were the old stones and the weeds and the moss that used to fill its cracks and crannies. Gone too the scent of primroses from the woods, the wild hordes of daffodils, the feathery grasses and the bracken fronds. The grass was shaved, the lawn edges sharp, the daffodils tamed to decorative clumps. Even the smell that drifted in through the open windows was a pale controlled ghost of those heavenly spring smells of two decades ago.

Getting out of the car, Amelia stood for a moment looking down towards the southern tip of the distant lake.

'Wonderful, isn't it, Lady Haybury, what these clever people have done?' The Rector came up noiselessly and stood beside her. 'When you think of how busy the Squadron Leader is at the Air Ministry. And when you think of what a wilderness this place was! I expect you've seen inside the house?'

'Not recently.'

'Then you have a treat in store!' He waved his hand towards the façade where windows now glittered in what had been empty sockets, towards the entrance now sporting a handsome door, flanked by two shrubs in ornamental pots. A murmur of voices leaked out from the hall. 'Everyone is inside drinking cocktails,' the Rector told her, scrutinising her face sideways as if unsure how she would take such dissipated news. 'Apparently it is the latest fashion. They seem rather strange and sickly to me, but then I'm no connoisseur.'

He opened the glass inner door for her. The air smelled of cigarette smoke and expensive perfume and the hall seemed filled with cloche hats in every imaginable colour, and long cigarette holders all in black.

Everyone seemed to turn towards Amelia, smiling deferentially. The doctor's wife and the Rector's wife said, 'Good morning, Lady Haybury.' The Bishop's wife kissed her cheek and said, 'How lovely to see you, Amelia.'

And then they all parted like the Red Sea itself.

A long awful tunnel opened up in front of her, and there at the end of it was James's wife. A short dark-eyed woman with her black hair cut in a straight fringe and bob, whom at first Amelia thought was rather stout, but as she reached her and took her hand, she saw that Marie was pregnant.

Why should I mind? Amelia asked herself. What business is it of mine? James had married this French woman. He was not a man to be coerced. Presumably therefore he was in love with her. And she must learn to accept that fact.

'Have you settled in happily?' Amelia asked her in a breathless voice quite unlike her own.

'I have settled in, yes, thank you.' Mrs March enunciated slowly and with a rather charming accent, but her tone was flat and her smile wintry. Her face was thin, well-sculpted and fine-boned, and should have been attractive in a vivacious way. Instead there was a chill aura of melancholy. The eyes lacked depth. Until, turning to make some banal remark, Amelia surprised a look in them, fixed on her own face, of deep devouring hatred.

'I was earlier remarking to Lady Haybury,' the Rector returned to the pair of them, sensing constraint, 'that you and the Squadron Leader have done such a splendid job on the house and grounds.'

'Thank you.'

Perhaps she is lonely, Amelia thought. Perhaps she is devoted to James and missing his presence.

The Rector smiled. 'And does the Squadron Leader still manage to come home regularly?'

Amelia watched the woman's expression carefully. Surely her face would light up at the mention of James! Instead, her expression resumed its look of total blankness. 'Every weekend,' she replied in a flat toneless voice. 'In fact, I'm expecting him later this evening. He is a devoted husband and father.'

It sounded like a carelessly written obituary notice, Amelia told herself. And hard on the heels of that thought, a sudden realisation – all this misery and she doesn't even love him.

The room felt stiflingly hot. The cigarette smoke stung her eyes. The cocktails tasted vile. Excusing herself from the Rector and walking towards the cloakroom, she opened the French doors in the corridor that led on to the rear terrace.

At first she had meant to do no more than take in a few gulps of fresh air and wipe her eyes and then tidy her make-up in the cloakroom. But at the bottom of the green slope she could see the midday sun sparkling on the lake. Despite the manicured lawns that now intervened, she was drawn irresistibly towards it. Her high thin heels made holes in the watered grass which no doubt the gardener would swear about, but she didn't care. She felt a sense of relief and escape. The hum of busy polite voices faded behind her. In a couple of minutes a clump of rhododendrons hid her from view, and in as many more she had reached what savage pruning had left of the reeds.

Despite the dampness of the grass, she sat down and clasped her hands round her knees, while she conjured memories of herself and James, watching the swans, casting their bread on what had turned out to be such troubled barren waters.

There were no cygnets visible, but five mallards had come down on to the water. Amelia closed her eyes, letting her mind and memory drift back over the years. After a few moments she heard the sound of quick small footsteps coming through the grass at the north end of the lake.

Suddenly there appeared, coming down the slope, a little toddler with black hair in ringlets. She held what looked like a lump of bread in her hand, and she kept casting anxious looks over her shoulder as if to see if she was being followed.

It was the same steep slope that James and she had lain on nearly twenty years ago, when the cygnets nested and where the water was deep. The child crouched by the water's edge and began crumbling the bread. Amelia was about fifty yards away, but she could see the absorbed expression on the round face. She could see to the firm jaw, the tender mouth. She could even see a faint resemblance to Charles. James's child, Amelia thought in anguish and envy.

'Careful!' she called automatically to the child, as the ducks swam up quacking and the child leaned further forward. But the child didn't seem to hear what she said, though she heard the voice and looked up. Like that, the resemblance to James and Charles was unmistakable.

'Careful!' Amelia called again. Another duck had swum up and the child lost interest in Amelia. She became absorbed in tossing a crumb as far out into the lake as possible so that the farthest, most timid, duck could reach it.

'Be careful! Don't lean forward like that!'

But the child took no notice. Amelia got to her feet, kicked off her shoes and began to hurry round the shore. Before she could reach the child, there was a splash. Not pausing to hitch up the skirt of her dress, Amelia waded in.

The ducks flew off in a furious clamour. Amelia pushed swiftly across the corner of the lake, through the turgid green water, her feet slipping on the weedy bottom, scooped up the child, pushed her on to the bank and scrambled out beside her.

In all the time, the child seemed too shocked to let out any cry at all. She coughed and spluttered and retched. Her face streamed with lake water. Her vivid blue eyes brimmed with tears. There were skeins of weed caught in her sodden ringlets, minute discs of green duckweed on her lashes. Simultaneously the child and Amelia seemed to realise how easily she could have drowned. The tears turned into sobs of fright. Amelia caught her to her, hugging her, crooning to her, rocking her in her arms, kissing the wet cheeks and the sodden hair.

'*Qui es tu?*' the child asked when her sobs had quieted. She held herself a little away from Amelia staring up, her eyes wide.

'Amelia. *Je suis Anglaise.* Can you speak English?'

'Yes, Madame. My father is English.'

'And what is your name?'

'Marianne.'

'What are you doing, Marianne, out here on your own? It is very dangerous. The lake is deep. Has your Nanny not told you?'

The child nodded. 'But she does not like to feed ducks. And I do.'

Amelia smiled. 'So do I.'

'Please, Madame, do not tell her! She will smack me.'

After a moment's thought, Amelia said, 'So long as you promise never, *never* to come here on your own again?'

'All right.'

'Then let me take off your wet dress and wring it out. If we spread it to dry in the sun . . . '

Gently Amelia unfastened the minute buttons of the child's dress. At thirty-five I am becoming middle-aged and broody she told herself, surprised at the wave of maternal pleasure. The child's petticoat was sopping too, so were her liberty bodice and knickers. Amelia wrung them out and spread them over a rhododendron bush to dry in the hot sun.

'*Your* dress too, Madame,' the child said.

Amelia took off her own dress and laid it on the grass, and then in inspiration she took off her petticoat. The top was still quite dry. She used it to towel the little girl's legs. Then she sat her on her knee with her arm round her. The tendrils of damp hair smelled sweet. The sun shone warmly on her own bare neck and shoulders. Bees droned. The ducks came back to the lake as if nothing had happened and were quarrelling over the remaining crumbs. The child put her head against Amelia's shoulder and dozed off to sleep. Her body went limp and heavy. The moment was almost unbearably sweet. Amelia closed her eyes and held her face up to the sun.

Then a shadow fell over her glowing eyelids. James stood looking at them,

234

his face a strange mixture of amusement, anger, concern and pain.

'What on earth . . . ?'

'Father.' The child was awake immediately at the sound of his voice. She scrambled to her feet, her arms outstretched to him. 'I fell in and Amelia pulled me out. And my dress is dry. Nearly.' She seized her clothes. 'Please, Father don't tell Nanny or Maman. *Please!*'

'I shall make no promises, Marianne,' he said sternly.

'*Please.*'

He waved her to silence. At the same time he flung Amelia a cross look as if she had brought the child there in the first place.

'Have you thanked Amelia, Marianne?'

'Yes. I mean, no.' Marianne threw her arms round Amelia's neck and kissed her.

'Thank you, Amelia,' James said stiffly, still frowning.

'I'll put her clothes on. They still feel a bit damp. I should get her Nanny to . . .'

'I expect,' James said, 'she will get smacked and sent to bed.'

'Oh, no!' Amelia protested. 'Please, no!' She looked up from her fastening of the buttons. 'I couldn't bear it. Please.' And throwing truth to the winds, 'It was *all* my fault.'

He nodded, unsmiling, and said he had already assumed that to be the case. He scooped up her dress and handed it to her. 'Can you get home all right, Amelia?'

'Perfectly all right, thank you. I drove over. My car is in the drive.'

'Then say goodbye to Amelia, Marianne.'

'*Au revoir*, Amelia.' The child continued waving over his shoulder, till, as they began the slope up to the house, the little face crumpled. Amelia could hear her sobs, and James's stern 'That's enough, Marianne! You know perfectly well. If you disobey, you must be punished.'

A wave of protective anger swept over Amelia. She got to her feet and regardless of her undignified appearance, called after him, 'You are becomig just like your mother, James! Unbending! Self-righteous!' And to herself, 'always resenting me.'

The child looked wide-eyed at Amelia, her sobs interrupted by surprise. Had Amelia been told that one day she would resent that child with every bit as much bitterness as James's mother resented her, she would have laughed it to scorn.

But the laughter that day was James's. He suddenly turned round. 'Amelia,' he laughed, 'if only you could see how ridiculous you look!'

235

FOUR

'You look the perfect birdwoman, Amelia,' Ronald Cummings told her as they walked over to the little Avro 504 waiting for them on Eastleigh airfield.

Amelia had a sneaking idea that James would think she looked more ridiculous than ever. She was wearing a fur-lined helmet with flying goggles above her forehead and a long leather coat. She had always been about to learn to fly but had kept on postponing it, partly because she felt unsure of herself, partly because she had been altogether too busy. Now with the factory staff reduced to a handful of men and women from Jerningham village working on what subcontract work could be found, both she and Cummings had time on their hands. Not only that, Charles had written to say that he had saved enough for lessons and, in a spirit of friendly rivalry, she wanted to beat him to the flying ticket. Cummings had insisted he teach her himself at the Southampton flying club and had told her. 'Mark my words, you'll have a natural aptitude.'

To her surprise, she had. The little Avro responded to her every movement, like a well-trained horse. Once up in the sky, wheeling the nose round the horizon on steep turns, or exploring the canyons between clouds or climbing till she was gasping for breath and the earth below had shrunk to toyland, she immediately found confidence. Ronald's comforting comments through the Gosport tube – the rubber tube 'telephone' that connected the front and rear cockpits – certainly helped, but suddenly she felt the real joy that James always said was in flying.

Even landing was fun – getting closer and closer to the fields and little houses, hopping over the hedge like a jump and then tantalising the earth by holding off till the last moment. And stalling and spinning was just like being in a whirlwind merry-go-round. She would delay pushing the stick forward and putting on opposite rudder to get out of the spin so long that Ronald would get the wind up and call plaintively through the tube, 'Amelia . . .'

'You've got a nice pair of hands,' he told her after her third lesson. 'But now we come to the *really* difficult part . . . instrument flying. You've got to distrust your own feelings and emotions and rely only on the instruments.'

The only blind flying instruments were the wobbling needles of altimeter and airspeed indicator and the spirit level attitude gauge. It was all in getting the 'feel' of the aeroplane and becoming part of it. But into huge woolly clouds Amelia sailed and still emerged, still on course, still at the right height, still knowing where she was.

After her fourth lesson, she demanded to be sent solo.

'Too early, Amelia. You haven't had enough instruction.'

'But I have!'

Naturally he weakened. Naturally he let her go. She completed that solitary trip round the airfield with smoothness and panache. And then she demanded to take the test for her flying ticket.

'No, Amelia . . . you're being too impetuous.'

'I'm not.'

'You don't want to risk a failure just to beat Charles.'

'I won't fail.'

The test was arranged and she took it next day. The instructor was most impressed. When she told Charles she'd passed, far from being jealous he was enormously pleased.

Three weeks before, a man called Barnard had won the first 'King's Cup' – an annual race from London to Glasgow and back, set up by George V to encourage flying. 'And what are you going to do now, Mama?' Charles asked.

Immediately Amelia replied, 'I'm going to win next year's King's Cup.'

The Royal Family's interest in flying was in Frederick's opinion the direct cause of their invitation to the wedding of the Prince's younger brother, the Duke of York, to Lady Elizabeth Bowes-Lyon in Westminster Abbey that April. At last, his qualifications for Air Minister were being recognised. Baldwin who had so long ignored him would certainly take the royal hint. As he told Diana, his present lack of office was but a pause in his upward climb.

He decided that the town house – a luxury he had begun to feel was unnecessary in the economic climate – should not be disposed of until after the royal wedding. He would mark the occasion in loyal style, Amelia must give a large and lavish dinner party after the wedding. Diana Nazier would come, of course. So would many of their fellow wedding guests. That dinner was to be the most crucial of his life.

Aunt Sempner sniffed at the whole idea of it, when Amelia called briefly on their way back to give Frederick's aunt a quick account of how beautiful the bride looked and how loving the Duke. Frederick refused to leave the car. He sat fuming at the delay while Amelia described to Aunt Sempner the dresses, the hats, the shoes, who was there and who – to Aunt Sempner's cackling delight – wasn't.

'And now you've let yourself in for a dinner, you silly gal! It won't do any good. Frederick's passé. It's a different set now. Gay young things. Duff Cooper. Churchill. The Prince of Wales. A jazzy fast set. It's your own fault, you silly gal! You spend too long on those smelly aeroplanes. Did you get close enough to Queen Mary to see her face? Does she still enamel?'

'I couldn't see. She looked very handsome.'

Aunt Sempner gazed at her own pink and white enamelled face in her hand mirror till the impatient car horn from the street below brought Amelia to her feet.

'And how are my grand-nevvies, Amelia?'

'Very well.'

'Frederick tells me Charles is turning into a bounder,' Aunt Sempner called gleefully after her.

'He's not,' Amelia shouted back.

'A cad and a bounder!' Aunt Sempner's shrill laughter followed her to the street.

Frederick and Amelia made their way with difficulty back to Park Lane. Crowds of Londoners were converging on Buckingham Palace in a spontaneous display of affection. 'Leave yourself time to get decently ready,' Frederick consulted his watch. 'I don't want there to be any hitches tonight.'

Half an hour before the first guests arrived, as the crowd outside Buckingham Palace swelled to 100,000 and red, white and blue rockets soared into the night sky, Diana telephoned. With unnatural sweetness and humility, she asked Amelia if she might bring a friend to the dinner. 'He's tremendously interested in aviation. And very clever. One of these days, I feel sure he will achieve high office. He's so interested to meet you.'

Thus that night, quietly and without any warning bell sounding, Christopher Birdwood Thomson entered their lives, there to remain for the rest of his days.

'You two have so much in common,' Diana said as she introduced Christopher Thomson to Frederick, 'I *know* you'll be friends.'

Not a chance, Frederick thought, as he shook hands with the man. He was Labour to begin with. The electorate had had the good sense not to elect him in the 1922 general election, but he was still hanging round his friend Ramsay MacDonald. Born of a military family, he had served in the Indian Army and become a brigadier-general. He was writing a romantic novel and spoke like a Shakespearean actor. He was younger than Frederick – tall, dark and classically handsome. Lastly, the biggest blot of all on his escutcheon, he was a bachelor.

That dinner was not a success. Thomson talked the entire time. Diana hung on his every word. Apparently she had met him in the Air League, and he shared her passion for airships, though it became apparent that he knew very little about them. Even with that superficial interest in the airships, a strange character for Diana to take up with, in Fredericks's opinion.

He mused on that problem for months. Diana seemed to keep him more on the hop than ever. Vickers were trying to persuade the Conversative government to build six commercial airships to operate the Empire routes. Frederick was a member of the parliamentary lobby who were pushing this hard. But before any agreement could be reached, there was a general election and in came Ramsay MacDonald. Frederick was furious, particularly as he had lost half of his majority. But he was delighted that Christopher Birdwood Thomson didn't get into parliament at all. Then came the hammer blow. Wanting his friend in his Cabinet as Air Minister, MacDonald in the same cynical way that Lloyd-George had sold peerages, created him Lord. And the man had had the nerve to pick 'of Cardington', thus allying himself with the big RAF airship station near Bedford, from which had issued the ill-fated R38.

Worse – Diana openly expressed her delight. She lunched with the new peer at the House of Lords. 'Don't you see, Frederick, how valuable this is going to be for you and Jerningham?' she asked afterwards.

He did not. All he saw was that Thomson was advancing politically at an enormous rate and he was going backwards. He redoubled his efforts for private enterprise in the House. As a result, the airship lobby forced a compromise on the Prime Minister: Private enterprise could build its airship to be called the R100, and the government would build its airship to be called the R101.

'Now, Frederick . . . Christopher,' Diana said to them over drinks in her house before the three of them went to see Sheridan's *The Duenna* at the Lyric. 'You have *both* got what you wanted!'

Frederick saw rather more of Christopher than he desired – and rather less of Diana. True the Conservatives got back into power in November 1924 and Thomson left the Air Ministry. Just for a couple of weeks, hope stirred in Frederick's breast and Diana became suddenly very attentive. Then Baldwin chose Sir Samuel Hoare (who knew even less about aviation than Thomson) to be his Air Minister. And things returned to the rather uneasy threesome that had existed before, with Frederick never quite sure whether it was he or Christopher who was playing gooseberry.

To Frederick's gratification, Diana did make a great effort for Arthur, always her favourite. At her own expense she put on a dance for his eighteenth birthday on 11 January 1925. The young flappers with their bobbed hair and boyish figures in narrow skirts came in dozens to her house, together with an equal number of unattached young men, one of whom was Charles.

Charles had at last found himself a more permanent job as a mechanic with the new Imperial Airways, founded from the four surviving British airlines before they teetered into bankruptcy. What he really wanted, he told Amelia after he got his ticket, was a pilot's job but these were scarce. Airlines were moving slowly. Imperial only flew to Paris, Cologne, Amsterdam, Berlin and the Channel Islands. And even on a trip to Paris engines and weather were so unreliable that there was a one in twelve chance of a forced landing – the record was seventeen in one trip.

Diana's dance was a great success. The band was particularly good and the food delicious. Amelia enjoyed it because she saw Charles who seldom came down to Haybury those days. Charles enjoyed it because he rarely had the chance to do the Charleston and the Black Bottom. Always shy with girls, after six glasses of champagne, Arthur became positively merry. Frederick enjoyed playing mine genial host in Lady Nazier's house.

But romantically waltzing half the night with Diana, the person who enjoyed it most was Christopher Birdwood Thomson.

Neither Lord Thomson nor anyone else of political note came to the luncheon to celebrate Charles's 21st birthday. Frederick had let it be known that in such times of economic hardship, when his PM Stanley Baldwin was calling for sacrifice, it would be inappropriate to give the usual tenants' and workers' ball and the firework display and all that nonsense.

Nor did Charles want anything of the sort. But he agreed with surprising willingness to Amelia's suggestion that they should go *en famille* in her new model Rolls to the Red Lion in Salisbury for a quiet celebration. In the event, as no doubt Charles had guessed, it was just the two of them. Frederick was detained on political business in London. Arthur asked to be excused. He had the opportunity of a trip to Germany with a schoolfriend who was also going up to Oxford next term.

'Suits me!' Charles and Amelia clinked their glasses of champagne. He was in high spirits throughout the lunch, teasing and affectionate, exerting all his charm. He laughed, 'And now I can do exactly as I want.'

'You always have done,' Amelia sighed.

'Not really. Not by a long chalk.' But he appeared to be enjoying his job and was clocking up every flying hour that he could scrounge.

Three months ago, amongst the ecstatic London crowds, he'd watched the return of Alan Cobham and Sefton Brancker from their Rangoon flight. 'I was just as mad as the rest of them, Mama. I rushed over and shook Cobham's hand. I tried to get up the cheek to ask him if he needed a flight mechanic. But I didn't.'

Driving home through the forest, harking back perhaps to Arthur's very different birthday celebration, Charles asked Amelia, 'What d'you think of this Thomson fellow?'

'I'm not sure. I didn't altogether trust him. He's ambitious. Ruthless too.'

'More to the point, I suppose,' Charles said, 'what does Diana Nazier think of him?'

Amelia drew in her breath sharply. 'She doesn't confide in me.'

He laughed bitterly. 'No, I suppose not.' He stared at his mother's profile, and added in a low voice, 'She's not a patch on you.'

'Darling!' Amelia laughed with deliberate lightness. She took her hand off the wheel and covered his. 'You're biased. But, you're learning. How to hand out the dewdrops.' She gave an exaggerated sigh. 'You'll be a tremendous hit one day with the girls.'

'How do you know I'm not now!'

'*Are* you?'

'No. I've not time for flappers.'

She glanced sideways at his handsome profile, at the secretive wilful mouth, and the square chin. 'Dear Charles,' she said. 'I doubt they'll let you escape.'

He shrugged and shook his head. The wind through the open window whipped his thick dark hair over his forehead, and he ran his hand through it in a way so reminiscent of James that she caught her breath.

'And what if Diana Nazier allows Father to escape?'

She trod harder on the accelerator. The speedometer crept up to eighty. 'Easy, Mama.' He laughed. 'Or else pull the stick back and let's get airborne!'

A corner came up. She lifted her foot off the accelerator, and as they rounded it at a gentler speed, Charles said with his knack of saying the unsayable, 'Talking of escape, Mama, why don't you divorce?'

She had no idea how to reply. She drove on for a few hundred yards tight-lipped, smelling the sweet nostalgic scent of the heather and the first hay. They dipped into a hollow where cattle drank at a shallow stream. They splashed across the ford in silence.

'I used to wonder if you were waiting till Arthur and I were older.'

'Nothing so unselfish.'

'Well, then?'

'It wouldn't do.'

'Why?'

She shrugged.

'Things are changing, Mama.'

'Not enough.'

'Oh . . .' He made the single syllable very drawn out and interrogative, waiting for her to explain.

Suddenly she saw over the top of a clump of birches, a welcome diversion. A red and yellow box kite, gently cuffed by the wind – now fluttering upwards, now spiralling down.

'Look, Charles! A kite!'

'I can see, Mama.' He spoke drily, disappointed at the interruption in a talk he felt was long overdue between them, an exchange of at least diluted confidences, some explanation of much that he didn't understand.

'Do you remember?' She smiled, escaping his probing, 'You used to love flying kites. And I can remember when I was a little girl . . .'

She sighed, and passing a clump of trees, there ahead of them was a little girl and her nanny, hauling at the kite string caught in a bramble bush. She had grown, of course. But she was unmistakable. The black ringlets shone in the sun. Amelia could see the beautiful little profile, the determined stance of the small body.

'I hope you did better than she's doing,' Charles smiled, giving up his attempt to talk seriously to Amelia. But his mother wasn't listening. She had already taken her foot off the accelerator and trodden on the brake. The car halted just beside the gentle slope that was crowned by the clump of brambles.

'It's Marianne,' she said with a strange exultation in her voice. 'She's only a baby. Do go and help her, Charles, there's a good chap!'

Dear Charles. He was already out of the car, and striding up the slope towards them, smiling.

'Marianne!' Amelia called from the car leaning out and waving. 'It's me! Amelia!'

The little girl turned. But her gaze didn't go beyond Charles. Amelia saw him drop on to one knee beside her, speak softly and gently disentangle the strings from her fingers. Then he straightened and began to push his way into the thorn bush, winding up the string as he went till he reached the tangle and began carefully to free it.

The French nanny, obviously delighted at the unexpected arrival of such a handsome knight errant, fluttered round the thorn bush, throwing advice and thanks and smiles in a continuous waterfall of French and English.

Once the kite was freed, its strings drawn in and pulled to earth, Charles squatted down beside Marianne and showed her how to fold it.

I had never realised what a way he has with children, Amelia thought, seeing their two profiles cameoed against the thorn bushes, Marianne's trusting and eager, Charles's tender and affectionate. Almost as if they *knew*. Then the French nanny, determined not to be left out, bent down and joined in. There was a brief conclave, and the three of them came walking down the slope towards the car, Marianne holding Charles's hand.

'I said we would give them a lift to their gate, Mama, if that's all right? It's a long walk back to Cornford House for a little one.'

'Of course!' Amelia smiled, delighted. 'Jump in!'

Charles began the introductions, but Amelia said gaily, 'Oh, Marianne and I

241

are old friends!'

She said good afternoon to Mademoiselle, a pale, fluttery girl who was promptly packed into the rear seat of the car, alone except for the kite.

'Marianne asked if she could ride in the front,' Charles said. 'I said she could sit on my knee, if you didn't mind, Mama.'

'So long as you hold her tight,' Amelia said. 'Don't let her bang her head if I brake sharply.'

'Mama is a devilish driver,' Charles winked to Mademoiselle. 'She drives like the wind, then she sees a rabbit, and whoom! On go the brakes.' Mademoiselle and Marianne laughed. 'Bang go our heads!'

'I shall drive very slowly,' Amelia said. Not only so that Marianne wouldn't be hurt, though that was paramount, but also to prolong the sweetness of the moment. She kept stealing sideways glances at the two of them sitting beside her. Charles and Marianne. How right they looked together! How trusting! How she would like to have spirited them both away!

And then just before they reached the gates of Cornford House, Marianne looked down at Charles's hands clasping her. Her vivid blue eyes grew wide and tender.

'But Charles!' she spoke his name with a delightful French intonation. 'You have hurt yourself! You bleed. Your hand is all scratches where you got my kite.'

She lifted his hand impulsively to her lips, and kissed each scratch with smacking gusto.

'That feels fine now,' Charles laughed when she finally released it. 'It's healing already. You've kissed it all better.'

Dear Charles, dear Marianne, Amelia thought, bringing the car to a halt outside the immaculate gates of Cornford House. They each had something of James. She loved them both.

She turned to the round baby face held up to hers. She bent to kiss the tender lips, and then she saw a smear of Charles's blood on the corner of Marianne's pretty smiling mouth. Her own smile froze. Then Charles was lifting Marianne down from the running board, 'Here, Marianne! Before you go! Wipe your mouth.' Charles the kindly thoughtful elder brother handed her his handkerchief. 'It's quite clean, I promise.'

Amelia and Charles waved in unison as Marianne disappeared through the gates, still clutching Charles's handkerchief. She was reminded of Dr Randall, telling her when Marianne was born that she would break hearts one day.

'Isn't Marianne a sweet little child?' Amelia remarked as they reached home, and she rang the drawing-room bell for tea. 'Such a pretty sight!' She sank on to the sofa, spread her arms relaxedly on the upholstery and closed her eyes. 'It's been a lovely day! I so enjoyed it, darling. I hope you did?'

'I did, Mama. It couldn't have been better. Exactly what I wanted.' He drew a deep breath, perched himself on the edge of the chair nearest the sofa, and added, 'That's why I hate to spoil it for you.'

Amelia's eyes flew open at his tone. 'Then *don't! Don't* spoil it, Charles!'

'I'm sorry, Mama. But I have to.' He waited until yet another of Sarah's many nieces, a clumsy red-fingered stout-legged girl, had brought in the tea and been peremptorily dismissed by Amelia. Then he went on, 'You remember I said I didn't want to stay for ever being a mechanic?'

'Yes, I do. Of course. And if you'd like to —'

Charles held up his hand. 'Mama, if I might finish. I said I'd get my licence and then think things over. Well, I've thought. And I've made up my mind. I'm fed up with England. Fed up with their ideas of aviation. I'm off to America.'

'What absolute nonsense!' Amelia brandished the silver teapot angrily. 'It's not the Land of Promise it's supposed to be!'

'Aviation-wise its got a damned sight more promise than here.'

'Rubbish! Besides you won't know anyone. Your Aunt and Uncle are in Colombo now. They're hoping to get back to America eventually, but it may be years. So you haven't even them to go to.'

'I don't want them or need them. And I do know someone. I know Babe Reynolds.'

'Who?'

'My squadron commander in the RFC.'

'When you ran away before?' Amelia exclaimed, stung into bitterness.

'If you call it running away.'

'And is this another venture like that?'

'No. I've made plans this time. I've been in touch with Babe. He's earning a good living.'

'How?'

'In aviation.'

'How in aviation?'

'He's got his own air circus.'

She drew in a long breath, closed her eyes, and shook her head speechlessly. Then she said in a cracked scornful voice, 'Barnstorming? Flying upside-down? Wing-walking? Risking your neck for the fun of the crowd?'

But it was a losing battle. She knew that tightmouthed determined look on Charles's face just as she recognised it on James.

'When do you sail?' she asked stonily.

'Next week. But . . .' He came over and put both his hands on her shoulders. 'I'd like to go with your blessing. I doubt I'll have anyone else's.'

Impulsively she turned her head and kissed his hand as Marianne had done.

FIVE

Two weeks later, it was Babe Reynolds who was holding his hand – on the dockside at New York, and shaking it hard. Warm sunshine flooded the skyscrapers; Charles fell instantly in love with the place.

Compared with his schooldays and life at Haybury and the frustration of aviation in Britain, America felt like a breath of fresh air. Of course the circus wasn't much, Babe said apologetically. But then he had told Charles so in his letters. Charles had merely tried to make it sound successful to Amelia. The circus was a couple of old Jennies, but they'd made a down payment on a third and as soon as they'd got the rest of the dough, they'd be off to pick it up in Wyoming. They weren't exactly on the gravy train, Babe told him as they rattled over the cobbled dockside streets in his Ford car. But then they weren't in the bread queue either, and boy, was it ever the life!

They went straight to Roosevelt Field where they were putting on gala weekend shows, so that Charles could give the planes the once-over and meet Babe's side-kick, Ernst von Stromm.

'Sounds German.'

'Is German. And is he ever a good guy! Flew with Richthofen.'

Charles whistled, half-teasingly, half-impressed. 'The Red Baron! Need you say more?'

'Came over after the war. Saw the light. He can do anything with a plane short of making it talk. And he's working on that.'

The object of his praise was working on one of the aeroplanes when they drew up alongside and jumped out on to the grass. The Jennies were indeed old and showed the wounds of their battle for the public's capricious attention. A pair of well-muscled legs were visible from under the fuselage of the older one. Babe kicked each of the boot soles and called, 'Ernst, meet the kid I was telling you about!'

Von Stromm wriggled out and stood up. 'Hi,' he said, wiping his hands on an oily rag. He was a thick-set man with a close-cropped blond bullet head and pale grey eyes.

'He looked better when he had a moustache,' Babe said. 'But he's had to shave it for a new show we're putting on. Never been seen before. I tell you, kid, in this racket you've always gotta be one jump ahead.'

'I can't wait to see it!' Charles smiled, having his knuckles ground by Von Stromm's handshake.

'You'll see it Saturday. Saturday, Sunday and all the days of next week, if it wows them. If it doesn't we'll be hitting the trail.'

The show wowed them all right. It took place sharp at two-thirty to what

244

seemed to Charles a capacity audience. More stands and three marquees had been put up. There was a four-piece brass band and several stalls selling refreshments.

Charles made a beeline for a stall selling hot-dogs. He was ravenous. Breakfast had not been included in the accommodation Babe had booked for him in their dreary brownstone rooming house five minutes drive from the airfield.

'We'll eat well, I guess, tonight,' Babe said surveying the large audience. 'Have another hot-dog. Be my guest. We get cut price. Oh, and while we're up, get into the crowd. Find out what they like.'

They seemed to like it all, as far as Charles could hear. The crowd screamed and laughed and shouted and clapped everything – looping the loop, flying upside-down, Babe climbing on to the wing and pretending to be trying to tie his bootlaces. They loved it when the announcer asked for ladies' handkerchiefs to be held out. Then Von Stromm, leaning far out of the cockpit grasping a long lance, charged like a medieval knight and speared them out of the ladies' hands. But though the crowd oohed and aahed and clapped, there was perhaps something missing. A drop of blood, a moment of drama. Charles remembered his mother used to say the crowds flocked to Hendon hoping to see someone crash.

Having made a smooth landing with the rackety little Jenny, stopping and leaving the engine running, Von Stromm gestured that he was excessively thirsty. He disappeared into the crew tent adjoining the refreshment marquee.

The band struck up with popular interval tunes, till suddenly the music was interrupted. The announcer's voice shouted, loud and clear, 'Stop her! For Chrissake, stop her!'

The crowds in front of Charles all turned their heads in one direction. He stood on tiptoe and looked over them. He saw a woman in a short red dress and a coche hat, rounding the corner of the refreshment tent and running determinedly towards Von Stromm's Jenny.

'She's getting in! Stop her, I say!'

A motorbike, followed by Babe's battered Ford raced across the grass. But it was too late. Clambering on to the wing, the woman had swung herself into the cockpit. A collective gasp of horror went up from the stands, as the aircraft roared towards them. Now the crowds were flinging themselves flat on their faces, as just clearing the top of the stands, the little aircraft staggered drunkenly into the sky.

'A madwoman! A maniac!' the crowd whispered. Someone had seen her talking to a sinister-looking man, someone else had seen her drinking hooch. Babe Reynolds got out of his Ford and shook his fists in fury, as now the Jenny banked right on to one wingtip, turned back to the field, and flew so close to the ground that Babe had to throw himself flat.

He got to his feet at once and ran to the other Jenny. The crowd cheered its heart out as he got in and a mechanic swung the propeller. 'Keep calm, folks! Babe Reynolds will save you!'

At this point, a hat went round. Moved beyond words by Babe's gallant little Jenny pursuing and finally taking up formation with its lurching sister aircraft, the people dug deep into their pockets.

Babe had produced a megaphone and was addressing the woman in red. 'I

245

guess he's trying to calm her, folks! Now, you just stay calm yourselves! He's telling her how to land! Oh, my, oh, my! Sooner him than me! Now would you believe that? She's keeping it straight now. Give her a big hand, folks!'

Both aircraft could now be seen to be turning towards the field. 'Keep back! Give them room! This lady hasn't landed before! We don't want an accident!'

There was an exodus towards the perimeter. Charles stayed where he was, his eyes narrowed. Suddenly and without warning the first Jenny turned right over and flew upside-down.

'Oh, God! Oh, my!' the announcer wailed.

Everywhere women were screaming. The sound drowned the klaxon of the approaching police and the ambulance. The next moment, a figure in a red dress dropped out of the cockpit and fell towards the ground. The screams of the crowd became hysterical, as all eyes were fixed on the woman turning over and over like a falling leaf.

'I guess what we most feared has happened,' the announcer cried, as the red-dressed figure reached the ground. 'Oh, gee! Oh, my! Oh, God!'

The organisers of the show were already racing to the scene in a lorry with a load of large canvas screens. So were the police on motorbikes. So was an ambulance. So was Charles.

When he arrived the screens were already up. An argument was going on between the ambulancemen and the police and the organisers. As Charles pushed forward to see what it was all about, the pilotless plane zoomed lower and lower in ever decreasing circles.

People ducked their heads as the Jenny, its vacant cockpit clearly visible, danced and twirled just over the stands. Till when it seemed the crowds could bear the suspense no longer, Babe Reynolds came in to land. And as though Von Stromm had indeed taught the aircraft to talk, the pilotless Jenny tucked itself behind him like Mary's little lamb and followed him in.

Behind the screens, the police had their notebooks out and were writing furiously. The ambulancemen were shouting. The organisers had their hands outstretched as though in benediction, trying to calm everyone down. The painted eyes of the inflatable rubber dummy in the red dress, which was all that had fallen from the Jenny, watched it all unblinking from the ground. The apparently pilotless Jenny taxied up and stopped. From his crouched hiding position in the cockpit, also in a red dress, Von Stromm stepped out laughing.

Those of the crowd who saw what had happened laughed too. But the New York police did not. As they counted their handsome takings that night in the brownstone apartment house, Babe announced they would have to hit the road. There were so many counts on which the cops might fine them or impound their property that it just wasn't worth hanging around to find out. They would leave tomorrow for Wyoming to take possession of the third aircraft. Von Stromm would fly his Jenny, Charles would fly Babe's, and he himself would rattle down by road in the Ford. Then with the third Jenny, they would be a real team, the world was their oyster.

Before they went to bed that night, they decided to call themselves The Three Musketeers, and that golden California, the state with its twenty-two carat industries of stars and films, would be their destination.

Their route took them by way of every flat field or possible landing strip between Wyoming and California, and it took them over a year. While Charles flew upside-down so often he almost slept inverted, while he flew under bridges, on one wingtip, roped together with Babe or Von Stromm, only infrequent news came to him from home.

His mother wrote, of course, but he'd usually moved on to the next place before the letters arrived. Britain was in the midst of the General Strike. Arthur, his mother wrote angrily, had joined with other Oxford students in helping to break the strike by driving trains and trams. Frederick had done the same. Lady Nazier had been photographed peeling potatoes. Jerningham had not been too badly affected. They were still doing subcontracts for the Burney airship project. Enthusiastically she described being on the House of Commons' terrace with MPs to watch Alan Cobham land on the Thames after his trip to Australia and back. She thanked him for his postcards, told him to look after himself and asked him for more detailed news when he had the time.

He sent her a long letter just before Christmas, and a rather beautiful shawl he'd bought in Nevada. In February they made it into California to a small field, where they did stunts, gave rides, offered lessons. But the money wasn't coming in. Times were hard. Maybe the novelty was wearing off. Maybe they hadn't enough invention. They considered selling one of the Jennies, which were eating money, but the Ford was more saleable, so they sold that instead.

By April, they were broke. They got casual jobs on farms, working in bars. Babe had hardly a nickel to buy the newspaper. But when he did, somehow they all knew their luck had turned. There was a huge advertisement in the centre page. Zuckerman Inc were wanting stunt fliers for a new movie. The Three Musketeers flew into San Francisco airfield the next day and presented themselves at Mr Zuckerman's office.

It was a disappointment. It was a crumby little office up a narrow flight of stairs above a shed like a cardboard box which he called his studio. Mr Zuckerman had curly black hair, thick glasses and rosy red lips. He talked a lot. At times he wept. He'd been badly let down. His last stuntmen had chicken-livered out. Of course he could only pay a little. Hardly anything. But the movie, God bless it, was the thing. Did they feel like that? They did? Then they could give him a flying display and he just might take them on. The contract was drawn up straight away. All the while Mr Zuckerman talked about the movie and flying and cliffhangers and weepies. How as a young man he'd seen the famous aviator Beachey plunge t his death in San Francisco Sound. How there wasn't a dry eye amongst the crowds, how men took off their hats. And how Mr Zuckerman had felt a sacred trust to transmute that emotion into a real dollar-earning movie.

'Then I take it from there, friends,' he said, waving the contracts to dry the ink, 'and I figure that if you add to that cliffhanger weepie, a bit of,' he wiped his glasses, 'sex. Nothing offensive. Mary Pickford style. Then Holy Hill, you're on easy street.'

'How does this Mary Pickford style girl come in, Mr Zuckerman?' Babe asked warily.

'The girl gets taken up in the air by you, son. Has to climb out on to the wing.'
'Why?'

'Why? Because she's pursued by the villain. You'll meet him next week. You'll like him. Then you,' he pointed to Charles, 'take up the hero in your

247

airplane. Fly alongside and let him grab her off to safety.'

'To safety, Zuckerman? To her death more like!' Charles exclaimed indignantly. 'And ours!'

'It'll be OK.' Babe said. 'Nothing to it. I've done dicier acts in my time. Wha's she like? Sensible?'

'Sensible? Sylvia Sylvaine? Why, Holy Hill, that girl could run for president!'

'She'll need to do better'n that,' Babe said.

''Sides that, she's light as duck-fluff. Brave as a lion. You'll get her off one wing and on to another like she wasn't there!'

Apart from Von Stromm's objection that he had the dumb-bunny role of carrying the cameraman, the Three Musketeers expressed themselves perfectly satisfied.

And then, a week later, they met Sylvia Sylvaine.

Amelia was uneasy. Sometimes she seemed to pick up strange disturbing feelings about Charles, sudden certainties that he was in some sort of danger or need, hear his unspoken thoughts, the way she used to with James.

'I haven't heard from him since this.' Amelia handed Ronald Cummings a postcard Charles had sent weeks ago when The Three Musketeers had reached California. 'I hate this stunt flying! A moment's misjudgment and that's it! Wouldn't you worry?'

'I suppose I would,' Ronald stirred his coffee. 'But my main feeling when I hear of Charles,' Cummings smiled faintly, 'is one of envy.'

'Ronald!' Their relationship continued easy-going, relaxed and perfectly proper. His admiration was a soothing elixir for Frederick's bitter antipathy and for the buffetting of the unpredictable world outside.

'You don't really mean that! Why should you envy him?'

'I can think of quite a number of reasons,' he said lightly, the earnest expression of his brown eyes belying his tone. Amelia didn't invite him to name the reasons. One of them without doubt would be her devotion to Charles. Cummings never mentioned his own for her. But Amelia accepted unthinkingly that it was there, and that *he* would be there.

'He's in love with you, M'lady. He looks at you in that spoony-eyed way Burton the butcher used to look at me,' Sarah had said only that morning.

'You should have married Burton, Sarah. I told you you should.'

'Not on your life, M'lady! I wouldn't have big red butcher's hands mauling me, thank you! Anyway, he got tired of waiting.'

As Cummings would one day, Amelia thought. One of these days he would see she wasn't the perfect woman he thought. He would find out as Frederick had done. And off he would go.

'You don't mean you'd really like to be a stunt flyer, Ronald?'

'No. I wouldn't have the skill. Or the nerve. But I'd like the challenge. The excitement. I find airships uninspiring and airship parts even less so.'

'I know how you feel.' The goldbeater girls had christened the parts they made elephants' bloomers. And it was just like that, cutting enormous half-legs of underwear that could never convey the soaring beauty of flight as an aeroplane did.

'I'd love to do some competition flying. Find fame and fortune,' Cummings suggested wryly.

248

'Resurrect Ajax?'

'You will, mark my words!' He drained his cup, and said, 'Meantime, back to the drawing board.'

'Meantime,' she parodied his tone gently, 'with Charles up to God knows what and Arthur still at Oxford . . .' she didn't mention Frederick '. . . I hope you won't go off to find fame and fortune elsewhere.'

'It's hardly likely,' Cummings shot her a wry smile and shrugging his shoulders, leaned across and touched her hand. For a moment Amelia was afraid he was going to become what Sarah would have called spoony. But at that moment, a knock sounded on the outer door of her office. Relieved at the interruption, Amelia called, 'Come in!'

The door opened slowly, momentously, as if to prepare those within for sad tidngs. James put his head round. His face was unsmiling, his eyes sombre. There was a dark aura about him. He comes to tell me about death, Amelia thought, reading his mind as she had so often done in the old days. And in a wave of panic, it's about Charles. Charles has crashed. They have asked James to come and tell me. She covered her mouth with her clenched fist.

In as calm a voice as she could muster, she said after a moment, 'Good morning, James. I didn't know you were home. You know Ronald Cummings, of course?'

Stupid words, banal and stilted.

'I'm sorry,' James said, eyeing Cummings coldly. 'I thought you were alone.'

'She is. Just about. I was on the point of going.' Ronald jumped to his feet. Amelia almost put out a hand to detain him. She didn't feel strong enough to hear what James had to say. Until James actually put it into words it wouldn't be true. Instead, she waved to the chair Ronald had vacated.

'Sit down, James. It's bad news, isn't it?'

Almost immediately her commonsense reasserted itself. Who would ask James to break bad news to her? The answer was no one. If Charles were dead, she would know inside herself. And more practically, she would receive a telegraph message.

James still stood. He said, 'My mother died last night.'

'Oh, James, my dear,' Amelia was on her feet immediately. 'I'm so very sorry. I didn't know she was ill.' She felt a flood of guilt at her own selfishness and self-absorption. Poor old woman! How little she had ever done for her!

'She wasn't ill, happily for her. She simply felt rather faint before she went up to bed. She died during the night. Father was with her. It was as it should be.'

Impulsively Amelia put her arms round him. 'You were such a good son, James. Such a credit to her. You loved her, I know. But you mustn't grieve. She must have been so proud.'

She stood on tiptoe and kissed his cheek, murmuring disjointed phrases of consolation. It was so rare that she had ever comforted him.

'Dear Amelia,' he said gently, brushing her hair with his lips, then gazing down at her. For a moment his eyes looked naked. She saw in them his love for her, undiminished and undisguised. 'She was very proud of her grand-children,' James said. Immediately she was pierced with a sharper guilt.

'And the funeral?' Amelia asked tentatively, 'May I come to it?'

'Of course. That's what brought me to see you so soon. Didn't you wonder?'

She shook her head. It had seemed so right that he should come to her. 'Dear Amelia,' he said again. He ran his hand through his hair in that characteristic gesture when he found explanation difficult. 'Look, may we walk outside? I can tell you better, I think, in the fresh air.'

She nodded and he pulled open the office door for her. They stepped out on to the gravel, blinking their eyes in the sudden sunlight. Automatically without any conscious direction they began walking towards the slipway and the sea.

'My mother,' James said after several minutes' silence, 'left specific instructions about her possessions and funeral. She dreaded the workhouse and the paupers' funeral above everything else.'

'I know.'

'She left everything ready in the drawer. She felt Father, being a man, wouldn't know how it should be done.'

His mother had left binding cloths and two new pennies to put on her eyelids, but he didn't distress Amelia by telling her. He drew in a long breath. He rested a hand lightly on her arm, 'The difficult thing is that she asked to be buried near your mother. In those plots your family own, just outside the family mausoleum.'

'And your father objects?'

'No. Far from it. If that was her wish, then that's what he wants. He always hoped the sea would have him. And he wouldn't want her to lie alone.'

'Then who objects? Oh, I see! You reckon Frederick will.'

In the silence their feet brushed over the thick summer turf, crunched over another gravel path, on to more grass, disturbed a curlew and went on towards the sea.

'I hadn't thought about your husband. I wanted first to ask you.'

'I don't mind. Why should I? It's nice to think she loved my mother so much. And it's Jerningham property, not Haybury, so it isn't really up to Frederick to object.'

He would object of course. Of that she had little doubt. But she did not intend to impart that knowledge to James. 'Not that it matters where one's buried,' James said softly, taking her hand quite naturally. 'But I think I'd prefer to be like your Eustace Wilkinson.'

'Oh, James. Please don't,' she lifted his hand to her lips. 'Please don't talk about it. Poor old Eustace!'

'And Ajax? Is that buried too?'

She shrugged. Their abstracted walk had brought them within fifty yards of the slipway and the small hangar. 'Not quite. But almost.' She gave him a faint smile. 'With only a very slight hope of the resurrection.' She dipped into her pocket and brought out her keyring. 'Do you remember saying it was Eustace's resurrection?'

'Of course.'

'D'you want to see the last survivor of the many we built?' she asked breathlessly.

He nodded.

With difficulty she unlocked the hangar door. It was so long since anyone had been here that the latch was rusty and the two small high windows green with sea mould. But inside was that unmistakable mixture of doped silk, oil and petrol that carried them back to their youth again. Death and funerals and sadness were forgotten.

Hand in hand proprietorially, they walked round the craft, in and out of the dust-speckled sunbeams. He clambered inside the cockpit, smoothed his hands down the wing, inspected the undercarriage structure.

'You should get Cummings working on it, Amelia. You shouldn't let it rot here.'

'We've no orders.'

'They'll come.'

She laughed uncertainly, 'From where?'

'From the RAF for one. Trenchard's new idea for keeping the RAF out of the hands of the Army and the Navy is that we can police the Empire for a fraction of their cost. So that's what we're doing. And we'll need better aircraft. This design could be modified. A more powerful engine could be fitted. Overload fuel tanks. Eventually a retractable undercarriage. I'll make some notes for Cummings before I leave.'

'For where?'

'For my next posting.' He gave Amelia one of his sweet self-deprecating smiles. 'Iraq. Where all we've got are Bristol Fighters from the last war.'

'But isn't there a sort of war in Iraq?' She suddenly recalled again the fortuneteller's words at the Whitsun Fair, that war would have James in the end.

'We don't call it that.' He smiled at her expression. 'We call it preserving the peace.'

'But the tribesmen call it war.'

'Perhaps.'

'There's fighting, people getting killed?'

'Amelia!' He shook his head reprovingly. 'You mustn't . . .' He stopped dead.

In the constrained silence, she asked unhappily, 'Where will you be stationed?'

'Baghdad. Guarding the oil supply.'

She looked so distressed that he came over and put his hands on her shoulders. 'Marie is quite happy about my posting. I leave in five days' time. We've decided to close Cornford House. It seemed better that she and the children should live permanently in France while I'm away. They stay much of the time there as it is.' He paused. 'I'm grateful to you, Amelia, for considering Mother's request.'

It was his way of telling Amelia that she was not his first consideration. His way, though he came to ask a favour, of putting her in her place.

Naturally Frederick raised every possible objection. So great was his dislike of Mrs March's last request, that he travelled down to Haybury that night. He was disappointed that Arthur had not yet arrived home from Oxford, but slightly mollified when Amelia told him he was due the following day.

'You can send a decent wreath,' Frederick said as they sipped after-dinner brandy. 'And that's more than is called for. You may allow the servants to wear black armbands. But really, I doubt if anyone remembers her. I understand your mother only took her in in the first place out of charity. Born in the workhouse!'

'All the more reason.'

'To you perhaps, but not to me.'

'It happens to be Jerningham, not Haybury. What I think *is* important.'

'What you think always has been too important.'

'Not as important as what Diana Nazier thinks.'

'Leave Diana out of this.' He glared at her. 'If we have the blacksmith's wife, other villagers will ask to do the same. And it'll be the damned blacksmith himself next, wanting to come in.'

'I hardly think so. And anyway, I've said I've no objection . . .'

'Have you, by God! Then I must make it known to the March family that you have acted against my advice. The father must be made to see reason. Otherwise any Tom, Dick or Harry can make some nonsensical request to be buried here, there or anywhere.'

The following morning, Frederick continued his castigation. 'Why, Amelia, do you always manage to get us into the most impossible situations?'

Predictably the Rector came down on Frederick's side. The request was unusual, Mrs March a strange woman, and the Reverend Bingham was quite prepared to put it to Mr March that it was causing embarrassment to his betters. But Amelia found herself with an unexpected ally.

Arthur arrived home that afternoon. University life suited him. He had filled out. The delicacy of his features which had made him look too angelic for a boy had not coarsened but hardened. Perhaps he had spent too long in the shadow of Amelia's love for Charles, for now he had acquired confidence and substance. He was dressed rather self-consciously as a student of the '20s in Oxford bags and a white sweater. But he was good-looking in a slightly pinched way.

'I'm so glad to have you home,' Amelia said, slipping her arm through his, and ringing for more tea. Arthur looked surprised and gratified as if she had never said that enough before. Perhaps she hadn't.

'So am I,' Frederick said meaningly. 'Very glad. We've just had the Rector here. A fine kettle of fish your Mama has got us all into! Maybe you can get her to see some sense.'

As Arthur munched his way through a cucumber sandwich, Frederick gave him a highly biased account of Mrs March's request. Then he sat back in his chair with his eyes expectantly on his son's face, waiting for him to echo his views.

'Father,' Arthur said, putting his hands in the pockets of his ugly Oxford bags, and managing to look simultaneously very young and very judicial, 'you're being a frightful stuffed shirt!'

No one else but Diana Nazier could have said that to Frederick.

It was the beginning of Arthur's new relationship with his parents and the end of Frederick's opposition. 'Well, as long as you don't expect me to attend,' he said, firing a last round over his shoulder as he retreated. 'I have a very important meeting of the Burney Committee.'

He departed that night for London. The chosen grave was hastily dug. The funeral took place the next day. 'Why so miz, Mama?' Arthur came into her bedroom, as Sarah helped Amelia to dress. 'Don't go to the funeral if it affects you. It isn't that important.'

'She didn't even like you, M'lady,' Sarah whispered in her ear, with astringent and therapeutic effect. 'Couldn't stand the sight of you.'

'I'm not miserable at all, Arthur. I was only thinking of Charles. How I wish he were here! How I'd like him to have come. Wing Commander March was very good to him in France.'

'Charles doesn't share your opinion of his goodness, I can tell you.' Arthur sat himself down on a corner of the bed to watch Sarah brush his mother's still golden hair. 'He reckons March is an interfering upstart. Mind, Charles is an ungrateful bounder. No news of him, I suppose?'

'Apart from another postcard, no.'

'Even though Charles can't come, *I* can. I'll support you. What difference does it make?'

Amelia smiled at him in the mirror, genuinely touched. It would be the last time she saw James, she thought, for years. Maybe after Baghdad he would go on to some other overseas posting. Maybe it would be the last time for ever.

'At least they've got a fine day for it,' Sarah said, 'which is more than can be said for poor Queen Alexandra's funeral.'

Seeing the turnout, one could have almost thought it was for a queen. The village was aware of Mrs March's obsession and they were giving her a good send-off, poor woman. The coffin was covered in expensive wreaths from the family and the Hayburys, and the whole of the hearse was a riot of wild and cultivated blooms. All the curtains were lowered in the cottages and black ribbons hung on the doors. Three carriages drawn by black-plumed horses followed the hearse. Then there was the silent, shuffling procession of villagers. They had downed tools and turned out to a man.

When it was all over, when the dirt had rattled on the coffin lid and the Rector moved away, James and his father came over to Amelia. After thanking her, the older man turned to say something to Arthur. They moved a little distance away. James and Amelia were momentarily isolated.

'Amelia,' James said after a moment, 'my mother left you something.' He lifted her hand and dropped into it a thin Victorian ring made of gold, twisted with hair of much the same bright colour. 'She thought you ought to have it. It belonged to your mother and she gave it to mine.'

Amelia stood in silence, staring down at the ring resting on her open palm. Her first reaction was one of relief that the old lady hadn't hated her after all. Then she thought it looked like a wedding ring, worn thin with the years. It could have been their wedding ring. She shivered. She wished James hadn't given it to her here with the black-clad mourners for background and the only sound the chime of the grave-diggers' spades. Where the theme was death, not life and love.

'Keep it for me, James,' she said impulsively, thrusting it back into his hand. 'Give it to me some other time. Some happier time.'

She hurried over to join Arthur now standing alone. They returned to Haybury in silence. Pearson opened the door for them before they reached the top step. He looked at them both mournfully as if the funeral had indeed been a family one, and then in a hushed voice pregnant with sympathy, he said, 'A cable arrived for you from America, M'lady.'

On broken-down legs, he hobbled to the hall table, lifted the silver salver on which reposed the small yellow envelope that war had taught everyone to dread, and held the salver in front of her like some communion of grief.

So, after all, it had come. Amelia tore it open with trembling fingers. It had been despatched from Hollywood. She could hardly focus her eyes to read. Then she saw with a surge of relief that it was signed *Charles*.

It read *Marrying tomorrow. Whirlwind courtship. Fabulous girl. Dying to meet you.*

SIX

The marriage of Sylvia Sylvaine, Mr Zuckerman's hottest little number, to Charles Haybury, English upper-crust member of The Three Musketeers stunt team, promised to be a real weaver. It was as fast-moving as one of his own scripts, Mr Zuckerman told his publicity men. The public would just lap it up. Nothing they liked better than love at first sight.

In fact it had been nothing of the kind. All Three Musketeers had agreed when they met Sylvia Sylvaine that she was a liability. She was nineteen years old, with auburn hair and velvety brown eyes. Her mouth was so small and red and perfect that it looked as if it had been cut of shiny crimson paper and stuck on to her powdered lineless face. She was light and small and physically everythin Mr Zuckerman had promised. But instead of being brave as a lion she was as nervous as a kitten, and her teeth chattered all the way to Babe's aeroplane.

Babe was in two minds as to whether to call the whole thing off. But she wept at that idea, said Mr Zuckerman had promised this was her big chance, and that if she didn't do it, dozens of other girls would.

'What's the delay, boys?' Mr Zuckerman had rushed up. 'We've waited for the weather you wanted! Now what?'

Eventually the three aircraft had taken off. It was then that Charles discovered that fear of flying was pretty endemic at Zuckerman Studios. Sylvia Sylvaine's fears were as nothing compared to that of the strong man hero actor he carried in his aircraft.

Scarcely had Charles followed Babe Reynolds up into the sky above Beverly Hills than the actor – a great blonde Swede with a voice like an unoiled gate – began to throw up. 'Christ!' Charles had yelled. 'Pull yourself together!'

In his mirror, he could see that Von Stromm had taken off and was close behind him. Babe, anxious no doubt to get the whole ill-conceived adventure over as soon as possible, was already beginning to formate on his port wing.

'How the hell are you going to grab Sylvia whatsit if you can't hold yourself steady?'

Charles had leaned over the side, trying to signal to Babe that the whole thing should be called off.

But obviously Babe had reckoned he was asking him to hurry. There followed five nerve-scraping minutes while Babe eased his aircraft against Charles's wingtip, and the squeaky-voiced actor at last stopped heaving.

Out on to the wing had struggled the crouched form of Sylvia Sylvaine. The wind whipped her red hair, and glued her skirt against her legs. If Zuckerman wanted his actress to register terror, she was certainly doing it.

255

'OK,' Charles had shouted to the great hulk of an actor, 'out you get! This is it! *Out!*'

There was no answer. Meantime, Sylvia was inching her way along the wing, her eyes half-closed, her hands clinging hard to each strut.

'Get out, you bastard!'

'I can't.' The squeaky voice was scarcely a whisper. 'I can't!'

Now Sylvia was halfway down the wing. Babe was gesticulating from the other aircraft.

'You've got to go, you swine! She'll fall in a moment! I'll kill you if you don't!'

The actor simply shut his eyes. In that moment, Charles had lived a lifetime. He balanced risks, while aloud like a maniac he hurled insults at the actor, at Mr Zuckerman, at Hollywood, at himself. At the end of that moment, it seemed she had a fifty-one per cent chance if he went out and got her himself, against a nil chance if he did nothing.

She had been almost at the end of the wing. No one would be able to make her understand to go back again. She looked frozen with terror. In a trance. Almost ready to drop. Lashing the stick rigid, praying the Jenny would hold its course, Charles had clambered out, terrified the wing would tip under his weight. Long practised at wing-walking, he had reached her in five econds. The most difficult part was to prise her rigid body over the few inches of air, then drag her back over the now steeply slanting wing to the cockpit.

He had to land with her sitting on his knee, her brown eyes gazing up at him, huge with mingled horror and admiration. He had felt himself become as she saw him. He had felt that special tenderness of the protector towards the protected. He was consumed with rage towards Zuckerman and went storming into his office. Mr Zuckerman had produced a couple of bottles of hooch and then disappeared to see what the cameraman had got in the can.

The hooch had worked wonders for them all. By the time the first bottle was finished, Charles was convinced Sylvia was the prettiest and pluckiest girl he had ever met. When she disappeared unsteadily to powder her nose, he had let it be known to the other Musketeers that he would be seeing her home. On the way there in the studio car, she had told him of her childhood, how her stepfather beat her, how she had run away from home.

They were birds of a feather. He proposed to her that evening.

'So you can figure,' Mr Zuckerman told the pressmen, 'why I guess I feel like a father to this young couple!'

He had refused to allow the couple to rush off to some sheriff's office. The ceremony would take place in the studio. Open-handed on any matter from which studio publicity could be extracted and sentimental as only hard businessmen can be, Mr Zuckerman recalled that day in 1920 when Mary Pickford, the sweetheart of the silver screen, married Douglas Fairbanks. The marriage had been world headlines and had rocketted their box office returns. They had never looked back; now they'd formed United Artists with Charles Chaplin – and Mary wasn't half as pretty as Sylvia.

So on 20 May 1927, the day of the wedding, he had a lulu of an altar rigged up in front of a colossal paper church window in the studio. He had wanted to wheel in Charles's aircraft as well but the bridegroom had protested.

At five minutes to two, Mr Zuckerman snapped his fingers and the scene shifter who was operating the gramophone put on the wedding march. In came The Three Musketeers. They had refused to wear flying goggles and boots, which didn't please Mr Zuckerman, but it was too late to dart them more than a reproachful glance. They were followed by the Hollywood Padre, an impressive old gentleman with a mane of white hair and hooch-laden breath.

Charles himself was pale and beaming. Apart from moments of ecstasy in flight, he had rarely felt so happy in his life. Babe and Ernst had spent the previous day trying to talk him out of it. All he had done was to send a telegraph message to his mother, finalising it. Now he kept glancing over their shoulders for the first glimpse of his bride. She came in on the arm of the squeaky-voiced Swede, who had recovered his colour and aplomb again.

Her beauty was breathtaking. She had had the pick of the studio wardrobe, and the best hair and make-up artists. She wore a crinoline of white satin and tulle with a high mantilla of lace and pearls. Her appearance moved Mr Zuckerman to tears.

'I can't believe my luck,' Charles whispered, as he kissed his new wife on that tiny perfect mouth.

Mr Zuckerman couldn't believe his luck either. Coming out of the bright lights of the studio and about to step into the second of the waiting bridal procession Buicks, he saw Charles, having handed Sylvia into the beribboned car, pause. Newsboys were yelling themselves hoarse, and Charles, almost as excited, was running now to buy a paper.

The other two Musketeers rushed past him and did the same. Always one to be where the action was, Mr Zuckerman felt in his pocket for a nickel, and followed suit.

"Ere, Mister! Lindy does it!'

There it was. Headlines as big as Mr Zuckerman's right arm. *Lindy takes off to fly the Atlantic.* Spirit of St Louis *on her way to Paris.*

'Can't you see the headlines? All the publicity Lindy's getting and more.'

Lindbergh's 25-hour flight to Paris was over. The world had gone mad. Mr Zuckerman sat on a corner of the bed in the hotel suite. 'Honeymoon Atlantic flight! First woman over the pond! Star of the silver screen, Sylvia Sylvaine! And baronet's son, Charles Haybury! All financed by Uncle Zuckerman!'

Sylvia was delighted at the prospect of such publicity. 'Just so long as there's no wing-waling, Mr Zuckerman.'

'Hell, no! Jest straight flying, isn't that so, Charlie? Jest from New York to Ireland. Then home to London. Meet you upper-crust ma-in-law. Meet the King and Queen. Lindy's right in there, hobnobbing with royalty, presidents, dictators, and Charlie's as good a pilot any day!'

Charles had in fact no false modesty about either his flying ability or his experience. He was as good as anyone. Better than many people who had already made long distance attempts. He had what Babe called a natural pair of hands, and as much experience as Lindbergh. What he had lacked was money. And now miraculously, money was being offered him. It was like a dream come true. And he owed it to Sylvia as much as to Mr Zuckerman.

He saw little of her during the next few weeks – though when he did see her she was sweet, compliant and remarkably accomplished in bed. Her time was taken up in a studio publicity drive. She was photographed in flying kit, studying maps, in glamorous gowns for meeting the English aristocracy, in

257

tweeds for shooting parties, in riding habits, and in casual clothes supposedly checking dummy rations and equipment for the flight.

Charles and the other two Musketeers were even busier. They were almost as pleased as he was. And having decided that Charles's own aircraft was the best of the three to use, they stripped her down, and renewed every part that showed the slightest weakness. They tuned the engine. They pored over the load and balance sheet. They tested various types of overload petrol tanks. Ernst with his meticulous German thoroughness studied the meteorological records of the North Atlantic for the past ten years and worked out a weather pattern, and as an added safeguard provided Charles with a list of all trans-Atlantic liner sailings and their approximate projected positions – just in case. Babe devised a scheme for pinning flight data to Charles's knee, and Ernst a rubber cushion to make the seat more comfortable for the passenger.

'I'd sooner try it without a passenger,' Charles told Mr Zuckerman but the producer was adamant. 'No Sylvia, no deal. Not a red cent! You're sure of yourself son. So'm I. And never forget what the preacher said,' he wiped his eye, 'ye twain are one flesh. She's gotta go!'

Not that Sylvia showed any reluctance. She trusted Charles. She idolised him. She told the press so in every interview. And she got a good response. The Clean-up-Hollywood campaign was under way, and sweet girls like Mary Pickford and Sylvia Sylvaine were applauded by women's organisations, rampant against male lasciviousness.

A beautifully groomed Sylvia appeared on the little airstrip behind the studios at ten am on 20 July. The days were long, and flying into the sun there would be scarcely any night. A huge crowd had gathered – the shape, Mr Zuckerman earnestly prayed, of things to come.

Charles had had a slight argument with Sylvia – their first – over the baggage she wanted to take. He had turned a deaf ear to her blandishments. She could take nothing. Her trousseau must go by sea. Every ounce counted. Even a nightdress meant one less chocolate bar or a thimble of fuel, and many a pilot had come in on that. They took off to thunderous cheers and the breaking of the Stars and Stripes and the Union Jack from the studio flagpole.

The two Musketeers accompanied them in their aircraft as far as Omaha, the first stop on the trans-continental airmail route. The engine purred smoothly. Below them the countryside spread out in a golden summer haze. Next day, without accident or incident, Charles and Sylvia landed at New York airport. A crowd that would have thrilled even Mr Zuckerman awaited them. There were bouquets for Sylvia. Cameras clicked interminably, all the newspapers in New York carried headlines. And two days afterwards most of the 16,000 cinemas throughout the United States showed a film of their flight from Hollywood.

Asked what she would most like to do while she was in New York, Sylvia opted for a hair-do and a shopping spree, while Charles, mindful that crowds had broken off pieces of Lindbergh's aircraft, mounted guard over his aeroplane till it could be wheeled into shelter. Waiting for Sylvia to return, he visited the New York weather office and back at the hotel he studied the map of shipping positions which Ernst had prepared.

On 25 July Charles was up early to supervise the refuelling and filling of the extra tanks. Sylvia was out on the tarmac soon after him, gorgeously dressed in a cream shantung suit with green crocodile trimmings. At nine o'clock they climbed into the aircraft to all the ballyhoo of cheering, cameramen and spectators and ships sounding off their sirens. The engine started. Down the runway the heavy aircraft belted not as fast and as certainly as Charles would have liked, but reached take-off speed just before the end came up. He pulled back on the stick. Up came the nose, then with gluey slowness the rest of the aircraft. He pulled back hard, giving the engine everything it had. The aircraft staggered, gained a little height, wallowed, screamed unhappily, zigzagged to one side of a skyscraper, just avoided a bridge and suddenly plummetted into the grey waters of Flushing Bay.

Desperately, Charles seized Sylvia as the aircraft keeled over and the water rushed in. He felt himself go down still clutching her, then come up again, still holding her. The aircraft had completely turned turtle, but was still floating.

'Hold on, Sylvia!' He almost threw her across the wing, supporting her in the small of her back till he saw her hands fasten over it. Her teeth were chattering. Her long red hair clung to her head. Her make-up streaked her face in black and blue; tears mingled with the salt water. 'I can't swim,' she wailed.

'They'll have seen us! They'll be here! There's no danger. Just hang on!'

Eventually a motor launch appeared, so loaded with photographers that there seemed scarcely to be room for them. In a matter of minutes, Sylvia was hauled on board, then Charles. To Sylvia's manifest horror, the cameras clicked with wild enthusiasm. Sylvia stood it for a second. Then suddenly she lifted her clenched fist.

Charles, fearful that she would damage her image by alienating the pressmen, was about to step forward when he saw that her victim was him. With a surprisingly capable punch, she caught him in the midriff, and followed that blow with one to the side of the head and was about to lift her knee to kick him in the groin, when he side-stepped and fell back into the water.

'You lousy no-good failure!' she shouted after him. 'You damned Limey! You couldn't compete with Lindy! We're finished! Washed up! I never want to see your face again!'

Baronet's son ducks actress wife in Flushing Bay.

At the other end of Diana's elegant breakfast table, Frederick anxiously watched her read the newspaper headlines.

She said nothing for a long time. Then she put down the newspaper, raised her head and looked Frederick straight in the eye. 'And to think, Frederick,' she said, 'that a woman like that actress will one day bear the proud name of Lady Haybury!'

By that she gave him clearly to understand that the name Lady Haybury had been so debased it was no longer worth achieving. The name Lady Thomson, however, certainly was.

Though Thomson and the Labour party were out of office, he exerted tremendous influence on the building of the two airships: the government R101 under construction at Cardington and the private enterprise R100 at Howden.

The building of those airships had brought more work for Jerningham. The labour force doubled, but it brought little satisfaction to Amelia. She still flew every weekend at Southampton airfield, but she was tired of flying round the Hampshire countryside. Twice she had entered the King's Cup race, more for fun than anything else, but at least both times she had finished the course.

The forms for the next entry arrived on the same day as Charles's disastrous Atlantic attempt was splashed over the newspapers. Unlike Lady Nazier, Amelia's reaction was contained in her offhand remark to Cummings, 'I'm not going to enter the King's Cup this year.'

He looked up surprised. 'Why ever not?'

'I'm going to fly to Australia instead.'

There was a moment of horrified silence. Then Cummings asked. 'In what?'

'Ajax, of course!'

'I suppose your mind is made up?'

'Totally.'

'Nothing I can say . . . ?'

'Will stop me? Nothing.'

The news was kept from the board and the family. Cummings worked all hours on Ajax in the hangar, borrowing such fitters and riggers as he needed from the factory. He and Amelia made repeated visits to Rolls-Royce at Derby, and their technicians came down to Jerningham to give the engine a complete overhaul.

It was while they were at Derby that Amelia learned how far Jerningham had fallen behind modern aeroplanes with their forced concentration on airships. The idea she once fondly had of entering Ajax II with its 230 hp engine for the Venice Schneider Trophy that September was shown to be ludicrous. Mitchell was designing the Supermarine winner which had a Rolls-Royce engine of nearly four times that horsepower and a speed of 281 mph. And Rolls-Royce were concentrating on an engine nearly twice the horsepower of *that* engine.

Ajax II was ready by Christmas. For the first time, into Amelia's excitement there crept a solemn awareness of the magnitude of what she was undertaking. But far from weakening her resolve, it strengthened it.

'I wish Master Charles was home,' Sarah signed, as family and servants toasted absent friends. 'He'd make you see sense, m'lady.'

'Flushing Sound sense?' Amelia reminded her wryly.

'That was the silly actress's fault, M'lady. Not Master Charles's!'

By the end of January Cummings had tested the aircraft, given such intruction as he could to Amelia and sent her off solo. By mid-February, she was flying all over Britain. In March she visited the monocled Sir Sefton Brancker, still director of civil aviation, who had flown to India with Cobham three years before, and been given a mass of valuable advice interspersed with hints of the best restaurants and nightspots along the route. He had introduced her to Sir Alan Cobham, who went over in detail with her the route to Australia.

All had helped with advice, recommended staging posts, promised all their co-operation. A certain amount of finance for the trip was pleged by commercial firms. The Wakefield oil company was particularly generous. But Ajax II was owned by Jerningham aviation. Some of the expenses would have to be borne by them, and it was necessary to get the Board's permission. With mingled trepidation and almost unbearable excitement, Amelia wrote to James at RAF Baghdad, saying she was planning to use RAF staging posts in the Middle East for her trip and was hoping to see him. There was no reply.

But the reaction of the others – family and board – was *no*.

Now in his second year in Law at Oxford, Arthur begged her to think again. From Ceylon, her sister Victoria wrote to remind her that a woman's place was in the home, especially one who was fortunate enough to have children. Charles, now divorced in Reno and still working in the air circus, with no intention of coming home, telephoned her not to go. Frederick did likewise. It was the only time she ever knew Charles and Frederick to agree on anything.

The board voting looked lined up totally against her – Victoria against, Connaught Engineering against, Frederick against. And then on the eve of the board meeting in the lounge of her house in London Frederick told Diana of this new example of Amelia's 'lunacy'.

She'll just make an exhibition of herself . . . exactly like that wretched boy! Can't you see the headlines? 'Lady Haybury gets a ducking in the Persian Gulf!' Or 'Lady Haybury kidnapped by tribesmen'!'

They were having an early dinner before going to the theatre together. These days, to Frederick's great satisfaction, he was seeing more of Diana. Her attitude towards Christopher Thomson appeared to have cooled.

'Flying on her own across those waterless deserts! Over those mountains! Inside those storms!'

Instead of answering, Diana seemed to go off on a quite irrelevant tack. She gave a strange secretive smile. 'I see from the evening paper that they've given up all hope of finding the Honourable Elsie Mackay.'

He looked at her uncomprehendingly.

'The daughter of Lord Inchcape, Frederick. So sad! Set off last Wednesday to fly the Atlantic from east to west,' Diana sighed. 'And has not been seen since.'

'Silly woman!'

'Six months ago, Princess Lowenstein disappeared trying to fly the Atlantic.'

'Really?'

'Then there was Frances Grayson, Frederick. That American millionairess. She vanished on the same route.' Diana shook her head slowly from side to side. 'Aeroplanes are awfully unreliable things.'

He was looking at her intently now, no longer uncomprehending.

'And women do seem to have the most frightful luck in them.'

'So what do you think, Diana?'

'What do I think, Frederick?' She leaned over and kissed him sensuously on his parted lips. 'Well,' momentarily her little pointed tongue touched his, 'If Lady Haybury is so determined to fly all the way to Australia on her own —'

Her large green eyes regarded him with studied innocence, 'I don't see why we should stand in her way.'

SEVEN

'Goodbye, Amelia.'

Diana Nazier leaned forward to give her a kiss on the mouth which Amelia managed to turn into a brush against a powdered cheek. Frederick gave her a husbandly peck for the benefit of the photographers, Arthur an unexpectedly demonstrative hug. Lord Christopher Thomson had come to Croydon especially, so Diana informed her, to congratulate her on her pioneering spirit for the Empire and to tell her to look out for the airship mooring mast they were building for the R101 at Karachi. Sir Sefton Brancker screwed the monocle into his right eye and wished her 'All the luck in the world, my dear young lady.'

Walking over to Ajax – painted bright red so that it would show up if she was forced down in the desert – Amelia turned to wave to them all, cinecameramen, journalists, photographers. Aristocratic ladies, the *Daily Mail* had already headlined in that day's issue, were going in for sky trailblazing in a big way, Lady Heath still on her way to South Aafrica (after two and a half months) and Lady Bailey still doing the same route there and back. Now Lady Haybury off on her own in the wonderplane Ajax, determined to beat Squadron Leader Hinkler's record of 15½ days to Australia . . .

Amelia jumped up on to the fuselage and climbed into the cockpit. The mechanic swung the propeller. The Rolls-Royce coughed, caught and whirred a cool draught of early morning air back into her face. As she began taxying forward she waved again and blew a kiss, this time particularly to Ronald Cummings, standing away from the others and looking terribly anxious. As the day of her departure got nearer, he had become more nervous than any of them, telling her, 'Don't take any unnecessary risks, Amelia,' and 'Have a good rest every night' and 'Don't try too hard to beat Hinkler!', even joining with Arthur to say, 'Don't be too proud to give up.'

At the far end of the airfield, she wheeled round into the wind and did her cockpit check. Just for a few moments, as Ajax throbbed and quivered under her, she looked at the dawn cracking open the sky over the grimy chimneypots of Croydon and wondered almost dispassionately how many more dawns she would see.

Then she opened up the throttle, heard the reassuring roar of the Rolls-Royce, felt the push in the small of her back as the heavily laden Ajax bumped over the uneven grass, and then with an overwhelming sense of release and relief and commitment eased the wheels gently off the ground.

She was off – first stop Lyons, cruising at an economical 140 mph. Cummings had fitted an extra fuel tank giving her five hours' range. She had the best maps possible – the Middle East ones were known to be erratic – with the magnetic courses laid off on them. She carried two gallons of emergency water, rations of beef, malt, chocolate and a full set of spares, including a propeller, bolted inside the fuselage. Cobham had given her an RAF 'guley chit' that he had carried, a handkerchief with a printed promise in Arabic, Syrian and Kurdish that 'a ransom of RS 3000 will be paid if this pilot is returned to the nearest British post'. In case this was ineffective, she also carried a revolver and ammunition, on which Cummings had given her painstaking lessons.

As England grew smaller on the climb and finally disappeared, she felt an overwhelming sense of excitement and exhilaration. Flying quite alone in the sky she had always found to be a kind of communion. The air was quite still. The wings were rock-steady. The engine sounded out a reassuring music of strong rhythmic heartbeats.

Now she could see the Eiffel Tower ahead, its legs awash in the mists of the Seine. Then an hour and a half later, the dark smoke clouds from the factory chimneys of Lyons, when she landed on the grimy city airfield for refuelling. Here she had her first delay. The official needed to sign her numerous papers could not be found, and it was three hours later before she was back on her way again.

Then there was a headwind over the Alps, slowing her right down and throwing Ajax all over the sky. Down below white peaks jutted up from brown mountains wrinkled in shadow. Over Italy, it began to get dark; little lights pricked through mauve mist. Over on the right, she saw the fiery crater of Vesuvius. Paraffin glims had been lit on the airfield for her arrival at Bari. Under bright searchlights, Ajax was marshalled to the place of honour. A band played military marches. Smart officials in black shirts and white trousers – the first of Mussolini's new Fascist Italians that she had seen – smilingly escorted her to a waiting limousine and she was whisked off to the best suite in the best hotel. Here to her dismay she found a big reception awaiting her, followed by a banquet, with so many speeches she didn't get to bed till midnight.

Once again though, she was off at dawn – over the Adriatic to the dazzling blue waters of the Gulf of Corinth and then on to another good landing at Tate's aerodrome, Athens. If she could only reach Konia in Turkey by nightfall, she had a good chance of beating her schedule of five days to Karachi.

Athens had Ajax insected, refuelled, oil changed and all valve clearances checked within two hours. But back in the air over the Aegean, the weather turned suddenly sour. The cloud base came lower, and Amelia had to go down to 1000 feet to get under it. Worse, light spots of oil began to bedew the windscreen. Every time she wiped them clear with a cloth, back they came. Ever so slightly, the needle on the oil pressure gauge started flickering.

Over Samos, she nearly went back to Athens. Then a fan of sunlight suddenly shot through the greyness blanketing the coast of Turkey ahead. The oil pressure had settled. The stains on the windscreen became less frequent. She decided to risk it. The trouble was the high ground. Mountains rose up steeply on either side of her. She flew down ugly gorges and close to sheer cliff faces. Konia was 3500 feet above sea level and the cloud base was no more than 200 feet above the aerodrome when she arrived.

The Turkish mechanics found a connection had worked loose on an oil pipe which was soon fixed. But the meteorology service was practically nonexistent, and what there was of it couldn't speak English. All that she could gather was that the weather beyond the Euphrates on her next leg to Mosul might be stormy.

She tried to telephone Mosul, but it was impossible to get through. Stamboul was finally contacted, but could add nothing to what she had already been given. The Turks were full of friendly co-operation and insisted that she attend a party complete with Turkish music and Turkish coffee, but she managed to get away to her room in the local hotel by nine o'clock.

Next day dawned without a cloud in the sky. Greatly cheered, she took off, flying north of a jagged range of mountains round Ereglia. Three hours afterwards, from 5000 feet she saw the glistening snake of the Euphrates twenty miles ahead, and still no sign of any storms. And then suddenly she heard a dry cracking noise as though Ajax's windscreen had split.

Lowering her eyes, she scrutinised it. There was no sign of anything. The perspex was perfectly clear. Down below, the desert steamed. Even up here, it was baking. The air she breathed into her lungs was warm, as though it had been breathed before. She put her hand out of the cockpit and touched the metal cowlings. They were burning hot but the engine was running as sweetly as a sewing machine.

There was the scratching noise again! Louder this time, more insistent. Yet nothing showed. The windscreen remained as clear as crystal.

Then she looked down at the desert again. It was as though that flat yellow expanse had suddenly grown curls that spiralled up into the sky. They were swaying and bouncing and moving as though driven by a terrific wind. Dust devils! Hundreds of them, like yellow dervishes dancing!

And now the scratching sound on the windscreen identified itself. Sand – sand thrown up even to this height – grains of sand crawling like ants all over the perspex. No longer was there a dazzling blue horizon ahead. A great brown lump had grown right in her path.

She pushed the throttle fully forward and climbed. Seven, nine, eleven, thirteen . . .

The lump climbed too.

She would have to fly round it. Jamming on rudder and aileron, she turned to port. The lump turned to port too. Great tentacles of ochre cloud shot out like octopus arms as though trying to grab her. Ajax started shaking. The instruments were doing a dance in front of her. Sand blindfolded the windscreen.

I've got to go back, she thought. I'll have to turn and make for Aleppo. But when cautiously she put the port wing down, a huge updraught tilted it right up. Almost upside-down, she struggled to get straight. Her mouth had gone dry. She could feel her heart hammering. Sand was everywhere – in her eyes, her face, her nose.

Under her, Ajax had gone sloppy, wallowing round the sky, refusing to climb. Caught in the web of the storm, the aircraft was becoming paralysed. The desert, the sky, the wing tips, even the propeller only six feet in front of her became a poisonous-coloured blue.

Then suddenly she was suffocating in a hot cloak. She heard the propeller screaming above the stuttering of the engine. The next moment she was on her back. All she could see was the phosphorescent gleam of the altimeter numbers like tiny stars on a dark night.

6000 . . . 4000 . . . 2000.

She was falling, falling fast. Grains of sand were pinging all over the aircraft like millions of bullets. The engine had gone quite silent.

1000 . . . 500 . . .

Like the end of a dark tunnel, now there was just a flicker of light. She was coming under the bottom of the storm cloud. She could see the yellow smudge of ground below. She pulled back on the stick. Putting on hard right rudder, she straightened. Out of the corner of her left eye, through the rising sand, she glimpsed a huge black cliff face and shapes of rocks.

But she was right side up. The controls were still responding. And ahead was a muzzy snakeskin that appeared to be a dried river bed.

Desperately she struggled towards it. Half-blinded by sand, suddenly she felt the wheels connect, sink into something soft, slew right round and crumple.

James found Amelia's letter announcing her trip on his return from three weeks' detachment at a forward landing ground, patrolling the mountains of Iraq.

Here beside the ancient walled city of Mosul, with only an army co-operation squadron of ancient Bristol Fighters and a detachment of armoured cars, he was in sole command of a huge tract of wild and dangerous desert. His job was stamping out local wars before they became too large. His main headache was an old rogue called Sheikh Mahmoud, who would raid a village or commit some sabotage and be off before James even heard of it. All he could do was to keep regular patrols over likely trouble areas and try to spot the brigands galloping over the desert before they struck. It was one continual wily game of trying to keep one jump ahead.

The fuel pump had packed up on his flight back and he had had to hand pump over the mountains with his engine repeatedly cutting out. Sweat, oil and grime poured down his face as he slit open the envelope and read her letter.

His first reaction was fury. Typical Amelia, impetuous as ever, trying to compensate for Charles's lunatic Atlantic attempt! He went straight to the telephone and rang RAF HQ at Hinaidi aerodrome, Baghdad, to make sure they refused permission.

What they told him made his mood change completely. It was all too late. Not only was she on her way, but she had left Konia for Mosul eight hours ago. They had known her flight was on the cards, but she was early. They had tried to telephone to let him know, but as usual the tribesmen had cut the telephone wires and they had only just been repaired.

'She hasn't arrived.'

'Not to worry, old boy. Might have met a headwind.'

'Her fuel would be exhausted by now.'

'Might have turned back to Aleppo.'

'Might also have hit a sandstorm. I saw some hellish build-up as I came back.'

'Then you'd better send out —' but the telephone was already slammed down before the Senior Air Staff Officer had completed his sentence.

Through the baking heat, James ran back to the airfield. He shouted for his gunner and for the airmen to refuel his Brisfit. There were only five other serviceable aircraft and two were on the regular patrol to the south over the Wadi Haurun – a favourite incendiary ground for Sheikh Mahmoud.

Five minutes later, he led the remaining three off the baked mud of the airfield to make a search along Amelia's track.

None of them found anything. None of them saw anything except brown clouds and sand devils.

James came back to land in pitch darkness on the flickering paraffin flarepath at Mosul, and rang Hinaidi immediately.

'Still no news, old boy.'

The next day was a replica of that day. Still nothing. Still stifling hot. On the English radio, he heard Amelia had been reported missing. When he went to bed, the sheet was sopping, the pillow stuck to the back of his head.

He could hardly breathe, let alone sleep. He got up at three o'clock and walked up and down the sand outside the mess, staring at the stars.

All of them were out. A crescent moon was whitening the sand of the desert. At least all signs of storms had gone. The eastern sky began lightening. He got a cup of coffee from the kitchen where they were now preparing breakfast. As he was drinking it, alone in the ante-room, the duty batman came up to tell him there was someone outside wanting to see him.

The first thing he saw in the half-light was a camel. Then a figure in white flowing robes. Two bright black eyes glittered at him from a thin face with a pointed beard. Two brown hands came together in a kind of prayer. The head gave a little bow. 'Wing Commander March.'

'This is a surprise, Sheikh Mahmoud.'

'This is a pleasure, Wing Commander.' The Arab spoke very softly.

'Have you come at last to pay your fines and taxes?'

The Sheikh laughed. 'A poor man like me, Wing Commander? No income, no wealth! Nothing but this camel!'

'Then to what do I owe the pleasure of your company?'

'Because you are my friend.'

'I could put you in prison now.'

'I came for your benefit. You would never do that – *bradarĭck chaka akat* – to a friend doing a favour.'

'But so early in the morning?'

'Wing Commander, from afar I have come as fast as my camel can carry me to bring you – *dan wa basĭkĭ gring* – miraculous news!'

'And what news is that?'

'Wing Commander, one of my trusted tribesmen reported to me the morning of two days ago – *shtĕacki barz la asman* – a sight high in the heavens. A star, he told me. Bigger and brighter than the one over Bethlehem. But red, he said. Redder than the planet Nergal that you call Mars. And falling.'

'And where was this?'

'In the Helebja district. Up north.'

She would be well off track if she had come down there. But she might well have turned to port to try and circumnavigate the storm.

He said slowly, 'The direct opposite from where the oil pipeline at Wadi Haurun is?'

The Sheikh smiled. 'The Wing Commander is always right.'

'And you are suggesting that we would wish to investigate?'

'That is my surmise, All Highness.'

It's a trap, James thought. He's going to get the Brisfit patrol far away from the oil pipe. And then just to show us we're being too successful stopping the brigands raiding the villages, he's going to cut it so as to teach us a lesson. And it mightn't be Amelia at all. It mightn't be anything. Just something to send us away while he does his dirty deed.

'So we will be far away from the oil pipeline when you fire it?'

The Sheikh said reproachfully, 'To think we could contemplate such a thing, Highest!'

'You not only contemplate it. You frequently do it.'

The Sheikh shook his head and clucked his tongue.

'And what if there is nothing there?'

'Highest, I hold you in utmost respect. I would never send you on a fool's errand.'

James watched the Sheikh's face, highlighted now in the rising sun, as he considered his decision.

But his mind was already made up. 'Thank you for this information.'

The Sheikh bowed low again. 'It is a pleasure to be of service to such as the All Highest.'

Ten minutes later, led by James, all serviceable Brisfits took off on the dawn patrol. But instead of going south towards the oil pipeline, they all went north towards the mountains. Spread out at visibility distance, ten miles apart, they made a square search of the Helebja district.

They saw nothing. Back on the ground four hours later, James only waited to refuel before again they were airborne. This time they searched north, even further from Amelia's track. To and fro the fighters went in their square boxed pattern. The terrain was rough and the sand had started to blow again. It was difficult to see anything.

Then the sun started to sink. The quick violet dusk began. James was about to go home, when suddenly his heart gave a leap. Following the muddy bed of a river, his eyes had caught sight of a flash of red against the winding grey. Coming lower, he saw a fuselage, the left wing tilted up at a crazy angle.

'There she is!' his sergeant called out from the seat behind him.

Ten minutes later, coming precariously over rocks, he got the Brisfit down on the hard mud and rocketed wildly to a stop. He raced up the slope towards the escarpment leaving the sergeant far behind.

She's left, he thought at first. Done the worst thing possible. But then he saw a little wall of slate and sand put up under the outstretched wing. She had made a kind of desert igloo of it under which to shelter and against which the blown sand had piled up. He struggled towards the igloo, his boots sinking deep into the sand. His heart was hammering, and even the swish of his feet seemed unnaturally loud and laboured like footsteps in a nightmare. There was an ominous hushed and deathly silence about the igloo. A silence against which their engine must have been clearly heard. Why didn't she come out if she was still alive? Why hadn't she tried to attract their attention? He glanced up at the sky to see if he could spot any hovering vultures, and was faintly reassured when it remained an unbroken violet.

Despite that reassurance, he had to pause for a moment before ducking down to peer inside. Amelia was lying on her leather coat, her water bottle, an empty tin of biscuits and a half-eaten chocolate bar arranged round her. White sand had sifted lightly over her, in the folds of her coat, in her hair, the corners of her eyes, in her lashes and in her ears. Her face was a strange blotchy colour, her mouth cracked and purply red. He dropped on to his knees beside her and lifted her wrist to feel for a pulse.

Her eyes half-opened. She stared at him fixedly for a moment, so fixedly that he wondered if she could see at all. Then her lips parted in a smile of almost unbearable sweetness. 'James? Oh, James!' her voice was a dry crackly whisper, but she seemed totally unsurprised. She put her arms round his neck. His pent-up fears and emotions broke. He kissed her face, her neck, her sand-matted hair with wild relief. That seemed to surprise her more than his sudden appearance. In a dazed voice she asked, 'Am I still alive then, James? I thought I'd died and . . .' Her voice cracked before she could finish.

She didn't need to finish. He knew what she meant. He had seen death often enough. And years ago in the RFC mess, the Padre and MO had talked of 'the strange mercy', the hallucination wherein the dying often see the sight that is most desirable to them.

He was moved beyond words. All these years they had been loving at cross purposes. He set about moistening her lips with water from his flask, and at the same time asking a question that was not wholly about the flight, 'Why did you do it, Amelia?'

She turned her head away and didn't answer. He was glad when his sergeant gunner came labouring up.

Darkness was falling when they took off. Amelia they had fitted in on the sergeant's knee in the back cockpit. As they rose higher with the cool night air up to 6000 feet for the quickest way over the mountans to Mosul, James suddenly saw far to the south a tiny yellow flame and smiled, grimly.

No Star of Bethlehem this. No fool's errand, just as Sheikh Mahmoud had said. But accounts must be settled. Debts of honour must be paid.

An eye for an eye. A favour for a favour. A life for a flaming oil pipeline.

From then on, the fire and the pipeline engaged all his concern. As soon as they had landed he handed her over to the young RAF medical officer who met the plane in his battered old ambulance.

'Lady Haybury, this is Flight Lieutenant Bird. Naturally known as Dickie. Run the ruler over her, Dickie, and make sure there's no damage. And see she does what you tell her.'

Amelia was immediately told to lie down on one of the stretchers, while James disappeared into the velvety darkness, cursing Sheikh Mahmoud and all his works.

At sick quarters, there was a collapsible canvas bath where she was able to soak her body and wash her hair. Dickie and a fearsome Scots nursing sister called Sims examined her from head to toe, discovered no broken bones, nothing that a good long rest wouldn't heal. The doctor had to apply iodine, he was sorry, but wounds went septic very easily out here. Then Amelia was put to bed with a sedative, and went to sleep lulled by the groaning of a wooden waterwheel which Sims told her irrigated the station flowerbeds.

Halfway through the night she woke. Moonlight was streaming through the slatted blinds and with it a strange mixture of smells – dry earth, camel dung, engine oil and some lily-like scent from the irrigated gardens. Even before she saw the shadowy figure sitting by her bed, she knew that James was in the room.

She put out her hand and his fingers fastened over it. 'Dickie said you weren't in too bad shape.'

He loomed over her. She could just make out his face in the moonlight, the movement of his eyes.

'How was the fire?'

'It's under control.'

'Was it partly my fault?'

No.' He kissed her forehead. 'Now, go to sleep!'

He straightened. She caught his arm. 'Why did you come?'

'To tell you we've sent a message to RAF HQ for transmission to your husband.'

'Is that the only reason?'

'And to tell you that if Dickie agrees, we'll have you on your way in a couple of days.'

'As far as I'm concerned,' Dickie told her the following morning after her temperature and pulse had been duly recorded, 'I don't really agree with anything of the sort. Medically I suppose it's all right. But personally we'd all prefer you stayed.'

I'd like to stay too, she thought, staring out at the distant barrier of jagged mountains. They seemed to cut her off from England and Frederick as effectively as if she were in another world. Never again would she be so close to James in a world so removed from their own. A world in which she thought wryly, lay the confluence of the Tigris and Euphrates at Al Qurna, the reputed site of the Garden of Eden.

'A rather grubby palm-mat city,' Dickie said in reply to her question about it. 'Most of these places aren't what they're cracked up to be.'

That afternoon he allowed her to sit out on the verandah. Her clothes had been washed and pressed. The nursing sister brought them out a tray of tea with ambergris and halva, which was like Turkish delight. They watched a procession of camels go by. Dickie told her camels, according to local legend, wore such a supercilious expression because they knew the hundredth name of God which is hidden from men.

'What remains hidden from me,' Dickie returned to his favourite complaint, 'is why you have to return so quickly. With such indecent haste. The day after tomorrow, Wing Commander March says. He thinks your husband will be anxious.'

'Yes.'

'Presumably you're catching the boat from Basrah. I've asked the Wingco to let me drive you. We'll go quite close to Al Qurna.'

'That would be nice.'

'Mind you, everyone here's keen to meet you. And we'd hoped we could put on a party, before you went. These happily married men like the Wingco don't know what it feels like to be dancing always with Eileen.'

'Eileen?'

'I-lean-on the bar. So few women, you understand. Even Sims, bless her

269

heart, has a queue a score deep. The Wing Commander has a picture of his wife and his children on his desk. That keeps him straight and level.'

When two days later Amelia went to say goodbye to James in his office, she sat beside that picture.

'I wanted to thank you before I went. Everybody's been so kind. The fruit and the mimosa. All those flowers! Where did they get them?'

Her voice chattered on, her eyes irresistibly drawn to the picture. James's wife, serious-eyed and unsmiling. Marianne, prettier than ever, in a stiff school uniform. The young boy so like his mother.

'You've met my wife, of course,' James said, following her gaze. 'And Marianne.'

His voice was level and determinedly neutral, as if Amelia were some distant not greatly loved family acquaintance. 'But I don't think you ever saw Pierre.'

'Pierre? Not Peter?'

'Pierre. They're quite settled in now near their maternal grandfather.'

'They'll grow up French!'

'European.' He laughed at her with a trace of his old affectionate mockery. 'How insular you are, Amelia! Anyway, that's what to hope for. One world. Europe has had enough war. Besides, Marie disliked the British climate.'

'And the British people?'

'She found them cold, too.' He gave her one of his warning glances. Come no closer. Don't tread on my sacred ground.

But Amelia rushed straight over it. 'No doubt you make up for all their coldness.'

'I try, Amelia.'

'Do you love her then?' she asked in a low urgent voice.

'Of course I love her.' He spoke clearly and with great finality. 'Very much.' He picked up a sheaf of paper from his desk. 'These are your arrangements. As Dickie told you, the SS *Melbourne* calls at Basrah on Friday evening. I've told Dickie he can drive you there. See you on board. Your husband has telegraphed that he will meet the ship at Southampton.'

'Won't you drive me yourself?'

'No.'

'Why not?'

'Because I'm too busy and you have already wasted enough of my time.'

'That's not the reason at all!' She leaned across the desk. 'I'll tell you why not. You daren't take me. You daren't spend three hours alone with me. Because it's me you love, not her.'

For answer, he strode round and opened the office door. He did not shake her hand nor indeed even glance at her face.

'Goodbye, Amelia.'

EIGHT

Frederick's first words to Amelia as she stepped off the SS *Melbourne* at Southampton were 'Lady Heath flies from Capetown to Croydon, Lady Bailey successfully flies round Africa. Lady Haybury crashes in the desert.'

As he drove her to Haybury almost in silence, he was thinking: an impulsive fool for a wife, a clown for an heir. An aviation business that was now only a cottage industry, kept going by a few scraps of airship subcontracts obtained by his mistress. His personal fortune depleted by the sudden crash on Wall Street. His political career in ruins.

How much lower could a man get? And *none* of it was his doing!

Lord Christopher Thomson on the other hand, in spite of being in opposition, was doing very nicely. He had literary and diplomatic connections, moved in the fashionable circles of Proust. His romantic novel called *Smaranda* about fairy castles and witches and sacred mountains and buried treasure had been published. Nothing but fantasy. Pure dreams of gold.

He actually found Diana so deeply engrossed in the thing that she'd brought it with her to his flat. 'You must read this, Frederick. You'd enjoy it.'

He pretended to be looking forward to such a treat. That was the undignified position vis à vis Thomson into which he had been forced. While he attended a few aviation committees in connection with the R100 and R101, Sir Samuel Hoare was flying all over the place in the new Calcutta flying boat, Imperial Airway's answer to the airship for the All-Red-Route. And Thomson had become bosom friends with the French Air Minister (no doubt they talked about Proust all the time) and was literally dividing up world air routes with him.

'I've almost finished it. Another three pages and then I would like to be taken out to dinner.'

It was the first time he'd had the chance for weeks. 'Delighted, my dear.'

She finished the book. As she closed it, she looked up. 'Frederick, how *old* is your Aunt Sempner?'

'Ninety-three.'

'And is she as rich as they say she is?'

'Richer . . . much richer! Beyond the dreams of Smaranda . . .'

'Lady Sempner's nurse on the telephone, M'lady.' Down at Haybury, Pearson sighed lugubriously and added with the intimacy of an old and valued servant, 'I hope her old ladyship isn't about to peg it at last!'

This appeared not to be the case. Lady Sempner was not worse. Not as far as the nurse could see, and she'd nursed a lot of old people in her time. Lady Sempner was suddenly very lively. Quite like her old self. She was sitting out

271

in her chair and watching the crowds. The Prince of Wales was visiting some club with Lady Cunard and her friends, and people – Lady Sempner included – were trying to catch a glimpse of them. She had been visited by her hairdresser that afternoon and a beautician from the salon in Bond Street. She had put on her newest dress. Now she wanted to be visited. Not by any old fogey with one foot in the grave. But either by her nephew or Lady Haybury. This very evening. Tomorrow she might not feel up to it.

'I tried to telephone Sir Frederick at his club. But he had just left. And I wondered if you . . . '

'Of course. I'd be delighted. I'll come at once.'

It was no less than the truth. She was glad of the interruption to her routine. Life without the hope of James or Ajax seemed as uninspiring and grey as the balloon fabric that now filled the Jerningham sheds and snuffed out her hopes.

Amelia swept aside Sarah's protests that she would be too tired to drive up to London and back that night. 'Leave me a flask of coffee and some sandwiches, Sarah. I'll eat a piece of chicken before I go. I'm not a child. Nor am I an old woman.'

She pretended not to hear Sarah's muttered, 'You're well past forty!' She fastened up the buttons of her motoring jacket and stepped into her Rolls with a feeling of release. There was nothing so assuaging as speed. She pressed her foot hard on the accelerator, put down the windows and felt the fragrant air rush past her ears. The familiar miles winding away under her wheels spun her back deliciously and nostalgically, to other years and other drives across the forest, ghostly shadows flitting amongst the summer trees. It was almost with surprise, as if emerging from a warm dream, that she found herself in the outer suburbs of London, then dodging competently and daringly in and out of the traffic in central London. She arrived at Aunt Sempner's house in Upper Brook Street shortly after eight.

Aunt Sempner was still sitting out in her chair close to the window. Her sparse hair was freshly curled. 'The new Marcel method,' she told Amelia. Her face was set as usual in a thick pink and white mask, but her brown eyes burned with an unnatural and consuming brilliance.

'Well, come and let me see you, gal, after your Arabian adventure!' She held out a skinny claw, weighted down with all the largest rings she possessed.

Amelia bent to kiss the enamelled cheek. 'And how are you?'

'Careful, gal! Don't spoil m'face! It cost enough. I'm in fine fettle. Sit down.'

She waved Amelia to the chair that the nurse was holding out for her. 'And you can go down and get yourself some supper, Nurse. We won't need you. We're going to have a nice chat. Lady Haybury will ring for you before she leaves.'

'And how's my nephew?' Lady Sempner asked when the nurse had gone. The bright brown eyes regarded Amelia mischievously.

'Very well, I think.'

'You think? You don't know? That's because you don't see much of him. Nor do I. Nothing at all. But I hear a lot.'

'Gossip,' Amelia said sternly.

'Maybe. And what's wrong with gossip? It's the best possible way to find out what one's husband is up to. Frederick is very like his uncle. Men have it all their own way.'

272

Amelia said nothing.

'And what about my great-nevvies?'

'They're very well.'

'Is Charles still aerial clowning in America?'

'More or less.'

'I hear he and his father never got on. Hardly surprising is it, considering . . . ?'

She cocked a bright birdy look at Amelia and cracked her pink and white face mask in a cackle of laughter.

Amelia flushed. 'Considering what, Aunt Sempner?'

'Considering he's the eldest. Considering all the troubles he's caused his father. Considering he takes so much after you, while dear Arthur . . . '

Her wicked eyes tried to look innocent and failed. 'That's all I meant.'

'Arthur's certainly giving no trouble. He didn't do brilliantly at Oxford, but he did well enough. We like his friends. Now he's trying for the Bar.'

'Arthur does all the right things,' Aunt Sempner said warmly. 'Dear, boring Arthur!' She reached out a claw and grabbed Amelia's arm. 'Now what about you, gal? Tell me more of this flying caper of yours. Tell me about that dreadful crash, you silly girl! Tell me about your rescue! Was it by this frightful man March who used to live in Jerningham? I want to know everything that happened! And when you've finished, I'll tell you something you can do for me!'

Aunt Sempner picked up a mirror from the ormulu table beside her and examined her own weird individualistic appearance in it. She tweaked a sparse dyed curl, thin and dry as a Victorian doll's hair, into place before replacing the mirror with a self-satisfied smirk.

'Well, go on gal!' She clasped her hands together, permitting herself a small enamel cracking smile. 'What are you waiting for? I've been looking forward to this.'

She listened to Amelia's expurgated account, at first punctuating it with sniffs of disbelief or the occasional cackle of derisive laughter, then in total silence. Amelia stared out of the window avoiding the old woman's bright fixed gaze, remembering James's cold and stern goodbye.

'Then Frederick met me at Southampton, and the board decided that was the end of Ajax. So that's all there is to it really, Aunt Sempner,' Amelia said and turned.

Aunt Sempner's wide-eyed stare was still fixed on her face. But the eyes were filmed and unseeing. Her lips were turned upwards caught in a mocking smile, but the mouth had slackened.

Aunt Sempner was dead.

'Did she mention anything to you about her affairs?' Frederick asked when Amelia finally reached him by telephone.

'Nothing. I don't think she felt like dying. She seemed so full of life.'

'At ninety-three! Well, I only hope she left everything in order. She was financially very warm.' He was thinking, now I shall be very much richer than Christopher Thomson. 'And I am, after all, her eldest nephew.'

Aunt Sempner had in fact left everything in order, and specific instructions about her remains. Her body she had left to St George's Hospital for medical

273

research, a legacy which Frederick found somewhat distasteful but well in keeping with Aunt Sempner's unlovable character. It did, however, make arrangements easier and cheaper. There was a small memorial service at St Margaret's, Westminster. She wanted such of her friends as could get there without too much trouble to attend. But none of her distant relatives, just Frederick's family.

It augered well for the reading of the will which took place immediately afterwards. Arthur accompanied his parents to the solicitor's office purely as moral support, for he expected nothing. He had only visited his great-aunt on rare occasions and found her as his father did, a contentious and aggravating old lady.

In the event, neither he nor Charles was mentioned.

All Lady Sempner's huge fortune was left to one person . . . *to my dear Amelia, on condition she does with it exactly as she pleases without any interference from anyone, least of all from my nephew Frederick.*

NINE

Frederick was furious. He could not bring himself to speak to Amelia of his aunt's will. Amelia herself was at first astonished and then profoundly touched. Aunt Sempner had possessed her own cranky integrity, and Amelia had genuinely loved her. She was glad Aunt Sempner had recognised that fact.

For three weeks after the will was made public, Frederick did not see Diana. She went twice to Paris escorted, he suspected, by Christopher Thomson.

He had been thrown over. Aunt Sempner's will had been the last straw.

Diana was even cooler after the May 1929 election. Baldwin and the Conservatives were defeated. His own majority was cut to the bone. Back came Ramsay MacDonald as Labour Prime Minister. And back, too, came Lord Christopher Thomson as Secretary of State for Air.

Frederick received another setback when he heard that Amelia intended to put Aunt Sempner's entire fortune into building a seaplane to win the 1931 Schneider Trophy. He was so furious, he refused to come down for the board meeting, which Amelia chaired in his absence.

Meanwhile, the *Graf Zeppelin* flew round the world. The Germans established an airship service to North and South America. On 12 October, R101 edged reluctantly out of her hangar and the next day carried out her maiden flight, which was followed over the next month with other flights.

Christopher Thomson, in Frederick's view, considered it his private yacht. He had two staterooms knocked into one and used them as a private office to conduct his Air Ministry business. On one flight to Bedford, he took Diana Nazier with him.

When she saw Frederick on her return that evening, she was so radiant that he feared she was about to announce her engagement to Thomson. 'The R101 is magnificent!' she told him. 'A restaurant. A promenade deck. And a lovely lounge to foxtrot our way to India!'

India, he thought. Was there e reason for Thomson to be so passionately determined that the R101 should fly to India, while the R100 was scheduled to go to Canada?

Thomson had done most of his military service in India. He still had high diplomatic connections there. At that moment, his sister was touring the Middle East route to India. India was the place where he had spent the most time on his recent world tour with the French Minister of Aviation. Why India, Frederick was still thinking when he received an unexpected invitation.

The Secretary of State for Air requests the pleasure of your company on 3 November 1929 for luncheon on the airship R101, followed by a flight.

Seventy-two other MPs were also invited. So was Diana. So were six doctors

– at Sefton Brancker's request for the Director of Civil Aviation was regularly airsick and felt MPs might suffer similarly.

3 November was a cold blustery day. Frederick drove Diana up to Cardington. From miles away, they saw the R101 flying like a brave silver pennant from her mooring mast. They went up together in the electric lift. They stayed together while the party was shown round the airship. But luncheon in the white and gold dining-room separated them. To Frederick's annoyance, Diana had been put beside Thomson while he was at another table with Sefton Brancker.

On the outside envelope could be heard the steady drumming of continuous rain. Halfway through chicken, roast potatoes and peas Frederick observed that they appeared to be 'wallowing' rather a lot. The MP for Stainforth asked apprehensively, 'We're not flying, are we?'

Brancker screwed in his monocle and gave his short sharp laugh. 'Good heavens no, old boy! Soon will be though!'

'If I feel like this now,' said the MP, 'what will I feel like when we're flying?'

'Better,' Brancker said briskly. 'You'll feel better, old boy.'

'But will he?' said the MP from Clackburn sitting at the bottom of the table.

'Engines giving trouble, that's what I heard,' said the MP beside him.

A chorus now came from all sides of the table.

'Insufficient power.'

'Can't make it to India because of the heat.'

India again, Fredeick thought.

'So the proposal is to cut her in two and put in another gasbag.'

'Gentlemen, gentlemen!' Sefton Brancker held up his elegant hands. 'You are talking about a lady!'

'But is she a lady?'

The morale on the table had sunk. And then it was announced that because of the weather, regrettably they would not now be taking to the air; R101 would remain at the mast.

And with that news, the bonhommie on Sefton Brancker's table suddenly leapt. The subject of airships disappeared in jokes.

'Well is she a lady, Brancker?' asked the MP for Clackburn. '*You* should know!'

The Director of Civil Aviation was famous for his amours. 'A *perfect* lady.'

'What does Thomson say?' The MP for Clackburn turned his head to look at the top table where Christopher was deep in conversation with Diana. 'I see he's occupied with a lady always!'

'Bet he wishes she was Princess Bibesco.'

'Is that still on?'

'Of course! Thomson always did aim high.'

'But isn't she married to that Rumanian prince!'

Frederick had spent all the meal jealously watching Diana sparkling away with Thomson, but now he pricked up his ears. He had never even considered the possibility – with a beautiful woman like Diana clearly so interested – of another woman in Thomson's life, and princess at that. His mood changed completely. Suddenly he became positively expansive.

'She could never get a divorce from a prince!' said the MP from Stainforth.

'Why not?' the MP from Clackburn said. 'What does marriage matter these days, eh, Brancker?'

And wasn't that the important question, Frederick thought. People looked now at divorce differently. The Prince of Wales was setting a new tone. He was far from being as puritanical as his father. If Princess Bibesco didn't mind a divorce, why should Diana? Amelia had once actually asked for one. There was no other woman in *his* life, as there was with Thomson. Why shouldn't he get a divorce and marry Diana?

Frederick's good humour continued into the lounge and the coffee and liqueurs, to the thank-yous to Thomson at the head of the gangplank, to the long climb down the steps in the pouring afternoon rain.

He was on the top of his form on the trip with Diana back to London. In response, she was gay and warm and tender. His love, after all, was not nearly so hopeless as he had supposed.

That night, for the first time in months, Diana asked to stay. And when she gave him his au revoir kiss next morning, he asked impulsively, 'Diana, if I get a divorce, would you marry me?'

Certainly she didn't say yes, but neither did she say no. All she said was, 'I'd have to think very seriously about it, Frederick.'

She was still thinking about it when the R101 was cut in two and a new bag inserted. In its new version, the airship made a rather drunken appearance at Hendon in June 1930, as part of a bill that included incredible acrobatics by RAF pilots in old fighters. Frederick saw the Jerningham designer, Cummings, spending all his time trying to sell Amelia's new fighter, Ajax III, to officials, one of whom was that blacksmith fellow, March, now returned from Iraq and high up in the Air Ministry. He also saw Thomson with the Sultan of Jahore.

It was that sight which disturbed him out of his euphoria of the last few months. He had made further inquiries about Thomson and Princess Bibesco, and had been reassured by what he had discovered. Diana had been particularly charming and acquiescent. Last Christmas, he had given her an expensive emerald bracelet, and a matching ring later for her birthday.

But seeing Thomson and the rich Indiàn prince together awakened all his fears. It was the way India kept coming up that was beginning to haunt him. He was beginning to think that Thomson had some personal private plan for himself and India, so often were their names linked.

And then in the middle of July, there was talk of giving Dominion status to India. Lord Irwin was retiring. A man of considerable stature was required to succeed him as Viceroy and effect the transition. Frederick heard the name of Christopher Thomson mentioned.

He went straight to Diana's house, but she was out. Every day that week, he tried to see her, but it was as though she was purposely eluding him. He finally caught up with her on Sunday, coming out of evening service at St Margarets's. Escorting her back home in a taxi, he said, 'It's eight months since I asked you to marry me if I got a divorce. Surely you can give me your answer now?'

She seemed to hesitate.

'I love you, Diana. I love you and only you. Divorce these days is becoming more and more common and unremarked on. I could make the necessary arrangements. Your name need not come into it.'

'But what about Amelia?'

'She's been wanting a divorce from me for years.'

'And your political career? The Court is still very strict.'

'My political career would mean nothing if I had you, Diana.'

It was the wrong thing to say. Politics and marriage were too indissolubly mingled in her eyes ever to be unentwined. If Frederick had now lost all political ambition —

'It is to big a step to be taken lightly, Frederick.'

'I understand that.'

'And I wouldn't want you to give up your political life for me.'

'I wouldn't give it up, Diana. I'm not giving it up! I'm up to my neck in airship committees. Baldwin has practically promised that I shall be Secretary of State for Air when Ramsay MacDonald falls. I shall be on the R100 when she leaves for Montreal on 29 July!'

At least that impressed her. Spurred on, he did his best to be on board. But the R100 left for her highly successful flight without him. Standing alone on the grass at Howden, Frederick welcomed her home. That flight resulted in the ordering of R102. Now everyone was talking about R101's forthcoming flight to India.

Thomson had stipulated that the flight must take place in time for him to return in triumph to the Imperial Conference on 20 October. It was perfectly clear to many – including Frederick – that he saw himself riding a fairy chariot to the East and back as the future Viceroy of India.

Diana had become obsessed with India. She read books on India, had insisted on a visit with him to the Indian Exhibition. She bought Indian pictures, Indian carvings. Already, Frederick was convinced, she saw Thomson as Viceroy and herself as Vicereine.

Frederick went to see Baldwin. The world was financially crumbling. Britain was tottering on the edge of going off the gold standard. The Labour government was just about to fall. Why shouldn't he be the new Viceroy of India? The Hayburys were a distinguished family, and two of them had served with the East India Company.

Baldwin as usual gave no immediate consent. But he did agree to support Frederick going as passenger in the R101 to India, if there was room. Frederick went to the Air Ministry and Cardington to arrange his passage to India. He found both too preoccupied with their own troubles. It was doubtful whether the R101 would go to India at all, with or without Frederick. There were problems with the engines. Nowhere near enough tests had been carried out. There was no certificate of airworthiness.

But on 2 October, after a short test flight, preparations for her departure were made. Her fuel tanks were filled with diesel oil. The navigator drew his tracks across France. She was provisioned and a full load of water was taken on board. Sir Sefton Brancker was uneasy and pleaded for a postponement.

'If you're too scared to fly,' Thomson told him. 'There are many who want to take your place.'

It was in such an atmosphere that Frederick at last obtained his place on the passenger list. Not only Thomson, he told Diana, would be riding this vast

278

Arabian Nights' flying horse to the East, so would he. Not only was Thomson a potential Viceroy of India, so was he.

On the evening of 4 October, the passengers and their luggage arrived below the R101 on her mast at Cardington. Half a ton of red carpet was loaded. So were Thomson's trunks, supervised by his valet.

Frederick said goodbye to Diana and went up in the electric lift. Lord Thomson followed. An official came with the Certificate of Airworthiness only minutes before the engines were started.

Then slipping the mast, her nose dipped. Four and a half tons of water ballast were jettisoned before it rose. From the brightly lighted passenger lounge, Frederick waved cheerily to Diana and the crowd below. At 7.34 R101, her red and green navigation lights glinting on her international identification G-FAAW, set course south into the darkness.

International messages flashed her progress to the ground.

24.00 GMT. 15 miles SW of Abbeville. Average speed 33 knots. Wind 35 mph. Altimeter height 1500 feet. Weather intermittent rain. Cloud nimbus at 500 feet.

And later.

After an excellent supper our distinguished passengers smoked a final cigar, and have now gone to bed to rest after the excitement of their leavetaking. All essential services are functioning satisfactorily. The crew have settled down to a watchkeeping routine.

A position report was passed, followed by silence.

Then suddenly, a single stark message from the French air ministry.

G-FAAW a pris feu.

TEN

'Amelia?' The telephone ringing beside her bed in the cold early morning wakened her from an uneasy sleep. 'I'm afraid I have bad news.'

The voice was James's. His quiet sombre tone quenched her surprise, prepared her for what was to come. Just as the wind that had risen during the night and the rattle of the rain had prepared her too.

'We have had it confirmed here at Air Ministry that the R101 crashed near Beauvais. I wanted to tell you before anyone else did. Or before you heard it on the wireless. There were eight survivors. But Frederick, I regret, was not amongst them.'

She couldn't remember saying anything in reply. She remembered watching the rivulets of rain running down the windows, and the swaying of the poplar heads. But at some point James must have asked her where Charles and Arthur were because she heard herself giving him their addresses, and in the light of their subsequent arrival he must have undertaken to break the news to them. She could also remember asking James if she could go over to Beauvais, but he told her sharply, no, the RAF would see they were all brought home. And just before he rang off, he offered diffidently, 'My wife is still in France. She's about ninety kilometres from Beauvais . . . if there is anything she can do, she would of course —'

'No, nothing, thank you.'

Amelia got up and dressed. It was still not yet dawn. She walked through to the kitchens to break the news to the servants. They were sitting down to traditional Sunday breakfast. The kitchen smelled of bacon and fried eggs and freshly baked bread. They all looked up guiltily, some with their forks halfway to their mouths, as Amelia came in pale-faced and unsmiling. But she was spared the necessity of telling them. Pearson had switched on the wireless set and the music emanating from it was suddenly interrupted by an announcer's voice giving a newsflash of the R101 disaster.

Not everyone in England had wireless sets. But the news leaked out in rumour and by word of mouth. All through that awful Sunday, the news came in fragments. The airship, it was said, was still burning. The diesel oil the experts had promised wouldn't burn had soaked the earth and trees had ignited. The hydrogen had caught fire. The Sisters of Mercy from the Convent at Beauvais had kept an all-night vigil by the bodies. The concert room of the town hall at Bauvais was converted to a mortuary. To this the bodies were conveyed on carts strewn with flowers.

Later that day, Arthur arrived home. 'He should never have gone,' he said. 'What a waste of lives!'

It was a sentiment echoed with bitterness in Cardington and Bedford. Crowds besieged the offices of the local paper, begging for news.

Two more had died by Tuesday, when the 48 bodies were taken across the Channel by destroyer, and then by train to London to lie in state at Westminster.

Amelia and Arthur walked amongst the stream of people coming in out of the cold October air into the huge vaulted chamber of Westminster Hall. Poor Frederick, she thought sadly, lying now in that numbered coffin on that catalfalque usually reserved for kings. She was overcome with remorse and regret. She should have loved Frederick better. She did not allow herself to think of her widowhood, for with James married of what use was it to her? She longed for Charles's presence. He had cabled that he had booked his passage and would be with her for the funeral.

But before that there was the memorial service in the vast cold marble of St Paul's. The church was so full that crowds stood on the steps outside. Amelia caught sight of Diana Nazier, dressed in deepest but most becoming black, sitting in the second row of seats between sir John Simon and Sir Stafford Cripps and immediately behind the Prince of Wales. After the solemn service, Diana came over and stood beside Arthur to shake his Royal Highness's hand, and with the relatives of the dead to receive his unhappy embarrassed murmur of sympathy.

'Bear up, Mama!' Charles hugged Amelia to him when she met him off the *Berengaria* in Southampton. 'This ghastly pantomine will soon be over.'

He looked sunburned and thinner and frighteningly handsome. 'They were crazy to go. I wonder why Father felt he had to.' And in the same breath, 'I only wish that Nazier woman had gone with him!'

'Charles!' She slipped her hand through his arm. 'Don't say that! It's horrible!'

'Why is it horrible? He'd have wanted her with him surely?'

'Perhaps. I don't know.'

'Well, he loved her, didn't he?'

'I don't know. I don't want to know. I know I never want to see her again.'

'We won't have to after the funeral Mama. This will be the end of airships. She'll lose all interest in the Hayburys.'

He could not have been more wrong. For though the R101 disaster had dealt a crippling blow to the lobby, Lady Nazier had by no means lost interest in airships or the Hayburys.

'I shall see you perhaps at the November board meeting.' Lady Nazier brushed her veiled cheek against Amelia's as they waited for the funeral – that final nerve-scraping display of public grief – to begin.

The cortège was late. Crowds had poured to Euston station to see off the funeral train. Thousands had lined its route. There had been so many wreaths there was scarcely room for them. Even the engine that pulled the train had worn a special red, white and blue wreath, the gift of the London, Midland and Scottish railway. The procession had been miles long, taking two hours to arrive at the darkening churchyard.

There was a deathly smell of all those new turfs. As they waited for the official cortège, silent crowds massed on Cardington green. The bells in the church tower tolled endlessly, while over the village roofs, like Nemesis, peered the enormous caverns of the airship hangars.

'I get the feeling she knows something we don't, Mama,' Charles whispered, watching Lady Nazier take up a prominent position on the other side of the huge mass grave. 'She makes me uneasy.'

Arthur shot him a reproving stare. His grief for his father was genuine. Over the years, he had become gradually aware of his father's liaison with Lady Nazier. And though disapproving, he had accepted it, partly because his mother accepted it, partly because his father made no secret of his partiality for his second son. Now his father was no more than a handful of charred bones in an unnamed coffin, he felt distressed and uneasy and alone, aware that it was on Charles's arm that his mother leaned, to Sir Charles Haybury whom she would turn.

As if realising his thoughts, Amelia slipped a hand through his arm. While all those coffins were lowered, while the Bishop of St Albans pronounced the committal, while the silence was shattered by the salute of guns and the aircraft roared overhead, they seemed a united loving family. That illusion was shattered on their return to Haybury as abruptly as that solemn silence.

Mr Pearless, the family solicitor, had made it his business to come down from London and deliver the news in person.

'I know this will be no greater to your liking than it was to mine, Lady Haybury. But it is my duty to tell you the terms of your husband's will.'

Veiled though it was in the niceties of legal language, Frederick's hatred was undisguised.

All of which he died possessed was to be divided between Lady Diana Nazier and his beloved son Arthur, except that though the Haybury estate would pass to Arthur in toto, Amelia could have the occupancy during her lifetime. But Frederick's share of Jerningham Aviation would belong in equal parts to Arthur and Lady Nazier. That would leave Amelia with one third of the votes, Arthur, Diana, Victoria and Connaught Engineering with one sixth each. In so far as Lady Nazier and Connaught Engineering believed it a most suitable appointment, Arthur would assume the mantle of chairman of Jerningham Aviation.

To Charles I leave nothing – he had actually spelled it out.

It was indeed as if a charred and malevolent hand had reached out to stab him from the grave.

ELEVEN

If Amelia had nourished any hope that Arthur might share some of his inheritance with Charles, she was quickly disabused. Arthur, after consultation with Mr Peerless, had made known his intention of abiding by the strict and literal letter of his father's will. What his mother did with Haybury during her lifetime was naturally her concern. If she chose to have Charles stay there he could raise no objection. Arthur himself would like to feel it was still the family home and he could stay there as he chose. Nor would he object if Amelia took up Cummings's suggestion that Charles be engaged as test pilot on Ajax III now the prototype was nearing completion. Both Amelia and Arthur had expected Charles to slam out in high dudgeon after the will, but he had stood his ground.

A steady job was exactly what Charles needed. What he wouldn't get from Arthur was a single penny piece or a single favour in contradiction of their father's wishes. 'That's what you call brotherly love,' Charles said to Amelia, after yet another family conference a month after the funeral in the library at Haybury, at which Arthur had made his attitude only too clear. 'You'd think he was the older brother, not me.'

'He loves you really,' Amelia said, none too surely.

'Nonsense, Mama! He loved Father, I think, but even there he was ambivalent. He was always trying to pretend to himself that the Nazier business wasn't happening. That Nazier was just a charming friend. And apart from Father, I don't think Arthur's capable of loving anyone. Even himself.'

Harsh though the assessment was, it was one with which Arthur would probably have agreed. Certainly he was not aware of any love or loyalty towards Charles. All he hoped from his brother was that he wouldn't continue to embarrass him in the pursuit of his new political career, as he had certainly embarrassed their father.

For as soon as the proper interval had gone by, Arthur had been approached by the chairman of the local Conservative Party and asked if he would stand at the by-election which must follow.

Agreeing to stand for what was a comparatively safe seat, Arthur threw himself into cultivating it as if it were a marginal. He instituted a monthly meeting at Haybury and began what he called, to Charles's amusement, 'surgery', where constituents could come and air their troubles.

'I always get the feeling with Arthur,' Charles said to his mother, 'that he's looking for something and doesn't find it. Maybe because he's already got everything that anyone could want.'

Perhaps, Amelia thought with a little pang of guilt, Arthur was looking for the warm maternal love that she had never given him. Charles went on to say, 'But one thing I can tell you. It's no good both of us being at Haybury. We get on each other's nerves. I'd like to open up the flat at the factory, if you've no objections.'

He refurbished the bachelor flat at Jerningham but according to Cummings, he hardly ever slept in it.

'Not that I've the slightest complaint about him, Amelia,' Cummings said. 'He's a first class mechanic. And a brilliant pilot. He works like a slave, too. But he's more cut up than he lets on. If it hadn't been for you, I think he'd have gone straight back to the States after the funeral.'

'What makes you think that?'

'His attitude to everything over here.'

'He's keen on Ajax.'

'Certainly he is. And with the modifications he's tried out and with him flying it, I think we should enter for the Schneider Trophy.'

'Well, doesn't that give him something worth staying over here for?'

'Perhaps. But . . . ' Cummings chose his words carefully, 'your husband's will somehow shamed him, unmanned him.'

'I don't see why.' She paused, then said in an altered tone, 'It shamed me too, if you put it like that.'

Cummings stretched his hand across the desk and grasped hers. 'But not so much, surely.'

Whatever it was, and to what degree, it soon became clear that Charles was establishing his manhood by the time-honoured methods. The gay young things of London society took him to their hearts and their flat boyish bosoms. 1931 was heralded in by Sir Charles dancing in the Eros fountain with a saucer-eyed little flapper called, according to the *Daily Mirror*, Miss Prudence Lehmann.

In mid-January, he made that paper's headlines. *Sir Charles Haybury arrested in Soho nightclub. Baronet accompanies Kate Meyrick and society leader Laura Corrigan to Bow Street for questioning.*

'But according to Cummings,' Amelia said in answer to Arthur's angry thrusting of the paper under her nose, 'it doesn't affect his work.'

'Cummings would say anything you wanted to hear.'

'I don't agree.'

'And if it isn't affecting *his* work, it is assuredly affecting mine. It may have escaped your notice, Mama, but by-election polling takes place on 12 February.'

'That's unfair, Arthur. I've done my bit. I've had your committee here for dinner. I've given talks.'

'One.'

'I've offered the use of the car.'

'When Charles isn't using it.'

'And I've sat on the platform.'

'You've been a very decorative asset,' he said half-affectionately, half-bitterly.

On polling day he received a telegram of good wishes from Lady Nazier. He was nervously excited. For the first time there were three candidates – Conservative, Liberal and Labour. Passing through Jerningham on their way to vote, Amelia saw a red and white poster *Vote Labour* pinned on the forge door, 'That won't do old March or the Labour candidate any good,' Arthur observed. 'He'll still lose his deposit.'

There he was wrong – and the Conservative majority was again cut. He blamed Charles and his antics – so much so that Amelia and Sarah entered into a tacit but unspoken conspiracy to keep all but the *Times* from Arthur's notice. The more gossip-minded papers did not appear until later than that august publication and were brought in direct to Amelia, when Sarah came in, ostensibly to help her with her clothes.

'Have you seen this paragraph here, M'lady?' She passed the paper to Amelia to read. *A treasure hunt caused chaos at two a.m. outside Buckingham Palace yesterday when bright young people led by Sir Charles Haybury raided the sentry boxes and made off in their cars with the busbys of six Coldstream Guardsmen . . .'*

'Oh, I do wish he'd behave himself,' Amelia sighed.

'He's doing no harm, M'lady. All the society young people are like that these days. It's high spirits. There's not a bit of vice in that boy.'

'He's no longer a boy, even if he acts like one.'

'But it's better than being so starchy, as things were in your young day.'

A fortnight later, there was another snippet and three weeks after that: *A party organised by Elsa Maxwell, The American Michelin woman, centred round an imitation cow from which guests had to milk their own champagne. Celebrations ended abruptly when the body of Sir Charles Haybury was found at midnight sprawled over the library table, stabbed to the heart and covered in blood. A lady's handkerchief clearly embroidered with the letter P close by the body led to Lady Penelope Chatteris, the Marchioness of Paisley, and Miss Prudence Lehmann being locked in the butler's pantry to await the arrival of the police. Three officers were quickly on the scene only to discover the blood to be tomato ketchup . . .*

'D'you notice, M'lady, the names that keep cropping up?'

'Yes,' Amelia replied drily, 'Charles Haybury.'

'No, M'lady. The *girls'* names. Either Lady Penelope or Miss Prudence. One or other. I've made a note each time. So has Cook from her paper. They're well in front. The next one's Lady Crammond. And she's lengths behind.'

'You talk as if it's a horse race,' Amelia said irritably. 'Really, I wish he wouldn't carry on like this. It's all so useless!'

She made a point of going down to the hangar the next morning to see him at work. She took the newspaper with her and thrust it under his nose as Arthur had done. He glanced at it, shrugged his shoulders and laughed. 'It was a good party. The Maxwell woman's a genius. How she dreams these things up I'll never know.'

'Weren't the police furious?'

'No. The girls smoothed them down. And in no time they were milking the champagne cow with the best of them.'

'*Very* edifying!' Amelia exclaimed. 'It's a pity these bright young things haven't something more interesting and constructive to do.'

'That's the whole point of it, Mama. They haven't. They've got all the money they want. They're young. They don't have to work. So every party has to have a difference. Otherwise an ordinary party is such a frightful bore.'

'It's a wonder you can fly with the life you lead.'

'Then watch me, Mama! This afternoon, I shall put Ajax through her paces.

Watch and see if I can still fly!'

'I haven't felt so proud in years,' Amelia said to Cummings as she handed him back the binoculars.

They were standing on the concrete end of the slipway after watching Charles make a perfect landing in Ajax III. It was a cool May afternoon, but the sun shone intermittentlyfrom between fast blown white clouds, and the air was full of the smell of the sea.

In and out of those clouds, Charles had taken Ajax. He was showing off, of course. He had not been able to resist a few of the old circus tricks even at the risk of almost giving his mother a heart attack. He had turned Ajax on her back, rolled her, put her into a steep dive and pulled out just over their heads. He had taken her up to 18,000 feet and reached a speed of 180 mph one minute after take off.

Cummings had timed him streaking over the airfield on the flat and even with that southwesterly blowing, he'd reached 240 mph. He had made tight corners and steep climbs. He had literally thrown Ajax around the sky. Then he'd brought her in silkily on to the water, slowed and stopped beside the tender. Cutting the engine, he got into the motor boat and jumped eagerly on to the slipway.

'Well, Mama, *can* I still fly?'

'Just about.'

'And shall we still enter for the Schneider?'

'I don't see any reason why not. The board doesn't object. The only person who might conceivably do so is Diana Nazier and she seems to have lost interest these days.'

'She's in South America at the moment, I hear. On one of the *Graf Zeppelin* flights,' Cummings said. 'So she's out of the way. In any case, she'd be outvoted.'

'That's a relief.' Charles smiled. 'By the way, I was over at Calshot yesterday.'

'So soon after that hectic party?' Amelia smiled back teasingly.

'So soon. I was as fresh as a daisy. And they told me they're entering three Mitchell Supermarine seaplanes for the Schneider.'

Amelia pulled down the corners of her mouth. 'They're good, aren't they?'

'Bloody good. They've got the same engines as Ajax, but Ajax has the edge over them. More manoeuvrable. Faster.'

'Do you think they'll win, Charles, these Supermarines?'

'Not against Ajax.'

'Three of them. Three chances.'

'Still not against Ajax.'

Amelia smiled. 'I hope you're right.'

'I still think,' Charles said as the three of them walked towards the office block, 'that we might improve the performance by one of the Gamley carburettors. What do you think, Ronald? I've one or two other ideas to kick around.' Then turning to his mother, 'And if you really feel it might ioprove *my* performance, I'll eschew the bright young things in London till Schneider is, as they say, fought and won.'

286

Unfortunately, the bright young things did not eschew him. Never the one to do things by halves, nor to pursue the comfortable sensible middle of the road, Charles was reported by Cummings as leading an almost monastic life. When he wasn't poring with him over modifications for Ajax, he was tinkering in the hangar, or test flying the aircraft, or buzzing in the tender over to Hamble to see if he could pick up any hints from other pilots, and retiring to his bachelor flat to study and sleep.

His presence was sadly missed. Bright young voices on the telephone pursued him not only to his bachelor flat but to his office at the airfield, and finally getting more desperate, to Haybury Hall itself. He appeared to remain single-mindedly devoted to the Schneider race.

The organisers of that were having more han their fair share of trouble. And Charles, in common with the Supermarine pilots across the river, was afraid that the race might be cancelled and the opportunity to win the Trophy outright for Britain snatched from them. Britain had won the two previous years, and now only required this third year. But by early June, the French and Germans were objecting to certain new rules. The Americans decided not to compete. What had begun as a race to further civil transport was now rapidly becoming a political football centred on national pride and potential war machines. There was talk that the Supermarine could be easily adapted to a highly manoeuvrable warplane. As Sarah reported, Group Captain March from the Air Ministry had been down to look at the design and see her trials.

Week by week the Schneider situation worsened. Both the French and the Italian entries suffered serious crashes while practising, and were forced to withdraw. Then Ramsay MacDonald, having promised government support for running the race, withdrew it because of what he called, 'the deepening economic depression'. It was an unpopular decision. The *Daily Mail* discovered that Fred Montague, the Under-Secretary of State for Air, was a member of the Magicians' Circle. They reported this fact with the comment, *The disappearance of the Schneider Trophy appears to be one of his most amazing feats.*

'This year's Schneider Trophy seems fated,' Amelia sighed. 'Everybody's dropping out. I doubt it'll take place at all. Just when we have a good chance of winning it.'

'It'll take place, you mark my words.' Cummings said. 'Someone will come forward to put up the money.'

The benefactor was an unexpected one. Lady Houston, a rags-to-riches Cinderella and Fairy Godmother rolled into one, nobly stepped into the breach left by the government. Born in poverty in Camberwell, she had eventually married Sir Robert Houston and become the richest woman in Britain. She wrote out a cheque for £100,000 – the amount needed for Britain to take part.

And almost at the same time as the news was announced that the race would go forward, the telephone rang in Amelia's office. A young girl's voice apologised profusely for disturbing Lady Haybury, but she'd been trying to track down Charles, who appeared to be flying all the time or else fearfully unavailable, there was this simply stunning idea she had for her 21st birthday party and she did so hope Charles would be able to take part.

Her name, she said, was Prudence Lehmann.

A month later on the glorious 12 August came the day Charles would fly Ajax flat out. He had flown her each day of the previous week, each time increasing the throttle setting. Now he was satisfied that Ajax III was as good as he and Cummings could make her.

The weather was benign. It was sunny with just sufficient wind to break up the water and stop the glueing effect on the floats of flat calm. Just before seven that evening, Charles taxied Ajax away from the slipway out to the deep channel beyond Hurst Castle where the measured mile had been marked by red buoys. He took off to the west, made a low circle and came down, engine roaring, over the first buoy and on to the second.

Cummings was in the motor boat with Amelia, timing him. He clicked the stopwatch. '280 mph!' He pulled down the corners of his mouth.

The next run was 312. 'Better,' Cummings said.

Then came the third run. 'Good Lord!' Cummings exclaimed. '350!' Quite overcome with excitement, Cummings hugged Amelia, and they both waved so enthusiastically at Ajax that they almost overturned the boat.

Charles did six more runs – all above 350 – before alighting. He was obviously delighted, but keeping his excitement in check. 'I didn't even have her completely flat out,' he said, telling the mechanic to fill her up.

When Amelia said, 'We *must* celebrate! Come home for dinner, Charles. And you, Ronald. This is an occasion. We'll open some boring old champagne,' Charles laughed, but shook his head.

'We'll leave the celebration till after the Trophy race!'

'At least we can celebrate reaching *that* speed! Race or no race!'

'All right. I'll look in later after dinner for a drink,' Charles said. 'I want to hop over to Hamble to tell my friends the good news. And there's another friend I've promised to drop in on after that.'

They waited with him while Ajax was refueled. Then, with Amelia's hand resting lightly on Cummings' arm, they watched Charles take off into a golden evening sky. The sun was setting in ambers and saffron, behind long calm weather clouds. It gilded the underside of Ajax, turning it already the bright gold of the Trophy.

Exhilarated, confident, Amelia and Cummings drove back to Haybury. Arthur was there still in his city clothes.

'You're early,' Amelia smiled. 'I wasn't expecting you till after dinner. We're going to crack some champagne. We've had a most successful test run, haven't we, Ronald?'

Arthur recharged his glass from the whisky decanter and sipped it slowly. 'Really?'

'Charles will be here later on for a drink.'

'Really?'

'And how was London today?' Cummings asked dutifully. 'Hot?'

'Hot in more ways than one. Frantic. All the European banks are going bust. And the Treasury want us off the Gold Standard.'

Cummings whistled, and Amelia asked, 'Will we go off? And what does it mean if we do?'

'We won't. But,' he swirled his drink in his glass, 'it'll be another election.' He looked at his mother. 'You'll have to get out your blue rosette again, I fear.'

'And your friend Lady Nazier will have to send you another telegram,' she said tartly. The conversation subsided. By seven-thirty, they were all for different reasons beginning to look at the clock. Amelia because she had hoped Charles would have turned up by now, Cummings because he wanted to be at his desk early tomorrow, and Arthur because he was dog-tired and fed-up.

By eight, Amelia was worried. She telephoned Charles's flat in Jerningham. No one answered.

'Shall I ring my pals at Hamble?' Cummings suggested, 'See if we can hurry Charles up?'

But Charles apparently had already left Hamble.

Arthur was in the hall when the telephone rang. He could see at once from Pearson's face that it was yet more trouble. He took the receiver from him. It was the Petersfield police. There had been an accident. Aircraft or motor, Arthur had asked but they weren't sure. All they knew was that Sir Charles Haybury had been admitted to the town hospital. He was still alive, as far as they knew, but they had no news of his condition.

The next half-hour passed like a broken film. One moment Amelia was listening to Arthur, hearing words her mind refused to accept; seeing his face unnaturally pale and ridiculously angry. Then the film jerked on. She was in the car beside Arthur who was driving like the wind down dark deserted roads. Cummings had been peremptorily dismissed. Somehow, she hadn't wanted him. Only Arthur – angry, pious, pale-faced Arthur. He had taken charge, given her a shot of brandy, refused to allow her to drive.

'No, Mother! You're shocked. You may say you feel perfectly all right. But I feel btter. Don't worry! I'm not in the slightest shocked. Nor am I worried. Nor am I surprised. He'll be all right. Charles is *bound* to be all right. Charles comes out of things all right. It's other people he leaves in pieces.'

At Petersfield hospital, the night sister took them into a private ward.

'Will he be all right?' Amelia asked urgently.

'Oh, he'll live'

'Are his injuries serious?'

'Not considering. I'll talk to you before you go home.'

'Told you,' Arthur said gruffly, following her inside.

There was a dim light shining down on Charles's head. His eyes were closed, his left leg was encased in plaster and suspended from a traction trolley. Then Amelia saw, sitting on the other side of the bed, a small thin girl, in a sequined evening dress. She had enormous saucer eyes and a wide mouth as red as a freshly painted pillar box. As they came in, she gave them a quick smile and got up to offer her chair to Amelia. She was so small she came barely to Arthur's shoulder as he moved forward to take it from her.

'Is Charles all right?' Amelia asked the girl, peering down anxiously into his face.

'They say he's in no danger, Lady Haybury. He's showing signs of coming round apparently. They said I could sit with him.'

She paused. Closer to, her eyes were of a pale grey, fringed with heavily mascaraed eyelashes. Her face was a flat heart shape, over which her changing expressions flew with remarkable swiftness.

'I'm Prudence Lehmann,' she said, now meek and apologetic. 'I'm afraid all this is my fault.'

'What happened?'

'It was my 21st. And I had this stunning idea. Or it seemed stunning at the time. For Charles . . . well, to make it different. To land on the lake at Shotfield.' She broke off and looked from one to the other throwing up her small hands in horror at herself.

'Shotfield is your home, is it?' Arthur asked very quietly.

'Yes. And there's a decent sized lake with a colonnade sort of thing at the north end. But . . . well, Charles didn't want to do it. Didn't want to come at all. Said he could only stay half an hour, if he did come. But I, well . . . I . . . '· The enormous eyes filled with remorseful tears. 'I persuaded him. And I'm terribly, terribly sorry but his aeroplane . . . '

'Tell me about Charles first,' Amelia said.

'Apart from his leg and the concussion, it's just bruises. I had a long chat with Sister. They've been frightfully kind here.'

'Good. Now tell me about Ajax.'

'Well, the poor thing's in frightfully bad shape. You see there was this half-sunk punt . . . I should have remembered . . . '

She looked so distressed that Amelia found herself putting her arm comfortingly round the thin bare shoulders.

She was the comforter again, when twenty long minutes later Charles slowly opened his eyes. He stared half-focused from one to the other. His first words were, 'Sorry, Mama. Sorry, Prudence.'

He said nothing to Arthur. But Arthur, naturally and justifiedly, had plenty to say to him. 'I suppose you realise Mama has sunk every penny of Aunt Sempner's legacy into that aircraft you've just broken.'

Speeding home in the early hours of that morning, Arthur kept himself awake by a continuous vitriolic diatribe against Charles. 'What price your entry into Schneider now, Mother? What price your Ajax project? What price all those orders that were going to come in? What price Jerningham? What price my reputation? Charles has behaved like the rotter he is. You'll throw him off the Jerningham pay roll, even if I've got to canvas the votes of Diana Nazier and Aunt Victoria and Connaught Engineering.'

But as they neared Haybury, his anger took on a more bitter personal note, 'Whatever in this damned crazy world,' he exclaimed, 'makes a stunning girl like Prudence Lehmann fall for a swine like Charles?'

TWELVE

By 13 September, the day of the Schneider Trophy race, Charles's leg was knitting healthily, and with it the relationship between himself and the stunning Prudence Lehmann. Though Charles was still on crutches, the pair of them accompanied Amelia and Cummings to the Royal Yacht Club at Cowes to observe the race, which would begin at a pylon on a destroyer anchored off St Helen's Point.

If it had been left to Charles, he would have stayed at home to lick his wounds and his pride. He was ashamed and dispirited. It was almost unbearable to watch Supermarine win a race that Ajax could have won.

For after all the stops and starts and crashes and arguments, the race was in name only. Britain was the sole competitor. It would be a fly-over, the race a foregone conclusion so long as only one of the three Supermarines completed the seven laps of the measured course. And because this was the third year running, the Trophy, amid worldwide criticism of unfairness and rule-bending, would become Britain's for ever. That Ajax had reached a speed higher than Supermarines' made Amelia's disappointment that much more acute. But her feelings that morning, as Cummings edged the motor boat into the landing stage at the Yacht Club, were of James as much as of Ajax. It was so much their creation that this latest disaster to it had underlined her own sense of a malign and frustrating fate.

She was aware too that she had canalised her love for James into Ajax, and now that it was once more in ruins, her life again seemed completely empty. She had not seen him since he had telephoned to tell her about the R101 and Frederick. Cornford House had remained closed. From Sarah, Amelia learned that old Mr March went over there regularly to see it was kept aired, though it was unlikely that the family would return, despite the Group Captain's position at the Air Ministry. The climate suited the Comtesse and the two children were at school in France. The Group Captain lived at his club, and only occasionally visited his father. Even when Aircraft Procurement, James's own department, had sent down a team to look over Ajax, it had been led by an elderly wing commander, not by James.

Now as Cummings tied up, Amelia saw a large RAF tender close by. Without a doubt, James would come to the race to see the Supermarines. She steeled herself, though against what she didn't know.

In the clubhouse, it was already crowded, but she saw James as soon as Cummings pushed open the large glass double doors on to the terrace. He was talking animatedly with a group of RAF officers. Just for a moment, as she stood in the doorway, she watched him, savoured him somehow, the set of his head as he listened, the line of his jaw, the slightly wry smile.

Then his eyes met hers. Unprepared, a procession of fleeting expressions crossed his face. And she wondered why she had ever steeled herself, ever been afraid. She watched him excuse himself from the others and come towards her as naturally as if drawn down some invisible beam of light. 'I'm very sorry about Ajax,' he said to Amelia, as soon as he and Prudence had been introduced and Cummings had rushed off to find a waiter. 'You must be very disappointed.'

His dark blue eyes regarded her gently. His voice, his carefully controlled expression set the tone of the encounter – that of an old family friend commiserating.

'Yes,' Amelia smiled brightly. 'It was bad luck, wasn't it?'

'*Was* it?' James looked levelly at Charles. The old family friend with the right to speak sharply to the younger generation. How ironic, Amelia thought!

'It was bad luck, Group Captain March,' Prudence put in beguilingly, 'plus a large slice of my fault.'

'Yours?' Again that level look at Charles.

'Mine and no one else's, Group Captain.' Then aware perhaps of Charles's discomfiture, if not of Amelia's desire of a few moments alone with James, Prudence suddenly pointed. 'Oh, hooray! I can see a vacant bit of parapet over there. Shall Charles and I go and perch ourselves? Take the weight off his leg?'

'She seems to be taking Charles in hand,' James said, watching Prudence in her short navy dress insinuating herself through the crowd, with Charles obediently tagging on behind.

'I have a feeling,' Amelia smiled, 'that she will become my daughter-in-law.' Yours too, she thought.

'And do you approve?'

'Very much. She's not as flippant as she tries to pretend. And marriage should steady him.'

'It didn't before,' James said drily. 'After all, marriage can only work on the material it's got.'

Amelia held her head on one side. 'That sounds very profound and philosophical, James.'

She wanted desperately to ask him if *his* marriage worked, if the material *he* had was sufficient. But as quickly, she was ashamed. Instead she said, with genuine regret, 'You've never really liked Charles.'

'On the contrary, I have often admired him.'

Amelia laughed disbelievingly. 'How could you? You've succeeded. And he's failed.'

He didn't answer. She saw that he was staring at Charles and Prudence over the intervening throng. They were both now sitting on the parapet. Charles had his arm round Prudence's shoulders, while she was popping little cocktail canapes into his mouth. A fleeting tender expression softened James's mouth, and somehow Amelia knew he wasn't seeing Charles and Prudence at all, but themselves over the intervening years.

Then Cummings came up with a waiter in tow and the conversation became three-sided and less personal, though it became clear to James that Amelia's dependence on her manager had grown. That Cummings, in the nicest possible way, was but biding his time.

'I hear that Supermarine,' Cummings said to James, 'are going flat out for a world record. So even though it's a fly-over, the race should be exciting.'

James nodded. 'Should be.'

'I also hear you're watching the Supermarine with an eagle eye as a land fighter.'

'The same goes for Ajax. For God's sake, don't give it up now!'

'It's giving us up,' Amelia said wryly. 'It's a write off. Most of it has sunk to the bottom of Shotfield lake. And we haven't the money to build another.'

'The factory teeters on the edge of bankruptcy,' Cummings sighed. 'This wretched government . . .' The conversation continued on the safe ground of the iniquities of government, the depredations of the Disarmament Programme, the depressed state of industry.

'The trouble is,' James said, 'we can't afford to let our aircraft firms go broke, while Germany rearms.' He closed his lips tightly and said no more. The RAF was only too aware that Germany was secretly building bomber and fighter aircraft and training pilots in Poland. But the British public remained oblivous of its danger, still believing that flying was for the laughs and the spills.

'But surely another war's unthinkable!' Amelia exclaimed.

Her voice was punctuated by the roar of aircraft engines and the crack of the starting gun. James grasped her hand and rushed her towards the parapet as the first Supermarine gracefully took to the air. Everyone else was rushing to the parapet. They were just in time to see S1595 do its regulation pre-race take off and landing, and the necessary two minutes throttled back on the water. Then the Supermarine was off smoothly again towards the pylon on the destroyer anchored off St Helen's Point. James watched the aircraft complete its seven laps. Amelia had her own binoculars pressed to her eyes, admiring the clean lines of Mitchell's design, watching the turns carefully. The Supermarine was said to have some instability on the turns as well as on floats, but there was no sign of it now.

1595 completed her seven laps without mishap and returned. The second Supermarine took off and did exactly the same. The loudspeaker at the Yacht Club announced the Schneider Trophy had been won by Britain at a speed of 340.8 mph. The champagne corks popped. Even a fly-over victory was something to celebrate. In the midst of doom and gloom in the face of accusations of cheating and bad sportsmanship, the Schneider Trophy was Britain's outright.

'But if there *is* another war,' James said, slowly lowering his binoculars, as if war had been his line of thinking throughout the race, 'we've just seen the aircraft that might well save us.'

But if war comes again, Amelia thought, remembering the gipsy, I doubt anything will save you and me.

War or no war, nothing could save the Ramsay MacDonald government. It collapsed shortly after the Schneider Trophy race.

All over Europe banks failed and repudiated their debts. Huge sums of money were owed to British bankers, who in turn could not meet their liabilities. Montague Norman took the step of ordering ration books to be printed in case the pound failed. Arthur was among the Tory MPs pressing for protection. In the September budget, income tax was raised to five shillings in the pound, the dole was cut by ten per cent. But it was all to no avail – there was a run on the pound, and Britain was compelled to go off the Gold Standard.

On King George's initiative, the three party leaders were brought together to offer National Government to the country. Polling took place on 27 October. The National Party received the greatest landslide victory of all time. Arthur was elected by a healthy majority under his new ticket of National Conservative. But as the returning officer announced the result, Arthur was aware of an overwhelming feeling of loneliness and doubt.

'I wonder,' he said to his mother as they sipped a quiet drink in the library at Haybury, when the congratulations and thanks had all been exchanged, 'where it's all going to end.' He would have liked to talk to her, to reach out and come closer to her.

'Everything will work out, I expect,' she said vaguely, looking at her watch. She had never greatly interested herself in politics, or in him for that matter. Even now, as she walked over to the wireless set and switched on, it wasn't to hear the election results from the rest of the country, it wasn't to discover how Arthur's career was likely to go, but to find out if anything had been reported of the two RAF officers who had embarked that day in a Fairey monoplane from Cranwell on a direct flight to Egypt.

'I don't envy them,' she shivered. 'My God, I don't! You've no idea, Arthur!'

Arthur's sense of loneliness deepened. Unlike Charles, he had no close friends. Girls found him distant and difficult to know. Yet superficially he had everything. A safe seat in Parliament at twenty-four, a bright future, wealth, good looks or so he had been told often enough. Yet inside himself he was conscious of a total vacuum. A nothingness like unbroken silence, a lack of conviction and commitment. An inability perhaps to love and be loved. It was as if his mind worked coolly and mathematically and clinically but not his emotions. He envied his mother her passionate commitment to aviation.

'It's as if you're in love with flying,' he said, as she interrupted the news of the landslide victory results to ask Arthur who he thought would be the new Secretary of State for Air.

'What a strange thing to say!' she exclaimed, standing up and brushing the top of his head with her lips preparatory to bidding him good night.

But it was true. His mother had poured all the love and passion that should have been his father's into that. Perhaps he secretly desired to follow her footsteps, to engage his feelings and offer his commitment to something. The following day, conscientiously travelling up to the House immediately to take his seat, he found himself sitting next to a fellow MP whose political career was already being forecast as one of exceptional brilliance.

The MP's name was Oswald Mosley, known to his friends as Tom. Though Arthur had exchanged a few words with him in the past, they had never had a discussion. The discussion that followed that day showed Arthur how much Mosley and he had in common. The process of Arthur's commitment had begun.

'Mosley. Oswald Mosley. The chap with the patent leather hair and the black toothbrush on his lip. I didn't believe Mama when she told me. But it's true!' Charles hammered a tent prop into place. 'Arthur is going to appear on the same platform with Ossie! In Southampton! With a repulsive creature called Diana Nazier.'

'Is that the woman who's flying in the *Hindenburg*? I've seen her photograph in the *Tatler*.'

'That's her! That's Arthur's friend. My little angel-faced brother has become a Fascist!'

'He's too sweet and nice and proper to be a Fascist,' Prudence said lightly and laughed. She was wearing a thin pink pencil dress that showed off her boyish figure to perfection. 'But he'd look stunning in a black shirt!'

Charles and Prudence were at Eastleigh airfield near Southampton, where in three days' time, Charles would be taking part in Cobham's Air Circus. He had had a job with Sir Alan Cobham for three months, ever since his leg was out of plaster. Despite some stiffness, his flying was unimpaired; so was his inventiveness. His acts drew the crowds and he had travelled the length and breadth of the country. Seeing, as he told Prudence, a lot of things going on that he didn't like the look of.

He had seen poverty and deprivation and despair and had in common with Prudence and most of her bright young friends suddenly become fashionably leftwing. Prudence had christened him 'the Red Baronet'. And the name had stuck. He still enjoyed the work but he was living a hand to mouth existence on the periphery of flying. Others were accomplishing the real feats – Jim Mollison, Kingsford-Smith, Amelia Earhart. And though he might have a certain notoriety as The Red Baronet, he was also a broke one. Not that Prudence minded. Wherever the Circus flew, she joined him. She was never averse to mucking in, mending the costumes they used, or the drag they flew in, making tea and sandwiches and being a general dogsbody.

But Charles could never get her up into the air.

'I'm no intrepid aviator,' she always reminded him. 'I prefer to keep my feet on the ground.'

Certainly she had kept her feet on the ground as far as he was concerned. In the years he had known her he had got as far as kissing her and that was all. 'Poor progress,' he had reminded her only the evening before, 'considering I married my first wife the day after I met her.'

They were sitting on the steps of his caravan at Eastleigh. The evening was warm and sweet scented. He rested his hand on her bare shoulder, wondering if he should risk Alan Cobham's fury and invite her to stay.

'More fool you!'

'This time or last time?'

'You must work that out for yourself.'

Working it out, he had pulled her to him, kissed her with unsimulated ardour, holding her thin body hard against his own, teetering on the edge of declaring himself at least close to being in love. She had wriggled determinedly free, jumped to her feet, and said quite nicely and brightly but very firmly, 'I think you just made the wrong calculation.'

And now she was exactly the same as always with him. 'I think *Arthur's* made the wrong calculation,' Charles said, as Prudence handed him a coil of rope. 'He's not tough enough to be a Blackshirt. He's selfish but not ruthless. He'll look stunning, you're right. He's a pretty boy. Perfect tailor's dummy!'

'Now you're being horrid! I like Arthur. I really do!' But she said it without conviction as if she didn't like him at all and they both burst out laughing.

Prudence blinked her prominent grey eyes. 'What did your Mama say about this meeting?'

'Mama was absolutely disgusted. She was disgusted enough about him being a neo-Fascist. Going on about the last war and all that. And going on about Germany rearming. And what Winston Churchill had to say! But when she heard Arthur was to share the platform with Oswald right here in Southampton, it was too much. Right on her doorstep!'

'It's on Arthur's doorstep, too. Near his constituency.'

'True. But it won't do *him* any harm. A lot of people round here sympathise with Mosley. He has friends in high places. Mama thinks the meeting won't do the factory any good. The workers and all that. All dozen survivors of them. But really it's because she hates Fascism. She's a freethinker.'

'So am I!'

'So am I. Up to a point.' He measured out the space to the next tent prop. 'I believe in being free. That's about all. Free as air. Free from all politics. Free to do what I want.' He kissed the tip of her nose. 'And something tells me Fascists don't believe in that.'

'Then what are you going to do about it?' She handed him a hammer. 'Eh?'

'Nothing.'

He pointed to the tent prop, and she knelt on the grass and held it between her fingers while he swung the hammer.

'But doing nothing's so dull.' She shot him a provocative look. 'Stupifyingly dull! I haven't done anything exciting for ages and ages! Except help put up tents and wonder if you're going to crush my thumbs.'

'You've watched me fly.'

'*Watched*. I've watched you dressed up as an old lady, as a villain, as a baby flying with a bottle and as a grizzly bear. But I am not by nature a spectator, Charles. I want to *do* something.'

'Something such as what?'

'Something different. Margaret Challoner who was at Roedean with me marched with the Hunger Marchers.'

'That would do them a fat lot of good.'

'None,' she giggled. 'But it did wonders for *her*. She dined out on it for weeks. Her image was improved no end. And my friend Candida nearly got herself sent down from Oxford for distributing seditious pamphlets. And . . .'

'All right, my dear imprudent Prudence, spare me the catalogue! What do *you* want to do?'

It seemed nothing would satisfy her but that they should get themselves to Southampton, and put some questions to the platform that would make Arthur see the error of his ways.

Arthur had begun to see the error of his ways before the meeting began. It was held on a hot evening in September in the same drill hall from which James March had collected his father nearly thirty years before. The hall was now surplus to the requirements of an Army hit by the Labour Party's disarmament axe.

It was ill-ventilated and packed, not at all the sort of place where he would have expected Diana Nazier to appear. It smelled of sweat and greasy clothing

296

and a subtle discontented odour that seemed the physical manifestation of the nation's mood. But what disturbed Arthur were the phalanxes of Blackshirt bouncers, who ranged themselves round the sides of the hall and at the back of the platform.

Although Arthur agreed with most of Mosley's proposals, such as putting Britain first and controlled expansion to eradicate unemployment, he was disturbed by Tom's tendency to ally himself too much with Mussolini and Adolf Hitler.

Diana was also very pro-German. Just before she sat down on the platform beside Arthur, she brushed his cheek with her lips and said, 'So glad to see another friend of the new Germany, Arthur! Such a pity we don't see more of each other!'

'We miss you on the Jerningham board, Lady Nazier.'

Since Frederick's death, she had not made an appearance at meetings preferring to send her solictor to represent her. 'I am so very busy these days in Germany with the airships. And surely nothing really happens at Jerningham Aviation, now that Ajax is no more.'

'We're planning to build a new prototype.'

'With whose money?' she asked tartly. 'Or has your mother had another windfall?'

Before the meeting began, Tom Mosley had told them jubilantly that in the German elections, the Nazis had become the strongest single party in the Reichstag. 'Hitler will be Chancellor before long. Then there'll be no holding Germany, isn't that so, Diana? The Germans are our natural allies. We've got to work together. It's that or worldwide communism.'

There were obviously some Communists at the back of the hall, because no sooner had Mosley risen to his feet to speak than the heckling began. Mosley gave the new Fascist salute of the half-raised rigid arm which was too much a carbon copy of Mussolini's and Hitler's for Arthur's liking.

Some men at the back didn't like it either. They waved clenched fists in reply, and without the men uttering a word the bouncers moved in on them. There was a scuffle, and they were thrown out. At once, a familiar voice shouted, 'Where's your freedom of speech, brother?'

And on to his feet got Charles.

Arthur, sitting on the platform next but one to Mosley with the text of an eminently sensible and reasoned speech about the desirability of expanding Britain's armed forces, closed his eyes in embarrassment. Trust Charles! There was absolutely no doubt that he was doing this merely to annoy him, just as he had done so much to annoy and embarrass their father. His brother had never suffered a political conviction in his life.

Happily someone sitting next to Charles pulled him firmly back into his chair. Mosley, biting his lip with annoyance, began to address the meeting. His speech unfortunately paid little heed to British economics. He began by praising Mussolini, who had liquidated the Communist party in Italy, was modernising Rome, and at last making public transport work. Then he got on to Germany and Adolf Hitler, comparing the splendour of Hitler's Youth Movement with the dismal British Hunger Marchers.

Charles leapt to his feet again. 'I've fought against the Huns!' he yelled. 'If you go on like this, we'll be doing it again!'

Mosley snapped his fingers at a couple of bouncers. Arthur pretended not to see as they closed in on Charles. At that moment, all he hoped was that the bouncers would give his brother a rough ride. Then he saw the person next to Charles jump up. And to his horror, he saw the petite Prudence Lehmann, her head and shoulders just visible now she was standing, above the intervening rows.

His first indignant thought was that Charles should be thrashed for bringing her to a meeting like this, his second that he hardly recognised her. At Charles's bedside she had seemed such a pretty young thing. A bright butterfly. A nice unspoiled little rich girl. Now she had turned into a virago.

'Don't touch his arm, you bastards!' she shrieked at the bouncers and swung her enormous patent-leather handbag in their direction, as if she were swotting wasps. Then, turning to Mosley and the platform, she raised a puny white fist, 'You rotten lot of cowards! Nazis! How dare you talk of putting Britain first! You put Fascism first! Germany first! Italy first!'

Arthur was transfixed. Prudence's enormous eyes seemed to blaze right into him. He was hardly aware of the shouts in the audience as other people took up the cudgels – while from every side of the hall the bouncers closed in like big black blowflies.

'She's a damned Jewess,' one of the Blackshirts behind Arthur shouted. 'Throw her out! Give her what for!'

A couple had already reached her. Arthur's feelings were indescribable. He felt as if something that had been growing all his life suddenly burst inside his head. He had no logical plan. He simply found himself on his feet, shouting at the top of his voice for them to stop. He felt Diana Nazier tug impatiently at his jacket for him to sit down. He had a vision of Mosley, gripping the microphone, waiting tight-lipped for the fracas to finish, looking at him as if he were out of his mind.

As indeed he was. He simply elbowed Mosley and every one else aside. Mosley's microphone was knocked from his grasp by a hand that must have been his. Then Arthur leapt off the platform and went pushing and shoving and kicking his way through the throng.

There must have been a number of anti-Fascists there or else he hit and kicked harder than he knew, for the crowd let him through with a will. Then he reached the two Blackshirts who were manhandling Prudence. She was fighting like a wildcat, biting, scratching, twisting her feet round their legs, butting them in the groin, but getting back far more than she gave.

Arthur had never been one for fighting. But now he found himself punching the nearest thug right on his ugly chin with the purest enjoyment he had ever experienced. He saw the man's pale eyes go momentarily blank as his head jerked back. He grasped the second man round his neck with his right arm, and punched him in the ribs till he released his hold of Prudence. Someone from behind hit him a glancing blow on his head, making him bite halfway through his tongue.

Luckily the fight spread. There were sailors and dock workers and an army of unemployed in Southampton who were aching for a fight, and in minutes the whole hall was in an uproar. The microphone must have got broken. For Mosley was shouting through a megaphone, 'Break it up, lads! That's enough! Let them go! They've learned their lesson! Let's get on with the meeting!'

Somehow in the mêlée, bleeding from the mouth with his suit torn and minus one shoe, Arthur found himself outside, still clutching Prudence's arm. There was no sign of Charles. Prudence's left eye was rapidly closing. Her lower lip was swollen. He led her slowly over to the wall that edged the parade ground, and sat her down and stared at her, saying nothing.

Suddenly it had dawned on him that a commitment greater than any inspired by Mosley had begun. For the first time in his life, he was in love.

THIRTEEN

'My daughter has pestered me out of my life and wits,' said the tall silver-haired gentleman sitting opposite Amelia in the drawing-room at Haybury. 'She has reminded me that I should have a very bad conscience about your son Charles.'

Mr Stefan Lehmann had invited himself to lunch. He was a handsome man in his fifties. The son, he had told Amelia over lunch, of a Polish refugee. His father had made his vast fortune in banking and had bought himself into English society by his lavish parties and support for charities.

'I am not like my father,' he said. 'I prefer the quiet of the countryside and a little coastal sailing in my motor-cruiser. But,' with a gleam of parental pride in his eyes, 'I think Prudence has inherited some of her grandfather's tastes.'

'Why should you have a bad conscience about Charles?' Amelia asked him, refilling his coffee cup. She had taken an immediate liking to Mr Lehmann. He exuded a warm restrained strength. His rich urbanity was spiced with Slavonic extravagance of gesture. 'It's Charles who should have a bad conscience about Prudence. Taking her to that frightful Fascist meeting! Most dangerous as well as foolish!'

'Oh, *that*!' Mr Lehmann studied the end of his cigar. 'I imagine it was six of one and half-a-dozen of the other. No, no, no! What am I saying? Knowing my daughter, eleven of Prudence and one of Charles.'

Amelia laughed. 'You obviously don't know Charles!'

'Not well enough perhaps. But I hope in the fullness of time to know him better. It's certainly about Charles I wish to see you.' He looked keenly at Amelia, 'Charles and Ajax.'

'Oh!' Amelia was too astonished to say anything. She felt her cheeks colour in a way she should have got over decades ago.

'My dear daughter tells me,' Mr Lehmann went on, 'that I and my property did irreparable damage to both. Indeed more than that. She tells me I inflicted irreparable damage on the whole future of aviation.'

'Your daughter,' Amelia smiled, 'has a colourful way of expressing herself. But as I don't honestly know what she means, or how you can possibly have come into it, all I can say is it's not true.'

'She tells me Ajax would certainly have won the Schneider Trophy.'

Amelia shrugged. 'It's the old story of ifs and ands. Ajax might have. Equally Ajax might not have.'

'And that if it had, you would have got orders. Orders from the RAF. Orders from abroad. You would have gone on with Ajax's production.'

'That part's true. But it didn't win. Charles wrote the aircraft off. It was *entirely* his fault. And nothing whatever to do with you.'

'There I must beg to differ! It was our lake. Prudence has pointed out that if I supervised my estate properly, 'I'd have ensured there was no obstruction on it.'

Amelia shrugged.

'To wit, a half-sunken punt left there after one of the youngster's previous parties.'

'Even if it was,' Amelia said firmly, 'Charles had no right to land there in the first place.'

'He was invited. Prudence dearly wanted him there. It would be the making of the party. Every young people's party these days has to have a difference. You know that. Charles was hers.'

'He didn't have to do it.'

'Come, come, Lady Haybury! Prudence can be very persuasive.' His large eloquent eyes were deliberately meaningful. 'And they're fond of each other.'

'Even so, it's his job to see his landing is clear.'

'Six of one and half-a-dozen of the other?' He spread his well-shaped hands pleadingly.

'Eleven of Charles and one of Prudence. That's my final offer!' They both laughed. He leaned across to shake her hand and then held on to it.

'And now, Lady Haybury, will you let me do something which will help absolve my conscience and make Prudence and me very happy?'

'I really thought,' Amelia told Arthur the following day, 'that he was going to talk about a marriage settlement. It was quite obvious that he approved of the relationship. And Charles and Prudence have been going out together now for over eighteen months.'

'Nearly two years,' Arthur said shortly.

Charles was away in the north of England where the Cobham circus was performing. There was little doubt that Prudence was there too.

'Her father probably wishes to regularise the situation.' Arthur went on frowning. Then he added, 'Charles is a swine.'

Amelia sighed. Arthur sounded so pompous these days. No wonder he frightened off suitable girls. And he was so jealous of Charles, she hated having them both at home together.

'It's just that he's not the marrying kind now.'

'After his first performance, I'm glad you say he's not the marrying kind *now*. But he *is* the kind to compromise a girl like Prudence.'

'I thought your generation didn't think in terms of compromise.'

'Most of us still do. It's people like Charles . . . '

'Well, let's not talk about Charles. Let me tell you what Mr Lehmann said. Of course it'll have to be subject to board approval . . . '

'But having the board more or less in your pocket, you're sure of no problem.'

'Don't sound so waspish, Arthur! It's *good* news I'm telling you. Your money's in it as well as mine.'

'Money isn't everything,' Arthur said dourly.

'Not *everything*. But in business 99 per cent. Lack of it almost made us give up. Having it enables us to go on.'

'And Lehmann's going to buy his way in.'

'That's putting it crudely.'

'Is there any other uncrude way?'

'Of course. The way *he* put it. That he and his colleagues believe Ajax is a superb design. They've read copies of reports on her performance. They've sounded out aviation experts. They've managed to get hold of our balance sheets. Mr Lehmann feels that aviation is at last getting off the ground. He wants to invest. He wants a share in the equity. He's a banker. He's no fool.'

'Mr Lehmann is also a devoted father. And where his daughter is concerned he *is* a fool. He may talk about his father buying himself into Edwardian society. But that's what *he's* doing. He's buying himself a son-in-law. A titled son-in-law.'

'He's buying himself a share in one of the finest aircraft ever built. You should know that.' Amelia jumped to her feet in fury. 'And that's a frightful thing to say about Mr Lehmann and Prudence and Charles.'

'I exclude her.'

'You can't exclude her. Don't try to be chivalrous, please! She's the moving light in all this. She twists her father round her finger. Lehmann wants to back Ajax. I want him to. The board will want him to.'

'And Lehmann wants Charles for a son-in-law. You've said yourself you see it coming. So he's bringing it about. He's waving his magic wand. In this case, his wallet.'

'So you think we should turn Lehmann down?' Amelia demanded angrily.

'Of course not! The board should accept! With grateful grovelling thanks. Why should we object?'

'But you *are* objecting.'

Arthur tightened his lips as if it was the only way he could hold on to himself. He shook his head and walked stiffly to the door. 'I'm not really objecting. So long as the price is right,' he said, turning the handle. 'But one thing I *could* tell Lehmann, banker though he be . . . whatever he pays for Charles, it's a million times too high.'

Charles returned to the factory in the spring. But it was the family Prudence saw rather than Charles himself. Charles threw himself into work on the new Ajax. He virtually left home so to do. He furnished the old nursery wing at Jerningham with the bare essentials of living, plus a couple of large draughtsmen's tables, a bench for models and bookcases. Work on Ajax was beginning at an auspicious time. Wiley Post had just completed his first solo flight round the world in a Lockheed monoplane. Almost at the same time, the Mollisons were flying a de Havilland Dragon from Wales to Connecticut. The star of aviation was ascending.

Prudence made no attempt to interfere. Though she was a constant visitor to Haybury, rocketing up the drive in her Hispano-Suiza with a group of bright young things in tow, she contented herself with waiting till he came over at six-thirty to join them for a cocktail. Amelia watched with amusement. Either Prudence had been carefully schooled by her father not to interfere with his investment, or she was playing some devious game of her own, for she never tried to persuade Charles away from Ajax.

It was left to Arthur, if he was home, to squire the gay youngsters with their bobbed hair in bright bandanas and their short-short skirts round the rose gardens, or to make up a foursome on the tennis court.

Even Prudence's invitation to her twenty-third birthday party was given to Charles, Amelia noticed, with demure carelessness. 'Please come if you can, Charles darling. But if you're positively and absolutely immersed, I will understand.' She nibbled the cherry in the cocktail he had mixed for her as the three of them sat on the terrace in the heat of a late June evening.

This time, Prudence had driven over alone. 'Everyone's at Ascot,' she explained. 'But horses aren't for me. And anyway, party arrangements are rather pressing.'

'So's work I'm afraid, Prudence,' the new conscientious Charles shook his head. 'I'd love to, but —'

'He wouldn't love to at all, Lady Haybury,' Prudence smiled saucily at Amelia. 'He's afraid I'd get him to do something else frightful.'

'Well, I did break an aeroplane and a leg last time.' They exchanged affectionate looks. 'Parties like that come expensive.'

'The trouble is, dear Charles,' Prudence made her eloquent eyes very mournful, 'I am short of handsome men. A few deb's delights I *do* have. But they're no match for the girls.'

'That I believe!'

It was finally Amelia herself who suggested Arthur. 'He's too serious for a young man. Too conscientious,' she confided to Prudence. 'He needs taking out of himself.'

'He needs taking out of himself and never finding his way back,' Charles said.

'Don't be horrid, Charles! I like Arthur!' Prudence said in the usual vague unconvincing way she referred to Arthur. 'Of course I'll invite him, Lady Haybury. And I promise I won't get him to land on the lake!'

'Walking on the water is more angelic Arthur's forte.'

'Well, not even that,' Prudence smiled. 'Nothing too spectacular at this party. Freda Dudley Ward asked me if she could bring HRH. If the lake is used, it'll be only for the most unspectacular of bathing.'

Edward, Prince of Wales did not come. The lake was used. And the bathing was unspectacular in the sense that few wore any clothes. Arthur had come to the party with mixed feelings, well aware that he was a substitute for his brother. He was also distantly aware that Prudence was playing some deep and devious game of her own. Not that he loved her any less, whatever her machinations. He already knew that if he couldn't marry her – and it was obvious that he couldn't – then he wouldn't marry anyone else.

In his own quiet way, he had enjoyed the last few months since Charles's return. While his mother and Charles had been obsessed with the latest achievements in aviation – Colonel and Mrs Lindberg's flight from Gambia to Brazil, the establishment of the official French airline, Air France, and the extension of Imperial Airways Calcutta service to Rangoon, he had enjoyed his respite from constituency work in the company of Prudence.

He was not content to worship her from afar, but he realised this was all he would ever do. While wearing a facial expression of austere gravity, his inner self melted and revelled in the bright young things' foolish chatter, their teasing and the extravagance of their ways.

'I doubt you will want to come to the party, Arthur,' Prudence had said

303

diffidently. 'Do say if you don't. I shall quite understand.'

But Arthur had wanted to come. Once he was there, however, he had found the gay young things shrill and overpowering en masse. The noise at the party was like birds before the beaters. 'Arthur is dying to get away from you all and back to his serious parliamentary business,' Prudence said pertly, slipping a slender bare arm through his, dragging him away from a group of sycophantic men and scantily dressed girls.

'I could see you were bored rigid, Arthur my dear.' She pulled him towards an enormous room, where a five-piece band was playing. The dance was about as much to Arthur's taste as a trade union rally. He had a vivid impression of multicoloured little skirts, whirling around tight little bottoms and above uniform knees in flesh-pink stockings, before Prudence clasped him to her. 'Let's dance.'

'I can't Charleston,' he said.

'Nothing to it. I'll teach you. Watch me!'

Prudence was nothing if not an exhibitionist. He watched her tiny feet turning in and out of themselves, her knees touching, her knees spread, her dainty figure swaying this way and that, her little hands thrown up provocatively, her saucer eyes wide and wicked.

'Come on! Now let's do it together!'

They did it together.

She clapped her hands. 'Arthur, you did absolutely marvellously! But now, let's cool off!'

Thankfully he followed her out on to the terrace and into the soft fragrance of the August evening. The grass was springy under their feet, a light breeze stirred the heavily leafed trees. Hand in hand, alone, they walked towards the lake. Other dancers were already cooling off. Piles of clothes littered the shore and the floor of the colonnade. A few of the more prudish or prudent had kept on their underwear, but for the most part they were as naked and natural as water babies. Some of them had pushed out a punt and were diving from it into the water. The whole scene with the backdrop of Mr Lehmann's Greek colonnade had an almost classical quality as pale young arms cleaved through the water and slender naked forms chased each other across the edge of the lake.

'This is the best way of all to cool off,' Prudence said, and began wriggling out of her red silk dress.

Again Arthur was aware of that same feeling of something bursting in his head. He tore off his clothes. It was as if he was back at the meeting again, as he leapt across the shingle and followed her in.

After that, she was no longer leading him. They swam side by side with long purposeful strokes through the silky water, till the voices of the other bathers came from a safe distance away.

Here the lake was indented with narrow shingly coves edged with pine trees. 'We used to take pinics there,' Prudence said, almost diffidently. 'It's . . .'

But she didn't say what its virtue was. Already Arthur was turning towards it, and she followed, resting her hand on his arm as they hopped over the pebbles, and then letting him haul her on to the turf.

With a sigh as if she had come a long, long journey, she threw herself on the

304

turf, her arms spread wide. Her tiny perfect body glistened in the starlight. Her enormous eyes stared up at him. They held a strange mixture of emotions – determination, triumph, and now that it was about to happen, apprehension. But the over-riding emotion was, to his astonishment, love.

He sank down beside her and pulled her moist slippery body to him. It was small and she wriggled like an eel slipping under him. He found her mouth. His hands stroked her body. His fear of hurting her was overwhelmed by an intense need to capture and subjugate her. Her bare feet kicked and scrabbled at the turf. Her scream must have been heard across the lake.

Afterwards, they lay side by side staring up at the patterns of the pine trees against the stars. Her face was pale, still softly lit with remembered pleasure. His mind was blank, washed of thought, though distantly anxiety and guilt had begun to nibble at his quietness. Then Prudence sat up and leaned over him. Her eyes were vivid and bright again, her mouth pert. She bent and kissed him briefly.

'Now,' she said, kissing him again. 'Now my dear good Arthur! *Now* you will have to marry me!'

FOURTEEN

They were married at Shotfield in August of the following year. The weather was warm and the wedding lavish. If Stefan Lehmann was disappointed that he had not after all acquired a titled son-in-law he gave no sign of it. He bought Arthur and Prudence the house of their choice – after they had sold the small Westminster flat – in Hals Crescent. He made a handsome marriage settlement and was constantly on the telephone to Amelia or driving to Haybury to make sure that the arrangements were to her liking.

'Having no wife is a great disadvantage, Amelia. I lack feminine intuition in such matters.' They had become very quickly on Christian name terms. He told her that his wife had died when Prudence was three. He had not remarried. He had devoted himself to his daughter, and as she grew up she had repaid his devotion a thousand times. Amelia found him easy to talk to, easy to confide in: but she could not confide in him her one reservation about the wedding – its effect on Charles. He had greeted the announcement of the engagement at first with utter disbelief and then with anger.

'Why on earth does a girl like her want to marry a prune like Arthur?'

'Presumaby because they're in love with each other.'

'I wonder.'

Charles's manifest disbelief had made Amelia say sharply, 'Well, *you* had long enough to make up your mind!'

'Possibly.'

'If you loved her yourself, you should have said so. A girl like Prudence won't hang around for ever.'

He said nothing for a long time; then he said quietly, 'I was never sure. And this time I wanted to be.' He frowned. 'No doubt one of these days, I'd probably have got around to marrying her but . . .'

'But?'

'I always felt . . .' He hesitated and gave his mother one of his sweet oddly vulnerable smiles before continuing, 'that there was more to it than being jolly good friends, lovers even, though we weren't. More than getting on well together. That one day I'd meet someone else . . . almost as if there was someone else coming up through time . . .'

They were words which Amelia recognised not only as meaningful to herself but prescient for him. Afterwards, she was to remember them with choking bitterness. But at the time she was too busy to think about them. And shortly after that, Arthur asked Charles to be his best man and it fell to Amelia to turn his outright refusal into acceptance. 'Arthur has no really close friends,' she pleaded. 'None at all. Underneath he's very lonely. You know that. And anyway, it would please Prudence as well. I think she has a bad conscience about you.'

'And so she should have,' Sarah said on the morning of the wedding, as she helped Amelia to dress in a Chanel creation of blue shantung. Lehmann had insisted Amelia stay at Shotfield for the night, telling her he would be grateful for her company. The three of them, Amelia, Prudence and her father, had sat down to a sumptuous dinner. It had been as if they were already a family.

'It's my belief she's a clever miss. Oh, I know you're very fond of her, but it's true! She played one off against the other. I've talked to their cook. She says Miss Prudence has had her father round her finger since the day her mother died. Maybe she hoped to land Charles. Give him a push in the right direction. Nothing like losing something to make you want it. She *couldn't* really prefer Arthur.'

'I'm quite sure she does, Sarah.'

Sarah sniffed disbelievingly. 'Well,' she prophesied, 'if *she* doesn't want him, some other girl will. Charles'll get snapped up. Just like that.' She snapped her fingers. 'Maybe today. Weddings beget weddings. Weddings get people in that way of thinking, in a manner of speaking.'

Certainy Prudence's many and vivid girlfriends eyed Charles hungrily across the flower-filled church as he and Arthur awaited the arrival of the bride. Amelia, with Ronald Cummings supportively beside her, watched them in their Paris dresses and their Bond Street hats, wondering if any of them was the one whom with a typical naïvety he seemed to await. Yet who was she to find such a sentiment naïve?

Charles looked so heartbreakingly like a more polished, more nurtured James that Amelia found herself searching for a girl who resembled herself. A girl who would make her own love affair with James, now so manifestly dead, come alive in the second generation.

After the ceremony, Charles escorted the chief bridesmaid – Margaret Challoner, of hunger marching fame – from the church. But Margaret wouldn't do for him. She was large and capable, with a booming bossy voice and was anyway rumoured to be engaged to a diplomat, who was serving as Second Secretary with Henry Tyrell, now in Peking. Victoria had sent a wistful cable. How she wished Henry could get a posting nearer home!

Amelia left the church on the arm of Stefan Lehmann, with Ronald Cummings following in the crowd. The arm was a strong comforting one. Protectively, he waved away the over-intrusive photographers, wafted her easily and capably back to Shotfield Hall for the reception.

'You will never guess, Father,' Prudence laughed to him as they waited in the line-up to receive their guests, 'Candida said you were the most arrestingly handsome older man she'd ever seen!'

'That compliment is double-edged,' Stefan Lehmann squeezed his daughter's hand. 'But thank your gerontophilic friend.'

He raised dark brows humorously at Amelia. Amelia smiled back tenderly.

'But he *is* handsome and arresting, isn't he, Lady Haybury?' The bride peered eagerly forward.

'Very!' Amelia smiled, meaning it. No one shehad ever met had as much presence as Stefan Lehmann. No one except James had given her such a sense of complete well being. Partly it was his splendid physique, his eloquent eyes which managed to be both bold and soulful, his deep rich voice, his slightly exaggerated courtesy. She had remarked to Sarah after the first day she met him that he exuded a psychic aura of good living, a whiff of old port and cigar smoke. He made Amelia feel protected, cossetted, something precious to be looked after, while James had always made her feel challenged, drawn forward – protected, yes, but endangered too. It was the first time, Amelia thought, shaking innumerable hands and brushing innumerable powdered cheeks, that she had ever mentally compared James to anyone.

'Father is nuts on your mother,' the bride whispered to Arthur as they cut the enormous wedding cake. 'Have you seen the way the poor chump looks at her?'

Prudence was not the only one who had noticed. Driving Amelia home after the reception, encouraged by the fact that she had not stayed either for the young people's dance or the quiet dinner suggested by Mr Lehmann and strengthened by five glasses of champagne, Ronald Cummings picked the moment to ask Amelia to marry him.

She stared at him for a moment uncomprehendingly, as if a character in a well-known play had suddenly donned the wrong costume. Once begun on his long pent-up speech, he was unstoppable. He spoke of his unworthiness, then of his deep devotion. 'You must have been aware . . .?'

She had been aware. Of course she had been aware, and yet selfishly she had not allowed herself to be. Wanting his presence, his help, his affection, his loyalty, and yes, his devotion without having to offer anything at all in return.

'Is there someone else?' Ronald asked when she didn't answer.

She nodded.

'Lehmann?' He gave an angry little laugh. 'I should have asked you before. Things haven't been the same since the Great Benefactor appeared.'

'No.' Amelia shook her head vehemently. 'You're wrong.' Away from his physical presence, Stefan Lehmann faded. He was as insubstantial to her as his aura of cigar smoke. No one but James retained his reality. Beside James, everyone else was a shadow. And James she could not have. James had come up too soon in time, as Charles had fancifully put it. They had missed each other for ever. There was no going back.

'I shall never remarry, Ronald. Never! But thank you.'

'Never is a long time,' Ronald replied – reassured about Lehmann, faint hope reviving.

'Never, Ronald! No matter how long I live!'

The words were so recognisably true to her, and so sad that her eyes filled with tears. The future road seemed suddenly to stretch out in front of her long and barren and dolorous, like the landscape in a dream.

FIFTEEN

The apparently improved relationship between Charles and Arthur, politely displayed at the wedding, did not continue. Arthur as a dutiful son-in-law made it his over-zealous business to see that Charles did not waste Lehmann and partners' huge injection of capital. Stefan now took his seat on the board. With his financial expertise he was a valued member, under Arthur's chairmanship. The fact that Charles did not need his brother's prodding, the fact that he accepted a salary cut in line with teachers and public servants, made Arthur's attitude all the more infuriating. Charles was perfectly aware that he was being given an unexpected and undeserved second chance. He threw himself into the redesign and rebuilding of Ajax, his wild ways totally discarded.

He refused Lehmann's repeated invitations to crew his cruiser, *Shalom*. He was seen no more at the Bag of Nails and the Embassy Club. His name no longer appeared in Castlerosse's Sunday Log in the *Sunday Express* or any other column of the newspapers of Britain. They contented themselves with the doings of the newly wed Bryan Guinness and Diana Mitford, with Gladys Cooper's latest conquests, snippets about Lord Blandford and beauties like the Countess de Flairieu. The occasional photograph of HRH in a party with Mr and Mrs Herman Rogers and Mr and Mrs Ernest Simpson did occasionally slip through the net, but the British public remained on that subject, as with aerial warfare, blissfully uninformed.

'We never see Charles in London these days,' Prudence said on the telephone to Amelia with what sounded like a certain wistfulness, six months after the wedding. 'When are we going to meet the girl?'

That autumn, to her joy, Amelia was told that she was to become a grandmother. But there was still no sign of a girl for Charles; like James, he had suddenly become aware that sooner or later there was going to be a war. That Britain had to prepare, had to have a strong well-equipped air force. And that in turn led to more arguments with Arthur. Like the rest of Parliament, with the exception of Winston Churchill, Arthur seemed unable to see sufficiently clearly the danger that was staring them in the face.

'Thank God I live up in London!' Arthur said to Amelia as they drove back to Haybury for dinner after the first board meeting of 1936 on 20 January. 'Charles gets worse with age, rather than better. It's almost impossible for me to open my mouth without having an argument.'

Over dinner, seated between Lehmann and Cummings, Charles began pressing Arthur on his duty to speak up in the House of Commons on Britain's crying need for aeroplanes. 'I didn't read that you were on your feet supporting Churchill's speech the other day.'

'To which of Churchill's many speeches do you refer?' Arthur asked coldly.

Charles continued his attack. 'And were you in the House, dear brother, when Attlee had the crass stupidity to move a vote of censure against the programme for RAF expansion?'

'I was. I voted against the Lib/Lab motion of censure.'

Charles looked slightly mollified.

'In fact, I would suggest you worry less about politics, and more about the factory. There's not a hope of getting orders for Ajax at the moment. Till then, you run your side and I'll run mine.'

'Usually the boot's on the other foot. It's you that's breathing down my neck. Why haven't we more orders for Supermarine parts? Why do mechanics get paid living wages, instead of working for free? Why —'

'Gentlemen . . . boys . . . brothers . . .' Lehmann said, holding up his hands, smiling forbearingly. But it was Sarah who restored the peace on that occasion. Coming in importantly, she whispered to Amelia in a loud audible whisper. 'M'lady, we've had the wireless on in the servants' hall. There's an important announcement. Shall I switch on the set here?'

They were just in time to hear the bulletin from Sandringham, 'The King's life is moving peacefully to its close.' They sat for sevral minutes in silence, aware that a new era was about to begin. Arthur, with memories perhaps of his own father, was visibly moved.

Next day, Amelia listened with Sarah to the accession of King Edward VIII being proclaimed. And examined with Sarah, the day after, the picture of the King watching the proclamation from a window in St James's Palace. Beside the King stood an unnamed woman. Even Sarah, expert now in the female aristocracy, was unable to name her.

A feeling of uneasiness was abroad. Prudence telephoned a week later to say that she and Arthur had watched King George's body being brought from King's Cross to Westminster Hall. An ominous little incident had taken place. As the gun carriage with the coffin draped in the Royal Standard and surmounted by the Royal Crown, had turned into the Palace Yard, the Maltese cross on top of the crown had worked loose. Down had fallen that lovely emerald and diamond cross into the mud. The new King had been heard to exclaim. 'Christ! What will happen next?'

It was a sentiment that was to be repeated by his subjects many times in the months that followed.

But on 7 March, Amelia cared nothing for crowns or omens, or whatever was to happen next. Prudence gave birth to Rachel at noon on that day. In the general family rejoicing, Charles forebore to mention that almost at the exact time of her birth, Hitler had occupied the Rhineland and brought war that much nearer to Britain.

By the time that war again began looming over the horizon, the peaceful side of flying had flung a network of communication all over the world. Imperial Airways were running scheduled services to South Africa and Australia. Pan American were flying across the Pacific. Germany – the only country still operating airships after the American *Akron* and *Maçon* disasters – were maintaining a highly successful service across both the North and South

Atlantic with the *Graf Zeppelin* and the *Hindenburg*.

As though in perpetual conflict with its benign brother, the warlike side was also expanding. Mussolini had declared war on Abyssinia. Hitler had renounced the Versailles treaty and was building up a huge air force. Churchill had warned, 'We cannot have any anxieties comparable to the anxiety caused by German rearmament'.

But another anxiety *had* appeared – a constitutional crisis that was to shake the British throne. The new King Edward VIII was totally different from his father, with whom he had never got on. By the time he ascended the throne, an affair had developed with an American woman that was front page news on all world scandal-sheets except Britain's. Mrs Wallis Simpson had already been divorced once and now again had a husband.

All through 1936 nobody appeared to be talking about anything else. German Fascists continued to build up their forces; Italian Fascists annexed Abyssinia unopposed. With great difficulty, in the teeth of a vote of censure by Labour and Liberal parties denying the need for increased air armaments, Baldwin had put in hand a modest expansion of the Royal Air Force.

Still no orders for Ajax came to Jerningham. Charles was on to Arthur to push harder. His brother did make one speech in the rearmament debate, listened to from the gallery by Amelia and Charles.

'Too weak, Arthur! Too wishy-washy altogether!' Charles told him in disgust afterwards. 'We'll never get any orders for Ajax that way! The firm'll go bust at this rate. Even your father-in-law won't be able to keep it afloat!'

Charles went rampaging off on his own Ajax IV advertising campaign. On 27 June, he did an aerobatic display at Hendon that compared very favourably with the new Supermarine Spitfire, based on its Schneider Trophy design. But back on the ground afterwards, arguing with senior RAF officers, one of whom was the man March, he couldn't get anywhere. They were concentrating on the Spitfire and the Hurricane, they told him. No money for anything else.

On 18 July in Spain there was a revolt against the government led by General Franco. Germany and Italy hastened to send warplanes to him. Britain and the rest of Europe declared a policy of non-intervention. No military equipment would be allowed to go to either side. Charles was disgusted with the RAF, the government and particularly his brother.

'What are *you* doing about it?'

'What can I do about it?'

'Support Churchill.'

'That damned warmonger!'

'Well, at least he realises Germany's spoiling to have another crack at us.'

'What rubbish you talk, Charles!'

Prudence tried to get him to come to parties to meet some of her girlfriends, but he rarely turned up. He was determined to sell Ajax despite the general apathy. 'The only thing that interests anybody these days,' he told Amelia wryly, 'is the King's affair with Wally Simpson.'

While rumours of the King's intentions circulated, German rearmament and the agony of the Civil War in Spain were relegated to second place. Stanley Baldwin was photographed looking suitably grim and determined, the King looking defiant and romantically sad, the Archbishop of Canterbury looking suitably tenacious of the principle of no divorce for British queens. Mrs

311

Simpson was reported to have left the King's side and been smuggled to France. Schoolchildren exchanged jingles about the royal affair.

The shades of night were falling fast,
When through an Alpine village passed,
A Buick driven very fast,
And in the cushions at the back,
The famous Mrs Simpson sat . . .

The British public were reputedly divided between King and Constitution. There was talk of a King's party. Of the throne being in danger. Faint whispers of revolution.

Then in December, the constitutional crisis that had occupied the centre of the British stage for nearly a year was resolved quite quietly with the abdication of Edward VIII, and the accession of his brother George.

So was the future of Ajax. Reluctantly, the board decided to shelve all future plans for the aircraft. The prototype was relegated to the same hangar by the slipway in which Ajax II had been stored. Just before Christmas, Charles went up to London to have one last go at the Air Ministry on the ordering of Ajax.

He saw a door marked *Group Captain James March, DSO* but he passed it by. He was damned if he was going to knock on that door. From behind the door he did knock on, he was told that the money was simply not available. Nor was the government likely to increase the air estimates greatly in the next few years. No matter how good the aircraft, they could not buy it. He was banging his head against a brick wall.

Angry, frustrated and bitterly disappointed, Charles took himself off in search of a drink to an underground bar near Victoria, which he remembered from the old days. It was much favoured by pilots, and that evening it was packed. Subdued lighting cast a dim glow over the cellar. Charles said, 'Excuse me,' to the shadow of a man standing at the crowded counter. The man turned his head, and he saw Babe Reynolds. He was an older, battle-hardened Babe Reynolds. With an odd sense of inevitability, Charles heard him say he was on his way back to Spain to fight on the government side against a new and deadly breed of Hun.

'What do you fly?'
Babe smiled grimly, 'Anything I can lay my hands on.'
'Bad as that?'
'I guess so.'

The conversation about Spain came to an abrupt halt. Charles had the feeling Babe clammed up in case he might influence him. So instead of Spain they swapped news of the last six years. Ernst had married, bought a farm in Wisconsin and sold his share in the circus to Babe. The circus business wasn't what it was. A set-up called the Air Registration Board had brought in safety regulations. Whoever heard of a circus where you couldn't walk on the wing, nor fly less than 50 feet above the crowd? In return, Babe sympathised about Ajax and the hell of trying to sell it to an unappreciative government, wary of the peace-at-any-price lobby.

Babe didn't mention that the Spanish government was desperate for fighters, that open cities were being bombed for lack of them. Nor did he remind

Charles that as a schoolboy he couldn't wait to get into the war.

Yet somehow Charles saw it all. The irony of the British government's rejection of Ajax and the Spanish government's need of it, the threat to world peace of the Spanish conflict, the tragedy of the Spanish people.

In the months that followed he would have liked to think that those considerations triggered his action, that he saw the civil war as a threat to democracy. Or even that he saw it as the cockpit wherein to prove both Ajax and himself. But in fact, he suddenly felt with the most overpowering urgency that there was a war on and he couldn't wait to get stuck in.

Telling no one, he took off in Ajax next day.

'Just as before,' James said grimly. 'A war on, so Charles can't wait. Eighteen years and he hasn't learned his lesson. Hasn't grown up. And this time he steals Ajax as well.'

James's anger was controlled but nonetheless apparent. It reached towards Amelia, stopping just short of encompassing her, too, as she sat on the edge of a straight-backed chair in Group Captain March's office on the third floor of Adastral House. James's brows were lowered and his eyes frosty as he stood with his back to the empty fireplace, glowering down at her.

Then reminding himself of what it had cost her to come to him, and pierced by her strained pale face, he walked over and put his hand comfortingly on her shoulder. Impulsively she covered it with hers. They remained still and silent for a moment, timeless, like an Edwardian married couple in a photograph. Except that their eyes were fixed not into the camera but on the morning's *Daily Herald* now spread on James's desk and the banner headline, *Guernica*. Below was the line, *Red Baronet reported shot down.*

'I wondered if you had any news at all.' Amelia broke the silence and reluctantly released his hand. 'Even,' she finished stonily, 'if it's bad news.'

'The news about Charles is usually bad,' James said with an anger that was strangely therapeutic. 'If not bad for himself then bad for other people.'

'You sound like Arthur,' Amelia shot him a fragile smile, knowing James would not have spoken thus if the news were really bad. She began to feel she was coming alive again after all the cold miserable weeks since Charles had left.

'My sympathies are with Arthur. In the main,' James returned her smile with one of mild reproof. 'As far as Charles is concerned, we know he's alive. Very much so. Very much an embarrassment to His Majesty's Government.'

'Oh,' Amelia let out her breath in a single syllable of mingled relief, reproach and a luxuriance in that sustaining comfort only James could give her. She felt it round her as palpable as arms, and streaming within her body like new revivifying blood.

All that chilly spring she had resisted the temptation to seek it. Since the February night she had wakened to hear Ajax's engine dwindling south, she had realised where Charles had gone. Ronald Cummings had tried to pretend otherwise, had denied such a possibility to the Press and the Police, who for days haunted the factory and Haybury Hall.

Charles's letter from Matista saying he was trying to contact Babe Reynolds had come a month later and then the journalists of every nation seemed to have got hold of Charles's story. He was at Matista. He was at Teruel. He had defended this great stronghold. He had helped set fire to the prison. He had been in dogfights with Messerschmitts. Amelia discussed the newspaper reports with no one, not even Ronald Cummings. The Spanish Civil War which had lured Charles away was now bringing business to the factory. Slowly at first but with gathering momentum. When Amelia spoke to Ronald Cummings it was usually of business matters.

Only Sarah was allowed to comment, and that only occasionally, on the newspaper reports from the Civil War. Sara bought every newspaper she could lay her hands on. She kept a scrapbook. She regaled the staff in the servants' hall on the 'Red Baronet's exploits'. It was a red-eyed Sarah who had brought her this morning's *Daily Mail*. Sarah who had persuaded her to come straight up to London and try to see James.

'Was he shot down?' Amelia's eyes returned to the newspaper.

James nodded. 'Eventually. But not injured. Or so I'm told.'

'And Ajax?'

'Repairable – according to my information. And that's about all I can tell you.'

'Thank you, James,' she replied humbly, pulling on her gloves, smoothing the fingers, reluctant to go.

'Except for one thing, Amelia,' his dark brows met in a frown. James being severe again, she thought tenderly . . . longingly. 'Charles left this country illegally. He could be in trouble when he returns. But you must know that as well as I do.'

She sighed, and with the gaiety of relief, of gratitude, of pleasure now in these few moments together, said brightly, 'Yes I do know, Arthur tells me that. Frequently. Charles is an embarrassment to him. He damages his image – that's what he means. And I have spoiled Charles. That's what you mean, don't you? I have been a bad mother.' Expansive in her momentary happiness, her face was youthful, her smile at its most beguiling again. She shrugged in self-deprecation.

'Amelia, you don't think that at all. Nor for that matter do I. You are,' he sighed trying to think of the right word, 'yourself.' He spread his hands at the inadequacy of his vocabulary. They both laughed.

'But still a bad mother?' she asked him teasingly.

He looked at her, his eyes gentle. 'No. I don't blame you.' He shook his head slowly. A moment of exquisite tenderness trembled fragilely between them.

Then his expression suddenly hardened. 'I blame his father,' he said harshly. '*He* should have . . .' And then seeing the stricken look on her face, stopped abruptly.

'I'm sorry,' he went on after a moment, amazed that the mention of Frederick had still the power to deeply hurt her, 'I have absolutely no right to say what his father should or should not have done.'

She shook her head wordlessly and stood up. He took the hand she held out to him, and opened the door for her. 'I'll let you know if I hear anything more of Charles.'

She nodded, still without speaking. She knew James came out on to the landing and watched her slowly descend the staircase. But she could not remember leaving the building, or hailing a taxi and being driven to Waterloo.

Not until July did she have another letter from Charles and that was an

314

unhappy one. It was to say that his American friend, Babe Reynolds, had been killed near Madrid. Charles asked her to write to the third member of The Three Musketeers, Ernst Von Stromm. There was nothing more until two days before Christmas. Charles wrote a few lines on the back of an old luggage label. The Spanish War was muddle and mess, filth and starvation, disease and misery. Amelia didn't even show the letter to Sarah, cheerfully supervising the decoration of the twelve-foot Christmas tree.

Not until May did Amelia get the phone call from James which she had subconsciously known would come eventually. Hearing James's voice at the other end of the line, grave, sympathetic, but restrained, she was spun back through time to 1930 and the R101 and Frederick's death again.

But it was not death. Charles was injured. Quite seriously. But there would be no amputations or permanent injury. Charles's comrades had got him to hospital. He would recover. He had been interviewed by an American voluntary worker. Amelia might find him somewhat changed. But he would be home eventually.

Eventually. That was the word they had used whenever he asked them anything in the hospital. Eventually. Eventually he would be able to sit up. Eventually he would be able to stand. Eventually his leg would heal. Eventually he would be able to walk again. Eventually he would go back home to England.

Now eventually had come. Seated in a four-engined Imperial Airways Handley Page 42, Charles stared down at the grey-blue Channel, glimpsed the white cliffs and the green fields ahead. It seemed much more than a lifetime ago that he had crossed the Channel, by night and on a more southerly course, hell bent for Spain and war.

Well, he had had his bellyful of that now. His mind had become numbed to the horrors he had witnessed. But lying in that hospital bed, the numbness had worn off like the anaesthetic they'd given him when they operated to save his leg. Then the murders, he tortures, the rapes, the bestiality, the obscenities of cruelty, the degradations had revived to haunt every sleeping and waking mment.

There and then, aboard that slow-moving majestic aircraft he vowed he would never fight a war, never build aircraft for war again. Never. He feasted his eyes on the serenity of England, the Downs, the Sussex villages. After the parched waste of Spain, how fresh and fertile it looked. How far away, and yet how terrifyingly close.

Croydon gasworks as they came into land, still smelled the same. So did London. But the Thames gleamed in intermittent sunlight, and the taxi driver was solicitous of his stick and gammy leg. Waterloo was crowded. Paperboys were yelling about Hitler's threat to Czechoslovakia. He had an hour to wait for the train and he toyed with the idea of phoning his mother. But he wanted it to be a surprise. And he wanted her to see him all at once. As he was. Home but changed. A peaceful Charles. His lesson learned.

Arrived at Jerningham he went straight to Amelia's office. Ronald Cummings was sitting opposite her, facing the door. Seeing Charles first, he stretched across the desk and put his hand protectively over hers. Gently squeezing it, smiling, he said softly, 'The Red Baronet has come home.'

Immediately she turned, jumped to her feet and flung her arms round Charles's neck. She hugged him, laughing and crying at the same time. Charles almost wept himself at the manifest pain he had caused her.

Cummings shook his hand warmly and said, 'Welcome back. You've come at just the right time.'

The factory was now on a war footing. Faced with the growing crisis of Germany, the government, as in the Great War, was at last embracing its aircraft manufacturers. Aircraft 'shadow factories' – of which Jerningham was one – were financially guaranteed by the government. Everything produced for the war was on a cost-plus-profit basis. And the more Spitfire components Jerningham produced, the better.

In the days that followed, Sarah fussed maternally about his leg. He told her it was all right now – but he still walked with a slight limp. Almost hidden in a letter from Cape Town saying that a long last Henry had managed to get the Foreign Office to post him back to Washington and they were now on their way, Victoria briefly and a trifle tartly expressed her relief at Charles's return from Spain.

Stories were now leaking through of Nazi atrocities and the appalling treatment of Jews in Germany. At every possible chance in the House of Commons, Arthur spoke out forcefully on the massive need for arms to repel Hitler's hordes.

For two months Charles kept quiet. He spoke very little about Spain, beyond saying that war was madness and that the Spanish one was a particularly insane example. He went back to flying school and took all his engineer's licences, his pilot's licence, and his first class navigator's ticket. Then he suddenly announced to Arthur after lunch in the library at Haybury that Jerningham Aviation should plan for peace. The sky must be peaceful or it would be the end of the world. A British mission had gone to Washington to buy 400 American aircraft – mostly civil airliners of the type of the British Prime Minister flew back from Munich in – and were going to use them for bombers! His idea was an 18-seater twin-engined passenger airliner capable of being 'stretched' with the addition of more powerful engines.

Arthur immediately exploded. 'So you can fly off and crash again!'

'Flying is communication. Unless we communicate —'

'*Communicate*? Is that what you've been doing? Is that what Hitler's doing with the Luftwaffe? If we don't build more Spitfires and crush the Fascists, they'll—'

Charles snapped, 'Bit of a change!'

'What d'you mean?'

'From sitting on the platform with them!'

'Every time you come into my house, you —'

The library door opened. Framed in the lintel, Amelia asked, 'What's going on?'

'Charles! It's Charles again! Wants us to build civil aircraft. *Now!* With war just round the corner! I tell you, Mama —'

But the door had closed again. Amelia had gone.

SIXTEEN

Amelia swept past Sarah in the hall and to her curious, 'Going somewhere, M'lady?' answered peremptorily, 'Out!'

'In the car, M'lady?'

'No!'

Until that moment she had no idea where she was going or how. She simply wanted to get away from Haybury, from Jerningham, from the factory, from her sons, from their arguments, and from all this talk of war. The afternoon was overcast, the air oppressive and stifling.

She found herself in the kitchen. It was the hour when Cook took her nap, and the kitchen, all neatly scrubbed and polished, was silent except for the ticking of the clock. She went through into the pantry and lifted the lid off the stone bread bin. She helped herself to half a loaf, let herself out of the back door, crossed to the shed and wheeled out her bicycle.

Until she went swooping down the drive and had turned left, she pretended to herself that she had no idea where she was going. As if she were trying to forget that the lake drew her with its own special magnetism. Cycling to the crossroads and then left, she turned towards the old bridge at the back of Cornford House, dismounted at the far side and pushed her bicycle into the hedge. It was in full leaf, the pinky-green of the thorn and hazel lit by the white stars of dog roses. She pushed her way carefully through it, parted the strands of wire, and found the overgrown now untrodden path past the rear of Cornford House to the lake. She averted her eyes from the shuttered windows and the closed doors. Throughout the family's long absence in France, the house had been kept perfectly maintained, but it looked more deserted, more abandoned than in its derelict days when James and she had first come here.

The formal gardens, too, were scrupulously groomed, flowerbeds weeded, roses pruned, lawns razored. But nature had reclaimed the lake to its own abundant life. The feathery grass was blooming, the willows dipped their leafy branches in the water, and ranks of young reeds and rushes had thrust up from the slashed stumps of the old.

The swans were still there, and this year's cygnets had hatched. They were no bigger than little dabs of long-necked fluff swimming safely between the twin wings of the cob's wake. Amelia sat on the bank, watching the swans' gliding approach through the silky water. She wondered if this were the original pair which James and she had fed, as she tossed them the bread and waited for the lake to work its old familiar magic.

No magic worked. The swans, those fine examples James had pointed out to her of lifelong fidelity, squabbled over the bread, chased off a couple of

317

mallards, and swam around, eyeing her antagonistically. Nothing remained the same. James, Sarah had told her, was in France. There were rumours in the village that the family would never return.

Nor was Amelia herself the same. She was thirty-six years removed from the girl in the Edwardian dress who had first sat here. She was fifty-two, middle-aged and a grandmother. She sat clasping her knees, staring into the tarnished crystal of the lake, finding no solutions, only her shadowy silhouette distorted by the swans' wake. I am a failure, she thought. A failure as a wife, as a businesswoman and most of all as a mother. My sons will always resent each other because of what *I* have done.

Impatiently, she got to her feet. The cob, disturbed by her abrupt movement, raised its wings, extended its neck and hissed. The sound seemed so alien and hostile that she hurried away, head down towards the path, averting her eyes again from the house. Then a movement forced her to look up.

Someone had raised the window blinds. The sashes were open. The house took on an entirely different and friendlier aspect. Then she saw the front door stood wide, and a tall figure was framed in it, shading his eyes. Amelia stopped in her tracks and stared. It was as if the lake had been fooling her, pretending to reject her, and now it had worked the greatest magic of all.

James came slowly down the steps and across the gravel and grass. She had not forgotten how he walked, but she watched as if for the first time the quite unconscious grace with which he moved his large frame. 'I thought I saw a ghost,' he said lightly, coming up to her.

'A ghost of summers past?' She smiled.

He shook his head. There was a tense uneasy silence.

'I didn't know you were here,' Amelia said apologetically. 'I suppose I'm trespassing really. I'm sorry.'

'Don't be. Please. I *was* away. In France. I spend a great deal of time there. I arrived here,' he looked at his watch, 'ten minutes ago.'

She could think of nothing to say, and gently he put his fingers under her chin and tilted up her face, 'Why did *you* come, Amelia?'

'I wanted to sort myself out.'

He smiled. 'I doubt you'll ever do that, Amelia.'

'I needed to think.'

'About?'

'The family. What's best for them.'

But for the first time, James did not appear to be listening to her. Or if he heard her words, they spoke to him about his family, not hers. We no longer communicate, Amelia thought, on some deeper more mysterious level.

And as if he had been reading her mind, he said, 'I need to get things ready for my wife's return.' He jerked his head towards the house. 'I've come on ahead to make it nice for her. Air the rooms. Stock the larder.'

Amelia was shot through with a pang of jealousy so sharp and painful that she must have caught her breath. James suddenly seemed to become aware of her again.

'I'm sorry, Amelia,' he said with a stranger's courtesy, 'I should have asked you to come in. We've no provisions yet, but I believe there's still some wine . . .'

'No, no, thank you.' She shook her head vehemently. 'I must get back.'

He didn't argue. 'Where did you leave the car?'

'I didn't come by car. I left my bike at the back. On the old bridge.'

Just for a moment an unguarded vulnerable look softened his mouth. 'You don't change, Amelia.' He shook his head with mock exasperation. 'I'll walk up there with you.'

The path was too narrow and overgrown for them to walk side by side. 'When do you expect your wife to return?' Amelia asked casually over her shoulder.

'At the end of the month. Sooner, if I can arrange it. I shan't feel happy till she comes. But she's rather difficult to uproot. We have just rebuilt the house to her liking. She had just begun to enjoy it.'

Amelia nodded but said nothing.

'The original house was shelled in the First World War.'

'And there will be a second war. Is that what you think?'

'Yes.' They had reached the wire by the bridge. She suddenly remembered nearly eight years ago at Cowes when he had talked of war, and she had known that another war would be the end between them. But the end between James and herself had already come. There was no mistaking his concern for his wife. His mind was obsessed with her well-being and safety. Amelia could never again say as she had in Iraq, 'It is me you love!' The Comtesse had won him in the end.

'Don't bother to come with me through to the road, James,' she told him, lifting up one of the wires and ducking her head to scramble through. 'I'll say goodbye here . . . and I hope you're wrong about the war.'

Amelia's gift to her granddaughter on her third birthday was a gesture against the inevitability of war, an affirmation of her right to live, or at worst a hope that she would enjoy herself while she could. She had already suggested the idea vaguely to Prudence and not been repulsed, so the week after her unhappy meeting with James, she drove over to the Forest Stud five miles north of Jerningham, and chose a well-mannered grey gelding of eleven hands.

There was to be a family gathering for Rachel's birthday. Rachel was the one true bond between the brothers, the only subject upon which they both whole-heartedly agreed. The pony was kept out of sight in the stables while Sarah in her best cap and apron supervised the setting of nursery tea on the terrace. Arthur and Prudence with Rachel sitting between them arrived by car, as the cake was being placed in a shady spot under one of the umbrellas. Stefan Lehmann came shortly after them, carrying an enormous parcel in gold wrapping and ribbon. Charles was last, still grimy from the factory, rushing inside to wash, then reappearing to hoist Rachel on his shoulders and gallop round the garden.

It all seemed so peaceful, so timeless, war such an impossibility. Yet already the factory was on a full war footing. Anderson shelters and civilian gas masks were being issued. Czechoslovakia had become a German protectorate.

'Amelia has something up her sleeve,' Stefan whispered to his daughter as Rachel, taking her place of honour at the birthday table, and tearing open her grandfather's gold parcel, demanded to know what her grandmother had bought her.

'You must wait and see,' Amelia replied. She winked at Charles, then exclaimed with admiration at the huge golden-haired doll the parcel disclosed. 'Shall we put a chair next to you for her? What shall you call her?'

'What did *you* get me, Grandmama?'

'Grandmama is very busy,' Charles teased. 'She had no time to go to the shops.'

Rachel raised her beguiling blue eyes to Amelia, 'Didn't you get anything?'

Amelia had not the heart to continue the teasing. 'I managed to get you *something*. Not from the shops, Rachel. And I haven't been able to wrap it up nicely.'

Then when the cake had been sliced and passed round, Amelia caught Sarah's eye for the pre-arranged signal. Sarah sped off. Minutes later the grey gelding, already saddled and bridled, was led round by the groom. Till that moment, the talk had harmlessly centred round Rachel. They had exchanged suggestions about the doll's name, heard about her friends in London, the ducks in St James's Park. Conversation had been indulgent, polite, innocuous, not a word about the international situation, nor politics, nor plans for conscription.

Now a disbelieving silence fell. No one spoke. Then everyone spoke at once. Rachel demanded if this was it, this the present, this really hers, hers to keep, beginning to scream with desperate excitement. Charles loyally applauded Amelia's gift. Stefan echoed him, but with a note of reservation. Arthur and Prudence looked stunned.

'I thought you were joking, Mama,' Prudence blinked disbelievingly.

'I really must say, Mama,' Arthur pushed back his chair and stood up, the better to see the animal, 'I do think it's not the best time . . .'

Then the argument began.

'That's a churlish thing to say.' Charles jumped to his feet. 'You might at least say thank you.'

'What I meant, Mama, is that Rachel is far too young to own a pony.'

'I rode at two,' Charles snapped.

'Much good that did you! If I thought . . .' he glowered at Charles, 'that it would lead Rachel in your footsteps, I'd have it —'

One glance at his daughter's agonised face made him break off and finish grumpily, 'It's the wrong time to give her one.'

'But she can keep it here, darling. Or until you feel you want it. Then I shall see more of you. Or she can come and stay here on her own and I will teach her to ride.'

'What Arthur meant,' Prudence said gently, 'is that times are so uncertain.'

'With war imminent,' Arthur put in.

'What's the point of building for peace if we talk about war all the time?' Charles demanded.

'War, my dear brother, will happen whether you give it permission or not. We've guaranteed Poland now. There isn't going to be another Munich. If Hitler goes in, that's it!'

'Let's still hope he doesn't.'

'Christ! You sound like some mealy-mouthed pacifist. And to think you were the one that couldn't wait to go to war!'

'Well, I went, didn't I? And I saw! And I've had my stomach full! I'm nauseated!'

'And I'm nauseated —'

'Please,' It was Stefan who intervened. He put a hand on each of their arms. 'Sons,' he looked at them both with such affection that Amelia's heart warmed to him. 'This is Rachel's birthday party. The child will be distressed.'

But the child had skipped away from the angry adults to the big present. The groom had already lifted her into the saddle. She glanced around at the group under the umbrella only for approval.

'Let's go too, Mother,' Prudence pushed back her chair. 'Let's take Rachel for a ride. Leave the men to it. Father will keep the peace. He's so fond of you all. There's something else I want to talk to you about.'

She watched her mother-in-law's face as she checked the length of Rachel's stirrup leathers and showed her how to hold the reins. Then side by side, following the pony, she came quickly to the point, 'Arthur and I have a great favour we want to ask of you, Mother.' She paused. 'We know there is a great bond between you and Rachel. In the event of war, we want to ask you to take her for us to Aunt Victoria in Washington.'

The argument continued all evening, when Sarah had led Rachel off to bed. Never one to refuse a request from one of the family, Amelia at first rejected this one out of hand. In the event of war, her place was at Jerningham, at the factory, at Haybury near her family. She was outnumbered.

As a Member of Parliament Arthur was privy to much that was not known to the general public. The government expected bombing on a scale never seen before. A possible knock-out blow to London on the first day with up to 25,000 casualties. 'It'll be a hundred times worse than the Zeppelin raids, Mama,' Arthur said, 'and you remember them?'

'Of course, I remember them. Vividly. And of course, Rachel can't stay in London. Couldn't you bring her here, Prudence? No, of course, this will be designated a danger area too, I was forgetting.'

'Shotfield isn't far enough away from Portsmouth,' Stefan said, 'so that rules it out, too. There's a scheme to evacuate children to Canada. And to the country districts of England. It's all organised.'

'I would prefer she went to America,' Prudence said, 'and not to strangers. It's providential that Aunt Victoria and Uncle Henry are back there.'

Henry Tyrell's diplomatic career had taken him all over the world. But as he had always specialised in American affairs, the Foreign Office regarded him as one of their key men for the USA.

'I'd take her myself but my place is with Arthur. Besides, I've got my name down to drive ambulances. That's about all I'm good for,' she smiled. 'Driving. You should have seen me at the wheel after Charles whipped the guardsmen's bearskins!'

Charles shot her a faint smile in return. He refused to enter the argument. He was torn between a desire not to acknowledge the inevitability of war and a desire to safeguard his mother and his niece from such horrors as he had witnessed.

'But do we know how Victoria feels about all this? After all, she's not used to children.'

'We thought it out carefully, Mother. Arthur wrote three weeks ago to her. She cabled back most warmly. Nothing would please her more.'

'And am I supposed to kick my heels living off the fat of the land in America, while the rest of you stay here?'

'No, Mother. I know it hasn't escaped your notice that Pan American Airways are about to start a Yankee Clipper service to Europe. You could return on that.'

'It's no use dangling *that* as a carrot, Arthur. They'll suspend it if there's a war.'

'There'll be something.'

'Perhaps.'

Finally, long after midnight, agreement was reached. If war seemed imminent, Prudence would book Amelia and Rachel on the first available ship. Amelia would stay for a month until Rachel was settled in and then she would return. Arthur promised to pull strings to ensure her return by Yankee Clipper.

The following week, Amelia received an eager letter from Victoria. She wrote that while she prayed for peace, if war came, it would be like welcoming a grandchild of her own to have Rachel. Several of her friends were expecting British children. She felt sure Rachel would settle down happily, and to see Amelia again would be wonderful. Gradually Amelia began to accept that it might be a sensible arrangement. But as May gave way to a warm golden June, her reluctance to leave England increased. The forest had never looked more beautiful, yellow with gorse, the heather already in bud, the mares with foals at foot, the corn high.

She had never been busier, never felt herself more useful. Every available bit of hangar space at the factory was in use. The airship section was turning out barrage balloons. They had taken on more workers – men out of retirement, women and girls from the village. To considerable speculation, Cornford House, though now stocked and ready, remained empty, though the newly promoted Air Commodore March and a lady had been seen walking round it.

On 3 June, a squad of painters arrived down from Air Ministry and sprayed the hangars and offices with khaki and grey-green camouflage paint in curves and swirls, to disguise, Cummings said, the outline of the buildings and make them melt into the ground.

Two days after that, there came a consignment of green netting to cover outside equipment, blackout baffles for the vehicle headlamps and a sheaf of posters about gas drill. But life still went on as if the war wasn't going to happen. The Rector's wife was asking for gifts and home-made cakes for the church garden fête. Mr Bingham wrote in the parish magazine that the choir was short of choristers.

So Peace might yet prevail.

Amelia scanned the *Times* at breakfast every morning, hoping to see some sign of Hitler drawing back but there was none. Germany had followed her non-aggression pact with Denmark by another with Latvia and Estonia. There were accounts of brutalities in Czechoslovakia, and, ominously, discussions between the German and Italian Air Forces. And then, on the morning of 10 June, as Amelia folded the *Times* over yet more war news – pictures of twenty-year-olds training at Aldershot, the launching of a battleship – the deaths column caught her eye.

One name leapt out at her. *March. At her home in France, Marie, beloved wife of James, devoted mother of Marianne and Pierre.*

Amelia sent a brief formal letter conveying her condolences. It was difficult to write, the more so because now she recognised that James had loved Marie and would be bereft by her death, and might under the circumstances not wish to hear from Amelia. Her letter came out stiff and formal and impersonal.

James did not reply. Whatever had been between Amelia and himself was over. She had a feeling inside herself of finality and death, of entering an emotional limboland, where before there had always been thoughts and memories and fantasies of James.

Ronald Cummings watched her anxiously. She had seemed apathetic about the sudden blossoming of aviation – Pan American Airways establishing a fortnightly service between Port Washington and Marseilles and Port Washington and Foynes. Imperial Airways and Air France were pooling their resources on the London–Paris service, and a Lufthansa plane was about to open a service to Bangkok. Cummings attributed Amelia's apathy to the fact that, along with all these aviation dreams coming true, lay the shadow of a nightmare to come. July saw the formation of the Women's Auxiliary Air Force for duty with the RAF in wartime. Strategic talks began in Warsaw. The RAF were practising over France while French planes were seen over Britain.

Early in August, however, Amelia and Cummings were invited to Foynes to witness the departure of the Empire flying-boat *Caribou* on its inaugural mail and passenger flight to Canada and the USA.

'After all, we can claim to have some hand in it,' Cummings persuaded her.

'Ailerons and fuselage bolts!' Amelia smiled, 'Hardly much of a hand.'

But she agreed to go. The day was warm and the sea calm, the crowd tremendous and enthusiastic. There was a feeling that month that everyone should celebrate something. Cheer while one could. Eat, drink and be merry. And the sight of the enormous silver flying-boat rising from Southampton Water, was enough. Even Amelia was carried away, taking off her straw hat and waving it and cheering.

She seemed like her old self again as Cummings drove her back to Haybury. They had the top of the car rolled back and the wind whipped her bright hair.

'You look a young girl still,' Cummings said.

'But I'm not,' she smiled. 'I'm not even sure I'd want to be. Not if I had to live everything over again exactly as it was.'

'Not even on a day like this?'

'Maybe just for the day. No more.'

And then they were turning down through Jerningham High Street. The pollarded elms by the church were dark green against a summer sky. A large Citroën was parked between them and the forge. James, now in Air Commodore's uniform, was holding the door open for a slim dark-haired girl, who must surely be Marianne, while out of the forge cottage, old Mr March stepped on to the cobblestones to welcome them.

James had his hand on Marianne's shoulder as the Rolls drew level with them. They both turned. The smiles of greeting seemed to freeze simultaneously on their faces. James's expression immediately became one of

323

studied emptiness, but astonishingly a flicker of hostility twisted Marianne's pretty lips and narrowed her eyes.

Amelia sank back against the upholstery and closed her eyes. She didn't speak again until they reached Haybury. Just before they turned into the drive, Ronald looked sideways at her. She had said, he thought sadly, that she wouldn't want to be a young girl again. She no longer looked one. Now for the first time, she looked old.

'Young Marianne is going into the Women's Air Force,' Sarah said three days later. 'Old March was talking to my brother. When Pierre – fancy calling him Pierre! – when he finishes school, he's going to join up, too. So there's talk of not opening Cornford House, because they'll be all three going their separate ways.'

'When?'

'Any day. Marianne's staying a while. But the Air Commodore's off tomorrow.'

He made no effort to contact Amelia, on neither that visit nor subsequently.

Cornford House remained closed.

'You're not working too hard are you, Mama?' Charles asked, suddenly noticing how thin and haggard she looked, as he shared a quick sandwich lunch in Amelia's office. 'I know the news is bloody, but I still hope to God we get a reprieve.'

There was no reprieve. The noose tightened. Concrete gun posts appeared like giant mushrooms peeping out of bushes by the curves of the river. The Army established Bofors guns at the southern end of the airfield, and the roads were full of camouflaged vehicles. There was a practice blackout in London. Orders came for windows to be taped. The Ministry of Works put up another air-raid siren. Sandbags were issued.

On 23 August Germany, the professed arch-enemy of communism, signed a non-aggression pact with Soviet Russia, the professed arch-enemy of Nazism. Europe was doomed. The following day it was announced that an Anglo-Polish pact of mutual assistance had been signed in London. On 26, the Admiralty was authorised 'to adopt compulsory control of movements of merchant shipping'. And shortly after the evening news had been read on the wireless, the telephone rang at Haybury.

It was Prudence telling Amelia that she had been lucky enough to secure Rachel and Amelia a passage across the Atlantic for 1 September from Glasgow aboard the liner SS *Athenia*.

SEVENTEEN

Things moved fast then. On 24 August, Arthur was called to the House to enact the Emergency Powers (Defence) Bill. Army, Navy and RAF Reserves were called up. Ration books were issued. All Air Raid Precaution services were alerted.

On 31 August, Germany invaded Poland. Warsaw was devastated from the air. All Imperial Airways aircraft were evacuated to Whitchurch near Bristol. From sunset to dawn, a complete blackout was ordered. Amelia and Rachel, Arthur said, were going in the nick of time.

Waiting with the family in the darkness on the platform for the night train to Glasgow to come in, Amelia wished she was staying. King's Cross station looked cavernous and creepy. It was packed with evacuee children standing in silent groups, with gas-masks in cardboard boxes slung around their necks and their name and number pinned to their coats.

'What if they begin bombing immediately?' Prudence murmured to Amelia 'What if they bomb Glasgow before you sail?'

'Of course they won't penetrate as far as Glasgow!' Charles said. 'We've got our defences. And remember, war isn't here yet. There may be another Munich.'

'I hope to God not!' Arthur exclaimed. 'We can't turn back again now!'

Charles, mindful of his mother's distress, bit his lip and said nothing.

'Perhaps Hitler is bluffing,' Amelia said. 'Perhaps when he sees our determination, he'll have second thoughts.'

They were words for Prudence, now verging on tears, and Rachel wide-eyed and excited, not words for herself or her sons. She knew war would come and so did they. The train came into the platform. People were rushing forward, opening carriage doors.

'By the time it's sorted out, we shall be safely in America.' Amelia said, kissing Prudence goodbye. Then she clasped her sons briefly to her, wondering if she would see them again. By the time she came back to England, where would they be?

Then the guard sounded his whistle and Amelia lifted Rachel in. There were no tears. Rachel was enchanted with the dim blue lights. Amelia liked them too – they were so kind to ageing faces. Hanging briefly out of the window, she exchanged with her family the useless 'Take care', 'Have a good journey', 'Look after yourselves' and 'Write as often as you can'.

The carriage doors slammed. The guard's swinging lantern gleamed green. He gave a long blast from his whistle. There was a whoosh of white steam. The engine shrilled. The train lurched forward. The wheels clanked over the rails, gaining rhythmic speed. Red sparks danced past the window.

Clutching Rachel's hand, Amelia leaned out for the last glimpse. Prudence and the two men formed a little knot of solid darkness against the flickering half-light of the station. She could see their diminishing arms waving. Then a cloud of steam spirited them from her view.

Luckily, Rachel was too young and too excited to take in the sombreness of events and the finality of the parting. The novelty of the sleeping-car delighted her. She liked the small pillows and the narrow beds and the tiny washbasin and dressing-table. It was like a doll's house. The proximity of Amelia, always willing to read a story, was so much better than going to sleep in her large London nursery.

The car attendant was a lusty tattooed lad from Glasgow who had already volunteered for the Navy and said he couldn't wait to go. He brought them hot milk and ham sandwiches and some iced animal biscuits. Rachel, clutching Stefan's doll, was asleep before they reached Watford Junction.

Amelia couldn't sleep. She was weighed down with misery and apprehension, filled with horror of the coming war. She remembered the long-drawn-out sadness of the last one. The casualty lists. The panic about the Zeppelin raids. And now there were the new weapons of the air, which she in her own small way had helped to forge. What would come to the world through them? The atrocities that Charles had seen in Spain? The razing of cities? Total destruction? Was this what their bright dreams, their youthful obsession had been for? Her's and James's? Was this their *Things to Come*?

James. Therein lay her deepest and most crushing misery. It was finished and over. James was a widower, free to come to her, but he hadn't come. Their love was a myth, a fantasy created by herself. An Ibsenesque life-lie. Well, Ibsen was right. Take away the life-lie and you took away the happiness. She had rarely felt more unhappy and bereft, more certain of doom. Every mile of the train's progress took her further and more finally away. And towards something. What? She had a powerful feeling of being swept along in a dark tide. She shivered, though the night was oppressively warm. When the train slowed down for a red signal, she could hear the rumble of thunder above the hiss of the steam and the screech of metal joints.

She was still awake when the train clanked out of Crewe. A few miles further on, she held back the window blind with her finger and peeped out at the now moonlit countryside of Cheshire. She saw the thin spire of a church, black as soot against the paler sky. It was so like the spire at Jerningham, she ached to be home. Some primitive instinct cried out to her not to leave. She climbed back into her bunk, wishing for the hundredth time that she had not acceded to Prudence's urgency.

She must have fallen into a doze shortly after, for suddenly she was in a nightmare. She was trying to find Rachel and James in a tunnel of what seemed everlasting darkness. There was noise but no light. Screaming human voices, but no faces. She felt a great howling wind that choked her breath back into her lungs. Then suddenly she saw a glimmer of light at the end of the tunnel. She woke. Someone was knocking on the door. The tea tray rattled. Early light rimmed the window blind.

'We're just an hour out of Glasgow.' The attendant handed Rachel a glass of orange juice. 'And it's a lovely day. Should be a nice trip on the briny!'

Rachel was thrilled at having breakfast in the dining-car. She kept on asking for more orange juice, and she ate six pieces of toast. Purposely, Amelia didn't hurry. There was plenty of time – the *Athenia* wasn't sailing till noon, and it was only nine when they arrived at Glasgow station.

She sat for ten more minutes, watching the crowds, trying to catch sight of the newspaper headlines. Everything looked much the same. Nobody was looking anxiously up into the sky for bombers. Eventually, Amelia went back to their sleeping-car, collected their luggage, tipped the attendant, and got hold of a porter. Twenty minutes later, they were approaching the docks and at the far end of the quay, she caught sight of the liner with a tall black funnel with a white band round it.

'That's the *Athenia*,' the taximan told her.

It took them over two hours to get on board. There were queues of people, mostly American and Canadian tourists anxious to get home while they could. Customs and Immigration were being particularly careful. All the luggage was thoroughly searched.

When finally they did get on board, they found their cabin on the boat deck filled with roses from Stefan. Red roses in a little plinth-lit alcove on the left. Golden yellow roses tinged with pink on her dressing-table – peace roses. There was also a mysterious large parcel on Rachel's bed in Stefan's favourite gold paper. Its contents of jigsaw puzzles and cut-outs and a little furry monkey on a string kept Rachel amused while Amelia supervised the unpacking. Momentarily she forgot the war. The sun on the water sent nets of bright light over the cabin. The smell of the roses was overpoweringly sweet. Even the sight of her smart new clothes hanging in the cupboard all gave her a feeling almost as if she were going on a honeymoon instead . . .

Instead of what? Her brain refused to contemplate the stark foreboding of her subconscious mind.

They had lunch in the dining-room. Again Rachel was too excited and too interested in her new surroundings really to miss her mother. The purser told Amelia that they would be 'crammed to the gills'. There were so many people wanting to get back to North America that they were putting six in four berth cabins and some of the male passengers would have to sleep on deck.

Just after noon the ship's hooter sounded out. Over the tannoy came 'All ashore who are going ashore'. From the dockside, the skirl of a single piper, and a crowd waving handkerchiefs and singing 'Will ye no come back again?'.

In glorious sunshine *Athenia* sailed down the Clyde. Boat drill took place an hour out, and Rachel regarded her grey kapok lifejacket as a new and elegant coat. At lunch, all the stewards had gone out of their way to be kind. By the time they were halfway down the Firth, Amelia felt quite at home.

In Belfast though, occasional lights from the shore pricked out the dusk.

'Shocking blackout!' said a woman on deck near Amelia.

'Ah well, we're not at war yet.' her husband said. 'Pray God we never will be!'

There was an early supper for the children, after which Amelia gave Rachel a bath and put her to bed. But she was too excited to go to sleep, and it took four of Stefan's stories read slowly by Amelia before her eyes closed. The bugle went. The stewardess came in to say she would look after the child while Madame went to dinner, but Amelia didn't feel hungry. She just lay on her bunk and then had a shower and went to bed. Halfway through the night, she heard the clanging of the ship's telegraph and the *whoosh* of the propellers.

We're off over the Atlantic, she thought, thankful and sad at the same time. Rachel will soon be safe in America.

When she and Rachel went up on deck after breakfast in their cabin next morning, the first thing they saw on the horizon were the golden liver birds on the Liver building in Liverpool. *Athenia* had been diverted to take on board yet more passengers for America. She sailed again that afternoon. Rachel insisted Amelia ate with her at early supper. More of Stefan's stories followed, and it was past ten when the child finally went to sleep.

Next day was Sunday and Amelia took Rachel to the church service on deck. There was no mention of war. The padre prayed for peace. As usual at sea, the last hymn they sang was 'Eternal Father, strong to save'.

Then just as they were getting up to go, the Captain came foward to say that the Prime Minister would be speaking to the nation in five minutes time and the radio had been tuned in ready in the passenger lounge.

Amelia managed to get a seat and took Rachel on her knee. The lounge was crowded. People were standing round the walls and in the doorways. The subdued conversation died to nothing as eleven fifteen approached. There was just silence broken by the crackling static of the wireless. Then suddenly, Neville Chamberlain's voice, tired and sad.

'I am speaking to you from the cabinet room at number 10 Downing Street. This morning the British Ambassador in Berlin handed the German government a final note, stating that unless the British government heard from them by eleven o'clock that they were prepared at once to withdraw their troops from Poland, a state of war would exist between us. I have to tell you now that no such undertaking has been received, and that consequently this country is at war with Germany . . . '

It was so like last time, Amelia was thinking. Substitute Poland for Belgium and here it was, all over again. Now the national anthem was being played. Everyone in the lounge leapt to their feet. And then – standing at the far side at the very back, his head visible above the rest – suddenly she saw James.

He had already seen her and was staring at Amelia with an unguarded expression of delight and disbelief. It was an expression that wiped away all her miseries and doubts. For whatever reason he hadn't come to her, it was not because he had ceased to love her. It has taken a war to bring us together. Amelia thought, as they began to push their way through the throng towards each other.

It was wicked to be so happy. The day the world braced itself for another war, for more grief, more uncertainty, more horror, more death, more pain, all she could think was that fate had another, kinder side, and that she had never been so happy in her life. The sharp shock of war declared had torn away the last vestiges of restraint, hurled James and her together and spun them dizzily back to the beginning again.

Miraculously, it was not the ship's deck on which she walked with James's arm round her waist, and Rachel holding his free hand, but the heather of the forest. It was not the white wheeling gulls they were watching, but the faithful swans on the lake. It was not the Scottish mountains they saw, slowly diminishing, but the hills of the island, after that brief dizzy rise into the air thirty-six years ago. Poised on the knife edge of fear, fate had given them another chance.

A chance in which every moment was to be savoured and stored away. After lunch, at which they sat like a little family of three, they watched the bow wave sparkling white against the inky blue of the Atlantic. The children's stewardess had led all the children away to play games in the nursery, followed by a special jelly and ice-cream tea. They were alone. The sun was warm on their faces, the air soft, the engines throbbing steadily, the bow wave glittering and hushing past like millions of ice particles.

Pleasurably, gloatingly, they pointed out to each other the events which had guided their footsteps inevitably towards *Athenia*, and each other. James, now head of the Department of Aircraft Procurement was on his way to Lockheed in California to see what he could buy. He was hoping American aircraft could be flown from Montreal by British pilots on the Dominions' flying training scheme. Amelia talked about Victoria and Henry, about her fondness for Prudence, and Prudence's request that she take Rachel to them. She reminded James laughingly that she had told him Prudence would be her daughter-in-law, at the Schneider race, all those years ago.

'Ah, but you expected her to marry Charles, didn't you?' James teased her.

Amelia's smile faded. She had not yet told him about Charles. Just a little longer, and she would tell him. She tried to rehearse how she would tell him as she put Rachel to bed, as she changed into her favourite sapphire velvet dress, her silver slippers, and kissing Rachel goodnight, hurried out to rejoin James on deck.

The bugle for dinner was just sounding and darkness had fallen. The southeast wind had freshened, and a waxing moon shone silver on the rising waves. Blacked out completely, not even a lighted cigarette showing, very slightly, *Athenia* rolled.

Leaning on the rail, the moonlight casting their joined shadows on the heaving water, James pointed to the curve of the horizon ahead. Where dense black ocean met the night sky was the thinnest rim of sunset red. The promise of a fine day, James said, a smooth crossing. Life seemed beguilingly beautiful and serene. She had emerged from the tunnel of her nightmare. Behind them, the other passengers streamed in to dinner, chattering and laughing, wearing their pretty dresses and their evening suits. Amelia and James talked about their families.

'I remember Marianne so well,' Amelia said softly. The Marianne as a little girl, not the one outside the forge. But even her hostility then no longer mattered, and as if James read her thoughts, he said softly, 'I couldn't get in touch with you after Marie died.' He paused, 'I felt I had been . . . less than I should have been to her. I needed time to come to terms with myself.'

Amelia put his hand on her arm and squeezed it gently. After a moment she asked, 'And Pierre?'

'Now he's finished school he's come over to join the RAF. Few people in France had any illusions on what Hitler was going to do.'

'Arthur once had,' Amelia said. 'But that was years ago. He's seen the light now. As for Charles . . . '

'I read about Charles in Spain.' Always when he spoke of Charles, James's voice took on a tone of exasperated affection. 'Charles and Ajax. The Red Baronet got himself enough publicity.'

'He's come back totally against war.'

'Haven't we all?'

Amelia nodded and went on, 'Charles never does anything by halves. Along with our Spitfire contracts, he's got Cummings working on a civil version of Ajax for when it's all over.'

James smiled indulgently, 'He's very like you, Amelia.'

She paused for several dizzy heartbeats and then said clearly, 'He's also very like you, James.'

Now at last it was said. She looked away and stared at the curve of the bow wave, glowing phosphorescent now as darkness deepened. She waited for the storm to break over her. There was nothing but silence from James. She turned and stared at his tense profile, at the sensitive mouth, now set and firm and unreadable, at the strong jaw, and the straight nose, the eyes narrowed and shadowy in the moonlight. What was he thinking, feeling? What reproaches would he heap on her when he at last spoke?

But when he did, it was an agonised murmur of self-reproach. 'I should have known. Why didn't I guess?' And then to her, 'I'm very proud.' He put his arms round her and kissed her lips. After a moment, he asked quietly, 'Have you told him?'

She shook her head. 'No.'

'Then don't tell him till we can both tell him together.'

Unable to speak, she nodded her head. Behind them as if from another world, the bugle for the second sitting of dinner sounded. As the notes died away, James dipped into the inside pocket of his jacket, and brought out something which he held out to her on the open palm of his hand. It was the gold and hair ring which had belonged to her own mother and which James's mother had bequeathed to her.

'We can ask the captain to marry us, or we can wait till we land in America.' And teasingly with a trace of his old wry smile, 'I feel we should be married before we break the news to Charles.'

'I feel married to you already.' She held up her left hand. 'Put it on now. I want it now.'

He slid it on to her third finger and whispered softly, 'Till death us do part.'

'Longer than that,' she said. 'For ever and ever.'

He bent to kiss her. For a moment it seemed as if the kiss had brought about the end of the world. There was an explosion like the crack of doom. The night sky was alight as the torpedo struck. With a terrible screeching sound *Athenia* listed. The deck tilted. Everywhere there was darkness and people screaming as in her nightmare.

James's hand was in hers as they struggled to the cabin. In and out of great clouds of steam, people pushing, screaming that the lifeboats would be overcrowded, so many passengers. Another explosion sounded. They had Rachel out of bed. James's hands were helping dress her in warm clothing. Someone was banging on the cabin door. Shouting, 'Hurry! All passengers on deck.' James's hand held hers again, pulling her along the steep deck with Rachel on his shoulders. An officer with a megaphone was shouting, 'Women and children only!' And her own unrecognisable voice shrieking, 'No!'

James was giving Rachel to the seamen organising the starboard lifeboat. He was disentangling his hand from Amelia's.

'No,' she shrieked. 'I'm not going to leave you! I won't go!'

But his hand was gone and strangers' hands pushed her urgently after Rachel – away from the sinking deck and into the lifeboat.

BOOK FOUR

Shadows of the Evening
1939–45

ONE

The memorial service for Air Commodore March took place at Jerningham Church on 25 September, three weeks after the *Athenia* was sunk and when all hope of his survival and that of 112 other victims had been abandoned.

A Norwegian tanker bound for Boston had picked up Amelia and Rachel and the others in their lifeboat, but not before they had seen the U-boat suddenly surface. Then with its forward gun it sent shell after shell into the unarmed liner. She was already sinking, bows deep into the Atlantic. Now she began to slip lower. The bridge was awash. Then only that single funnel and the two masts showed above the waves. Just before dawn, they too disappeared and all that remained were the gulls screaming over spreading grey oil.

Safe in New York, Amelia prayed for news. Most of the survivors had been landed in Ireland – James surely would be amongst them. Victoria and her husband met them at the quayside. But they had no news. And despite the warmth and genuine affection of their reception, Amelia scarcely saw Rachel settled into Victoria's lovely house overlooking the Potomac river, before she was making plans to return.

'I *must* go home, Victoria!' There was no news anywhere of James. The company could tell her nothing. The Embassy could tell her nothing. 'Rachel has so obviously taken to you,' she pointed out to Victoria. 'She doesn't need me. It's you she wants to tuck her in at night. And I must go home. Now more than ever. There are things to be done that only I can do.'

'I would have thought one torpedoeing was enough without risking another,' Victoria had sighed.

As usual, Amelia was a jump ahead. She had no intention of spending another week as sea. One torpedoeing was indeed enough. Hadn't Victoria heard of the Imperial Airways flying-boat flights to Foynes and Hythe? Amelia herself had been at the inauguration. Jerningham had a contract for their spares. She could pull a few strings. She was so determined that Victoria gave up trying to persuade her to stay, though she refused to help her arrange what seemed an extremely dangerous flight, for the flying-boat was to be refuelled in mid-air over the Atlantic.

Not that danger ever deterred your mother, Victoria wrote in a long letter to Charles. *Indeed she will, God willing, probably arrive home in the* Caribou *before this letter. You will find her changed, shocked, aged in fact by the* Athenia *disaster.*

It was no less than the truth. When Charles picked her up at the jetty after her epic flight, he hardly recognised her thin figure stepping off the gang-plank.

'Darling Mama!' He threw his arms round her. 'I always seem to be meeting you off one adventure or another! But what have they done to you? You look half-starved!'

She looked around sadly at the grey shapes of warships at anchor in the Solent. A shoal of silver barrage balloons flew high over Southampton. There was barbed wire along the banks, and corrugated Anderson shelters in the gardens. More concrete blockhouses. The customs officers all carried gas-masks in cardboard boxes and the customs hall was full of posters warning against careless talk.

'Didn't they give you anything to eat on the flight?'

Her smile remained the same. But her cheeks were hollow, her eyes shadowed with grief.

'They fed me like a fighting cock,' she said. 'A six course meal in the restaurant. And they gave me one of the bunks to sleep on.'

'Well, you've certainly made family history,' he laughed, flinging her small weekend bag, the only luggage she had, into the boot of the car. 'The first of us to fly the Atlantic.'

'Only as a passenger.'

'And what was it like? The trip itself?'

'Exciting. Bumpy at times. But wonderful really.'

'Was it cold?'

'A bit. There was ice, too. We climbed to get out of it. And we heard lumps of it clanging against the fuselage.'

Charles pulled a face, as he started up the car engine. 'Not very nice.'

'The rest was fine. This morning was beautiful. We flew into the dawn. And last night we saw the Northern Lights.'

'You saw no German aircraft, I hope?'

She shook her head. 'No, thank God. I'd have felt like tearing them down with my bare hands.'

'It was sad about Air Commodore March.'

In a low voice, she said, 'He was still on the ship when they fired the shells into her.'

'So we heard.'

'He's presumed killed.'

'Yes.'

Her eyes filled with tears. Charles took his left hand off the wheel and covered her two hands folded in her lap. For the first time he noticed she was wearing on her wedding finger a little Victorian ring which he hadn't seen before.

'It must have been awful, Mama. The *Athenia*. I can understand how you feel. But,' he patted her hand comfortingly, 'it's all over now.'

'Yes, it's all over now,' she repeated in a voice of such utter desolation that he stared at her with concern. For several miles she kept silent, staring out at the concrete teeth of tank traps that now edged the wintry lanes. Then suddenly she said, 'But I still have you.'

He smiled reassuringly. 'Of course.'

'And you're going to stay at the factory?'

'I . . .' But it was no time to try to convey to his mother the turmoil and contradictions of his feelings. 'Tell me about *Caribou*,' he asked her. 'What was the take-off like? Heavy? Did you find out the pay load? Do you really think they'll make a go of an Atlantic service like that when the war's over?'

By the time they reached Haybury, Amelia seemed to have recovered some of her old vigour. Sarah was hovering in the hall to greet her, Tears streamed down her face. In the days that followed, she glued herself to Amelia like an anxious shadow.

Charles worried that news of the coming memorial service for Air Commodore March would distress his mother. But no. Amelia said that if old Mr March had not already begun the arrangements, she herself would have done. The village could do no less.

She insisted that the whole Haybury household and family attend. Not that any of them were reluctant. Prudence and Arthur were mindful of their debt to the Air Commodore. Without his assistance, who knew what might have happened to Rachel? Prudence had in fact written at length to Marianne, expressing their gratitude and sorrow. She had been a little hurt to receive only a formal printed reply in return.

'The poor girl would be grief stricken,' Amelia said to Prudence as they all drove together to the service in Charles's Riley. 'Her loss is so overwhelming.'

The memorial service was rather overwhelming too, Charles thought, driving slowly through the village as a stream of black clad men and women made their way to the church. The bell was tolling out its solemn funeral peal. All the shops were closed, the cottage windows shuttered. Someone had nailed a wreath to the forge door and the forge cottage was hung with black crêpe that looked as if it had come out of an old attic trunk. There were fresh wreaths, too, on the Great War cenotaph, the Union Jack hung at half-mast on the church flagpole. Tere was a guard of honour of airmen with new-looking uniforms and frighteningly young faces. And there were white waxy lilies on the purple-draped alter.

But there was no coffin, thank God, no gaping grave. Just an aching pervasive grief that seeped into one's bones like the damp September air.

'We thought, if you didn't mind, M'lady, the first row centre should be reserved for the bereaved family,' the verger whispered, as Charles with Amelia on his arm advanced up the flagstones of the aisle. 'They will be here presently.'

The second row centre was already filled with men in RAF uniform. Senior men with ribbons, their gold-acorned caps laid on the seat beside them. And behind them were the villagers. The church was full. But trained through generations of knowing their inequality in the sight of God's church, the villagers had filled the rear pews and left the first two centre and sides empty for the gentry.

The verger ushered Amelia and the Hayburys into the first side row beneath the lectern. Almost immediately the bereaved family arrived. Old Mr March, still upright and dauntless, was escorted on either side by his grandchildren. Both were in uniform. Pierre had a white band round the cap he carried, so he was trainee aircrew. The daughter wore the ill-fitting blue-grey of the WAAF. The peaked cap shadowed her face. The jacket flopped unbecomingly over her rather narrow shoulders. Her heavy black-laced shoes echoed ringingly down the aisle. Her thin legs were encased in black grey lisle stockings. Her thin sculpted face was blotchy with grief. As they passed within touching distance, she seemed suddenly aware of Charles's gaze. Her large blue eyes met his.

337

And suddenly, at this time of all times and in this place of all places, he was suddenly acutely and overwhelmingly aware of her. And never having had the slightest literary inclination, never to his knowledge ever having enjoyed a poem, certainly never having read one for pure pleasure, a single line leapt into Charles's mind, and seemed to brand itself on his brain . . . 'He never loved who loved not at first sight'.

Amelia was too absorbed in her grief to notice Charles's interest in Marianne March. She stood for the hymns and knelt for the prayers, dry-eyed and composed but an empty shell. The only life that still warmed her sprang from the ring. She kept twisting it on her finger as if it were a magic talisman, a lifeline. For I was his wife, she told herself. We were joined in the sight of whatever God there may be.

'Why could such a fine man not have been saved?' For a moment it was as if Amelia had shouted her indignant question to the Almighty aloud. But no, it was the voice of the Reverend Bingham, ringingly and rhetorically not only asking the question but answering it, explaining to his flock the inexplicable ways of God. It was undoubtedly so that the Air Commodore's life should be an example of self-sacrifice, so that others might follow in his footsteps, when self-sacrifice would be needed in this country as never before.

'*He* was needed,' Amelia whispered to herself. 'Damn the self-sacrifice!' But no one heard her.

The Rector waxed in earnest eloquence on how James had helped to save the women and children aboard the unarmed *Athenia*, after the cowardly and inhuman U-boat attack. A hero of the last war, a legend in the village, a source of pride to all who knew him, he had remained a hero to the end. Thanks be to God!

It was almost over. The congregation was rising for the last hymn . . . 'Abide with me'. Amelia sang with fervour and a strange yearning. Her voice roe sweet and clear above the rest, Prudence noticed, as if trying to pierce the hymn's fast falling eventide.

'Shine through the gloom and point me to the skies . . .'

'Poor Mother-in-law,' Prudence afterwards remarked to Arthur, they had unwittingly asked more of her than they ought to have done. The experience had aged her beyond belief.

The service ended with the national anthem. The hatless RAF officers stood rigidly to attention, Marianne at the salute. The last chords died away. They all began moving out into the overcast afternoon, slowly following Mr March and his grandchildren. Amelia and Charles with Prudence and Arthur after them, walked behind the bereaved family at a discreet distance.

The Rector waited in the porch to clasp each mourner's hand. 'I hope you did not mind, dear Lady Haybury,' he whispered in her ear.

'Mind?'

'That you were not in your accustomed family pew. This time, we felt . . .'

'I'm sure it was as the Air Commodore would have wished,' Amelia said, wondering what James would have thought of it all, wanting to rush back and beg even of the Reverend Bingham some reassurance that all this was not a charade, that something of James remained, however transmuted.

There was Charles, of course. She rested her hand on his arm as the heavy

338

quiet of the churchyard was pierced by the RAF trumpeter sounding the Last Post. Her fingers dug into his arm. And following the last dwindling note, the Reveille.

'Heaven's morning breaks and earth's vain shadows flee' – if only she could believe what they had sung in the hymn!

Then she saw Marianne cover her face with her free hand, her shoulders shake. She is the only one who grieves for James as deeply as I do, Amelia thought. No man, even his father, can grieve as much as we do. It was almost as if Mariane had become the daughter Amelia had never had. She felt suffused with love and compassion for her. Impulsively, Amelia hurried forward and put her arm round the girl's shoulders.

'Dear Marianne,' she whispered, 'I know how you feel. But please don't grieve. Your father . . .'

The girl whipped round and stared into Amelia's face, at first with disbelief and then with anger. With a quick jerk, she freed herself from Amelia's comforting arm, and squared her shoulders. 'Thank you, Lady Haybury,' her eyes blazed, 'but I don't need your sympathy.'

Amelia was suddenly aware that Charles had come up, that his hand rested on her arm. Had she not known better, she would have thought that it rested there restrainingly, as if telling her not to say anything she might be sorry for. 'Marianne,' Charles said in a gentle and unfamiliar tone.

Marianne rounded fiercely on him. 'Nor do I want your sympathy either, Sir Charles,' she snapped bitterly. 'You should never have come. You —'

She broke off suddenly, pushed her way past them and hurried towards the lych gate.

'Well,' Amelia drew in a long sighing breath, and turned towards Charles. But he had left her side and was striding after Marianne.

Charles caught Marianne up just outside the churchyard. She was getting into a small red MG. The hood was rolled back. He rested one foot on the running-board, and said, 'Listen, Marianne, please.'

'Go away,' she pulled the driver's door shut behind her, and shoved the key into the ignition. 'I don't want to talk to you. Leave me alone.' She switched on and revved the engine. 'Take your foot off the running-board! I warn you! I'm going! I'll move off with you on it if you don't!'

In answer, and with careful timing, he swung his legs over the top of the passenger door and slid into the passenger seat as she hurtled off.

'Damn you!'

She made as if to stand on the brake. But he put his hand on her arm. 'Please don't, Marianne. Just listen to me. I want to talk to you. You're upset. Just give me a chance.'

'Why?' She flashed a sideways angry look at him. 'Why should I give you a chance? And anyway, a chance for what?'

'To get to know you.'

'I don't want to know you.'

'How d'you know that?'

'I know your family. Your reputation.'

'My reputation for what?'

'Just your reputation.'

339

He laughed, 'And that's enough?'

'More than enough.' She gave a faint smile. The angry mouth softened. Even under the awful WAAF hat, she was suddenly beautiful.

'Where are we going?' he asked, as the hedgerows thick with blackberries and rosehips whipped by less fiercely.

'I'm going home. To Cornford House. Our housekeeper has got a buffet ready.' Then she added hastily, 'For those mourners who have come a distance.'

'Don't worry, I wasn't inviting myself.'

'I didn't mean that. Not altogether. Father used to laugh at that sort of thing. The funeral spread,' she laughed hollowly herself. 'And I didn't want your family,' she said with an abrupt return to her anger. 'I didn't want them at all.'

'You mean my mother?'

'Yes. Mostly your mother.'

'Why? And why were you rude to her? She only meant to be kind.'

'She couldn't be kind.'

'Rubbish! She's nearly always kind. You don't know what you're talking about. You're being childish and rude.'

'If that's your attitude, you can get out.' She had taken her foot off the accelerator for the turning into the drive of Cornford House. Now she pressed the brake.

'I'm not getting out till you promise me one thing.'

'What? Access to my father's papers so that your factory can steal anything that's worth stealing?'

'Hardly. Is that what you think my mother did?'

'According to *my* mother, yes.'

'Then you couldn't be more wrong there either.'

She turned the car slowly into the drive, and then asked, 'So what is it you want me to promise?'

'To see me again.'

She shot him a strange look in which anger, bewilderment and helplessness mingled. 'Why should I see you again?'

He leaned towards her. 'Because you want to.'

'I do *not*. You're the last person I'd want to see again.'

'Liar!'

Her mouth tightened. 'I'm not in the habit of lying,' she said. 'I've only seen you twice and that's enough.'

He laughed. 'So you do remember!'

'Of course. It was years ago. But I remember.'

'You were a nice little girl then.'

'I've changed.'

'So I would hope.'

She darted him a look more teasing than hostile. 'So have you. You've changed.'

'For the better?' he suggested. 'You liked me then after all. You liked me very much.'

She neither agreed nor disagreed. She brought the car to a skilful halt outside the front door.

'I won't ask you in,' she said 'Because . . .'

'That's all right. Just tell me where to find you and when I can see you, then I'll go. Otherwise I'll hang round till the others arrive.'

She drew in a deep breath, pulled the key out of the ignition and dropped it in her pocket. 'I'm at the Air Ministry at the moment,' she said. 'Extension 375.'

'May I take you out to dinner?'

'Perhaps.'

'Don't sound so enthusiastic.' He opened the car door and got out.

He walked beside her to the front door of Cornford House and opened it for her. 'And where shall you be, Sir Charles?' she asked. 'Shall you be staying at the factory? In a civilian capacity? Still working on Ajax?'

'That's right, Marianne. I shall stay at the factory. Working on the peacetime version.'

But already he knew that that was untrue. Past history. As he walked down the drive of Cornford House, past the faint glimmer of the distant lake, he knew he couldn't stay at home building for a peace that might never come. War was here. Like it or not, he was involved. Marianne was involved. The wings of the dove were no match for the excitement and passion that stirred his blood as never before.

'I simply can't believe it!' Amelia cried to Charles when he told her of his intentions. 'I refuse to believe it! That your conversion to peace should be so shallow!'

The trouble was that she did believe it. Not only did she believe it. She had foreseen it. War was in Charles's blood. His conversion to peace had been no doubt for other and more devious reasons than a hate for war.

'Hating war, indeed!' She warmed to her indignation as her own cool logic told her it was inevitable. She was, as Sarah would have said, spitting against the wind. 'Designing a civil airliner! Building for the future!'

'But don't you see, Mama, if we lose the war, there'll be no future. Spain was a foretaste.'

'Spain was supposed to be your catharsis.'

'So it was! Build for peace, yes. I thought peace was possible. So did millions of other people.'

'I'm not interested in other people.'

'Remember Oxford? The motion not to fight for King or country? Now they're falling over themselves to volunteer.'

'They were children. You're old enough to know better.'

'I'm old enough to fight better.'

'Perhaps.'

'Certainly to train them better.'

Amelia snorted scornfully.

'And I'll be fighting the same bloody set-up I was fighting in Spain. Nazis. Fascists.'

'And a lot of good that did!'

'Because we didn't stop them *then*. This time we must!'

'The war to end wars!' Amelia exclaimed derisively.

He shrugged. 'I don't know about that, Mama,' he said soberly.

'Well I *do*! It's always the same. It's always the war to end wars.'

'I thought since the *Athenia* . . . you felt . . . well, bitter.'

'I feel more than bitter,' she said promptly. 'I feel hatred. If the Germans invaded, I'd kill them if I could. But I know that my feelings are wicked, and that war is wicked. And I still don't want . . .'

Her lips trembled. She was about to say 'you to join up', but she bit back the words, and snapped dismissingly as if she were tired of the subject, 'Oh, do what you want! What you feel you must! Don't let's argue! If it's any consolation to you, I knew you'd go.'

He cupped her face in his hands and kissed her forehead. 'Thanks, Mama.'

'Charles,' she asked as if on sudden impulse, 'this joining up . . . it isn't anything to do with the March girl is it? Marianne?'

He caught his breath. He could not have answered that question truthfully even to himself. How much Marianne had to do with his decision, he really didn't know. How many people, come to that, did know the real reasons that tipped the balance into this or that? Besides, it seemed important to his mother that Marianne should not have influenced him, and his mother had had enough to put up with today without Marianne.

So he let out his breath in a laugh of almost unfeigned amusement. 'Good Lord, Mama, whatever gave you that idea?'

'You ran after her at the service.'

'I felt sorry for her.'

'Yes,' Amelia said, momentarily deflected, 'so did I. Very sorry.' She stood for a moment, her eyes lowered, her expression maternal and compassionate. Then she looked up at him and remarked for the first time since the service, 'But you spent a long time with her.'

'Is this a cross-examination?' he asked her teasingly.

'Not really, I'm just remarking that you did.'

'No, Mama, I did not. I accompanied her to Cornford House in her car. There she gave me the order of the boot. And from there, I thumbed a lift back to Haybury. Is my alibi all right?'

'I thought,' Amelia said slowly, 'that she looked very touching in her uniform.'

'Did you, Mama?' Charles shrugged carelessly, and added convincingly, 'Personally, I don't like women in uniform.'

Marianne was wearing a new officer's uniform when Charles met her in London on a cold October evening, three weeks later. The sun had set behind long charcoal grey clouds. But there was still a diffused gloaming. The windows of the buildings on either side down Kingsway were scrupulously blacked out. Cars with baffled headlamps patterned the road with thin pencils of light. It was homegoing time. The buses were crowded, the pavements full.

'I hardly recognised you,' Charles said, a minute after Marianne emerged from the sandbagged entrance to Adastral House.

That wasn't true. He would have recognised her thin figure, her graceful walk, the set of her head, anywhere. He had watched from the shadows for a moment as she paused before stepping on to the pavement. He had savoured the moment, feeling again that sense of inevitability, of homecoming, as if all his life he had subconsciously been waiting for her to emerge through time towards him.

'I recognised you,' she said. She drew a deep breath as if she was about to add something, then changed her mind. She seemed quite pleased to see him, less hostile. Perhaps her loneliness had caught up with her, and she was glad of even his familiar face.

On the telephone when they made the arrangements Charles had suggested he take her to Quaglino's for dinner, where there was a floor show and they could dance afterwards. 'And how did you get such rapid promotion?' Charles asked her teasingly, when they had at last got a taxi and were crawling down the Strand. 'A commission already?'

She smiled frugally in return and replied, 'By merit, of course.'

He felt a twinge of irrational and painful jealousy. 'No doubt the officer who recognised your merit was a man?'

'Quite wrong! A woman. A stout old lady with a wheezy chest who is the Squadron Officer in charge of personnel. She told me I was officer material.' Her smile deepened. 'She told everyone who sounded their aitches in the right place exactly the same.'

Charles smiled. 'The French aren't known for that virtue.'

'I must have been very British that day. Anyway, they gave us a week's course of lectures. Mostly on hygiene. *Et voilà*. The old boy network, my father would have said. He hated it.'

As they were getting out of the taxi at Quaglino's a sudden thought struck Charles. 'Does that mean you'll be posted somewhere?'

'Probably.'

'Where to?'

She shrugged. 'Wherever they're prepared to take WAAFs instead of men. I've asked for Fighter Command. Because of Pierre. He's being trained for fighters. It'd be nice to get on the same station.'

He frowned. 'It might be anywhere in the country.'

He brooded over that unwelcome thought, as they hitched themselves on to stools in front of the bar and he asked what she would drink. He recommended the barman's gin fizz.

'You've been before?'

'In the bad old days, quite often. Long before your time.'

She smiled.

He sat for a while, stirring his drink and saying nothing. 'May I come and see you, if you're posted?'

'If you want to.'

'You know I want to.' He touched her hand. 'Don't frown. Are you still feeling anti-me?'

She seemed to weigh her reply. 'Anti and pro.' She gave her quick frugal smile.

'You are a most undissembling person,' he said suddenly.

She stared at him over the rim of her glass.

'Why are you anti-me, Marianne? Because your mother disliked mine?'

'That's one reason.' She took a gulp of her gin fizz.

'And the other?'

'I'm afraid.'

'Afraid of what?'

'Afraid of you.'

There seemed no immediate reply he could give to that.

343

'You are a womaniser,' she said quite tenderly but seriously in explanation.

'Not any more.' He caught hold of her hand. He blurted out there and then without intending to, like some callow youth, 'There's only you now, Marianne.'

She put the tip of her finger over his lips and shook her head. 'You say that, but —'

'I say that and I mean it.'

'But you have had so many affaires, you must have said that very often. To *many* women. And you have been married. I read about that in the papers. And soon I will go away, and you will meet someone else.'

'Soon I will go away too,' he said, stung into sudden anger. 'I've joined up. I expect my papers any day.'

Her eyes widened and she asked gravely, 'Why do you tell me like that?' Her cheeks flushed. 'Why are you so angry?'

He shrugged his shoulders. 'Because I can't get through to you.'

It was only hours and several stiff drinks later, when they were foxtrotting around the crowded little dance floor that he could even begin to try to explain.

'I'm sorry,' he said between bursts from the saxophone, 'for so many damned things.'

'About me?'

'About us.'

She held herself a little away from him and looked up into his eyes. 'Why?'

It was so difficult to put what he wanted to say into words. His usual easy manner dried up. This was not really the time or place. The band was excelling itself. They were beating out a ghastly tune called 'We'll hang out our washing on the Siegfried Line' – patriotic but inappropriate. Spotlights fingered the sweating faces of the dancers, most of them uniformed. They briefly lit Marianne's lifted eyes, her parted lips.

'I feel as if I've just found you,' he said huskily. 'And I don't want you sent off to one end of the country and me to the other.'

She said nothing. 'I feel there is a bond between us,' he said. 'Don't you feel that?'

He hadn't expected her to agree. But to his surprise she nodded. She stayed in his arms when the music stopped with a roll of drums. Then as they walked back to their table, she whispered, 'That is the reason I am afraid.'

TWO

'I am afraid for Charles,' Amelia told Cummings, three weeks later as they drafted an advertisement for more jig and tool makers. The orders for spares were streaming in, the factory almost bursting at the seams. 'He will no doubt find the RAF very different from the RFC.'

Charles's call-up papers had come through that morning. He was to report to the Receiving Wing at Babbacombe in Devon on 5 December 1939. He had expected, after all his experience, to go straight on to Spitfires, and he had cursed when he read them. 'Good God, they're sending me right through the mill as though I'd never left the ground!'

'He doesn't take kindly to being sent where he doesn't want to go,' Ronald said from the other side of the desk. 'But then who does?'

He smiled at her gently as he had done for so many years. Sometimes she wondered what went on behind those eyes, how he *really* saw her these days. The factory was full of pretty girls with bright red lips and tight skirts. They were so short of hands that they sent a bus to the surrounding countryside to pick them up. They had a canteen and a medical hut run by a tall attractive nurse, and the canteen supervisor, a woman of about forty, plainly adored Ronald.

'But where does he want to go? That's what I ask myself.'

'If I know Charles,' Ronald smiled, 'into the thick of it.'

'Not that there's much thick to be in at the moment,' Amelia said, and added, 'Thank God.'

'Amen to that!' Cummings sighed. 'Though I doubt Charles would agree.'

'He's such a strange mixture! He wants to be in it and he doesn't. He wants the fun, but he doesn't want the discipline.'

'And who's to blame him?'

'I blame him,' Amelia replied with a sharpness she no longer felt. Her talk to Ronald Cummings was no more than a safety valve, a letting off of emotional steam. She had been worried about Charles, but she had come to terms with his plans. She had accepted that Charles should join up, bowed her head to the inevitable, been rather proud that he might well be setting course for a distinguished RAF career. Following in his father's footsteps, keeping James's memory alive. Though she didn't need Charles to do that. She had been thankful, too, that the posting was for some distance away. Not that she any more feared his interest in Marianne. That had died like his interest in so many girls, if indeed it had existed at all. Only three days ago, she had seen him in laughing conversation with the first aid nurse, heard him say, as he left her, 'I'll buy you a drink on that.'

No, his interest in Marianne had been no more than a figment of her own guilty imagination. But Amelia had spent several sleepless nights torturing herself with the grim choice that would lie before her if Charles did fall seriously in love with Marianne. Could she ever bring herself to tell him, tell them both, come to that? Bring the world so completely down about Charles's ears? Shatter that austerely beautiful face of Marianne's into misery, contempt, rejection of her father as well as of herself? But worst of all to discredit James's memor, to tarnish his glowing reputation. And then to go through all the legal tangles which Charles and Marianne would insist upon of declaring Charles a bastard and ensuring that the title went to Arthur. Yet rather than let them marry, she supposed she would have to do exactly that.

The thought had been so frightening to her that all through November she found herself watching Charles like a hawk, almost spying on him, terrified that she would discover he had been in contact with Marianne. Several times she had brought up the subject of Charles to Cummings. But that was no new thing. In many ways Cummings was like a second father to Charles. And if Cummings ever tired of the subject he gave no sign.

'I often think Charles must be lonely in his flat,' Amelia had said probingly to Cummings on several occasions. 'It's all books, and plans and aeroplanes. He has so few visitors.'

'Apart from you and me,' Cummings replied, 'none. But then he works so hard.'

'Of course occasionally he goes up to London, doesn't he?'

'Mostly business. I think he really wants to get as much work in on Ajax as he can before his call-up, Amelia!'

Her anxieties had been assuaged. And now the call-up had come.

'When does he go?' Cummings asked.

'A week tomorrow.'

But in fact Charles left two days early. 'I've someone to see in London before I disappear into the Far West,' he told his mother that night at dinner. In a sudden access of affection and relief, she had asked Ronald to join them. It was a cosy family meal of three.

'Devon isn't very far from here, darling.'

'Nevertheless before I disappear into the Wild and Woolly.'

'Who darling? Who is it you have to see?'

'Now that's a very personal question,' Charles winked at Ronald. 'You are getting to be a very nosy old lady, Mama.'

'I object to that,' Cummings smiled. 'Your mother will never be old.'

'You note, Mama, that he didn't defend you on the nosy score.'

They all laughed, and still laughing, Charles added, 'But as you are obviously dying of curiosity, Mama, I'll tell you. Ronald asked me to see a chap from de Havilland about some new oil filters they've dreamed up. He lives just outside London.'

Ronald nodded. 'That's true.'

It was indeed the truth. But not the whole truth. Why he should keep Marianne from his mother, Charles was never sure. Instinct really. A sense that she both liked and disliked the girl. The sins of the mother presumably. The Comtesse had never liked his mother, nor she her. On the other hand, he loved Marianne. Of that he was sure. For his last night of civilian freedom he

346

booked himself into a hotel in Bloomsbury. Before he left Jerningham, he telephoned Marianne. He told her he was going into the RAF and arranged to meet her there. It was a small hotel, discreet and comfortable enough. They had dined there together the week before. This time she brought a small overnight bag with her.

As they sat sipping gin fizzes at a mahogany table in the lounge, that overnight bag sat on the floor between them like an unexploded bomb. Finally Charles took Marianne's hand in both of his and asked softly, 'Are you meaning to stay, Marianne?'

'If you want me to.'

'I want you to and I want you more than anything else in the world.'

'I'm off duty tomorrow. I don't have to get back,' she said not looking at him. 'You see, I'm posted too. It seems . . . '

She wanted to say that it seemed whatever fate had their destinies in charge was pulling them apart. But it was altogether too difficult and too emotional to enunciate, though she felt that destiny with profound certainty.

'Where are you posted to, Marianne?'

'Eleven group. Biggin Hill, where Pierre is.'

'Kent,' he said thoughtfully. 'About twelve miles south of London. It could be worse. Only a couple of hundred miles from Babbacombe.' He smiled wryly, 'And it'll make me all the keener to get on fighters.'

'Don't be. Please! Pierre is enough. I'd be so afraid for you.'

Charles said nothing for a moment. Then he stood up. 'I'll see if I can book you a room.'

She shot him a quick half-apprehensive, half-tender look and then nodded. He walked over to the glassed-in reception, and moments later returned, and dropped a key in her lap. 'Room 304.'

'Is it on the same floor as yours?'

He shook his head and sat down in the chair opposite her. Leaning forward, once again he took both her hands. 'We'll go out somewhere tomorrow, Marianne. We'll drive into the country. Have lunch at a pub. But,' he drew her hands closer to him and went on softly, 'but tonight would be the first time, wouldn't it? For you?'

'Yes,' she breathed, after a long pause.

'But it wouldn't be for me, Marianne. And somehow when it does happen with us, I want it to be different, I want you to be certain. Us both to be certain.'

'Don't you love me enough?'

'It's because I love you too much. Too much for my own good.'

He suddenly realised that they were the truest and the saddest words he had ever spoken.

347

THREE

Aircraftman Second Class Haybury, C, marched up and down the esplanade at Babbacombe, saluted, listened to Air Force law in a pierrots' pavilion, and never once glimpsed an aeroplane.

After four weeks of this at two shillings a day pay, he went to Initial Training Wing at the Palace Hotel at Paignton for another two months, listened to lectures in ex-cinemas and flashed rude messages in Morse with Aldis lamps across the promenade. Then he went up to Prestwick Elementary Flying Training School where they tried to keep him as an instructor on Tiger Moths for the rest of the war.

'No,' he said firmly. 'I've opted for fighters.'

With an *Exceptional* assessment he was posted to Drem near Edinburgh to do his Service flying on yellow painted American Harvards.

The Phony War proceeded as undramatically as Charles's RAF career. Bomber Command still dropped leaflets; Coastal Command and the Navy sank precious few U-boats.

In early spring, Arthur wrote, *I have decided I must do something more direct about the war. So naturally I have opted for the Senior Service . . .*

Charles wrote back, *God help the Navy! Remember, it won't be anything like sailing* Shalom.

On 9 April 1940, the Phony War ended abruptly. German tanks crossed the Danish frontier. German warships and troops poured into Oslo, Kristiansand, Stavanger and Narvik. A month later, 89 German divisions invaded Holland and Belgium. The Luftwaffe obliterated Rotterdam. The Battle of France began – and a fortnight later was virtually over.

In the historic railway carriage at Compiègne where the Germans had signed the surrender terms 22 years before, the French surrendered to the Nazis. The entire British Expeditionary Force was trapped between Rundstedt's ten panzer divisions and the sea. Since everything was clearly lost, only a miracle could save Britain now.

'Save the British Army,' the Admiralty flashed out. 'Operation Dynamo to commence.'

Stefan Lehmann was at Shotfield preparing for another group of Jewish refugees when the telephone rang. Within the hour he was driving down to *Shalom's* berth at Hamble. And within two hours, he was nosing his ship out down the Hamble river into the slight chop of Southampton Water. He was in good company. Already a flotilla of little boats were making their way seaward. The RAF tenders from Calshot, were well ahead. There were ferries and fishing boats, lifeboats and tugs. A silent purposeful armada. Somewhere over there, no doubt, Amelia would be fuming that Jerningham Aviation had disposed of its tender. He smiled to himself with sad resignation as he guided *Shalom* into the free channel, and catching the stronger east wind, she bucked like the fragile racy little craft she was. He knew Amelia needed him; more than Prudence did at the moment. And none of the considerable riches and success that had come his way was as precious to Stefan Lehmann as the privilege of being needed. If death came today, and he was mindful that well it might, he had no great fear of it. He feared the agonies, the gross degradations, the atrocities his compatriots had undergone. If they allowed him to snatch one man only from such in return for his own life he would make the exchange gladly. Were it not for Amelia, he would be sailing with eagerness to participate, to avenge his race, almost with lightness of spirit, young again.

As it was, he watched the flash of exploding bombs on the starboard horizon with narrowed eyes, and a cool calculating appraisal of his chance of survival. Two days, the Admiralty had said, we'll need you for two days, after that evacuation will be impossible. After two days would there be none of this swelling armada of little boats left?

Lest that were so, Lehmann had told his secretary to cancel all his appointments for the coming week. Only his dinner engagement with Amelia in three days time had he told her to leave. He had been looking forward for weeks to entertaining her at Shotfield. He would continue to look forward to it, he told himself, as he ran under the shelter of the chalk cliff and into Dover harbour.

Here was a confusion of ships, of eager amateurs so British that he almost wept. Finally, he was given a Bren gun, cans of extra fuel and orders to proceed by the direct route to Dunkirk. There he was to sail as close in as he could, pick up as many men, and feed them to the ferry boats which because of their deeper draught would be lying offshore. Then just as he was trying to get *Shalom* out of the mêlée, an officer with a megaphone came along the jetty, and summoned all boat owners back to the shed. Orders had been received to abandon the short route during daylight hours. Route Y, via Ostend, Ewinte Buoy, and Zuydecoote Pass must be used.

'87 bloody miles,' the owner of a fragile wooden bungey-boat swore helplessly, jerking his thumb towards the explosions across the channel, 'and what the hell's waiting at the other end?'

What seemed like the whole German Army and Air Force was waiting. The scene, with the town ablaze and the great gun emplacements firing, was so reminiscent of Lehmann's childhood idea of hell that for a moment his heart stood still, his hand faltered on the throttle. He had become accustomed to the crump of bombs, the flash of explosions, the gunfire on the long journey over. But this . . .

It seemed so hopeless, so hideous, a cause so lost that he felt like one of his own pathetic refugees at Shotfield, wanting only to escape from an insane horror he could not mitigate. He wanted escape from the great billowing smoke, from the blaze of what must be the oil farm, from the tumult, from the boom of the great gun emplacements at Calais, escape even from the forest of soldiers on the gun-raked beach and that long wooden pier where the men were queuing for such little boats as his.

349

And as if to prove that he, rich businessman turned saviour, could do absolutely nothing, one of the offshore ferries, which the little boats were feeding, received a direct hit. Up it went in a shattering orange explosion, gouts of crimson fire and black smoke. The sky above was full of its débris. *Shalom* rocked, and almost overturned. Shattered bodies floated on the water.

Staring transfixed, Lehmann suddenly saw a hand grasp the side of *Shalom*; an arm inside a torn sleeve came out of the waves. He found himself pulling on board a young soldier with a bandaged head. 'Thank God! Thank God you've come, sir!' The soldier flopped on to the boards of *Shalom*, vomiting. He just had time to say, 'There's more coming, sir. Hang on, sir,' and jerked his head towards a line of soldiers that were swimming towards *Shalom*. Then he died.

From then on, Lehmann worked like a man possessed. In fact he was possessed. Possessed of hatred, possessed of love, possessed of outrage, possessed of pride. He felt at one with his Shotfield refugees, suffering now as they had suffered, at one with the soldiers he carried to the waiting ships, more distantly and more sweetly with Prudence and Rachel and Amelia and her sons.

Night fell. The supply officer from the *Duchess of Fife* dropped him cans of fuel, some bully beef sandwiches and a bottle of beer. He couldn't remember feeling hungry or thirsty. The night lit by fires was as bright as day, but the Stukas and the Messerschmitts bothered them less. He couldn't remember feeling afraid, even when machine-gun bullets raked across *Shalom* and one grazed his shoulder. He couldn't count how many days, or nights, or hours he was over there.

All he could count was how many soldiers he lifted off that jetty, and all he could calculate was how long *Shalom* was likely to last. His businessman's brain totting up lives instead of profits, assessing *Shalom*'s strength instead of the market places. Even when *Shalom* was holed just below the water-line he couldn't feel anything. The men of the *Duchess of Fife* hauled him on board along with the soldiers he carried, and an hour later they were setting course for Dover.

There he was handed trousers and sweater and a railway warrant to London. He went straight to his St James's club where he always kept a change of clothing and where he resumed his rich urbane businessman's role again. He slept the clock round, summoned the club barber and ate a leisurely breakfast. He was very tempted to call on Prudence, but he feared she would winkle out of him the events of the past three days before his rich urbane role was completely back in place again.

He would never be able to talk of Dunkirk to anyone, even Prudence or Amelia. So he strolled alone in St James's Park, half in and half out of his role, his eyes feasting on sunlit sandbagged London going about its business, the axe poised, the invasion forces gathering.

Then he ordered a car to take him straight to Shotfield and found, not altogether to his surprise, that Amelia had arrived early for dinner.

Dunkirk and the evacuation and the threat of invasion were, however, tacitly ignored. Amelia was looking thinner but particularly beautiful. She wore her golden hair in its own version of what coiffeurists called The Victory Roll – in her case lightly swept back from her temples and gathered into a chignon at the nape of her neck. Her dress was pre-war blue velvet brought up

350

to date by Sarah's clever fingers. Two diamonds were pinned into her chignon, a diamond necklace clasped her throat. She had dressed up for him.

'I've brought you a photograph of Rachel,' she said. 'Victoria sent it via the diplomatic bag.'

But she had brought him much more. There was a shadow in her eyes as if she knew and understood. There was a respect of a different sort, an acknowledgement that he was perhaps nearer the man she sought than she had at first supposed him to be. And though throughout dinner the conversation remained on the family, when she kissed him goodbye she suddenly put her arms round him and hugged him.

'You make me feel very humble,' she said softly.

And for the first time he seriously began to hope.

Hope was the sustenance of the British people that summer – hope and a grim determination inspired by Churchill's oratory: 'Even though large tracts of Europe and many old and famous States have fallen or may fall into the grip of the Gestapo and all the odious apparatus of Nazi rule, we shall not flag or fail. We shall go on to the end. We shall fight in France, we shall fight on the seas and oceans, we shall fight with growing confidence and growing strength in the air, we shall defend our island, whatever the cost may be. We shall fight on the beaches, we shall fight in the fields and in the streets, we shall fight in the hills; we shall never surrender, and even if, which I do not for a moment believe, this island or a large part of it were subjugated and starving, then our Empire beyond the seas, armed and guarded by the British Fleet, would carry on the struggle, until, in God's good time, the new world, with all its power and might, steps forth to the rescue and the liberation of the old.'

The tattered remnants of the British Expeditionary Force – 338,226 men – had been rescued from Dunkirk. And though Churchill had solemnly pointed out that this was not a victory, nevertheless the sight of the train loads of men, many wounded, many barefoot, and all of them famished sent a feeling of profound relief almost of euphoria through the nation.

A euphoria despite the knowledge that Hitler's invasion forces were poised. More concrete tank traps were thrown up along the main roadways. Curving Sussex rivers acquired gunposts. Schoolboys widenedstreams to impede the Germans. Farmers dragged old tractors and machinery on to the verges. Trees were felled ready to throw across the road. Signposts and bus destinations were removed. The ringing of church bells was banned except to announce invasion. And the government distributed a leaflet entitled *If the Invader Comes* to every home. *Do not give a German anything*, it said. *Do not tell him anything. Hide your food and bicycles. Hide your maps.*

'I'd do more to the Jerries than hide the food and maps from them,' a scornful Sarah exclaimed as she and Amelia sorted through the gun-room and the kitchen for every available weapon.

Sarah took an armful of knives and choppers down to the butcher to be sharpened. Arthur wrote from Lossiemouth, Charles from Drem, both fuming at their own inaction.

Then in the fine long summer days the Luftwaffe began the softening up process for Operation Sealion, the invasion. They had mustered an immense force of 3500 aircraft on 400 airfields across the Channel. They began cautiously

351

with tip-and-run raids on Channel ports and radar posts, then penetrated deeper to fighter airfields, until, on 12 August, they launched *Adler Tag*, Eagle Day, and the Battle of Britain had begun.

Marianne March was just putting on her uniform ready for the afternoon shift, when she heard the usual, 'Enemy Aircraft in the vicinity' warning for the third time since midnight, and rushing over to her bedroom window, saw the Hurricanes and Spitfires skimming the hangar roof. Pierre's aircraft G-George was second to take off, almost nudging his flight commander's wing. Typical Pierre.

She resumed the fastening on of her blue collar and the knotting of her black tie. Her hands were unsteady. She hated it when Pierre was scrambled. She sometimes wished they were not on the same station together. 'You try to protect Pierre too much,' her father had once said. 'Loving sometimes means renouncing.' Strange words, sad, she had thought at the time. But then, as she grew up, she had recognised that though she and her father were very close, there was some part of him she would never know.

And what would her father have thought of her love for Charles she wondered, fastening her jacket and pulling the peaked blue cap down over her springy dark hair. The cap bore the same velvet and gilt badge as her father's. She ran her finger round it wistfully, and then hearing the Bofors guns starting up, shouldered her respirator and steel helmet, to hurry over to Ops before it got too hot.

She was just passing the mess office when the orderly said, 'Phone call for you, Ma'am. I'll put it through to number one box.'

As soon as she lifted the receiver she heard, with a lift of her heart, Charles's eager voice. 'Marianne? I'm in London. I've finished at Drem. I've got a 48-hour pass. I'm coming down to Biggin. Can you book me a room in the Mess?'

'I'll try. I'm just going on duty.'

They were interrupted by the operator at the min PBX saying sharply, 'Sorry, Sir. Must cut you off. Line needed operationally.' Then the phone went dead.

Yes, the Messing Officer said, they could fit in one visiting officer, providing the Mess was still standing in what looked like being, he peered through the criss-cross taping of the windows, a bit nearer home.

That last night's raid had been a bit nearer home was clear as Marianne walked the short distance to operations. There was a bomb crater along the perimeter track. It ran at one point close to the road. Blast had half-demolished the little newsagent's shop. The proprietor and his wife were sweeping up outside. They had already made a huge notice, *More open than usual*.

It was the sort of British sense of humour her mother and brother most hated. Marianne sometimes wondered why Pierre, who felt himself so deeply French, had not gone into the French Air Force. Certainly he had embraced the French view that the evacuation of Dunkirk was a British betrayal of the French. And certainly his contempt for the British was as nothing compared with his dislike of Charles and all the Hayburys. She scanned the sky for signs of the Hurricanes and Spitfires returning. But apart from the fluffy white puffs from the Bofors guns, the sky was as empty as a glass bowl.

By now the tannoy voice boomed out from every loudspeaker, 'Enemy aircraft approaching the airfield. Take cover.'

Almost at once, aircraft appeared like flies out of the glassy blue. Every gun on the airfield began firing. Up came a cloud of dandelion puffs. As she dived down the sandbagged entrance of Ops, she heard the first bomb fall.

'Bags of action on the table.' Section Officer Rawson jerked her head at the green rectangular table surrounded by plotters with long cues. She got out of her chair, stretched and handed her earphones to Marianne. 'What's it like out there?'

'Just hotting up. You'll need your tin hat on. Mind how you go.'

'Oh, not to worry.' Rawson gave the Controller an elaborate salute. 'If one's got your number on it, that's it. See you this evening in the Mess for housey-housey.'

They never saw each other again.

Taking up her position overlooking the sector table, Marianne looked at the squadron board. She found the name March and G-George. Then momentarily the board blurred. She saw a chalk cross. The words *Aircraft destroyed category 3*. Forcing herself to read on, she saw *Pilot unhurt*.

Her WAAF sergeant came over with a mug of tea and whispered, 'Flying Officer March telephoned in. Baled out near Hawkinge. Requested transport.'

How like perverse, self-contained Pierre, Marianne thought. Anyone else would have tried to phone her too, but not Pierre. She sipped her tea, thankful he was safe. Now she watched the 170 bandits that had crossed the Kent coast moving into the Tunbridge Wells/Kenley area. The plotters were shunting and gathering the counter blocks, their pretty made-up faces as inscrutable as croupiers at Monte Carlo. For her eighteenth birthday her mother had taken her there for the weekend. Her mother had stayed there with her first husband. Marianne had hated every minute of it, as she had hated her mother's devotion to the memory of her first husband, hated the way she had made their home a monument to him.

Now that home once more was in ruins; Pierre had flown over Château Saguenac before Dunkirk. The house had been shelled again. He blamed the British Army.

'Angels three to Red Leader. Bandits at twelve o'clock high. Heavy escort.'

'Ease formation. Choose your own target.'

Almost immediately, softened by the thick concrete roof of operations, came the crump of bombs. The Controller vectored in 253 Squadron. The pieces on the board moved rapidly, like flotillas of little boats going this way and that.

'Tallyho. Giving chase.' Then another voice, 'You're on fire.' The air crackled with voices.

It was stifling in Operations. The Controller wiped the sweat off his brow. An airwoman brought round more mugs of tea heavily laced with Nestlé's milk. Marianne looked at her watch, trying not to think of Charles.

In some odd way she had been trying to put him out of her mind ever since she could remember. She had never quite understood the reason for her mother's hatred of the Hayburys. It was something to do with the cheating of her father over an aircraft design. That and Lady Haybury's coldness to her mother. As a schoolgirl, Marianne had read of Charles's exploits, and vividly remembered his kindness to her as a child. She had alternately imagined that she loved and hated him. That he was her hero and her Nemesis.

'Bandits approaching the field. Getting a bit too warm,' the Controller sighed as a flight of Dorniers thrust towards them. The counters had hardly been moved when the bombing started.

And then the somehow unbelievable, the moment everyone thinks will never happen to them. There was a deafening explosion as the concrete roof was ripped apart. Everything was plunged into a roaring darkness. Marianne felt herself flung into space. The whole world was falling on top of her. Everywhere was heaving and crashing. Her mouth and nose were choked with rubble. Something caught her on the side of her head. Something else pinioned her down.

Dimly, in her last conscious moment she realised that Operations had received a direct hit, and that she would probably die. Yet all she could really think was how sad and bereft Charles would be.

Just outside Kenley, the train from London suddenly ground to a stop. Putting his head out of the carriage window, Charles saw a pillar of smoke rising from the hill ahead.

'Looks like Biggin Hill's getting it,' said the only other occupant of the compartment. 'Now we'll be stuck for hours.'

'Not me,' Charles opened the carriage door, dropped down on the track, ran to the level crossing gates and out on to the road. There he tried to thumb a lift, but like the train, all the traffic seemed to have come to a stop. As he again started running, high above his head he could see the vapour-trail whorls of dogfights. Over on the left, three Ju88s started diving, and seconds later, he heard the crump of bombs.

Panting and out of breath, he tried to run faster but it was dusk by the time he reached the guardroom. A bright orange glow lit up the whole airfield. Shadows were moving in the half-darkness. Voices shouted. He saw ambulances, two fire engines, a string of lorries.

He still went on running. Past a dark Station Headquarters in ruins. Past a shell of a barrack-block. Past an MT section ghostly with gutted bowsers. He turned left towards Operations.

There was nothing there. Just a rubble of brick and concrete. Firemen were hosing water over burning wood. A Service policeman shouted something unintelligible. He shouted back. 'What's happened?'

'Direct hit an hour ago.'

'The Ops staff? The WAAF?'

The man simply shrugged his shoulders. He didn't know. The figures materialising out of the darkness didn't know either.

The whole station had turned into a nightmare. Charles felt numb, devoid of feeling. Only his legs, moving like pistons, propelled him like an automaton. Yellow slits of headlights shone like cats' eyes through the blackout, as a van came towards him.

'Section Officer March?' he asked of the driver. 'D'you know what's happened to her?'

'Not her. But her brother's been shot down. A van's gone to pick him up.'

The guards at the gate shook their heads when he asked. So did a despatch rider. At last in the Officers' Mess, lit only by candles, someone told him, 'Section Officer March . . . I saw her after the Ops Room was hit. She's all right.

They've moved everyone to some place in the village . . . Still carrying on.'

Relieved at least to have news of her, he went out to look where it could be. He searched for RAF cars, RAF personal going in and out of some door of the black blocks of houses and shops. But in the blackout it was hopeless. Round eleven, he went back to the Mess. At least they'd got the electricity back on again.

By now she would surely be off duty. But she wasn't in the lounge, nor in the bar of the ladies' room. He found out her room number from the mess corporal and went up to the first floor.

He knocked on the door of the room at the far end of the corridor.

There was no reply. So he just opened the door and went in.

Though it was empty, there was an aura of her in the room that was quite unmistakable. By the window was the same RAF issue white coverletted bed on its black lacquered legs. Opposite was the same dressing table, on which were a silver-backed brush, some make-up jars, a photograph of her father in uniform. On the bedside table, an old snapshot of himslf in sportscoat and flannels.

He stood for a few minutes, looking round imagining her there. Then he lay down on the bed with his hands behind his head, his eyes up on the dark ceiling, waiting.

He had no idea what time it was when he heard the footsteps coming down the linoleum of the corridor. They came to just outside the door, then they stopped.

He held his breath and closed his eyes. It mightn't be her. It might be some other WAAF officer looking for her, come to collect her things. And then there'd be yet another addition to the saga of Charles Haybury, caught this time red-handed in a WAAF's bed.

He heard the door handle turn, the click as the light went on. He opened his eyes, and saw Marianne standing above him. 'Charles!' She shook her head. Her battle dress uniform was streaked with dirt. There was a cut on her left cheekbone. Her face was pale, her eyes very dark and almost hysterically bright. He swung his feet off the bed. Putting his hand on her shoulder, he kissed her lightly. 'Sorry! Did I give you a fright?'

'No. Not a fright. I didn't expect to see you.' She sat on the edge of the bed, rumpling her hand through her hair distractedly and wearily. 'What time is it? My watch got broken.'

'One fifteen. Have you had something to eat?'

She nodded. 'The Sally Ann van came round.'

'I looked everywhere for you. They said Ops had had a direct hit. I blew my top. I began running round everywhere like a chicken without its head. Couldn't find anyone that seemed to know anything.' He sat down beside her and took her hand. 'Then I found a bod who said you all got out alive.'

'They set up another Ops room at the far end of the village. In a grocer's.' She laughed shrilly. 'You should have seen the Controller doing his stuff on a counter full of dried egg and tins of Spam,' her laughter rose to a high note and shivered into a flood of tears. 'My WAAF sergeant's arm was blown off,' she sobbed on to his shoulder, 'and Rawson got the chop.'

He tried to smooth her dark hair. It was full of grit and rubble and bits of plaster. At the thought of her near escape, he pulled her tightly to him, murmuring incoherent endearments.

'Would you like me to go now?' He stroked her cheek with his forefinger. 'Now I know you're safe.'

'No. Stay.' She grabbed his hand, and held on to it.

'If we're found we'll both get court-martialled.'

'We won't get found. They're all in bed. Sleeping while they can.'

'When are you on again?'

'Ten. I did a double shift.'

'Who gets called first in the WAAF Mess?'

'The Orderly Officer at seven. She won't come in here. No one disturbs the Ops people.'

'You've had someone in before?' he teased her.

She looked so astonished, so wide-eyed and indignant that he said immediately, 'I was only kidding.'

'I never know when you are and when you're not. My mother and Pierre never teased. My father sometimes but not often. Do you know, I can never remember my mother really laughing. That is one of the things I like about you . . .'

'Love about me,' he corrected.

'Love about you,' she repeated. 'That you begin to laugh with your eyes and then with your mouth.'

'How very interesting I sound! Tell me more.'

She shook her head.

'In that case,' he said, 'I shall tell you something. You're to lie down and try to get some sleep. The bastards may be back tomorrow again.'

She put her hand up to her head. 'I've got to see if there's any water to wash my hair. Then I'll put on my dressing gown and lie on the bed, if you will.'

'Too risky.'

'I'll risk it if you will. I'll risk a court martial.'

He was going to say, it's not just a court martial, but the strain of day and night had somehow made her a vulnerable young girl again. Chastely and sedately, therefore, as an old married couple, they lay side by side on the narrow bed. Within seconds, he heard her breathing grow deep and regular. Then he himself must have drifted off to sleep.

The night was quiet. But his subconscious mind must have been alert for any troublesome sound for suddenly he was awake. He heard sharp regular footsteps coming down the corridor. Light was rimming the blackout at the window. Somewhere distantly an NCO was bellowing.

The footsteps came nearer, paused outside the door. Charles felt himself break out into a sweat as knuckles rapped on the panels. Marianne's eyes flew open. The knock sounded again. A man's voice called 'Marianne? Are you there? Marianne?'

'Pierre!' Marianne breathed in Charles's ear. 'Oh, my God!'

Her eyes went wildly round the bare room looking for some hiding place. But the handle was already turning. The door was pushed back. A dark head came round, saying again, 'Marianne?'

Then the head became as still as a snake's. Narrow brown eyes glittered malevolently at Charles. The door was kicked wider. 'My God! *You!* You

356

bloody bastard! What the hell are you doing in here?'

He seemed to fling himself on top of Charles, grabbing him by his shirt before he had time to get up. The two of them fell off the bed and began rolling on the floor, Pierre shouting at the top of his voice, kicking and punching. Charles managed to free his right hand and slammed his jaw, but he couldn't get enough swing behind his fist. Pierre brought his knee up to Charles's stomach and was trying to get his fingers in his eyes. Marianne leapt off the bed and was struggling to part them, shouting now in English, now in French.

This time, no one heard the approaching footsteps. The noise of the fight drowned everything until a deep penetrating contralto swelling from the depth of a righteously heaving bosom demanded, 'March! What, my girl, is the meaning of this disgraceful display?'

The WAAF Queen Bee resplendent in red dressing gown and pink slippers, hair pinned up under a white slumber-net, stood in the doorway, more imposing and formidable than any crowned queen. The two men got sheepishly to their feet. The Queen Bee, having demanded an explanation, refused to listen to it.

There were no enemy raids on Biggin Hill that day, and there was time for the three of them to make their explanations to the Station Commander. He listened carefully to them. He tore a strip off them, one by one, and pronounced that he wasn't going to waste the RAF's time and money with charges against them. But they weren't to think the matter would be left there. These things had a habit of catching up. Perhaps it was pure coincidence, or perhaps he spoke no less than the truth. Within a month, Pierre was detached to a lonely squadron in Orkney and Charles to his fury was posted to Limavady in Northern Ireland on Lysanders. Whilst, most obviously connected of all to that unfortunate episode, Marianne was asked to present herself at the Station Adjutant's office.

'Had a signal about you from Air Ministry,' he told her. 'How would you like to make better use of your French?'

FOUR

'How would I like to make better use of my French?'

Those days, like everyone else at Biggin Hill, she felt too tired to think. The golden hazy days of September were passing in what seemed like constant squadron readiness, in the constant ebb and flow of Bandits and Angels on the sector table, in snatched meals and even more snatched sleep. No sooner did the Spitfires and Hurricanes land to re-fuel and re-arm than they were off again. The Luftwaffe was using fighter-bombers now in high level sweeps across the South East in daylight attacks on the airfields. London had been severely bombed by day and provincial cities by night. And in the midst of all this, Air Ministry in its wisdom wanted to know like some overzealous schoolmaster if Section Officer March would like to make better use of her French!

It was all so typically muddled and British. No wonder her mother had found her father so very difficult to understand!

'That's what it says here, m'dear. Our code and cypher queen never gets the message wrong, does she?'

'D'you know what it means?' Marianne asked the adjutant.

'Haven't a clue, dear girl. That's all I got from them. You're to be asked that question. How would you like to make better use of your French?'

'A better use than swearing at my brother?' Marianne asked with a faint smile.

'There's no better use than that,' the adjutant replied gravely. 'Especially knowing your brother. But that is, no doubt, what the chairbornes in Kingsway had in mind.'

'And you've no idea what the work might be?'

'Writing French menus for the generals' luncheons, perhaps? Explaining to de Gaulle why he can't wear a crown and move into Buckingham Palace yet awhile? Sorry. You being half-French you probably like him.'

'Not particularly.'

'Anyway, you can always be like the captain's daughter, and tell them Up you. I can signal back and say no.'

Marianne paused for a moment. Then she said, 'Tell them yes.' She walked to the door and saluted. As an afterthought, she added, 'I wonder if it might be something to do with interrogating the Free French Forces?'

'Could be. Anyway you'll hear in due course, if Jerry lets us live that long. And if the signal doesn't end up in the Laugh and Tear Up File.'

Marianne was beginning to think that was where it had ended up, as autumn gave way to winter, and as air-raids continued but the threat of invasion receded. Now small but fierce attacks were being made on the aircraft factories round Southampton, and in the Filton area of Bristol, as well as the heavier blitzes on the industrial cities.

How was Lady Haybury in all this? Marianne wondered, reading a letter from Charles in which he fumed about his so-called exile in Northern Ireland. Marianne wished that she herself could break through the mistrust her mother had engendered in her towards Lady Haybury, and feel again the warm friendliness she remembered towards her as a child.

Pierre's mistrust of the Haybury family would never be assuaged. He wrote repeatedly from Orkney, blaming Charles, taking it upon himself as head of the family now, to forbid her to see him, adding, *The PT instructor up here was a professional boxer in civvy street. Next time I meet Haybury, he'll wonder what has hit him.*

Marianne, busy with the plotting of hit-and-run raiders, was thankful that the Irish Sea and the Pentland Firth separated the two people she loved most in the world. But winter was cold and grim without them. Goering intensified the night blitzes. Even the Corpo Aero Italiano made a brief appearance in November on the sector table. And led by Heinkel Pathfinders, German bombers penetrated to Birmingham and the Midlands. In the middle of November 437 German aircraft guided by their X-Gerat navigational aid almost razed Coventry to the ground.

The world as reflected in the skies above Kent and on the green of the plotting table seemed full of bandits. In the second week of December both Charles and Pierre wrote to say they had been unlucky in the Christmas leave draw. Marianne herself spent Christmas Eve on duty.

No Bandits showed on the plot that night. Ironically, as the station choir at Biggin Hill sang 'Silent Night, Holy Night', round all the sections in return for lashings of rum, the British and German bombers remained grounded. Liquor flowed freely on and off duty. Returning to her room at six am on Christmas Day, Marianne found a note from the adjutant on her bed, saying she was required for interview on 30 December in London. He would give her the address over Christmas lunch, and she must please destroy this note.

'I should go the day before,' the adjutant suggested as the officers served the customary roast turkey and Christmas pudding to the other ranks. 'Take in a flick. Then go to 7 Portman Place at nine next morning and ask for Mr Jobling. And don't get talked into doing anything you don't want to do.'

Marianne arrived in London late on the damp Sunday afternoon. It was the first time she had been in the city since she was there with Charles, and it felt empty and cheerless without him. She booked in at the service women's hostel in Buckingham Gate, ate a dried egg omelette at Lyon's Corner House, and then took herself to the Odeon. The opening credits had barely faded before the red light of the air-raid warning showed beside the screen. The film was interrupted while a slide was put on. *An air-raid warning has just been sounded. If you wish to leave the cinema please do so as quietly as possible. Those who wish to remain may do so at their own risk. The film now continues.*

Few people left. A false optimism that Goering was about to change his tactics momentarily lulled the capital. Besides even with drink short and cigarettes like gold dust, it was still the Christmas season. A few servicemen let off steam by hurling a stream of mild obscenities. Then the film recommenced.

Everyone settled down. The bombing started almost at once, distant at first, then it came swiftly nearer. The screen shimmered like a cracked mirror. The building shook. There was the sound of falling masonry. Someone must have turned the sound up louder because the actors' voices suddenly boomed out. But their efforts were like the Dutch boy's finger in the dyke. The crashings and boomings penetrated the jolly dialogue. One by one, then four by four, then in a steady stream, the audience left. Marianne stayed put. Since the raid on Biggin Hill she had a horror of being buried alive under the débris. But the débris itself seemed to penetrate the cinema. Bits of plaster kept falling down. Her nostrils were filled with the smell of dust and rubble and of what smelled like the stench of a broken sewer.

She clenched her fists and forced her eyes on the screen till the last unreal embrace, the final swell of canned Hollywood music. Then the curtains hastily closed. The swaying lights went up. An accelerated version of the national anthem was played to a tiny audience of hardened survivors. One of them, a man of about twenty-eight in Army officer's uniform followed close on Marianne's heels into the street outside.

In the intermittent light there was broken glass everywhere. The pavement was wet. A sewer had burst. Effluent spurted from an uncovered manhole. Ambulances and fire engines hurtled backwards and forwards. Gangs of men in steel helmets ran with hoses. All London appeared to be blazing. Beneath the criss-crossing of ghostly searchlights, the eastern sky flamed a deadly dark orange. Only the top of the dome of St Paul's retained its solid black silhouette. The noise was deafening. Ack-ack guns rattled. Spent cartridges showered down. There was the sickening crump of bombs, the thrum of engines.

'Take cover! Get down to that shelter!' A warden blew his whistle and gave Marianne an exasperated shove in the small of her back. She skidded along the wet pavement. A hand steadied her. She turned round to look into the face of the Army officer who had followed her out of the cinema.

'Are you going to take shelter?' he pointed to the sandbagged entrance into which people now were hurrying.

'No.' She shook her head. 'I haven't far to go. I'd rather get back.'

Under a small toothbrush moustache a slight smile curved his lips. 'If we stand here much longer,' he said drily, 'the journey will be to Kingdom Come.' He drew her hand through his arm. 'Come on. Put your tin hat on and show me the way to go home.'

Together they darted across the road, and dodged from doorway to doorway. They were whistled at by ARP wardens, but keeping a sharp look-out for falling débris they negotiated Trafalgar Square safely. Then they made a quick bolt down Buckingham Gate. Breathless, they arrived at the doorway of the service women's hostel, and said goodnight. In the half-light she studied his face briefly. It was an open, young, uncomplicated face. They never exchanged names, nor did he ask if he could see her again.

The following morning Marianne was awake early. A pall of smoke hung over the city. There was an acrid smell of burning. The streets were still choked with rubble and broken glass. Marianne walked. She arrived punctually at nine at the doorway of a tall innocent-looking house. She paused on the steps to wipe the grey dust off her shoes and was shown by a civilian janitor into a small, sparsely furnished office on the second floor.

A short bald-headed man in a dark suit was sitting behind a bare trestle table. He bade her take the wooden chair opposite him. It all looked very impermanent and hastily assembled. There was no filing cabinet, no files, no typewriter, no books, no charts. Nothing. He asked her polite rather disinterested questions about her journey, when she'd come up to London, where she'd stayed, how she liked Biggin Hill, whether she had made any close friends, gradually working back to her parents and her childhood in France. Her own feelings for France. Her mother's feelings for her country. Could she describe her mother? Where was her mother buried? Had she seen a photo of her grandfather? He asked her innumerable, seemingly irrelevant questions in French, and listened to her replies with his head held appraisingly on one side. Then, he made the only positive remark of the interview, that the work might involve some danger. 'Could you cope with danger, Miss March?'

'I think so.'

'Would you wish to undertake dangerous work?'

'Yes.'

He nodded several times but made no comment. Then he stood up to indicate that the interview was over.

'Naturally, Miss March, you will not mention this interview to anyone.' He saw her to the door of the office, told her she would hear from them in due course. Halfway down the stairs, she heard other footsteps descending. She leaned over the banisters. She was just in time to see her acquaintance from the previous night, the youthful-faced Army officer, leaving by the front door.

The months went by and she heard nothing.

The raids on Britain caused 33,000 casualties in three months. In the spring, Greece and Crete had been lost. The Germans had occupied Yugoslavia.

During this time, still at Biggin Hill, Marianne had decided that she hadn't got through the interview. They didn't want her. Had she but known it, a long and intense argument had been going on in official circles as to whether it was right to employ girls in such dangerous work. However in June, just as the Germans invaded Russia, she was again summoned to the adjutant's office and told that Mr Jobling would like to see her again. This time she should pack a small suitcase. The selection procedure might take several days.

'Selection procedure for what?' Marianne asked the adjutant.

'Haven't a clue, dear girl. Putting the wooden chips in raspberry jam most likely. Ask Mr Jobling. He'll tell you as good a lie as the next one.'

This time, when she was shown into his bare little office, Mr Jobling was more eloquent and forthcoming. He quoted Churchill's directive, 'Now set Europe ablaze,' adding with melancholy humour, 'and though it may seem to the uninitiated that Hitler has perversely set Britain ablaze, Europe is the target and we may possibly have a hand in the pyrotechnics.'

This time he seemed to know the minutiae of her background. He knew that her mother had been devoted to her first husband, that she had asked to be buried with him. He knew Pierre was still in Orkney, that she heard from him every week, that Pierre had a quick temper. He knew about Marianne's relationship with Charles, and asked her if she intended to marry him.

'He hasn't asked me.'

361

'And if he does?'

'Then I would think about it. But only then. And . . . '

'And you certainly wouldn't tell me, is that what you were going to say?'

'More or less.'

'Fair enough.' Mr Jobling then changed the subject back to the war effort. He spoke of the brutality of the Nazis, their methods of interrogation, the different thresholds of pain which individuals could endure. And only towards the end of the interview, how would she feel about returning to Occupied France.

'As a spy?'

'It is not for me to answer questions. Just to ask them. How would you feel?'

'I would like that,' she replied.

'But you want time to consider it?'

'No, I'm certain.'

'You wouldn't feel any impending matrimonial entanglement might hamper you?'

She shook her head. 'In any case, we wouldn't marry till the end of the war.'

'Well,' once again he got up to indicate the interview was over. 'We shall see how you get on in the next few days. There's a transport waiting outside. You will be taken to a house in the country. It will all be very painless and comfortable, I promise you. At the end of that time, you will be told whether or not your services will be required. And you will again have the option of changing your mind.'

He saw her to the door and opened it for her. Once again she descended the stone steps of this strangely innocuous-looking house. This time no one preceded her through the front door. A large Hillman car was waiting outside. The corporal driver took her bag and stowed it in the boot. There were already three other cases inside. In the car sat two men in civilian clothes and the ubiquitous Army officer. He made no acknowledgement that he had ever seen her before and after a few moments of staring at his blue-eyed innocent face, she wondered if she was mistaken.

They arrived that evening at a country house in Surrey. They were met by a tall man with a walrus moustache, who looked like a retired Army colonel but who was dressed in a tweed suit and a yellow cravat and who introduced himself as Captain Ventnor. Two other groups of four had just arrived and were sorting their bags out in the hall. Their stay would be for two days, Captain Ventnor told them. They must regard it as an informal weekend. They would find the food good, the beds comfortable, the liquor plentiful. At the end of that weekend some of them would return to their units. Others would be invited to stay. If they had letters they wished to write, they would not mention this place. Nor would they post any mail in the village. They would leave letters in the box in the hall, from whence they would be collected and censored.

Marianne wrote therefore with great circumspection to Charles, saying she was on a course. He would have no reason to doubt this. The WAAF were now organising numerous courses especially for those who like herself had been thrown in at the deep end without any training. She missed him, she said, and was looking forward to his leave. But her circumspection forced a chilly note into her letter. Her spontaneity, her warmth and affection were missing. There were no little anecdotes. Nothing personal.

Reading it in Limavady on a blustery afternoon, the message that seemed to come over loud and clear to Charles from between those carefully written lines was that Marianne's affection for him had cooled. Possibly she had met someone else. That lunchtime he waylaid John Forrester, his CO, in the Mess bar, and demanded when the hell they were going to get out of this dump.

'Dump, laddie?' said Forrester, ten years his junior. 'You don't know you're born! Guiness galore! Real eggs with yolks.' He raised his tankard. 'Here, have another pint!'

In sheer desperation to keep his mind off Marianne, Charles worked his off duty time in the hangars. He helped with the inspections. He watched eagerly for the mail. To make matters worse, Southampton was heavily bombed on the 7 and 8 July, and he was edgy till he heard from Amelia that nothing of any consequence had dropped at Haybury or near the factory. When, at the end of that month, Charles received another letter from Marianne, this time asking him to write to her at a Post Office box number because she had now been posted from Biggin Hill, his suspicions deepened. But it was some months later before the real blow fell.

Marianne was among those invited to stay when the weekend was over. With the unwanted recruits gone, Captain Ventnor became more precise and more formidable. A programme of intensive training began at once. Their objective was more openly declared. To infiltrate Europe, and help organise the Resistance.

To this end, their old names and their old identities would be discarded. They would be given a set of new identities for varying occasions. The Monday of the following week began with physical training, hill climbing, tree climbing, running before breakfast along the Hog's Back, learning how to fall as if from a parachute. The physical exercises were followed up with classroom work. They pored over maps. They learned Morse code and ciphering. They memorised the geography of specified areas of France. Towards the end of the week, they did target practice, stalking and silent killing. She did not see the blue-eyed Army officer.

Care of the Post Office box number, a disgruntled letter arrived from Charles: *You don't sound like yourself at all. Pierre hasn't been getting at you again, has he? Or are you whooping it up with someone I ought to know about?*

She wrote back and answered, *Neither. I haven't seen Pierre. I think I've forgotten how to whoop it up. It's simply that I'm worked off my feet.*

That was certainly true. She ached from head to foot. She shared a bedroom with a silent very withdrawn woman who was the widow of a French naval officer. They were both too tired and too wary of exchanging anything that might seem remotely like an indiscretion to talk at night.

And then after six weeks Marianne was told her group was transferred again. With mingled feelings of pleasure and foreboding, Marianne found herself less than a dozen miles from her old home at a small manor house five miles north of Beaulieu. And this time the ubiquitous Army officer was in her group. Not as a trainee but as staff. He was known as Jean-Paul. She was not told his surname. Only that from now on the training would intensify and that he would be her mentor. 'And,' he said with that same small bright smile under the toothbrush moustache, 'your tormentor.'

Marianne was assigned the area of Chartres. Cover stories and identities were prepared for her. She was taught how to leave bombs, how to dynamite a railway track, how to bury a body. The torment began after she had been at the manor house for three days when she was wakened out of a deep sleep. A light was shining in her eyes. Jean-Paul thrust the torch full into her face and demanded to know who she was. When she hesitated, he slapped her across her mouth.

She began her first cover story. He questioned her. She stumbled. He hit her again.

The next night he left her in peace. But after that it was every night, till her first cover story was perfect. By day, she had to stalk him through the streets of Southampton as he dived down sidestreets, melted into crowds, became almost in a single second totally invisible. Then alternate days, he stalked her.

At first she found him almost impossible to shake off. Then, as the weeks went by, she became more proficient. Till finally she could melt into the background with almost the same skill as Jean-Paul.

It was on a fine afternoon in late autumn that Marianne performed her last act of eluding Jean-Paul. Her assignment was to be dropped on the Totton Road and to reach the Dolphin Hotel in Bar Gate without interception from Jean-Paul. She had a specified route to follow. She also had to leave an imitation bomb in the Town Hall. She had then to buy a ticket from a certain cinema, buy a paper from a certain newsvendor, leave an envelope in a certain hairdresser's shop. Then proceed to the Dolphin Hotel, into the lounge bar, and order two dry Martinis before Jean-Paul could waylay her. Marianne had just thrust open the door of the lounge when she saw Lady Haybury and a tall Jewish gentleman in close conversation.

Marianne was so appalled at seeing her that she stopped in her tracks, unsure what to do.

Lady Haybury looked up and met her eyes. A variety of expressions crossed her face. She smiled tentatively. Marianne's expression remained frozen. Then she turned on her heel. She hurried to the ladies' cloakroom, splashed her face with cold water and tried to think what to do. Minutes later, when she emerged. Jean-Paul put his hand on her arm.

'Caught you!'

Despite her protests he insisted on taking her into the bar for a drink.

'I can't. There's someone in there I know.'

'All the more reason.'

'To what?'

'To make everything look above board.' He pulled her hand through his arm. 'You'll have to learn to carry off worse than this.'

'But this is rather personal.'

'Still more reason.' He opened the door. On the pretext of brushing her ear with his lips, he whispered, 'You and I don't have anything rather personal till this war is over.' Then aloud, he asked, 'And what are you drinking tonight, darling?'

Lady Haybury made no effort to make Marianne acknowledge her. She was acutely aware of the girl's embarrassment. She and Mr Lehmann sipped their aperitifs and then went upstairs to dine. But the following day she wrote to Charles, not in malice, but like someone trying to scotch the last vapours of a troublesome ghost. *I saw Marianne March yesterday at the Dolphin in Southampton. She had with her such a nice-looking and attentive Army man. They seemed very absorbed in one another. I have often thought that she must be very lonely. It would be nice if they were to marry.*

It would indeed. She would most fervently wish them well. As for Charles, she was sure – or almost sure – that he had forgotten about Marianne.

The letter arrived in Limavady three days later. Had Charles not the previous night received a typewritten slip to the effect that he and Forrester were posted to Stanton on the mainland for special duties, he would have gone AWOL, war or no war, till he had sorted out what was happening to Marianne.

FIVE

Arriving at Liverpool docks from Limavady, Charles parted company from Forrester, who was off to whoop it up in London, and heaved himself and his kit on to the first train south.

He had already written a terse note to Marianne at her box number, asking her to meet him at the Dolphin Hotel in Southampton and giving her a date and time. He added, with a bitterness unusual to him, that he had chosen that particular venue as it appeared to be a great favourite of hers.

The train was crowded with servicemen and women. Charles shared a compartment with several Army types, whom he looked upon balefully, and a young naval lieutenant, on posting from Gourock. They talked sporadically, but not about the gloomy war news. The Germans were in sight of Moscow. Besieged Malta was being pulverised. Sinkings in the Atlantic were mounting. Charles asked him if by any chance in his travels he had come across a type called Arthur Haybury.

The lieutenant looked at Charles suspiciously, 'Why? Is he some relation of yours?'

'Very distant. You've met him I take it?'

'Once or twice.'

'Flourishing, is he?

'As the proverbial tree. Last time I saw him, he was PA to the Admiral.'

'That sounds like the Arthur Haybury I know.'

Charles smiled, But the world of Arthur Haybury and of his mother for that matter, seemed a long way away. Arriving in Southampton, he got a taxi to the hotel. For a moment, he toyed with the idea of phoning his mother, then discarded it. He wanted to leave himself entirely free.

At the Dolphin, he booked a room without difficulty. He enquired rather fearfully if there was a message for him, and was relieved to be told there was nothing. He hurried out into the street, found a florist that was still open and bought a bunch of flowers. He went up to his bedroom, bathed and shaved, and returned downstairs to the bar on the stroke of six.

Every time the door opened he jumped. He smoked endlessly. At seven he ordered a gin fizz to keep the barman happy, but he left it untouched. There were several Army types tanking up. He eyed them suspiciously, wondering if one of those was Marianne's. At eight, he went along to reception saying indignantly, 'Look, there must have been a message, and you've forgotten to give it to me.'

The grey-haired woman in reception denied the charge indignantly. 'Shall you be taking dinner, Sir? The dining-room closes in a moment.'

'No,' he said petulantly. 'I'll be going out for a few minutes.'

Hands thrust in his pockets, he walked the blacked-out streets, angrily composing his accusations to Marianne, sometimes even getting so carried away that he spoke out loud. But nobody heard and nobody cared. Marianne didn't care either. He felt sickened and miserable.

He returned an hour later, to be greeted by the triumphant lady receptionist. 'Flight Lieutenant Haybury, your message has come at last. You see no one forgot to give it to you! The lady is unable to keep the appointment you suggested. She will do her best for tomorrow. But is unable to promise.' The underlying message seemed abundantly clear without the receptionist's little smirk. Charles went to the bar, then went drunk to bed.

He woke to the chambermaid shaking him on the shoulder and saying apologetically, 'There's a lady downstairs says she wants to see you.'

He put his head under the cold shower, dragged a razor over his face, threw on his clothes and ran downstairs.

Marianne was standing in the hall. He saw her face, wide-eyed, upturned and eager, and for one delirious moment it seemed that the very poise of her body, the tender appealing expression of her face proclaimed she loved him and longed for him. She took a step towards him, her arms spread, her face breaking into one of her rare wide smiles. 'Charles!' Her voice sang with welcome. The time between should have dissolved, but he had nursed his worry and his grievance too long. About to jump down the last three stairs and take her in his arms, his anger slowed him. He sauntered towards her and said coldly, 'Hello, Marianne. So you managed to get here at last.'

Her hands dropped to her side, her smile froze.

'Thanks for the welcome!' she said.

'Don't mention it. Thanks for mine. Delayed though it be. I love waiting around in a dreary hotel for someone who doesn't turn up. Oh, sorry, I shouldn't have said dreary, you like this place, don't you?'

'Now you're being childish.'

'Am I?'

'Yes. And spiteful.'

'And what are you being? What have you been up to?' he shouted. 'Who've you been carrying on with while I'm away?' He suddenly became aware that they were both shouting, that the receptionist was enjoying the scene with undisguised interest. 'Come on,' he took Marianne's arm roughly. 'Let's get out of here.'

The street was crowded. A pale winter sun, the colour of egg white, shone faintly. They threaded their way amongst women pushing prams, groups of servicemen and couples arm-in-arm. Charles tried to hold on to Marianne's arm, but with remarkable agility she twisted it out of his grasp, walking beside him then but out of range as if at any moment she would dart off and leave him.

'I thought you'd be pleased to see me!' she said reproachfully. 'It was you who suggested it.'

'I'd things to sort out with you.'

'What things?'

'Your strange behaviour.'

'It's your mother, isn't it? *She* wrote to you, didn't she? She'd seen me.'

'Quite rightly.'

'Quite wrongly! She hates me! She doesn't want me to have anything to do with you. I saw it in her eyes. She was so *glad*! So glad to think she'd caught me. It made her evening.'

'Rubbish! And anyway, I had my suspicions before.'

'Suspicions of what, for heaven's sake?'

'Of you. And other men.'

She stopped in her tracks and clenched her fists. 'How dare you!'

'I dare because,' he grabbed her wrist and pulled her into the doorway of a café, 'because I love you,' he finished thickly, and kissed her on the mouth. She returned his kiss tight-lipped at first, unwillingly and angrily, and then with a passion that made his blood race.

'Listen, Marianne,' he said shakily, when she finally pulled away from him. 'We can't go on like this . . . being separated . . . ' But before he had time to finish the sentence, she took a step back out of the doorway, turned and disappeared.

Her disappearance was abrupt and uncanny. He began running in the direction she seemed to have gone. He searched the length and breadth of the busy street. He peered in shops. He searched the faces of a queue which had formed up outside a butcher's shop. He ran up and down a cinema queue.

Finally, he went into the park and sat down on a deserted bench. He sat dejectedly, his head bowed, his hands hanging loose. He had been there for no more than a quarter of an hour when Marianne came and sat beside him. She put her hand on his arm and said, 'I'm sorry.'

He said nothing. He didn't ask her how she had found him or how she had disappeared. But suddenly he knew. Those two events clicked together in his mind.

'You got so angry before I could explain,' she said. 'I didn't know how to begin. Or if I could explain. I just wanted to be on my own to try to think what to say to you.'

'You don't have to,' he said. 'At least not all of it. The Army type isn't a boyfriend, is he?'

'Of course he isn't. You don't think I'm as disloyal as that, do you?'

'I know you're not. But people can change.'

'*I* don't. *I* shall never change.'

'He's a colleague, isn't he?'

'Yes.'

'A colleague for what?'

'I can't say.'

'Not even to me?'

She looked at him mutely and he said heavily, 'It's OK, I won't press you. So it's something highly secret. So secret you have to use a box number. And you're half-French, bilingual. It doesn't take an Einstein to add two and two there.' He paused. 'Why?' He rounded on her sharply and suddenly. 'Why Marianne? Why do this to us?'

'Christ!' she answered equally angrily again. '*You* ask *me*? *You*? Of all people. Oh, it's perfectly all right for you to get into action. You bind enough about getting on fighters. What about *me*? What about *my* feelings? What about *my* father? And my mother? I want to go back . . . I want to do something useful there.'

'So that's what it is.' He said nothing for several moments. 'You're going to be dropped. Parachuted in?'

'I didn't say so.'

'You didn't have to. Anyway, I'm hardly likely to bruit it around.' He drew a long breath. 'It's your bloody French blood. The French are impossible.' She said nothing and he went on, 'I didn't think they sent women.'

'Now they do. They're less noticeable. Men of military age attract attention.'

'And they reckon you wouldn't?'

'Much less so.'

'And what are you supposed to do when you get there?'

'That I don't know.'

'Christ,' he said, shaking his head, unable to begin to express his emotions. 'And how the hell did you land yourself up in this? Why didn't you ask *me* first?'

'It just happened. I was approached. It was a way of using my French they said. And you weren't here to ask.'

Charles put his head in his hands and groaned. 'D'you know I'd rather you *had* been having an affair with that Army type. I'd rather my mother had been right,' he exclaimed bitterly after a moment. 'At least I could have beaten hell out of him.'

'You wouldn't do that. Not really, would you?' she said, cupping his face in her hands and kissing him slowly, and with a strange innocent sensuality.

This time it was he who drew away. 'Yes, really,' he said. He found himself shaking with anger. 'Didn't you know what this could do to *me*?'

'What does your flying do to *me*?'

'That's not the same. A man's expected —'

'A man's expected to what?'

'To fight.'

'But why?'

'I don't know. All I know is that you've put yourself at risk, so you've done the most bloody awful thing to me that you could have done.'

He almost hated her then for the future pain she would cause him. He had not known it was possible to care so desperately and to be so afraid for anyone.

They sat in silence. Far away children played on the park swings. There was the hum of the encircling traffic. But the seat was sheltered by rhododendrons and laurels. They were contained in their own unhappy peace.

'Maybe the war will be over before I ever get there.'

'Oh, very likely!' Charles clenched his fists. 'This war will go on for years!' He drew a deep breath. 'Have you any idea when you'll go?'

She shook her head. 'Not for ages. There's still more training after we leave here. But,' she looked at her watch, 'I have to go back to the centre soon.'

'I'll take you there.'

'No, you mustn't.'

'Why not?'

'It's a secret place.'

'Where?'

369

'I can't tell you.'

He gritted his teeth. 'Shall I see you tomorrow, then? I shall have to go back after that.'

'I can't, darling. I'm sorry. I shouldn't really have come today.'

'The brown job objected did he?' he asked bitterly. 'Is it going to be like this from now on? Meeting just long enough to have a bloody row?'

Her eyes filled with tears. 'Oh, Charles, don't be like that.'

The tears streamed down her face. Absurdly he was reminded of her as a little girl all those years ago. Immediately his anger dissolved. He flung his arms round her, pressing her body close to him, kissing her mouth, her eyes, her hair, her neck. She responded wildly and almost desperately. 'Come back to the hotel,' he said thickly. 'Now. Come to my room. I love you. I want you. Now.'

'I can't. I must get back. But I'll get leave soon. They've told us. In a few weeks when we finish here. Then I'll come to you. And it'll be all right then, I promise.'

SIX

Charles joined Forrester in London, and they travelled together by train to Stanton. A Hillman car was waiting for them at the station.

The transport took them into apparently deserted countryside. There was no sign of the usual RAF watertower on legs, no sign of hangars or runways or barrack blocks. The sun had set, but it was not yet quite dark. The sky to the west shone a watery yellow, sending a faint shimmer over the flat ploughed fields flooded after a month's rain. It was a depressing landscape in tune with Charles's mood. As they turned the corner of a winding lane, a guardroom suddenly emerged from a farm hedge. Usually so lax, service police surrounded the car, demanded their identity cards and searched them and their baggage.

'This place stinks,' Forrester said. 'Literally and allegorically!' The driver took them past cowsheds, a pond complete with ducks, a hen run, turnip fields, a muckyard and a dilapidated farmhouse.

'What d'you suppose this place really is?' Charles asked, as having been allocated suspiciously comfortable rooms, they descended to an equally comfortable bar for the pre-dinner noggin. The Mess was full of pilots – experienced ones by the number of gong ribbons, with a handful of Army officers and a few civilians. All looked well-fed, as if in a country house retreat. No one was talking flying. The hangar doors were firmly closed.

'And why all the guards?' Charles asked. 'You saw them, I suppose?'

'I counted five outside one cowshed, laddie! Not to mention a couple defending the manure heap. Could this be typical RAF planning?'

Both of them had begun to suspect. Perhaps Charles after his meeting with Marianne was more alive to the way events in Europe were moving. Perhaps he already felt a glimmer of their inevitably conjoined fates. He was more suspicious still, as going for a stroll behind the Mess after dinner, he came to an ordinary telephone box. Thinking that he might now telephone his mother, he discovered the box to be padlocked. Then as he lay awake that night going over in his mind both the strangeness of RAF Stanton and the frustration of his last meeting with Marianne, he heard the sound of aircraft engines. Padding to the window, cautiously raising the blackout an inch, he looked out.

The moon was in its third quarter and clear of any cloud. It flooded the countryside with its pale light. By it was clearly visible the familiar black shape of a Lysander, rising astonishingly out of what appeared to be a field of brussels sprouts.

Again, like a dark kaleidoscope, the pieces of his life shifted into shape and pattern. It was little surprise to him when, in the morning, the CO summoned Forrester and him to his office and, after saying, 'I suppose by now you're

371

wondering what all this is about,' told them that they were in the Moon Squadron where every word was *Top Secret*.

During the next two weeks, Charles found out why.

Like any normal airfield, there *were* runways – but narrow ones between the turnips and brussels sprouts so from the air they looked like roads. The thatched farmyard barns concealed Operations, Intelligence Offices and store-houses. Up in the haylofts were rows of shelves for parachutes, changing rooms, wardrobes full of continental clothes and shoes, stocks of Gauloise cigarettes, Michelin maps, safes full of forged papers, rows of little transmitter and receiver radios. Right at the far end, always double-padlocked even in this secret area, was the armoury, filled with light automatic weapons. There was a little room where people referred to as 'Joes' turned out their pockets before departing in the little Lysanders and where they received in return their tablet – a suicide pill guaranteed to kill in six seconds.

A mile down the road, was a heavily guarded country house called Hansell's Hall, where these 'Joes' had a brief idyll of comfort and good food before they left. These were under the orders of an organisation called Special Operations Executive, with headquarters in Baker Street.

The young men sent by SOE to Hansell's Hall spent their time playing games – tennis, croquet, ping-pong, cards – until the moonlit night when a Hillman with all its windows blacked out conveyed them, two by two, to the door of Operations. Here they would be given their final briefing, their radio equip-ment, their knives and revolvers, their poison, then off they would go in a Moon Squadron Lysander, leaving all trace of their previous identities behind.

'Clean out your pockets, ladies and gentlemen! Don't leave a penny behind! Give till it hurts!'

So spoke the young man with the Brylcreemed brown hair who stood on the Wings for Victory platform in Hyde Park. Beside him , to her surprise, Amelia saw Lady Diana Nazier.

But a changed Diana Nazier, one swathed in pale mink, not the black leather coat she had been photographed in a few years ago when she flew in German airships with her German friends. Today she sported a red, white and blue rosette in the lapel of her mink. There was a silver model of a Spitfire beside the platform, and in front of it there were young innocent-faced RAF men holding collecting tins.

'I hate her!' Amelia said to Cummings, shivering with anger.

Ronald had brought her up to spend Sunday afternoon in London followed by dinner at the Dorchester. 'We'll have a stroll in the park and then an unrationed meal. You need a change,' he had said.

These days she was unusually depressed. She felt in her bones that something was wrong with Charles. She rarely heard from Arthur, though her long phone calls to Prudence were a great comfort. And – a perennial, unassuageable grief – she missed James in every nerve of her being.

The war news, too, was bad. The Vichy government in France had allowed the Japanese their bases in Indo-China. Singapore was in peril. Russia wanted supplies from Britain, which meant Arthur might go on that long dangerous convoy to Murmansk.

372

'Thank heavens Diana Nazier doesn't come in person to our board meetings,' Ronald said, taking Amelia's arm.

'Thank you, Gerald Saville!'

Diana was on her feet, leading the clapping. The smooth young man carefully pinched up the knees of his trousers and sat down.

'Who is Saville?' Amelia asked.

Ronald shrugged. 'From his pinstripe suit, I'd say a merchant banker.'

'Then Stefan Lehmann will know him.'

'I doubt it.' He began to lead her away. 'What you need is a drink, Amelia. I'm going to take you into the Dorchester and clean out my pockets, you mark my words, and spend every penny on the very best brandy.'

But the brandy somehow failed to warm that deathly chill Amelia felt inside herself. 'If we lost the war,' Amelia said suddenly, 'it would be people like Diana Nazier we'd find bobbing to the top and taking charge.'

It was the first time she had ever allowed herself to consider the possibility of defeat. James, she thought, would have been ashamed of her. Two hours and three brandies later, the lounge of the Dorchester became suddenly silent. There was an important news item, the waiter whispered to Ronald. The radio was being put on for the benefit of their guests.

The news was indeed important. Following a lightning Japanese airborne attack on the US base at Pearl Harbor in which two battleships had been sunk, many aircraft destroyed and thousands of casualties inflicted, the United States was at war with Japan and the Axis powers.

Amelia and Ronald sat for several minutes in profound silence. Then Cummings clasped her hand and said, 'You mark my words, Amelia . . . the tide has turned. The worst is over.'

The worst was not over.

The battleships *Repulse* and the *Prince of Wales* were sunk by the Japanese. Singapore fell. Besieged Malta was starving. At Stanton, where Charles and Forrester spent their time training on easy trips just inside the French coast, two Lysanders were shot down near Fontainebleau with their 'Joes' on board and another disappeared over the Channel. While they waited impatiently to do more difficult operations, they beat up the local pubs and went into Bedford in a clapped-out old Austin that Forrester had bought.

It was not till February that they were given trips deep into enemy territory. Charles began dropping human cargoes everywher – in France, Belgium, Holland, even Germany. With them, he dropped boxes of explosives, submachine-guns, wireless transmitters, after landing on pocket-handkerchief size fields lit by four tiny torches.

After dropping one load, he would pick up another and fly home – agents, Maquis whom the Gestapo were pursuing, spies, French soldiers coming to join de Gaulle. One night, he brought back two agents who had been tortured by the SS. One died before he managed to land at Stanton.

One comfort was that he had heard that the old argument that women shouldn't be dropped into enemy-occupied territory had come up again at headquaters. Certainly no women had yet made an appearance at Hansell's Hall. Then, suddenly, a girl with fair hair arrived. The argument had clearly been resolved. Forrester dropped her near Amiens. Other girls followed. He longed to find out what Marianne was doing. Her letters to him were guarded, and his to her contained nothing about his activities. But he constantly wrote. *When can we meet? How about coming to Haybury?* And then as spring arrived, *Do you think we can spend Easter together?*

She wrote back saying, *I doubt I shall be here at Easter.*

The night he received that letter, he was having a drink with Forrester in the bar when Forrester suggested a stroll up to Hansell's Hall for a game of ping-pong.

They strolled to the games' room. The door was half-open, and there could just be heard the quick pit-pat exchange of celluloid ball by wooden bats. An Army captain and a WAAF officer were utterly concentrating on a sharp rally.

Then the Army officer hit too hard. The ball landed wide. The man called, 'You're too good for me, Lisette.'

The WAAF officer swung round to catch the bouncing ball.

It was Marianne.

'We've finished.' The girl called Lisette gave him a non-committal smile and handed him her bat. 'You can have the table now.'

The Army officer came up to join her. As they walked out through the door, she said, 'You can have your revenge after supper, Jean-Paul!'

'Shall we play for service?' Forrester called across the net, and when Charles missed the ball completely, added derisively, 'You'll have to do better than that!'

Charles lost the first six points. He was hardly aware of the ball. All his mind was concentrated on the fact that the moment he had hoped would never arrive had come – and gone. Marianne had come to Stanton . . .

How soon would she be gone?

'My game! What's up, Charles? Gone blind?'

Not a flicker of recognition had crossed her face, though she could have not had the slightest idea she might find him here, while he had known of the possibility for months. Training? Or after all these months had the memory of him faded? Was this Army chap the same character Mama had seen her with?

Charles said, 'Too many late nights.'

'Too much booze, you mean! You owe me a quid.'

'Want another game?'

'No, thanks. Bit peckish. Let's go and have supper.'

She was sitting at the far table, talking with the Army officer. She saw him come in, then quickly looked away.

Through tomato soup, shepherd's pie and prunes and custard, Forrester soliloquised on about some woman he'd met on his last trip to London.

'How about coming up to town next Saturday, and I'll ask her to bring a friend?'

'No, thanks.'

When they went into the ante-room, she had already finished her coffee. He manoeuvred Forrester close to where they were sitting, knowing his CO would be unable to resist chatting up a woman.

'Anyone for tennis?' Forrester said to the girl called Lisette, pointing his lighted cigarette languidly at the rain pouring down outside.

'Not exactly the weather.' Though he might look like a Frog, the Army officer spoke perfect English. 'We were wondering whether there was a cinema on the camp?'

'In one word . . . no. But there's a fleapit in Bedford and I happen to have a couple of gallons in the old banger if you'd care to – '

'No . . . no.'

' – accompany my friend and me there.'

The Army officer looked at the girl. She gave the slightest inclination of her head. 'Thanks.' They both stood up. 'By the way, my name is Jean-Paul and this is Lisette.'

'I'm John Forrester and this laddie is Charles Haybury.'

She gave him a charming smile. Charles tried to smile back.

Forrester said, 'Off you go and get your coat, Lisette. We'll get ours and meet you in the hall.'

Outside the Mess, on the pretence of keeping her out of the rain, Charles bundled her into the back seat and then got in beside her.

'Lisette would be more comfortable with me at the front, Charles.'

'She's safer here at the back with me, John.'

Charles put out his hand and took hers. Up front, Forrester chattered away as the car wound damply through the winding lanes.

'You two are remarkable quiet at the back.'

'We're perfectly happy, thank you, John.'

And so they were – for the moment. Just for this short time, the future need not be looked at. Tomorrow was a long way off. This was today. The future, like *mañana*, might never come. The past —

Suddenly the past slid out sideways from between the trunks of misty trees. No signposts, no place names. Neither he nor anyone else in the car had any idea where they were. And then in the slight light from the hooded headlights, ust past a triangle of sodden grass, he recognised a curved stone wall, saw the gravestones and the wet grey shadow of a church tower.

Cardington – Cardington churchyard. Immediately he was back in the past, standing beside his mother watching his father's remains and those of the other victims of the R101 slowly descend into that vast hole in the ground . . .

He shivered.

Forrester was still chattering. Jean-Paul was politely listening. The view meant nothing to them, nor what had happened here eleven years ago. Marianne —

Charles took his eyes away from the scene outside, and looked at her. Her profile gave nothing away. Only a momentary tightening of her hand on his told him that some sensitive awareness had caught that tremor and was answering it.

Then the car was through Cardington village, was rounding the corner into the suburbs of Bedford, turned off sharply into the car park of the Odeon.

'Judy Garland in *The Wizard of Oz*.' Forrester read out the poster. 'Anybody seen it?'

Nobody had. In they trooped. Charles bought the tickets and, leading the way, escorted her through the powder-and-cigarette-smoke scented darkness into the back row of the stalls. Like a guardian angel, the Army officer took up position on Marianne's other side.

The main film had already started.

A girl with an oval face surrounded by the little inhabitants of Oz was dancing down a cobbled street, singing, 'We're off to see the wizard! The wonderful wizard of Oz . . .'

Charles stared at the screen – saying nothing, only aware of the pressure of her hand gripping his.

The picture suddenly began crackling at the edges, wobbled, stopped. The moving figures froze. Then there was total darkness. Whistling started, followed by the lights coming up.

'Film's broken,' Forrester announced. 'Anybody want a lemonade to drown their sorrows? Everybody? Right . . .'

He and Jean-Paul set off to join the queue in the aisle that led to the usherette carrying a trayful of lemonade and ices. Charles said to her, 'When are you going?'

'Tomorrow night.'

'Lysander or Halifax?'

'Lysander.'

Forrester held two glasses of pale green liquid in front of them. 'One for you, Lisette, and one for the little laddie.'

A minute later, the lights went off. On came the picture again and flickered uneventfully to its happy ending. Nobody said much on the trip back to Stanton. The future seemed to hang over all of them.

'Night, Lisette. Night, Jean-Paul.'

'Goodnight.'

Charles watched her go up the stairs behind the Army officer, hoping she would look back but she didn't.

On their way back to the Officers' Mess, Charles said, 'OK if I take your trip tomorrow, John?'

'Why?'

'Just happens to be more convenient.'

'Ha-ha!'

'Thanks, John, I knew you'd understand.'

Next day, it was still raining. Since he was flying that night, Charles did not have to go down to flights. Briefing was at eleven o'clock. The weather had cleared – he would much prefer it cloudy. There was a full moon bringing up the flat Bedfordshire countryside like day.

He walked to Operations, partly because it was such a glorious night, mostly to compose his mind. The air smelled of damp honeysuckle and wild roses. Just outside the aerodrome, amongst the cow parsley and the barley, he saw the tiny red blob, and stopping, he picked the scarlet pimpernel – for luck.

Operations reeked of tobacco smoke. Destination was near Chartres. Three white lights to land. No particular problems, the intelligence officer said. Usual reception committee. Colours of the day, two red cartridges.

The black Hillman was waiting by his Lysander when finally he emerged from Operations. As he walked across the tarmac, the rear door opened and she got out.

She was wearing a beautifully cut grey flannel costume, the skirt inches longer than was being worn in England, black hat, black shoes and carrying a black handbag – the typical smart Parisienne. Behind her came the Army officer in a very French raincoat. From the boot, airmen began unloading ammunition and stores – submachine-guns, revolvers, small bombs and grenades – and putting them in the aircraft.

He raised his hand casually. 'Hello, again.'

'Hello,' she said.

'Sleep all right?'

'Fine.'

'Bit better weather tonight.'

'Yes.'

'Your turn to sit in the back with Lisette tonight, Jean-Paul.'

'That's right.'

Charles held the ladder for her. 'OK, jump in!'

Five minutes later, propeller ticking idly over, they taxied sedately to the head of the runway.

'Here we go then!'

The engine roared. Heavier than usual, nevertheless the Lysander left the ground almost immediately and went into a slow climbing turn to port.

Charles called back to them, 'ETA Chartres three twenty-two.'

As they slipped past moonlit Cambridge all he could think of to say was, 'There should be a flask of coffee behind me, if anyone feels like a cuppa.'

Nobody did. They'd be feeling much like him, he thought. The Jean-Paul chap looked sombre. Just before crossing the coast of England, he turned to Marianne and produced the little scarlet flower he had picked from the hedgerow and gave it to her. 'For luck!'

It was a simple gesture, the sort of thing, in such circumstances, any pilot might have done to any passenger. But even before she had time to say anything Jean-Paul took it away. 'I'm afraid she can't have it.'

'Why ever not?'

'Scarlet pimpernels don't grow in the Chartres area. If it was found on her, there would be questions.'

A sensible reason; he should be grateful such forethought surrounded her. But this rejection struck a cold note. 'I'm sorry,' he said. 'I should have thought.'

Then he turned his attention to his flying, throttled back and dived down to nought feet above the moonlit surface of the Channel.

Over on the left now was the Le Havre peninsula and the pale halo of Normandy. 'Coming up to the enemy coast,' he told them. 'May have to jink a bit.'

Vaulting over a hill he followed a deserted road, detoured a town, plunged along a forest track, kicked the Lizzie round to avoid a farmhouse, all the time penetrating deeper into France.

'I can see the cathedral now,' Jean-Paul said.

Swinging well to the left of the city, Charles climbed. 'Shout if you see an L of white lights,' he told them.

They leaned forward over him. Momentarily Marianne put her hand on his shoulder. He saw a wood, a railway line, the garden of some château, an avenue of trees.

Marianne called out, 'There!' He kicked on left rudder, saw the lights almost beneath them, slammed down full flap, throttled right back.

377

With a *chop-chop-chop* of the windmilling propeller, the Lysander descended, swung round the trunk of a poplar, slipped over a dark hedge, softly brushed the grass with its wheels and had stopped by the second light, engine still ticking over.

Like ghosts in the moonlight, two men and a woman came running forward. The exit of the Lysander was opened. Marianne and Jean-Paul jumped out. Within a minute, ammunition and stores had been unloaded.

'Good luck . . .' Charles whispered, *'au revoir!'*

Everyone round the Lysander suddenly disappeared except for a man ahead with a torch who was waving him round. Every moment he was here was a danger to them – they wanted him off and away.

He wheeled round and slowly taxied back to the first light of the L. As he turned into the wind, he saw they had brought bicycles and Marianne was already riding one, going further and further away from him, becoming more shadowy every second as she bumped unevely over the moonlit grass towards a gate at the far end of the field.

SEVEN

On the moonlit nights that followed, Charles saw dozens of such figures disappearing into the shadows of Occupied Europe. Regularly he descended quietly, dropped Resistance workers, and took out other uncommunicative figures, who immediately on arrival at Stanton were swept off for questioning in the black Hillman.

During 1942, these 'Joes' were joined by surviving members of bomber crews who had been handed down the escape route to him. As the war hung in the balance, the RAF stepped up its bombing. Hamburg, Düisberg and the Ruhr, Düsseldorf, Wilhelmshaven, Osnabrück were pounded, though with heavy losses. Two USAAF groups equipped with Boeing B17 Flying Fortresses had arrived in England, and shortly afterwards were bombing railway targets at Amiens. But the German fighters and ack-ack took their toll.

Increasingly, it was shotdown crews who scrambled into the Lysander. And increasingly, after the Dieppe raid, the Lysanders failed to elude the probings of the now heavily reinforced searchlights and the firing of the much stronger ack-ack defences. How was this greater vigilance by the enemy going to affect Marianne's chances? How was she even to escape the raids of our own bombers, Charles thought bitterly as summer dwindled with the bad news outweighing the good. Malta was besieged, bombed day and night. Eastern and northern England were still being regularly raided at night by the Luftwaffe. Rommel had launched a fierce attack on the Eighth Army and reached the gates of Cairo. U-boat packs were still sinking vital shipping in the Atlantic. Air Commodore the Duke of Kent and all but one of the occupants of a flying boat were killed when their Sunderland flew into a Scottish mountain.

In early autumn, Cummings wrote to Charles that he had heard via the aeronautical grapevine that a jet-engined aircraft had made its first flight in the USA. It was made by the Bell Aircraft Corporation of Buffalo, and was powered by engines developed from Whittle's British design. This was on a fighter, but jet propulsion must be considered for a later mark of the civil aviation Ajax when peace came. And had he any experience of the fog-burning device called Fido?

Although Montgomery won the battle of El Alamein, peace and Ajax were a long way away. Charles found it difficult to think of anything but would it be Marianne he was picking up tonight? Always it was other faces, smiling with relief in the faint glow of light. The net seemed to be tightening about her. Within days of Operation Torch, the Allied invasion of French North Africa, German and Italian troops entered Unoccupied France. So that back door of

379

slipping from Occupied to Unoccupied France if urgent need arose, was closed to her.

Bringing back a middle-aged Frenchwoman at the end of November, Charles found himself breaking the Lysander pilots' rigid rule, and whispering to her, as he handed her the thermos of coffee, 'Have you any news of the girl Lisette?'

She shrugged and shook her head. But she squeezed his arm, and her eyes looked so sympathetic and sad that he almost wept.

It was the quiet self-contained kindliness of the Joes that was almost as unnerving as the flak. Though the French were supposed to be such a volatile demonstrative race, never did he see any display of emotion. That they were so was shown in simple, moving ways. Picking up two Resistance workers on 15 December, he saw they carried a crate. It was of champagne. *Bon Noël* was written beneath the Cross of Lorraine.

It was on that same trip that the contact handed him a thick package with the instructions that he was to deliver it personally to SOE HQ in Baker Street.

'A buckshee trip to London. Shopping spree thrown in. Some people have all the luck.' forrester asked with simulated envy, 'What'll you do? Pick up some floozie and take her to the Miramar?'

'Possibly,' Charles smiled. 'Or I might just make it the Savoy.'

In fact he did more or less that. Because of the apparent importance of his mission, he was driven up to Baker Street in the black Hillman, and shown into an office where an anonymous man in a grey flannel suit asked him the exact time of the pick-up, the exact words the contact had used, told him to forget he had ever been to his office and then he was dismissed. As he left, the man smiled faintly and said, 'Enjoy the champagne!' It was the only indication, Charles thought, that he was human.

No one that afternoon in those darkening streets seemed to be human. Anonymous crowds were hurrying into the tube station on their way home from work. The blue lit buses looked packed with subhuman bundles. Searchlights were playing behind the dome of St Paul's. The whole capital seemed unknown and uncaring.

He tried to think of anyone he knew in London at this particular moment. But everyone he knew was in the Forces. He considered the possibility of catching a train to Haybury. But sore and sad as he was about Marianne, he couldn't face Amelia's possible probing. In the end, he was just toying with the idea of going straight back to Stanton when he thought of Prudence.

He went into Baker Street station and managed to find a telephone box that actually worked. He wondered why he hadn't thought of her before. But he knew why he hadn't. His relationship with Prudence was a delicate one, difficult to describe even to himself. Of course she was probably out or on duty, he thought, giving her number to the operator. The phone rang for a long time and he was on the point of hanging up, when the line clicked open.

Her voice, her cautious, 'Hello?' moved him strangely. Like so many people these days it was conditioned to such a caustic mixture of fear and hope.

'Charles here, Pru. Hope you didn't think it might be Arthur. I'm up in London. Just a brief visit. And I wondered —'

'Oh, my dear!' There was no mistaking her delight. 'What a lovely surprise!

How did you manage it? Are you on leave? Not embarkation, I hope? No, I didn't think it might be Arthur. I've just had a letter fom him. Do you know he's actually seen Rachel. Tell you all about him when I see you. I am going to see you, aren't I?'

When he could get another word in, he said, 'That was the idea. That's why I rang.'

'Oh, good! *Wonderful*! Where? When?'

'I was going to ask you that. I didn't know how you were fixed. Whether you are on duty or going out.'

'I was. I am. I mean, I was on duty till just before you rang. I was in my bath. All five inches of it. And I was going out, but I won't if you'd rather not.'

'Out where?'

'To the Savoy.'

'Who with?'

'Oh, my dear brother-in-law, you don't have to ask me that! With no one in particular. With a whole crowd. You remember Margaret Challoner at my wedding . . . ?'

'The hunger marcher?'

'The same. With her and her hsband and masses of types. Some of the other drivers. Bods on leave. Etcetera. Anyway, can you come round to the flat? And we'll take it from there?' She made kissing sounds into the telephone before she hung up and said, 'Dear Charles, how sweet it was of you to ring!'

She was still in the same ebullient mood when he arrived at Hals Crescent. She was dressed in a black sequined evening gown that left her shoulders bare and showed her neat little ankles. She was wearing very high heels, and her hair was piled up on top of her head in sausage curls. Her face was thinner, her eyes shadowed, and as if to make up for the pinchedness of her face, her lips were pillar-box red and her cheeks thickly rouged. She looked exactly like a little girl dressed up in her mother's clothes.

'You look stunning,' he said, kissing her cheek.

'And you look thin. Are they working you too hard?'

'I'm practically running the war.'

'You look it.' She poured him a stiff Scotch. 'Now tell me what you'd like to do? Have a meal quietly somewhere, Jerry permitting? Or go and whoop it up at the Savoy? The nice thing about the Savoy is they have a damned good shelter, so you can continue the party even if Jerry drops in.'

For various reasons, the leat of which was his own inclination, Charles chose to go along and whoop it up at the Savoy. There, to the music of Carol Gibbons and the Savoy Hotel Orpheans, he held Prudence in his arms as in what seemed another existence he had held Marianne.

'You were going to tell me about Rachel and Arthur?' Charles reminded her.

'So I was. Rachel first. Arthur's on a frigate called *Eglantine*. God knows where, but they did put in for a you-know-what at Boston. Phoned Aunt Victoria and she and Uncle Henry brought Rachel to meet him. Rachel cried. Didn't recognise him. Upset Arthur a bit. But she's fine. Looked very bonny.'

'Is Arthur on the Atlantic now?'

She shook her head. 'From what I gather he's got himself to the other side of the world, reading between the lines. No leave for months, he writes.'

She looked suddenly sad.

'He'll be all right,' Charles said. 'Did I ever tell you I ran into a chap on the train who knew him? Said he was in the pink. You're in more danger here than he is, Pru.'

As if to give credence to words he wasn't sure were true, the air-raid sirens went. But no one seemed to take any notice. The band played its smooth way on. 'Thank you so much for that lovely weekend', 'These foolish things', 'Wish me luck as you wave me goodbye' . . .

All the smoochy sentimental tunes that made the couples cling tightly together under the soft lights. No bombs were falling. They all seemed to move in a softly lit sweet-smelling oasis. Prudence looked up at him. 'You seem sad, Charles?'

He shook his head, 'I haven't felt happier in months.'

'That could mean anything.' Her eyes searched his face. 'What's her name?'

'Why do women always think it's a woman?'

'Because it always is.'

'That's the vanity of women.'

'It's not. It's the law of nature.'

'This time's the exception.'

'Liar,' she said. But she didn't press him.

Two foxtrots later, she tackled him from another angle. 'You're not worrying about your mother, are you?'

'No,' he held her away from him worriedly. 'Should I be? She writes very cheerfully. So does Cummings.'

Pru shook her head. 'I didn't mean that you should. I simply wondered. Elderly parent and all that, one does worry. I worry about my father.' She smiled wryly. 'I think of them as my trinity of worries. Arthur, Rachel and my father.'

Charles was astonished at how fiercely he envied that blessed trinity. When she went on, 'I often wonder why he doesn't ask your mother to marry him. He's so fond of her. And it would make us so much of a family,' he felt as if she were talking of a world into which, for some reason, he could never enter.

It was not only Charles who thought he was being excluded from a particular world. That was exactly what Stefan Lehmann was thinking as he drove down from Shotfield to Haybury that New Year's Eve.

Beneath the mellow and urbane smoothness of his business manner was hidden a diffidence in his personal relationships. That side had previously been totally fulfilled by a very happy marriage. After his wife had died, he had tried to fill the void with a continuous involvement in his many activities which had been vastly increased by the war. What spare time he had from organising factories for the maximum effort against Germany he still devoted to the welfare of Jewish refugees. That Christmas he had spent on his own supervising a new aircraft shadow factory in Northumberland. He had posted his presents to Prudence and Amelia – the ones to Rachel had gone months before – and had phoned them on Christmas Day, but it wasn't enough. So for New Year's Eve – since Prudence was on duty – he had decided to surprise Amelia and give himself a treat.

Now he drove fast, skirting Southampton – no searchlights, no flak, only the barrage balloons tinged yellow by the moonlight – eager to reach Haybury and see Amelia. Even though I am seven years older – nothing when you come to think of it – she and I are the surviving Edwardians. Of our little circle, only she and I can remember not only what it was like before this war, but before the Great War and indeed before the Boer War. And even though she is so enterprising and courageous, in these difficult days certainly she is leaning more on me . . .

Which is just as it should be, he said to himself as he brought the car to a halt outside the Hall. 1942 had been pretty gloomy. Terrible Allied ship losses through U-boats; 24 ships sunk on the PQ17 convoy to Russia of which, he was pretty sure though his son-in-law said nothing, HMS *Eglantine* had been one of the escorts. But 1943 – surely he could have his own dreams and hopes? – might turn out to be an *annus mirabilis* . . .

Taking the bottle of champagne he had brought down from the back of the car, he ran up the steps and rang the bell. It was Amelia herself who opened the door. 'Stefan . . . what a lovely surprise!'

'I thought we owed it to ourselves,' he said, after they had kissed, 'to bring in the New Year together.'

'Stefan . . . how thoughtful! I *am* glad. Just leave your coat . . . Pearson'll collect it eventually . . . and come on into the library.'

He was already going over in his mind what he was going to say. In the dark room the only illumination was the blazing fire at the end.

'Stefan!' A figure had risen from the armchair to the left of the hearth and now came over to shake hands. 'How nice to see you!'

'Ronald and I,' Amelia said, 'have just had a little New Year's Eve supper. Now let me get Cook to —'

'No, Amelia, thank you. I've had something.'

In the end, he had a plate of cold turkey and a slice of Cook's eggless fatless chocolate cake on a tray. Then they talked about the past year and what chances there were of a Second Front and the overthrow of Hitler in the year to come.

'Mark my words, the Nazzis' – Ronald had taken on Churchill's pronunciation and he rolled the word round his tongue with relish – 'are on the run!'

Were they, Amelia was thinking as she stared into the fire. And even if they were, might not they produce some horrifying backlash against us? That was what old Mr March had prophesied when she had taken his Christmas present down to the forge. He had had no news of Marianne. Pierre had gone to the Mediterranean and had taken part in the invasion of French North Africa.

And what about her children, he had asked. What news of them? She had been able to tell him just as little. What exactly *was* Arthur doing in the Navy? What exactly *was* Charles doing in the RAF? What dangers had Prudence run during the Blitz when London was on fire? All three of them were so flippant.

She looked across at Stefan sitting on the other side of the fire from her and caught his eye and realised that he was thinking exactly the same. She smiled at him, and he smiled back. We have so much in common, she thought. Rachel, at least she's all right. But those other three, they are all hostages to fortune. Let them be safe – that is all he and I are wishing for 1943.

The grandfather clock in the corner struck midnight.

'Happy New Year, Amelia!' Stefan took her in his arms and smiled and kissed her. 'May 1943 be an *annus mirabilis*!'

But he had not, after all, spoken the words that were closest to his heart.

383

1943 stated with a bang. At Stalingrad, Field Marshal von Paulus and the whole German Sixth Army surrendered to the Russians.

'Didn't I say the Nazzis were on the run?' Ronald said. 'Now, Amelia, we must look to the future. We must plan for peace. We must hurry up with Ajax V!'

The building of the civil airliner prototype had indeed been a lifeline. There was something to look forward to beyond the war. Impressed with the Lysander's slow speed – particularly useful for small rough grass airfields – Charles had devised leading edge flaps that would increase its lift and shorten its landing run. There was still at leastthree years' work before it would be flying, but both Charles and Cummings were excited at the basic design and the way it could be 'stretched' to build larger versions.

Now the government had also the foresight to look forward to peace, too. As, night after night, hundreds of Halifaxes and Lancasters pounded Hamburg, Berlin and the Ruhr, continuing the destruction wrought by USAAF Liberators and Fortresses by day, the Air Ministry did not wholly absorb itself with building bombers. A group of experts called the Brabazon Committee had detailed Britain's civil airliner requirements for peace, and interested aircraft manufacturers were invited to a secret meeting on 10 July at the Ministry to discuss the proposals.

Amongst the many reserved seats for representatives of Handley-Page, Avro, Airspeed and De Havilland appeared three labelled Jerningham Aviation. They were occupied by Amelia, Cummings and Charles who had come down from Stanton specially. The hall was packed. Everyone listened intently.

To Charles's surprise, the ideas presented were imaginative: a non-stop Atlantic airliner; a medium sized turbo-prop 30-seater; a pure jet for the Empire routes; and a small eight-to-ten seater for feeder services. He was particularly interested in hearing that jet engines with turbos but no propellers were going to go ahead so fast. The first British jet, the Gloster fighter, had already flown, and such a quick transition to peace he wholeheartedly supported.

He came out of the meeting elated. Ajax, he said, in various modified versions and with different engines, could be adapted to most of the requirements. Amelia was pleased he was in such good spirits. Cummings had to go back to the factory straight after the meeting, and she and Charles went to the Trocadero for a drink and then dinner. The place was packed with men and women in uniform. The atmosphere behind the blackout curtains was thick with the smell of Camel cigarettes and Gauloises.

'It's nice to have a long chat with you, Charles,' she said as they lingered over coffee. 'But when are you coming to Haybury for leave? Surely it's long overdue?'

'Busy, Mama. You know how it is.'

'What exactly do you do?'

'Oh, stooging over the sea. General dogsbody work.'

'Then why can you never get away?' She looked at him and smiled. 'Some girl, I suppose?'

Charles went on stirring his coffee.

'I'm not prying. Just a normal mother's instinct. And it's time you married.'

He looked up and gave her one of his sudden sweet smiles. 'What about you, Mama?'

She laughed. In content and good humour they lingered over another cup of coffee before it was time for Charles to catch his train. 'We'll get a taxi and first drop you at Waterloo, Mama.'

It had begun to rain and the taxi wheels swished through puddles along the dark streets. But sitting beside Charles inside the cab, it was warm and dry and comforting. With a feeling of closeness and well-being to everyone, as the taxi swung into Waterloo station, Amelia asked, 'I wonder what the March children are doing now, Charles? Have you ever bumped into Pierre in the RAF? Do you ever hear anything of Marianne?'

EIGHT

One dark autumn night with leaves and rain blowing into his face, Charles left the duty office where he'd just spent an uneventful four hour standby shift, and began walking across the airfield for his usual natter with Stubbs in the hangar.

Buffetted by the wind, its red and green lights blurred by low mist and cloud, a Lysander was on the circuit. It was Forrester again, hogging the trips, Charles thought, stepping into a puddle and cursing. His temper these days was short. The last months had gone slowly. If it hadn't been for long friendship with Forrester and his new one with Stubbs, the engineering officer, he'd have gone round the twist. He had learned a lot about engineering and design from Stubbs. He always did his own daily inspection on Lysanders now.

'You're getting too serious in your old age, laddie,' Forrester had chided him. 'Take some leave!' Charles never did. He was afraid to go away from Stanton in case some word filtered through from Marianne. His constant hope was that one day he would be sent to pick her up, his constant dread that via some returning agent, he would hear that she'd been killed or taken prisoner.

The papers and the wireless that summer were full of Nazi brutalities. Charles was haunted by that poison pill she carried. Sometimes, dropping off into an uneasy sleep at night, he dreamed she'd taken it. Sometimes he would wake to the wind howling round the corners of the mess with the awful certainty that he'd heard her scream out.

The wind never ceased, he thought bitterly one autumn evening, watching Forrester taxi, cut the engine, and jump out on to the tarmac. Almost at once the car was there. It was the usual Hillman with the black drawn blinds. Its headlamps slewed round to light the way for the passengers. The aircraft exit swung open. Two figures jumped out. They ran bent double under the wing and across the beam.

The first was a man in a woollen cap. The second was Marianne.

They were into the car and the doors slammed before Charles had time to recover. As the Hillman began to accelerate, Charles rushed forward. He managed to bang on the window as it turned round.

A finger parted the rear black curtains. Briefly a ghostly white face glanced out. His heart leapt.

The whole world, the whole war seemed suddenly wonderful and winnable. Now he was acutely aware that the tide was turning. Italy had changed sides and had declared war on Germany. The Russians were advancing. Berlin was being pounded. With luck, soon France would be liberated – and Marianne's war would be over.

He felt his shoulder gripped. He looked round to see Forrester's gauntletted hand shaking his shoulder, Forrester's reproving face framed by his helmet.

'I'll forget I saw that, laddie. That un-British don't-you-know expression of welcome home Lisette. For Christ's sake, laddie, keep off the Joes, or you'll find yourself in Queer Street! Posted quicker than a letter!'

'Where've they taken her to?'

Forrester shrugged. Then added grudgingly, 'Debriefing at Baker Street, I imagine.'

'Then what?'

'How the hell should I know, laddie? Now I suppose you're going to bind away about leave?'

'You're always telling me to beat it up to town.'

'Not with one of the Joes.' He shook his head and yawned. 'Well, I'm for Intelligence. And then shut-eye.'

For the next sixteen hours, Charles was on tenterhooks. Then just on lunchtime, he was summoned from the bar to the Mess telephone. His mouth was dry when he picked up the receiver. Marianne's voice was cool, clear and matter of fact. She was in London shopping for the next few days. Was there any chance of him joining her?

They met at the same Bloomsbury hotel that evening.

'How did you manage to wangle it so quickly?' Marianne asked breathlessly after their first ecstatic hug in the foyer. He could feel the thinness of her body through her uniform. She looked older, but happy, and infinitely more beautiful. He was suddenly hopeful because she was wearing her WAAF uniform. It seemed so signify to him the end of her SOE work, the return to normal duties and what in 1943 passed for safety.

'My CO was glad to see the back of me.'

She laughed and kissed his cheek. 'That I don't believe.'

'He was. I've been a pain in the neck.' He gripped her hand. 'I've missed you.'

She returned the pressure of his fingers but said nothing.

'How's the brown job?' Charles asked as he took his bag upstairs and went into the first of the adjoining rooms. The blackout was already up. He switched on the bedside lamp.

'I don't know.' She sat on the corner of his bed, watching him unpack. 'Let's go out and dance,' she suggested as he took out a clean shirt and laid it on the bed. 'The Embassy? The Café Royal? Somewhere like that?'

Charles nodded, but returned to the subject of the brown job. 'Is he still out there?'

She shrugged. 'I honestly don't know.'

'Thou shalt not talk . . . the SOE motto. Even to me.' He gave an odd little smile, then came and sat on the bed beside her. He took both her hands. 'But *you* won't be going back, will you?'

'I don't know that either.'

'You sound as if you wouldn't mind. You can't *want* to go back?'

'I do. More than ever.'

She cupped his face in her hands an kissed his lips slowly as if physically seeking his understanding of something she found difficult to express in words. 'I like it,' she said, her eyes searching his face. 'At times I'm actually happy.'

'Well *I'm not!*'

'It gets into your blood, Charles. It becomes a way of life. I've an organisation. Friends. *Real* friends.'

He took her hands down from his face. He felt excluded, resentful, jealous. Crossly he began to pull off his tie and unbutton his shirt. 'Where do *I* figure?'

'Here.' She put her hand to her heart in a gesture that might have been theatrical, but which her manifest sincerity robbed of all artifice. He suddenly was over come with love. He put his arms round her, kissing her wildly and longingly. Her kisses were warm, spontaneous and uninhibited. He felt a terrible surge of physical desire. He pulled her down on to the bed, and began unfastening the brass buttons of her jacket. She brushed aside his clumsy fingers, and undressed herself modestly and neatly, folding her clothes, then, pausing to flick off the lamp, jumped into the bed beside him.

He had a momentary vision photographed for ever on his memory of her, thin as a child, her white skin almost incandescent in the lamplight. Then he was clasping her to him. He felt her small body tremble.

'Are you afraid?'

'Not really.'

She rubbed her cheek against his chest.

'I'm afraid,' he said, 'afraid to hurt you.' But all the time he was speaking, he was battling against his own urgent physical necessity, reminding himself of her youth and her need for gentleness.

He felt her flinch. But her arms came round him, pressing him tightly to her. Her rapid breath fanned his neck. For a moment they seemed to reach some never-ending plane of unison and unity. Distantly he was aware that the sirens had sounded, and later, as they lay side by side, that a heavy ack-ack barrage was going up. He didn't care. Nothing seemed important but his necessity to be at one with Marianne, to merge his being with hers. When the bombers came nearer and the hotel shook, he thought with luxurious melancholy that it would be the way to go.

They stayed in the hotel for three days, going out for the occasional meals, for a stroll along the Embankment in the sunlight, for a lunchtime session in a pub. They avoided Shepherd's and the other well-known haunts of the RAF, keeping to small unfashionable places.

The last days of October dwindled hopefully. The war news held the promise of victory. American Liberators striking from Italian airfields were bombing targets in Austria and Southern Germany. And though throughout those blissful days of that Indian summer, bombs dropped sporadically on London and the South East, the tide of war had turned. The end was in sight.

Then at breakfast on the fifth day, Marianne announced that she would be returning to Stanton that afternoon.

'How do you know that?' Charles asked indignantly. 'You haven't had a phone call or a letter.'

'I knew all along.'

'Christ! And you kept it to yourself!'

She reached across the table and touched his hand. 'I didn't want to spoil it.'

'Will you be sent away soon?'

'No.' She shook her head. 'They gave me five days, that's all. They're always tight-fisted about leave. I'll probably be on retraining. I'll be at Stanton for ages. It'll be like you and your CO. You'll be glad to see the back of me.'

'Never!' He leaned across the table, and took both her hands. 'But in case I do, let's get married!'

She laughed and shook her head.

'Seriously,' he said softly.

'Seriously,' she echoed, mocking but tender.

'We could get a special licence. Marry in Stanton. I'd feel we belonged.'

'We don't need to get married to feel that.'

'But if that's what *I* want, Marianne?'

'Then . . . ' she nodded vigorously without finishing, her eyes wide and glowing. 'Yes'.

'Shall you tell Pierre?' he asked, now excited as a schoolboy.

She smiled wryly. 'Not till the ceremony's over.'

'You reckon he'll blow his top?'

'You know Pierre.'

'You don't mind my telling Mama?'

After some hesitation Marianne said, 'Of course not.'

'I'll go to Haybury tonight. Break the glad tidings. Join you at Stanton in a couple of days. Mama may want to come to the ceremony.'

'Perhaps.'

'She'll be delighted. She always had a soft spot for you, Marianne.'

'She has managed to grow a corn over it.' Marianne put down her napkin and pushed back her chair. Thoughtfully, as if this were of prime importance in her mind, she said, 'Be very careful how you explain Jean-Paul. Even to her. Say he was the brother of a friend. Or just a passing fancy.'

On their way to Liverpool Street station, he insisted on stopping at the only jeweller's shop they could find open. It was standing rather forlornly on its own. The other shops on either side had been demolished by blast.

'But I'm not allowed to wear any jewellery,' she protested as they stared in through the criss-cross taping of the window, and lowering her voice said, 'because of tracing its origin.'

'I want the pleasure of putting it on your finger,' he said, and she allowed him to lead her inside.

The sallow-faced youth behind the counter was the only witness of that act.

Marianne was still wearing the ring when Charles saw her off at the station. He saw it glittering like a spark on her finger till the track curved, and a white cloud of steam blotted it from view.

'Darling, how marvellous to see you! What a wonderful surprise!'

Amelia had heard the taxi draw up and parted the blackout curtain just enough to see Charles jump out. She had run to the door before the butler could open it.

'Sarah will be furious, she's off for the evening. Pearson, see what can be rustled up in the kitchen!'

Amelia kept repeating, 'What a wonderful surprise, darling!'

'It's wonderful to be home, Mama.' Charles smiled and walked over to the sideboard to recharge his glass. His mother seemed so delighted, so maternal, so close that he couldn't wait to tell her his news.

'But darling, Mama, I have yet another wonderful surprise for you!'

'Well, don't tell me for a moment! Let me digest the nice surprise of seeing you! Then let me guess.' She sat down on the edge of her chair. 'Pearson, bring in some more logs! And fetch a bottle of the '08 port. I thought you were never going to get leave.' Amelia went on excitedly. 'They must have worked you awfully hard. Though you're looking quite well on it. A little thin. Is that what the surprise is? You've got a gong?'

He laughed. 'Dearest Mama! Not on Lysanders! I'm not really in a gong-getting neck of the woods. Guess again!'

'You've been posted down here? Cummings was very impressed with those modifications, by the way. You'll get in some more work on Ajax? You must spend a day with Ronald. And if you've been posted round here, he'll be delighted.'

'Wrong again! Cold.'

'You've got promotion? Another ring?'

'Wrong! But warmer! Think of the word ring! Not round my sleeve, but round . . .'

He held up a finger.

'Darling!' Amelia jumped to her feet. 'You're getting married!'

He stood up, put his arms round her and kissed her. 'Are you pleased?'

'Delighted. Now you'll really have to settle down. And it's high time. You're thirty-nine. Who is she? Where did you meet her? Why didn't you bring her with you?'

'You'll see her very soon. And you'll be more pleased than ever when you hear who she is!'

'Who?' A cold finger seemed then to touch Amelia's heart. But even so, she was not prepared for the catastrophe.

'Marianne. Marianne March. You always liked her.'

'I *never* liked her.' Amelia stamped her foot in fury. 'She was a sweet little girl. But that was all. I like children. *All* children. But she grew up into a cold scheming woman.'

'How dare you talk like that, Mama!' He clenched his fists. 'To me. When you know I love her!'

'More fool you! Though you don't know the meaning of the word! Nor does she!'

'And you do, I suppose?'

'Yes.'

Amelia took a deep breath and tried to compose herself. 'See it from my point of view. She's not at all the girl I'd have chosen for you!'

'Christ!' Charles exploded, draining his port and slamming the glass down on the library table. 'How old do you think I bloody well am? See it from *your* point of view? You *have* no point of view!'

'I'm your mother,' Amelia said, leaning on the chimney-piece and trying to sort through the appalling jumble in her own mind.

'No one is denying it. What I *am* denying is your right to interfere in my life.'

'I have a right to consideration.'

'And that you damned well get!'

'After all, it won't be the first mistaken marriage you've made!'

'Being spiteful won't help, Mama.'

'Nor will marrying Marianne!'

She was aware she was making a mess of the whole scene.

'You're just being a spiteful possessive old woman!'

'Wrong! I'm *not* possessive. It's not that I don't want you to marry! I don't want you to marry *her*!'

'You know nothing of her.'

'I know more than you do. The whole family hates ours.'

'Probably with cause.'

'You saw how rude she was at her father's funeral.'

'She was upset.'

'And I told you I saw her with that Army man. Who was *he*?'

'Just a casual friend.'

'They weren't acting casually.'

'She might have said that about you and Lehmann.'

'Then she'd have been lying. Again.'

A sudden look of pure hatred flickered in Charles's eyes. 'If you're going to talk like that, Mama, I'm going!'

He strode furiously towards the door.

'I'm sorry,' Amelia said chokily, walking towards him, hand outstretched placatingly. 'I'm not doing this well. But there was something between them, I swear! I saw it in his eyes! They were in love!'

'Shut up, Mama!'

'And even if they weren't, you *can't* marry her! *Anyone* but *her*!'

'Shut up, Mama!' he gritted warningly through his teeth. 'I'm going!'

But she wouldn't shut up. She came towards him and put a restraining hand on his arm.

'I'll tell you exactly why.' She gripped his arm. 'And I won't let you go till you've heard it.'

He looked down at her contorted face, almost unrecognisable, at her thin hand gripping his arm, and suddenly he hated her. He tore her fingers off his arm, and pushed her so hard she staggered backwards.

'Damn you, Mama!' he threw over his shoulder. 'I hope I never see you again!'

He slammed the front door behind him. He walked till he came to the main road and thumbed a lift going north. He meant what he said. He hoped never to see Amelia again. But when he arrived at Stanton at lunchtime the next day, it was Marianne he was not to see again.

A drop had taken place. She had already gone.

NINE

'I'll be seeing you in all the old familiar places . . .'

The wireless turned out the sentimental songs all through that snowy winter, while everyone speculated on when the Allies would start the Second Front.

Stalin was demanding it of Churchill and Roosevelt. De Gaulle was antagonising the Allied generals with his insistence. The vast army assembled in Britain under Eisenhower was raring to go. No one awaited the Second Front more eagerly than Charles Haybury. He studied the map of Europe, particularly the position of Chartres. Less than a hundred miles away from the French coast, surely it was bound to be one of the first places to be liberated!

Alone in his room, he lay on his bed, night after night listening to the six o'clock news. 'During last night and throughout today, Allied aircraft attacked railways, bridges, airfields and coastal batteries in Northern France.'

Obviously softening up the German defences in preparation for the invasion. The same sort of announcement was made continually. 'Yesterday 360 Liberators of the USAAF bombed Dieppe, Boulogne and Calais.'

They were plastering the Channel ports. That was where Eisenhower would strike. 'Last night, large formations of Lancasters dropped bombs on enemy installations on the Cherbourg peninsula.'

'Where d'you think they're going to land?' he asked Forrester, drinking at the bar counter.

Forrester shrugged. 'Search me, old boy.'

'Dunkirk, I reckon,' Stubbs said.

'When?'

'Oh, not till it's better weather. You can't expect Eisenhower to budge in this sort of stuff. Been raining for days! If I was Eisenhower, I'd wait till summer.'

'The *summer!*'

'Here, Charles, no need to blow your top. You're not Eisenhower. Neither am I, thank God. Have another drink?'

In May, the weather was better. The news was better too. The Moon Squadron was busy. So was the Resistance. Stories of their exploits filtered through – German troop trains blown up, bridges sabotaged, shotdown Allied pilots smuggled to safety. Chartres was far enough from the Channel not to be affected by Allied bombings, and it seemed to Charles, still listening on the wireless, that they were concentrating on the ports.

'Yesterday afternoon, RAF Typhoons and USAAF Mustangs shot up and bombed enemy positions at St Malo and Dinard.'

Next day, RAF Bostons did the same. The Americans attacked Caen, then

Rouen. They seemed to be edging closer to Chartres every day. And now the bombing was round the clock.

Charles's mood changed to one of excitement. It would be any day now. Forrester was betting on early June. 'Yesterday afternoon, Hurricanes and Mustangs attacked gun emplacements at Dieppe and Cherbourg.'

Dieppe was certainly closer to Britain. But it might be Cherbourg. They would have to have a port. A harbour would be their first objective. Might be Boulogne. Might be Le Havre . . .

In the event, it was none of them. In the greatest secrecy, huge concrete blocks of artificial harbour were made in different places throughout Britain. And at six-thirty am on 6 June 1944, they were towed across the Channel together with the warships and invasion barges, and dropped to form an artificial port on the beaches at Arromanches.

Charles flew all that day artillery spotting for the Navy, shelling German positions along the beachhead. From 5000 feet, he watched hundreds of landing-craft move in, saw squadrons of Dakotas dropping parachutists, followed the mass formations of gliders descending into France. All that week, he had a grandstand view of the battle, reporting developments over the radio-telepone. The strangest development of all was a pilotless aeroplane he saw streaking along with its tail on fire. Minutes afterwards, there was an explosion. A German rocket, Intelligence told him – a V1, already christened doodlebug and already being shot down.

Coming back to Stanton on the evening of 13 June, very cheerful, he was just going into Intelligence to report when John Forrester stopped him. 'Charles —'

He turned round.

'Radio message from Chartres. Last night, four of the Resistance were captured. One of them was Lisette.'

He sat in Intelligence, listening.

Marianne and the other three, one of them the man called Jean-Paul, were in Chartres prison. Two-way radio communication had been established with the Resistance and all information had been passed to Baker Street and the Air Ministry. The activities of Jean-Paul and Marianne were known to the Germans, who had realised that the four they had captured could tell them the names and addresses of the other Resistance workers in the cell. Torture would be used to get the names. Operations had been told it was imperative that a rescue should be mounted immediately.

'How?' Charles asked.

'I obviously don't know the details of ther end of it,' Forrester said.

'When?'

'Tonight.'

'What time?'

'Two am. Same Chartres rendezvous.'

'Departure time here?'

'Midnight.'

Charles began planning the flight immediately, getting the maps laid out and the tracks drawn, talking to the met officer, phoning Air Ministry for the latest information, speaking to the French section of SOE.

Coded messages had been flashing between Chartres and Baker Street. The

Air Ministry had approved the flight, provided it was routed via Le Havre – well east of the invasion beaches.

SOE had a contact in Chartres prison – a civil prisoner who was a trusty and could obtain access to cell keys. The prisoners' cells would be unlocked at the vital time of eleven o'clock when the guards changed and the garbage lorry left the prison. The lorry would take the four of them to the pick-up field.

On the BBC news in French at seven, amongst a string of other messages were the cryptic words *Mes cousins sont restés là-bas*.

It was on. Both sides had OKed time and place. Then the weather began to give trouble. Certainly a moon, but rain was forecast over northern France.

Round ten, Charles walked to the airfield, carefully checked over Lysander Freddie with the flight sergeant, saw all unnecessary weight had been removed, went back into intelligence to read up the latest reports: more 88-millimetre flak at Harfleur at the mouth of the Seine, a Ju88 night fighter squadron at Choigny.

'Signal to land . . . a triangle of three white lights– downwind end. Don't land . . . a series of red flashes,' the Intelligence Officer told him. 'Wait . . . two long dashes. Usual three white lights for the flarepath.'

Now a string of things to do occupied him. Turning out his pockets, going up to the armoury and choosing a light Sten gun with six drums of ammunition. Picking up the latest met flimsy. Getting the final OK from Baker Street. Walking with Forrester out to the silent black Lysander.

'Good luck, Charles.'

'Thanks.'

It was a relief to be inside the cockpit. A relief to press the starter button, listen to the wheezing of the big Pegasus engine, watch the propeller suddenly spin into life.

He opened the side window and waved the chocks away. It had already begun to rain. Rivulets of water ran down over his dark windscreen as he taxied past the duckpond to the end of the runway.

A Polish Liberator took off before him. He watched its landing lights skelter down the runway, lift off into the night. Now it was his turn. A smudge of watery green Very cartridge momentarily illuminated the control tower. He opened the throttle. F Freddie gave a little waggle of its tail, groaned, arthritically moved forward, then quickly gathered speed.

Not bad – airborne in 400 yards with a full load of fuel. Should be able to lift four passengers off from the field at Chartres – provided the southeast wind stays.

He set 195° on the compass, watched the needle settle between the lubberlines. Far south was London, a solitary searchlight enamelled the low stratus yellow, glinted on the fat bellies of barrage balloons.

Nothing much happening. No flak, no bomb flashes. No doubt the Luftwaffe were too occupied with the invasion beaches. He saw no other activity, no lights, no dark shadows of aircraft, nothing till a pale half-moon pierced the cloud and lit up the bay round Worthing.

The moon stayed with him across the Channel as he flew just above the sea. Its reflection bounced up and down like a ball on the wave tops, oddly comforting. Every now and again, a great burst of rain splattered all over the glasshouse. Then everything was clear again, with the Lysander cutting quickly through the night and the engine singing sweetly.

Gunfire over to the southwest. Searchlights too. A Lancaster caught in the cone of three beams. Against the yellow bead curtain of heavy flak, he could just make out the tiny shapes of ships and barges.

French coast already. He inched round the promontory, swung away from Le Havre, entered the Seine estuary just above the water.

There was nothing moving. Nothing there. Still blessedly intermittent the moon gave him little lamplight flashes to guide him on his way.

Not a gun fired. Not a searchlight moved. He saw only small signs of life: a car with hooded headlamps crossing a bridge, the tiny glow of a stove on a barge he flew over, a trickle of wash behind a steamer. The river like a long winding pipe sucked him along.

A little huddle of spire and houses in sudden moonlight. He looked down at the map strapped on his knee. Amfreville, time to turn starboard and branch off along the river Eure. He edged closer to the right bank. Here was the intersection! He recognised the tower on the hilltop. He turned just before the moon was doused by another bucketful of rain. Dark – pitch dark. He eased the stick back, flew forward blind and prayed. The little phosphorescent numbers and needles on the instruments glowed at him reassuringly.

Ten past one – he was early. He pulled the throttle back, practically hung on the prop. That way at least he had more time to avoid things. A dark poplar came out of nowhere like a sword from above. He swung the nose to port, lifted the right wing. Telephone wires now – a whole long line of them inches below his wheels. He pulled the nose up sharply, skimmed a rooftop, crawled up the side of a hill.

One twenty-eight – and here was the town of Maintenon. Another clue came from the moon on the spire and a glint on the railway lines to Chartres. The rain had stopped. In this gloaming he could almost imagine he was a train, his wheels practically running along the tracks. Nine carriages were snaking just below him now. He saw the fire in the driver's cab, smelled the acrid coal smoke.

One forty-six. He couldn't be more than fifteen miles from the field. On his left, he could see the twin spires of Chartres cathedral.

One fifty-five – and there was the field all right. He recognised that hill south of it, the twist of road by the line of poplars. No lights – but he was early. Engine cut right back, hardly making a sound, like a dark moth, he began circling. He was relieved, glad to be here, ready to come down the moment they wanted him.

A light! Then another!

He picked up the gun and put it across his knee, just in case. Then turning on one wingtip into wind, he came lower. Still only *two* lights. *Three* in a triangle was the signal. But the flarepath of white lights was there.

He hesitated, then put on more throttle and went up again into the sky. Strange! Still only two lights.

He peered at the clock. Three minutes *after* two. But still no sign from the ground that they were going to put out the right signal.

What should he do? He made another circuit of the field, to make up his mind. He could imagine Marianne and the others down there, waiting for him. One of the torches had gone wrong – that's what it could be! A bulb or a

395

battery. If there was an emergency, they would have sent red flashes. He couldn't simply fly away.

He made another circuit. Still only two lights, and now it was six minutes past. Rendezvous had to be effected straightaway. Every second waiting was dangerous for them.

Into wind again, decisively he chopped the throttle. He turned the safety switch on the Sten from *safe* to *fire*. Noiselessly the Lysander glided down, practically brushed the top of the hedge with its wheels.

At the first light, he was down. Bumping across the grass, the little aircraft slowed.

A shadowy figure was running towards im. Then another! Two more! Four, just as they said!

He began taxying to meet them. And now through the windscreen, he could see the first figure clearly – slight, in a dark cloak.

Marianne!

He had already opened the window. Stopping, he held out his left arm for her. Followed closely by the others the figure reached the aircraft, was running up to the door when the wind blew the cloak aside.

In the tiny light from the last flare, Charles caught the glint of an Iron Cross.

He pulled the trigger on the Sten and pushed the throttle wide open. The man staggered, crumpled against the moving wing.

Now suddenly it was as light as day. The searchlights shone straight into his eyes. Lines of white tracer poured across the field. A dozen figures were racing towards him. At full throttle, still firing the Sten from the open window, he charged them. Like a whirling of dervish knives, the Lysander's propellers cut them down.

They scattered, fell to the ground. The aircraft wheels bumped over them, tried to rise. Red tracer now, criss-crossing the air in front of him. He heard the bullets rip into the duralumin. The engine coughed. He felt a sudden searing pain in his chest.

Ahead was the hedge, glittering silver in the searchlights. He pulled back with all his might.

The wheels left the ground, bumped back, lifted up again. Tilted to port, staggering, the wounded Lysander leapt the hedge, steadied itself and followed by tracer and searchlights, limped back into the night.

TEN

Charles spent the next three months in hospital. He did not tell Amelia, nor send her any message. He could not forgive himself for not rescuing Marianne. And, quite unfairly, he blamed his mother.

Amelia was in despair. What, she wondered would James have thought of the clumsy way in which she had handled their son. Sarah didn't help. She went around pursing her lips, asking impatiently, 'No news yet, M'lady, from Sir Charles?'

Sitting in the library at Haybury with the last unopened letter returned from Charles, she telephoned Prudence. Her daughter-in-law's sleepy voice answered her. No, Mother-in-law needn't apologise. Prudence hadn't been on night duty. No, the doodlebugs weren't keeping her too busy. Devastating when they fell. But their area hadn't been too bad so far. And anyway you heard them. Engine like a motorbike getting louder all the time. When it coughs and cuts, you take cover. The taxi drivers were marvellous at giving warning. Sounding their horns when they came. What had kept Prudence out so late was nothing to do with doodlebugs. She'd been to a splendid party at the Savoy. A schoolfriend's husband had just arrived home from the Middle East. No, she hadn't had any news of Arthur. But from what Prudence could read between the lines of his last letter from Gourock, she reckoned Arthur would be needing his balaclava helmet and snow boots. Prudence sounded gay, brittle, immensely flip, and underneath desperately worried.

She seemed to welcome Amelia's suggestion that she contact Charles, see how he was, find out if he was married.

'Married! Charles? Good Lord! You're joking, you don't really think so?'

'He was threatening to the last time I saw him.'

'Threatening? Oh,' Prudence drew out the single syllable meaningfully. And then asked crisply, 'Shotgun wedding?'

'I sincerely hope not.'

'You hope no wedding at all, Mama?'

'I do indeed.'

'You don't approve?'

'I strongly disapprove!'

'And you told him so?'

'I told him and we quarrelled.'

'Naturally, Mama. If you told him, you *would* quarrel. Charles being Charles.'

'But I've written and explained. Or tried to explain. But Charles won't relent. It's as if he hates me. I can't bear it,' Amelia finished lamely. 'With the war and

397

never knowing . . .' Her voice faltered and trailed away before the unsayable.

'Could you bear it if he had already married her?' Prudence asked.

'No.'

'But you still want me to find out.'

'Please.'

Prudence asked her mother-in-law no more questions. She undertook to ring Amelia as soon as she'd seen Charles. But in the meantime Amelia was not to worry. Charles was not the kind to keep up a grudge, and she doubted very much if any girl, after the Sylvia episode, would get him to the altar again. He was probably whooping it up in Bedfordshire. These pilots were real honeypots to the girls. Like that silly song – 'He wears a pair of silver wings' – Amelia could have Prudence's personal promise that she would get Charles to end his sulks and see he came down at long last to Haybury.

Prudence rang ten days later to report only partial success. She had dined with Charles at the Embassy. No, he hadn't shown any reluctance to come. He had looked thinner and older. He had seemed genuinely pleased to see her. Affectionate and sweet. 'You know how Charles can be!' Till she had asked him point blank, Prudence style, if he was married.

'Then I thought he was going to walk out on me. But he didn't. And after a while he just answered very quietly. "No, unfortunately."'

Amelia let out a long sigh.

'Now I come to the rather awful bit, Mother-in-law.' Her voice shook. 'It was Marianne March he wanted to marry and Mama,' Prudence swallowed. Then she said, 'She's *dead*.'

At first Amelia refused to believe her.

'How awful. How tragic.' Amelia was overcome with remorse, horror, sadness and a terrible shaming relief.

'How? When? How did it happen?'

'That I don't know.'

'Does Charles?'

'I don't know. But that's why, Mama,' Prudence went on slowly, 'he doesn't feel he wants to come to Haybury at the moment.' Neutral though her daughter-in-law's tone was her sympathies now clearly lay with Charles. 'He really loved her. Really. I'm sure of that. But he'll get over it. I'll keep on at him. Business is slack at the moment. They say the buzz bombs are easing off. I might go up and see him at Stanton.'

But almost immediately, business, as Prudence put it, hotted up. Perversely, the very day after Mr Duncan Sandys, chairman of the Counter Measure's Committee against German secret weapons had announced, 'Except possibly for a few last shots, the Battle of London is over', the first V2 rocket roared over London and exploded at Chiswick.

More of these German secret weapons followed almost daily. Prudence was too busy, too preoccupied, too tired, to ring Amelia. For the first two weeks of the V2 attacks, the government left the strange bangs unexplained to the public at large. Then in Parliament, Prime Minister Churchill stated that for weeks, 'the enemy has been using his new weapon, the long range rocket'.

When Amelia telephoned Prudence it was to find out how she herself was. If she was safe. Not too overworked. Charles was never mentioned. There was still no letter from Arthur.

'I always hate November, Amelia told Ronald Cummings, when he remarked that she seemed listless, quite unaffected by their record output, the letter of congratulation from Beaverbrook, and quite uninterested in Cummings' own current passion – the jet engine. 'I feel as if I'm weighted down.'

'War weary?' Cummings sighed.

'Worse than that. As if I was about to get some bad news.'

When the news came, it was far from bad. Amelia returned the following week from the factory to see a taxi outside the front door at Haybury and Arthur getting out of it.

'We docked at Southampton,' he told her when she released him. 'So I thought I might call in on my way to London. I'll get this taxi chap to take me on. Prudence doesn't know I'm here yet. Don't tell her! I want it to be a surprise!'

He stayed only long enough for a drink and to say hello to Sarah. Then just as he was leaving, shyly, apologetically almost, 'Oh, by the way, there's another little surprise . . .'

Arthur had been awarded the DSO. The investiture was in a week's time. Amelia would be able to go as well as Prudence. Stefan Lehmann was sure to insist that there was a family celebration.

Charles would have to come. Fate seemed to have dealt Amelia a trump card at last.

Stefan Lehmann in his self-appointed role as honorary head of the family booked a table at the Savoy, for the evening of 6 December, and undertook to drive Amelia to Hals Crescent two hours before the investiture.

Amelia found Prudence radiant and Arthur pale-faced and nervous. He had, Prudence said, been singularly uncommunicative about how he got the award. All the same, he relished the idea of being one up on Charles, and couldn't wait to see Charles's face.

'And is Charles coming this evening?' Amelia asked her as she nibbled a sandwich she was almost too excited to swallow.

'Of course, Mama! He's due to arrive at King's Cross at five forty-five. We thought it would be nice if Father and you picked him up at the station and brought him to the Savoy. We'll join you there.'

Dear Prudence, Amelia thought, as Arthur drove them both to Buckingham Palace. A breaking of the ice at the station with Stefan there to see that the quick-tempered mother and son came to no harm. Then the warmth of the evening's celebration to bring about the thaw. She stared out at the cold December afternoon. There was a grey-pink sky over London. Already lights glowed in the shop windows. London was now on a dimout instead of the total blackout, but there were bomb holes and bomb damage everywhere. Queues, shabby people. And a depressing sense that with this sudden German break out in the Ardennes the war would end as slowly as it had begun.

Then they were turning down the Mall towards Buckingham Palace. Briskly at first past the bare winter trees. Then slowing. Another queue here for the entrance.

Amelia spun back through time to herself forty years ago. A girl of eighteen, already marred, hiding her pregnancy. About to be presented by dear Aunt Sempner.

Gone were the carriages, the plumes and the elegant white-clad ladies. Gone the huge hair-dos, the enamelled faces. Gone the flunkeys and the dowagers. Tarmac had replaced the wooden blocks of the roadway. Petrol fumes and bomb dust replaced the smell of horses, carriage oil, white lilies, perfume and horse dung. The taxis and cars were filled with men in uniform, the only women were wives and mothers. There were ack-ack posts in the park. The iron railings and gates had been ripped up supposedly to make guns. There were sandbags outside all the buildings, and fire-watchers on the roofs. But the Palace, only slightly damaged by its six bombs, loomed formidably the same.

The same and not the same, Amelia thought, following one of the same breed of incredibly handsome aides who whisked the relatives of the men up the curving staircase she had climbed all those years ago. The carpets looked a little shabbier, and the windows were taped against bomb blast. The paintings had been taken away for safe custody and there were fire buckets and stirrup pumps in strategic places. But it was still overwhelmingly regal.

A different king of course. A king paler than the young men lined up to be decorated, nervous and gentle-faced. Much less formidable than his father or grandfather. He seemed to spend a long time talking to Arthur. Amelia and Prudence exchanged pleased proud glances.

Then it was all over. They were out in the cold afternoon air. There was a handful of pressmen photographing groups, the recipient in the middle showing his medal, the proud family around him, to appear in the *Times*, the *Tatler* and the *Bystander*. As they were about to get into the car, something streaked across the sky. Amelia heard an enormous crackling sound followed by deep echoing rumbles.

'Hitler saluting the family hero!' Prudence smiled as she removed her smart little hat and settled herself in the car. 'It's just a V2 Mama! Not to worry! It's miles away. Is it the first you've seen?'

'And the last I hope!' Amelia smiled abstractedly, her mind already on the coming meeting with Charles.

'Knowing Charles, he may not turn up at all,' Amelia said to Stefan as she shivered in the cold cavern of King's Cross station. It was crowded with troops. The train was late.

'Oh, he'll come,' Lehmann paced up and down. 'It's a proud day for the family. He won't miss this.' He smiled fondly, 'Arthur said His Majesty was most kind. Most interested. He has a great future, that boy,' adding after a pause, 'both boys have.' He stood on tiptoe. 'Ah, here it comes now!'

A plume of steam reflecting pink from the engine fire appeared at the far end of the cavern like a reluctant ghost. The red bumper light gleamed. There came the powerful peaceful roar of the engine and the clank of metal wheels. It halted for a moment just before the platform as if to tantalise them, and then clanked forward hissing to a standstill on platform one. Immediately its blinded doors were thrown open and servicemen and women spilled out, kit-bags and luggage thumped on to the concrete.

Charles was one of the first off, but Amelia hardly recognised him. Despite Pru's remarks on the telephone she was unprepared. He looked so much older and thinner. The bright spark of vitality that had seemed so much him had died. He looked older than James had ever done.

He kissed her coolly on the cheek, shook Stefan's hand, murmured that it was good of him to have gone to all this trouble, received Lehmann's sincere, unaffected reply that it was an honour to be allowed so to do.

Stefan also took it upon himself to maintain the conversation on their way to the Savoy. Beyond a cold, 'You're looking well, Mama,' Charles had not addressed a single word to Amelia. He asked Lehmann how things were at the Ministry and not altogether humorously when were they going to come up with a decent British transport aircraft. Lehmann replied with good humour. With Amelia's permission he lit a cigar. He talked about Shotfield and the Jewish refugees. He told them amusing anecdotes. There had been a rumour in the village that one of the refugees was a fifth columnist. Lights were reported to have been seen. Signalling to the German bombers, the Local Defence Volunteers reckoned. But, in fact, a courting couple.

Charles and Amelia listened politely but inattentively. Charles gazed out at the half-lit streets. Amelia studied her son's withdrawn expression.

'He's come in name only,' Amelia thought. When they arrived at the Savoy she went into the powder room to freshen her makeup. There was no sign yet of Prudence. It will take more than the celebration of Arthur's DSO to make Charles melt. But he would be better when the others came, she told herself nervously.

'They're late,' Lehmann sighed, consulting his heavy gold watch. 'Twenty minutes late. But then,' with an indulgent smile, 'they're allowed to be. We are not. I suggest we go in. We have my own special table.'

And his own magnificent flower arrangement and champagne chilling on ice. Better than that, he had his own jubilation, his smooth unfailing flow of conversation. His kindly questions first to Amelia, then to Charles. The running of Haybury, the running of the factory, staff problems, rationing, shortages, his questions were unending and seemingly interested. What had been Charles opinion of the Arnhem landing? How serious was this German breakthrough in the Ardennes? Did Charles really think there was any future in this jet engine? The Ministry advisers were inclined to pooh-pooh it. Had Charles thought what he would do when the war was over? But less and less were his fine eloquent eyes on their faces as they replied. More and more did they stray towards the glass entrance doors.

At eight o'clock Stefan ordered a round of drinks. 'I don't think, under the circumstances,' he said almost apologetically to those empty chairs, 'they can object if we have a drink without them.'

At nine, the head waiter's smile began to look pinched. 'You must be very hungry,' Stefan murmured to Amelia. 'We shall begin whenever you wish.'

'Let's wait.'

'For how long?' Charles asked, not unkindly. For the first time that evening, he met her gaze with eyes that were not cold and hostile. Yet far from reassuring Amelia, his look touched a muffled chord of panic.

'Till they come.'

Charles shrugged and said no more. At nine-thirty, as if he could bear it no longer, Stefan rose from the table to telephone the flat. 'Something must be detaining them,' he said smoothly. 'They can hardly have forgotten.'

He returned five minutes later to say the number was out of order. He and Charles exchanged looks.

'It may mean nothing.' Stefan finished uncertainly.

Charles stood up. 'I'll go round and find out.'

'No. You stay with your mother.'

But Charles was already striding to the door.

'I don't want to be stayed with,' Amelia shook off Stefan's hand. The hand was trembling. She grasped it with her own.

'We'll take my car. You drive. You'll be quicker.' Stefan handed Charles the keys.

'The telephone lines may be damaged.' Stefan murmured, as they sped towards Knightsbridge. 'Or there's a burst. Or an unexploded bomb. Or a gas leak. And they couldn't let us know because of the phone being out of order . . .'

Even before he finished speaking they could see a pillar of paler dust against the night sky to the left of Knightsbridge. They could smell the choking rubble, the strange sappy smell of scorched trees, the reek of gas. An ambulance streaked towards them coming from the direction of the dust column, its thin headlamps making a zigzag lightning pattern over the street which ran with rivulets of water.

Then they turned the corner. The entrance to the crescent was blocked off. There was a big Danger sign. The barrier was manned by a warden in a black steel ARP helmet and black oilskins. Only Charles's uniform got them past the barrier.

It was something out of a painting of hell. Number 12 Hals Crescent had vanished into a pile of rubble. Over it, men in steel helmets crawled and dug like blowflies. Fountains of water played on number 12's neighbours, themselves gaping and blackened and torn. The laurels were burned to crisps. Everywhere people were shouting and directing and running. Another ambulance was racing off as they stood aghast.

A direct hit three hours ago, a warden snarled, fed up with grief and bodies and stricken relatives. Yes, trying to shake his arm free from Charles's grasp, a V bloody 2! No one got away with it! They were still digging. But there was no hope. None. They'd had the sniffer round. The chap who could smell if there was anyone alive, or it was just dead bodies. There was no one left. They'd got a naval officer, or rather what was left of him, out and a girl. Dead! Dead as mutton!

The dark flickering stinking world spun out of Amelia's control. She was falling. James had caught her. She was in his arms. No, in Charles's arms. He was holding her tight. Kissing her. They were reconciled. Just as James and she had been reconciled.

But oh, God, at what a price!

ELEVEN

Amelia spent Christmas that year in her office at the factory. Charles came home on leave and Stefan Lehmann drove over from Shotfield. They needed each other's company, but by common consent none of them wanted the traditional celebrations. Nor did Cummings.

With peace looming, they held an ad hoc board meeting for the civil version of Ajax on Christmas afternoon. Watching the other three, Cummings felt almost excluded. Sorrow had drawn them tightly together. He had never seen them so close. Nor had the Ajax project served a better, more therapeutic, purpose. It was as if they huddled together on an emotional raft that was Ajax. The three of them haunted the factory. Charles was bubbling over with ideas for modifications, Amelia with possibilities of marketing and government contracts, Lehmann with offers of more capital injection.

'Apart from Rachel,' he said, when Amelia thanked him, but told him he had already sunk enough into the factory, 'I have nothing on which I wish to spend it. Had you not taken her to America, I would not have had her either.'

They spent an equally quiet New Year, welcoming in 1945, with Charles's bitter, 'Surely it can't be as bad as the year that has just gone!'

It opened with the last attack of the war by a large German bomber force. It was against British and American aircraft on the ground at airfields in Holland and Belgium, and the raid was amply compensated for by the Americans bombing the railways at Kessel, Coblenz and Gottingen. Every day of the New Year brought news of Allied bmbings, from Nagoya and Bangkok to behind the German salient in the Ardennes. There, the enemy was falling back. 'I shall always feel,' said Field Marshal Montgomery that month, 'that Runstedt was beaten by the good fighting qualities of the American soldiers and by the team work of the Allies.'

Victory was in the air. And though it was a hollow sorrowful victory for the Hayburys and Stefan Lehmann, they had, in Ajax, at least something to build for in the peace when it came. There were few people in Jerningham and Haybury who hadn't suffered in some way. Many of them had gone into the Royal Artillery and were in the D-Day landings. Sarah's nephew had been killed in the Ardennes offensive, a nephew-in-law taken prisoner in Greece.

'And I hear young Pierre March is a POW too, so his grandfather said.'

Making it her business to call in at the forge on a trumped-up excuse about hose clips, Amelia found the old man sad but undaunted. He was still working. The forge was spotlessly clean. Business was poor, but he had more than enough. His son had seen to that. He kept working because that was his wish. He talked to her about Pierre, shot down on a tactical sweep behind the

German lines. He looked forward to him being released with the Allied advance. Neither mentioned Marianne.

Nor had Charles. It seemed to Amelia that he was sustaining himself with false and painful hopes. She was wrong. Charles was as certain that Marianne was dead as he was that he himself still unfortunately lived and breathed. When, at the end of February, Forrester bought him a beer and said, not looking him in the eye, that he'd talked to one of the Joes he'd brought back the night before, Charles knew exactly what Forrester was going to tell him. That the girl they'd called Lisette had got the chop.

He asked him quite steadily, 'When?' And he was absurdly glad that she had been killed before he had attempted that abortive rescue, that at least he had done the best for her he could. He also managed to ask Forrester if he knew how she'd been killed, but Forrester wasn't sure. Firing squad, he thought. The Wing Commander stayed in the bar with him that night till they were both paralytic. After that, Forrester saw Charles was doing more than twice his normal share of ops. Once again work became his interest as well as his solace.

Besides, the work at Stanton was changing. As the Allies advanced, so more German prisoner-of-war camps were being opened up, and operations were geared to peace. Now the Lancasters and Halifaxes and Mosquitos and even the little Lysanders brought in loads of returning Army, Navy and RAF prisoners. There were still a few returning Joes amongst them, distinguishable by their silence and lack of exuberance. But the service prisoners were wild with excitement, some of them flinging themselves on the moist Bedfordshire ground to kiss it.

Volunteers from the Stanton personnel dished them out hot food and drink and Woodbines and tots of rum, no matter what hour of the day or night they landed.

Then as the missile sites in Holland were destroyed, and the army of occupation fell back, the extent of the starvation of the Dutch population became apparent. The quickest way to relieve it was by air. Every available aircraft was stacked with food parcels. Charles and Forrester took the first two Lysanders low over the North Sea, skimming above the sand dunes to where a Union Jack was spread out. There, as slowly as they could, they tipped out the parcels, terrified that some over-eager child would get hit by one.

There were children no bigger than Marianne when he first met her, so thin that he could hardly bear to see them. Children no older than his niece was now, but who looked older than his mother. They jumped and waved and blew him kisses. Over 9000 tons of food and clothing were dropped by the RAF Commands.

Those trips had the most profound effect on Charles. More than Churchill's announcement in the House of Commons of Germany's unconditional surrender. More than VE Day which Charles spent on his own, walking round the airfield watching the food parcels being loaded into the bombers.

Going home on three weeks' leave shortly afterwards, Charles said to Amelia, 'That sort of thing is what flying's meant for. Relieving distress. Bringing people together. For peace.' He said that he had applied to the RAF for early release to work on Ajax. He spent that leave almost entirely with Cummings in the air. Cummings wanted him again as test pilot; Amelia hardly saw him. Not that she minded. The war was over. With Stefan Lehmann's support, they had survived their own family catastrophe. Ajax had borne them up, but now that the boys were coming home, she felt the loss of James more keenly again.

Charles went back to Stanton for his last stint with the RAF before demobilisation, arriving very late on the last day of May. The end of the war had not improved the punctuality of the trains. Before going to bed, he went over to the noticeboard and looked at the next day's orders – just in case.

He was not on the flying detail. No training. He was just turning away when his eye was caught by a piece on the bottom. General Court Martial to be held in the Officer's Mess ante-room at nine thirty.

Officers of the court: Group Captain M.S. Ruthven, President. Squadron Leader F.E. Aylmer, Squadron Leader C. Haybury, Squadron Leader J. Cragge, Flight Lieutenant W.N. Everett members.

BOOK FIVE

Night into Day
1945–

ONE

Next morning, he slept in. Remembering the court martial, he put on his Best Blue, and went straight into the dining-room to grab a cup of tea. It was there to his horror that he learned from Stubbs the name of the accused – Pierre March.

'What's the charge? Beating someone up?' Charles asked, remembering Biggin Hill.

'Worse than that! Half-killed a chap. A fellow POW. An Army type. Seems March thought he had something to do with his sister's death.'

Charles felt as though Stubbs had just kicked him in the midriff. He put down his tea cup, his hands trembling. Taking his silence for interest, Stubbs went on, 'This brown job was taken prisoner with her. March reckons he betrayed her.'

'Christ!' Charles said, got up and walked out.

It was minutes before he could compose himself sufficiently to go in to meet the other members of the court. Now after the shock, he was wracked with contrary thoughts and emotions. Would March object to him? Should he ask to be stood down?

No! He was damned if he would! He owed it to Marianne to sit on that court. It was the last possible act he could do for her. Still white-faced, he joined the others. He knew none of them. Group Captain Ruthven was from Bomber Command Headquarters. Cragge was a Coastal pilot. Aylmer was from Air Ministry and Everett was in admin. The Judge Advocate's department had sent a prosecutor, now arrayed in wig and gown.

'With a name like that I can't understand why he isn't in the Free French Air Force,' said the Group Captain.

'With a name like that,' Charles retorted, 'of course he would go to the RAF. As you may remember, Air Commodore March was a very brave and distinguished officer.'

The remark was drowned in a long spiel from the representative of the Judge Advocate's department on procedure. Then they were hurried into the ante-room and took their places behind a green baize-covered table at the far end. In came the Station Warrant Officer with a ceremonial sword in its scabbard, reverently unsheathed it and laid it parallel with the table, pointed away from where the accused would be positioned.

Smaller tables had been arranged for accused and escort, defending and prosecuting counsels, a card table for the clerk. Behind, chairs were arranged in rows for visitors and officers under instruction.

Gradually, the room filled up. At nine-thirty am exactly, the court was sworn in, one by one. 'I swear by Almighty God,' Charles said, holding up a blue bound Bible in his right hand, 'that I will well and truly try the accused before the court according to the evidence, and that I will duly administer justice according to the Air Force Act without partiality or affection . . . and I do further swear that I will not divulge the sentence of the court until it is duly confirmed, and I do further swear that I will not on any account, at any time whatsoever, disclose or discover the vote or opinion of any particular member of this court martial . . .'

And I also swear, Charles said to himself, that I will do my damnedest to get Pierre acquitted.

Eventually the outside door was opened by the SWO. Accompanied by his escort, hatless, Pierre March came in. He looked much the same as ever. That same rather long face, those bright black eyes below the cropped brown hair. The eyes searched the room, stopped dead at him, then moved round the other members of the court, finally fixing themselves unblinkingly on the president.

The official proceedings commenced. The President asked, 'Are you Flight Lieutenant March, P, 63661?'

'I am.'

'You were serving in the Tactical Air Force when you were shot down on 29 May 1944?'

'Yes.'

'You were then in a prisoner-of-war camp till freed by the British advance?'

'Yes.'

'When you were brought to Orly with other POWs for transportation in a Halifax.'

'Yes.'

'Now I want you to look carefully at the members of the court. Do you object to any of them?'

Pierre's eyes met Charles's directly.

Is he going to be fool enough to object to me, Charles wondered. He must know there's nothing for him to object to. Quite the opposite. Whatever he's done, I'd have done more. Whatever he felt for Marianne, I felt more. How could I ever blame him?

Pierre must have come to that same conclusion for he raised no objection.

'You have copies of the charges?'

'Yes.'

'You are charged under Section 36 of the Air Force Act regarding behaviour prejudicial to good order and discipline in that you caused grievous bodily harm to Colonel X, an officer of the Free French Forces. Do you plead guilty or not guilty?'

'Not guilty.'

The President whispered something to the dark-suited figure in wig and gown. Then he said, 'Now we will proceed to the prosecution's case.'

The Judge Advocate rose. 'Call Colonel X.'

A man in khaki French Army uniform had to be helped to a chair in front of the table. A white bandage covered his neck and jaw, his right eye was puffed up, his face badly bruised – but Charles could still recognise him as the man he knew as Jean-Paul, whom he had dropped with Marianne at Chartres that first time.

'You are an SOE officer?'

'Yes.'

'You operated with the Resistance in the Chartres area?'

'Yes.'

'On 12 June 1944, you were captured together with three other members of the cell, and put in Chartres prison?'

'Yes.'

'After six months there, you were transported to Ravensbruck?'

'Yes.'

'And you were freed by the American advance?'

'Yes.'

'And brought to Orly with other POWs for transportation to Stanton in a Halifax?'

'Yes.'

'On that flight, you sat next to the accused?'

'Yes.'

'He spoke to you?'

'Yes. In very good French. He asked me where I was imprisoned, I told him Chartres.'

'He realised you were an SOE officer?'

'Yes.'

'What happened then?'

'We got talking. I asked him his name. March, he said.'

'That meant something to you?'

'Yes. My special charge was a brave young woman called Marianne March.'

'You were dropped with her in the Chartres area?'

'Yes.'

'And operated with her?'

'For many months.'

'She was one of the Resistance network who were arrested with you and put in Chartres prison?'

'Yes.'

'The Germans wanted the names of the other members?'

'Yes.'

'You were all questioned?'

'Yes.'

'Tortured?'

'Yes.'

'But nobody said anything?'

'No.'

'However an escape was planned and organised?'

'Yes.'

'The four of you were going to be picked up on a field near Chartres?'

'Yes.'

'But the plan misfired?'

'Yes.'

'In fact, Marianne March and two of your other companions were shot that afternoon?'

'Yes.'

'And it was the Germans who met the plane in?'

411

'So I understand.'

'In fact, the plan had been betrayed?'

'Yes.'

'You are not at liberty to say by whom?'

'No.'

'And in the Halifax, when the accused told you his name, you realised that Marianne March might have been a relative?'

'Yes.'

'You said nothing?'

'No.'

'Then what happened?'

'Through the portholes of the plane, we all suddenly saw the Kent coast. Everybody cheered. Except him.'

'And what did he do?'

'He said, "I had a sister in the SOE."'

'And what did you say?'

'Nothing.'

'And then?'

'He went on, "I don't suppose you knew her?"'

'And what did you say?'

'Nothing.'

'And afterwards?'

'He said, "I hope she's all right I haven't heard any news of her."'

'And what did you do then?'

There was a long silence. Then the Colonel said, 'I told him.'

'What did you tell him?'

'What I've told you.'

'And what did he do?'

'He listened perfectly calmly.'

'Did he say anything?'

'He just sat silent.'

'And what did you say?'

Sadly Colonel X shrugged his shoulders. 'What could I say? The usual things. I'm sorry . . .'

'And then what happened?'

'Just after we landed at Stanton he said to me, "Why didn't they shoot you?"'

'And what did you say?'

'That I didn't know.'

'What did he say to that?'

'Nothing. He just went off to be interrogated.'

'But you saw him again?'

'Yes.'

'When was that?'

'After dinner that night, in the ante-room at Stanton. He suddenly came in and saw me sitting by the window. And he came over and I said, "Hello, aren't you having any coffee?" And he didn't answer. He didn't say anything. He just hit me.'

'Had he been drinking?'

'No.'

'What did you do?'

'I tried to get up, but he went on hitting me. Till people dragged him off. The next thing I knew, I was in a hospital bed.'

'And that's all you remember?'

'Yes.'

'Do you think the accused may have jumped to the conclusion that it was you who betrayed them?'

'Perhaps.'

There was a long silence.

'Did you?'

The President sharply interrupted. 'There is no need for the witness to answer that question. The Colonel is a distinguished officer in the French Army with long service behind the enemy lines in the Resistance. There is not the slightest suspicion that he gave the enemy any information.' He paused, 'Has the defence any questions?'

'None, sir.'

'Then that is all, Colonel . . . thank you.'

The Colonel was helped to a seat at the back of the court. A number of officers were then called who were in the ante-room and witnessed the assault, all of them saying much the same. A doctor from the hospital went through a list of injuries – broken jaw, concussion, damage to the retina of the left eye. For none of these witnesses did the accused have any questions.

Finally defence counsel rose. 'Sir, the assault is admitted, but under extreme provocation. As you know, the accused has been held in prison for nearly a year. Suddenly he was confronted with news of his sister's death in circumstances that are beyond describing. *Someone* betrayed them. You may well think it impulsive to jump to the conclusion that it was Colonel X, but put yourself in the accused's position. He had been given a shock sufficient to unhinge anyone.'

The President leaned forward over the table. 'Are you meaning to imply that the accused was insane?'

'No, sir. Momentarily knocked off balance.'

'Unpremeditated?'

'Exactly!'

There was a long pause. Then the President asked very slowly, 'But how can it have been unpremeditated when there was a five-hour interval between the accused being told and the assault?'

Defence counsel murmured something about 'delayed action shock'. Then prosecution and defence gave their last speeches, before the court retired to consider their verdict.

Before they had even sat down in the room they had been shown into, Charles knew what that would be.

'Such behaviour,' the flight lieutenant from admin said, 'is not that of an officer and a gentleman.'

'Whatever the defence may say about shock,' said the President, 'no RAF officer can be excused for going berserk in that manner.'

'Particularly against a man like Colonel X,' Aylmer from Air Ministry pointed out. 'Such an excellent record.'

413

'An acquittal would reflect so badly on him,' Cragge said.

'An acquittal?' The President raised his head. 'Who said anything about an acquittal? The assault is not disputed.'

'But there *were* extenuating circumstances.' Charles said. 'The defence is perfectly right.'

'What do others think?' asked the President.

No one else had anything to say.

'Nobody appears to agree with you, Haybury.'

'In that situation, which of us would have acted differently?'

The President raised his brows. 'Is there any need to discuss the matter further? No? Then shall we vote? What's your verdict, Aylmer?'

'Guilty.'

'Everett?'

'Guilty.'

'Cragge?'

'Guilty.'

'And I say Not Guilty!'

'How can you say that, Haybury?'

Charles said slowly, 'If I'd had a shock like that . . . if I'd heard what March heard in those same circumstances . . . I'd have hit him too.'

'But he half-killed the man!'

'I *would* have killed him!'

There was a shocked silence. Eventually, the President said, 'My vote is guilty. Four to one.' He paused. 'And the sentence?'

Charles said immediately. 'If you bring in a guilty verdict, at least appreciate the diminished responsibility.'

'Don't let us forget,' Everett said, 'that if this case had appeared before a civil court the charge would be Grievous Bodily Harm and the sentence would be prison.'

'And don't let us forget the victim,' Aylmer put in.

'Leniency would condone,' said Cragge.

'Prison,' Everett repeated. 'A period in prison —'

'He's *been* in prison!' Charles said hotly. 'Over a year in prison!' He turned towards the Group Captain. 'And I will not, Sir, be associated with an inhuman sentence on a man who has fought with us against inhumanity! This is plainly a case of reduced responsibility. In the circumstances, he didn't know what he was doing!'

'But he ought to have done,' Everett objected.

When Flight Lieutenant Pierre March was again brought in to stand hatless before the court, the sword was pointed straight at him.

And the sentence was: *Dismissed the Service.*

TWO

It was Charles Haybury's doing – Pierre had not the slightest doubt of that.

Alone in his room, after the court martial was over, he had laid on his bed for twenty-four hours, too stunned to think.

Now it was late afternoon – time he was moving. He swung his legs off the bed, walked over to the basin in the corner, washed and began shaving.

He had not expected the verdict. He had expected the court to understand. How could they do otherwise? The son of a man who had given his life to the RFC and RAF. An officer who had fought in the Battle of Britain. A man who had spent nearly a year as a POW. And then suddenly to hear his sister had been executed from a man who himself had escaped the firing squad!

That was why he had not objected to Charles when he had seen him as one of his judges. In spite of his feelings against the Hayburys in general and against Charles in particular, because of Marianne he had been sure that he would have been on his side. In his shoes, Charles would have done the same thing. Of course the man who had survived had betrayed her! Or course he had half-killed him!

Marianne had told him very little of her feelings for Charles, but then she had always been withdrawn, more like their father, where he was like their mother. But what he had seen had been enough to convince him that there was a relationship between them. His mother would have hated the idea, hating all things Haybury. His father had remained a remote figure, a legend who had shot down a Zeppelin in a plane that was built on his own design – which had been stolen by the Hayburys for their Jerningham Aviation.

And now, true to the family character, Haybury had betrayed him. All his pride in being named after his mother's first husband – a shadowy saint where his own father had been a shadowy hero – called for vengeance. He finished shaving. He took a last look at the face, haggard but still determined, in the mirror. Then he dressed, packed his few belongings into a kitbag went downstairs and cashed a small cheque at the PMC's office, and then walked to station headquarters to finalise the arrangements for his demise.

The squadron leader admin tried to be kind. He said the sentence was subject to confirmation, implying that there was still hope. Pierre brushed aside the words, signed the necessary documents. 'Would you like any money? You will be credited with back-pay for your POW service.'

'No.'

'A railway warrant?'

'I don't want anything from the RAF.'

A fine drizzle was falling when he went outside, but he did not notice it. He walked past the hangars towards the main gate and the road – to go to somewhere but where he had no idea. Passing stores he stared balefully at the notices pasted on the wall. *Careless Talk, Dig for Victory, What to do in the event of an unexpected V1 or V2.*

V, he thought. V for Victory with Churchill's two fingers up, that's the only thing they understand about V. He had all the Frenchman's contempt for the British – for their attitude, their arrogance, their total ignorance of every language but their own. But V stood for *Vergeltungswaffe*. Not that the British would be any the wiser!

V for Vengeance. Vengeance against everything Haybury. And now there was only him to carry it out. He refused to count the old blacksmith. Like his mother, he resented the humiliating connection. Pierre hated Cornford House. He hated Jerningham. He had no desire to go there now.

It was in this mood that he rounded the corner of the camouflaged hangar and saw an old Dakota come trundling up to the control tower. It bore no squadron markings. All that was painted on its side was the letter Q.

Both propellers creaked to a stop. The door was flung open. A ladder appeared. Down came a hefty girl in dark blue tunic and trousers – the uniform of the Air Transport Auxiliary. He saw a big round face, plump red cheeks, untidy auburn hair on which the blue forage cap was set at a careless angle.

'Hey,' she called out in an accent you could cut with a knife. 'Hey, you! Any petrol round here, lad?'

'Are you talking to me?'

'I am that.' She took off her cap and ran her fat fingers through her hair. 'Queenie's a thirsty lass and I've miles to go.'

'Tell that to Flying Control,' he said curtly.

He had never seen a less prepossessing female. Then turning away towards the gate, on an impulse, he asked, 'Where are you going?'

'Whitchurch.'

Bristol's civil airport – where BOAC were now based. It was somewhere to go. He would save the rail fare. And the drizzle had turned to rain.

'Can you give me a lift?'

'In Queenie? Well, I might if you get me petrol!'

So it was arranged. Twenty minutes later, refuelled, checked out at Control, he sat beside her in the co-pilot's seat, watching two surprisingly competent hands start up the engines, move the throttles forward, taxi to the head of the runway, stop.

She lifted up her microphone, 'Tower clearance, please.'

One minute later, they were airborne.

On the way to Whitchurch they exchanged names.

'They call me Joycie,' she told him. 'Joycie Ogden. Any need to tell you where I come from?'

'Where?'

'Yorkshire. West Riding.'

'My name's March.'

'What's your Christian name?'

'Pierre.'

'Pierre not Peter?'

'I'm more French than English.' He diverted the conversation from personal questions. 'Why are you going to Whitchurch?'

She thumped the control column. 'To try to sell this old girl to BOAC. ATA's getting rid of all its planes.'

So were the Air Force. They flew over fields full of Fortresses, Liberators, Lancasters, Halifaxes, coralled like cattle. Half of BOAC's 169 aircraft were at Hurn and half at Whitchurch – nineteen types fitted with nineteen types of engine.

As the Dakota neared Whitchurch, ragged stratus hung over the ground. A southwesterly wind was bringing in sleety rain off the Bristol Channel. Old Queenie began bucking in the uneven air like a frightened horse.

'You're cleared to land,' Whitchurch tower told them. 'But mind the wind. It's right across 33.'

Joycie's face remained expressionless. The big red hands enveloped the throttles, gently eased them back. Queenie quietened, then began meekly descending. Just over the hedge, Joycie checked and flared, edged the nose right up, then kicked off half the drift.

The squeak of the tyres on the soaking runway was like the mewing of a new-born kitten. 'Good landing,' Pierre said.

It was more than that. In its own way, it was a work of art. But Joycie's face still remained expressionless as she began her after landing check. Watching the movements of the big red hands on the levers and the switches, Pierre thought how sure they were, how competent and capable. Even old Queenie, now coming up to the ramp on her very best behaviour, seemed to know they could be trusted utterly.

Even so, nobody seemed to want the old Dakota. Joycie tried all the offices – administration and engineering. Nobody was impressed with Queenie. The most she could get by way of an answer was that they would have a closer look over the aircraft, and might make an offer by the weekend if London was agreeable.

Joycie rang ATA who told her to stay in Bristol to await BOAC's decision. Since Pierre also had to find a roof over his head for the night, they took the BOAC bus into town and registered at a small commercial hotel in Clifton.

THREE

'As I see it,' Joycie said in the Bristol pub five days later. 'Nobody wants any of us. The three of us are redundant.' She took a long swig of her beer. 'And two of us – Queenie and me – are damned near being obsolescent.'

BOAC had said they didn't want the Dakota. They were concentrating what purchasing power they had on a long-range four-engined aircraft, the old Liberators, the new Lockheed Constellations and the Yorks.

Pierre smiled for the first time in weeks. He drained his glass and Joycie hooked it up with her own and said, 'My round.'

He didn't argue. He had the not unpleasant feeling you get sometimes when you are caught in a jetstream. When he came to think of it his meeting with Joycie had been exactly that. She had scooped him up and away off the dung heap, to a new life.

'There,' she said, 'sup up.' She set the tankard in front of him. 'As I was saying. The RAF doesn't want you, love.'

'Damn them!' He raised his tankard.

'Sod them.' She clinked her's with it. 'And the ATA doesn't want me.'

'Has no *work* for *you*. The whole caboodle's washed up. That's different. *You* haven't been thrown out.' He hid his face in the mug. 'Disgraced.'

'Boils down to the same in the end, Pete.' She was the only person who had ever called him by that ghastly diminutive. No one else would have dared. Yet coming from her, it suited him, suited them both. It suited his new life, though what that was he didn't know. 'No work, no job, Pete. And there'll be lots of us that won't be saying roll on civvy street. Come demob everyone's going to be looking for a pitch. We should be thankful, I suppose that we're not for the knacker's yard like poor Queenie.'

She sighed heavily. BOAC had suggested Queenie was fit only to be cannibalised. And with that in mind they could accommodate her in a large field south of the perimeter where other redundant aircraft were waiting break-up.

'Once they don't need you any more it's curtains. That's the way of it now, you've copped your clog.' Joycie drew her fingers across her throat. 'Like Queenie.'

'It's not a living thing!' Pierre reminded her, as, to his astonishment, discomfort and annoyance, a tear trickled from the corner of Joycie's grey eyes.

She wiped it from her cheek with the back of her hand glancing at him apologetically, but said stoutly, 'Happen it's not to you. But it is to me.'

'Nonsense.'

'I tell you it is.'

'Sheer sentimentality!'

'No. It's not. I've flown her in some bloody awful conditions. She's saved my bacon more than once.'

'Well, you can't save her now.'

'But there's years of life in her. Like me.' She half-laughed, half-cried. 'I'd buy her myself if I had the necessary.'

'And what on earth would you do with her.'

She shrugged. 'I dunno.'

Neither of them said anything more on the subject till it was Joycie's turn again. The beer was good. Pierre began to feel life might yet be good.

'You and I could start a little freight service,' Pierre said. 'That'll be the thing now.'

'Using what for brass?'

'You haven't any?' he asked her.

'Enough for a few more pints.'

'Family money?'

'Nay, lad! You have to be joking! Oh, I see, because I was a private pilot you thought I'd a rich daddy who paid for flying lessons. Some Yorkshire mill-owner type? Sorry, Pete. The mill part's right enough. My dad was a sorter. Tops and noils. Does that mean owt to you? Thought not. Smelly job. Stinks like dirty hair.' She laughed. 'He did me proud though. Sent me to the Gregg Secretarial School after I left Grange Road Secondary. Then I got a job with the tramways. They had a depot at Stanningly. Not far from Yeadon. Once my dad took me to see Clem Sohn, the birdman – had a five bob flight in an aircraft. That did it – saved every penny for lessons. Did without dinners. Learned quite quickly.'

'You're a good pilot,' he said. 'A natural.'

'Aye,' she said without the slightest vanity, 'I know.'

'We'd make a good team. Purely business,' he added hastily, as she turned her curiously clear eyes towards him questioningly.

'Oh, I wasn't getting any romantic ideas,' she said crisply. 'I lost them a long, long time ago. But what the bloody hell. It's all beer talk. You can't start a business without brass.'

He nodded.

Joycie sighed, 'We couldn't even rustle up a loan.'

'But,' Pierre said, as he came back from the bar with his round, '*I've* got a bit of money coming to me. *I* could raise quite a proportion of the wind.'

In the cold sober light of the following morning, after another not very comfortable night at the hotel, his plan began to gel. The more he thought about it, the better he liked it. A little airline of his own, with Joycie and himself as the pilots. As a start he wrote to his solicitors instructing them to put Cornford House up for immediate sale.

'I want you to come with me, Sarah, I don't want to go alone.'

'I don't see why you've got to go at all, M'lady!' Sarah answered crossly. These days she had been promoted to housekeeper. But her real role was Amelia's companion, her confidante, her most trusted friend and mentor. Amelia needed her. The war had drained her, taken so much. Yet she dreaded the problems of peace.

419

'You don't *have* to see,' Amelia snapped. 'You're not paid to see. I'm simply telling you. I want you with me at the Cornford House sale.'

Sarah sniffed. It was a warm August morning. The air was filled with birdsong and the distant hum of reapers. The war in Europe was over. The crowds had danced in the streets, the beer had flowed, the boys were beginning to come home. Very slowly life was beginning to return to normal. Sarah had been intending to sit in the sun to finish a nightgown for her youngest niece, which she was making out of parachute silk obtained by Amelia. Life went on. Her niece widowed at Dunkirk was marrying again.

'Anyway, there's nothing there that *you* could want, M'lady.'

'You don't know *what* I want, Sarah.'

'Stands to reason. There'll be nothing worth having. The son'll have taken anything that's worth anything.'

'I'd like a memento,' Amelia said, more to herself than to Sarah.

Sarah leapt on it. 'Of *what* might I ask, M'lady?'

'No. You might *not* ask, Sarah.'

Indeed Amelia would not have known how to answer the question even to herself. The selling of Cornford House was the end of an era. After today perhaps she would never again be able to return to reinforce her memory of James.

'I would have thought,' Sarah went on unabashed, 'that you wouldn't want to touch *anything* to do with that horrible Pierre March. Not with a barge pole and rubber gloves. The things he's said about Sir Charles!'

'He was in an emotional state. I think the Air Force was very hard on him.'

'Not hard enough, if you ask me. Sir Charles took that court martial to heart. He's only beginning to perk up now, in my opinion. Roll on the real end of the war, I say. The sooner those sneaky yellow little Japs get their come-uppance the better and we can get him home for good.'

But it was only Ajax would get Charles home again. The wheel had come full circle. Charles's commitment had returned to Ajax. He spent almost every spare moment of his leaves and what 48-hour passes he could manage working with Ronald Cummings.

'And thank heaven we *have* Ajax,' Cummings had said. The war contracts dried up almost overnight. As Whitehall decorated itself with flags and red, white and blue bunting, out had come the cancellation notices of government contracts. Already there was talk of aircraft firms going bankrupt.

A new government had come to power in July. The victory crowds which besieged Buckingham Palace in thankfulness for deliverance immediately dismissed the architect of that victory, Winston Churchill. At the beginning of August Prime Minister Attlee appointed Lord Winster as Minister for Civil Aviation, which indicated aviation was to be accorded some importance, but no one knew whether the Labour government would be better or worse than Churchill's in taking Britain into the airborne age.

And what would everyone fly?

Towards the end of the war, Britain had relied heavily on American aircraft. Would it continue to do so in the coming years? On one of his leaves last month Charles had been up to see the Gloster-Whittle E28 Pioneer which had made the first British jet-propelled flight in 1941. Charles had come back a convert to jet propulsion.

420

'I don't at all like the idea of being *blown* along,' Amelia had protested. 'It isn't natural.'

'That's precisely what it is, Mama. Natural. More natural than grinding your way into the air. Didn't you tell me designers used to study sycamore pods? Insects? Birds?'

'Sycamore pods and birds and insects don't have a great roaring burning jet behind them, Charles.'

'I tell you Mama, it's better than petrol. Less moving parts than piston engines. Less to go wrong.'

It seemed, though, there was always something to go wrong in aircraft design. Always something they had forgotten or overlooked to produce that seeming anomaly, the heavier-than-air craft that would handle like a bird and stand up like a battleship to the buffeting of the skies. Not that things were going wrong yet with Ajax V. Both Cummings and Charles now had test flown the airliner prototype. The two turbo-prop engines were quiet and economical. She was easy to fly, responsive and coming in so slowly she was a dream to land. Some hint of that original little Ajax could be seen in the tall tail, the cutback of the wings.

'This year, next year,' Charles had said, 'the orders will come pouring in.'

Amelia hadn't finished the jingle for him: 'Sometime, never'. She had seen too much of the ups and downs of civil aviation and government awarding of contracts to be optimistic. She was afraid of how they should go on. The future was so uncertain. And with James's death she had lost her star.

She sighed. She became aware that Sarah was watching her with her habitual expression of impatient tenderness. 'I'm sorry, Sarah,' she smiled. 'I was just thinking of what you were saying. About Charles. He *is* only now beginning to look better. But I don't think it's anything to do with the court martial. I think he's fed up with the war. As you say, roll on victory in Japan. He has applied for early release. Because of the firm. And Arthur . . . ' her voice shook. 'The family problems that have to be settled. Rachel. Sometime Mr Lehmann and I want to go over to see her. Decide what's best for her. Then there's the finance for the Ajax airliner to be thought of . . . ' she picked up her handbag, ' . . . what capital investment we can afford . . . '

'That's why I can't understand you wasting time going to Cornford House. With all *your* problems, M'lady.'

Amelia tightened her mouth reprovingly but said nothing. That of course, was why she had to go. Because she had all those problems, she needed to get as close as she could to James.

Cornford House still retained something of James. The grounds had been allowed to run wild, the lake choked with reeds and willows, then the whole hastily shaved and brutally tidied by contractors for the sale. Amelia slowed the car and gazed sadly down across the bald patched lawns to the unplugged lake. There was no sign of the swans.

No sign of the Countess's ornate jars beside the front doors. A 'Sale this day' label was stuck on the glass. The hall was crowded with would-be buyers. Today the sale was of the contents. Tomorrow, the property itself. All the furniture was numbered. A bright-eyed red-lipped girl sat behind a card table selling catalogues.

It was difficult to think of James here. Or in the reception rooms. Amelia wondered if anything of his remained, among the birdy-eyed predators examining that sideboard for woodworm and those leather chairs for rot and mould. Over the years Pierre must have removed the most personal items belonging to his parents. The rooms for the most part were furnished in the Countess's rather ornate style – heavy brocade curtains in swags and loops, Louis Quinze furniture, Limoges bowls and figures. But James's study was so much his that it was as if his unseen hand had reached out to touch her. Amelia felt such a mixture of agony and sweetness, such a rush of contradictory emotions that her face drained of colour. The auctioneer's young assistant rushed up with a chair, and to Sarah's delight, asked her if the old lady would like to sit down.

'Old lady, indeed!' Amelia fanned herself with her catalogue, 'It's the heat that's all.'

She looked round at James's bookcases, at his desk, at his swivel chair, worn where his arms had rested, as if by staring at them long enough could evoke him. But the more she tried the more elusive did he become. She was simply aware now of a great emptiness.

Sarah was right. She had been foolish to come.

'We'll kick off in here,' the assistant appeared at Amelia's elbow with a glass of water. 'If I pull your chair over here, you'll be right under the auctioneer's nose.'

It was a doubtful privilege. The auctioneer had a loud voice and a heavy hand on the gavel. Amelia's head throbbed. By the time everyone had crowded into the study the heat was intense. Her escape was cut off by rows of sweating people in chairs and the dealers lounging against the walls. She tried to think of James. To see him again by the lake just visible as a grey glaze through the trees. To see him carrying off little Marianne. Poor Marianne. Charles had never spoken of what had happened to her. Only that she was dead.

'I think you should go, M'lady,' Sarah said severely. 'you look the colour of skimmed milk. There's nothing you want here. Can't be. You've got all the desks and bookcases you could possibly need.'

And just as Amelia was about to agree, suddenly she saw it. Sitting on the top of the dusty bookcase, numbered 53 in black on a white tag, that first model of Ajax which James had ever made. It looked such a small scrap now, bent wire rusting, silk half-rotten. It was hard to believe that it had changed so many lives.

'No,' she hissed at Sarah. 'I don't intend to go. I am perfectly comfortable. You go outside if you wish. There is something I want. I'm going to bid.'

Silently, acting what she called dumb saucy, Sarah raised her eyes to the ceiling, but remained silent. After several more items had come under the hammer Sarah asked heavily, 'When, M'lady? When do you intend to bid?'

'Wait and see.'

'Before lunch, M'lady?'

'Probably. The prices are cheap, don't you think?' A walnut bookcase was knocked down for three pounds.

'People haven't the money to throw about.' Sarah grunted.

'Four pounds for that rug. That's cheap.'

'Not specially. Which lot are *you* going to bid for, M'lady?'

The assistant's hands were already closing round it. 'Lot 53,' came the auctioneer's unenthusiastic voice. 'What am I bid. What is it worth?'

No one bid. Amelia suddenly found herself unable to speak. 'Come, come, come,' said the auctioneer. 'It must be worth something to someone. No one. Not one of you?'

As he turned to his assistant to say, 'Take it away,' Amelia found her voice. 'Fifty pounds,' she gasped.

There was a titter of disbelieving laughter. The auctioneer cupped his ear towards Amelia. 'Did you say fifty, Madam?'

Amelia nodded vigorously. The titter of laughter became louder. The pink-faced assistant stood on tiptoe to whisper at the auctioneer. Amelia heard the murmur, 'Not feeling well. Doesn't know what she's . . . Dotty old lady.'

'Fifty pounds,' Amelia repeated firmly.

'Fifty pounds. Will anyone improve on that? Or will it be fifty pounds for a maiden bid?' the auctioneer deciding it was less embarrassing to continue, raised his gavel. 'Going to the lady in the front.'

'Fifty-five.' A deep male voice came from the back. A voice familiar and yet unfamiliar.

There was another rustle of astonishment.

'Sixty,' Amelia said promptly.

'Sixty-five,' the deep voice.

'Seventy!'

'Please, M'lady,' Sarah's fingers plucked at Amelia's sleeve, her voice almost tearful. 'You don't know what you're doing. It's the heat . . . you're not feeling well.'

'Seventy-five!'

'Eighty!' Now the study was humming with interest.

Dealers were exchanging worried whispered speculation as to what the hidden value of the item could be. Was it of some precious substance they had overlooked? Was it an *objet d'art*? Was it something to do with Lindbergh?

The auctioneer, aware that prices so far had been low and pleased that he now had two eccentrics instead of one, happily encouraged the price to climb. Finally the model was knocked down to Amelia for five hundred pounds.

'You're mad, M'lady!' Sarah whispered. 'Stark staring raving mad. My niece could buy a house and furnish it for that price. What d'you want with that bit of rubbish? Where'll you put it? What shall you do with it?'

Amelia didn't answer. She was craning her neck to see who her opponent had been. Who could possibly have wanted that model of Ajax as much as she did? The only possibility was Pierre. And yet Pierre would have sorted through the contents before any auction began. Despite Sarah's entreaties and dire warnings, Amelia stayed till the lunch interval, when the kindly auctioneer's assistant allowed her to write a cheque and claim her prize. The young man who had bid against Amelia was leaning against the panelling of the study as they left. He surveyed them with a sardonic smile. He wore grey flannel trousers and a blue polo necked shirt. To the half-familiar voice was added a half-familiar dark thin face.

'Pierre? Are you Pierre March?' Amelia asked going up to him.

'Yes, Lady Haybury.'

She began to say, 'I'm so very sorry about your sister. You must be very proud of her.' She got no further than, 'I'm very sorry . . . ' Then she held up the model and finished, 'I hope you're not too disappointed.'

'Disappointed? About what, Lady Haybury?'

'About this. The model.'

He gave up an unpleasant little laugh. His narrow dark eyes snapped. 'You don't suppose I *wanted* it, Lady Haybury?'

'Of course I do.'

'Then I'm sorry to disabuse you. I had every opportunity to take whatever things I wanted. That,' he stabbed a scornful finger at the bits of silk and rusting wire, 'was not amongst them.'

'I thought perhaps you had changed your mind.'

'On that.' He shook his dark head. 'No.'

'Then why did you bid?'

'Because you wanted it. And . . . '

'And?'

'And I wanted the money.'

'You mean you forced Her Ladyship up?' Sarah accused indignantly.

'I mean exactly what I said. I need money. A lot of money. And you, Lady Haybury, are providing me with some of it. For a business I'm starting. An aviation business.'

'Well, of all the cheek!' Sarah began till Amelia kicked her sharply on the ankle.

Amelia herself remained silent. She turned away from Pierre with a brief nod. She was afraid to speak. Not because she was angry, but because her reaction would have spoiled his perverse triumph and shocked Sarah.

For the first time in years she was almost happy. She clutched the model tightly. Momentarily she had found James again. It was right somehow that indirectly she was helping his son with his enterprise. Dimly, a pattern seemed to disclose itself. She returned to Haybury untouched and undeterred by Sarah's what-did-I-tell-you monologue. She set the model on her bedside table, and slept soundly, as if her life had taken on a new and satisfying dimension.

The following morning, like a reinforcement of her optimism, the news broke – Japan was suing for surrender. Two secret and deadly bombs had been dropped on Hiroshima and Nagasaki. The towns had been devastated. The Japanese brought suddenly to their knees.

The first reaction was of immense and thankful relief. Some of the horrors and degradations of the Japanese POW camps had leaked through. The thought of the returning men produced a wild euphoria. The bunting was unrolled again, and the street parties organised.

It was Charles who, not for the first time, shattered Amelia's optimism. On leave at Haybury for VJ Day, his mood was sombre. He voiced a thin undercurrent of anxiety that tugged uneasily beneath the national rejoicing. 'We've taken the lid off the nuclear box, Mama. From now on, the world will be poised on the edge of a holocaust.'

FOUR

That same day on Durdham Down, Pete March and Joycie Ogden were also considering the implications of VJ day. Theirs was a purely financial discussion. The war in Japan had ended rather sooner than they expected. How would this sudden peace affect them and their infant enterprise, which in honour of the event they were calling Victory Airways.

They stopped for a moment to watch the dancing under the chestnut trees. Some pretty girls, short of partners, shouted at Pete and beckoned him over. 'Go if you want to,' she told him. 'Enjoy yourself. I don't mind.'

But he shook his head and went on discussing their peacetime operations. Most of the RAF transports would be on trooping, especially now that Japan had surrendered. A large number of Coastal Command aircraft and crews had been turned over to Transport Command for this purpose.

'We'll never get onto trooping. We'll have to start off with freight.'

They had brought the Dakota for £2500 which was more than both of them had in the world, including the sale of Cornford House which (apart from the lucky £500 on the worthless model sold to Lady Haybury) had been bitterly disappointing. The estate agent had told Pete's solicitor that such houses as Cornford were now a drug in the market. No one wanted them. What money people had was going on labour-saving little houses.

Their bank manager had yesterday agreed, however, to advance them a further £2000 on the security of the Dakota. Joycie had spent the morning working on the engines, and had managed to hire a rigger to go through the airframe. 'He won't find much wrong with her, though. She's sound as a bell, old an' all as she is. But I've told him to do what's necessary.'

Pete was well aware that he was somewhat of a liability without his pilot's and navigation licences. But he had had a slip from Kingsway House telling him to report there for the examination in ten days' time. Until then, he would just have to act what he called the dogsbody, and what she called the brain of the enterprise.

'Even if we three are outcasts, Pete,' Joycie had said when she first suggested the name. 'You, me and Queenie. We'll show'em who's going to win in the end. We'll show 'em who are the conquerors.'

By them she meant men as a whole, the whole male sex. It wasn't that she disliked men. It was just that she disliked what men did. They were the arch exploiters. After using women to help win the war, they didn't want women in peacetime aviation. They were not at all sure they wanted them as airline stewardesses. Women, they said, would distract the men. They would cause all kinds of complications. Certainly they could not possibly consider them as pilots.

'We'll show them all right,' Pete had said, meaning by 'them' the Haybury family about whom he had told her very little.

They stopped their stroll at the refreshment tent where free beer was being handed out. They got themselves a mug each and clinked them together, saying 'Victory.'

'We'll need to fly to somewhere close to begin with where they've not been touched by war.'

'Eire, d'you mean?'

'Exactly.' Pete nodded his head. They stood for a moment watching a rocket splinter into a hundred stars in the dark sky. Their hearts lifted. The future seemed suddenly bright. 'Dublin. Irish steaks! We could sell them to the restaurants in the city centre. We could bring other stuff as well. Butter, cheese, bacon.'

'Owt that's rationed?'

'Right. The whole country's browned off with ration books. We'll bring back soft fruit in season. Cream. Asparagus. Flowers. Prawns. Oysters. Lobsters.'

'And what'll we take over? It'll have to be a two way load, Pete, otherwise it'd work out too expensive.'

They thought for a while, as they wandered through the brightly lit streets thronged with people. 'War surplus stuff?' Joycie suggested. 'Tents? Blankets? Socks? Gum boots? Cameras? Parachutes?'

'It's not a bad idea, Joycie. We might get the odd revolver too.'

'We'd get everything cheap. Some of it they're just chucking on to muck-heaps.'

'It's worth giving a try. War surplus to be flown out. Luxury goods in. Seems sensible.'

'Agreed then. Pete?'

'Agreed, Joycie. It won't make us rich. But at least we should stay even.'

But they didn't. War surplus goods of the kind the Irish wanted proved more expensive than they had realised. Queenie was indeed a thirsty aircraft and the fuel bills were high. Landing fees soared, and Whitchurch put up the rent of their hangar space. Times generally were hard. Unemployment reached record proportions. The restaurants would not pay the prices they asked, knowing full well they could knock them down if they waited long enough. One after another the little airlines which had started on gratuities and savings went bust. Victory Airways hung on by the skin of its teeth, and the help of a shrewd bank manager.

Interested by this combination of French thrift and Yorkshire canniness, impressed by their economics (they lived strictly platonically in two rooms in a Brislington boarding house on the edge of Whitchurch), he doubled and then trebled their overdraft.

'You reckon we can carry corn then?' Joycie asked him drily when he agreed to this further loan.

As a southerner, he was not quite sure what she meant. But he got the gist. 'As a businessman,' he smiled, 'I am certain, Miss Ogden, that for two people in partnership as determined as you are, something is bound to turn up.'

'It will,' Joycie said cheerfully, 'if not this year, then next.'

But the first few months of 1946 only brought another loss to the March family. Old Mr March passed quietly away in his sleep. Joycie sent flowers but neither could spare the time to attend the funeral.

It was not till the summer that Victory Airways got the break which they and their bank manager felt they deserved. It followed the granting of independence to India. Almost at once, massacres broke out between Moslems and Hindus.

Operation Pakistan carried 43,500 Moslems from Indian areas to their new country and Hindus from those areas back to India; approximately 3876 of these were carried by Q Queenie, which Pete and Joycie took turns to command. The figure was approximate because they were never quite sure how many had squeezed in before they managed to close the doors against the seething crowds clamouring to get in. Sometimes they had to taxi the Dakota at speed, zigzagging to shake off the people who clung to the wings and tail. They saw crying children left by their parents, distraught mothers separated from their families.

At Hyderabad there was a particularly unpleasant incident. Escaping Hindus were swarming up the passenger steps into an already overloaded Queenie, when a huge crowd of Moslems surrounded the field and began firing. A screaming hoard of Indians were climbing up in front of the propeller, getting on to the wings, while at the rear, others were climbing on to the tailplane. Pete yelled at them through the open window but they took no notice. He started the propellers. That made not the slightest difference. Bullets starting zinging inches away from the fuselage. One shattered Joycie's windscreen.

With both of them still yelling through the cockpit windows, Pete started taxying forward slowly. Sick with fear, milling in circles, the crowd gave way only gradually. Pete simply increased the power and, quite relentlessly, the propellers whirling like knives, he cut his way through and took off.

'It was the only thing to do,' he told Joycie when finally they were airborne and winging towards India. 'It was them or us.'

It was a lesson in his ruthlessness that she was to remember.

No sooner had that resettlement been effected than the Russians closed the railways into Berlin on 4 May 1948. The Allies used canals. The Russians closed those. The city was on the verge of being starved out.

So the Americans, French and British began to fly in food, oil, petrol, coal, clothes, all necessities. Yorks, Hastings, Halifax, Skymaster, Dakota and Tudor aircraft, watched by red starred Mig fighters, waiting to pounce on any that breached the corridor.

At one minute intervals, they were brought into Tempelhof and Gatow by Flying Control. If the bomber stream against Germany was the first mass-scheduling of aircraft, the Berlin airlift was the first mass controlling of them for take-off and landing at airports.

One of the Dakotas was Q Queenie, hired by the British government at £140 an hour, with danger-money of £10 extra because the loads they carried were petrol. Every day, Pete and Joycie worked ten, twelve, sometimes fourteen hours. Pete pushed both them and Q Queenie to the limits. Flying sometimes almost in formation with Yorks or Halifaxes, he would increase the power, edge ahead, jostle his way into Tempelhof before them. Once on the ground, he would push his way forward to get first in the unloading queue, and then be off again empty to get another load.

There was another incident which had certain similarities to the Hyderabad take off. In a drizzling October dusk ninety miles west of Tempelhof, Pete was taking Queenie down on the descent when a shadowy Hudson pushed its way in front of them. Furious, Pete slammed the throttles hard against the stops. The other aircraft followed suit. In and out of cloud, fighting for position, they descended neck and neck. Again and again, their wingtips were inches away. Pete interrupted on the R/T to get tower clearance first, slammed down his wheels, triumphantly won the race.

The Hudson put in a complaint to the Berlin authorities, actually showed them tyre marks on his wings. But by that time, Queenie was off again to England for another load. That was one of the few times that Joycie remonstrated with him.

'But you've got to do these things, Joycie,' he told her. 'You've got to do it if you're going to win.'

There were other things that had to be done in that same endeavour. He wanted her to share a room on night stops, because a double was cheaper than two singles. Joycie flatly and puritanically refused unless they were married. It was the first time marriage had been mentioned between them. Nevertheless on 8 April 1949, they went to the Bristol Registry Office and were married.

The marriage was witnessed by the next couple waiting outside. There was no best man. No bridesmaids. No guests. No honeymoon. They were given one present – a bottle of champagne from the manager of Barclays Bank, together with a deposit account bank statement that showed them £5307 6s 8d in the black.

Juan Trippe, who built up Pan American Airways from nothing to the biggest airline in the world, had reputedly gone to the office on his wedding day. There was no office for Peter March to go to, so he stayed in the lounge of the Brislington boarding house, discussing with Joycie their next move.

Queenie would have to be retired. She was too small and too old. But with what to replace her? The problem was there were no suitable British aircraft. The Tudor, Ambassador, Elizabethan, the huge Princess flying boats, had either failed or were clearly failing.

'Finally,' Peter said reluctantly, 'we want something modern. Piston engines are out. Jets are the next step. Before pure jets, the only thing is the jet prop. Then we don't want something too big because we need flexibility. It's the sun these holiday people will want – Spain and the Mediterranean. But we may have to use it for internal UK work. And the only thing that can give us that flexibility is the Ajax V.'

She had, of course, seen pictures, knew its specifications, but little else. 'They're built in the New Forest?'

'That's right. At Jerningham. By a family called the Hayburys.'

They obtained mortgage guarantees from their accommodating bank manager, and wrote a careful letter to the Ajax Aircraft division of Jerningham Aviation, asking for an option on one Ajax 18-seater, subject to the usual provisos and guarantees, and enclosing ten per cent of the purchase price.

They received an acknowledgement from Cummings, saying that their

428

request for an option would come up at the next board meeting. 'It's an unexpectedly cold letter to a customer, wouldn't you say, Joycie?'

'No one can say it's enthusiastic.'

'Jerningham is a close Haybury concern. The directors are almost all family. But I've heard on my visits to other aircraft manufacturers that there is one thorn in their flesh. A Lady Nazier. There's no harm in writing to her, just in case the board gets bloody-minded about selling us an Ajax . . .'

FIVE

'Diana!' Amelia took hold of the bony hand in its black lace glove. 'It's been such a long time since we saw you!'

'Since dear Frederick's funeral.'

Cummings came up, smiling. 'This is an unusual pleasure, Lady Nazier, to have you at a board meeting.'

Before, she had always sent her solicitor or some favoured young man with strict instructions to vote against everything. Jerningham Aviation still managed to remain a family business – an almost feudal relic in an industry that was being nationalised and gargantuanised all round them. Lehmann and Amelia owned a quarter of the equity each. Rachel had inherited one eighth from Arthur. Victoria still owned an eighth. Connaught Engineering invariably cast its eighth in with Lehmann. Only a tiny eighth outside this formidable alliance belonged to Lady Nazier, and till today she seemed to have lost most of her interest in the business.

'Does this bode trouble?' Amelia whispered to Cummings. 'She's not to be trusted.'

Back came the whisper, 'We can but wait and see.'

The typists laid out plates of biscuits and offered tea. They all sat down. Amelia said, 'Can we have the minutes of the last meeting?'

The company secretary read them out. 'Any objections?'

Lady Nazier opened her mouth, but to everyone's relief said nothing.

'First item on the agenda . . . financial situation.'

She turned to Stefan. In his best banker's manner, Lehmann read out the latest balance sheet, circulated copies and congratulated the sales department on the healthy state of the order book now they were in production.

Surely Diana's going to ask about the huge overdraft, Amelia thought. She must have some reason for coming. Diana never does anything without a motive. But there was not a sound from the end of the table.

'Aircraft situation?'

On safe ground, Charles was at his surest. He began explaining graphs and Amelia's mind wandered. He was getting more like James every day. More serious, more responsible, infinitely dear. A pleasant room this – the best in the house with a lovely view down over the lawns to the Solent and beyond to the Island. It had been her parents' bedroom. She was the only person here, she thought, who would remember. There had been a four-poster bed against that far wall. That nick in the mantelpiece was where she had thrown a silver candlestick at Victoria. The elms outside were the same, now just coming into leaf.

'Flying trials?'

'Well,' Charles smiled sweetly across the table at his mother. 'No less a person that the chairman of the company flew the Ajax prototype yesterday and pronounced herself delighted.'

Amelia nodded and smiled. 'She's everything Charles said she'd be.'

For a moment Amelia paused, remembering her contrary emotions. Her feeling of pride when Ajax V was wheeled out, the big turbo-prop engines jutting out just the right amount for her wings, the neat flight-deck windows matched by the line of portholes that stretched down the blue and white fuselage above her swept-back wings.

All great manufacturers stamp themselves on their aircraft, and so it was with Ajax. Minute fragments – something about the shape, the mien, the character – brought back James's first flimsy butterfly of silks and bamboo. Ajax was still James's aircraft, his immortality and she loved it.

Charles had opened the door for her. 'Hop in, Mama.'

She walked up the steps, entered the cabin with its rows of seats, smelled the new carpet and the new upholstery, stepped through into the flight deck, paused beside the navigator's table, was about to sit down in the co-pilot's position, when Charles said, 'You're doing the take off!'

'I couldn't, Charles!'

She had hardly piloted for years, only a few times since coming back from the desert. There hadn't been a Jerningham aircraft for one thing. And then, she simply hadn't felt like it, fearful she might break it. Gingerly she got into the lefthand seat. Gingerly she held the controls. Gingerly she pushed the throttles forward. Gingerly she lifted the nosewheel.

She was not conscious of when the wheels left the ground. Just for a moment, it wasn't Charles who sat beside her but James, as Ajax soared effortlessly up into the sunlight.

Amelia was suddenly aware that Charles had stopped talking and was looking towards her.

'Next item on the agenda . . . orders.' She pulled herself back to the present. 'Twenty options to date accepted. One —' she hesitated. The last thing she wanted was to underline it in any way. '– is unsuitable.'

Immediately she saw Diana's eyes rise from the golden pool of the table like two little bright green fish.

'Our order is recommended to the board for refusal.'

'By whom?' asked Diana Nazier.

'The technical committee.'

'In other words, Sir Charles Haybury?'

'By no means,' Cummings protested. 'Myself, the assistant designer, all the managers and shop stewards, all voiced the same opinion.'

'A unanimous decision to refuse,' said Lehmann.

'For what reason?' Diana persisted.

'Insufficient supporting technical staff,' Lehmann went on. 'No guarantees of adequate servicing. This is a complicated and sophisticated aeroplane' – his rich banker's drawl was so smooth, so unruffled, so *authoritative* – 'and must be serviced to a high degree of professional competence. The Ajax is for the big airlines. An accident at this stage of development by faulty airline maintenance would not just kill the aeroplane' – he raised his voice to give exactly the right

431

emphasis – 'it would kill the company.'

'And what is the name of this suspect airline?'

'Victory, Lady Nazier.'

'Victory, eh? I like the name!'

'It's not really an airline at all,' Cummings contributed. 'A one-horse outfit that made a lot of money on the Berlin Airlift and is now too big for its boots. Run, I believe, by a husband and wife who have pilot's and engineer's licences.'

'And what is the name of this ambitious pair?'

Determinedly Lehmann again took the reins. 'Their name is March, Lady Nazier.'

The green eyes blazed at him triumphantly. 'The Marches were always an enterprising family. And sitting here in the heart of March country, how can we refuse?'

She knew, Amelia thought. She knew all along. Pierre must have written to her to drum up support. That's the reason why she's here today. She herself had been perfectly willing in the circumstances to allow the option, but Charles had been adamant. Something well below the surface had caused such antagonism. Brothers and half-brothers had reputations for fighting from Cain and Abel onwards.

'Couldn't we give them help?'

'We haven't the staff to spare, Lady Nazier.'

The two voices – one deep and quiet, one shrill and loud – continued uninterrupted.

'Why are you sure that there would be an accident?'

'One can be sure of nothing, Lady Nazier. But the accident rate of the charter companies is higher than that of scheduled airlines.'

'I have never heard of an aircraft firm refusing a sale!'

'There have been quite a number.'

Each objection stalled, everything kept at a low key. Finally, a vote taken. Predictably, Lady Nazier's one eighth was the only vote against.

Amelia shot Stefan a grateful look. As usual, he had taken on a difficult problem and turned it into an easy one. He did so with all her problems. Except of course the problem of Charles's lonely life. She had often told Stefan she wished Charles would go out more often, meet some nice girls, marry one of them, have children. But Stefan had simply shrugged his shoulders.

'You don't think he'll ever marry again?'

He had smiled at her rather sweetly and sadly. 'I think that trait is in the family.'

Sarah was always on to her to marry Stefan. 'Sometimes I think you're blind, M'lady! He's a good catch. It'd be the best thing for you! And for Rachel! You know Mr Lehmann's always wanting to go to America to see her. She must wonder if you love her.'

'I have promised to go with him next year, Sarah,' she had snapped. 'And now . . . mind your own business!'

Amelia began stacking her papers, but now Lady Nazier produced one final sally. 'I am left with an uncomfortable impression that the board's business is decided before the board meets!'

Everyone laughed. The meeting closed quietly. Diana Nazier accepted a glass of champagne to toast the future of Ajax. Then she made her farewells in a burst of cordiality, handshakes all round for the men and kisses on both cheeks for Amelia.

'*Au revoir*, my dear!'

So the day ended perfectly happily.

That *au revoir* bothered her slightly, but driving her home Charles scoffed at any ulterior meaning behind the remark. 'You're seeing too many bogies, Mama! Just a storm in a teacup that's now blown over. Now Ajax is all set to be a winner!'

She said as much to Sarah on Sunday night, after she had returned from spending the weekend with her relatives in the village.

But Sarah was strangely quiet.

That Monday, the local newspaper carried the headlines: *Local firm rejects local hero's son. Jerningham Aviation refuse wonder plane to sole March survivor.*

SIX

'Bastards!' Pete exclaimed, skimming through the letter. 'Bastards!' He clenched his fists. 'Bastards! I'll show them they can't do this to me.'

'What's up, Peter?' The question was largely rhetorical. Joycie had seen the long white envelope with Jerningham Aviation on the back, and had guessed it brought their decision on the Ajax order. The rest was clear from Pete's expression. In all the five years she had known him she had never seen him as angry as this.

Of course, she knew he had a temper. He got impatient with delays and sometimes he took it out on Queenie and sometimes on her. He would say the aircraft was too slow, too sluggish, was an old cow. Then he would slam the controls left, right, up, down and poor old Queenie would lurch round the sky like a chicken with its head cut off.

He never called her names like that, he was too polite. But he looked at her sometimes as if he thought them. He was looking at her now as if thinking what a stupid old cow she was not to know what was up.

'Is it business or personal?' she asked.

'Business, of course.' He darted her a bitter look through his narrowed eyes as if to say they never spoke of anything else. What else but business would he possibly discuss with her? Business in fact represented seventy per cent of their conversation – lengths of runways, visual aids, centres of gravity, met forecasts. The house, food, money, represented the other thirty per cent.

Occasionally Joycie, who had a profound respect for the stars, both navigationally and astrologically, would read aloud their horoscopes. Sagittarius, the Archer, under dark all-powerful Jupiter for him, the Crab under the unlikely maternal Moon for her.

'May I read it?' He still sat with his clenched fist on the letter. Irritably he passed it to her. She read it slowly and phlegmatically. At the end, she shrugged and said stolidly, 'So what, Peter? If they don't want to sell to us, then tell them to get stuffed.'

'You don't understand!' He stood up and began pacing the room. Outside, it was a soft spring morning but he saw none of it.

'Mebbe we could pick up another secondhand Dak? They're going cheap.'

'Don't be more stupid than you can help, Joycie!' He snatched the letter from her hand, scrunched it up and hurled it across the room. 'What you don't realise is that I have a *right* to an Ajax. And not to just one. To all of them. That bloody aircraft is more mine than it is theirs!'

Out it all came then. The whole story. The beginnings were lost in the mists of time. But one thing was sure. Or so Pete said. The basic design of Ajax belonged to *his* father. *His.* Somehow he had been done out of it by the Hayburys while his father was serving his country in the RFC. His mother had told him. His father was a poor man but in his own way he was a genius. The Hayburys had exploited all that. Robbed him. Made him dependent on *her* money or what the Huns had left of it. That was why his mother hated them. Now they had the nerve to refuse to allow him even to buy one of *his own father's* design.

'Guilty conscience,' Joycie suggested with just the right measure of stolidity and sympathy.

'I doubt any of them has ever had a conscience,' Pete snorted. 'Because it isn't just stealing Ajax. God, no! That's only the beginning. I never told you about my sister, did I?'

'Marianne? No, not a lot. I gathered . . . ' she put her big hand sympathetically on his arm.

'You gathered she was killed?' he exclaimed bitterly. 'Oh, she was killed! Murdered.'

'By . . . ?' Her shrewd eyes looked disbelievingly wide. She was thinking she never knew anyone could hate quite as bitterly as this.

'Oh, not Haybury. Not *exactly*.'

'Who then?'

'By a mixture of Nazi brutality and British incompetence. She was taken prisoner. Someone betrayed her.'

'Haybury?'

Pete shook his head. 'No. But Haybury was supposed to try to rescue her. Made a balls-up of it. He's a fool and a coward. If I didn't hate him for Ajax I'd hate him for that.'

'So you should,' she said judiciously.

'And that's why I was court martialled. For hitting the chap I thought had shopped her.'

'Shame.' She patted his hand. 'A bloody, sodding shame.'

'And Haybury got me found guilty.'

'Christ! The swine. Still, he'll come to a bad end. That sort do. God damn them!'

If her native shrewdness told her that there were most likely two if not three sides to the story, she chose not to hear. Pete was like no one she had ever met before. He was a Jekyll and Hyde, a bewitching mixture of charm and violence. A phenomenon. A devil sometimes. A genius like his father, though in a different way. She would do anything, be anything for him. Anything.

'And any road,' she added comfortingly, 'it hasn't worked out too bad, has it?'

It was the wrong thing to say. It brought his temper back in all its fury. It had worked out badly. He hadn't yet laid a finger on Ajax.

At nine that night, as a bit of relief, she suggested they go to a pub called the Wine Vaults at the end of their street. It was a dark and rather poky place, but they had a cellar of good French wines that she knew Pete appreciated.

Now they sat silent and alone. Pete was drinking an iced Bergerac. She drank beer. The Vaults had one large window but no curtains. Above the street lights and above the roofs of the houses opposite arched a dark blue sky pierced with thousands of stars.

'Let go, Peter. Don't fret yourself,' Joycie said as he went on and on about the Hayburys. 'It'll work out. It's what's in our stars. *Que sera sera.*'

'You have the vilest accent,' he said, looking at her as if he hated her as much as the Hayburys.

'Accent or no accent it's true,' she said stubbornly. She knew suddenly something else was true, though she didn't say it aloud. That day it was as if she'd been on a journey to the very centre of Pete. Like the Jules Verne journey to the centre of the earth. And reaching it today she knew what lay at the very core of his being. Not another civilisation, far from it. Not molten rock and fire but something like it. She sighed to herself. It was hatred. Herself unused to hatred except a vague resentment of men, she digested this discovery in silence. Then she took her discovery a step further. If hatred was the core of his being, what was the cornerstone of their marriage? She drained her tankard to the last dreg. What did that make their joint enterprise, the bright star of their lives. Revenge against the Hayburys of course. Revenge.

She put her hand on his arm. 'But don't you worry, lad. Our stars are in the ascendant. You'll get your Ajax. And not just one.' She patted his arm. 'They all really belong to you. We'll get even with the Hayburys. We'll get the whole damned Jerningham factory one of these days!'

Pete scowled, but said nothing. When the barman called, 'Time gentlemen please,' he still said nothing. Joycie looked at him sideways. In its own way, she thought resignedly, hate was just as thick a bond in marriage as love. And if revenge was what her husband wanted, then revenge he should have.

'You've just got to be patient,' she said soothingly. 'We must bide our time. You Sagittarians are too fiery. It's a good thing you married a Crab. Crabs lose their claws sooner than let go.'

She looked down at her bricks of hands, and clenched them. After a while, to her surprise, Pete took one and held it almost tenderly as they sat in a peaceful silence. Then suddenly, they got up with one accord and hand in hand – Sagittarius and Crab – walked out under the stars to go about their business.

A business in which they were suddenly joined the following morning by a welcome ally. A thick letter arrived for Pete containing a veritable quiverful of arrows. First there was the cutting from the *Hampshire Gazette* about the son of the local war hero being denied an Ajax. Then there were the pieces the national press had taken up. Best of all, there was an enclosing letter signed Diana Nazier, deploring the action of the board in refusing an Ajax, and suggesting that it might be to their mutual advantage to meet.

Sagittarius and Crab looked at each other over the breakfast table. Both recognised that a powerful star had just joined them in their isolated little firmament.

SEVEN

A vaster firmament of stars glittered through the portholes of the British Overseas Airways Stratocruiser G-MACE as her four 3500 hp Wright engines ground a track at 29,000 feet across the icy North Atlantic sky. Huddled inside her mink coat, Amelia pointed them out like old friends to Stefan Lehmann as he sat in the seat beside her, lightly holding her hand.

It was close to two on the morning of 26 January. All the other passengers, replete with their first class silver service dinner of turtle soup, cold Inverness salmon, carved baron of beef and peach melba, had either been tucked in the upper bunks, or swaddled in blankets and settled to sleep. The lights had been switched to a dim nursery blue. But Stefan and Amelia were too excited to sleep.

Lehmann, who had made all the arrangements and had wanted to give Amelia every luxury, had suggested booking bunks. But Amelia had refused. She didn't want to miss anything. She wanted to savour every detail of the journey – to see the take off from Heathrow, and again, after refuelling at Prestwick, to feel even the bumpiness as they went in and out of the cumulus build-ups, to notice every star, every finger of the Northern Lights, every electric flicker of St Elmo's fire.

'Of course she won't recognise us,' Amelia turned away from her contemplation of the frosty brilliance of Arcturus, and the pink crystal of Betelgeuse and returned to the object of their journey, Rachel. Their, the grandparents, first glimpse of her since the war, since . . . Amelia closed her eyes, her mind refusing for the moment to go back further. 'We'll be like strangers.'

'We certainly couldn't have left it any longer. I sometimes reproach myself with having left it so long.'

'We've been so busy,' Amelia murmured. But it was more than that. She had needed to wait till she could see James's death in a different perspective, till she could fight her way through the tragedy of that awful September night and glimpse at least a landscape beyond.

'I wish Victoria could have seen her way clear to bringing Rachel to us. After all Rachel's home is really in England. We are her guardians.'

'Victoria is busy too. She has to do a lot of entertaining.' Indeed Victoria, from her letters, seemed to have one continuous round of social engagements.

Henry, much to their mutual delight, on his retirement from the diplomatic service, had landed a plum job at the United Nations in New York. They had bought a house in Vermont and rented a Fifth Avenue apartment. They were able, as Victoria constantly wrote, to provide Rachel with an excellent background. 'And she has been very good to Rachel.'

'That I don't deny. But Rachel is thirteen. Nearly fourteen. And if she's going to receive an English education.'

'Stefan. You don't give a damn about an English education. She's probably had a far better, more cosmopolitan one. It isn't her education you want, Stefan. You want Rachel.'

'Is that so reprehensible?'

'You know it isn't. I want her too. But I know you wouldn't have wanted her when she was small.'

'Obviously not. She needed a mother then. But now . . .' He sighed. 'At my age, time goes very fast.'

'At *your* age, what nonsense!'

'I'm getting old.'

'You're in your prime.'

'Late sixties. Very late. Pushing seventy.'

'Late sixties, early sixties, what's the difference?'

'Do you mean that, Amelia?' He leaned closer to her and studied her face, his dark eyes eloquent.

'I simply mean that I'm getting on too. I'm sixty-three.'

'Yet you have never looked more beautiful.'

'It's the blue lights,' Amelia smiled. 'They're becoming. You can only see a ghostly me.' But she didn't feel ghostly. She felt vigorous and young again. Life was taking a turn for the better. Three turns. Like a lucky trefoil. Firstly Charles was restored to his old self again. Secondly Ajax was out of the red. All indications were that it would scoop a hefty share of the home market. At the last board meeting, which took place only three weeks ago, Charles had given a masterly and most encouraging report. Indeed, it was because of that meeting when the other board members had actually cheered, that Stefan had persuaded Amelia to take this long-promised, much-postponed, very overdue trip to America. They would stay for two weeks with Victoria and Henry in Vermont and some time in New York, and get to know Rachel. They would discuss with Victoria the child's immediate future. Arrange for her to come to Haybury or Shotfield. School perhaps at Roedean or Cheltenham. Rachel being of course the third leaf in Amelia's trefoil of happiness.

That on the reverse of that trefoil might already be the maggots of contention, Amelia refused to acknowledge to herself. It was a joyful journey they were making. Her mind went tremulously back to Rachel and that night on the *Athenia*, their rescue, their landing as survivors in Boston, and she ached to gather the child to her again.

'I wonder who Rachel will take after?' Stefan murmured, waving for the stewardess to recharge his glass of brandy.

Victoria had sent photographs with conscientious regularity. Rachel in a bobbly hat on skis. Rachel riding an elephant at the Zoo. Rachel off to summer camp. But photographs showed so little.

'I expect we shall see a little of both Prudence and Arthur in her. But don't expect too much, Stefan. She may have become very much Victoria's child.'

In fact Rachel appeared to be nobody's child. Flanked on either side by Victoria and Henry – both white-haired, unmistakably old, but unmistakably British – upright, elegant and stiff. Rachel – large and clumsy in ski pants, woolly cap and lumber jacket – slouched and loomed like a reluctant cuckoo on exercise out of the nest.

'I can see Victoria!' Amelia had exclaimed as they emerged from the customs' shed at Idlewild into the snow filled bite of the New York air. 'That's Victoria over there.' She grabbed Lehmann's arm and pointed. 'No, she isn't like her photo. But it *is* Victoria. She's older that's all. We all are. Look, she's waving. And that's Henry. And that must be Rachel . . . heavens, how she's grown.'

It was a masterly understatement, Lehmann thought. He wondered how his dainty quicksilver Prudence, his pocket Venus, had produced such a strapping lass. Closer too, the child had an unwelcoming, overfed face. When that face finally broke into a smile of perfunctory welcome they saw the poor child wore a heavy brace over large front teeth. Nevertheless once inside the Cadillac, which by dint of its CD plates Henry had managed to bring right up to the shed, Lehmann was able to see traces of Prudence in her daughter.

'You have your dear mother's chin.' Rachel was sitting between Lehmann and Amelia in the back of the Cadillac, and he slipped an arm round the child's shoulder. 'Prudence was always very determined. Always knew her own mind. Are you very determined, Rachel?'

'My goodness, yes!' Victoria turned round from the front seat and tried laughingly to reply for her. But the child replied for herself. Pulling away from Lehmann's affectionate arm, she sat forward and spoke her first words to them since their greeting. 'Grandmother Haybury, Grandfather Lehmann,' she nodded at each of them. 'Since you ask, yes I am determined. And just in case Aunt Victoria hasn't told you, I'm determined *not* to leave here for England. My home is right here.'

Taken aback, Amelia thought, the child feels we've neglected her. Trying hastily to be tactful, she laughed airily, 'Rachel, darling! It's *much* too early to start talking plans. We've only just arrived.'

'I guess that's why we've got to, Grandmother Haybury. Talk plans. I want to know right away. If you've come for a visit, that's fine. We're happy to have you. But if you've come to take me away . . .' Frosty blue eyes stared directly into Amelia's, the adolescent voice never faltered, the braced mouth looked muzzled, dangerous. 'Then we don't want you. You'd best get the next aeroplane back home.'

For a moment no one said anything. Henry trod harder on the accelerator. Houses, apartment blocks, shop signs, whipped past the windows in a grey brown mulch. Amelia was too surprised, too angry, too hurt to speak.

'Really,' Henry said mildly after much too long, 'that's rather going it, Rachel! I think you should apologise to your grandmother.'

'Yes, darling,' Victoria reiterated weakly. 'You should. In fact you must. Your grandmother is our guest.'

But it was Lehmann who most surprised Amelia. He said nothing at all. Yet he looked at Rachel with a strange not unrespectful expression on his face.

And yet I am angry for Stefan's sake more than my own. He always set such store by Rachel. I guessed how things might be, Amelia told herself, as they arrived at the gracious colonial-style mansion on the lakeshore. There was a log fire crackling in the polished hall. The huge picture windows at the back showed the flat snow-covered lawn sloping gently to the frozen lake. Three or

439

four children were skating, and in the middle distance behind, could be seen the dark serrated climb of the pine forests against a pale clear sky of arctic blue.

Amelia could imagine the smell of those forests, the quiet, the sense of total unsullied freedom. She turned impulsively to her granddaughter and smiled. 'I don't wonder you don't want to leave all this.' She tried to take Rachel's hand and kiss that plump spotty face. But Rachel's hand was unresponsive.

'It's my family I don't want to leave,' Rachel replied stonily, then she walked over to kiss the top of Victoria's head.

'But Rachel, my dear,' Lehmann came over from the window and spoke in his caressing voice, 'we would never force you to come to us. Never try to get you to do anything against your will. *Would* we, Amelia?'

'Of course not.'

'Grandmother Haybury doesn't sound very sure.'

'We want only what's best for you,' Stefan said quickly. 'For you to be happy.'

'Do you promise that, Grandfather? I'm happy here.'

'Of course.'

Clumsily a determined woman parodying a child, Rachel put her arms round his waist, and kissed his cheek. The battle for Rachel is over without a shot being fired, Amelia thought, as she settled into the comfortable bed that night. Stefan will be so disappointed.

She slept uneasily. The scream of a fox wakened her before dawn. She lay there thinking again. This time her thoughts were not of Stefan's disappointment, but that one day Rachel would inherit Haybury, a good deal of Jerningham and the Ajax project besides.

Amelia as usual underestimated Lehmann. If he was disappointed he gave no sign. He was urbane and affectionate, radiating bonhommie and good spirits. The cold crystalline air agreed with him. He loved the smell of the pines, the food, the whole atmosphere. He looked vigorous and healthy.

Victoria and Henry made sure their guests' programme was full and varied. They had so many friends who wanted to meet them. Rachel had so many friends too. There was a formal reception at the United Nations, there were theatre parties and dinners. Word had got around the banking fraternity that Lehmann was in America and the telephone did not stop ringing with invitations. It was a dizzy first week that left Amelia exhausted and left no time to talk further about Rachel.

'This is far more fun than being in England in January. See the papers did you, Amelia? Wet and foggy. Miserable. Not to mention a very tricky election looming,' Lehmann said as the three of them drove in Rachel's horse-drawn sleigh to a teenager's party nine days after their arrival.

The horses' hooves beat softly over the packed snow. The sleigh carried a chime of bells and lanterns that sent iridescent flashes over the snow. 'Do you remember your first pony at Haybury?' Amelia asked her granddaughter.

Rachel shook her head.

'Surely you remember us all being there for your party? I remember it as if it were yesterday.' Lehmann smiled.

'Vaguely. I seem to remember *you*, Grandfather.' She smiled back up at him.

Since his capitulation that first night, she treated him with a measure of affection. Amelia she kept at arm's length.

She doesn't take to me any more than she did at the beginning of this visit, Amelia thought as she packed her bag for the return.

'Rachel, darling, kiss Grandmother Haybury goodbye,' Victoria ordered as they stood outside the immigration barrier at Idlewild. Obediently Rachel brushed Amelia's cheeks with unyielding lips. Then she threw her arms round Lehmann's neck, till he laughed with embarrassed delight and said, 'Here, young lady. Don't strangle me.'

'Please don't let it be so long before you come again,' Victoria said politely.

'I promise it won't be.' Stefan waved a fond farewell, turning as they walked down the terminal building for his last glimpse of them. 'You've given us far too good a time. You've made us so welcome.'

Settled in the aircraft seat beside Amelia again, he dabbed his eyes with his handkerchief emotionally. 'It was wonderful, was it not, Amelia? Quite unforgettable.' He peered out of the porthole across the white waste of snow between the runways to see if he could distinguish Rachel waving.

'Yes,' Amelia replied without total conviction. 'But I shall be glad to get home.'

'Home,' Lehmann repeated the last word with a dry inflection. And then added sadly, 'Shotfield will seem very empty.'

'You're not disappointed, are you?' Amelia asked after a moment, listening to the engines start up one by one and the packed lumps of snow flick back like bullets. 'About Rachel?'

'Quite the reverse. She's a fine girl. Her own person.' He helped himself to a barley sugar from the stewardess's proffered basket and crunched it happily. 'I always told Prudence one's children never cease to educate one. Grand-children even more so.'

'Perhaps you're right,' Amelia nodded as the engines roared, and the aircraft taxied round the perimeter track to the runway head. The light was fading, the evening sky heavy and grey. She felt a gentle homesickness and melancholy, a sense of life's transitoriness. The visit so eagerly looked forward to had vanished. It had been happy enough, yes. But neither, surely, had found what they sought? 'She isn't like either of them is she?' Amelia said.

'Hardly at all,' Stefan agreed. 'Frankly I don't see anything of Arthur in her. Not one little bit. A look occasionally of Prudence. But in temperament she's extraordinarily like me.'

Amelia said nothing. She watched the runway lamps flick past under the port wing till they were one thin yellow ribbon. The roaring engine note quietened. The earth fell away. The grey sky gathered them up like some huge brooding goose. Amelia had a last glimpse down below of the distant Manhattan skyline, toy-sized black cutouts pricked with miniscule lights. Then everything outside was muffled in feathery grey.

'There is nothing for me in Shotfield!' Lehmann announced suddenly, the words wrenched out of him as if the take-off had been catalytic, an emotional wrenching away from a peopled landscape to this grey wilderness. 'Nothing. Not a soul.'

But perhaps the real catalyst was something more prosaic and practical.

441

Halfway across the Atlantic, in the early hours of that Friday morning, the first election results were broadcast and picked up on the flightdeck radio of their Stratocruiser.

By breakfast-time, when the captain did his customary round of the passengers, the trend was clear. 'Well, Sir,' Captain Jones said wryly to Lehmann, 'it looks as if we shall be having yet another spell of Socialist government.' He had the results written down on a piece of paper which he showed Stefan. 'I wonder how that will affect us all?'

Amelia looked up at the Captain's face with its little grizzled goatee beard, and knew instinctively that he had just brought news that would change her life. Half an hour later, when a magnificent red dawn had broken, Lehmann took her hand, told her that he had come to a decision. He had finished with England, that all his instincts, all his inclinations, all his loyalties drew him to America. There would be much more future for him there. Besides he wanted to spend what years remained to him getting to know Rachel. She was his heir. Everything.

'I shall miss you very much,' Amelia replied feeling his eyes on her face searchingly and expectantly. 'More than I can say.'

'But you don't have to miss me, Amelia. This isn't just for me. Rachel is your grandchild as well. I want you to come, too. Amelia, God knows this is neither the time nor the place! Nevertheless, I am asking you to become my wife.'

EIGHT

A proposal of a different kind was sparked off by Diana's letter to Pierre, enclosing the press cuttings. Pierre had written back, inviting her to lunch at the Ritz. She was spending the winter in Bermuda but eventually the meeting was arranged. Pierre brought Joycie. Deferentially, a foot behind Lady Nazier, was a man.

The green eyes were still as alert and glittering as ever, darting over the faces of Pete and Joycie – assessing, calculating, planning.

'Lady Nazier, I did appreciate you writing.'

'My dear boy, I thought you had been treated so badly! Particularly since, as I understand it, Ajax was your father's original design.' She turned to the man by her side. 'This is Gerald Saville, an old friend and my trusted financial adviser.'

And what else, was Joycie's shrewd reaction, but she said nothing and simply smiled. Gerald Saville was sleek-haired and good-looking, perhaps twenty-five years younger than Diana Nazier. Pete had looked her up in *Who's Who* before their meeting, but no date of birth was given. For the last twenty years, so the entry said, she had been concerned with various aspects of aviation, particularly airships, which had been her life-long interest. She also had connections with certain finance companies and was clearly very well-heeled.

Pete fussed over seats, menu, wine list – as though this was the sort of thing he did all the time. That it wasn't was evident to Diana Nazier before they were halfway through their *hors d'oeuvres*. So was Pierre March's hatred of the Hayburys. They got on very well together.

Gerald and Pierre did most of the talking and it was all about business – Pierre's certainty of an explosion in the aviation tourist industry, of the search for the sun by Northern Europeans who spent so much of their lives under grey skies. He spoke of Suntara Travel and its connection with his old Dakota, of expanding business already in these difficult times. He elaborated on his hiring of tourist aircraft, how instead he wanted to buy modern aircraft, packing in many more seats and cutting fare prices to the bone.

As he talked, the two women continued to size each other up. Just as in politics, Diana Nazier was thinking, it was the woman who was important, so it was in business. And this girl was tough. While Joycie was thinking that under that smiling facelift and below those green eyes there lurked an ambition as relentless as Pete's. But for what? And why at her time of life, when it was evident that as far as material things were concerned she had everything? What was the driving force?

The meal continued. Pete showed his knowledge of French food and particularly French wines. By the time they reached the dessert, it was Gerald Saville who was doing the talking – and everybody was very friendly.

'What is missing in your business, Pete . . . I can call you Pete, can't I? I notice Joycie calls you that . . . is a finance company. You're making profits, right? Fine, but you're making profits on both the small airline *and* the tourist business. What you need is a finance company which would lend out the profits you don't want. Then your own money can travel round in a nice tight circle, with no leaks into the Inland Revenue.'

The whole matter was decided over coffee and liqueurs. A finance company would be set up – Fortress Finance, that sounded strong and safe. All the arrangements would be left to Gerald, and he would manage it with Pete as chairman. The airline and the tourist side could be allowed to expand as business demands dictated.

And certainly, he must buy a modern airliner.

'Why Ajax, Pete?' Diana Nazier suddenly asked. 'Why Jerningham Aviation?'

By this time, Pete felt expansive and talked at length. But it was not so much on Ajax and Jerningham Aviation, but on the Hayburys. He had always wanted to own an aircraft manufacturing company, he said. There were certain aspects of the Hayburys which had been difficult as regards his own family in the past. Ajax was, as Diana had pointed out, his heritage – and there had been other things too. And when you looked at the matter dispassionately, what was missing businesswise in their excellent trinity – airline, tourist offices, finance company – was a factory to make the aeroplanes they wanted.

He did not talk loosely. He was shrewd enough to be discreet. But Diana Nazier was even more discreet and said nothing. Even so, when they made their effusive farewells, Joycie knew what was the driving force that made Lady Nazier's ambition as relentless as Pete's.

They both hated the Hayburys.

The Fortress Finance Company was founded with Gerald Saville as manager.

The money they were going to use to buy Ajax was invested in this company. The bookings made by the Suntara Travel agencies would be carried in Victory Airways aircraft and the profits made would be ploughed into Fortress and immediately lent out. Linked loosely together, no one outside could really be aware who was in control. Victory would borrow from Fortress; Suntara would always be expanding and never have a profit; Fortress would rarely have any money to tax.

Meanwhile, around them the British civil aviation business shivered. Half a dozen small skytramp firms which had invested in transport aircraft to jump on the Berlin bandwagon had gone bust. One operator, remembering the war posters asking housewives to send their old pots and pans to help make new planes, now survived by reversing the process, putting all his engines, spares and ex-RAF Haltons into a huge pit and selling the aluminium off to manufacturers to make pots and pans. Others were reduced to giving joyrides round London Airport.

On the scheduled airlines, matters were even worse. A York had disappeared in what was to become known as the Bermuda Triangle. There were other disasters. A Tudor called *Star Tiger* followed her – *her fate remains a mystery* said the accident report. BEA and BOAC struggled forward with unsuitable aircraft, the long-range airline having to buy American.

Gradually it was becoming evident that as the British Empire dissolved, the new empire was the sky – and it was becoming practically all American.

America was the place to be.

Once he had decided on America, Stefan Lehmann did not allow the grass of England to grow under his feet. He was as like his daughter, Amelia thought, once his mind was made up, he acted. Shotfield House was put up for sale in the spring of 1951. Nominees were appointed for his business and charitable interests. Amelia was introduced to a middle-aged solicitor, who looked like a Benedictine monk and who would sit as proxy for Stefan on the Jerningham Aviation board.

Over in America, Victoria constituted herself as his house agent. She scoured the real estate offices and had already five properties she wanted him to view, within striking distance of theirs. Until Stefan made up his mind, he would of course stay with them. Rachel was reported as delighted and only regretful that Amelia was not coming too. Amelia had her doubts about Rachel's regret.

'Have *you* any doubts about it yourself, M'lady? That's more to the point! You could marry him tomorrow, you know. Go over with him.'

'Shall you, Mama?' Charles asked her much the same question. 'There's nothing to keep you here if you want to go? Jerningham's on its feet.'

'For the present.'

'All right. On its feet *for the present*. The order book's healthy. More than we can cope with. Tomorrow the wind can change, yes. But I'm talking of *now*.'

'You're still here.'

'I don't intend to spend my whole life here. Aviation's a big business. A world business. I might well not stay in one little corner for ever.'

'Even so this is my home.'

'Home is people, Mama. And Stefan would make you a good husband. He'd look after you.'

'How d'you know he wants to?'

Charles smiled. 'Everyone knows he wants to. And if you want my advice I think you'd be silly to turn him down.'

Increasingly, as that chilly spring gave way to a warm summer, Amelia lay awake at night turning over Charles's advice and Stefan's proposal. Dearly as Charles loved her, he believed her to suffer from that malady common to Englishwomen, overpossessiveness of their sons. 'Everyone must learn to let go of the people they love,' he told her often.

Sadly it was James she couldn't let go, not Charles. James who still lived and breathed in the environs of Jerningham. James who, in memory at least, she could resurrect all around her. She could never leave him.

'Think of getting away from the remains of rationing and austerity! Think of warm houses!' Stefan smiled invitingly, two weeks before his departure, as they dined alone at Haybury. 'Think of all the fun we could have together with Rachel. It's still not too late to change your mind. I can still get you a seat on the Monarch service. It's just a matter of ringing BOAC.'

She didn't change her mind. In the middle of June, she saw Stefan off from Heathrow Airport. The airport was an impermanent looking jumble of newly put-up buildings, marquees, tents and wooden huts. Concrete was being put down, earth turned. That graveyard smell of freshly dug earth mixed with the sickly sweet one of petrol fumes and raw concrete.

The parting seemed immediately final and heartrending. She was suddenly aware that she might never see him again, suddenly aware of how fond she was of him, how much she had relied and leaned on him.

'Dear Stefan,' she said thickly, putting her hand on his arm. If he had asked her to change her mind then, she might well have done so, but he was checking in his pocket for a gold bracelet he had bought to take to Rachel, and his eyes were abstracted.

'Dear Amelia,' he replied vaguely, 'I shall miss you.'

The moment passed.

'You'll come back for visits, won't you, Stefan?'

'Of course, my dear. And you'll come to us too.'

She watched till the Stratocruiser took off into the clear blue sky, till it became a snow white cross, and then a speck – and then nothing.

Gerald, Pete and Joycie toured England, looking for likely aircraft for Victory Airways. Driving over from Whitchurch to Filton, they watched the enormous eight-engined Brabazon being towed out of its cathedral of a hangar. They watched it lumber into the air.

'It flies as slowly as a pterodactyl,' was Pete's comment. 'No good for anything.'

As for the Bristol Britannia – the big turbo-prop passenger carrier that was supposed to capture the nonstop Atlantic travel – it was already three years behind schedule.

They went down to Hythe to look at the old Empire boats. 'Look at those huge hulls that have to be hauled through the air!' Pete said. 'Just because the British were a naval nation, they hung sentimentally on to them. They're going, just like the Empire they're named after!'

They went to Hatfield and saw the beautiful streamlined de Havilland Comet, first civil jet airliner with its four Ghost engines sunk smoothly into the wings, streak at 500 miles an hour across the blue sky.

'They'll have trouble,' Pete prophesied.

British aviation, they decided, was in what Gerald called 'disarray'. 'Victory Airways still better lie low.'

BOAC continued to operate American Stratocruisers and Constellations on an Atlantic route that was expanding by 17 per cent a year. Even so, both government airlines went deeper into the red.

So did Jerningham Aviation.

All the confidential board papers now found their way via Gerald Saville, who deputised for Diana Nazier, to Pete and Joycie. They read them with avid interest.

Jet-prop engines were giving trouble in icing conditions. The certificate of airworthiness was temporarily withdrawn. Lehmann had made a strong appeal to the board 'To explore further sources of finance'. The nationalised airlines had explored further sources of aircraft in their famine, and had come

446

up with a real British compromise – an American DC4 built in Canada with British Rolls Royce engines, the Argonaut. Amelia pointed out to the board that the first of these hybrids to be delivered was called Ajax – 'a happy omen'.

Victory still only had old Queenie, so was still hiring other aircraft which was getting increasingly difficult. Pete was getting restless, although Suntara Travel was making money hand over fist. He and Joycie had moved from Whitchurch to Hurn where Queenie was now serviced. They had bought a very nice modern house on the Bournemouth cliffs. He felt the urge to expand, to buy, to invest – before high inflation arrived, as he was sure it would.

'Hang on before buying,' Gerald Saville said, 'wait!'

It was during that protracted period of apparent indecision that Joycie began saying to Pete that it was time they started a family.

I have a new family, Stefan wrote to Amelia. *And it's wonderful.*

She heard from him regularly. Throughout that year she received the most happy letters. He had taken on a new lease of life, he wrote. He felt young again. He sent photographs of Rachel and of the house he had bought in Vermont. Victoria and Rachel had helped him choose the furnishings. His granddaughter was a great companion to him.

At the end of October, he wrote that Rachel and he had motored to Montreal to see the arrival of Princess Elizabeth and the Duke of Edinburgh aboard the Stratocruiser flagship *Canopus*.

This was the first time royalty had crossed the Atlantic in a civil airliner. *You ought to have been there at Dorval airport, Amelia. The crowds went wild. It's difficult to think flying has blossomed like this in our lifetime. I took Rachel back by way of the Laurentians, and we stayed the night in a little inn high up near St Agathe called the Chanticleer.*

Life was obviously good. The only cloud on the horizon was Henry's state of health. In mid-January, shortly after King George had been operated on for a lung re-section Henry entered the Mayo Clinic for a similar operation. He never recovered consciousness. Amelia spoke several times to both Victoria and Stefan on the trans-Atlantic telephone. 'I could never have survived without Stefan,' Victoria sobbed. 'He has been such a tower of strength.'

That year, which had begun so sadly, continued on a melancholy note. King George VI died. The new Queen Elizabeth flew back from Africa to ascend the throne. She returned from Nanyuki aboard a DC3 of East Africa Airways and thence by BOAC Argonaut, arriving, symbolically it seemed to many, into her new realm by air.

All over the world now, airlines were expanding, and aircraft manufacturers were building bigger and faster. Everyone was experimenting, designing, borrowing, canvassing, to be in on the great travel boom.

Thal this boom in air travel carried with it the seeds of the smaller airplane builders' destruction began to be apparent. As on the television set Charles had bought Amelia, they watched the inaugural flight on 2 May of the Comet leaving London airport for Johannesburg, Charles said softly, 'Ajax will have difficulty competing with this.'

The new jet's success showed that this was what the travelling public wanted and would demand. But there was still much to be learned on compression, on pressurisation effects and on metal fatigue. Such research was beyond Jerningham. But the board considered the designing of a pure jet Ajax. Cummings and Charles and their two new assistants worked on possible designs.

'You mark my words, they put the Comets back into service too soon. They haven't got over their teething troubles. Not by a long way yet.' And early in 1954, his words came tragically true. On 10 January, BOAC's Comet G-ALYP, homebound from Rome, disintegrated in the sky above Elba, with the loss of everyone on board. In April, disaster struck again.

'We must wait to see the results of their tests before we sink any more money ourselves in a pure jet version,' Cummings advised at the next board meeting. It was a dismal one, full of strangers. Stefan Lehmann's deputy, the monk-like solicitor read his adverse financial report like the last chapters of Job. Amelia longed for Stefan to be at her side, easing her problems, exuding comfort and well-being. He had been in America for over three years now and though his letters were regular and as warm as ever, he had still not made the long promised visit to see her.

Amelia was quite glad for once of Gerald Saville's smooth, confident presence. He at least urged more, not less, borrowing. Backing their judgment, he called it, standing up to the big boys, like de Havilland and Bristol. It was decided that research for the stretched pure jet Ajax would go on.

'I hope to God we're doing the right thing,' Cummings said to Amelia, as they watched Charles take off on yet another delivery flight this time to Scottish Aviation at Prestwick. Orders were coming steadily in, though customers were slow in paying. The next three Ajaxes were for Egyptian airlines, and the two after that for South Africa.

'Of course we're doing the right thing, Ronald! What on earth do you mean?'

'I mean if we stretch our financial resources too far, we expose ourselves to the money-lenders.' He smiled at her wistfully. 'You know Amelia, I never thought I'd say what I'm about to say now, but I'd be far happier if Lehmann were here.'

'So would I, Ronald. Though I'm not so timid as you are. Nor will Stefan be. And he's promised to fly over for the 1955 AGM.' Amelia smiled with eager anticipation. 'He says he might even bring Rachel with him. I shall put on a dance for her.'

But Stefan Lehmann never came. Six weeks before the board meeting Victoria telephoned in deep distress. Stefan Lehmann was dead. He had suffered a massive cerebral haemorrhage while playing golf. The end had been swift, the doctor said. They must all take what comfort they could from that. But how could any of them comfort themselves, Amelia cried silently to herself. Stefan had always been the comforter, always the strong arm to lean upon, the hand to guide. She would never know a man of his compassion and stature again. Her heart went out to Rachel. She and Victoria were yet again supporting one another.

Grief-stricken herself, Amelia was on the point of flying over to offer them what comfort she could, when a serious crisis at the factory came up. Orders for eight Ajax airliners had been cancelled because of monetary tension in the Middle East and it looked as if Ronald Cummings's fears could well be realised.

NINE

The wind of the Suez crisis that blew ill on Jerningham blew warm and sweet on Victory Airways. Peter March obtained a large contract, ferrying troops to the Middle East.

All through August and September Joycie flew that trooping contract with him in Queenie, but it was a different Joycie – more apprehensive, more irritable, more tired. The Suntara Travel agencies put in accounts for 1955–6 showing a 96 per cent increase in turnover. The huge profits had gone straight into the Fortress Finance company where Gerald Saville reported another highly successful year.

At the beginning of October, just home from Malta, she flopped down in front of the fire and said, 'Christ, I'm knackered!'

'Have a drink.'

His sovereign and only remedy.

That she should become tired never seemed to enter his head. Though flying hour regulations had now been introduced, he did not consider they applied to Victory. He himself was tireless, making do easily with five hours sleep a night.

He was a man with a star. She was a woman with the same star – that was his view. Sagittarius and Crab, together now with Lady Nazier and Gerald Saville, were proceeding steadily against their target – the Hayburys.

'Peter —'

He was already at the sideboard, preparing his alchemy. 'Yes?'

'Couldn't we take on another pilot?'

'Whatever for?'

'Make it easier.'

'Why? The two of us can cope.'

'Can't we afford another chap?'

'Of course we can!'

'Well, then?'

'I don't want anyone else.' He saw to it that each of his tourist enterprises had its own manager. He himself only provided the grand supervisory design. 'Staff are nothing but a damned nuisance.'

'We'll have to take on staff *some day*.'

He passed over to her a glass half-full of whisky. 'That evil day we must postpone as long as possible.'

She said carefully. 'It can't be postponed very much longer.'

'What d'you mean?'

'I won't be able to carry on much longer.'

He paused with his glass halfway to his lips and stared at her fixedly, narrow-eyed.

'I'm going to have a baby.'

He slammed down his drink. 'You're *what*?

'You heard.'

'I don't believe it! You're mistaken!'

'I'm not.'

'You must be.'

She shook her head.

'Go to a doctor.'

'I don't need to go to a doctor. I've known for months. I'd have told you before only —'

'You're wrong! We take precautions.'

'Not . . . *always*.'

'*You*!'

She saw his eyes blaze. 'You've tricked me! You've cheated! You —'

'I told you I wanted a child,' she said coldly. 'But you wouldn't listen. Not yet, you said. Like you say when I want more staff. I knew that soon it'd be too late. I'm getting on. Oh, Pete . . . ' she looked at him hopefully, 'it's wonderful really!'

'Get rid of it!'

This time, her eyes blazed. They had the first real row of their married lives. For ten minutes, their future, the future of Victory Airways, Fortress Finance, Suntara Travel shivered. The sword over the Hayburys lifted.

And then Pete recovered himself.

Love for him was business. It could be analysed quite coldly into figures. And those figures spelled that plus Joycie added up to success and minus Joycie to failure. And he had not the slightest intention of failing – in business or in his campaign against the Hayburys.

'How much longer d'you think you can go on flying, Joycie?'

Autumn came, and Joycie was still flying. The demand for trooping had reached unexpected levels. On 30 October, the British and French governments sent an ultimatum to Israel and Egypt who were again locked in battle on the Sinai peninsula, calling on them to cease hostilities and withdraw their forces to a distance of ten miles east and west respectively of the Suez Canal. On that same day, Pete had at last signed up a Dakota pilot to take her place in a week's time, and Joycie was sitting in the righthand seat of Queenie as they still called her in spite of the phonetic alphabet change. They were flying back empty after dropping 26 Marines in Malta, and were now 60 miles south of the Hampshire coast.

A sunset of red and gold smoked across the western horizon. 'Q Queenie cleared to descend to 8000 feet.'

Pete picked up his microphone. 'Descending to eight.'

'Forecast Hurn from 22.00 . . . cloudbase 600 feet. Visibility one mile in rain. Wind southwest, gusting 30.'

'Weather closing in.' Pete looked at his watch. 'Quarter past nine.' He pushed the throttle forward. 'Better get a move on.'

'Are you going to try to beat it in?'

'Yes.'

He never liked bad weather landings. 'Would you like me to do the landing?'

'In *your* condition.' He was quite huffy about it. 'No.' And then, 'Queenie at eight requesting six.'

He didn't want to be stuck up here, having to do a long instrument letdown.

'Negative six. Maintain eight.'

That irritated him. Handflying Queenie, now he began to treat her roughly. They whooshed through a cloud, jinked to the left in turbulence.

'It's all right,' she said. 'No need to panic.'

That irritated him too. Since they had already decided that this would be her last flight before staying on the ground, she wanted it to be a good one. She asked pacifically, 'Been a nice trip.'

'So far.'

'That landing of yours at Malta was a corker.'

Like all pilots, he liked being complimented on his landings. He picked up his microphone. 'Control . . . latest weather at Hurn?'

'Latest weather . . . cloudbase 900, visibility one mile, worsening.'

'Bloody stuff!'

Grey cloud mushed against the windscreen, leaving a splatter of rain on the perspex. Pete leaned forward in his seat, anxiously staring into the gathering darkness ahead.

'Navigation lights?'

'On,' she told him.

He picked up the microphone. 'Control, can I have six now?'

'Negative. Maintain 8000.'

He swore. She could feel his feet, never still, on her set of rudder pedals. He kept moving the ailerons as though he had to move something to relieve the tension that she could feel building up inside him.

'Now . . . cleared to six!'

He gave a sigh of relief, pushed the nose down hard. Half a minute later, he was reporting at six, requesting four.

'Negative four. Maintain six.'

In gaps through the overcast could just be seen the white chalk ghosts of the Needles. 'We can see the Isle of Wight.'

'Do you want to cancel instrument flight rules?'

'Negative. Still too cloudy.'

'Then maintain six.'

He swore under his breath. She put out her hand and touched his. In answer, he gave her a stiff smile.

'They're being too particular! There's nothing around!'

'You don't know.'

'If there was, we'd hear them on the R/T.' He pushed the nose further down. The altimeter unwound past 6000, 5500. 'I believe we can get under the stuff, and then we could go visual flight rules.'

The cloud was certainly thinning. They could see scraps of sea below. At 4500 feet, they emerged from cloud.

'Told you!' He picked up his microphone, but before he could call Control, they were back in the stuff again. The old Dakota began bucketing around. The port wing dropped. They fell lower and lower, past 4500 feet to 4000.

451

Suddenly she saw a hazy red light. A ghostly shape materialised dead ahead. She felt the jerk as Pete pulled the stick back. Up went the port wing in an almost vertical turn.

There was a terrible rending sound. The Dakota was back in cloud – on her side, engines screaming, rain pouring over the windscreen. Pete was shouting at her. Queenie was trying to roll over and over on her back. With all her might, on her set of controls she tried to pull the wing up, jammed her leg hard on the right rudder in an effort to get level. Out of the corner of her eye, she saw the altimeter – 300, 200, 100, the needle still rotating anticlockwise.

Then with a crack like thunder, Queenie hit the water and split right open.

They had landed in the shallows, a hundred yards from the beach at Mudeford. Neither of them was really hurt, though Joycie had banged her head against the instrument panel.

Clinging together in their Mae Wests, half-swimming, half-walking, they struggled out of the water.

'Didn't you see?' Peter demanded.

She lay on the sand, still panting, too exhausted to say anything. 'It was an Ajax! A bloody Ajax! The bastard clipped our wing! Bloody lucky we didn't go right over! I tell you this, Joycie —'

She had fainted. They took her to Bournemouth Hospital. She would be all right, they told him. But as regards the baby . . . well, they couldn't be so certain.

What *was* certain was that it *had* been an Ajax. They told him so in Hurn Control Tower when he stumped up, furious, to see them. The pilot was on test trials in an Ajax bought by Pakistan, the controller said. He says a Dakota came up on his starboard side out of cloud and nicked four feet off his tailplane. He had the greatest difficulty making it home.

'He was lucky to make it home! My aircraft, my *only* aircraft, is now lying a total wreck in the sea!'

'What height were you flying?'

'6000, of course! The height I was cleared to!'

'He says he was four. The height *he* was cleared to.'

'He's wrong!'

'Are you *sure* you were at six?'

'Of course I'm sure!'

'He's certain he was at four.'

'Then he's lying.' His eyes glittered in the white face. 'What's his name?'

'Charles Haybury.'

He clenched his hands. 'It would be! By God, it would be! I'll go and see him tonight. I'll —'

They managed to restrain him from going. The doctor pronounced him suffering from shock and he spent the night in the airport sick quarters, but he was up early in the morning. He rang Jerningham Aviation, but there was only a night-watchman there. No, Sir Charles hadn't come in yet. He was still at Haybury Hall.

He took a taxi, but by the time he arrived, Charles had left for the factory. He saw Amelia and told her his story. '6000 feet, Lady Haybury! I was at 6000 feet.

452

My wife was with me! We had just checked the altimeter.'

'Mr March, my son tells me he was at four.'

'He couldn't possibly have been.'

'He swears he was.'

'But he was alone, Lady Haybury. There were two of us in the cockpit. *Two*.'

Just for a second she saw Pierre draw up his shoulders, the way James used to, his mouth tighten. Her voice faltered. 'There must be some mistake . . . '

'Yes, Lady Haybury, there *was* a mistake. Your son's.'

'No, Mr March. He was adamant.'

'Naturally. When people are in the wrong, they usually are!'

'I'm quite sure he wasn't wrong.' She drew a deep breath. 'I think you should see my son.'

'That is precisely what I came for, Lady Haybury. I came to —'

He clenched his fists and then shrugged, changing his tactics. 'It isn't that I don't understand your point of view. And his. But he was alone in the cockpit. It's easy to overlook an instrument. It's easy to have your attention diverted when you're doing checks. I've found that myself.'

Now he actually smiled, albeit ruefully. He became disarmingly frank. 'I'm not really blaming him. It could have happened to anyone. I'm just thankful no one was killed.' He paused and said quietly, 'At least I hope to God no one was killed.'

That brought Amelia to her feet, her eyes wide. Then he told her the story about the unborn baby, and about Joycie in hospital. The effect on Amelia was electric. How badly hurt was she? How many months pregnant? Could she go to the hospital to see her? Was he sure she was having the best possible treatment?

It was easy after that to slip sideways into the fact that Queenie was a write-off. 'Of course it's the kiss of death for the firm. We can't fly without an aircraft. But what *I* worry most about is the effect on Joycie of that too. It'll break her heart. Our little firm means so much to her.'

He could see his story had gone straight to Lady Haybury's heart. She followed every word he said, her vivid blue eyes fixed on his face. Yet all she could think of was that this was James's only grandchild and it might die.

Before Pierre left to return to Joycie's side, he had secured Amelia's promise that she would do everything she could to help him to secure an Ajax to replace Queenie.

In the circumstances, it seemed the least she could do.

'You don't honestly mean you told March he could have an option on the next Ajax?'

Amelia nodded.

'What on earth possessed you?'

Charles had arrived back from the factory hours later. He and Cummings had been in the hangar, going over the damage to Ajax, and had come to the conclusion that it could be repaired within the week. He had been pleased with Ajax's quick and positive response in what had been a potentially lethal situation. He had also checked with the coastguards and police about the other aircraft, and found to mingled relief and dismay that, though no one had been seriously hurt, it belonged to Pierre March.

Putting the receiver down, he had remarked wryly to Cummings, 'That name always spells trouble!'

Now this.

'It was because of the baby,' Amelia said.

'It was because of *what*?' Charles paused in the act of pouring himself a large Scotch and frowned at her over his shoulder. As soon as she told him she realised he couldn't be expected to understand. More and more, Ajax had become Charles's baby. The only one she was sure he would ever have.

'What the hell has the baby to do with letting him have an Ajax? And what is March doing allowing his wife to fly when she's like that?'

'Don't be angry, Charles! I know it sounds sentimental.'

'Sentimental!' he exclaimed when she tried to explain. 'It's sheer lunacy. You are the chairman of an important company and you have no right to make such off-the-cuff decisions!'

'Now you're trying to say I'm too old for the job!' she bridled.

'I am not saying anything of the kind! I am saying you acted in a thoroughly irresponsible manner. Age has nothing to do with it.'

'I *am* getting old,' she said quietly. 'But it wasn't that. Both he and I were shocked. Upset. I was thankful it was no worse. So was he! But he was dreadfully worried about his wife and the baby.'

'I doubt that.'

'That's very uncharitable of you.'

Charles took a swig of his Scotch. 'You don't know Pierre March as I do!'

'You have never told me how well you know him,' she countered.

'Nevertheless, you should have seen he was putting on an act.'

'Why? Obviously he would be worried. And not just about his wife. Worried about supporting her and the baby. He only had that one Dakota. He'll go broke without an aeroplane.'

'Then let him buy another.'

'Just like that?'

'Just like that.'

'He wants an Ajax.'

'Too bad.'

'I think,' Amelia said stubbornly, 'that he should have one.'

'Then you are absolutely wrong.' Charles drained his glass and speaking with carefully controlled anger went on, 'I'll tell you why though it should be obvious. First,' he held up one finger, 'Pierre March is a two-faced lying bastard with an outsize chip on both shoulders. If we give him an Ajax, he'll make damned sure it gives us trouble.'

His mother drew a deep breath and tightened her lips but said nothing.

'Secondly, and right now to me most importantly, he'll let it be known that *you*, the chairman of Jerningham, have immediately promised him an Ajax.'

'So?'

'So! Mama, don't be naïve! That is tantamount to admitting our liability. *My* liability. To admitting that I was at the wrong height.'

'I don't see that it is.'

'If you don't, everyone else most certainly will.'

She hesitated and Charles went on, 'He was at the wrong height. He is totally in the wrong. But *your* action has made that sound very doubtful. He'll make it known to the accident investigators just what you have promised him. He'll swear he was at the correct height.'

'He did say that he and his wife had just checked their altitude . . . '

'God, Mama!' he exploded. '*You* think it was my fault! There we go. That's the beginning!'

'Of course I don't.'

'Well then, is it his fault? One of us *must* be lying! You can't get away from that.'

Amelia said nothing.

'Do you think I am lying?'

'No.'

'Then it must be him, mustn't it? I told you he was a two-faced lying bastard.'

'Oh, please, Charles!' Cornered she covered her faced with her hands. 'Don't be so harsh! Then she said the unforgivable, 'Isn't it for other *personal* reasons that you're so harsh?'

'What do you mean, Mama?' he asked in a cold deadly voice that should have warned her.

'I mean because . . . because you were so fond of his sister . . . and . . . he didn't . . . and I didn't . . . ' Her voice trailed away. His anger was somehow palpable. It seemed to force the breath back into her chest.

Watching him walk stiffly out of the room, she remembered that dreadful row over Marianne all those years ago. Now she must seem to have allied herself with Pierre against him again.

She sat down at the table and buried her head in her hands.

'Whatever have you done now, M'lady?'

Where Charles had been, now Sarah stood, her arms crossed over her chest. Amelia simply shook her head.

'Well, whatever it is, M'lady, by the look on Sir Charles's face, you'd best get about undoing it.'

It was what Amelia had already decided herself. The next day, she persuaded Cummings to go over and see Pierre at Bournemouth, where he tried for hours to persuade him that he didn't want an Ajax. He tried in vain.

The company secretary then wrote to Victory Airways telling them that circumstances now demanded the full purchase price for a firm option. The company secretary assured her that Victory would not be able to produce the money just like that. But three days later came a cheque for the full amount.

Amelia saw nothing of Charles. Two men arrived down from the Board of Trade accident investigation department to examine the wreckage and ask endless questions. They were patient, methodical and sympathetic. They were confident that this would be a simple enquiry and there would not be a public one.

'Nevertheless,' Cummings spoke up firmly at the next board meeting, 'I cannot stress too strongly that if this company is eager to provide a substitute aircraft, it gives the impression of believing itself to be in the wrong. We all know that the company is the injured party, that Sir Charles was flying totally correctly, in accordance with all the rules of the air. And at his allotted altitude.'

Only Lady Nazier failed to nod her head. When it was her turn to speak, she said in her rasping voice, 'This option should have been allowed years ago. In the present circumstances we can do no other than approve.'

The monk-like solicitor whom Stefan Lehmann had appointed as his proxy and who for the time being continued for his estate, pointed out the company's need for more orders, especially cash orders.

'Are there any other observations?'

There were none. The vote was taken. The motion was carried. 'I might as well tell you,' Charles leapt to his feet, 'I shall not continue to serve this board. You have shown a total lack of trust in me. I feel my useful work here is therefore over. I tender my resignation.'

Charles had already left Jerningham with the barest peck on Amelia's cheek and not even the promise to write by the time Cummings showed her a long official-looking paper.

It was entitled, *Report on Accident Investigation to Dakota Q of Victory Airways and Ajax K of Jerningham Aviation.*

Amelia, her hands trembling nervously, skimmed quickly through the technical report until she came to the summary of the findings *The cause of the accident was pilot error. The Ajax pilot was flying at an altitude that had not been allotted, thus causing the collision with the Dakota at its correct altitude which ensued.*

'Charles saw it before he left,' Cummings said, gently taking the report from her. 'He didn't seem unduly cast down. You must not distress yourself.'

Amelia said nothing. There are two things now, she thought, for which Charles will never forgive me, this and Marianne. Sitting, still silent, opposite Cummings at her desk she tried to strike one of her bargains with the Almighty. Let me live long enough to tell Charles how sorry I am, and you can have Ajax and the whole factory in exchange.

TEN

To Pete and Joycie March: God's gift of a son – William.

That was the birth notice Joycie put in the papers. The wreckage of Queenie was sold the same day for three times what they paid for her, an event which Pete found much more interesting.

The fact that the baby had been given the name of William was a matter of indifference to Pete. He would have preferred him to be called Pierre so as to continue the French connection. It was Joycie who wanted plain William, now the apple of her eye.

He was not the apple of Pete's. He had not wanted the child, felt no need for him. Like civil aviation he had made enormous strides. He now had a string of tourist agencies, a 'shadow' airline whereby he hired tourist aircraft, and a very successful finance company. More important still, he had managed to deal Charles Haybury the body blow he richly deserved by buying an Ajax airliner against the Haybury wishes and getting him blamed for the accident.

Now was the time to consolidate those gains, and make a real push. The arrival of William was therefore unfortunately timed, and Joycie's undue interest with the baby he regarded as a defection. From now on, for total loyalty and support, he would have to look elsewhere.

He did not have to look far. Since that memorable lunch at the Ritz, he and Gerald Saville had got on extremely well. Both had much the same outlook in life. Both had an enormous capacity for work. Both had similar aims. If Gerald did not share the obsession against the Hayburys, at least through Lady Nazier's influence, he helped pursue the fight vigorously.

The four of them – Joycie and he, Diana and Gerald – regularly met for what Pete called 'a business lunch'. Quite what the relationship was, he did not know. Nor did he care. A year ago, he had thought they might marry, but Joycie was sure they wouldn't – and they hadn't. All that was important was that Diana supported Gerald. And Gerald supported him.

With Joycie out of the running, it was natural that he and Gerald should become the main partners in their growing business enterprise. All the secret Jerningham Aviation board papers were of course passed on by Gerald who had been given power of attorney of all Diana's interests and took her place on the board. It was through his persuasive power, even in enemy territory, that Victory Airways received its first Ajax even earlier than expected – in April 1957. It was immediately put to work. Two aircrews were taken on by the airline and were worked day and night flying tourist trips. Due to so many other commitments, Pete gave up flying and took on the managing of what was clearly going to be an ever-expanding airline.

Nevertheless he wanted more Ajaxes – particularly the new stretched variety into which fifty tourist seats could be densely packed. And here he was blocked. Ajaxes were being flown by BEA, Air France, Lufthansa, American Airlines, Braniff, Air Italia, Iberia – and now many developing countries were building up prestige airlines and had put their names down on the order book.

All well ahead of Victory Airways.

Peter and Gerald met alone for lunch in the Ritz to discuss the situation. Jerningham were not doing particularly well, due to the cost of abortive research into fitting pure-jet engines into Ajax. They decided to try Connaught Engineering to find out whether they would sell out at a reasonable price.

The price was more than reasonable. Connaught Engineering reckoned they were well out of aviation in the present world situation.

At the next board meeting, a man called Jock Tyler made his appearance as the director controlling the ex-Connaught shares. Between them, March's two deputies controlled a quarter of the Jerningham equity.

The news of Lehmann's death had made little impression on either March or Saville. They knew practically nothing of Lehmann's background and family connections. They had always presumed that he would have business associates to whom his Jerningham interests would descend.

Pete March had already agreed that either he or Gerald would go to America to make a thorough exploration of what they were doing in civil aviation in 1958. After all, in spite of a gallant first by the Comet IV, American 707s and DC8 jets virtually ruled the long-range air routes of the world.

And then came the final probate of Stefan Lehmann's will. Everything he owned, including his share of Jerningham Aviation, he left to his only surviving relative – his granddaughter Rachel. With the eighth she had inherited from her father, they learned that Rachel Haybury now owned three-eighths of the Jerningham equity.

Gerald Saville was on the next Pan American 707 out of London Airport.

Arithmetic moves fast.

'He'll be back!' Amelia had said, in the first few days after Charles had left, reiterating it less surely as the weeks went by.

'That he won't be!' Sarah growled back, as winter came. 'Not this time! You've gone too far, M'lady. You've sided against him.' Adding melodramatically, 'With the enemy.'

'Enemy! Rubbish! Anyway, he always comes crawling back.'

'That he doesn't. *He* doesn't know how to crawl. It's other people that know how to do that.'

'Me, I suppose you mean?'

'Yes, you! Crawling to that swine March. That awful man. Getting Sir Charles blamed. No wonder he was upset.'

'You get beyond yourself, Sarah! One of these days you will go just a step too far.'

'Not me, M'lady. It's *you* goes too far. It's just *me* you blame.'

Perhaps she was right, for over the miserable months of early 1958 it was Sarah who took the brunt of Amelia's distress. She complained of her often to Cummings – Sarah's bossiness, Sarah's intractability, Sarah's impertinence – watching him run his hands through his thin white hair, as he tried to think of a

458

tactful way of steering her.

'We're all getting old, Amelia,' he sighed. 'A bit demanding. Set in our ways.'

'I wouldn't object at all if Sarah were set in her ways,' Amelia replied dryly. 'It is the very fact that she is not that I am objecting to. She knows her place well enough. She's been well trained. But she simply refuses to stay in it. Sometimes, I think she sees herself as the head of the Haybury family.'

'Surely not! It's just that she was always so fond of Charles.'

'She spoiled him.'

'But in a kind way.'

'Kind, yes, I don't doubt, at the time. But whether it was kind in the long run . . .' Amelia sighed.

'That's what's really bugging you, isn't it, Amelia? Not Sarah at all. Charles.'

'Perhaps.'

'No word from him, I suppose?'

'I've no idea. *I've* had no word from him, if that's what you mean. Sarah, I suspect, writes.'

'To where?'

'According to the postmistress, some box number in Australia.'

'And you mind?'

Amelia shook her head. 'Neither Charles nor I are good at climbing down.'

'You don't like admitting you're wrong.'

'I wasn't wrong.'

'You might have been a little wrong, Amelia.'

'Nonsense!'

'Everyone is wrong sometimes. Even you. You don't have enough people to argue with you. You're on your own too much. That's why Sarah gets on your nerves! There are lots of other things you should be thinking of.'

'Such as Jerningham Aviation?'

'Exactly, Amelia.' He paused. 'The board's trying to think too big.'

'You mean Gerald Saville?'

'Anybody connected with Lady Nazier is suspect in my view.'

'Oh she's just an old lady like me now!'

'You'll never be old, Amelia.' He paused. 'But she can still do us harm. And I've never liked *him*!'

'Gerald's all right.'

'Smooth certainly. But I think, from the way he supports Victory that he's thick with Pete March.'

'I doubt it.'

'Do you ever see the Marches?'

'No.' Amelia paused. 'Not after the crash.'

'I'm sure he lied.'

'I'm sure he did . . . *now*.'

'You know sometimes . . .' Ronald stopped and looked at her anxiously. 'I hope you don't mind me saying this, Amelia . . . but I have a feeling Pete March menaces Jerningham Aviation.'

'Ronald, how can he? The Hayburys *control* the business!'

'All the same, Amelia, that's the feeling I have. And I have a feeling Saville's in with them somewhere. The way he tries to get us to expand —'

459

'But aviation *is* expanding!'

Certainly that was true. Three and a half million passengers passed through London Airport, and the number was expected to quadruple in ten years. Transatlantic passengers were increasing by twenty per cent a year. Soon the luxury ships would become simply tourist attractions. The age of the big jet 707 and the DC8 had begun, and the Russians were just about to launch a rocket into space.

'We've got to go carefully, Amelia. We're only a tiny firm.' He paused. 'And you're too concerned over Charles, Amelia.' He smiled at her uncertainly. 'You don't mind me saying that, as an old friend?'

He hadn't mentioned again the possibility of marriage. Indeed since that day after Arthur's wedding, he had never spoken to her of it. Over the years, Cummings had become more and more the bachelor, devoted to his job, rather smug with his smart office and the ever-increasing band of underlings. On more than one occasion, he looked round the factory site and remarked to Amelia, 'Who would ever have thought that we would have come so far?' He was still Amelia's friend, in many ways her closest and dearest and most trusted. Yet it remained that. Just after his sixty-fifth birthday, the board had asked him if he wished to retire, but the prospect had thrown him into such panic that the subject, like his proposal to Amelia, had not been brought up again.

'Of course I don't mind, Ronald,' Amelia smiled back at him. 'I value your opinions. But I could do with less of Sarah. We rattle around in that house too much. We'll end up hating each other. Mistrusting each other. Rivals,' she laughed uncertainly, 'for Charles's affections.'

'Why don't you ask Sarah if she *is* writing to him? It would be nice to have news, surely?'

'Of course I'm writing to him M'lady!' Sarah snapped when Amelia taxed her. 'Someone's got to behave like a human being! I write. I send him parcels. He sends his love, by the way.'

'And I suppose you send mine?'

'I do, M'lady. Regular as clockwork. Though I sometimes wonder if you've got any to spare.'

'How is he?' Amelia asked reluctantly.

'Fine. Fit as a fiddle. Enjoying life.'

'Where?'

'As if you didn't know, M'lady. As if you hadn't been spying on me! Asking at the Post Office if I buy stamps for Australia. Some ladies don't behave like ladies but just like plain nosy-parkers!'

'How does Charles like Australia?'

'Loves it, M'lady. All free and easy. None of that what he calls bullshit. They're all mad on aviation. People hop on aeroplanes like we do on buses.'

'He isn't in that again, is he?'

'The flying business? You know he is!'

'He's too old.'

'If you aren't, he isn't. You're still hanging on. The board hasn't managed to retire *you*, M'lady. Not yet.'

'And I haven't retired *you*, Sarah. Remember that. Though sometimes . . .'

'M'lady, I'm *five* years younger than you. And I've lived a different sort of life. And —'

'Be quiet, Sarah! What sort of job has Charles got?'

'Pilot, of course. Big spaces in Australia, he says. Opening up the outback. A man's life, he says. No women. Just men flying and roughing it.'

But man's life or whatever, less than another year went by before Sarah came in with Amelia's breakfast brandishing a letter from Charles announcing, Amelia would never guess what, that he had met and married an Australian girl.

A letter direct to Amelia followed a few days afterwards. Charles made no mention of the quarrel. He wrote about his job flying jets in Western Airways, about Australia and about his wife, Fenella.

'Fenella!' Sarah exclaimed, reading over Amelia's shoulder with her irritating familiarity. 'Don't like the name. Sounds like a herb.'

'Fenella. Not fennel, Sarah.'

'Oh, beg pardon. Fen – ella. Is that better, M'lady? I still don't like the name.'

'You're jealous. You really are, Sarah!' Amelia replied. 'You're possessive of Charles! You see him as your personal property! Anyway,' she folded the letter away before Sarah, who was a slow reader, whispering every word to herself, could reach the end, 'she's having a baby.'

'Shotgun wedding, is it M'lady?'

'He doesn't say so.'

'She must be years younger than him.'

'Probably. The older they get the younger they like them.'

'That's true enough, M'lady.' Sarah sighed. 'How did he meet her?'

'He says she was a stewardess.'

'Quite common then.'

Amelia shrugged. 'I've no idea. Not necessarily. But,' with difficulty she kept her voice steady, 'apparently he's hoping for a transfer to Western Airways transoceanic division. In which case, he might get a trip home.'

For some reason at that point, Sarah the irritating, the bossy, the irascible, began to weep.

'Of course, Sarah's pushing seventy,' Amelia told Cummings, when she had passed on to him the glad tidings of Charles's possible return and Sarah's reaction to it. 'Old people get weepy. I've offered her a retirement cottage in the village, and told her just to come in when she feels like it. But she told me she'd see *me* out.'

Cummings said sadly, 'I dread the day you offer *me* a cottage in the village,' and they both laughed. 'We all want to see you and Charles reconciled,' he went on. The sentence trailed as if it should have continued with 'Before . . .'

Before what? Amelia shivered. Before we die? What else was there to do before?

We are all old, Amelia thought. The world is moving on too fast for our ageing feet. We have difficulty keeping up. Technology is just too clever and complicated now. Aviation has outstripped our vision. Big as we are, we are not big enough or prosperous enough to keep up. It is as if our ideas are solidified, crystallised, fossilised in the era of our splendour, our youth.

461

We need Charles back. We need Charles and Charles's son – it would be a son. Already she felt her dynastic impulses stirring. They would keep the factory going. Hold on by the tips of their fingers, and skin of their teeth. Charles would come back. He would be persuaded to take over Jerningham again. There were many aviation experts in the business older than him; most of them less experienced. His son would be an incentive to him.

In the months before Charles's baby was born, the board called two emergency meetings. As a result of the first, a market research project was commissioned to look into how Jerningham was to keep its head above water in the sudden new recession. There were too many big jets flying. The second considered the subsequent gloomy report and also brought to the board's attention a tentative interest on the part of the Bristol Aircraft company, which might if encouraged eventually lead to a takeover bid. The government was set on a civil aviation policy of amalgamation. Big was beautiful.

Fired by her new hope, Amelia succeeded in winning time and maintaining independence. On Gerald Saville's proposal, it was agreed that they would proceed with plans for a bigger turbo-prop version of Ajax. It would mean the raising of a new loan, which Ronald Cummings shook his head over. The more we raise, the more we put ourselves in other people's hands, he warned. Control might one of these days slip away. But Amelia hardly listened.

At the end of March 1962 Charles's son would be born. She had written to tell him to be sure and cable her. The postmistress had been alerted to telephone the contents of the cable through, either to Haybury or to Jerningham depending on the time of day.

The cable arrived when Amelia was taking her morning coffee break with Ronald Cummings in his smart carpeted office next door to hers, which was in a new management wing, proudly called by Cummings Mahogany Corridor and christened by the youthful zestful generation of designers, the geriatric wing.

The news seemed quite unbelievable. The baby was a daughter. Even the fact that the girl was to be called Kate Amelia in no way softened Amelia towards her. Nor did Cummings' wry 'After all, *you* were a girl. She may be as interested as you were.'

A girl was an incredible disappointment. She would never take to her.

'Well, at least they're coming home to show her to you,' Sarah said.

The birth of the girl was no disappointment to her. She took on a new lease of life as she bullied the two maids, the cook and the gardener which were all they employed these days at Haybury. She would have both of them to spoil, Sir Charles and little Kate. Only six months old, the nicest possible age, all soft and round and cuddly, Sarah ecstasised. The wife, Fenella, was a nuisance but Sarah had no doubt she would be able to cut her down to her colonial size.

She persuaded Amelia to have the old nursery repainted for their arrival, dug in the attic to find old toys, sewed new curtains for the windows, made Cook bake fruitcakes, boil marmalade, smoke ham as if they were catering for an army. She also took to embroidering and smocking baby clothes which somehow irritated Amelia profoundly. 'They're only due to stay a fortnight,' she reminded Sarah.

'Well, that remains to be seen, doesn't it, M'lady? When this Fennel girl . . .'

'Fenella. You know perfectly well what her name is.'

'Well then, Fen–ella, that right, M'lady? When Fenella sees the sort of background Sir Charles comes from, she'll most likely want to stay. She'll recognise a good thing when she's on to it. She'll never have dreamed of a civilised life like this. We'll convince her. And Sir Charles always did love his home. When he's treated properly in it, that is.'

Amelia did not take issue with her. It was so much in line with her own thinking that she could disregard Sarah's impertinences. She simply said crossly and loftily, 'Life isn't as simple as you seem to think.'

'May I come with you to the airport to meet them?' Sarah asked, adding slyly when Amelia hesitated, 'I promised Sir Charles I wouldn't let you drive these days on your own. Not up to London.'

'I am a much better driver than Charles will ever be,' Amelia replied. 'And I don't need you mollycoddling me. But you can come, if you must. It'll do you good to get out.'

She was glad of Sarah's company. She had not driven up to Heathrow for years, and its concrete complications almost overwhelmed her. Huge blocks, huge hangars, huge warehouses were mushrooming everywhere. There were wide ribbons of fast-moving roads, underpasses, overpasses, glaring signs and imperative arrows.

'It's unrecognisable,' Amelia murmured, turning the nose of the Rolls cautiously off the Great West Road, following a humpy airport bus in through a wide gateway.

'Life goes on, M'lady,' Sarah said sententiously. She was almost as enchanted by Amelia's nervousness as she was by the excitement of the occasion. She sat bolt upright in the front seat, clasping her handbag, a new felt hat set on her still dark hair, her bright eyes peering this way and that, and yet at the same time managing to keep an officious eye on Amelia's driving.

'Not that way!' she protested, tearing her eyes from a Comet taking off. 'Incoming flights, that way, M'lady! I said to Sir Charles the last time, *and* he agreed, *you* should wear your spectacles for driving. It's just vanity stops you, M'lady. There now, can you read *that* sign?' She pointed to a notice about ten feet tall. 'We go to the left. To the car park. Then we'll have to stay in the terminal. We're hours and hours early. We'll have a very long time to wait.'

That wasn't so. Even before Amelia had reached the enquiry desk, she felt an electric prescience of disaster. 'Flight AK 304 from Darwin, Madam?' The traffic girl's expression became blank, a pale moon-face to be for ever imprinted on Amelia's memory. A cold hand touched her heart. 'Not due for several hours,' the traffic girl swallowed uncomfortably, playing for time.

'Has it *left* on time?' Amelia asked sharply.

'Yes, Madam. But I think it's delayed. If you just wait a moment, I'll find out the latest information.'

She rose from her seat, whispered to another girl. The other girl turned her youthful face towards Amelia. It was unbearably sympathetic. The moon-faced assistant disappeared behind a frosted-glass door. Amelia could see a shadow of her gesticulating. Minutes later, she reappeared accompanied by a tall thin traffic officer in navy blue uniform with four gold bars round his sleeve. The uniform, the solemn face, the earnest manner, reminded Amelia of Arthur.

463

'May I have your name please, Madam?' he asked without preamble, not looking Amelia directly in the eye.

'Haybury.'

'Are you a relation , Madam?'

'Of whom? And why do you ask? Why don't you just tell me when the flight is due?' Amelia heard her own voice rise, shrill with panic.

People glanced in their direction. Now the moon-faced girl was also avoiding her eyes, as if she had begun to suffer some dreaded disease.

'Something's the matter! You've got to tell me!'

The traffic girl looked at the traffic officer.

'I *know* there's something wrong!'

At a nod from the traffic officer, the girl lifted the hatch of the counter and stood back. Amelia and Sarah were conducted towards the frosted-glass door. The officer with the four gold bars held Amelia lightly under the elbow, steadying her, not allowing her to escape. It was as if he knew she wanted to turn and run, to refuse to go through that door. It was as if beyond it lay something she had been dreading all her life, her own private hell, which part of her knew would one day come to overwhelm her.

Then the man's hand was on the knob of the door, and she summoned all her strength to walk through it with dignity.

'I'm afraid,' he said, closing the door behind them, 'that I have some rather worrying news.'

It wasn't quite as bad as she had feared. The danger was grave. But Charles was still alive. So were the rest of the crew and passengers.

'Whether or not we get them down alive hangs in the balance.'

Three quarters of an hour after the Western Airways 707 AK304 had taken off from Karachi, they told her, a telephone message had been received by the Company's representatives at the airport to the effect that a bomb was on board and a ransom of a million dollars in gold was demanded. The bomb had an altitude fuse and would detonate at 7500 feet. Unless something was done, the aircraft would not be able to descend below that altitude in order to land. Everyone in it would be imprisoned up in the sky.

The message had been relayed to Captain Haybury, who had immediately begun a search of the aircraft, while the company prepared to accede to the terrorists' demands. A rendezvous near a Karachi bank was arranged – but the Pakistan government stepped in and refused to sanction the giving of the ransom. They believed, particularly as now a message had been received from the aircraft that no bomb could be found, that it was a hoax. Even if it wasn't, they pointed out that the altitude of the airfield at Addis Ababa in Ethiopia was over 8000 feet. If he landed there, he would be above the detonating altitude.

Captain Haybury had been diverted to land at Addis Ababa.

'We're pretty sure everything will be all right, Lady Haybury. Your son has a tremendous reputation in the company.'

'If it's humanly possible,' she said, 'Charles will bring them down safely.'

Seventy-five years had dimmed but not quenched Amelia's optimism. Charles was experienced, skilful, courageous. In a tough situation, Charles was unbeatable. Besides, the whole world was trying to help him. And what was he pitted against?

'A maniac,' the traffic officer answered the query in her mind. 'In our own ways, these days we're all faced in lesser degree with that.'

He talked for the sake of talking, faced with two old ladies who God knew might have a heart attack on him at any moment, who had to be allowed to hope, and yet who also had to be prepared, if necessary, for the worst. 'We're all at the mercy of some madman. But the airways now especially. The trouble is this, if I can explain it to you.'

He found Lady Haybury remarkably intelligent and perceptive. Yes, she knew how an aircraft operated. She didn't have to have it explained to her. 'When will he arrive at Addis Ababa?' Amelia asked.

'In half an hour's time. He will then circle as they continue the search till the moment when his fuel is almost exhausted and he has to land. The airfield is already alerted. All other traffic diverted. Every airport, every tracking post, every ship is on the alert. There's a great network helping your son, Lady Haybury.'

It's like the war all over again, Amelia thought. A madman – and the world joins hands. Too late.

She tried to rise from her chair, staggered and straightened herself. She walked to the map of the Middle East and Africa on the wall opposite. She shook off the traffic officer's hand and stood in front of it. The map was a blur, not altogether of dimmed eyesight. She took out her glasses, put them on and studied it.

'There's Addis,' the traffic officer pointed out unnecessarily.

'It's their only chance?'

'Yes.'

'And if the bomb itself isn't accurately set?' She took off her glasses and stared at him with those frightening eyes.

He looked at the floor. 'As I said, Lady Haybury, it's their only chance. They're in constant contact. The crew may find the bomb. There may not *be a* bomb. Then the police may trace the madman. You never know.' He cleared his throat. 'Now would you like some coffee? We haven't told anyone else.' A ghost of a smile crossed his face. 'You were so insistent. We have set aside a room for relatives and friends . . .'

'Thank you,' Amelia said. 'But I'm not leaving *here*. You brought me in here. And here I stay. Till I know. We'll sit over there in the corner. We won't disturb anyone. Coffee would be nice. But not if it means leaving here.'

She pulled her chair into the far corner just by the teleprinter. Sarah, mute and white-faced stood looking at the map beside her.

'I know, sir,' Amelia heard the traffic officer say on the telephone. 'It's very difficult. Very embarrassing. But I can't throw them out by physical force. That would look terrible.' There was a pause while he listened. 'Is that the latest, sir?'

He put down the receiver. 'Ops have just had a signal that the search for the bomb continues. But no joy so far. A German ship reported seeing the 707 at 12,000 feet over the Red Sea.'

The time passed slowly by. Amelia sat quite still, staring out of the window. Then suddenly the teleprinter clacked, the traffic officer read aloud, 'AK304 will land at Addis at twenty to eight local time.'

Amelia's eyes went to the clock, moon-faced and white like the traffic girl of ill omen. 'Ten minutes from now,' the traffic officer said. 'We'll keep our fingers crossed for them.'

Amelia clasped her hands. She tried to pray, but she was too frightened. No coherent thoughts or prayers would form in her mind. She could think of nothing with which to bribe the Almighty. What would He or anyone else want with the stub-end of her life? What virtue could she promise? What sacrifice compared to this?

The clock was an electric one and it crept stealthily with a jerky sound that wasn't a tick, just a thief's, a maniac's footfall, inch by inch. To the final desolation. Five minutes went by. Sarah had her eyes closed, her lips visibly moving. Four minutes, three minutes, two, one. Nothing.

Amelia suddenly covered her face with her hands and wept. She needed no mechanical transmission of news, no ringing of the telephone, no chattering teleprinter to tell her of the disaster, not even a hand on her shoulder, nor a human voice. She knew inside herself. She was more certain of that than of the room around her.

They tried to tell her of course. They were kind and dutiful and sympathetic. 'Lady Haybury, do you understand?' Someone shook her lightly by the shoulder. 'Can you hear what we say?' She looked up at them blankly, and said 'Yes, I understand.'

The bomb had detonated as they were about thirty feet from the runway. Everyone on board was killed.

For the first time in my life, Amelia thought, I am glad I am old, that I shall soon be dead. Life has defeated me. There is no one and nothing I need to live for. She clasped Sarah's hand, released it to sip a cup of something that was probably tea. She waved away the brandy, and the services of a man with wispy white hair who was the doctor and another who introduced himself as the Padre. As His self-styled representative on earth, she wanted to tell him she hated God and all His works, His terrible way of catching up with you in the end. But she was too tired.

After what seemed a very long time, she was being told that her car had been brought round and a driver provided to take her home.

'Home.' That deceiving tender word that now meant nothing!

Well, that was another thing she no longer cared about. She was done. Finished and glad of it. She rose from her chair.

It was then the hateful teleprinter clacked again. The *coup de grâce*. God, damn Him, had not finished with her!

'Lady Haybury.' The traffic officer advanced at her with the torn-off message in his hand and a strange expression on his face, 'It seems there was just one survivor of the crash,' and, speaking quickly lest she jump to false hopes, 'a baby. The stewardess was holding her at the back. Addis Ababa believe she is your granddaughter.'

ELEVEN

'I could never love her. How could you expect me to? I don't want her! I'm too old! Too tired,' Amelia said to Sarah, six weeks later.

Those weeks had passed like a nightmare, tortured, terrifying, unbelievable. Vivid fragments of them lodged painfully in her mind as time floated her on. The memorial service with only Cummings remaining to support Sarah and herself. Life was nothing but a succession of funerals and memorials, milestones, gravestones.

'Of course you can love her, if you let yourself, M'lady!' Sarah replied briskly. 'You must love her!'

'*Must!* You can't love to order.'

'Yes, you can.'

'*I can't.*'

'It's wicked not to!'

Amelia exclaimed bitterly, 'Wicked! That's a stupid word! I don't care what's wicked and what isn't!'

She looked at Sarah balefully. The baby had been Sarah's salvation. She who had loved Charles almost as much as Amelia had done, had with indecent haste transferred that love to his daughter. 'That's what *he'd* have wanted you to do! Sir Charles! It's no good loving the dead till you're half-crazy!' She hugged the baby to her. 'Do something for the living!'

It was a pretty cuddly little thing with large blue eyes and golden brown hair. 'Like you, M'lady.' Sarah had tried pointing out ingratiatingly. 'The spitting image!'

'I hope not,' Amelia said bitterly, 'I'd love her even less.'

As six weeks developed into six months, the likeness increased. 'Children often skip a generation, take after their grandmas,' Sarah said. 'Hold her a minute while I just brush her hair, will you, M'lady?' Sarah was adept at overcoming Amelia's antipathy. She herself was so irritatingly in her element. A baby in the house, and no parents to bother her.

She it was who made all the arrangements. She it was who engaged her youngest niece, a stout widow now of nearly fifty, as nurse and great-niece of eighteen as nursery-maid. Sarah had been on her own shopping spree up to Harrods, and bought a muslin hung cot and a layette of vastly expensive clothes.

'You're just living through what you didn't have,' Amelia said bitterly. 'You always wanted a baby without . . .'

'Without, M'lady?'

Amelia pursed her lips.

467

'Say it, M'lady. I don't care! Without the husband, you mean? Well, so why not? I never wanted a man, I don't deny it. I saw too much of my poor old mother.'

And I have seen too much of too many things, Amelia thought, but said nothing. On one point only were Sarah and she agreed. They wanted no Norland-trained nanny as Victoria had written to suggest, and indeed had offered to provide. Finance was strained at Jerningham of course. Amelia these days took only a limited interest in the Jerningham factory. She left all that to Ronald. She still attended board meetings. She still acted as chairman. But it was Gerald Saville and Cummings who really ran the business.

Victoria had heard from Cummings that times were bad, the company struggling to keep its head above water in the face of huge aircraft corporations. *We are in a familiar dilemma, he had written. We need to be bigger to compete. But if we borrow too much and things take a further downturn, we will find ourselves either in the hands of the government or the moneylenders.*

Victoria wrote in her shaky hand to Amelia offering whatever small help she could provide. It would be, as she put it, a thank-offering for the years with Rachel. It would be for leaving her behind, Amelia thought, and not bringing her back to England. Victoria was now crippled with arthritis, but Rachel was such a comfort. She was engaged to be married to such a nice executive, somewhat older than she was. A divorcé, the innocent party of course. Would Amelia feel able to make the journey for Rachel's wedding?

Amelia sent a handsome silver salver, but did not feel able. Nor was she particularly interested that Rachel's husband, Frank Walton, was in the American aircraft industry. As she now rarely set foot inside her office at Jerningham, she could not be interested in any executive working for some distant corporation called Lockheed.

Victoria sent lavish photographs of the wedding. Sarah, going beyond herself as usual, rescued them from Amelia's desk drawer and had the best of them framed but Amelia never glanced in their direction, never glanced, it seemed to Sarah, in anyone's direction. Her blue eyes had a clouded unfocussed look. She walked in the grounds erect and seemingly unbowed, but she never went beyond the lodge gates, saw no visitors except Cummings.

He came twice a week to report to her. Dismal news, she could be excused for not listening to it. She seemed to look through him and beyond him. She made no comment except just before Christmas 1963, when Charles had been dead over a year and Cummings was reporting a big trading loss. Then she said bitterly, her eyes not focussed on Cummings but beyond as if talking to someone else altogether, 'So none of it was worthwhile! None!'

'None of this is worthwhile either,' she said to Sarah as Sarah decorated a tree in the old nursery. 'It's nonsense! Christmas means nothing to me. It's a waste of money we can ill afford. All these new baubles and lights. The baby's too young to appreciate it.'

'That she's not, M'lady! She sees more than you think. Look at that,' as the baby crawled towards the pile of baubles, 'look at that clever girl!'

'Mind she doesn't stuff them in her mouth,' Amelia eyed the child coldly. 'And shouldn't she be walking by now? You feed her too much. She's too fat.'

'Well, I suppose we should be grateful for your notice, M'lady. Very grateful! But no, she isn't too fat. Dr Randall said . . .'

'Good Lord, *that* old fool!'

'The *son*, M'lady.' And under her breath, 'It's not him that's the old fool!'

'I don't suppose he's any better than his father. His father was a fool too.'

'Well, *he* says, M'lady, that Kate Amelia . . .'

'Can't you just call her Kate? The two names sound silly!'

'As Your Ladyship pleases. *He* says Kate Amelia, beg pardon, *Kate* is the perfect size and the perfect weight.' Sarah scooped Kate up from the floor and pressed her to her. 'Just feel, M'lady, she's solid and firm!'

'No, thank you. I've done my days of dandling babies.'

'The trouble is some old ladies can't abide girls. They're jealous of them M'lady. They know they've lost their looks, and they can't bear little girl babies with all the fun in front of them.'

'Thank you, Sarah. I don't want to hear any more.'

'And I don't give a tinker's cuss what you want to hear or don't want to hear, my fine lady.' Sarah's wrinkled face flooded angry red. She put her hands on her hips, pushed her face pugnaciously forward. 'You're going to get a piece of my mind before you make yourself die of boredom and this poor mite shrivel for want of a bit of love!'

The two old ladies faced each other furiously, oblivious of everything else. Till in one of those sudden bursts of infant progress, Kate Amelia staggered to her feet, took her first uncertain steps forward and grabbed a branch of the shallowly potted Christmas tree. The whole overladen tree tottered over her. Sarah whipped round quickly to straighten it, clasping the trunk with both her hands. Amelia made a dart for the baby and gathered her up before the fir tree fell over her.

There was no danger at all, but Amelia hugged the child as if she had been snatched from the jaws of death.

Only it wasn't the child who had been snatched. It was herself. The jaws were very close still, of course, but a lifeline tugged her back. She looked down at the blue eyes so like her own, and knew suddenly that this was perhaps the most precious child of them all.

'So Sarah is displaced,' Cummings smiled, as Amelia, renewed in strength and health and concentration, faced him again across his office table for the ritual of their mid-morning coffee. Old habits had been restored as if never interrupted. Amelia was older by ten times as many as the fifteen months since she had been regularly in her office. She was thinner and more wrinkled. But the concentration was back in the blue eyes, her brain was as needle-sharp, her step as firm, her voice as incisive.

'Sarah has not so much been displaced as moved over a fraction. She is still first in Kate Amelia's affections.'

Which was quite untrue, as they both knew. It was Amelia's affection the baby sought. Amelia she ran to, Amelia's hand she held at night through the bars of the cot before she fell asleep.

'Naturally the poor mite has to make up for lost time,' Sarah muttered. 'You didn't give her much love in the first twelve months!' But it was more than that. Much more – a strange empathy, a mutual identification that locked them together, and which perhaps subconsciously Amelia had fought against in that awful year after Charles was killed. 'I couldn't bear to love someone so much

469

and lose them again. I must learn not to love.'

'That's what life's all about, M'lady,' Sarah said, dismissing Amelia's attempted explanation.

'And what do you know about it, Sarah?'

She didn't deign to answer; Sarah as usual was right. Life was loving and losing. Losing people, losing things, losing ambitions, losing battles. The battle for the survival of the Jerningham factory was on. Amelia had resumed her interest and her fight. She must leave something of Ajax and the factory for James's granddaughter and her own. In a distant mystical way she was working again with James.

For Cummings's part, that morning in early March 1964 he couldn't wait to get off the subject of Kate Amelia and on to the new Ajax.

'There is no way, Amelia, that we can continue the project without an injection of new capital. That's for a start. We need someone to come along not just with thousands or hundreds of thousands but with millions! We've got good staff, but we haven't got the money for them. We've got the premises, but we need them altering and expanding. We need to think ten years ahead. And then we need to design and get orders for ten years ahead! The days of wire and string and silk and the seat of one's pants have gone for good!'

'I know that. I can think ahead. And you can design ahead. But the money? Where do we get that?'

'The well-known cry of British aircraft makers.'

'The government won't give it, will they?'

'Not a hope in hell! What they're encouraging is mergers. An aeroplane's a huge undertaking now, it needs huge corporations. United we stand, divided we fall. That's the thinking.'

'What are you leading up to, Ronald?'

'There have been feelers.'

'Who from?'

'Solent for one, Westley for another.'

'Creep in under their blanket?'

'It could be worse.'

'How?'

'They'd probably develop Ajax better than we ever could.'

'Or kill it off.'

'Either's a possibility.'

'Over my dead body,' Amelia exclaimed and then remembered wryly that dead was what she had wanted to be not so long ago, and the Lord was known for providing you with exactly what you wanted the moment you had ceased to want it.

Cummings voiced a near paraphrase of her thoughts. 'We're both getting on. We're no spring chickens, Amelia. Nor are we King Canute. We can't order back the tide.'

'Tides can turn.'

He smiled, 'And turn again. And sweep you away.'

But Amelia remained as firm as a rock in her newfound purpose in life. With encouragement from Gerald Saville, she called an extra board meeting and was not cast down by the pessimists. She went directly against Cummings's advice and with Saville's help arranged a revolving credit agreement with six banks, whereby the company could borrow and repay as its needs dictated. She did her own public relations work, calling on likely customers for Ajax. The sheer pertinacity, charm and the novelty of such a sprightly old lady won her some success.

Civil aviation was still expanding at twenty per cent a year, and the world was ringed with air routes. And now automation linked up with aviation. The radio officer on the crew had long since been dispensed with. Now the navigator was disappearing – his place taken by the inertial navigation system which produced latitude and longitude automatically. Autoland systems had been developed whereby aircraft could take off or land in thick fog. Everything was becoming more complicated – and therefore bigger and more costly.

Grudgingly, at the end of the summer Cummings admitted that the outlook was improving. They had nine firm orders for the stretched Ajax. By the spring of 1965, the number had risen to twelve. Amelia joined Gerald Saville in talking optimistically of the Farnborough Air Show, maybe even Paris, of raising yet another loan.

'This may be just an Indian summer, Amelia,' Cummings pointed out. 'The trend is against us.'

But as summer gave way to autumn and winter, interest in Ajax continued. The aviation papers praised its performance. It was described as a first class example of Britain at its best. In direct contradiction of the accounts department's advice but on Gerald Saville's urging, Amelia gave the workforce a Christmas bonus.

Christmas at Haybury was celebrated in the traditional style. Kate Amelia was old enough and young enough to make the celebrations mystically sweet for the aged family that surrounded her. After Christmas service and Christmas lunch, Amelia telephoned Victoria, and spoke one by one to the family gathered there. Rachel and Rachel's husband Frank and son Evan. Even Amelia felt a pang of guilt at having almost forgotten her other granddaughter, now no more than an Americanised voice at the other end of the trans-Atlantic cable.

'We thought we might take a trip to Europe, Grandmother, before my stepson Evan starts high school. Frank is interested in some of the European factories . . .'

'And in ours too, I hope.'

'Oh, yes, very! I'd also like to show Haybury to Frank. So if you'll have us some time . . .'

Vague invitations were issued and accepted. 1966 dawned full of family peace and promise. *You might have got the impression from Rachel that I wasn't so very interested in Jerningham, but indeed I am,* Frank took it upon himself to write to Amelia direct. *Any time I can be of assistance over here just you let me know. I'll always root for you, advertise for you, do whatever you want, you only have to call.* The letter went on to sound an ominous note about everything going huge and corporate over there and small firms being pushed to the wall, but Amelia chose not to hear, just as she chose not to think about Rachel's eventual ownership of Haybury.

The warm tone strengthened Amelia's dawning sense of well-being. Family feuds and quarrels were over; Rachel was well and happy; Kate Amelia blossomed into childhood. What if it was only an Indian summer? Life went on

471

despite all the gravestone-milestones. A generation died. But another came to take its place. Even the factory tottered on. And though she knew now by name only a handful of its staff and their functions, it was there and she and Cummings were there.

'For how long, I wonder, Amelia?' Cummings said soberly in reply to her remark that hot summer. The world was tense and uneasy again. Once more there were rumours of global war.

'For how long? Which do you mean? For how long can the factory totter on? Or for how long shall we be here?'

Cummings smiled wryly. 'Both.'

'You will be here, Ronald, till you decide you want to go. The board have agreed that unanimously. Till you decide you want to put your feet up and make model aeroplanes in your rose garden.'

'It might be considerably more profitable.'

'And I shall be here till they carry me out.'

'Suffragette style?'

'Suffragette or stiff,' Amelia smiled.

'But you don't answer about the factory, Amelia.'

'Because you know more about it than I do.'

'Well, one ray of hope, those British United chaps who came down today were interested. But then I'm interested in lots of things I haven't the wherewithal to buy. So it may mean nothing. You did your stuff, Amelia. They were enchanted by you. The real grand old lady, handing out the teacups.'

'Thanks, Ronald,' Amelia said drily and pushed back her chair from the desk.

'You look tired, Amelia. It's been a long day. I should go home and get to bed early. It's Friday tomorrow. Why not stay at Haybury? Rest up.'

'If you take the day off as well, I might.' She stared across the desk at him. He too looked suddenly old and tired. She reached her hand out and touched his, and he squeezed it with a sudden sad and fierce emotion.

'I might. I might stay late tonight, get this lot finished and go birdwatching tomorrow. I doubt they'd miss me. Now *you* see *you* get that early night!'

She did not get to bed early. Kate Amelia wasn't well. Sarah met her with the news as soon as she opened the nursery door. 'It's nothing, M'lady. Just that beastly polio injection Dr Randall gave her. Sir Charles was the same with his smallpox vaccination. She's flushed I grant you, but her temperature's only slightly up.'

'How much up?'

'99.8. There, poor babe! She's fretful,' as Kate Amelia sat up in the cot and held out her arms, her red face puckered. 'But she'll be pleased now she's got you.'

Kate Amelia finally dozed off to sleep about midnight, still holding Amelia's hand. Sarah undertook to sleep the rest of the night in the nursery. 'Not that there's any real cause to, M'lady. She'll be right as rain in the morning, no cause to look alarmed.'

But for some inexplicable reason, Amelia was alarmed and uneasy. At first she put her uneasiness down to the thundery pressure of the night, the airlessness even with the large windows open wide. Then to her own overtiredness, that jangled state of being when body and mind seemed too

472

tense to sleep. Then memory. She kept thinking of Charles at that age, flushed and ill in London, and suddenly found herself reliving all the terrors she felt then of infant disease and mortality. Somewhere she had read of fatal reactions to prophylactic injections, of encephalitis, meningitis, brain damage . . .

She was aware again of the vulnerability of life, of death waiting to claim all the people she really loved. She could almost feel death fluttering round the house.

'I am becoming a silly fearful old woman, just when I need to be strong,' she told herself, going down into the deserted kitchen to heat some milk. She took up a glass for Sarah and one for herself. Sarah was still sitting bolt upright near Kate Amelia's bed. Amelia drew up another chair. They drank the milk sitting close together, warming their old hands round the beakers, though the night remained stifling, like elderly children whom the grim reaper had overlooked.

At two o'clock, Amelia forced herself to go to bed. But she was awake again at six. The cloud had lifted. The morning was fine. She felt clear-eyed and clear-headed. She padded immediately along to the nursery. Kate Amelia was sipping orange juice and chattering happily to Sarah. Her arm was no longer sore, her face its usual delicate pink.

'Isn't she a clever girl, Grandmother?' Sarah beamed. 'She's cool as a cucumber again! I told you not to worry.'

In the clear light of morning, everything looked less worrying and splendid. Amelia felt in tune with the day. Rested and refreshed, another minor crisis passed. Far too alert and energetic to take the day off. She breakfasted with relish, and took her Mini out of the garage. There were spangled cobwebs on the hedges as she went down the drive. There were still a few pale heads of the honeysuckle's second blooming to set off the red of the unripe blackberries and the round knotty convolvulus fruits. The air smelled of hay and harvested corn, heather and green hazelnuts.

On such a morning, surely one could believe that the tide had turned, that even huge aviation problems were surmountable, that in some mysterious way James was very near to her?

Amelia stopped the Mini in her usual place. She was amused to see that Ronald Cummings's car was also in its appointed space. So he hadn't taken the day off either! Birdwatching indeed! She combed her hair in her own office, and leaving her handbag to show her secretary when she arrived that she was in, she walked down the mahogany corridor to tax Ronald with his duplicity.

He was sitting at his desk as usual with his back to the door. 'Ronald,' she began. But he didn't turn at the sound of her words. 'Ronald,' she repeated, anxiety changing her tone.

Then she saw he was sitting at a strange uncomfortable angle. She put her hand on his shoulder, and even at that light touch, his body lurched sideways. His cheek was cold, his eyes filmed. He was still clenching his pen in his right hand. The paper he had been working on ended in an agonised almost unreadable scrawl.

When what seemed hours later help had come and Ronald's body was taken away, Amelia stared down at that scrawl. The last two words she finally deciphered as *get help* – though whether he meant in his agony for himself or for the factory or for her, she didn't know.

TWELVE

Help came immediately. Gerald Saville took charge and was a tower of strength.

'Leave everything to me, Amelia,' he said, and she was glad to do so. These days aeroplanes and aviation finance were becoming so complicated and interwoven with other disciplines, it was safer to leave it to the experts.

Business was becoming worldwide and interconnected. Organisations were convoluted. Who owned what and why was becoming increasingly difficult to decipher. While Victory Airways and their cheap holiday trips to Spain could easily be recognised, as with the Suntara Travel and Fortress Finance, few would have the patience or the ability to trace their present proprietor to a big French banking concern called Securité, to whose head office in Paris Monsieur March was a constant visitor.

'We shall, of course, have to employ someone to take Cummings's place,' Gerald Saville told her. 'Things are very difficult at present. Poor old Ronald! He was wonderful, of course, but he couldn't have left us at a worse time.'

This message he emphasised at the next board meeting. Then things became more difficult. On Amelia's eightieth birthday, she had a surprise present – a huge bouquet of red roses from Gerald Saville. But two days later came a not so welcome postcript. 'You've been a marvellous chairman, Amelia,' Gerald told her with a smile. 'Eighty years old. Not even Juan Trippe went on in charge of Pan American World Airways that long!'

Over the weeks there were repeated reminders of all the work she was doing, and hints that it was all too much for her. Finally, Gerald Saville came right out with it. 'I do think, Amelia you should be taking things easier. Being chairman is too much for you!'

'I'll think about it, Gerald,' she retorted.

'Please don't get me wrong, Amelia. It's you I'm thinking of.'

Others had also been thinking about Amelia and Jerningham Aviation. Certain items in the minutes, and information from their proxy on the board had worried Rachel and Frank Walton. Hurried reorganisations – business and family – were made. A friend moved in to keep Victoria company.

The next thing Amelia knew was that Rachel, Frank and Evan would be coming over to Haybury – and not just for a visit – as soon as it could be arranged.

'You're quite knocked off your perch again, M'lady,' Sarah said in a rather frighteningly kindly tone. 'Rest yourself! Let other people do the thinking for you. They know more about it than you do. You don't want to end up like poor Mr Cummings. And he was a good few years younger than you, you know.'

'I know, Sarah. I know.' But she spoke without her usual tartness and that alarmed Sarah. 'And I thought the tide had turned.'

'Well, maybe it has, M'lady. You have to look on the bright side. Mr Cummings was a good age.'

'Early seventies. Not such a big age these days.'

'Well, he was no young pippin. He worked hard.'

'Too hard.'

'He loved his job, M'lady. He died in harness. Most of us'd like that. And it'll be lovely to have Miss Rachel and her husband over. I think it's wonderful Mr Frank's coming to help you out. Blood's thicker than water, and that's true now. He might be even better than Mr Cummings. The Yanks are clever. And there's more in it for him, as they say these days. Then it's a young family for Kate Amelia. The boy'll be a nice playmate.'

'He's years older, Sarah. At least six years.'

'Well, later on, if they do stay over here, it'll be someone to take her to parties . . . that sort of thing, M'lady. Anyway, I'm looking forward to it, if you're not.'

In her increasingly vague way, Amelia *was* looking forward to it. Just as much perhaps as Sarah. She knew her hands were slipping on the reins, and she longed for young capable ones to take over. Her personal sorrow at Ronald's death had been so much greater and more profound than she would ever have thought. Indeed she had never really thought of losing him. He was an institution, a part of her life, and besides all that, younger than her. He was to be there as long as she needed him. As the board had agreed, irremovable. She should have known better.

Now without him and his interpretation, the factory became more of an unknown territory, the mechanics, the costing, the administration, the politics of modern aviation, a maze in which she lost herself. She went into her office as little as possible. She avoided the workshops. She gave letters to the works manager or her own secretary to answer. She allowed herself to be simply told that Frank would be arriving to take Ronald's place – or tacitly her own as chairman – on 1 January 1967. She was dimly aware that working his notice out to his present employer, the letting of the house and the planning of Evan's education naturally delayed him.

'And we'll have to think of *our* preparations won't we, M'lady? Where shall they live? Should Sir Charles's flat be enlarged for them? Oh, it's no good shaking your head, M'lady! Some decisions have got to be taken, and you'll have to take them!'

But if Amelia took them, she was hardly aware of it. She had never realised how easy it could be to take decisions without thinking. A nod here, a shake of the head there. No thought, no weighing the pros and cons. She drifted through that autumn like the mist itself, the days undefined and gently sorrowing, her life decaying.

The arrival of Rachel, Frank and Evan on a cold late December afternoon changed all that.

'My goodness me, M'lady! She's easy on the eye,' Sarah whispered in Amelia's ear as they peeped through the drawing-room window at the family disembarking from the Mercedes outside the Haybury front door. 'You never told me she was such a looker!'

She jerked her indignant head at the figure of Rachel, swaddled in a mink coat, the pale winter sun gleaming on her ash-blonde hair.

'She wasn't. Not then. Not last time I saw her. She was plump and spotty and she had a brace on her teeth.'

'She's made up for lost time. Real model's figure, eh! *He* looks nice. In a cuddly sort of way.'

Mistakenly as it turned out, it was Frank Amelia was studying, as if he would be the one to wield power. She saw a well-built, slightly balding, slightly portly man in his late thirties, one hand resting on his young son's shoulder, the other round Rachel. They presented a good well-omened picture. Amelia took to him at once.

Even before she had hurried out into the hall, waved imperiously for Sarah to open the front door, and then stood framed in the doorway, her arms wide in welcome, she had decided she liked Frank. Rachel had made a good marriage, despite Victoria's fears. He was a good solid citizen.

'Welcome to Haybury!' Amelia smiled, allowing herself to be swallowed in Frank's enthusiastic embrace. Close to, he had warm golden brown eyes, a kindly mouth and a ready smile. She thought rather shakily, as he released her, she had forgotten how good it felt to be in a man's strong arms.

He pushed his son forward. 'And this is Evan.'

'Hi!' The boy too, she took to. He had his father's eyes, his rather puggy jaw, a short nose and bright smile. But there was underneath a reserve which she found interesting.

'I hope you'll like it here, Evan,' she said, shaking his hand.

'Of course we shall!' It was her granddaughter Rachel who answered for her stepson. Close to, she was even more sensational. The ugly duckling into the pure white swan. She kissed Amelia lightly on the cheek. She smelled exquisite and expensive.

'I see her in you, and you in her,' Frank said as if sensing Amelia wasn't sure. 'I can see we're going to be one happy family.'

'You've grown into a very beautiful woman,' Amelia said. She put her hands on both Rachel's shoulders. 'Let me look at you!'

'She's very like you,' Frank repeated, his eyes going from one to the other. It was so obvious that he worshipped Rachel that Amelia felt a pang of unjustifiable envy. 'She has your mouth, Lady Haybury.'

'She's like her father too,' Amelia studied the perfect sculptured features, the fine skin, all accentuated by the most exquisite make-up. Nothing about Rachel was less than perfect. Amelia found herself studying her granddaughter for some physical flaw, as if finding it would make her more human and lovable.

'Grandfather Lehmann used to tell me I was very like my mother,' Rachel divested herself of her coat, and handed it to Sarah.

'If you'll excuse my saying it, M'lady, Miss Rachel's also very like her grandfather, dear Sir Frederick.'

Sarah smiled like some foolish sentimental old servant. Only Amelia recognised that Sarah had declared her enmity towards Rachel.

It was to become mutual.

'Let me show you to your rooms,' Amelia smiled. 'We had thought . . . '

'We?'

'Sarah and I.' And when Rachel raised her finely plucked brows, 'Sarah is now my housekeeper and confidante.'

'I can actually dimly remember you, Sarah,' Rachel turned to her rather condescendingly. 'You were nursery-maid for a time.'

'That is correct, madame.'

'You were always bossy then, I remember. You haven't changed.' She paused, 'Well Grandmother, what was it you and Sarah thought?'

'That you might have felt we were all too much on top of each other here at Haybury. That you might prefer to live at the Jerningham flat.'

'Uncle Charles's flat?'

'Yes.'

'Oh, no,' Rachel laughed. 'I wouldn't have liked that at all! Living over the shop, as it were. Besides, it wouldn't be big enough.'

'We were going to have it enlarged.'

'Much enlarged,' Sarah put in doggedly.

'Why bother?' Rachel walked up the hall towards the staircase. 'After all, this is home now. My home.' She put a manicured hand on Amelia's arm. 'For though we all hope you'll live for a thousand years, dear Grandmother, this place eventually is *mine*.'

'You never explained that to me, M'lady! Never, never, never!' Sarah clacked her knitting needles in time to her words. Kate Amelia was asleep, the nursery nightlight glowed softly, the fire was banked down. Sarah kept her voice lowered to a hoarse hiss.

'You get above yourself again, Sarah. Why in God's name should *I* explain my financial affairs to *you*? What's it got to do with you? You're a household servant.'

'*Housekeeper*, M'lady, beg pardon! *And* confidante. You said it yourself just a few days ago, when Princess Maude arrived.'

'And that just means I talk to you when *I* feel like it! I, Sarah, not *you*! Besides, you wouldn't understand money matters.'

'I bet I understand them a sight better than you! I know what balancing a household budget means! I know what it means for every farthing to count. I doubt you could add up a column of figures right.'

'You're just being rude now, Sarah! No wonder I can't tell you things. Anyway, it was common knowledge that Arthur inherited Haybury and I merely had the life interest.'

'I thought you could still pass it on.'

'There, you see! You can't understand these things. You're not legally educated. Not educated at all, really. I can't pass it on. That's quite definite! Quite unalterable!'

'Haybury goes when you go?'

'Yes.'

'Just like that?'

'Just like that.'

'To whom might I ask?'

'You know damned well! So what's the point of asking?'

'To Princess Maude?'

477

'Yes.'

'Mr Arthur could've left a will leaving some of it to you.'

'Well, he didn't. He didn't expect to die before me.'

'And I suppose Princess Maude got Mr Lehmann's money as well?'

'Naturally.'

'Every penny?'

'Every red cent.'

'Even his share in Jerningham?'

'Yes.'

'Isn't that a bit difficult?'

'I don't see why.'

'You should've married Mr Lehmann!' Sarah stabbed a knitting needle through the ball of wool and sighed heavily. 'You could've done. He wanted you to. He was a real gentleman.'

'I didn't love him. So how could I?'

'Because someone's got to provide for Kate Amelia, poor babe! What's going to happen to *her*?'

'I don't know.'

'No money! No parents! No home!'

'Oh, it's not as bad as that, Sarah, I don't think.'

'Have you ever really given it a thought, M'lady?'

'I gave it a lot of thought to it at one time, Sarah. But lately — '

'Lately you've let things go. You don't have to tell me. Let yourself get old.'

'Perhaps you're right.'

'And do you really think Princess Maude'll let her stay on? Once *you've* shuffled off?'

'That I don't know. Contrary to your opinion, I'm sure Rachel is a nice girl. Maybe she thinks we neglected her early on. But anyway, I've long since ceased to forecast how people will behave in given situations.'

'Well, you think about it now! You try and guess!'

For several nights after that talk with Sarah, Amelia lay awake trying to answer that question. She never succeeded in answering it. But it did most marvellously compose and strengthen her own will to live and for Jerningham to continue.

THIRTEEN

In that will to live she was assisted by her step-great-grandson, Evan. He seemed at first an unlikely ally. 'I never expected to see a son of mine playing that game,' Frank said to Amelia on a hot afternoon that first August when he came across the two of them playing a leisurely round of croquet.

'Evan is being kind and polite to an old lady,' Amelia smiled, adjusting the brim of her floppy straw hat. Evan had been enrolled at a school in Winchester and they were now halfway through the summer holidays. Amelia and Evan had spent a lot of that holiday together. 'We've also been flying kites on the forest, and I drove him to the motor museum at Beaulieu.'

'No kidding? Well, that's great!' Indeed Frank could not be more pleased at this turn of events. Times were more than tricky at the factory, and the kindest thing anyone could do was to keep Amelia out of the way. Frank had taken over his wife's interests in the factory, and been elected general manager on the family votes. Rachel was far more interested in the London and Paris shops than she was in aircraft factories. Her taste was exquisite and, particularly in jewellery, expensive.

As for Amelia, she insisted on taking her place as chairman at board meetings, although she rarely said anything on the items on the agenda and everything was done by Gerald and Frank. The finance items were particularly difficult. All over the world, the big airlines and aircraft manufacturers – particularly the Americans – were spending large sums of money. Nine months before Frank arrived in England, Pan American signed a contract for 25 Boeing 747 Jumbo's at a cost of $525 million. These vast aircraft, weighing 325 tons each, could carry 404 passengers at 550 mph. Unless you were big, you hadn't a chance.

'Jerningham is much too small,' Frank confided to his wife. 'And then there's the Labour government. All this red tape plus nationalisation hanging over our heads. Fortunately Gerald Saville knows his way around. He has some particularly good finance contacts with a French house called Securité.'

Sitting at the board meetings, Amelia had recognised how Ronald Cummings had interpreted the aviation world for her. How it had moved much further forward and left her far behind. Unable to follow, she had at times found her concentration going altogether, had several times dozed off to sleep. As the months went by, she began to follow a little better with practice. But no sooner had she grasped one point or one development than they were on to the next, rationalisation, nationalisation, siphoning off, buying in, contracting out, wing loadings, insurance factors, union practices, closed shop, picketting, seat spaces, IATA regulations. Her head reeled. It was like trying to keep a slippery foothold while being swept along by a strong tide.

But she was in her own way not unhappy. Frank, she was sure, would save Jerningham. He was strong and vigorous and clever. Ajax would go on. It was her testament to James, her gift to Kate. Rachel was not nearly such a hard person as Sarah declared.

'Dear Grandmother,' Rachel said sweetly enough and often enough, 'you are much too lenient with your servants! Especially Sarah. She is, after all, only an ignorant village woman. You take much too much notice of her opinions. Nor is she good for young Kate. She spoils her.'

Young Kate. There was the sun, the moon, the centre of Amelia's happiness. Kate was a bonny child, the spit, as Sarah said, of Amelia herself, but precocious as only a child entirely surrounded by aged people can be. Reluctantly, Amelia had allowed Rachel to persuade her to send Kate to school when she was six. 'No, Grandmother. Don't get a governess! Let her play with children of her own age!'

'She's jealous, M'lady! Princess Maude is. Eaten up with it! Can't bear to see how much you love that child because she thinks you never loved her! Wants her out of the house! And talking of the house, I hope you've noticed how she's trying to take over the running of Haybury? Did you see that new-fangled stuff she's bought for the kitchen? Tried to tell Cook the other day what we should have for dinner! Tried to tell me that she was expecting guests and would I be there to take the ladies to her room? I said, "Madame, I shall take orders from Lady Haybury and no one else and —"'

'Oh, shut up, Sarah! We've all got to live together. Don't make life difficult!'

'If I'm making life difficult, M'lady, I can always retire.'

It was Sarah's constant threat. Only with the two children did Amelia find herself completely at peace. Sarah was jealous, of course. 'We always did like the boys, didn't we, M'lady?' she would mutter darkly, as she helped Amelia put on her coat for some outing with Evan. 'Poor little Kate Amelia has quite had her nose put out of joint!'

'You know that's not true. Kate is *everything* to me! Everything!' But in the end, for the sake of peace and quiet, she began to take Kate along as well, even on outings and expeditions that would hardly appeal to a girl. So as the months went by, off Kate went to museums, to stock-car racing, to football matches, to village cricket, to birdwatching. She learned how to handle a boat, to keep a straight bat, to shoot arrows, to make models.

'It's the quaintest sight in the world to see them,' Frank remarked to his beautiful Rachel, 'the old lady and the two youngsters! But they keep her out of mischief!'

It was a strange and mutually satisfying trio. Each gave to the other two something of what they needed. To Kate, Evan was like a breath of fresh air and youth, a kindly adventurous playmate such as had previously only existed in her imagination. To Evan, the young-old little girl was a soothing admiring and very adaptable companion after the hideously detestable ways of his English schoolmates. He had made few friends since he came over to England. And at Winchester, he saw little prospect of ever making any. To Amelia, they both gave love. She was an anachronism which only extreme youth could fully savour. They liked her trembly old hands that could be so comforting and gentle. Her myopic blue eyes missed the dirt and the pimples and the untidiness that other eyes saw and other voices remarked upon. They enjoyed her quick laugh, her sudden brightening, and they revelled in the stories of her youth, and the exploits of Sir Charles, the Red Baronet.

They believed few of them. They did not believe that she had flown in a homemade aeroplane made out of undergarment silk, or that she had met famous aviators, been forced down in the desert and rescued by a handsome aviator. Nor that she had dropped the ashes of some poor old man overboard quite close to the very place they were then sailing their little boat. They had doubts of her accounts of the races round the Isle of Wight and the huge flying boats that flew round the world from Hythe. But they liked to pretend they believed her, and would press her for more. Sometimes she had a strange way of talking, as if they weren't just a trio, but as if a fourth person were present. Someone called James to whom she referred occasionally for confirmation on some point which they patently disbelieved. 'Isn't that so, James?' she would say. 'You'll bear me out?'

Kate of course couldn't hear too many stories about her father. How he had run away from school to fight in the Great War. How he had wingwalked and barnstormed and even been in films, had fought in the Spanish Civil War and had brought down Fascist planes.

And then as the months melted into years and the friendship of the trio changed but deepened, Amelia began to dream her dreams again. Frank would build up Jerningham. Evan and Kate would grow up and marry. The family would be united. Kate's home and future would be made secure.

FOURTEEN

The little family of Amelia, Kate and Evan played in the garden at Haybury, looking up every now and then at the big aeroplanes cruising majestically across the sky.

Lying back in a deckchair at dusk, Amelia would watch the bright red, white and green brooches of lights move against the stars, catch sight of a long rope of vapour trail coloured bright pink above the grey gloaming at 30,000 feet.

Evan knew all the different types and so did Kate – which was more than Amelia did. She listened to the high shrill sound of the jets and was reminded of the wind in the wires of Ajax. From this little Garden of Eden in the New Forest where for her it had all begun, serenely she watched the triumph of aviation.

'Civil aviation is the greatest instrument ever forged for international solidarity' – Winston Churchill's words, but Charles's sentiments exactly. And it was going from strength to strength in a universe that was making such marvellous progress. On 21 July 1969, watched by 600 million people on television – three of them were Amelia, Kate and Evan – Neil Armstrong climbed backwards out of his spacecraft and set foot on the moon, saying 'That's one small step for a man, one giant leap for mankind.' A year afterwards, they watched the first big Jumbo jet spread its silver wings above them on a flight over the forest to Hurn. And two years later – perhaps the biggest thrill of all – she was invited to be one of a special group of passengers in the supersonic Concorde that flew at 60,000 feet at 1250 miles an hour.

Frank drove her to Fairford airfield, together with Rachel, Evan and Kate for the big moment. She was quite composed, though inwardly excited. Press photographers were there taking pictures as she climbed the steps into the passenger cabin. At altitude, she looked down at the earth so far below, the strange purple light on the horizon, touched the portholes and found them strangely hot, drank tea out of a Royal Doulton china cup.

One of the young stewardesses took her up front to the flight deck. The captain and the crew knew all about her. The Grand Old Lady of Aviation, the Press had called her. They asked about the early days – about Rheims and Hendon and her flight over the desert. They insisted that she climb into the lefthand seat, take the controls – and there she was, flying straight and level, banking and climbing, diving as she had done all those years ago with Charles in Ajax V.

Evan didn't believe it, of course. Neither did Kate. As they drove back to Haybury, they could hardly swallow their laughter. 'Happy, Grandmother?'

Rachel asked her that night in the drawing-room, after she had kissed the children goodnight.

'Happy, now, my dear, and content.'

The content, she began to notice, was not evident these days in Frank. She had been pleased that Frank and Gerald Saville, who knew more about Jerningham Aviation now than anybody else, should have so immediately hit it off. They had become good friends. Gerald often came over with Frank to Haybury after finishing at the factory. At the board meetings she attended, there always appeared to be harmony.

Then the aviation peak boiled over. Too many huge Jumbos were operating for the passenger demand. As many empty seats as passengers flew the world's air routes. The big operators began to lose money – a lot of money – each year. Pan American were around $35 million in the red. The pattern was prevalent throughout the industry. Amelia noticed Frank was working later and later. It became evident that Jerningham Aviation was also losing money steadily, becoming deeper and deeper in debt to the French banking consortium Securité.

'Nothing to worry about Frank,' Gerald Saville reassured him. 'These recessions come and go.'

But this one got worse. The biggest holiday air transport business, Court Line, went bankrupt. Then came the fuel crisis. First a fuel shortage. Then the price of it doubling, trebling, quadrupling. Finally industrial unrest. Strikes – even at Jerningham. And inflation an annual 30 per cent.

Clearly Frank was very far from content. So was Rachel. Things at Haybury were altogether too quiet for her. Evan was now at Winchester, and Rachel was persuading Amelia to send Kate to boarding school.

'She's not what you call the maternal type, is she, M'lady? That's the tenth time this month our Princess Maude's been to London,' Sarah said, 'not to mention three trips to Paris. Wonder to me why she ever bothers to come back here.'

Certainly Rachel seemed to return more and more reluctantly, always with new clothes and furs and jewels. She's an obsessive spender, Amelia thought.

'I've heard tell she's running up bills all over the place,' Sarah murmured darkly.

'She's a rich woman,' Amelia replied. 'She has no need to run up bills.'

'The way she spends she does. Have you seen some of her furs? And she expects me to look after her clothes. I nearly said to her the other day —'

'Don't,' Amelia forbade sharply. 'Whatever you were going to say, *don't*.'

Despite her warnings, the antagonism between Sarah and Rachel was never far off boiling point. 'You are too easy with that impertinent old woman,' Rachel objected shortly after her return from her latest trip to London. 'It's not what she says, Grandmother, it's how she looks! I've never known anyone who could be so sassy without ever opening her mouth.'

And then came the news that Victoria was ill. Rachel was on the trans-Atlantic telephone to the hospital every day. She fretted. She loves her, Amelia thought, more than anyone else. More even than she loves Frank.

'If you ask me, I think her place is at Miss Victoria's side,' Sarah said piously.

'No one is asking you,' Amelia replied. But already she knew it was the beginning of the end. If Rachel wanted to return, that would be it.

The final straw as far as Frank was concerned was the Labour government's declared aviation policy of no competition. That announcement coincided with an offer to Frank of one of the big executive positions in the American Boeing Corporation. Amelia had always liked Frank. So had the employees of Jerningham Aviation but she could sympathise that he and Rachel wanted to return to America. He broke the news to her perfectly openly, told her how sorry he was in many ways, invited her comments. She had none. She understood perfectly, she said. She would miss them all. She loved having them. Frank took hold of her hand and squeezed it. 'We'll come back often. We've had a good time.'

'You've had a hard time,' she corrected.

'Well, times are tough. I don't pretend I wouldn't have liked to leave Jerningham Aviation in better shape. But all aviation firms are the same these days. Look at Pan American. A $319 million loss in nine years! We're not really in such a bad way. And in Gerald Saville we're leaving a first class man with all aspects of the business at his fingertips.'

Amelia nodded.

'There's just one other thing,' Frank hesitated a little before proceeding. 'It's impossible to keep an eye on things across 3500 miles of Atlantic. We found that before we came here. We did have three-eighths of the equity, but Rachel,' he smiled indulgently, 'has already disposed of a little. After much heart-searching, it does seem that the sensible thing to do is to sell the rest.'

'Who to?' Amelia asked.

'Not to any old individual or organisation. We wouldn't agree to that. The person who buys must have Jerningham interests at heart and really know the business. A pretty tall order particularly as he has to have access to consortium finance for the equity. We're all lucky really in having that very person actually on the doorstep in Gerald Saville . . . '

So now the packing was done, there remained only the farewells.

'It's Master Evan I shall be sorry to see go,' Sarah whispered meaningfully, as Amelia and she stood surrounded by suitcases in the hall at Haybury, waiting for Rachel and Frank to descend.

The taxi taking them to London Airport had arrived. At the top of the entrance steps, just visible through the window, stood the object of Sarah's sorrow, Evan. Beside him stood Kate. They both looked disconsolate.

'I shall be sorry to see Mr Walton go too, of course. But young Master Evan,' Sarah sighed mistily, 'has been such a lovely companion for Miss Kate.'

Amelia said nothing.

'If only they could stayed a few more years . . . '

Amelia still said nothing.

'Not that I was getting silly ideas about them like some people.'

'I don't know what you're talking about, Sarah. You're getting garrulous in your old age. Ah, here's Rachel now! And Frank! My dears,' she went towards them her hands outstretched for the last farewells. 'Give my love to Victoria.'

'Now you just let us know if there's anything you want, you hear?' Frank kissed Amelia warmly.

'We shall come back for visits, Grandmother.' Rachel pecked her on the cheek, held her arm lightly as they walked down the steps to the waiting taxi. Hand in hand behind them came Evan and Kate. Clumsily at the taxi door, Evan bent and kissed Kate's upturned face, tears cascading down her cheeks.

'Come back soon,' Kate whispered.

'Real soon.'

Then the taxi started up. Evan waved frantically.

'It'll be lovely to have the house to ourselves again, M'lady. And you'll soon find other friends, Miss Kate,' Sarah said cheerfully.

But the house seemed suddenly very empty. The three of them rattled around in the big rooms and the long corridors. Kate didn't find other friends. And Amelia seemed to become more vague and dreamy as the days went by.

While in contrast to the quiet within the house, outside was a steadily increasing volume of activity.

FIFTEEN

Lorries, vans, cars streamed along the road to Jerningham. New sheds, a hangar, another workshop, an extension of the runway, dozens of prefabricated buildings went up. Sarah came back from her day off in Jerningham to report big developments afoot. Amelia took hardly any notice.

To Sarah's 'Hasn't Mr Saville told you anything about it, M'lady?' Amelia shrugged and murmured that she supposed he had been much too busy.

'Too busy to come round here at all, M'lady. We never see him now the Waltons have gone.'

Not that Sarah or Amelia minded. And on Gerald Saville's part, he didn't seem to mind that she attended few board meetings now. Jerningham receded from her mind to a hallowed distance where big things were going on which she didn't nowadays have to bother her head about.

Whenever anyone asked her how things were at Jerningham, she would use the new fashionable phrase being used to describe anything and everything, but which seemed to describe Jerningham especially well: 'ticking over'. Occasionally Frank telephoned from America, on rare occasions Rachel. Once, shortly after he went off to Yale, Evan spoke to her and asked if he might have a word with young Kate. A few months later he sent Kate an odd-looking pin which she wore on her school tie, and in her stock when she went riding.

To Amelia's dim eyes, Kate seemed to grow more beautiful each day. She seemed content enough with her aged grandmother and Sarah. Life, like the factory, seemed to be ticking over. Amelia rarely thought about money. But when she did, it was to reassure herself that with the factory doing so well, Kate would be well provided for. Amelia was a bit hazy as to where Kate would live after she herself had died, and more and more she dreamed of what she had decided was the perfect solution – that Evan would return. He might well have fallen in love with Kate as a little girl, the way Charles had fallen in love with Marianne.

Amelia looked eagerly through the mail when Sarah brought it in with her breakfast, hoping for letters from America. On 14 October there was a letter from Gerald Saville, inviting her to attend a board meeting on the last day of the month at 10 am. As a postscript, he had written that he felt she ought to come if she possibly felt able, and if her health permitted.

'I haven't got one foot in the grave yet,' Amelia exclaimed, 'I'm not some doddering old fool.'

Sarah pointedly said nothing.

At nine-thirty sharp on the morning of 31 October, a company car driven by a strange young chauffeur drove up to Haybury Hall for Amelia. 'I don't like it,

M'lady,' Sarah said suddenly peering into Amelia's face. 'You sure you got all your wits about you this morning?'

'Quite sure thank you, Sarah. Are you sure you've got yours? If so, see your great-niece gives Miss Kate's room a better clean for the weekend.'

Restored and reassured by Sarah's cross expression, Amelia embarked on her last journey to Jerningham.

Apart from the fact that they were all, with the exception of Gerald Saville, strangers, the board meeting proceeded as usual. The company secretary plodded through the minutes. Those minutes were full of half-remembered names, Fortress Finance and Suntara Travel and full of strange expressions which she no longer understood. Everyone else seemed to understand them though. The acceptance of the minutes was proposed and seconded.

'And now we come to the business of today's meeting,' Gerald Saville shot Amelia a strange look, 'the election of our new chairman.'

Amelia tried hard to keep her wits about her, but her tired old brain refused to function with the swiftness and dexterity of these middle-aged men's.

'First I should make clear,' Gerald smiled at her briefly, 'that the consortium for which I bought Mr and Mrs Walton's equity, through Securité, was a tripartite organisation consisting of Fortress Finance, Suntara Travel,' his smile towards Amelia became more reassuring, 'and,' he paused, 'Victory Airways.'

The name at first meant no more than a chord of memory lightly touched. Victory Airways. Of course. Now memory reverberated. The collision with Charles. Charles's being blamed. Charles going to Australia. She heard the rest only as words without real meaning. She stared at Gerald Saville's face blankly.

'As a result, the chairman of those companies, having obtained Lady Nazier's share of the equity, has now overall control.'

This piece of information seemed to be a matter for congratulation to the assembled strangers. They all smiled. 'So therefore I feel that without further ado, I should invite him to take over this board meeting.'

The smiling faces all nodded.

Amelia heard her own cracked voice ask, 'Is he here?' The middle-aged men all smiled again as if she had asked something very funny or very silly, and Gerald Saville answered soothingly, 'Oh, yes, Lady Haybury. He has been waiting in my office till the preliminaries were disposed of. I shall fetch him in now. There will be no need to introduce him to you. He is an old friend of yours.'

And there, almost before she had time to take a sip of water and blink her eyes, stood Pierre March. James's only surviving child. The man she hated now more than anyone else in the world, come back like some evil genius into her life after all these years. She didn't even try to hear the rest. Pierre was elected chairman and symbolically his first task – or was it his first pleasure? – was to vote her off the board.

Dismissed from my own board, she thought, as some little clerk conducted her pityingly downstairs, to the waiting car. Pierre March has come back into my life to destroy what James and I began and Charles continued. He hated us all and now he has won.

But she was getting so old she could no longer feel the therapeutic warmth of real anger. She tried to rekindle the dying embers inside herself. But all she could feel was fear for Kate. Returning in the car to Haybury staring at the back of the chauffeur's head, she tried to strike the last bargain of her lifetime with the poker-faced Almighty. 'I'll not weep for all I've lost at Jerningham, if you make Evan come back for Kate.'

SIXTEEN

'He'll be back,' Amelia said suddenly, sitting bolt upright in her chair, pushing back the sunhat Kate had insisted she wear.

'Who'll be back, Grandmother?' Kate asked anxiously, peering into Amelia's face, her bright blue eyes alert as they so often were these days.

'Why Evan, of course,' Amelia replied testily. 'Evan will be back!'

'I doubt it,' Kate replied. These days she had grown almost as beautiful as her cousin Rachel. More beautiful to some biased views, which included her grandmother and Sarah. Where Rachel's beauty was of a chinalike perfection, Kate's was lit by humour and warmth, and a mysterious tremulous quality more beautiful than any physical perfection. That she had also grown into the image of Amelia, almost the reincarnation of Amelia, was another fact constantly harped upon by Sarah.

'I see you in her more every day,' Sarah would remark, as she helped Amelia to dress and get out into the garden. It was a beautiful garden and it was rare that Amelia travelled beyond it. She had reached the age when every day was a bonus. Something to be thankful for, savoured and enjoyed. And if possible repeated.

'Doesn't Evan write to you?' Amelia took off her sun-glasses and frowned at her granddaughter.

'Oh, yes,' Kate smiled. 'You know quite well he does!' She kissed the top of Amelia's head. 'You're an inquisitive old thing! Now put your hat on!' She placed the wide-brimmed straw hat carefully on Amelia's still thick, still beautifully groomed white hair. 'We don't want you getting sunstroke.'

'*And* he telephones you. He used to telephone me when you were at school to ask how you were.'

Kate blew a disbelieving irreverent noise with her lips, and watched her grandmother thoughtfully. She had inherited more than Amelia's looks. She had inherited also a good deal of her temperament. Though in Kate, Amelia's impulsiveness was tempered with a certain shrewdness and maturity. Apart from Sarah, her grandmother was the only person in the world Kate loved. She wanted to please her and she could see the way the wind was blowing.

How much of the precarious situation in which they lived her grandmother was aware of, Kate didn't know. What she did know was that it was uncomfortable living near the now hugely expanding factory, with the rich March family their enemies. And, if Sarah were to be believed, Rachel was just waiting her opportunity when Amelia died to come in and claim Haybury.

Not that Kate wanted Amelia to realise. She would do anything, even go along with Amelia's romantic fantasies of Evan and herself, rather than distress her grandmother. She felt protective towards her, as if their roles were reversed and Amelia were the child and herself the grandmother.

Kate had her own ideas of life. She was old for her age and self-sufficient because she had had to be. She had stoutly fought her grandmother over the question of schooling. Not because she hadn't wanted to go to boarding-school, but because she was afraid to leave her grandmother. Eventually, Kate had been allowed to attend Godolphin School in Salisbury as a weekly boarder. She hated leaving even for the five days each week. Sarah had strict instructions to telephone Kate if Amelia was the slightest bit ill or off-colour.

Despite her anxiety for her grandmother, Kate had done well academically. She had managed to get ten 'O' levels last summer and was now studying for 'A' levels in maths, chemistry and physics. Hopefully, she would go on to university. But after that she wasn't sure. She wasn't sure what she wanted to be or do.

'I knew exactly what I wanted to do at your age,' Amelia said suddenly, as if she had been following her granddaughter's train of thought as she sat on the lawn beside her. 'I wanted to fly. To build an aeroplane and fly it.'

'That was all right then. But it's been done.'

'There are always new developments,' Amelia said vaguely, fanning herself with her newspaper. She glanced up at the clear sky arching above.

'I don't want to be a spacewoman, Grandmother,' Kate laughed, 'if that's what you mean. Too lonely! Too claustrophobic, I'd hate it!'

'I didn't mean that. Just flying itself. New techniques. New machines . . . ' her voice trailed away, as it so often did these days, her eyes became unfocussed. Then she said, resummoning her concentration, 'You heard they've built a whole new development wing, those wretched Marches, at Jerningham?'

'Yes. You told me.'

'A new stretched version of Ajax. But Sarah says they're running into problems. Things aren't what they were.'

'Sarah hears a lot of things.' They both smiled indulgently.

'She's showing her age,' Amelia said.

'Very much so.'

'I suddenly saw her the other day coming up the steps, and I thought to myself, my God, Sarah, you are really ancient.' Amelia sighed and added suddenly, 'I am too.'

Kate clasped her blue-veined hand. 'Nonsense!'

'I also heard from my solicitors that March has been trying to buy some Haybury land.'

Kate clicked her tongue sympathetically.

'I hate that man!' Amelia growled. 'Hate him! Who would have thought he would have been as treacherous as he was! I don't like the feeling of him coming nearer and nearer. Closing in. It's bad enough with Rachel. But with him as well.'

'Why should you care, Grandmother? It's yours for as long as you live.'

'That's not the same as mine outright.'

'But even if it were yours outright, you couldn't take it with you. Why worry?'

'I worry about *you*.' They were back to square one again. Why did

Grandmother choose to spoil this lovely hot August morning? The bees were humming in the roses, the air was full of the smell of the forest beyond and the sea in front – the scent of heather and gorse and the first hay harvest, the sky arched in unclouded blue, except for the white snail-trails of two high-flying jets.

The present was peaceful and plenteous. And if the present was trapped by the past and the future, rather like she and her grandmother were trapped at Haybury by the enmity of the Marches and the acquisitiveness of Rachel, why worry about it today? Her grandmother was alive and still well. Kate herself was young and healthy.

'Then *don't* worry about me!' Kate shook her grandmother's hand lightly and playfully. 'You look after yourself and I'll be all right. I'm seventeen. You've fed me and clothed me and housed me and loved me. Now I can look after myself.'

'Seventeen is a very vulnerable age.'

'Rubbish! I like being seventeen.'

'But when *I* was seventeen —'

'In *Edwardian* times, Grandmother!'

'At least I knew what I wanted. And if *you* don't know what you want, how can I help you to get it?'

'You can't.' Kate took both Amelia's hands and stared into her face. 'And anyway, did *you* get what you wanted?'

Amelia's blue eyes clouded. She took a long time about answering. 'Some of it. No one ever gets all.'

'Did you get the most important?'

Amelia didn't reply, then she said slowly, 'You and Evan have a lot in common, Kate. And one day, as I said, he'll be back. You'll marry young like I did. I feel it in my bones . . . '

She finished vaguely, her mind wandering as it so often did these days between past and present, between fact and fantasy. Surely Evan had told her on the trans-Atlantic telephone that he was coming over to England just as soon as he had got his degree? Adding with special significant emphasis, 'I hope Kate Amelia will be there. I guess she's the only girl in the world for me!'

Of course he had said it. And of course she had told Kate he had said it. Because she distinctly remembered Kate smiling that secret smile as if she already knew, and was saying nothing. Or as if she knew Amelia was dreaming again.

' . . . you're made for each other,' Amelia finished.

'I doubt that's true,' Kate sighed, and shook her head. 'I doubt anyone's ever made for anyone. The theory doesn't hold water, Grandmother. There are so many permutations. Mathematically, probably hundreds . . . a *thousand* mates would do equally well.'

'Don't give me your schoolroom logic,' Amelia said frowning. And then with a touch of her sharp wit, 'But if a thousand will do for you, Evan will do better than the nine hundred and ninety-nine others.'

Opening her mouth to say, 'I don't want Evan or the others,' Kate was spared what would have undoubtedly caused her grandmother great disappointment, for their eyes were suddenly filled by an extraordinary contraption that came silently over the farthest belt of fir trees. To Kate it was a white triangular sail on a tricycle undercarriage with a windmilling propeller driven by two sets of cycle pedals. To Amelia's dimmer eyes, it was like a great white dove.

Amelia whipped off her sunglasses, took off her shady sunhat and struggled to her feet. She swayed with the sudden movement. Her heartbeat fluttered. She screwed up her eyes as the shape came staggering unevenly downwards towards them. The garden seemed to shimmer in a heat haze, the ground shook.

Time stood breathlessly still. She was aware of the overpoweringly sweet smell of the roses, the blinding of the morning sun.

Everything seemed to swim around her. The world spun on its axis. She gripped the edge of the chair and closed her eyes momentarily and when she opened them she was a young girl again. She was alone in the garden. The dove or whatever had come down to earth in the meadow beyond the ha-ha. Kate was racing across the garden towards it, to embrace her destiny, Amelia remembered thinking. Or was it her own?

The white dove was an aeroplane of sorts, so like the old ones, the ones James and she had struggled over, that for a moment she actually wondered if she had died and if that was herself running down the garden. People said that was how it was. People who had come back from heart attacks and dying momentarily under surgery. You watched your body, you sat on top of a wardrobe and watched people trying to revive you, or you wandered for a moment in your most desired places. Gardeners saw beautiful flowers. Maybe she saw her aeroplane.

But no, she was alive. She felt dry-mouthed and very faint. And she heard her granddaughter shriek out, 'Are you all right?' to someone in the contraption. 'My God, are you sure?'

Just for a moment, Amelia thought wistfully turning the old gold ring on her finger round and round, she had half expected James to step out of it. Then her heart nearly did stop. For out of it did step a thick-set young man with black hair, who walked and moved and was exactly like him.

Amelia subsided into the chair. Perhaps she dozed, perhaps she fainted. Amelia didn't know. Time came and went. Past and present merged. But she was alert and awake and present again as she heard their footsteps rustling towards her over the lawn. Trembling, she put on her sunglasses. She needed them not to shield the expression in her own eyes, but to shield something dazzling in theirs as the two young faces looked down into her own.

'Statistics are always wrong, aren't they? You were wrong, were you not?' she wanted to say suddenly to her granddaughter. 'There aren't hundreds who would do equally well.' But she felt too weak, too overcome. And then she heard the young man who looked so like James say apologetically and gently, 'I'm very sorry to trespass, Lady Haybury. I do hope I didn't startle you, but this machine of mine is a bit unpredictable.' He stretched out a hand towards her. 'I'm awfully glad to meet you. I've heard a lot about you. Admired you. My name is William.'

'March,' Amelia finished for him. 'William March.'

'That's right, we're neighbours.'

'Of sorts,' Amelia said.

'I live over at Jerningham. At least part of the time.' His mouth tightened, his dark blue eyes became frosty. He doesn't get on with his father, she thought. The old story. But he'll be more than a match for Pierre. Aloud, she said, 'My old home.'

'Yes. I'm in the flat. My parents still live at Bournemouth.' He paused, and peered worriedly into her face. 'Are you sure I didn't frighten you, Lady Haybury?'

'Nothing frightens Grandmother,' Kate said proudly.

'Certainly not that!' Amelia jerked her head towards the contraption in the meadow. 'And what part, young man, do you play in the factory?'

'I'm an engineer. But I'm not going to stay at Jerningham. I'll strike out on my own. The sooner the better. That,' he smiled and jerked his thumb at the plane, 'is what I build in my spare time.'

Amelia took off her sunglasses, screwed up her eyes and studied it frowning, 'What do you call it?'

'It's an unpowered craft. There's been a competition. You may not have heard of it. For the first flight of an aircraft propelled solely by human effort.'

'I've heard of it,' Amelia said sharply tapping her newspaper. 'I can read. But you've missed the prize across the Channel! The Gossamer Albatross won that!'

'But Lady Haybury,' his deep rich voice became full of a familiar enthusiasm, the dark blue eyes sparkled, in the remembered way. 'There is still the prize for the first to carry a passenger!'

'Yes,' she sighed. 'You should have had that. You won that really.'

She seemed to be speaking to someone else, to this shadowy man called James whose name Kate often heard. But now her audience paid no attention to her actual words. They noticed only her sweet suddenly girlish smile. She seemed to become young again. The enmity with the Marches appeared for the moment to be forgotten. William went on enthusiastically, 'I couldn't just manage it on my own. I need another pedal-pusher.'

'You Marches!' Amelia exclaimed trenchantly. 'You're so impatient!'

'That's what my poor mother says,' William looked for a moment as if he might have said more and then clamped his mouth shut as James used to do, 'about my father. He believes in big and quick. He doesn't think much of my aeroplane. Nor me. But there are many possibilities. We could put a little engine on and make it a sky runabout. Or a solar motor powered through the sun. Flying for fun . . . that's what *I* want from my Ajax.'

'Have you damaged it?'

'Nothing I can't fix. If you want it off your land, I can either stay and do it, or —' Again that look came into his eyes, 'Ask my father.'

'Certainly not! I won't have him on my land!'

William said nothing, but Amelia suddenly saw everything. In the fullness of time Pierre would be overthrown by his own son. The Ajax project would begin afresh.

'Grandmother,' Kate said tentatively, 'William and I were talking about it as we walked up.'

'Oh, it's William already, is it?'

'Yes, Grandmother. Would it worry you terribly if I helped him repair it, then . . . ' she swallowed, 'crew it?'

'D'you mean go up in that thing?'

'I won't take her if you don't want me to, Lady Haybury. You've had enough worry today. But I would take the utmost tremendous care of her, if you felt you could trust me . . .

They stood side by side looking down at her. They didn't hold hands. They didn't even touch. But already . . . already the wheel had come full circle. Amelia suddenly crooked her finger for William to bend over her, as if she wanted to whisper in his ear. But when he did so, she said nothing. She simply kissed him gently on the cheek, and waved the two of them away.

Half an hour later, William came rushing back to say breathlessly, 'Everything's fixed, Lady Haybury! Kate's been an enormous help. She's quite a mechanic. If you're sure you don't want to change your mind about her coming with me? Just say the word if you do.'

But she neither saw nor heard him. At least, not as William. She saw James come for her at last. When he put out his hand to wave, she stretched both hers towards him and he seemed to take them. The white bird shape seemed to come closer to her. She had the strange sensation of simultaneously being in it and watching it.

She felt its sudden release from the pull of the earth. She felt James beside her. They were soaring upwards together. And at the same time, she was watching the white wings rise over the treetops and melt into what seemed to her closing eyes to be a vast eternal all-embracing blue.